To the Walls of France

Martin McDowell

Published in 2020 by FeedARead.com Publishing – Arts Council funded

First Edition –

A CIP catalogue record for this title is available from the British Library.

Dedication

To my wife, Doreen, and children, Amy and Steven,
who are so indulgent of my tedious
Napoleonic obsession!

And Dave Wood, History teacher colleague. Dave - ever in our memory.

Acknowledgments
The History of the Peninsular War- Volumes IV and V - Sir Charles Oman
Waterloo - Mark Adkin
Costello. The True Story of a Peninsular War Riflemen - Eileen Hathaway
An Atlas of the Peninsular War - Ian Robertson
Peninsular War Atlas – Col. Nick Lipscombe
The Peninsular War – Charles Esdaile

During the campaigns described in this volume:-
The 105th are in place of:
40th Foot (2nd) Somerset – "The Excellers". "The Fighting Fortieth"
This Regiment fought in every major of the whole Peninsular War, from 1807 to 1814, then at Waterloo and throughout the American Wars post and prior to that.

Books by the same author.

105th Series - Worth Their Colours
- Close to the Colours
- The Plains of Talavera
- The Walls of Badajoz

A Question of Duty – a novel set in Nelson's Navy, post Trafalgar

Cover Picture
– Incident on the Peninsula by Chris Collingwood
British 15th Light dragoons (and Hussars) and 16th Light Dragoons engage the French 1st Provincial Chasseurs during the Peninsula War

List of Characters

105th Privates and NCOs

Light Company – 1st Section

Snr. Sgt. Ethan Ellis, Cprl. Ezekiel Saunders, Chosen Man John Davey, Privates Tom Miles, Joe Pike, Nat Solomon, Len Bailey, John Byford, Bill Turner.

Three Company (Colour)

Colour Sgt. Jed Deakin, Regimental Colour.
Colour Sgt. Harry Bennet, King's Colour.
Sgt. Obediah Hill, Sgt. Henry Nicholls, Cprl. Toby Halfway.

Regimental Sergeant Major Cyrus Gibney

Grenadiers – 1st Section.

Sgt. Arthur Bennett

Grenadiers – 2nd Section

Sgt. Luke Ridgway

Colonel's Staff

Sgt. Herbert Bryce – Colonel's Clerk and servant.
Bugler Edward 'Bugle' Bates.
Reverend Thomas Albright – Regimental Chaplain.
Surgeon George Pearce

Servants

Private Percival Sedgwicke – Chaplain's Assistant.
Private Sidney Morrison – Light Company
Private Arthur Binns – Grenadier Company.

Followers

Mulcahey family, adopted by Col. Sgt. Jed Deakin

Bridie Mulcahey, mother. Kevin 16, Bridie's son. Sinead, 14, Bridie's daughter.
Eirin Byford (nee Mulcahey) 19, Bridie's daughter and married to John Byford.
Jedediah Byford – Eirin's baby son (father Lt. Stuart Maltby – killed at Cuidad Rodrigo).

Nicholls family, Father – Sgt. Henry Nicholls

Nellie Nicholls, mother. Daughters - Sally, 16. Trudie, 14. Violet, 12.

Consuela Saunders – wife to Ezekiel

Family in England of rank and file

Mary Pike (nee O'Keefe – Bridie's youngest sister) – wife to Joe Pike, son Thomas

Molly Davey, common-law wife to John. Children – Tilly 14. Infants John and Rachel.

105th Officers

Colonel Sir Ambrose Brockenhurst MP.

Colonel's ADC Major St John Slade (later Colour Company)

Senior Major Padraigh O'Hare. Junior Major Henry Carr.

Grenadier Company.

Cpt. Lord Charles Carravoy. 1 Sec. Lt. Royston D'Villiers.
2 Sec. Lt. Simon Ameshurst.

Three (Colour) Company

Cpt. Joshua Heaviside. Later Junior Major

1 Section Lt. Lionel Farquharson. 2 Section Lt. Leonard Howarth

Light Company

Cpt. Nathaniel Drake. 1 Sec. Lt. Luttrel Bettridge. 2 Sec. Lt. Richard Shakeshaft.

Two Company

Cpt. Reginald Charters

Ensigns.

Ensign Henri Rasenne, King's Colour.

Ensign Patrick Mulcahey (son of Bridie), Regimental Colour.

Relatives and wives in England

Jane Carr – wife to Major Henry Carr

Cecily Drake – wife to Captain Nathaniel Drake

Lady Constance Fynings – Aunt to Jane.

Cavalry Division

General Stapleton-Cotton – Division Commander

Major-General Le Marchant – 3rd & 4th Dragoons,
5th Dragoon Guards

Col. Bocks' Brigade – 1st & 2nd Dragoons, King's German Legion.

Col. V. Alten's Brigade – 1st Hussars King's German Legion
14th Light Dragoons.

Col. G. Anson's Brigade – 11th Light Dragoons (Col. Lionel Piers)

12th Light Dragoons (Col. Richmond Stockton)

16th Light Dragoons

Colonel George Withers

Major Arthur Johnson

One Squadron - Captain Lucius Tavender

A Troop - Cornet Harry Smythe

Sgt. Ned Shelby

B Troop - Cornet Ben Faversham

Two Squadron - Captain Samuel Oakwood

C Troop - Cornet Willoughby Carr

Sgt. Septimus Baxter, Cpl. Jim Makepeace,

Troopers Len Spivey, Percy Nunney.

D Troop - Cornet Douglas Peterson

Sgt. Desty

Three Squadron - Captain Somers-Cocks

Four Squadron - Captain Myers

Major Engagements

Battle of Salamanca

4th Division, Gen. Sir G. Lowry-Cole,

Brigadier W. Anson's Brigade:-

3/27th Inniskilling, (Col. Daniel Creet)

5/60th Rifles - 1 Company (Capt. Thomas Bairns)

105th Wessex – Colonel Sir Ambrose Brockenhurst.

Brigadier Ellis' Brigade – 1/7th, 1/23rd, 1/48th.

Siege of Burgos

16th Light Dragoons – G. Anson's Bgde,

with 11th & 12th Light Dragoons

Battles of Vitoria, Roncesvalles and Sorauren

4th Division, Gen. Sir G. Lowry-Cole.

Brigadier W. Anson's Brigade:-

105th Wessex, 3/27th Inniskilling, 1/48th Northamptonshire,

2nd Provisional Battalion (2/31st & 2/66th),

5/60th Rifles - 1 Company

Brigadier Ellis' Brigade – 1/7th, 1/23rd, 1/48th.

Prologue

Jean Dulongue, erstwhile citizen of France, sat his sturdy horse within the shelter of a copse of oak. The leaves above him were just feeling their way into Spring, many now large enough to rustle softly in the mild breeze, but not enough to mask the sounds that came up to him from below. The copse crowned a prominent hill giving good cover as he observed what seemed an endless column of marching men, accompanied by artillery, vehicles, wagons, horses, sheep and cattle, the requirements of a vast army, all passing beneath him on a road that ran, with few curves, to the town of Prienai. Either side of the town ran the excessive curves and loops of the River Neman, the natural border with Russia.

Dulongue had emigrated to England with his family when they were forced to flee The Terror, but now he posed as a French victualler, with all the necessary papers, all expertly forged. He had ridden the length of the column for days, counting battalions and batteries and recording crucial details, to the extent that he was now running out of pencil, such had been the size of the task. What he was trying to record now were the number of nationalities within that endless column. He had seen every colour of uniform possible, bar the red of England and he was now convinced that almost every European nation was represented, bar England, Prussia and Austria. He now sized the army at 500,000 men, the largest seen on European soil for centuries, all now poised on the edge of Russia.

Dulongue was intelligent and a thinker, given often to philosophising and, as he sat his good horse, he could not help but think that here were hundreds of thousands of men, dragged from their homes to march hundreds of miles to the borders of remote Russia. This a country at the opposite end of Europe to France, from where Russia could not realistically pose any serious threat, yet here Bonaparte stood, poised to invade yet another country, for the simple reason that he now felt the enterprise was wholly possible, one that would extend his empire across Europe, to this furthest extent.

Dulongue decided that it was now time to take what he had discovered up to Gdansk on the Polish coast, a port practically independent of Bonaparte, from where he could find a neutral ship that could begin his journey back to England. One final look revealed a distant shaft of sunlight glinting on hundreds of polished cavalry helmets to further confirm what he now knew, before he turned his horse away, that this was an army of vast power and potential, but there came at least one cheering thought. In Spain, Bonaparte's armies were under severe pressure, such that the Allies under Wellington had now captured the two vital border fortresses, Cuidad Rodrigo and now Badajoz. The French grip on the Peninsula was gradually being prised away, piece by piece.

Chapter One

The Chase

Captain Nathaniel Drake, Light Company, 105th Foot, The Prince of Wales Own Wessex Regiment, looked ruefully at the significant bulge in the sole of his right boot, this alarming feature caused by upward pressure from within by his middle finger. His brows came together at the thought of marching any further on such suspect footwear, when the light from the door was blocked by the arrival of one of his Lieutenants, one Richard Shakeshaft, him of One Section. Drake looked up to see the tall, young, but nevertheless scarred and veteran member of his Company.

"Have we been here before?"

The reply was somewhat impatient.

"Yes! At least three times."

"What's it called?'

"Castello Branco."

Drake nodded, more resignedly than in agreement.

"Should've remembered, the number of times we've been up and down this track from North to South and vice versa."

Drake could not have enquired from a more qualified person than Shakeshaft, him the recorder of the 'doings' of the 105th, through sketches and an accurate diary.

"Seems a bit more knocked about than the last place we hurried through. For that, memory also fails."

Shakeshaft pulled forward the awkward chinstrap of his shako, removed the headgear and placed it near the door. Drake was sitting on the sole item of furniture in the hovel; a rough bench.

"True, it is. Clausel's Division of Marmont's were here for three days. And you well know their nasty habits!"

Drake sighed and changed the subject.

"How many weeks since we actually took Badajoz?"

"More like days! Eleven."

Drake sighed again.

"And he's forced marched us up to here to try and cut off Marmont, who's been roaming about West of Cuidad, making a nuisance of himself."

Now it was Shakeshaft's turn to nod his head several times.

"That's what's being said."

"And we left Badajoz when?"

"Four days after taking it, the twelfth of April, year of our Lord 1812."

More than slightly incredulous, Drake then turned to more important matters.

"How are the men? Our wounded? Bearing up?"

"My walking wounded? Well enough. Three are back in the transport, hoping to recover."

"And Two Section?"

"Much the same is my guess, but ask Ellis."

Drake's jaw clamped upwards, remembering the feeble wave given by Lieutenant Rushby as he was born away on a cart to the coast and then England, nursing a severe bayonet wound inflicted on the battlements of Badajoz. Senior Sergeant Ethan Ellis now ran Two Section until an Officer replacement arrived. He returned to his original concern.

"Give these boots to Morrison, will you, please? They won't last another day. I'm told he knows of a cobbler in Colour who can do repairs. Using bits of French saddle".

He threw the boots towards him and Shakeshaft gathered the pair to then disappear, at which point Drake noticed the alarming hole in his left sock.

There was no such worry over boots and kit, as both mess groups of Colour Sergeant Jedediah Deakin and Chosen Man John Davey piled into the building with which they were familiar from previous campaigns and it now claimed for themselves. Most of what they wore on their feet, around their legs and now swinging from their backs were French, eagerly pillaged from any French dead of any past conflict. Soon all were sat around the walls, whilst their Followers, these women mostly within

Deakin's group, started a fire in the wide grate, using the dry kindling that all carried within their packs. First to comment was the inevitably belligerent Tom Miles.

"Straight off a siege and straight into this! Forced march, just in case and some hopes. All knows the Frogs marches quicker'n us."

The huge Corporal Ezekiel Saunders, almost asleep as he waited for the rations to be cooked, opened one eye and turned to the scowling Miles.

"Shuddup and start enjoying yourself!"

All grinned at the put-down of Miles, always ill-tempered and at odds with someone about something, or just anything, in this case a march of almost 150 miles in five days over Portuguese roads.
Miles slumped back, having vented his spleen; he was as tired as anyone. However, all looked up as Eirin Byford, now five months pregnant, was helped through the door and onto a bench quickly vacated by her husband, John Byford, the 'educated, gentlemen-ranker' of the Light Company. The

From Badajoz to Salamanca

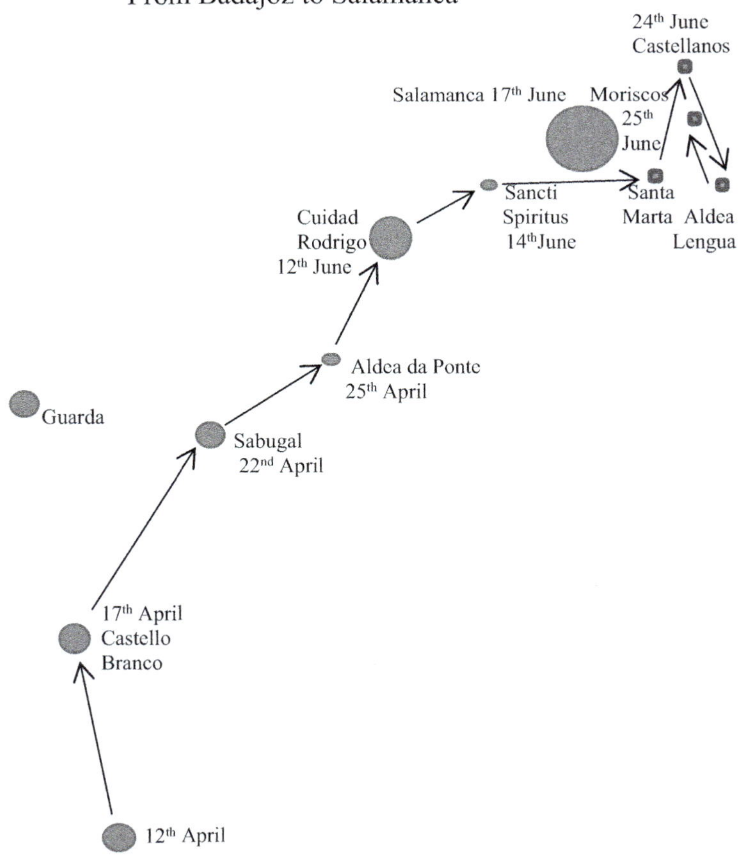

anxiety in his face was matched by that of her mother, the very Irish Bridie Mulcahey 'army-wife' to Jed Deakin, and the enquiry was troubled and heartfelt.

"How are you, now, Eirin darlin'? Has it been a better day, for you now?"

Eirin, pale and wan, sat and shook her head. She had been riding in the cart of the Battalion Chaplain, one Reverend Thomas Albright and so she had been helped through the door by the Chaplain's Assistant, Percival Sedgwicke, who replied for her as she was eased onto the seat.

"Not so good a day, I'm afraid to say. Too sick to eat much, but she slept most of the day, which cannot be a bad thing."

Equally as well educated as Byford, Sedgwicke was, however, a convicted thief and de-frocked Priest, condemned to serve in the army 'for the duration'. However, hopeless line soldier as he had proved to be, he had gravitated to the post of servant to the Battalion Chaplain when the 105th gained such a notable figure, this when awarded their Colours for the first time. Highly popular with the men, although personally somewhat discomfited by his full acceptance by such as these, his own background being almost aristocratic. His family were several social levels above most of the ranks, but he was most certainly welcome amongst this group of soldiers, but the welcome was spoken this time by the other 'mother' of the group, the fiercesome, equally Irish as Bridie, but often kindly, Nelly Nicholls, church married wife to Henry Nicholls.

"Well, 'tis most kind of you now, Parson darlin', so it is, to be bringing Eirin up here to us, so careful like."

She studied the grate and the good fire, with the hot griddle pan over it with dough-cakes now cooking, all formed and ready from ingredients combined whilst they marched, to speed the process of providing immediate food before cooking the main rations. A kettle alongside was now near boiling.

"So now, Parson, will you not take a small cake and a drop of tea with us? 'Tis almost ready, now."

'Parson' Sedgwicke needed no further persuasion. Bridie's dough-cakes were a treat in themselves and so he found a place along the wall with the others, the space made for him by Jed Deakin, the NCO who had escorted him from Frome Gaol to Taunton Barracks, almost seven years ago. Chosen Man John Davey, convicted poacher, had been another 'King's Hard Bargain' and part of that sad, shackled group, but now, after all they had been through, it seemed like another century.

However, the present and what it was bringing, was very much on the mind of the two Commanders of the 105th, Major Padraigh O'Hare, now in his early fifties, a thorough veteran, a calm sage and a source of experienced wisdom. His companion was Brevet-Major Henry Carr, now in his late twenties and almost the opposite, a ruthless, often irritable, but a thoroughly professional soldier, determined to prosecute this war in the most competent and capable manner possible, this being the most likely route to arriving safely home to his wife, Jane Carr, married to Henry much against her Father's wishes. Both O'Hare and Carr now ran the Battalion, now that their beloved Colonel Bertram Lacey had deservedly retired after the horrors of the siege of Badajoz. At that moment, both were studying a map of Portugal, with deep concern on their faces. It was very clear that where they were, was only half-way to where Wellington wanted them to be. No words needed to be spoken as Carr stabbed his finger, in order, onto Badajoz, Castello Branco and then Guarda, central to what they knew as the 'Northern corridor', the space between mountain ranges that gave passage between Northern Portugal and Central Spain. Carr looked at O'Hare.

"What chance of cutting off Marmont?"

O'Hare shook his head, the mass of grey hair swaying with the motion. His accent was broad country Irish.

"I wouldn't put even an each-way bet on it!"

Carr nodded, resignedly.

"Right! Let's get around the men. It's our job to drive them, but we must do what we can to keep them going. Kit, transport, rations, wounded and all the rest of it."

O'Hare rolled up the map and gave it to Sergeant Herbert Bryce, the Colonel's Secretary.

"How long till food?"

"Give it half an hour, Sir. It's chicken. I picked up a couple on the way."

However, Carr's brows still came together, the anxiety remained still.

"About the best news I've had these past days."

However, the news did improve that evening in that Wellington was allowing them to rest for two days. However, on the third day the bugles sounded to form column of march, but as soon as it was formed the grim-faced Sergeant Ethan Ellis marched back down the column to the Followers and spoke immediately to Bridie and Nellie.

"Get the childers on the far side of the cart. The left. What's waiting up there is not a pretty sight."

Chaplain's Assistant Sedgwicke, then holding the reins of the two mules, turned and looked down from the front seat.

"Why Sergeant? What has taken place?"

Ellis eased his Baker rifle on his shoulder.

"Beresford's shot some Portuguese Ensign of Militia for deserting his troops. Trant's Portuguese was beaten by Marmont at Guarda and this one hurried off out of it. Too hurried for Beresford's liking, so he's had him shot and he's still up there now. No-one's bothered to cut him down."

There was no need for Ellis to say anything more, because all had been overheard by Bridie and Nellie and so Ellis hurried off and the two women shepherded their brood to the left-hand side of the cart, which now contained Eirin. The 'childers' were two, Bridie's Sinead, the last of her two daughters now that her eldest, Mary, was married to Joe Pike of John Davey's mess and now back in England. The second was Bridie's only son remaining with their group, Kevin, because the eldest son, Patrick, was now a 105th Ensign. Nellie's three were also ushered round, Sally, Trudie and Violet, all remaining close to their Mother, but behind her Mother's back, Sally placing herself suspiciously close to Kevin. The column started off and within minutes they came to the Town Square, where, hanging gruesomely upright against a post were the mangled remains of the Militia Officer, his body and face wholly disfigured by the impact of 12 three-quarter inch musket balls at 12 paces range. At the reins, Sedgwicke gave the scene barely a glance and he concerned himself to distract his sensitive and unworldly Superior, the Reverend Thomas Albright with the sight of the Town Church, although close to the size of many English Cathedrals.

"The Town Church, Sir. The Spanish certainly do their best to do justice to the worship of Our Good Lord, even in so lowly a place as this, would you not say, Sir?"

The Reverend Albright's brows came together. Castello' Church was not all that impressive in terms of Spanish dimensions, but much ornamented with delicate stonework and so he decided that this feature was the one which had drawn Sedgwicke to his opinion. They were both High Church and so Albright smiled kindly and turned his head as he sat the front bench besides Sedgwicke.

"I am not inclined towards disagreement, Private."

Sedgwicke smiled at the thought, "the evil deed has passed us by".

All had averted their gaze as they passed, bar one, for at the head of the 105th column, there marched the Grenadier Company whose Captain, Lord Charles Carravoy, was most pleased with the spectacle, this confirming his predilection for firm discipline and his high opinion of General William Carr Beresford, who plainly held 'old school' attitudes to those within the ranks.

oOo

Nothing else so disturbing was seen further to the North. Merely 30 odd miles as the Portuguese road ran, another column was making its way Northwards, only this one mounted. It was made up from the 16th Light Dragoons, part of Brigadier G. Anson's Brigade of Horse, their brother Regiments being the 11th and 12th, these also Light Dragoons. As if Infantry Major Henry Carr did not have enough to worry about, being in joint command of a whole Battalion, the ranks of the 16th contained a special Cornet, one Willoughby Carr, Henry's younger brother and his only contact with his estranged family. Younger Carr was the Cornet commanding C Troop of Two Squadron, as the 16th organized themselves, all Squadrons being given numbers in sequence, all Troops with letters in sequence, throughout the Regiment.

At that moment Elder Carr should have no worries for his brother, for at that moment they were at an easy trot on the road to Sabugal, the scene of a minor battle during early April 1811, almost two years previous. What jolted the Troopers of the 16th from thoughts of their rumps and their stomachs was a galloper coming back down their column from the Hussars of the King's German Legion, these an elite Brigade of cavalry some way ahead. No-one attempted any questions, the uniform revealed him to be KGL, but a galloper meant news, even as he disappeared in a cloud of dust and the news was not long in arriving. The galloper had stopped at the head of their column before their Brigadier and had spoken the correct words of English, before saluting and riding on. At the head of the column was the 16th's Colonel, George Withers, with his Major Arthur Johnson. Then came the Captain of One Squadron, Lucius Tavender. Behind him was a Sergeant, one Ned Shelby of A Troop, One Squadron, who eased his horse forward to just behind Tavender to overhear. Within seconds the message was winging its way down the column, they were catching up to Marmont, even if the infantry were not. Another half hour of progress and matters began to develop even further. Again, within the earshot of Ned Shelby, the Cavalry Division Commander, General Stapleton-Cotton arrived and ordered Brigadier Anson to give him two Squadrons to go forward to begin the relief of Alten's Brigade, the 14th Light Dragoons and the 1st KGL Hussars, who had been in the van for two days, often skirmishing with Marmont's outlying vedettes. The first two Squadrons were Tavender's One and that of Carr, Two, his Squadron Captain being Samuel Oakwood. The 180 odd Troopers put spurs to their horses and hurried forward at a good canter. An hour brought them to within five miles of Sabugal, but Alten's KGL Regiment had not yet departed and Captain

Tavender, him being the Senior, thought himself entitled enough and so he eased his horse further forward as Stapleton-Cotton was apprised of the situation by a KGL Major.

He learned little other than the fairly obvious that Marmont had his Light Cavalry out as a screen between himself and the approaching Wellington, but all French forces seemed to be moving in the direction of Cuidad Rodrigo, held at that moment for the Allies by a mixed Spanish and Portuguese garrison. However, Tavender was not in the best of moods. In the hope of advancing his own career, throughout the ride he had done his best to engage in conversation with Stapleton-Cotton, the fourth in line to command the whole army behind Lord Wellington, General Hill and General Graham, but he had received in reply nothing that could be described as conversation, merely grunts and dismissive gestures. Thus, ill-tempered and alone, he allowed his horse to water at the small stream that ran through the tiny hamlet and he remained standing there, awaiting orders. In contrast, his men and the KGL were mingling together and doing their best to communicate, mostly by gestures and eager trading. The KGL were well respected throughout the Allied army and so amity and comradeship required little encouragement. Just so for Captain Oakwood and his two Cornets, Willoughby Carr and Douglas Peterson, all now watering their own horses alongside a Captain of the 1st KGL Hussars. He was the first to bow and introduce himself.

"Good afternoon. I am Captain Arnt Schengen."

The three introduced themselves and then Peterson asked the obvious question.

"What have you seen of the Johnnies? Do they seem up for the fight?"

Schengen smiled.

"I would say yes. Marmont has raided deep into Portugal, whilst we were in the South and this has made them feel good about themselves, I am thinking. These are veterans, they know how to do what they do and they feel as good about themselves as any French here. That's my own impression."

It was Oakwood who replied.

"So, our next meeting with them will not be easy."

Schengen nodded.

"I would say so. This is not a beaten army. Far from it. They are as aggressive as ever."

However, Carr was now puzzled.

"You speak very good English."

Schengen grinned and nodded.

"Perhaps because I am Dutch. Many of us speak English and it is no bad thing if you are to serve in Wellington's army."

All three of the 16th grinned, but then the bugle sounded for the KGL to form column of march and so Schengen pulled his horse away and mounted.

"Well, good luck. Keep a good lookout. These Frans know what they are about."

The KGL departed shortly after and Stapleton-Cotton called over his two Captains, Tavender and Oakwood to issue orders and soon the two Squadrons of the 16th had parted company to perform the duties they were trained and equipped for, to roam the countryside, making good use of their eyes and ears to find and report on their enemy. Throughout an hour of roaming the hills, they saw no-one but Portuguese peasants, who nevertheless waved enthusiastically and cried out 'Viva Ingleses! Viva Vellinton!" However, this pleasant post-Noon sojourn changed when, riding along the edge of a shallow valley, Sergeant Baxter pointed directly across from where they were.

"Sir. Coming out of that small valley on the opposite side."

Carr followed Baxter's pointed arm to expand his telescope and through it he saw a column of brown and grey clad horsemen splashing through the brook that came down into the main valley to feed the main stream there. The horsemen had seen them first and were soon climbing up the valley side to meet them. Baxter studied their progress.

"Guerrillas, Sir?"

Carr nodded.

"Yes. Called Ordenanza in Portugal. Rebels as far as the French are concerned and therefore shot or hung or worse if caught. I'll give these credit for risking that. They may have news or captured despatches. They do us a great service with what they discover."

However, there was nothing. The column swerved right, giving the watching Troop nothing more than a wave, but grim, hard faces were common throughout as they hurried past.

oOo

It was the following day that the Allied infantry entered Sabugal in the shape of General Picton's Third Division, which included the 105th. Sabugal itself was familiar to them, as also were the depressing sights all around which so often followed a period of French occupation. The great majority of the buildings were wrecked and pillaged, but what was worse were the number of inhabitants lying dead against walls that were all too suitable for executions, also several more hanging from trees and now being cut down by angry Portuguese citizens, all this being accompanied by the piteous cries and wailing from local womenfolk. Plainly the last of the French had not long gone, judging by their angry shouts at Picton's marching Battalions.

"Voces sao muito atrasdados, Ingleses"

Saunders turned to his marching companion, John Byford.

"What they saying, Byfe?"

Byford screwed up his face before answering.

"Something about being late. Too late, I'd say."

The Third Division pounded on through the town, following Picton's orders for a forced march. Beyond Sabugal the small villages were more welcoming and less wrecked, as commented on by Carr to O'Hare.

"Not much damage or suffering here. Perhaps the great hurry that he's placed upon us has done some good. Pushed on the Johnnies before they can wreak their usual mischief."

O'Hare nodded agreement as he waved to acknowledge the clapping Portuguese and another cry of "Viva a Inglaterra." However, at the far end of the 105th column, at the place of the Light Company, Drake was alongside Shakeshaft and not so sure of that conclusion as the two Officers up at the van.

"This insane hurry. Is it doing any good? A Captain in the 74th told me that Marmont's already over the Agueda at Cuidad and falling back to Salamanca! Much more of this and I'll be spending another shilling on shoe leather."

Shakeshaft nodded and grinned. He was busy recording the day in his diary, including what they had just seen in Sabugal.

The following day the diary was again opened to record the town of Fuente Guinaldo, a place much used by Wellington and his army during the previous year and again, as for that time, the 105th were sent to camp in the fields outside. The good condition of the town was not lost on Colour Sergeant Jed Deakin, now sat smoking with his long-time comrade, Corporal Toby Halfway.

"Seems like this place has been lucky again, Tobe. No damage nor stringings up in this place. Frog's must've took another road."

Halfway tamped down the smouldering tobacco in his pipe with a very stained forefinger.

"You b'ain't wrong there, Jed. Seems like just luck, whether these in these parts don't get their homes wrecked and God knows what done to their selves and their family. Just luck."

Halfway sucked on his pipe and blew out a cloud of smoke.

"At least here I feels like I'm on the right side."

Deakin nodded slow agreement.

"No argument from me. Remember when we was in the Norfolks, before we got shipwrecked, and we was chasin' Feinians all around Ireland, burnin' homes and whatnot. That didn't feel like bein' on the right side!"

"True, Jed. At least this is what can be called proper soldierin', an' not actin' like a squad of Bow Street Runners. Here, we'n in with a good crew, John an' Zeke an' whatnot. Even Tom! But he's old Norfolk, so he's forgive a lot. An' a good set of Followers. You've taken up with Bridie! A catch thur', an' that's the truth."

Deakin grinned and nodded. He had taken on the Mulcahy family when Bridie's husband was killed at the battle of Maida six years before and they had remained together ever since. Only just approaching early middle-age, Bridie remained an Irish beauty. With that, both emptied their pipes and stood up to return to their camp-fires. Rations had kept up with their march and they expected a good supper.

However, at that moment the circumstances of the goodmen Deakin and Halfway were about to undergo a significant change. It began with a letter arriving at the Headquarters of General Picton that the 45th Nottinghamshires were about to rejoin his Division and so he had to decide which of his existing Regiments was to join the 4th Division under General Lowry-Cole, which was one Battalion short. He had made his decision. Although he well knew the quality of the 105th, he never had any liking for their now departed Colonel, Bertram Lacey, nor Major Henry Carr, nor the Regiment as a whole since one of their ranks had told him to "Go take his bad mouth and use it somewhere else", this whilst the 105th were protecting terrified citizens after the capture of Cuidad Rodrigo. Picton's foul language was infamous throughout the army and, ever one to bear a grudge, he had sent one of his ADCs to fetch Major Carr. In response, the same was at that moment stood outside Picton's room in one of the better houses of Fuente, the previous occupants now being confined to one room, but they were far from discontent having been handsomely paid.

Carr knocked and waited. A loud 'Enter', caused him to lift the latch and march in. Carr well knew Picton's dislike of him and so he maintained strict formality, coming to attention and reeling off a perfect salute, with his shako held within his left forearm.

"You sent for me, Sir."

Carr moved not one muscle, neither in his face nor in the rest of his body, as Picton studied him with barely concealed dislike and he wasted no time.

"My 45th are coming back to the war, which means I have one Battalion too many and Lowry-Cole's 4th has one too few. W. Anson's

Brigade specifically. You'll be joining them. You leave in the morning. They're up further at Aldea da Ponte."

He allowed the words to sink in.

"Any comment?"

Carr remained rigidly at attention.

"None, Sir, no. Other than the hope that we have given good service, Sir."

He paused.

"To your Third Division, that is, Sir. As part of the Third we gained the battle honour of Fuentes D'Onoro and we'll not forget that, Sir. One further thing, we were in General Lowry-Cole's Brigade at Maida, Sir. It will be good to renew his acquaintance."

Picton could not let the remark go by, seeing there a mild insult even if none was intended. His eyes narrowed.

"When you were just a Provisional ragtag crew?"

"Yes Sir. After that we became the 105th Wessex, Sir. The Prince of Wales Own. A bit of a change, Sir."

Picton nodded, his face remaining surly, then he sat forward and reached for some papers.

"These are for you, Carr. Nothing to do with me now. Probably the usual stuff for requisitioning and whatnot, but there is one there that may mean a particular change in your circumstances."

Carr took the letters as offered, pushed them behind his shako, took one step back, saluted and spun on his heel to then leave the room. Back in his tent he opened last the one that was plainly of greater significance, this coming from Horse Guards. He broke the seal, read it and then banged his head on the table three times, such that Sergeant Bryce came running in.

"Sir! Are you all right, Sir?"

Carr folded his arms and sighed heavily.

"I have to say not really, Sergeant, but just how bad that turns out to be remains to be seen."

It was a surprise to all when, mid-morning of the next day, the bugles sounded for the 105th to form column of march to get to Aldea da Ponte. That they were leaving their camping ground was not too unwelcome an event, because it may mean a better billet, one under shelter. Therefore, all marched out briskly enough, inevitably trading as they passed the usual insults with the 88th Connaught Rangers, their foes of long standing, but the handshakes with their Colonel John Wallace by Carr and O'Hare were fierce and sincere. Once on the road, Carr showed O'Hare the Horse Guards letter. The reaction was a non-committal grin and the swaying of the leonine head from side to side. Carr took the letter back.

"You weren't there. It happened back in England, after Talavera."

Feeling the urgent need to share the disturbing news with someone, Carr fell out of the column and hurried back to the last Company in the column, the Light, where he found Drake in his place. When Drake was shown the letter, it elicited two words.

"Oh God!"

The day was dying when they reached Aldea da Ponte and there were no cosy billets, the 4th Division had taken them all in a village smaller than Fuente Guinaldo, such that even good camping ground was in short supply. Nevertheless, in the semi-dark the 105th set up camp and Carr and O'Hare set off to find General Lowry-Cole's Headquarters. There were too few buildings to make the choice difficult and it was made very obvious by the two Redcoat sentries stood outside. They quickly entered through a door solid but unkempt, into the usual Iberian hallway of high ceiling, whitewashed walls and the smell of onions and garlic. A Captain was sat behind a desk, plainly in the act of closing for the day, but the approach of two Majors halted his preparations and he stood to receive both. Carr wasted no time, this was also to be the final event of his day.

"Majors O'Hare and Carr of the 105th Foot. We are to join the 4th Division, or so we have been told and therefore we are reporting here, at the earliest opportunity and so we require to see the General, if he is still available."

The Captain remained standing and pointed further down the passageway, that ran alongside the heavy mahogany staircase.

"I'm sure he still is, Sirs. He has not passed by me, not as yet. Second door on the left, Sirs."

Carr nodded his thanks and both hurried to the door and knocked. It was immediately opened by the Colonel of the 27th Inniskillings. Both entered, came to the attention before the General and saluted. Both Carr and O'Hare remarked within themselves how much he had changed since he was their Brigadier at Maida in summer 1806. He could have been Wellington's twin, tall, thin with a long angular face, but there the comparison ran out. Whilst Wellington was clearly bright and energetic, the Peninsular years had plainly taken their toll on Lowry-Cole, the vivid signs being the sad eyes and down-turned mouth. He was a man much worn down by five years of the travails of the Peninsular Campaign. Carr took one pace forward and placed Picton's letter on the desk.

"105th Foot, Sir. General Picton has ordered us to report to you, with a view to joining your Division."

Lowry-Cole picked up the letter as if intending to read it, but did not do so, instead replacing it on the desk. Yet still he said nothing and so Carr continued with what he had planned to say.

"We were in your Brigade at Maida, Sir. Over there on the left. I hope you remember us, Sir."

The memory brought a small flicker of cheer to Lowry-Cole's face and with the memory he reached out his hand to both.

"Indeed I do! I remember you both and your good Colonel. Is he no longer with you?"

"No, Sir. Our Colonel Lacey retired immediately after taking Badajoz, Sir. Myself and Major O'Hare here, are currently in command."

With that, the General's face fell, but his voice remained welcoming.

"Well, I'm pleased to see you both again and to welcome you to the Division. You'll be in Anson's Brigade, it's fortuitous that Creet of the 27th is here. He's Anson's too!"

He brightened still further.

"The old 'Rag and Bone Boys'! We could not do better."

He looked behind to the 27th Colonel.

"So, may I introduce Colonel Creet of the 27th? You've heard of these, Daniel?"

Carr and O'Hare turned to find Creet immediately offering to shake the hand of both as he greeted both.

"Indeed I have, Sir. A strong addition to our Brigade. Anson will be pleased."

Lowry-Cole nodded and actually smiled.

"Well, we can make further acquaintances and introductions on the morrow. There's Captain Bairns of our Rifle Company, from the Fifth Sixtieth, but enough for today, I feel."

The pair took that to be their cue to leave and so they saluted and departed. Outside, it was O'Hare who voiced the opinion of both.

"Well, he's feeling the strain! There was the look all over him."

Carr nodded. He well understood 'the look.

"No surprise. The 4th Division lost almost 1,000 men at the main breach."

Where the 'main breach' was, needed to no further explanation for O'Hare, who instead added his own detail.

"And he was wounded at Albuera."

The response from Carr was a wry look and a long sigh.

oOo

The following morning Carr was sat in his tent, at one of the few pieces of Battalion furniture, attempting paperwork at a table that served both as desk and dining table. He was examining one of Picton's letters when Sergeant Bryce knocked on the tentpole and stood in the entrance.

"I think you'd better come out, Sir, there's quite a cavalcade coming into the camp."

Carr dropped the paper, gave a deep, heartfelt and knowledgeable sigh and followed Bryce outside. His eyes followed the worn grass that marked the central route through their camp and there, part way up, were two Redcoated Officers, one with a large bicorn hat worn 'fore and aft' and both mounted on unnecessarily large horses. Behind came a civilian riding a mule and behind him half a dozen of what could only be described as bearers, carrying a variety of bundles and luggage. One bundle so large it needed two to carry it on a pole between them. Carr did not take his eyes off the spectacle but spoke softly to Bryce.

"You'd best fetch Major O'Hare."

Carr studied the approaching group, comparing what he saw with his memory of Autumn 1809, when he had returned to England during the period of inactivity after the battle of Talavera and married his dearest Jane Perry. The two figures in front required no introduction, the most imposing being Colonel of Militia Sir Ambrose Brockenhurst MP and the other Major of Militia, St. John Slade. The Colonel's face appeared a little more bucolic than Carr remembered, probably reddened by an excess of fortified wine, but Brockenhurst remained an evidently powerful man, good looking as middle-age makes some men, but a stern face with a tight, grim mouth and staring, yet narrow, eyes, under overly dark, projecting brows. His companion was of much slighter build, although equally as tall, but what distinguished him from his companion was his expression, not aggressive as with Brockenhurst, but one of pure disdain, even contempt, for all that he perceived within eyesight, as though being in the presence of such had to be endured and only with much sufferance. His mouth described a significant downward curve, whilst his eyes peered from narrowed sockets in a pale face adorned with pale brows above which pale hair protruded down from an immaculate shako, its plate burnished bright. There was nothing in what Carr saw that gave him any comfort regarding what was to come, either immediately or in the future. When they were separated by 12 paces distance, Carr came to the attention and saluted. The return was delayed and dismissive, a wave of the riding crop. Bryce motioned the two sentries at the entrance to the Headquarters tent to run forward and hold the bridles of both horses.

Carr saw little point in being welcoming nor pleasant, but remained at attention, as Brockenhurst dismounted, handed his gloves and crop to the civilian who had been riding the mule, but who was now stood attentively just behind Brockenhurst's right shoulder. Brockenhurst then approached, wearing a grin that could only be described as one of triumph on his face, speaking the syllables of both words slowly and carefully.

"Major Carr!"

"Sir."

"So this is the 1st Battalion 105th ?"

"Sir,"

"All of them?"

"Sir."

"How many?"

"24 Officers, 558 men, Sir. I was hoping that you would be bringing some replacements. We lost many at both sieges, Sir."

Brockenhurst grinned, but with little mirth.

"Right behind me, Carr. 78 Militia, trained by me. It was all a bit of a rush, had to pack up and get myself out here, what with your Colonel Lacey wandering off like that, but they are here. As am I."

He paused to allow the threatening words spoken in a very assertive tone to sink in, before gesturing with his left forefinger over his shoulder.

"You remember Major Slade."

Carr's head moved not an inch. He continued to stare the regulation stare, over his superior Officer's left shoulder.

"I do, Sir."

However, at that moment Padraigh O'Hare arrived and only then did Carr move.

"Colonel Brockenhurst, please allow me to present our Senior Major, Padraigh O'Hare."

O'Hare made the mistake of walking forward with his hand outstretched, but Brockenhurst gave him barely a glance, before returning to Carr, leaving O'Hare in an embarrassed quandary, which he rectified by coming to attention and using the hand to salute. It was in huge contrast to the reception they received in the Divisional Headquarters of no less than their own Major-General. Brockenhurst continued with Carr, but with O'Hare as the subject.

"Irish, I presume."

Carr felt his anger rising at this curt dismissal of a genuine veteran soldier who had seen more actual, bloody and desperate action than Brockenhurst could ever imagine.

"Many of us are. Sir!"

Brockenhurst nodded dismissively.

"Just so! Now, where are my quarters?"

"I afraid there are no quarters, Sir. At least not here. Such is only allocated if we are billeted in a small town. Or larger."

A flicker of annoyance passed over Brockenhurst's face, but he soon recovered, his left hand moving to his sword hilt.

"No matter."

He turned to Slade.

"No matter, eh Slade? We'll just have to try out that tent we brought with us from England. Should do, nicely quartered up as it is."

He returned to Carr, his voice and expression curt, harsh and disdainful.

"Parade the men."

"Yes Sir, immediately, but first, Sir, may I enquire what role you intend to allocate to Major Slade?"

Brockenhurst stared hard at Carr, expecting an argument.

"An ADC to me, Carr. My aide and messenger around the place. That is to be his position within the Battalion. You regard a message spoken to you by him to be an order from me. Clear?"

"Yes Sir. I understand perfectly the status of an ADC when they arrive from our Generals. Sir."

If Brockenhurst appreciated the sarcasm in Carr's reply he did not show it.

"Full parade, Carr. Half an hour."

Brockenhurst and Slade, now walked off, followed by their horses and the bearers of their baggage. O'Hare looked at Carr.

"What in the name of Jesus, Joseph and Mary, was that all about?'

Carr looked at him with deep concern.

"I'll tell you later. Over a drink. And we'll need it!"

It was Sergeant Ellis who brought the news to the mess areas of Deakin and Davey.

"The new Colonel's arrived and I don't like the look. He wants a full parade right away."

Even as Ellis spoke the bugle was sounding 'Fall in', and men were running from all directions to form up in their ten Companies. Within a few more minutes Regimental Sergeant Major Cyrus Gibney, a huge, imposing Yorkshireman, RSM in every way, was stood before the centre of the line at the Colour Company, Number Three. He drew one deep breath.

"Parade!"

All came to 'Order arms', the butt of their weapon against their right boot.

"Paraade! Shoulder arms."

Almost as one, the weapons swung through the movements, to finish on each right shoulder. That done, Gibney turned to Brockenhurst, him just arrived and up on his horse, with Slade mounted beside him.

"Parade ready for inspection. Sir."

Brockenhurst ignored him and looked down at Carr and O'Hare, both on foot.

"We'll start with the Grenadiers, I think."

That required a slow walk to the right of the line, where stood Carravoy, out before his men, with Section Lieutenants, Royston D'Villiers and Simon Ameshurst, stood out just behind him, but before their own Sections. The slow progress began and they had not got as far as the Colour Company in the centre, before Brockenhurst made his first comment.

"They look a mess, Carr!"

Walking beside Brockenhurst's right boot, Carr could not hold back his reply.

"Sir. They have just come from a siege, barely two weeks since and then a forced march!"

The reply was another question.

"And where are their stocks?"

The question horrified Carr, for Brockenhurst to be concerned with the stiff leather collar that forced the men's heads up to a straight-ahead position and held it there.

"At a guess, Sir, in the bottom of their packs, where they stay whilst on active campaign."

"That is about to change! Next parade, stocks to be worn,"

Carr was never one to be overly concerned about the creature comforts of the men, but he well knew the discomforts that would be caused by wearing the stock and, to him, the pain and discomfort it created sapped energy which meant slower marching.

"Sir! The stock is a parade ground item. We often ask the men to march 25 miles, sometimes more, with full kit, usually 60 pounds weight, Sir. In heat! Frankly, Sir, adding to the men's discomfort makes them less effective, for us. Sir!"

Brockenhurst did not even turn towards him.

"You heard my order, Major."

The ensuing silence was broken only by the plod of the horses' hooves on the thick turf, until they came to the Light Company at the far left. Brockenhurst leaned forward in his saddle, his brows closing.

"What kind of weapon is that, which these carry?"

Anxiety grew within Carr.

"It's a Baker rifle, Sir. Now issued to all Rifle Battalions. It is more accurate for marksmen work and skirmishing, Sir."

"Who said it should replace the good old Brown Bess? You are not a Rifle Battalion. And how did you get them?"

"Our Colonel Lacey obtained them, Sir. Prior to our posting to Sicily. We used them first at Maida."

He turned to Slade.

"Sort of spoils the parade, St. John, would you not say? Looks a lot shorter than what they should be carrying. Perhaps we should do something about that. What, Slade?"

Slade leaned forward over the pommel of his saddle, his mouth narrowing into a reptilian smile.

"I'd say you have the right if it, Sir."

Carr was close to panic.

"Sir, I beg you. The Baker should remain their weapon. It is more accurate for the situation in which they meet the French. It makes them much more effective for skirmishing. On top, Sir, our Light Company are often called upon to support our Rifles because they have the Baker. It would not look good if we refuse such a request, always from a General, when we reply that we have now discarded the Baker and therefore we would be of little supportive use. Sir."

At the mention of a General's request, which it would very foolish to refuse, Brockenhurst immediately changed the subject.

"I brought a new Lieutenant out with me. Our Luttrel Bettridge. From a good family. My nephew."

"Sir?"

"He fell ill on our journey across country. We left him in some Inn two days ago. I would expect him soon and expect him to fill the gap in your Light Company, here."

The empty space before One Section was obvious and Carr could only make hopeful enquiries.

"Is he aware of Light Infantry tactics, Sir?'

"No, but he'll learn."

"With respect, Sir, would it not be preferable to move a Lieutenant from one of the Line Companies and have him learn the basics there?"

"No! And tell the men to find their stocks. Or be docked their pay!"

Carr was further horrified at such an order, but he could only turn to RSM Gibney, who appeared equally alarmed.

"Pass the word, please, RSM."

The parade broke up and as they returned to their camps there was only one topic of conversation, that of the obvious and soon to come order, that they would be required to wear the hated stock, on the next parade. Once back within their mess-area back-packs were emptied and the stiff, black leather item was retrieved, always at the bottom. It was the usually mild Zeke Saunders who passed judgement.

"Bastard! I expect to wear this if I'm up before the King or such, but not when chasing Johnny up and around the country. Does he expect us to fight still wearing this damned thing?"

The question concerned them all. The stock prevented all movement of the head; up, down and sideways.

"Johnny's Jumpin' Jacks don't have to wear such as this."

He waved it in the air, the back laces twirling round. The 'Jumping Jacks' he spoke of were the feared and very capable French Voltigeurs and Tirailleurs whom they often had to face when in action out between both armies during any serious conflict. Jed Deakin, close by, looked sadly at his own. During his own 20 odd years in the army, he had served under some martinets, fanatical about appearance, but never one who required his men to wear so restrictive a parade item when on active service. He shook his head and looked at Halfway.

"This one's special."

Halfway nodded and thrust his own stock into his pack, but now placing it near the top.

Meanwhile, in a mood that matched that of his men, Carr and O'Hare were sharing a drink, some of O'Hare's Irish whiskey. Once the spirit had been poured, O'Hare began with a question.

"I take it you've encountered him before?"

Carr drank half his glass.

"Yes. After Talavera I went back to England with Drake to get some Militia. He was their Colonel and St. John Slade the Major. Tavender was back there then and the three of them, Tavender, Brockenhurst and Jane's father, did their best to stop us marrying, me and Jane. Brockenhurst is an MP and threatened to raise the question in the House because Jane's father objected so thoroughly. I would have been required to sail back here before the question had had time to go through the House and probably been rejected or wherever, so no marriage. I would have needed to go back. Tavender wanted her instead, you remember him?"

O'Hare took a sip and grinned.

"I do! But you did marry her, so something must have transpired."

Carr's face became stern.

"Brockenhurst had some illegal scheme. I discovered that he had been requisitioning far too many cartridges for the size of his Militia, three times too much, but I didn't know to what purpose. I threatened him with a Horse Guards investigation and then told the story I had heard about some Militia Colonel who had sold military cartridges to manufacturers of game-shot. Cheap for them when they are re-cast as bird shot and lucrative for the Colonel. That Colonel got banged up. In wartime Brockenhurst could be for the gallows-dance as a saboteur or some such. He dropped his idea about the House of Commons, shut up and I got married."

O'Hare laughed.

"That's some story, but it's no surprise that he has it in for you."

Carr nodded and smiled ruefully as he finished his drink.

"Time will tell for that one."

However, the time came soon enough in the shape of St John Slade, walking boldly into their tent.

"Colonel Brockenhurst wants to see you. Right away!"

Carr looked at O'Hare and drained his glass.

"No time at all. He must mean me!"

He stood and brushed past Slade, leaving him being blankly stared at by O'Hare, until the pointlessness of remaining became painfully obvious and so he left to follow Carr, who was now far ahead and heading for an imposing canvas structure, the pegs for which were just then being finally hammered in. There was no sentry and so Carr entered to find Brockenhurst sat behind an imposing but collapsible desk. Inside was an arrangement that reminded Carr of what he had read regarding the tents of nomadic Arabs, their Sheikhs in particular; tents that were large, with screens and partitions creating at least three separate 'rooms'. He brought himself to the attention but did not salute, nor say any word, but Brockenhurst was eager to begin.

"Carr! I am your Colonel and you are my subordinate."

Carr's brows narrowed.

"There was no need to summon me here to tell me that, Sir, and occupy the time of us both!"

Brockenhurst angered.

"Insubordination such as that will land you in trouble, Carr. I am a Member and have influence at Horse Guards. You just remember that!"

With no reply from Carr, he continued.

"There is history between us, Carr. I have not forgotten that ridiculous concoction of a story that you threatened me with back in England. You may have felt successful with your pack of lies there, but it will not be so here."

A pause whilst he delivered his best hard stare.

"So, when I give you an order, you move! At your best speed, understood? With no argument."

Carr gave his disrespectful half smile, more an indifferent smirk, such as had so annoyed authority and privilege throughout his life and the effect on Brockenhurst was no different.

"Of course, Sir. What else? If we are to beat the French, there can be no delay nor any form of shilly-shallying about. Sir!"

During the pause, whilst Brockenhurst struggled with the best words to respond, Carr took the opportunity, even if Brockenhurst wished to say more.

"If that's all, Sir, I have some returns to prepare for our Brigadier, Sir William Anson. You may have heard of him. Also, our Divisional General, Sir Lowry-Cole. We stood together against shot and shell, at Maida. Sir. That was an actual battle! French Voltiguers and all! We stood against a whole Battalion of them."

With that, Carr regarded his Colonel no more, turned on his heel and marched out.

oOo

The order they had been hoping for came the next day, conveyed to Carr by the excited Nat Drake as Carr sat in the Headquarters tent, sorting paperwork into that which Bryce could deal with and that which required the attention of both himself and O'Hare. Drake and Carr were good friends, each had been the other's Best Man at their weddings and they had been comrades since the 105th came together in Taunton as the 5th Detachments, a collection of criminals, Militia and the survivors of the 9th Foot's shipwreck. Thus, there was no need for Sirs nor salutes.

"Have you heard?'

Carr was already curious at the sudden entrance.

"We're marching. Going after Marmont. He's somewhere close to Salamanca and tomorrow we're on our way. Back into Spain!"

Carr grinned ruefully.

"Oh good. Our trips there have been so diverting! Such a pleasure!"

Drake smiled at his good friend, despite the difference in their ranks, as Carr continued.

"Do you think I can assume that our good Colonel has been informed?"

"You can. I'd say you were the last to know. Being merely a Major!"

"He cannot be too happy about dismantling his canvas castle. He's only been here two days."

Drake gave an airy laugh.

"Don't worry on his account. He's got at least three servants doing that for him, one Archie Lackenham being the leader amongst that crew. A civilian."

Carr nodded and sighed and then remembered something more important.

"Your replacement Lieutenant that came out with the pair, but didn't arrive with Brockenhurst. One Luttrel Bettridge. Any sign of him?"

Drake shook his head.

"No. None."

Carr's brows came together in puzzlement.

"His name? Is that a Christian name plus surname, or a double-barrelled surname?"

Drake shook his head, his face a picture of total ignorance.

"I've no idea and finding out means talking to that odious St. John Slade. His label is Christian-name plus a surname, in case you forgot and talking to him for more than ten seconds is an offence against my religion!"

Now Carr did genuinely laugh.

"Didn't think you had much of one."

Drake immediately displayed mock umbrage.

"What are you talking about? A good Christian boy like me, who always says his prayers.

Carr grinned.

"Yes. Mostly when French shot is flying about!"

Drake's face settled into an expression of reluctant agreement.

"Yes, well. That may provide some extra incentive."

Carr smiled but then stood up and donned his tunic.

"Right, to business, getting ready to move. Have we got Gibney onto this?"

"Yes. He was the first that O'Hare told."

Carr face and voice became serious.

"Thank God for Padraigh. We are going to need what he can bring to the table. Very much."

oOo

The dawn found Henry Carr at the rear of the 105th column finally giving attention to what he had no time for the previous day. The 105th had two transport wagons for rations, supplies and ammunition and these required an inspection, but cursory was all that was required. All four Waggoneers were veteran and well knew the requirements of keeping up with a rapidly marching column, not least the well-being of their eight draught horses. The next gave him some anxiety, this being the cart of the Reverend Albright and his Assistant, Private Percival Sedgwicke. Although both were well meaning, this he knew, but that fact alone did not create confidence and he could only hope that they were ready and could immediately accompany the Battalion's departure. He found both still packing their possessions and placing cases and boxes carefully into the cart.

"Reverend Albright. Is all well? Will you be able to move with the rest of us?"

Albright spun around, as quickly as his bulk and age would allow.

"Major Carr! Hmmm, well, I can only thank you for your concern. I'm sure we will be ready at the appointed time."

He then turned to Sedgwicke.

"May I have confidence in that, Private?'

Carr knew that Sedgwicke was, if anything, the veteran of the two and he gave more credence to Sedgwicke's reply.

"Given fifteen minutes, Sir, I would say yes."

Carr nodded and moved to pass on, but Albright slightly blocked his passage and so he stopped.

"Major Carr, I have been meaning to raise this point with you for some time, in as much as I miss many of the Officer Corps at my Sunday Services. I may say the attendance of yourself would go a long way to encouraging such attendance from the remainder."

Irritation grew within Carr. He had never been much of a Believer and this would be an additional duty that Albright was suggesting to him, on top of the need to perform as two Executive Officers undertaking what had previously taken three, before Lacey's departure. He had no confidence in Brockenhurst being prepared to do his share of the administration. Nevertheless, he did not feel able to be dismissive of their kindly Reverend.

"If I can, Reverend, but you know we are about to embark on a major campaign, which will keep us all busy, and many Officers are of different persuasions. Captain Heaviside, for example, is strict Methodist and Major O'Hare a lifelong Catholic. For some, their religious persuasion will keep them from attending."

Carr hoped that would finish the discussion, but he was wrong. Albright felt there to be room for constructive discussion to overcome any differences.

"Yes, Major, but I would wish to point out that I conduct what could be very accurately described as wholly neutral, such that ...."

At this point Sedgwicke intervened. He appreciated the urgency of the moment and well knew Albright's failure to understand the question of priorities.

"I'm sure the Major would wish to discuss this further, Sir, but as he says, we are soon to depart and must first look to our own more earthly affairs. Sir."

Albright's face immediately registered his confusion, which Carr took to be his chance and so a nod to Albright and then one to Private Sedgwicke for his helpful understanding, sent him on his way. Sedgwicke then brought his Officer fully to the issue at hand.

"Now, Sir. I must see to our mules, if you could just finish the last of your packing, then the cart is loaded and ready and then we are in the Major's good books. We would not want to delay departure or, even worse, be left behind."

Albright nodded agreement and bumbled off to see Carr stood quite near, but he attempted no more discussion because Eirin was approaching the cart, expecting a place for the coming journey. The party passed Carr quite close, the patient being helped by Bridie and Nellie and what came next from the usually 'stuffshirt' Carr, astonished them both.

"I hope the term with your daughter is progressing well, Mrs Mulcahy?"

Whilst still supporting Eirin, Bridie did her best to curtsy.

"Well as can be expected, your Honour, we thank you for your concern."

"She rides in the Reverend's cart, I take it."

"She does, Sir, and grateful we are to the Reverend. Good kind man that he is."

"And Surgeon Pearce. Had he been in attendance?"

"He has, Sir, and he is as well pleased as can be expected."

"Indeed! Well, if there is any way that you think I can help, you only have to ask. Please do not hesitate. You will call upon me, will you not?"

More astonishment registered on the faces of all three, but it was quickly hidden, and it was Nellie who this time replied.

"That's the kindest thought, Major Carr, Sir, but we do hope to get through this with the littlest bother to your good self. And others, of course. Tis only the birthing of a bairn, after all."

Carr grinned at the dismissive comment, so then, now boldened, she felt able to ask a question.

"Do you expect us to be a long time about this new business, your Honour? Goin' again into Spain."

"I do, Mrs. Nicholls. It could be that we will never be back here again!"

"A Blessing on that, Sir, and our true thanks to you."

Carr nodded and walked on, this time along the column of Followers and what he saw gave him confidence. He appreciated what they did for the Battalion, all there now being ready to move and all women much festooned, as were the children, with back-packs, pots, pans, skillets and boxes. Satisfied, Carr returned to the head of the column. Bugles were sounding for 'column of march'.

The standard twenty-mile march brought them to the walls of Cuidad Rodrigo and joyous celebrations could be seen on the walls, with British and Spanish flags flying from every high point. Carr and O'Hare now riding, out of choice remaining significantly behind Brockenhurst and Slade, saw fit to remark on which they saw.

"Seems our appearance has cheered them up, Padraigh."

O'Hare gave a broad smile.

"And no wonder. They've seen Marmont's whole army marching by within cannon-shot, knowing he could be willing to give the walls a try, with us thoroughly occupied down South."

Soon they were crossing the Agueda by the long, low bridge, but the parapet was hidden behind cheering crowds. Then they were marching along the front of the battlements, the sight of these and the slopes either side, bringing back vivid memories of one February night of that year. Their column was turned off the road by a well-mounted and well-helmeted Provost and they broke column in the wide fields beyond to the North. Their camp was hardly set up, when an ADC arrived with a message for Brockenhurst, who broke the seal, read the brief contents and showed it to Slade.

"Tell Carr and O'Hare. We'll need them to show us where this San Francisco place is. Make that clear."

The note was an invitation from their Brigadier Sir William Anson, for his Colonels and Majors to dine with him that evening. In response, Carr and O'Hare presented themselves at Brockenhurst's tent, where both he and Slade were waiting. There was no greeting, instead a blunt question.

"You know the way?"

O'Hare answered.

"We do, only too well."

The significance of the last words brought no response and so Carr and O'Hare walked ahead, wishing for no form of interaction.

Anson's Headquarters was a substantial house, it little damaged from the recent siege, sited opposite the Convent, which had now sprung to life despite unrepaired damage, judging by the chanting voices of the Nuns emanating from the lower side windows as they approached. Inside the Headquarters building they handed over their gloves and shakoes to be immediately offered a glass of white wine. Both Carr and O'Hare found the light wine quite refreshing, but one swallow caused St. John Slade's face to screw up in distaste and Brockenhurst held his glass up to the light. Carr and O'Hare walked further in and presented themselves to their Brigadier. As the Senior, O'Hare did the introductions as this was the first time they had met with Anson.

"Sir William. May we introduce ourselves. I am Major Padraigh O'Hare, and this is Major Henry Carr. Of the 105th, Sir."

Anson was a thick-set man, above average height, perhaps early fifties but his wide face broke into a welcoming grin as he vigorously shook the hands of both.

"The 105th! The old 'Rag and Bone Boys', 'Wearers of the Green', what!"

Carr grinned.

"Some call us that, Sir."

Anson patted Carr on the arm.

"And not unkindly, that I know. Now ...."

He turned to an ADC.

"Phelps! See that these two get a drink. Something better than that infant's piss they first had."

He turned back to Carr and O'Hare, nodding vigorously.

"Enjoy your meal here. I feel we're in for the long haul. There won't be many like it, if I'm any judge of the coming campaign."

Carr grinned and nodded.

"Not for the first time, Sir."

As they moved away they found their passage blocked by Brockenhurst and Slade.

"I would have thought that you would have had the good manners to introduce us, Carr!"

Carr stared straight back.

"Well yes and no, Sir. You see, this is our first time of meeting our Brigadier ourselves, and you did both seem somewhat pre-occupied with the issue of the wine."

With that he bowed and walked on to make a straight line for Colonel Creet of the 27th, there to be introduced to Captain Thomas Bairns in the contrasting uniform of the 60th Rifles. The conversation was pleasant and mostly professional, when the gong sounded and they all entered a square room, with high ceiling but no paintings, merely the sign of what had been their places on the wall, this a slightly darker shade to the pale distemper. The room showed no signs of being any kind of family room and so Carr turned to Creet.

"Sir. What was this place?"

"Some kind of gallery, I believe, but all artwork now long removed and built into the collection of some French General. Perhaps even Boney's brother, the King of Spain, El Rey Joseph himself."

Carr took his place and studied the walls and their dark patches further. This was his first appreciation of French looting and plundering of Spanish artistic valuables, a practice that the French had been indulging in since first they had marched into Spain. Then he lowered his gaze to see that Brockenhurst and Slade were directly opposite, but the table was wide and so he averted his eyes and engaged Bairns in conversation about the coastline and villages of North Wales.

The food was Spanish, fish, chicken and sausage with a kind of fruit custard to follow. The port and nuts circulated, then Anson clinked his glass.

"Gentlemen. The Loyal Toast."

He looked at Bairns.

"Captain! I feel that must be you."

Bairns grinned and stood, because as the most junior Officer present, he was required to make the toast.

"Sirs. Please charge your glasses."

The port decanters slid around at great pace to the necessary diner and Bairns raised his glass and all stood.

"The Loyal Toast."

At this prompt, all stood.

"Gentlemen. The King."

The response was made and all drank to then sit and now the conversation could now become professional, in their case military. St. John Slade immediately threw out a question to no-one in particular.

"Who are all those women and children that followed us today. Local whores and beggars? I found them quite distasteful."

It was a less than accurate description of his true feelings, because what he saw at the rear of their column, when he took himself there, appalled him; all coarse, chattering women, heavily clothed and shod, all with complexions tanned to the shade of leather, something quite beyond his experience. It was O'Hare who answered first, motivated by anger at the terms he had used, but he remained calm and factual.

"We call them Followers, Major, because that is what they do, follow the Battalion almost wherever we go. All have a husband amongst our ranks, or Father, in some cases. They cook, sew, mend and tend. To the wounded, that is. I would go so far as to say we could not function without them. As you will probably find out for yourself, in time."

He turned to Carr, who was equally angry.

"Anything to add, Major?"

"Just this. At Talavera many were killed whilst tending the wounded right behind our firing line. Behind the feet of our men as they loaded and fired. At Vimeiro many of our wounded were dragged to safety by them running forward and pulling them back between the French assaults. There's many as are still alive because of their knowledge of how to stem blood flow."

He paused.

"So, I'll leave it to you, now, Major, to decide if whores and beggars are the best terms to apply. I personally have much appreciation and respect for them. For them all, I would add. Often they endure hardships beyond those of our own, them being so much more vulnerable. If you can bring yourself to do it, you would do well to enquire about the retreat to Coruna."

Slade could now feel the looks of disapproval being delivered in his direction by all within earshot, but Brockenhurst came to his rescue by changing the subject.

"I'm told that this summer will be a time of 'serious conclusion', meaning, I take it, the end of the war."

It was Creet, sat alongside O'Hare, who answered.

"I feel you have been badly informed, Sir Ambrose. This will not end the war, even if we significantly beat Marmont in the coming months. The French have almost a quarter of a million men in Spain, whilst we have about 70,000, up to 100,000 if you count the Spanish who are our Allies, but, I fear, to little effect. They put army after army into the field, credit them for that, but usually with little success."

He allowed the numbers to sink in.

"If we beat Marmont, even crush him, there are plenty more French to come against us, and plenty more beyond the Pyrenees."

Brockenhurst's brows narrowed. There was worry behind his eyes.

"And if they beat us?"

Creet grinned.

"Then it's back to Torres Vedras! If we can get back down there in time."

Again the pause.

"Or a sea evacuation, as was after Coruna."

He turned to O'Hare.

"You saw a bit of that, O'Hare? Didn't you?'

O'Hare nodded.

"Indeed! A bit too much. Both myself and Major Carr."

A flicker of worry passed over the faces of both Brockenhurst and Slade, until it was broken by a Colonel three places up.

"Brockenhurst! The port lies with you!"

Gratefully, Sir Ambrose slid the decanter in the correct direction.

Meanwhile, in the 105th camping ground, whilst their Officers dined in comfort and splendour, the rank and file of the 105th were making serious use of goose-grease. All needed some such salve to ease the chaffing from the first day of wearing their stocks whilst on the march.

oOo

The long and far from silent infantry column, wound its way around the North of Cuidad Rodrigo, musically, in that Wellington had ordered all the bands to play. All the citizens were cheering for all they were worth and the local Bishop had organised a choir to sing hymns of thanks and praise to all things Spiritual, as Wellington's men marched rhythmically onto the Salamanca highway and away from the town. However, it was far from the case for the Light Cavalry of Brigadiers George Anson and Victor Alten. Both Brigades had been required to leave long before dawn and scout ahead, acting as a mobile and responsive screen, the less the French knew of Wellington leaving Cuidad Rodrigo the better. Theirs was a more solitary progress as the first two Squadrons of the 16th eased their way forward, both maintaining sight of each other across a road that ran Eastwards through the tangle of wooded hills to the North of the main Salamanca 'chausee'. Oakwood's Squadron were on the Northern side and it was himself who called a halt when a column of Ordenanza emerged from the trees some two hundred yards ahead. It was Cornet Willoughby Carr who first managed some recognition as the column trotted closer.

"That's Julian Sanchez himself, Sir. 'El Charro' as he is often called. I saw him back in May 1811. I know that because it was just before Fuentes D'Onoro. He came up through Barba del Puerco, huge gorge that is, which separated us from.........."

Oakwood lost patience.

"Yes Willoughby. Some other time. You are certain of who they are, now? This isn't some French ruse?"

"Oh no Sir. That's him. Same sheepskin, I'd say, but it looks as if he's wearing a French hat, but back to front, it looks like."

Oakwood held his men steady in column as Sanchez and his men approached. The hat on the Ordenanza's head was indeed odd, the badge at the back, but their attention was soon distracted by a predatory smile from brilliant white teeth beneath an impressive black moustache. Above this, in a dark brown face, his eyes glinted black/brown, piercing and cheerless. This time, in contrast to 1811, he had enough English to speak for himself.

"Hola inglés! I have French dog for you!"

He turned to wave his arm forward and a rider broke out of the column, pulling a French horse with a Dragoon slumped over the saddle.

The horse was led up to Oakwood and the reins handed over, at which point the Dragoon slid off the saddle and onto the ground. Carr immediately dismounted, as did Baxter and Makepeace and they turned the Frenchman over to see a gaping wound, probably a sword cut, in the side of his head. Sanchez, totally unconcerned that the Frenchman may now be dead from his fall, pointed down at him.

"He has letters, there in saddle. We not kill because you like to ask of him, si?"

Oakwood nodded.

"Our thanks, Senor Sanchez, for both the letters and the prisoner."

Sanchez nodded and swung round his horse, but he did not ride off immediately, instead he turned in his saddle to again look at Oakwood.

"This time we send them out, si? Esta peste francesa!"

Oakwood had no idea what the final words meant, but he was sure it was motivated by extreme hatred of the French, however, whilst Oakwood considered, El Charro was gone and his men with him. Meanwhile Carr was giving the Frenchman some water and bathing his wound. Baxter produced a bandage and that was soon applied, such that the man could sit up. Oakwood, meanwhile had opened the French saddlebags to extract a bundle of papers. Then Tavender arrived from the far side.

"What have we here?"

"A French courier, captured by the Ordenanza. Both him and some papers. We have to get them back."

Tavender looked down at the man, now sat with his head between his knees.

"Right. I'll do that. Get him back on his horse."

Oakwood looked at him intently.

"That's not wise. You are needed to command your Squadron. Carr here has one of our best mounts, he can take him back with a Sergeant. You should remain here, Lucius. Who knows what we will meet next and, anyway, Anson is out with us and he will be more than curious as to why you left your whole Squadron, just to take back a prisoner."

Oakwood had voiced the obvious arguments, but he well knew Tavender's motive. To draw favourable attention to himself as the deliverer of a valuable captive and some even more valuable French despatches, but he had not finished.

"Besides, he's my prisoner!"

Tavender looked daggers at Oakwood, but, although he was the Senior Captain of the 16th, Oakwood held sway for matters involving his own Squadron. Tavender nodded curtly, his face black from ill temper and he spurred his horse away. Oakwood turned to Carr, but did not fail to notice the grins of approval from his men sat behind, who had heard every word.

"Right Willloughby. Get him on his horse, take Baxter with you and get him back to the main road. You'll find our main column there, I feel sure."

Then his voice hardened.

"Do not come back out to try and find us. Stay until we come back in, which I suspect will be this evening, when we need to report."

With that he waved his men forward, leaving Baxter and Carr to hoist the man onto his horse, but he was plainly unsteady, his face a sickly white and his wound still bleeding beneath the bandage. Another swallow of water helped, then Baxter mounted his own horse.

"Best I take the reins, Sir, in case this charger decides to bolt. Best if you ride alongside, Sir. Keep him steady like."

Carr handed him the reins, mounted his own horse and placed himself alongside. They began a slow walk, then Carr turned to examine the condition of the Frenchman who, to Carr's surprise, began speaking.

"I am grateful to you both."

"You speak English!"

"I do. I spent some time as a youth in your city of Chester."

Carr's eyebrows shot up.

"Chester! I know it well. My home is not too far from there."

The result was a weak smile.

"Yes, and I must say again how grateful I am to you."

Carr said nothing as to why he should be so grateful, because he knew well enough what usually happened to French couriers. Instead, he grasped the man's arm to ensure he remained in the saddle. There were several miles to go, which he filled with endless prattle about Chester and its County, whilst the Frenchman remained in a sink of despair knowing that he had been captured and that his precious despatches were now in enemy hands.

At that moment, back in the main column on the chausee, the 105th Foot knew well enough who their enemy was, their new Colonel, a name that was cursed with every mile that they paced out beyond Cuidad Rodrigo and also with every sore chafe their almost new stocks gave to their necks. So, it came as both a surprise and a relief when, early afternoon, they were brought to a halt alongside a large village that seemed to have a road running to and from it in every direction. Their Brigadier William Anson rode back and stopped at the 105th group of Officers.

"We pause here. Could be for two or three days. The Peer is not happy that he knows enough about Johnny's doings before he goes any further and so he's waiting for whatever our Lights and the Guerrillas can find out."

Carr overheard all and turned to Carravoy, marching just behind. He pointed to an inviting meadow which he wished to claim before any other Battalion did.

"Charles. Lead them off over there. Beyond that stream. Tell Gibney to get things organised."

There was no salute from Carravoy in response, but Carr did not expect one and so he turned away. He had a duty to his Colonel, distasteful as it was, to await any of his requirements that may apply to him at that moment. However, from Brockenhurst there came nothing, rather he was looking around somewhat bemusedly himself, rather surprised at the speed with which the whole army column was breaking up and spreading out and he then turned around to see his own command disappearing into the distance. However, all seemed well enough and so he turned back towards his servant close by, the mysterious Lackenham.

"Lackenham! Get our tent up from the baggage at the rear. We'll have it set up."

As Lackenham hurried his mule away, Carr decided that Brockenhurst had no real concerns and so he turned his own mount to see about his own domestic affairs and soon the efficient Sergeant Bryce had all in place such that Carr and O'Hare were quickly at their leisure outside their own tent with no delay and O'Hare was puffing contentedly on his pipe.

"A pause for intelligence! Is that what this is about?"

Carr stretched back in his chair.

"Whatever it may be, it suits me just perfectly, provided we can keep out of our good Colonel's doings and his concerns."

The following day, mid-morning saw the pair sat in the same chairs outside the same tent, but this time more diverted, as remarked on by O'Hare.

"Seems like our Chief's disposing of his army."

The sight before them was the popular Lieutenant General Hill, with a full Staff, marching South with two Brigades. Carr folded his arms and remarked further on Wellington's strategy.

"He's got Graham up North with the 1st and 6th Divisions. Grand strategy seems to be the order of the moment."

However, Battalion minutiae soon intervened on their sojourn with the arrival of Sergeant Bryce.

"Sirs, you'd best come. There's an addition to the usual ration wagons."

Both stood and walked to where they could see the newly arrived transport, but there were at least two extra. On the way, Bryce handed a letter to O'Hare, as it was addressed to him. O'Hare broke the seal, read it, grinned and then handed it to Carr, producing the same response, with the addition of "The Old Devil."

He turned to Bryce.

"Get Captain Drake and John Davey."

The covers were being thrown back when the pair arrived to find several long boxes, one of which was opened to reveal racks of Baker rifles. One was handed down by the Waggoneer to Carr who handed it to Davey.

"Compliments of our old Colonel, Davey. A new pattern, so he informs us. What do you think?"

Davey took the weapon, examined it briefly, before bringing it up to his shoulder to sight along the barrel. He lowered it and smiled.

"They've dropped the stock, Sir. It feels better and gives a better sighting."

He looked again at the lock and then down the barrel.

"The lock looks different and there's extra rifling."

He looked at Drake, then back to Carr.

"A better weapon, Sir."

Carr grinned.

"Right. That one's yours. Get a service kit before you go."

He turned to Drake.

"Nat, get these given out and the old one's collected. Do it quietly, I don't need to tell you why."

As Drake and Davey hurried off to organise their Company to receive such a gift from their old Colonel, O'Hare and Carr walked back to their tent, when O'Hare looked at Carr, his voice more than a little accusing.

"Do it quietly and I don't need to tell you why!"

Carr's face became serious.

"Yes, and so do you. Brockenhurst has no need to know. Unless it's on a man's shoulder or at 'present arms', he wouldn't know a Baker from a broomstick! On top, anything from Lacey, Brockenhurst is liable to tip over a cliff."

Within an hour all of Drake's Light Company had the new pattern Baker, but Drake was in a quandary as it what to do with the old rifles, all now stacked in groups of six close to his tent. Such should not be wasted and, remembering 'do it quietly' he took himself to the Grenadier camp and approached Captain Lord Charles Carravoy.

"Charles! Up to you, of course, but mine have been given new Baker rifles. Would you like yours to have the old. Still good, of course."

The vehement response was immediate, but, seeing as this was Carravoy, somewhat predictable. The Lord pulled himself up to his full height, with his hands clasped behind his back. He rose once on the balls of his feet before speaking.

"So, you think it desirable that my Company, the Grenadier, should be armed with your cast-offs! I think not, Captain Drake."

Lieutenant Ameshurst was stood listening and his face dissolved in shock and surprise, such that there came an outburst that was almost insubordinate.

"Sir! The whole army knows the Baker to be a better weapon. The men would like it, Sir."

Carravoy turned on him.

"We are Grenadiers! Shock troops, trained for assault, not to go jumping about in the space between opposing forces. The Brown Bess with a bayonet is perfectly adequate for us. That's final!"

Drake took a step back, somewhat surprised himself at the intensity of Carravoy's refusal.

"Very well, Charles. It's just that I thought I'd give you the first offer."

The reply was a curt nod and so Drake hurried off to Reginald Charters of Two Company, who could not say yes quick enough.

The following day, Deakin and Davey walked into their mess area with two rabbits and a hare, trapped in the fields alongside the forest. Once there, Deakin stood in the centre, very perplexed.

"Where's the women."

Zeke Saunders looked up from reinforcing the stitching on his French backpack.

"Taking a bath in the river upstream. Our Anson organised it for them, a long way upstream."

Deakin grinned ruefully.

"And where's Tom Miles?"

A figure rolled over from behind two boxes.

"I be yer, thanks very much, and I know what you'm both thinkin' an' you'm wrong! I b'ain't one as goes peerin' at the womenfolk from the bushes when they goes off to take a wash. I'll thank you to know that, Colour Sergeant Deakin!"

Deakin threw his tobacco pouch at him.

"All right, all right, don't get too far up on your high horse! Here, have some of that. Thing is, we all knows where the women are. 'Specially those as is single, and there's a fair number of they, after Badajoz. So, as often as not, that's where we'n most likely to find thee!"

Miles, genuinely offended, helped himself to a big slug of tobacco and crammed it into his pipe, but still with more to say.

"That's as may be, but not in that way, sneakin' up when they all gets a chance to have a good wash, which only comes once in a blue moon!"

As the pouch was tossed back, his face showed that his irritable nature had not been wholly appeased, but Jed Deakin was so well used to Tom Miles that he chuckled slightly to himself before replying.

"So, don't you tell me that you've not thought of hitchin' up with one of our widows. You knows the way it works as well as I do."

Before Miles could answer, Saunders spoke again.

"Perhaps, but there's his reputation stood in the way! I'd say that 'tis only us as've got the patience to put up with him."

Now thoroughly out of sorts, Miles sat on a pile of logs and blew out a huge cloud of smoke. At that point he was hit by a spare length of Spanish sausage that Saunders had thrown at him.

"There! That you eat, not smoke."

Somewhat appeased by the gesture, Miles took a bite, then added some army biscuit. The sight of his Sergeant and Corporal grinning indulgently at him, did heal his sorely wounded self-appreciation a little further.

oOo

Richard Shakeshaft opened his diary to record the entry for that day and it once more occurred to him that it would be the same as that for the last two entries; 'Camped at Santi Spiritus'. On this occasion he felt the need to at least add something that would make this day, the 15th June, a little different. "All pleased to hear that General Hill has captured the bridge at Almarez. Now we have better links with our forces in the South. All hope to move forward soon."

Early the following morning, events were in motion that would grant his wish, the same wish that was dwelling with many others. Lowry-Cole had called all his Senior Officers together, senior down as far as Senior Major and for that reason O'Hare was stood at the back of the town Church, whilst all Colonels and Brigadiers were allowed to sit. The arrival of Lowry-Cole distracted him from a comparison of Spanish churches, their sumptuousness in marked contrast to the equally devout, but practically sparse by comparison, Catholic places of worship that he had left behind in Ireland. Lowry-Cole stood at The Crossing, the join of the aisle, the transept and the chancel. Behind, sat a Priest, presumably somewhat fearful as to what harm may transpire in his Church from so many 'not of the Faith', all now crowding his pews. However, Lowry-Cole wasted no time and O'Hare thought he looked brighter and simply less 'worn down.'

"Some captured despatches were brought in some days ago. All were in cipher, but there's an Officer at Headquarters back in Cuidad, a Captain Scovell, to whom we must give all credit, he de-ciphered the lot and we now know that Marmont is isolated. Soult is where Albuera has pushed him, down South and El Rey Joseph Bonaparte wants Marmont to operate more up North, but that he is refusing to do so, therefore, as far as El Rey is concerned, Marmont can fetch for himself, he's on his own. However, I must point out, he is still possesses a substantial force of veterans."

He paused in order to give extra weight to his next words.

"So, tomorrow make preparations, because the following day, 17th June, we move on Salamanca. An important day! The initiative is with us, a last."

Then he looked around the 'congregation'.

"For those of you new to Spain, be informed. June in Castille and Leon, where we are, is closer to an African desert than anything we have at home. Prepare your men for such."

His salute was the signal to dismiss, which some returned, including O'Hare, who left the church quickly, not wishing to accompany Brockenhurst back to the 105th camp. Once in their Headquarters tent, O'Hare found Carr, tunic off, shirt unbuttoned and enjoying morning coffee and rolls.

"We're going. Tomorrow."

Carr poured a cup for O'Hare.

"To Salamanca?"

O'Hare nodded.

"And he's warned us about the heat."

At that moment Brockenhurst burst in and saw O'Hare with Carr. He stared at O'Hare, but gave not a glance to Carr.

"You've told him?"

O'Hare could only assume that the 'him' referred to Carr.

"Sir."

"Right. I leave the arrangements to you both."

With that he was gone and the tent-flaps, by gravity, closed behind him. Neither of the pair said another word, they simply shook their heads for a few moments, in disbelief, if not despair, before finishing their food and drink, then they took themselves off to their own tents to make their own preparations. Once in his tent, Lackenham handed Brockenhurst a letter, unsealed. It was quickly unfolded to find that it came from the Battalion Surgeon, George Pearce. He had heard about the order for the men to wear their stocks and he urged Brockenhurst to rescind the order. He was concerned over the possibility of losing men because of heatstroke. Brockenhurst screwed it up and threw it on the cooking fire outside.

Orders for arrangements were not required for a Regiment as veteran as the 105th, all that was required was some warning and all Sergeants and most Captains and Lieutenants would make the inspections. Therefore, to that end, Light Company Senior Sergeant Ethan Ellis arrived in the mess area of John Davey soon after breakfast, some of which was still in the pot, as leftovers, and Bridie spoke to him before he could say a word.

"Ethan, have you eaten at all well, this breakfast?"

He shook his head and immediately Bridie held out her hand for his plate, so he reached around and pulled it off his backpack. Bridie spooned out a portion and he turned to face Davey and Saunders, speaking between mouthfuls.

"We're on the road tomorrow. You've heard?"

Both nodded, but Davey replied.

"We have."

"Any worries?"

"No, we'll be ready."

Ellis nodded and turned to Jed Deakin, sat by his own fire with Bridie, toddler Jed, who was Eirin's firstborn, fathered by an Officer now dead, and Nellie's three daughters.

"Jed have you heard? New boots have arrived."

Deakin looked up.

"I've not! Best get ours over then, for the issue."

They moved amongst the men of their Companies, Ellis around the Light and Deakin around the Colour and soon there was a long, but quickly moving queue at a wagon where pairs of boots were given out, but with no reference to shoe size. It was not long before Joe Pike stood with Tom Miles, each now with a pair of boots in their hands, and they used the wagon as a prop whilst they tried them on. Miles was content with the fit, but Pike was not.

"They're too big, Tom."

Miles rapidly became impatient with his young messmate.

"Well, you knows what to do! Go and do some swappin'! Find a cove as is bigger'n you and probably needs a larger pair."

Resigned and disappointed, Pike did as he was bid and soon he did find a Grenadier who found Pike's pair a perfect fit, but it required two more exchanges before Pike achieved anything like the same. Boots now on their feet, they joined the others and returned to their camp to find Nellie just arriving back from the meat ration issue and in a very bad temper.

"That Betty Barker! I'll swing for her, so I will. She'll not let up, always saying that we gets better because of some scheme of signalling to get a good piece from the Sergeant as is doin' the issue."

The 'piece' of salt beef was unwrapped from her apron and showed to Bridie, whose face showed that she was none too impressed with the quality, scheme or no scheme. However, Nellie had not yet finished her invective.

"She's a cow, so she is. A rotten, moaning miserable cow, as won't let up."

Bridie immediately spoke in support of her good friend.

"That she is! And she's not Barker no more, although she may be church married to that gobshite Neet, but he's deserted. Gone! She's took up with a Corporal in Number Four. Sure, the name escapes me!"

All around had been listening and all that had heard, laughed softly and shook their heads. The verdict spoken by Jed Deakin.

"A Corporal in Four! Well, all the good luck from all the Saints to him!"

However, the atmosphere reversed again, when Bert Bryce arrived in their mess area.

"Letter for John."

The small, grey/white letter was handed to John Davey and he pulled it open, breaking the seal. The writing was neat and well ordered, but most of it unintelligible to the half literate Davey.

"Where's John?"

It was Bridie who knew.

"Back with Eirin and Parson, at the wagon."

Both were quickly summoned by Nellie's Violet and the letter was given to Byford to read. A letter from Tilly, John Davey's 'adopted' daughter even though he was not married to her Mother, Molly, was a major event for both mess groups. Both were back in Gloucestershire, on a small holding with John Davey's Mother, housing his 'wife' Molly, Davey's new son, John, and Joe Pike's wife, Mary and their son Thomas. Such a letter halted most activities and mere concerns for new boots and the quality of rations were no exceptions. Tilly had been taught to read and write by Sedgwick, hence his presence there, but it was John Byford who was reading it out, not a long communication, because the army forbade anything too bulky.

Dear John,

We would all like you to write as soon as you can. We have heard about the terrible battles and all of us are very worried that you are all right and all my old friends and uncles there with you. We were glad to hear that Zeke has got married and that Eirin is expecting. We hope that all is going well there and you are getting enough food. Our little smallholding is doing well with us selling eggs and chickens at the local market. Pigs too are bringing in useful coin. A merchant is happy to buy from us and he takes what we can sell him to Gloucester. Your son John is growing up and is a good runner, especially after he has been stealing apples. He goes to Sunday School and the lady there is learning him his letters. Me, I go to school every day in Cirencester. Our new Vicar, the Reverend Ledley has persuaded our Squire to help with the fees and the Reverend funds the rest. We are all well, even though a fever was going round the village, which carried some off, but it didn't come near us. I have to finish now, space is running out, but just to say that there is a home waiting for you, John and any of your good friends when this horrid war finally ends. Love to you, and to all there with you. May God keep you safe and return you to us whole and well.

Tilly.

The last sentences created a profound silence that lasted several seconds, as Byford lowered the letter, in a silence broken only by quick sobs and long, deep sighs as the words conjured images of a rural home, far from any warfare. Byford folded the paper and handed it to John Davey, who immediately slipped it into his tunic pocket. Then Gibney's broad Yorkshire tones brought them back to the present. Even he had halted as he passed by knowing this was a letter from Tilly.

"Raht! Let's all be about what needs adoin' of. Dawn will see us out of here. And it's stocks still, tha' knows. Me an' all."

The following day was already hot when the bugles sounded early for 'column of march'. The 105th were formed and ready on the main road, behind the 27th and Carr and O'Hare were bestride their horses behind Brockenhurst and Slade, when the former turned around to O'Hare.

"Have the men 'left face'!

The order was clear, if patently absurd, given that they could be required to move off at any time, but O'Hare had no choice but to obey and so he turned to Gibney.

"Left face."

The order was bellowed out and all spun smartly to their left. With that, Brockenhurst and Slade rode slowly down the ranks, examining each Company. They passed the first, the Grenadiers, then they came to the Colour Company, second in the column. Once there, Slade dismounted and entered the ranks to insert his middle finger down behind the stock of several men. He then looked up at Brockenhurst.

"Too slack! All of them!"

Brockenhurst's face angered, but the order was being called out down the column to move off. Gibney quickly gave the order to 'right face' and the 105th turned again and marched off. Soon all were feeling the heat, Carr and O'Hare included, even though mounted, the thick serge of their tunics quickly turning into a very uncomfortable source of warmth that sent beads of sweat down their backs and down their faces. Jed Deakin, marching behind his Captain Joshua Heaviside and his Lieutenant Lionel Farquarson, with Toby Halfway immediately behind him, were all soon making use of their canteens. He could feel the sweat running down inside his own stock and soreness was growing under his chin.

"At this rate, Tobe, we'n goin' to have men falling out from the heat. Losin' men afore we've even fired a shot."

Halfway took a meagre swallow from his canteen before answering.

"Sun stroke, does they call it? Makes sense. We'll soon be callin' it that ourselves, when lads starts to keel over."

Marching not far ahead, their Captain, the popular, even if ever lugubrious, Joshua Heaviside, felt anger rising within himself. As a Captain, his uniform had merely a stiff collar, but stocky and enduring as he was, he knew that Deakin was speaking the truth, especially as the rate of march was far from leisurely. He was badly feeling the heat himself, with his own backpack as an extra source of discomfort. It was common and well known throughout the Regiment, that with him, any comment on any situation usually came in the form of a Bible quote, and this was no different, in fact, this time there came two, spoken more to himself than to any audience.

"Whoever sows injustice will reap calamity and the rod of his fury will fail. Proverbs, 22, 8."

They marched on, but Heaviside was not content. There came forth another, this even more condemnatory in his fiercely Methodist mind.

"The fear of the Lord is the beginning of knowledge, fools despise wisdom and instruction. Proverbs, 1, 7."

Deakin, who had overheard, turned to look at RSM Gibney, marching in his place immediately alongside the Colour Party.

"Seems our Captain is none too happy with how things is goin', Sar' Major. But this b'ain't good!"

Gibney had never, in all his years as a soldier, made any criticism of any superior Officer, either by word or gesture and he did not do so now. However, he did look at Deakin with an expression that thoroughly conveyed what he would not put into words, that he was in total agreement, as one veteran soldier to another.

Three hours of marching saw the Regiments ahead coming to a halt and so Brockenhurst held up his hand for the 105th to halt also. O'Hare was only too aware of the discomfort of the men and called out in the hope of giving respite as quickly as possible.

"Fall out, Sir?"

Brockenhurst turned.

"Yes, but Colour Company to stand fast."

Again, O'Hare had no choice and he turned his horse back to place himself beside the ranks of the Colour Company as the order to 'Fall out', was given, but O'Hare had a counter-order.

"Colour Company. Stand fast!"

Then Brockenhurst and Slade arrived and Brockenhurst began to 'put things right', or at least as he saw it.

"Each man to tighten the stock strings of the man in front!"

It being a flogging offence to disobey, each man began the hateful task of re-lacing the stock of the man in front. This had gone on for over a minute when Lowry-Cole cantered up with his full Staff, concerned that one of his Companies was still on the road. When he saw what was taking place, he rose up on his stirrups and turned to Brockenhurst, his face thunderous.

"What the Devil is this Colonel? Have you gone mad?"

Brockenhurst was given no time to answer.

"This is insane! Parade stocks are not to be worn on campaign. Not, do you hear me? Not at any time, even in chilly weather, never mind this heat."

He fixed Brockenhurst with a withering look.

"Give the order! This instant!"

Brockenhurst's face looked as though his head were about to explode.

"I am a Member of Parliament and well known in Horse Guards."

It was Lowry-Cole who exploded.

"I do not give one good Goddamn who you are or who you know. You are my subordinate, I mere Colonel in my Division and I have given you an order."

Brockenhurst could not bring himself to give the order but he knew who could.

"Slade!"

At less than a shout, Slade gave the order.

"Remove stocks and fall out."

Throughout the Company the men that were once lacing were now unlacing and soon there was not one black leather object to the seen, all had disappeared from the necks of the 105th. That evening, after their

20 odd miles of marching, in final camp for the night, songs were quickly composed and sung or chanted in praise of 'good old Gally Lowry-Cole', but perhaps one of the better was composed by John Byford;

"Come and sing a song for old Lowry-Cole.
Let all that's here now bless his soul.
Our stocks was on, but now they're gone,
'Cos good old Lowry said, "That's wrong!"

This was sung to the Regimental tune of Bright Camp, accompanied by Tom Miles on the Jew's Harp and Len Bailey on the 'spoons', but it was sung loudest and longest around the mess-fires closest to Brockenhurst's Bedouin palace. However, perhaps the final word came from Captain Joshua Heaviside as he spoke his evening prayer into the sunset, kneeling before his plain cross and the images of his wife and two daughters.

"A wise man's heart inclines him to the right, but a fool's heart to the left. Ecclesiates 10, verse 2."

His prayer said and judgment made, he took himself off to his tent, unlike many, erected in the centre of his Company.

The following day brought no change in the pace of their march, nor in the direction, but Carr and O'Hare, both mounted were afforded a better view to either side and O'Hare voiced the thoughts of both.

"So, he's made further dispositions and it seems we are the centre column!"

Carr nodded.

"Lucky us! It means we keep to the best road."

Seen in the distance across the expanse of the plain, under the arching blue sky, both to their left and their right were columns of Redcoats, Heavy Cavalry and artillery. O'Hare spoke further of what he knew, pointing left.

"That's Picton out there!"

Carr turned towards him, his face blank.

"Fine, as long as I'm over here. So that must be Graham out over there."

He pointed right to a similar column in the distance, all now keeping pace with each other.

"And we are under? Not that anyone tells us too much."

"Beresford. With the Light Division in the lead."

"As he chooses, but we must stop for water soon. If the Peer has half a brain, he'll call the halts at water, as though we were crossing a desert."

O'Hare looked at him.

"I'd say he has a bit more than half. You should have more faith."

O'Hare's hopes appeared accurate, as each Battalion was allowed to halt and fall out when they came to a suitable stream, it guarded by Provosts who prevented anyone from wading in and stirring up contaminating mud.

In thus fashion they marched, rest, food and water being paramount in the heat. Six days after they started, just before the mid-day meal, Beresford came hurrying back, coming finally to the 105th, the last Battalion in the 4th Division column, but the 27th were already leaving them behind, moving forward at pace. He stopped at Brockenhurst, whom he did not know.

"Double time, Colonel. We're up to the Johnnies, our cavalry has met theirs. Bock's KGL had a minor action with some Chasseurs. Wellington wants infantry support."

A Drummer arrived to beat out the time and the 105th hurried forward, following the 27th. Carr decided that a change was needed in their order if they were to go into action and he had noticed that the 27th were already doing what had just occurred to him.

"I'll get the Lights up."

He dropped back to the final Company in their column.

"Nat! We could be in action. Our cavalry have met theirs and so who knows what comes next. They'll probably call for Light Companies, so you may have to run forward. Go up one section each side."

Within minutes the conversation had been relayed back, to produce an eager hope within Miles.

"Cavalry action. Could mean boots and blankets."

It was Davey who all but killed the optimism.

"Some hopes! There's two Divisions between us and there. All will have been well picked over by the time we gets there."

And so it proved to be, the Light Company were ordered up, but only to the head of their own Division, no further. When they finally arrived at the scene of the action, there was merely a row of dead bodies, mostly French, and some lone, bareback horses, now hobbled, but grazing the still green grass. Of boots on the bodies, or blankets, saddles and bridles, there was no sign. They reformed and marched on and that evening even Shakeshaft could not put a name to where they were but the Followers and rations arrived soon after making camp and so at least they all enjoyed a good meal. All the time no one could fail to notice the camp fires of the other two columns, the light of their fires winking repeatedly as men and sentries moved across the line of the light.

It was Graham's infantry column that gave Anson's Light Dragoons their bearings as, throughout the following day, they tracked across the hills to the South. When Oakwood's Squadron were directed still further to the South, they were joined by a mounted Guerrilla column led almost inevitably by Julian Sanchez himself.

The hardened veteran cavalrymen of the 16th could not look without admiration at the tight column of well clothed men on well cared for horses. Each man carried a light carbine slung across his right shoulder. Sanchez came up to Carr and Oakwood, his face a fearsome grin in his leathern face and the grin widened to one of recognition.

"Hola Teniente. I remember now when you I see. At Barba del Puerco. You are well, si?"

A brown hand, missing one finger, was extended and Carr took it, before it was extended to Oakwood, who grasped it warmly.

"This time we push them out, all, si. Estos viles franceses."

He spat on the ground after the words, his command of English deserting him when it came to insulting the French. Oakwood grinned at him as Sanchez looked up.

"Do you have any news, Senor?"

Sanchez' face split into a grin, taking his moustache further across his face.

"News, si! The franceses have gone from Salamanca. They leave some in the ...... how you say?"

He turned to one of his men.

"Fortelezas, en ingles."

The man grinned.

"Forts!"

Sanchez turned back, an amused expression across his face.

"Si, in forts they have left some men. But all others, go. Afrancensados also."

Oakwood nodded.

"Have you told our army?"

"No. I go now. You are first to know."

Carr felt that some gesture should be made and so he offered Sanchez a drink from his canteen, which was accepted and he took a long pull.

"Gracias, Teniente."

Then Carr had a thought.

"Do you know a Guerrilla leader called Mateo?"

The grin reappeared.

"Ignasias Mateo! Si, I know. Him down South. Is my cousin. How you know him?"

"I was captured by the French down there and he rescued me. I'm grateful."

"Si, and lucky too, Teniente. You say prayer, si, because God loves you!"

With that he handed back the canteen and waved his men forward.

"Go with God, Ingleses!"

Hours later, Jed Deakin, of the infantry, found out from Ted 'Bugle' Bates.

"The Frogs've gone out of Salamanca. Just a few left in some forts. No bustin' into that place then."

Deakin nodded.

"Good news, that, Ted, I've had enough of sieges. One is too many, never mind two!"

At that moment, the relief from any possible siege had thoroughly brightened Nat Drake's mood, but not enough to dispel another source of anxiety, because sat in front of him in the Light Company tent was his new Lieutenant, one Luttrel Bettridge, just arrived, having at last caught up with the column. Across the table from him, sat a youth who could classically be described as 'callow', this soon confirmed by his answers to the next questions. The anxious youngster subconsciously fingered his right cuff, his face more than a little stressed, having ridden through the vast camp of the centre column, making several hopeful but useless enquires, regarding the whereabouts of the 105th.

"How old are you?"

"Seventeen."

"I am your superior Officer!"

"Sorry. Sir."

"What do you know of Light Infantry work?"

"Nothing, Sir."

Drake sighed.

"I'll lend you a book. No, I'll give you a book. Keep it and read it."

He exhaled a deep breath.

"What is Colonel Brockenhurst to you?

"He's my uncle, Sir."

Drake spoke to one side.

"Which explains a lot!"

Another deep breath.

"Now listen, Luttrel. That is your Christian name, is it not?"

"Yes Sir."

"Now listen! You are in command of the most experienced, the most capable and, in many cases, the toughest men in this Regiment, in fact in this army. What they do not know about Light Infantry work is probably not worth knowing. On top, they have no time for fools who could put their lives at risk from ignorant stupidity. In fact, I have heard of such being shot, by their own men, their arrogance and ignorance creating too great a danger!"

He allowed the words to sink in as an expression that crossed the boundary between puzzlement and outright fear now occupied Bettridge's face. Drake paused further and then continued.

"I am giving you One Section with Sergeant Ethan Ellis, the best soldier I have ever come across. Were he the Officer in command, I would have no qualms nor concerns. What he advises you to do, you do! Without hesitation!"

He fixed him with a hard stare, which caused the youth to blink several times.

"Do anything different to what he advises and you and your Section, perhaps even the whole Company, could get wiped out! In which case, I would be very dismayed with you!"

The slight humour was lost on Bettridge, who was feeling more and more out of his depth by the second, so he simply nodded, which prompted Drake's last question.

"Are both your parents back in England?"

"Yes Sir."

"See that you write to them!"

Drake now stood.

"Right. I'll take you to meet Sergeant Ellis."

oOo

Salamanca was something new. Cities such as Lisbon, Oporto, Elvas and Cuidad Rodrigo had often been marched through, even visited, but here was a major Spanish city that was new to them all. For Beresford's central column, the city lay to their left, both theirs and Graham's columns having been directed far South, because the guns of the French held forts thoroughly commanded the single bridge. This was solid and Roman, across the River Tormes on the city's South side and Beresford's column was further out by a mile beyond that. Picton's Division was required to take an even wider sweep South. Carr and O'Hare were enjoying the leisurely walk of their horses, as the view of the towers and spires of Salamanca changed their arrangement as they progressed. O'Hare made first comment.

"One of the first Universities in Europe was created here."

Carr was somewhat shocked.

"You've been reading up!"

"Yes. Found a book at Anson's Headquarters. It has two Cathedrals, the newest built around 1350."

Carr sighed.

"Spare me anymore, especially as, at some time, while it seems not this time, we may have to knock the place to pieces!"

They rode on in silence, still enjoying the view in the bright Summer sunshine, until Carr changed the subject.

"Our new Light Company Lieutenant has arrived."

"And?"

"Clueless! And he's our Colonel's nephew. Drake's put him with One Section, Sergeant Ellis. What else could he do?"

O'Hare nodded.

"There's some good men in there."

"And a lot of villains too!"

O'Hare made no reply to such an only too accurate statement.

At that moment the said Sergeant Ellis was marching at the head, but to the right, of his Company, beside Chosen Man John Davey. He had been inflicted, as he would put it, with several inexperienced Officers before, many of whom had purchased their Commission and, for that simple, monetary reason were now in command of perhaps 100 men. However, this one looked the worst. So thin it seemed he would be blown yards away by a strong gust of wind and Ellis could swear that he found his sword on his left side so heavy that he was walking lop-sided to his right, where the strap came over his shoulder. When introduced, this Bettridge had been unable to say a word and so Ellis simply took a step back, said, "Very good, Sir", to Drake, saluted and left, to go and break the news to his men and work out their plans for self-preservation. The only reassurance he had was to look left at the men marching besides him, any of whom he would trust in any tight situation.

It was a long march to get to the far side of the city, but all the way every Spanish man, woman or child that they met cheered and clapped. Eventually, having passed the city, they turned North, which meant fording the Tormes and Shakeshaft was grateful to see that the village there had a name board; Santa Marta. He also recorded that the river was so low that no one, unless they slipped over, got wet above their knees. Even though the two columns, theirs and Graham's, marched side by side through the shallow water and it was almost full dark before both made camp with the lights of Graham's camp very visible merely yards from their own. The Followers arrived but it was too late for a meal and so all gratefully prepared to sleep.

With the early dawn, events quickly gathered pace, with Jed Deakin being shaken awake by Bridie.

"Jed, the orders come. Us to go back to Salamanca. Does that mean there's goin' to be a battle, Jed?"

Deakin shook his head several times and then splashed some water onto his face from the bucket Bridie was holding.

"Not necessarily, love. What it means is that we'n now up close to the French and we could be needin' to do a lot of quick marchin' an' general jumpin' about. You'm best back in the city. "Tis better billets for one thing."

He peeled back his blanket from his legs and reached for his boots.

"Now get the breakfast done. That's the issue now."

He stood up and stretched, to then look both ways and what he saw did much to confirm what Bridie had said. Wellington's whole army was stretched out on a long ridge, this not so high, but a prominence just the same. He found his tunic and buttoned it as he realised why the increase in the army's size and he spoke it out loud.

"Picton's must have come up in the night."

The others were coming awake around him, John Byford with Eirin and also Zeke Saunders with his wife of but a few months, a Portuguese girl named Consuela, who had become good friends with Bridie and Nellie. The order began to circulate for the Followers to leave quickly and it became very clear what these two pairs meant to each other, amongst the last to break their farewell embrace and one of the many to turn several times to wave what could be a last good-bye. However, the last word came from Nellie to her husband Henry, she pointing to the pot as she turned away.

"Right, well, there's a good fill stew left in that pot. That'll last for a day and more without your snouts in it too deep. So now I'm on my way so see that you don't get your gombeen-self killed!"

Many who overheard, smiled at the typical parting between the two, however, Noon came but no orders and so the whole army remained in their mess areas, talking, or watching the Light cavalry come and go. Many Officers, however, had an aid to the naked eye and O'Hare, Carr and Drake shared Drake's superior instrument. Soon it was Carr's turn and he used the telescope and pointed.

"Sight to the right of that lone barn out there, I swear I can see a smudge of blue on that horizon."

O'Hare took it from him.

"I believe you, but from memory I do also believe that in hot weather the French wear white!"

He took the instrument and sighted it to where he was told.

"You may be right, but their cavalry don't. So, evidently, we're stuck here for the rest of this day, unless Marmont throws his whole army into columns and comes doubling at us over that flat expanse out there."

Thus, was the day spent, in idle conversation and activities, but there did arrive some conflict of sorts come mid-afternoon, although it was very one sided. Wellington was patrolling his ridge when he came to the 105th with its very prominent feature of Brockenhurst's tent, it having been erected, without much serious thought, on the forward side of the ridge. Wellington halted at the entrance and met Luttrel Bettridge coming out.

"You, Sir! Whose is this?"

"My uncle's, Sir."

"Your uncle's! Why, is he on a family visit?"

"Why no, Sir. He is the Colonel of the 105th. He sleeps here, Sir."

Wellington sat back in the saddle, mostly, but not completely in mock astonishment.

"The 105th, by God!"

The astonishment continued, but for the briefest seconds.

"So, fetch him out!"

Bettridge hurried back inside and muffled speech could be heard from behind the thick, marine quality canvas. Eventually, Brockenhurst emerged, with no tunic, merely in his shirtsleeves, but Wellington had a much greater issue than improper dress, with which he was much exercised

"This dwelling can be seen for miles! Marking our positions for the enemy. Take it down. If you must sleep in such as this, take it further back."

Brockenhurst stood and stared at Wellington, for some seconds, but too long for his Commander in Chief, who repeated the order in a flat, but menacing, voice.

"Now, Colonel. Now. This instant."

Brockenhurst well remembered his defeat at the hands of Lowry-Cole and, whilst inwardly raging, he submitted immediately to the orders of this even higher, in fact ultimate, rank. He nodded vigorously then turned to Lackenham who had also emerged by now.

"See that it's done."

Wellington then sat forward, folding his arms over the pommel of his saddle.

"So, you are the Colonel of my Hundred and Fifth. How did this come about?"

Brockenhurst drew himself up to his full height. Here was an opportunity to regain some dignity.

"I am the Colonel of the 2nd Battalion."

Wellington's face turned to scorn. This made no favourable impression on him.

"Militia, eh, and come out now when you think it's all just about over and going to be easy! Now that we have 'the keys'."

Wellington cared not if Brockenhurst understood the term 'keys', meaning possession of both Badajoz and Cuidad Rodrigo and so he delivered a final glower and moved on.

It proved to be another sweltering night on the ridge and all there woke short of sleep and thirsty, but behind the ridge all were well provided for with rations and so they settled to another day of eating, watching and speculating. However, for Anson's 14th Light Dragoons and Clinton's 6th Division there came one welcome order which immediately dispelled the boredom. Both were to prepare themselves for a parade, a triumphant entry into Salamanca. Amongst the cavalry, many Cornets and Captains of the 14th hurried amongst the 12th and 16th hoping to borrow whichever piece of uniform or harness would look better than the one they had. The parade road into Salamanca ran up from the village of Moriscos to cross the ridge and there came much jeering and catcalling as the two chosen units of the army marched along the ridge to the crossing, progressing through all other units positioned along its length. However, all fell silent when Wellington and his whole Staff arrived to lead the parade off. With bands playing and burnished harness jingling, off they all went towards the towers and spires of the grateful city. It was during the evening that the 14th returned, to gratefully return what had been borrowed, but all Cornets and Captains were mercilessly plied with questions as to what had happened, One Cornet of the 14th's One Squadron, named Vivian Preston, painted the most amusing and vivid picture.

"The place went mad! You cannot imagine such a thing, all the cheering and thronging, whilst all the time the Old Boy was doing his best to write orders for the capture of the two forts, but he couldn't! The women were the worst, all crowding up and threatening to pull him off his horse, they were so grateful. Picton and Stapleton-Cotton had to effect a rescue. Several times."

The following morning, with the full sun now risen, the same three Officers of the previous day, made their fruitless study of the horizon, then, with the folding of the telescope, came the sound of guns battering the forts, then they saw the familiar accessory for any siege, remarked on by Drake.

"Just like Badajoz and good luck to them."

The cause of the comment was the Rifle Companies of the 4th Division, filing back towards Salamanca, their role required there only too well known, to get as close as they could to the walls to put accurate rifle fire through the embrasures and suppress the French reply. The ironic 'good luck' addition came because the defenders always had the advantage of height which had caused the loss of several Riflemen during the previous two sieges. Then came something even less welcome, in the shape of Brockenhurst's servant, Archie Lackenham.

"The Colonel requires your attendance for luncheon."

The bald statement caused Carr to bridle immediately, but all three simply nodded and Lackenham departed, for Carr to finally give vent to his feelings.

"Nothing like, 'request the pleasure' or 'would you care', just a simple order to come and eat with the damned man."

Drake grinned openly.

"Well, on this occasion I can only express my gratitude for my lack of advancement."

He grinned.

"Such as this can only be for Majors!"

At this O'Hare turned to Carr with a half-smile on his face.

"Well, look at the possibilities. This could mean a thawing in our relations."

Carr dismissed the idea with a brief scowl, but at the acknowledged time for lunch they appeared at the tent and knocked on the tent post. Lackenham ushered them in and they found the three already seated at a sizeable trestle table, Brockenhurst at the head with Slade and Betteridge either side. There was no welcome, other than Brockenhurst waving at two vacant seats either side of the table. Carr and O'Hare took their places and the meal began, accompanied by the local wine, the food arriving via two Spanish servants and the wine being poured by Lackenham. The meat was mutton and Carr dwelt a while on how much it must have cost, because conversation was sparse, bar such as "pass the salt". O'Hare was much more inclined to conviviality during such occasions and so he asked a convivial question.

"How are you finding the sights of Spain, compared to those of home?"

The use of the plural 'you', produced only one response, that from Slade.

"I would say that this country is utterly backward!"

At this Carr felt much inclined to argue, if only mildly.

"You may be correct, Major, if a little unkind. This country has been at war, in one form or another for six years. Under French occupation, the impact of which we have seen all too often. It must make a difference."

By now the food had been consumed and cleared, but there came no response. Carr thought of enquiring over the loyal toast, but thought better of prolonging what was now a tedious and strained affair, until Brockenhurst spoke out.

"Do you think there will be a battle?"

O'Hare nodded.

"Yes. Several, before we get home."

"I am meaning soon."

"Well, yes Sir. I expected one right here. We are drawn up and ready. Rumour has it that Marmont, as we speak, is weaker than us. Wellington may well decide to spring forward from here."

"So, the battle could be in what form?"

Carr looked at O'Hare from across the table, the expression on his face conveying his opinion that the question was absurd, but he felt obliged to attempt an answer.

"Well, Sir, until now we have always stood on the defensive. They send attack columns at us and our lines wrap themselves around the heads and blast them back to where they came from."

He paused to judge the reaction, but saw only three blank faces, so he continued.

"Major O'Hare may disagree, but I feel that, with us advancing into Spain, it may well be us that does the advancing on the next battlefield. Up to their positions, that is. If anything does happen here, that'll be the form it takes, in my opinion."

O'Hare nodded.

"I agree. The time may well have arrived when we can no longer rely on them coming at us. They know that we are unbeatable on a good defensive position. They'll not try that any more. It'll be up to us to take the initiative!"

Slade sat forward.

"Us to attack? Walking at them?"

Carr nodded.

"Yes, Major. That's about the size of it. It'll be one or the other this time, either us going up to them, or vice versa, but my money's on the former."

Slade sat back. The idea had become all too vivid, then Bettridge spoke up.

"What's that we can hear?"

O'Hare turned to him.

"Bombardment. Of the forts."

"It sounds ferocious!"

By now Carr had lost patience.

"Well it isn't! Nothing like intense enough. We don't have the ordnance. We did not bring it with us from Cuidad. Taking those forts will not be a simple matter. It will cost lives."

With that, Carr stood up and O'Hare did likewise and Carr turned to Brockenhurst.

"Thank you for the invitation, Sir, and thank you for the delicious food, but we both have duties to attend to. I for one, must inspect the pickets, which are some way out, you understand."

Both put on their shakoes, saluted to three blank faces and left. Outside, Carr was still irate.

"I can imagine a warmer atmosphere in an Eskimoe's igloo!"

O'Hare was more understanding.

"I think, perhaps, our three are beginning to realise just how much they do not know. Beginning to wonder what they have got themselves into and wish to correct their ignorance. If so, for that we should be grateful."

Carr nodded.

"Perhaps! Anyway, any of that whisky left of yours? I could use a measure after that."

O'Hare turned left and steered Carr towards his tent.

oOo

The bugle notes for alarm cut through the camp, causing all in the 16th to throw off their blankets and rapidly don their boot and tunics. Oakwood was amongst the first to arrive at Colonel Withers tent.

"Sir. What are your orders?"

Withers was busy buttoning his own jacket.

"Get yours into column of fours and get them out before our line. We'll get together out there and see what Anson or Stapleton-Cotton wants. I've got no orders, but I do know that all our vedettes have been driven in by a strong French cavalry screen. Just get yours out there as soon as you can."

Oakwood ran back to find Carr and Peterson at his own tent, obviously awaiting orders.

"Both Troops, column of fours. In line ahead, yours first, Carr."

Within minutes the four Squadron columns of the 16th were cantering down the slope in front of Picton's Divisions. Withers had been right, they soon had the 11th and the 12th Light Hussars alongside, with Anson now galloping up. His three Colonels, Withers, Piers of the 11th and Stockton of the 12th cantered over to meet Anson to receive their orders, which, when they came, were very much less than specific.

"Marmont's coming on! We don't know in what form, we only know he's coming forward. Stapleton-Cotton wants us to find out what we can. We're to scout to the North, we'll have Alten's 14th and KGL to our right."

Anson's voice betrayed his anxiety, but his orders were now clear.

"We are the extreme left, so, Piers, take your 11th and go far enough North to be certain there's nothing there. At least for the moment. When you're sure come back and support Stockton in the centre. Withers, maintain touch with Alten on our right. Take no risks! None! We should not lose a man, we are only here to find out."

All three saluted and rejoined their Regiments where Withers found his Squadrons all in columns line-abreast, Number One on the left, across to Four on the right. He waved his men forward at a brisk trot. The hooves pounded on the hard, high-summer earth as the four columns each of 60 plus men, eased their way forward, those in the van hearing nothing of the hooves nor the jingling harness as they concentrated forward, straining their eyes through the growing heat haze. It did not take 15 minutes before they saw what was advancing towards them and Withers held up his hand to call a halt and his Captains came up to him.

"You can see what I can. It looks like three columns. Each a Division strong, I'd say. Could be more."

He pointed to each.

"One there, opposite Stockton's 12th, one there opposite Alten's and what I make out to be another, much further South."

Tavender had focused his telescope.

"Yes Sir, a third much further down."

By now Withers was using his own telescope.

"They have a multiplicity of cavalry. Swarms of them!"

He paused and thought.

"We need to gauge their strength. We'll go for the one opposite Alten there. His KGL will be attempting the same, but we'll try from our side. Right, as we are but 100 yard spread. Expect no more than a brisk trot, I don't like all these Frog Hussars."

The 16th moved on, the four Squadrons easing apart to a distance of 100 yards, but they had gone no more than half a mile before what looked like a whole Brigade of French Light cavalry converged across their path. The bugler with Withers sounded the halt and they obeyed and then waited. What was surprising is that the French did also, for some long time, such that the Noon sun reduced their shadows to mere inches and Withers began to remember that his men had hurtled out of camp with no breakfast and now there they were, almost two miles before their own lines, halted and watching the equally static French. His Captains were with him, also Major Johnson. By now Withers had used his own telescope over three dozen times and he handed it to his Major.

"Arthur. It's my impression that all three columns have stopped. What's your opinion?"

Johnson focused it for himself on all three, folded the instrument and gave his opinion as he handed it back.

"I agree!"

Withers nodded.

"Right. The men can dismount and eat what they have. Tavender! Send one of yours back to tell Headquarters that the French have stopped. We see three heavy columns, both horse and foot, but accurate strength is impossible to tell."

As Cornet Smythe galloped off at Tavender's behest, the word was circulated that they could eat, an invitation that meant nothing to Cornet Carr as he had nothing, but his Sergeant Baxter came to his rescue.

"Here Sir, a bit of dried beef and a biscuit. Take my advice, Sir, always keep something in your saddlebag, if 'tis only biscuit. The likes of us is often too far out from rations."

Carr accepted the two items gratefully and began to chew on the hard beef, but for the rest of the day, they did not move, neither did the French. Withers sent back for some rations, but little could be brought forward on the spare horses. Despite that, Withers turned to Johnson.

"We've no choice, we stay here and make camp. Looks like Johnny's doing the same."

Camp fires were now growing in number in the direction from where they had last seen the French cavalry before the growing darkness hid them from sight.

"Set pickets."

Carr's Troop were one of the first for the duty and so they walked their horses forward for 300 paces and halted, remaining dismounted. Baxter remained with Carr and dispensed his wisdom.

"It's about now that Johnny'll come out checking for us as we does for them, Sir. We needs to stay awake. I'll walk our line as you should too, Sir. Keep our boys on the job."

Two hours ticked by and in the distance they heard their French equivalents exchanging calls. At around ten Tavender arrived, as Senior Captain he had responsibility for pickets. Baxter and Carr were stood together, but Tavender approached Carr and spoke an order that had Baxter grinding his teeth with anger.

"We need to take a look, Carr. To check just where they are. Take a man and ease your way forward. I do believe they've gone and left their fires
burning!"

Tavender might be genuine, or it might be yet another threat to Carr, which angered Baxter greatly. Tavender might have some issue with Carr, that was his affair, but Baxter cared more for the life of his accompanying men than he did for the life of any Officer and here was Tavender threatening the life of one of his lads in order to imperil Carr!

Tavender might have the ambition to put Carr in the ground, but one of his was not losing their life because of it. He intervened strongly, feeling that he could, he was, after all, a Senior Sergeant.

"No need for that, Sir. They're still there, at least their pickets are."

Tavender looked at him.

"How do you know that, Sergeant."

"Just listen, Sir. All our horses is whinnying to those of the French. They're calling to each other, Sir, they can smell each other on the wind."

Tavender was incensed.

"You expect me to believe that, Sergeant?"

"I do Sir, and, with your permission, I'll go forward myself and prove it."

There was no reply from Tavender to Baxter's gamble and so Carr spoke up.

"They are there, Sir. I took a bit of a stroll forward myself a while ago and I heard their call, "Tout va bien ici. Vive l'Empereur."

Tavender now ground his own teeth, but there was nothing more he could say that would sound reasonable. He had got an answer to the concerns he voiced, he could say no more. He turned and led his horse back to the main camp.

Back on the ridge, the main army endured another hot night, this made more uncomfortable by the anxiety of sleeping in line, in uniform, weapons close-by. Anson's two Battalions of the 4th Division were in the very centre of the Allied line, with the 105th on the left of the 27th. Dawn enabled them to see the rest of their Brigade, Bairns' Company of Rifles, these revealed by the rising sun, were some 400 yards before the main line, some on sentry far out before, with their comrades still taking what rest they could and remaining prone on the ground. Wellington allowed hot food to be cooked and consumed, so the last of Nellie's stew was consumed with hot tea. The only sound was that of the guns back in Salamanca, their crews still doing their best with inadequate ordnance for the task they had been given. For all that day, they remained in battle formation, the only change being that the guns fell silent. Eventually, the word came forward, this from Heaviside to Deakin's enquiry.

"Our guns have run out of shot, Colour Sergeant. Wisdom is with the aged, and understanding in length of days. Job, 12, 12."

The reply was a mystery to Deakin, but, as always, he could manage some manner of sensible reply.

"Yes Sir, I'm sure that's about the long and the short of it, Sir."

Standing in position throughout the day made all expect the afternoon to be the same, until the cavalry came galloping out of the heat haze, and the orders rang out all along the ridge "Stand to, stand to". All scrambled to their feet and set their weapons beside their right boot at 'order arms'. Staff Officers galloped out before the line, but not so far as to lose the height advantage of the ridge and all studied the distance through telescopes and then galloped back. Some time passed and the line was allowed to sit, then some French offensive action did appear, but in the form of several field batteries. They came under fire from the Allied batteries on the ridge before they could unlimber themselves, but soon cannon shot were humming above their heads. Carr ran along the line, shouting as he ran, worried that the French batteries were concentrating on the centre, where the 4th Division were.

"Lie down! Lie down!"

As he ran, he passed Brockenhurst and Slade both sat their horses. Seeing his men lowering themselves from their ordered ranks to lie on the ground, Brockenhurst shouted above their heads.

"What the Devil is this, Carr. Have the men stand up. Stand up, d'you hear?"

Carr halted, he had to, but at that moment, Lowry-Cole cantered by to call out to Brockenhurst.

"Well done, Colonel. Anticipated my order to lie down. Well done!"

Carr barely supressed a laugh, nor did he fail to notice the grins of the Colour Company stood before him. He continued along the line, bidding the remainder of the 105th to lie flat. On the far left, Luttrel Bettridge was flat on the ground alongside Sergeant Ellis.

"Is this correct, Sergeant? To lie down in the face of the enemy."

"Better this than to make yourself a full target for a cannonball, Sir. Best make yourself comfortable, Sir. We could be here some time."

From somewhere along the line they suddenly heard screaming and Bettridge looked back at Ellis, whose face taking on a 'sagelike' expression.

"Not all stays lucky, Sir."

The artillery exchange remained until the early evening, with most on the ridge elevating themselves to see the results whilst still remaining prone. Coinciding with the evening meal, the French brought their horses forward and hitched up their guns, leaving three wrecked upon the plain, destroyed by accurate Allied roundshot. With the French departure, the 4th Division were allowed to stand, which brought forth a pointed comment from John Davey.

"Now that's what I call perfect timing. We must remember to thank the Johnnies for allowing us our evening meal in peace."

Ingredients were quickly thrown into their mess stewpot above a quickly kindled fire and a hot stew was quickly prepared. That eaten, with biscuits, they all sat and smoked and looked towards the French and it was not long before the bugle notes of 'Stand-to' rang out again. Davey's keen eyes had seen why.

"Johnny's come back! He needed his tea time, just like us."

He was correct, only this time it was artillery accompanied by infantry. Carr and O'Hare studied the advance through their telescopes. Both saw the tell-tale yellow tassels and high yellow plumes decorating their wide topped shakoes.

"Voltiguers! Heading for the village."

O'Hare nodded agreement.

"He'll not allow that!"

O'Hare was correct. Within a minute a whole Battalion was running forward from the 7th Division's position to their right. Both were now used their telescopes.

"Who?"

O'Hare trawled through his memory of Regimental facings, in which knowledge he took great pride.

"Light Infantry wings. Blue to green facings. I could be wrong but I'd say the Durhams. Of the 7th."

"Right or wrong, they're making a race of it. That village Moriscos is a good half mile in front."

Only mildly anxious that they would lose the race, as the Durhams ran forward, therefore only mild relief was generated when they disappeared into the village buildings before the French. Carr turned to O'Hare.

"What's your bet they'll hold it. That's a Brigade coming at them."

O'Hare grinned.

"The odds aren't worth it. They'll hold."

They continued to watch as the first attack was repulsed and fell back, then the French field guns arrived again and began to batter the village and also bombard the line on the ridge. The Allied batteries gave a furious response and cannon-shot filled the air, two shot actually colliding. Before he ran along the line again to order 'lie down', Carr grinned at O'Hare.

"Perhaps I should have laid a bet. Shorter odds now!"

Jed Deakin was lying down in position, with his 'wife's son Ensign Patrick Mulcahey lying on one side, with the Regimental Colour still in its case beside him, and Deakin had Toby Halfway on the other side. All three were staring forward, their chins on their folded arms. Cannon shot continued to buzz and humm overhead, some ploughing the turf before them, but Deakin was looking further out.

"He's having another go, Tobe!"

Halfway had already seen for himself another cloud of Voltiguer's sprinting for Morisco village for all to be suddenly shrouded in smoke from the Durham volleys. Halfway delivered his judgment.

"That's brought down too many of 'em. They'll not get in!"

Deakin rolled slightly to his left, the better able to see what was happening to his right.

"Here's a caper, Tobe. Take a look at that."

What Halfway was being invited to watch was Wellington and the whole of his Senior Staff walking their horses slowly down the road that led to Morisco.

"They're all there, Tobe. Graham, 'Daddy' Hill, Beresford, that foul mouthed Picton and a half dozen others."

Further along the line, Carr was stood with Nat Drake and both had noticed the 'sally forward', it first commented on by Drake.

"Well that's very noble of our Senior Officers to go forward and drawn the enemy's fire!"

Carr did not reply, but merely stood shaking his head at the spectacle, as Wellington held out a map, at the same time pointing around and beyond as he spoke to his Seniors, seemingly explaining what he wanted them to do, were they to advance. They watched this for a minute or two and then Drake continued.

"It won't be long before the Johnny Gunners will see what we can and alter their intentions.

Carr turned his attention to the French field-guns out before them and Drake was right. Those closest to the road were rapidly swinging around and then being loaded. Soon round shot was ploughing up the ground near the group and within seconds all were galloping back up the ridge. Deakin could not help but chuckle as he spoke softly to himself.

"There you are, Sirs. Have a dose yourselves."

He resumed his study of Morisco, but a glance to his left revealed his Ensign fast asleep. He smiled paternally.

"Fair enough, son. There's not much else to do."

The 'else to do' was to watch a third French attack on Morisco fail, then an ADC galloped along the road to the village and the Durhams doubled back, unmolested by French field-guns who were galloping in the opposite direction back to their own lines. Then, many minutes later, all saw the Voltiguers hurry forward again to take possession of the undefended village. However, the same as most on the ridge, Carr and Drake were unconcerned and then both heard a horse behind them to see an ADC from Anson rein in where they were.

"Stand the men down, but they sleep in position."

It was Drake who saw the humour.

"Stand the men down! They're already lying down. Shouldn't he be saying stand the men up?"

Carr grinned wryly, placed his hand of Drake's arm and both walked off to where the Light Company tent was. A cup of Morrison's tea was suddenly very welcome.

oOo

"Well, at least they've given us a change of view!"

"And perhaps a more interesting job!"

"What? More than sitting on a horse and peering through telescopes. Not difficult."

"Well, the peering bit is still there!"

The reply to Oakwood's first comment came from Major Johnson as he peered through a powerful telescope set up on a frame. He waved his hand in a downward motion and Cornet Willoughby Carr turned the handle on the frame to lower the line of sight. He stopped when Johnson held out his hand flat in front of him, then made a small adjustment to the focussing. Behind them stood four members of Two Squadron, Sergeant Baxter, Corporal Makepeace and Troopers Nunney and Spivey. These had been tasked with carrying the heavy equipment out to the vantage point on the more advanced ridge they had now been ordered to patrol, ordered forward on the previous day. The change had put all into a good mood, with Oakwood and Johnson now becoming firm friends.

Oakwood pointed downwards,

"What's that place, nearest? Alongside the river"

Johnson consulted a piece of paper.

"Aldea Longua. There's a ford there."

"And the other? Furthest?

"Huerta. There's lots of fords there."

Oakwood twisted his mouth in wry humour.

"I'm sure they're very grateful for that!"

Johnson stood up fully and used his own telescope. Nothing like as powerful as that on the frame, but far easier to sweep across the landscape. The nearest Allied force was a smudge of red amongst the sun faded brown and green fields about half a mile across the River Tormes, directly opposite Aldea Longua. They were plainly there to guard against any French crossing at Huerta, but from down there they could not see what Johnson could see. He screwed his face as he pressed his eye to his own telescope, then he returned to the heavier version on its cradle.

"That's cavalry plus more. Lots of it moving South to get to Huerta, I'll wager."

He stood up.

"We know that Johnny's pulled right back. Out of Morisco and further. What's your opinion, Oakwood."

Two Squadron's Captain needed but seconds at the large instrument before he also stood up."

"Cavalry! Yes, but not alone."

The judgment was interrupted by Corporal Makepeace.

"Sir. Beg pardon, Sir, but there's riders coming up. Looks like Staff."

All three at the telescope turned to see what they recognised as Wellington himself approaching with Beresford, three Aides-de-Camp and six Dragoons as escort. The whole party at the telescope sprang to attention, but Wellington was too anxious to use the instrument himself and his wiry frame almost leaped out of the saddle. As he hurried up he looked at Johnson.

"Report, Major."

"Cavalry at least, Sir. Moving towards Huerta."

A look of concern passed across the aquiline face, before he bent to the eyepiece. A minute's study, then he turned to Beresford.

"That's more than just cavalry."

He pointed across the river to the red 'smudge', dancing in the heat haze.

"Bock is down there at the fords and won't hold them. Marmont reconnoitred yesterday with some Hussars and now he's going full."

He looked at one of his ADC's

"Marchment! To General Graham. Get over the Tormes at Santa Marta with the 1st and 7th Divisions, deploy there and hold. He is to take Le Marchant and a battery."

As one ADC hurried off, Wellington turned to another.

"Wakefield! To Lowry-Cole and Leith. Lowry-Cole's at Castellanos above Moriscos. They should be there, I sent them there yesterday. Leith's at Moriscos. Both to march down to Aldea Lengua. They may have to cross here."

He returned to his horse, but spoke to Johnson as he moved.

"Keep watch Major. Anything new, get a message to Stapleton-Cotton."

All three saluted, but Wellington was already into his saddle and riding away. Oakwood looked at Johnson.

"For how long?"

"Until this day's business is done!"

"I'm hungry already."

In response to the order to the Lowry-Cole's 4th Division, almost an hour later, the Light Company of the 105th were the first to arrive at the heights above the village of Aldea Lengua. Seeing nothing on their side of the Tormes and hoping for something to eat, it being Noon, Drake looked at Luttrel Bettridge, him plainly worn out by the hurried march of the Light Infantry of the whole Division.

"So, there you are, Luttrel! Welcome to the infantry. Marched hither and thither without much explanation, so much so that we lose track of where we are."

Carr was up with them and using his telescope.

"And the freezing, soaking and starving. Don't forget that!"

Drake added his own.

"And the boredom! But right now it's the starving bit that's worrying me!"

Carr had been studying the French column beyond the river moving across his sight from the left.

"They must have come over at Huerta, not here."

He folded his telescope and thrust it into his tunic pocket.

"Well, here we have a grandstand seat for the spectacle and we have much to be grateful for. At least we're not at the forts. There was another failure last night."

The afternoon wore on and the main bodies of Graham's two Divisions arrived to deny the French the Santa Marta fords across the Tormes. What the 105th saw, stationary up on their perch, was the heavy French column come up to Le Marchant's Dragoons, these some way forward from the infantry, to immediately be heavily assaulted by Le Marchant's accompanying field-guns. Thus opposed, the French halted and returned the way they had come, re-crossing the Tormes at Huerta.

Drake folded his arms.

"Well, I'd call that one paltry effort from this much vaunted so-called veteran army. They're given a village, abandon it next day, next day pull right back, this day cross a river and then scuttle off back over it."

Carr was unimpressed by Drake's verdict.

"Don't speak too soon. He's trying something and at least he's getting his boots wet in the attempt.

Soon the order came to return to the ridge above Moriscos and it was through the evening gloom that both the 4th and 5th Divisions of Lowry-Cole and Leith marched across the bare plain to their old positions. As they rode back Brockenhurst was in a foul mood and, not being a man used to restrain his speech if his thoughts merited it, he gave full vent to his feelings, these still being wounded by the incident with his tent. Slade was the audience.

"Move here, move there, move somewhere else, with no rhyme nor reason! Does the damn man know what he's doing? We'll be worn down with marching before we've fired a shot."

Carr, with O'Hare, was riding just behind and he felt the need to answer, even though Brockenhurst had been speaking to Slade.

"If I may, Sir, and perhaps this will help your understanding, this marching comes as no surprise, really. In open country such as this, each Commander will manoeuvre in the hope of his opponent making a mistake. That will involve a great deal of marching, Sir. If that helps."

Brockenhurst did not deign to turn around.

"And has a mistake been made?"

"I'd say not, Sir, which means a great deal of marching lies ahead. For both sides."

oOo

Chapter Two

Salamanca.
"By God, that will do!"

From his office, high at the rear of an unremarkable building composed of offices, Colonel John Waters looked down on the bright summer scene beneath him in Dean's Yard, a precinct of Westminster Abbey. The high summer green of the leaves and that of the immaculate lawn, drew barely any of his attention, neither did the unworldly Clerics, innocently strolling the quadrangle which was exclusively their precinct for exercise and ecumenical deliberation. Waters' thoughts were lodged hundreds of miles distant, drawn there by the report from his most trusted Agent, Jean Dulongue. He had journeyed through Sweden and Norway to reach London and the report, now more than two weeks' old, was on Waters' desk, read by him several times.

In the room sat his equally trusted Assistant, Redeemed Radipole, although no one ever used what seemed to many to be his most absurd, clumsy and even presumptive, Christian name. Whilst Radipole could be described as slightly built and immaculately turned out, Waters was every inch an experienced soldier. This an impression not only produced by the fact that he habitually wore his army uniform, this of a full Colonel, his tunic displaying the brass throat gorget, both epaulettes and wide collars, opened and turned back to reveal the pale yellow of the 12th Foot, The East Sussex. However, the impression of a veteran, vastly experienced soldier was mostly produced by a faraway look within eyes that had seen too much, much of it disastrous, these eyes set in a face that rarely displayed any humour. He was in his late forties, but 'old soldier' also came from the fact of a complexion that had not yet lost the deep-seated tan of campaign and also from his serious, concerned expression, this most clearly reflected in the downward turn of his mouth. He was one of Wellington's most trusted Intelligence Officers, as often roaming French-held territory in Spain, as he was in his office in Great Smith Street.

Radipole stood obediently by the door, deigning not to sit whilst his Chief stood, a sheaf of papers held in a slender hand protruding from an immaculate white cuff. His calm expression contrasted with the fierce intelligence behind his pale green eyes as he mulled over his own thoughts and examined possibilities. He had also read Dulongue's report.

No words were spoken between the two, because they were waiting for their own Department Head, this being the even more grizzled veteran, General Sir Henry Livermore, Secretary to the Commander in Chief and Waters turned from the window when he heard

Livermore's battlefield voice speaking to the sentry on the landing below. Within seconds, Livermore entered and the three occupied the seats in the room. It was Livermore who began.

"So, Boney's gone into Russia with 500,000 men, which must be a fair proportion of all the men in Europe able to serve, never mind France. What do we think?"

Waters had been thinking of his answer since receiving the report and he had two conclusions.

"First, he will beat the Russians and take Moscow, but with appalling casualties on both sides. Second, he crossed the Neman late June which means he'll be in Moscow something like mid-September, perhaps later. Even if the Russians make peace, or if they don't, he'll still have an army in Russia that he's got to feed and give shelter to, especially with the Russian winter coming on. The Russian army is limitless, whilst getting to Moscow will cost him 200,000 men. If the Russians do make peace, then he can pull his army out and still have one, of sorts. If they do not and he has to remain there so as not to concede defeat himself and feel humiliated, he will lose his army. Nothing survives a Russian winter, except perhaps the Russians!"

No humour crossed Livermore's face as he assembled his own thoughts.

"Whatever, seems clear that he cannot remain in Russia and he'll come out with a damn sight fewer men than when he went in. What are the implications of that, for us?"

"No more reinforcements for his brother Joseph in Spain, or perhaps even troops being taken away from there."

Livermore was unconvinced.

"But that only if he is forced to keep fighting after his withdrawal. If the Russians don't follow him out and there isn't another Coalition of his enemies, he may be able to hang on to Poland and all the rest of it with little more than a show of intent on the borders.

Livermore sat back after his words, as though exhausted, but he continued with his own assessment, almost spat out at higher volume.

"Coalitions! A Sixth, I can't see it, when Boney beat the previous five into dust."

Waters sat forward.

"That's for the Politicians, the Commander in Chief and the Minister for War. We subsidised our Allies for those five, but now there are no bones about it, if we want to take advantage of this, a huge mistake on his part, in my view, then a sixth is imperative."

Livermore made no reply and so Waters continued.

"If we want to ensure that Boney is not left alone, making it difficult for him to send forces to his brother El Rey and thereby keep

Spain as well as most of Europe, then we must unite our Allies against him. This is the opportunity to get shot of him and if the Politicians want that, then we have to dip into our national pocket again."

Livermore looked at the floor and pondered, whilst fingering the hole in his left ear at the end of a furrow across the side of his face, this inflicted by a grapeshot at the battle of Camden during the Revolutionary Wars.

"Of one thing you are right, whatever happens, he will come back with a damn sight less of an army than he went in, but a Sixth Coalition, after the humiliation of the previous five. That's another thing entirely and wholly less predictable.'

Waters nodded his head and then looked around Livermore to Radipole.

"Your thoughts, Radipole?"

Radipole sat upright, his face remaining expressionless.

"I agree with everything you have said Colonel, apart from one thing. Whilst Napoleon has an army, however sparse and ill equipped, he will keep fighting. Someone! He cannot stop himself. Perhaps not a coalition, but someone."

He took a deep breath.

"For that he will ask King Joseph for troops and Joseph will refuse to send them. He will say that he needs them all to hold down Spain and to fight us. If we can do something to give Joseph less of an excuse to keep all his forces and even give Napoleon good reason to take some from him, then that will aid our forces in Spain."

Waters grinned slightly.

"And you have a scheme?"

Radipole nodded slightly, the only physical gesture he ever used.

"Yes, broad brush as yet, but it starts in the Americas. High tension now exists across our Canadian border with the Americans, now that they've declared war on us, back in mid-June. Soon this will turn to open warfare, probably with them invading us. They are not strong enough to make any serious inroads and, in all likelihood, fail to hold onto their gains. When they are repulsed or withdraw, if we can convince the Americans that we are going to build a substantial force of our own in Canada, such as could retaliate with an invasion of our own, then that is our way in, to influence French thinking. Faced with that threat across the Great Lakes, then the Americans will appeal to France, their ally, for help. They know that toe-to-toe we take some beating, so for them it is unlikely to end well. France will do nothing, of course, but if the Americans and the French are convinced that part of the invasion force will come from our forces in Spain, then El Rey will have no excuse to hang on to all his troops."

Waters smiled, whilst Livermore looked astonished at such a scheme from someone so thoroughly unmilitary, then he turned to Waters.

"You know, that could work!"

Waters nodded.

"Yes Sir, it could and so, if you agree, then we'll get that going, if you can get to work on the Politicians!"

oOo

On the same day, but in a very different climate, as part of Beresford's centre column, the 105th marched the road down to Moriscos. Before them stretched the hot, wholly uninviting plain, in the distance of which, their road disappeared into a shimmering heat haze. Carr and O'Hare were content to march on foot, which further divorced them from Brockenhurst and Slade, both habitually riding at the front of the 105th column. Conversation between the two began as small-talk, Carr first to O'Hare.

"Did you get into Salamanca?"

"No, I did not. A pity in one way but not in another."

"How so?"

"There is much to see, but during the opportunity I did have, I declined. The last of the forts was burning fiercely and did so for some days, filling the place with smoke. Did you?"

"No, our two up there found extra duties for me."

O'Hare laughed.

"Sorry to hear that, but there's one piece of good news. Boney's gone into Russia."

Carr looked full at him.

"How can that be so good, if he knocks Russia out of any coalition before its even been formed? The Treaty that ended the Fourth caused Russia to declare war on us!"

Thinking that to be a very tenuous conclusion in the present situation, O'Hare screwed his face.

"I don't agree. Do you remember what Lacey said when we were on our way to Bath to get our new Colours after Corunna. The war will last eight years, unless Boney makes a mistake. He's made one, in my opinion. Lacey knew his stuff, and he put it at six, with the mistake. Two years less of this is more than welcome for me."

Carr nodded and his mouth managed a 'perhaps' smile, but he made no reply, because they were now passing through the remains of Morisco and the British dead had all been buried, they could see what looked to be around 30 graves close by. The French dead were simply laid out in rows, all now black with decomposition, but nevertheless, the inhabitants of Morisco, all now returned, were pulling at their clothing. Both Carr and O'Hare were glad when the spectacle was behind them and the conversation turned to more immediate, military matters.

"You know where we're going?"

O'Hare nodded.

"Yes, got it from Creet of the 27th. Up to the Douro! Marmont's pulled back behind it"

Carr then turned to O'Hare, almost in amusement.

"Much of a river, this Douro, is it?"

Carr received his answer when he accompanied all the Light Companies of the 4th Division as they marched into the town of Tordesillas, over a long Roman bridge that spanned that wide but summer sparse river. They had left the rest of the 4th Division in the village of Rueda, five miles behind them. All that the ancient town of Tordesillas meant to them, was a long, straight, main road, that led directly North, running between high, three storey buildings. These cast down shade upon the marching seven Light Companies of the 4th and not only shade, also flowers of all kinds were thrown upon them by the girls and ladies of the town, from the high balconies above. This inevitably aroused the interest of Tom Miles, marching alongside Joe Pike, John Davey and Zeke Saunders.

"What's the chance of a bit of a stop, some ways up, so's we can better give these ladies a chance to show how much they appreciates our comin' through yer?"

Davey laughed.

"About as much chance as a snowball in a hot kettle! We're through here, so I've heard, up to find Johnny."

"B'ain't that the cavalry's job?"

Saunders pointed to a group of mounted Staff Officers in the square which they had now entered.

"There's General Anson over there. When you get the chance, I'm sure he'll give you a full explanation. And a shilling and a swig of his brandy!"

Subdued laughter came from all around as they marched on, but Carr himself would have appreciated some explanation. He was marching with Drake and St. John Slade, the latter there 'for experience', because Carr was as much concerned by Slade's inexperience as he was over that of Bettridge already there with the Light Company. There was another reason why Carr had come forward himself to supervise the 'military education' of the pair, not the least because Brockenhurst had been making extra demands on him, often fuelled by Spanish brandy, the evidence for which often stood in rows outside Brockenhurst's tent each morning.

Carr was not the Commander of this Light 'half' Battalion of the 4th Division, the role had been given to Creet of the 27th and so later, when decisions were required, the two marched together out through the shambles and hovels of Tordesillas that formed the outskirts of any Spanish town. Creet was a rare thing, an Irish Colonel of an Irish Regiment and he had achieved that position by sheer capability and the fighting abilities of his men. As such, a 'soldier's soldier', he asked for advice from anyone whom he thought could provide it and Carr was no exception.

"Can you see what I can, Major? I'd say that's our place."

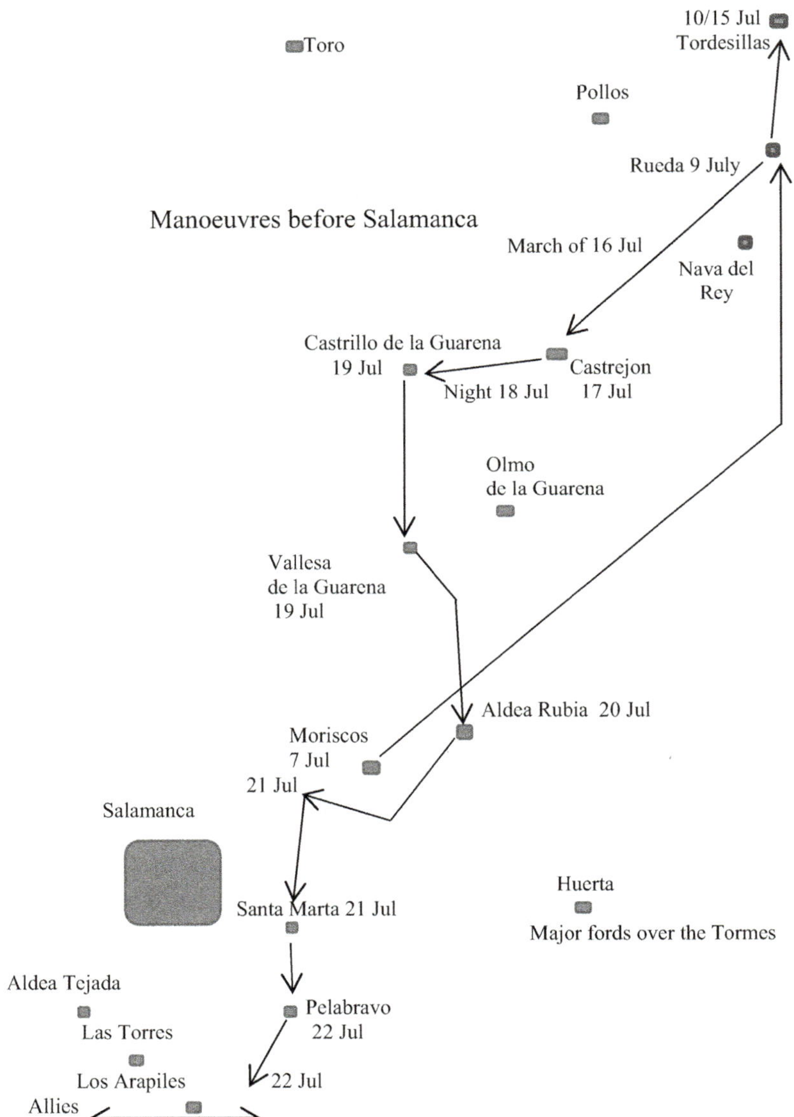

⟷ French

"I can, Sir, and I agree. Such a prominence cannot be ignored." Less than a mile from the last hovel, to the right of the road was a prominent hill, prominent atop a ridge that crossed the road. Within an hour, the Light Companies were sat around their campfires on the town side of the hill, whilst their pickets stood guard on what was likely to be the French side.

As darkness fell, Carr collected Bettridge and Slade and with them toured their picket line. What struck both as they heard Carr exchange comments with the men, who replied as though to an equal, was the men's demeanour, not just their appearance. This was almost tramp like, but both
were taken by confident way all the men stood, Baker rifle in the crook of their left arm, staring forward into the night, faces serious, set and determined, offering their opinions whilst Carr listened. It struck both, but Slade especially, that they discussed their situation with Carr as men who thoroughly knew their trade. Coarse, surly and intimidating they may look, but he could not avoid some gratitude and reassurance that such as these wore the same uniform as himself and belonged to the same Battalion. When Carr was content with the picket's positioning and he had explained all to Slade and Bettridge, he took both to a higher part of the ridge and bade them look into the far distance.

"What can you see?"

It was Bettridge who answered.

"Lots of lights. Another town?"

"No, Luttrel. That's Marmont's army. He'll be coming forward again, of that you can be certain. He's been given an army big enough and veteran enough such that Napoleon expects him to drive us into the sea. Learn all you can, both of you. On your competence could depend the fate of the whole Battalion, even the Brigade. And beyond that!"

This established, Carr walked away, leaving the pair staring into the night, alone with their own thoughts, these thoroughly occupied by the myriad fires of the enemy and what the proximity of such an army, of such a size, implied for them.

After a day of picket rotation, during the following evening, Ellis brought welcome news, to the Davey and Saunders groups.

"Get packed for an early move, we're out of here at dawn. We're being relieved and getting back to Rueda. I hear the Followers are up which probably means rations too."

As the Light Companies marched away, Carr was the last to leave the ridge, which remained in the hands of Bairn's Rifles and the

Company of Brunswick Oels of Ellis' Brigade, this their duty until their relief arrived. Who their relief was to be, was only revealed after they had crossed the Douro. It was Anson's Brigade of Light Dragoons and young Carr begged a minute to stop as he could see his elder brother stood between some houses waiting for the road to clear. The warmth of their greeting was genuine and for all to see, as Cornet Carr dismounted to embrace his brother, him a Major. Then Cornet Carr shook hands with Drake, both equally pleased to renew acquaintance, but it was the elder who hurried things along, seeing the whole cavalry Brigade almost over the bridge.

"Are you well. No diseases?"

"None so far. You?"

"No. Must be Mrs Maits' cooking, made us all immune!"

Cornet Carr laughed.

"We're going up. Have you just come from there?"

"Yes, but have you heard from home?"

'Yes, here!"

The Cornet pulled out a letter from his tunic pocket.

"Came last week. Hang onto it until next time!"

With that he was back into his saddle and his wave farewell was as genuine as his grin. Not so for Captain Tavender, who ground his teeth in anger and frustration at the scene of the happy reunion. His hatred for both only deepened.

The march back was five miles at Light infantry pace and Slade plainly was not in condition, whilst Bettridge, of a lighter frame, clearly was. Bettridge dropped back in the column to march alongside Shakeshaft, seeing in him a sympathetic soul and indeed he was, even though in another world of experience compared to this new companion, although he was a mere two years his senior. Shakeshaft being of equal rank, Bettridge regarded him as a priceless mine of information.

"How long have you been with the 105th?"

"Oh, since we landed in Portugal, August of the year eight."

Bettridge quickly did the maths. Four didn't seem so long a period.

"What battles have you been in?"

Shakeshaft's brows came together.

"Right, let's see, here we start with Rolica, then comes Vimeiro, retreat to Coruna, Coruna itself, Oporto, although not really a battle, Talavera, Busaco, and Fuentes. Don't think I've left any out! Oh – Sabugal I suppose. And of course, both sieges."

A look of shock came over Bettridge's face and the ghastly thought, "What if a number such as that still remained in the future?"

Shakeshaft took pity when he saw the fear and anxiety in Bettridge's face and he felt the need to say more, in the form of good advice.

"Look, what you are is an Officer in the Light Company, that's a cut above what's expected of you in the Line. So, when out taking on their skirmishers, two things, keep moving and take Ellis' advice. In fact, you could just leave it to him and watch and learn. He doesn't do anything silly or risky. Second, if it comes to a fire fight, us opposed to them and in line, there's only one thing the men expect of you, well two, really. Set an example by standing in the front rank and call the half-Company volleys when the smoke's cleared, 'front rank or rear rank'. You do that if your Captain's down, take over your Section at least. That's what they expect of a decent Officer. Manage that, and you'll be alright."

For the rest of the journey back to Rueda, 'alright' was the last thing Bettridge felt, not least from the business of 'calling half-Company volleys', about which he had not one clue.

Several days later, out on an expanse of scrubland North of the Douro that had cooled not one degree, Cornet Carr looked across at Peterson, writing his own diary, using his right leg hooked over his saddle as a writing surface.

"How many days have we had of this?"

Peterson counted them.

"Five!"

"And you've recorded what!"

Peterson looked again.

"10th, nothing, 11th, saw hoof sprints with French shoes, 12th, nothing, 13th, French cavalry in the distance, 14th nothing."

"And what's your bet on what this day will bring?"

"Three to two, nothing!"

At that very minute he was proved wrong, this arriving in the shape of Major Johnson and the diary was hastily thrust into his pocket.

"French infantry are over the Douro at Toro. They repaired the bridge there. The French infantry that were positioned at Pollos, upstream of Toro, are marching down to join them and presumably cross their bridge. What was up here with us at Tordesillas is also marching downstream to join. The Brigade's to get back to Tordesillas and scout South of the river to see if the French really have gone. 11th, 12th, then us at the rear. All Squadrons in column. Johnny may have sent cavalry to Tordesillas to seize the bridge. There's only a few Companies of our Lights holding it."

It was a fierce canter back across the open plain to Tordesillas, with all who could, these being mostly Officers alongside the column, looking anxiously North in the direction from which the French should appear if they had any intensions on Tordesillas bridge, but nothing was seen. Finally, they came to Tordesillas itself and clattered through the empty streets to finally arrive at the long bridge and then cross, observing disconsolate citizens at the North end ready to become refuges and alert Light Infantry at the South, these mounting a final guard. At the head of his Troop, Carr enquired of Baxter.

"Is this being blown up, Sergeant."

Baxter knew what he needed to see if that was the case.

"Don't look like it, Sir. Not if the Frogs is moving downstream away from this."

The sound of their horses hooves changed to that caused by hard baked earth and Brigade turned right and rode in the direction of the French manoeuvre. They maintained a leisurely trot through the pleasant countryside of open fields, open woods and olive groves, with the river to their right, which they all gazed over, anxious for any view of the French. An hour's ride brought them to Pollos, built on a slope that afforded a good view of the river, the fords there and beyond. There the Brigade halted, whilst all Officers used their telescope to examine the view Northwards over the river, but not for long, because there was nothing to be seen. Soon the telescopes throughout the column were hurriedly lowered as Anson ordered continue onwards and so they did, at a brisk trot. Because the Brigade was 'on alert', Peterson was required to be behind Carr's men at the head of his own Troop, therefore Carr had no-one else to remark to other than Baxter.

"Pretty village, that. Sergeant."

The Midlands accent came rumbling back.

"As you say, Sir, but all things in these parts is a bit too tense for prettiness!"

However, they had not been on the road for more than ten minutes, before they saw Captain James Myers of Four Squadron, normally positioned at the rear, gallop up beside them and fling five words over his shoulder to Oakwood as he hurried past.

"Johnny cavalry on the other side!"

Within five minutes a halt had been called and soon after the order came down the Brigade column, 'about turn' and 'trot on', which they did, to then see Anson himself gallop up alongside the 16th', hurrying back to Pollos. Once back in the village, they saw what Myers must have seen first, just after leaving the village. A whole French Corps, in three Divisional columns, was now marching towards Pollos. A screen of French Hussars were already under half a mile from the fords, these just upstream of the village. Within minutes the whole Brigade column had wheeled right and away from the river, thankfully onto a good road, the direction due South.

At that same moment the 4th Division were beginning a forced march Southwards themselves, back from Rueda. They had hurriedly broken camp and had just departed, obeying orders from Wellington himself, by ill-luck just when the Light Company arrived at the end of their own march back from Tordesillas, arriving with the darkness having served two days up there on picket at the bridge. This meant that they found themselves at the beginning of another hard march and so Carr hurried to the head of the 105th column to find out what was afoot. There was no choice but to ask O'Hare.

"What's the panic?"

O'Hare turned to look at him.

"Panic's the word! What I've got from Creet is that two French Divisions, at least, plus cavalry have repaired the bridge that Picton blew up at Toro and they are over and marching on Salamanca. Forget Divisions, probably a whole Corps. The panic comes because we are scattered all over to cover the Douro, whereas Johnny's got over the greater of his at one particular place."

Carr let out a deep sigh.

"This is not going well! Where at we marching to?"

"The whole Division is marching on a place called Castrejon de Trebancos, if I've got that right."

The march lasted all night, through a silent landscape, where the only view available to convince them that they were not walking through some endless tunnel of darkness, was that of the silhouetted horizon against a myriad of stars. As dawn was breaking they entered Castrejon, where Carr remarked to O'Hare.

"Good job we arrived in daylight. Seeing this place now, we could have blinked and missed it!"

O'Hare nodded.

"If this is a village, what's a hamlet?"

However, there was no time to discuss the town geography of Spain as they were hurried through it, over a dry river bed and onto a ridge where they found cavalry and infantry already drawn up. A quick enquiry from the directing Provost as to who was already on the ridge, drew an accurate reply.

"General Anson's Light Cavalry just arrived, Sir, and the Light Division. General Wellington's up there as well."

Carr looked at O'Hare, his look conveying all. If 'The Peer' was where they were, then things were getting serious. They were directed to the right of the Light Division and all slumped down to sleep. Even the Followers took their rest, all content that food could wait until later, all except Carr and O'Hare, who knew what was coming when Slade rode up to them.

"Colonel Brockenhurst wants to see you immediately!"

Carr was in no good mood.

"Having trouble pitching his tent, is he?"

There was no reply as Slade trotted back and the pair followed his direction. Where he halted, they found Brockenhurst, studying what looked like an order. They both saluted and waited, but the look of concern on Brockenhurst's face was plain to see as he raised the paper, then lowered it.

"This is from Lowry-Cole. The French have crossed at Toro, Pollos and Tordesillas, the last now at Rueda, where we've just come from. We are the Rearguard, us and the Light Division. With Anson's Light cavalry out as a screen."

The pair stared at him, making no reply, but Brockenhurst stared back, until Carr broke the silence.

"Yes Sir. Very good, Sir. Thank you for that."

Yet more staring, until Carr asked for orders.

"Should we make the arrangements, Sir?"

Finally, a reply.

"For what?"

"For a battle, Sir!"

The look of dread on their Colonel's face intensified, but Carr continued.

"Are there any more orders regarding that, Sir?'

Carr pointed at the letter. Brockenhurst raised the paper again, but again not far enough to read it.

"It says that all baggage and Followers are to be sent back to Salamanca."

"Very good, Sir, but I'd say we can give our Followers a few hours rest and allow them to cook our men a meal before they go."

Brockenhurst surprisingly nodded consent, but Carr could not resist the temptation.

"The order about baggage, Sir. Would that not include your tent. Sir?"

The look of dread turned to thunder, but the pair saluted and made off. They needed some sleep themselves, both expected to be in action before the next nightfall.

However, little sleep was afforded to them. Almost straight away, Lowry-Cole's ADCs galloped through their camp, calling for them to form into battle line. Developments were obvious, the Light Division were marching back towards Castrejon as support for G. Anson's cavalry who were already on their way there. Carr noticed the 16th within

Anson's Brigade, the distinctive dark blue and red tunic, and the black shako with the red and white tuft at the front. He thought he could pick out his brother, but could not be sure. He made no further attempt because RSM Gibney had approached.

"The Followers, Sir. Can they make a meal afore they takes off?"

Carr turned towards him, Gibney at full attention.

"Have you not been told that they are to go?"

"No Sir."

"Then yes, Sar' Major. I'm sure there will be time."

When permission arrived, Nelly Nicholls took charge.

"Right. Now. All is to go into the pot to leave a good supply for after when we've gone."

Bridie was already cubing up the salt beef and Sally was pounding up biscuit to thicken the stew. Tom Miles, excused line duties for a while to help hurry up the food, was slicing up potatoes and onions, accompanied by a comment from Nellie, whilst she stripped off some sage leaves from their stalk, fixing him with a sideways look of thorough disapproval.

"Sure, it'll take more than an onion to make him cry!"

This brought an immediate retort from Miles.

"You complain when it don't get done! 'Till then, you leaves I be!"

Bridie reached over to administer a consoling pat on the back, then, with her own preparations done, she supervised Trudie dividing up the flour. All was undertaken alone from the men, who now stood in line looking down the slope to Castrejon, where the Light Division and the cavalry had by now disappeared into a cloud of dust of their own making. Within the hour, the stew was eaten and the remainder poured and poked into French water bottles, these better for transport, having a superior 'stopper'. With the flour in their knapsacks, all was done and now came the parting. All was as familiar as before but genuine and emotional for all that. For some reason, Bridie clung to Jed for a little longer.

"Will there be a battle, Jed?"

"Yes, love, and a big one."

He saw the anxious look come into her eyes.

"But I'll be alright. Me and the lads, don't we always see each other through?"

With that, she detached herself, her left hand finally running down the front of his tunic, over the row of brass buttons. Soon all Followers were collected at Chaplain Albright's cart and, with final waves of hands and handkerchiefs, they marched off on the good, straight road to Salamanca, two days away.

Almost two miles forward from the ridge, Oakwood had risen on his stirrups and closed his telescope.

"There they are!"

Carr looked at him, then at the light blue smudge in the distance.

"How many?"

Oakwood grinned.

"Lots!"

"What will we do?"

Oakwood looked again in the direction of the French.

"Well, if Anson knows his business, he'll go up to the French, tempt them forward and then lead them onto those very capable boys of the Light Division formed up behind us."

The order came, 'Troops in line abreast. Two ranks." The order was obeyed, but, when formed up, the Brigade did not move. They sat their line and watched the approaching French Light cavalry, a multiplicity of uniform colours decorating their whole line as they came forward. The British cavalry were too tempting a target, because if they could be hit whilst remaining static then they would suffer a major defeat, so the French came on, their speed of charge increasing all the time. Carr sat his horse, more than a little bemused, so he looked at Baxter.

"Wait for the bugle, Sir. It'll be 'about turn', then 'Columns by Troops' as we ride back. Sir."

And so it was. With the French 300 yards off, at full charge, the bugle sounded, all wheeled their horses and cantered back, forming into narrow Troop columns as they went, back to the line of the Light Division. This superb Division were formed in columns of Sections providing intervals through which the 16th rode. Within seconds the Sections broke apart and formed into line to meet the oncoming French cavalry and Carr heard the first volleys crash out. Anson's men turned and formed again behind the infantry line to see them delivering controlled volleys into the stunned French. Smoke shrouded all, but the line did not buckle or even bend and it took but three minutes before the line fell silent, the smoke drifting away to reveal French cavalry in full retreat. Both infantry and cavalry remained in the same position for a further hour, whilst the Lights gathered what food, drink and valuables were available from the French dead. Some horses were brought back to Anson's line, most with N26ème embroidered into a corner of their saddle blanket.

Back on the ridge, being Wellington's main rearguard, the 4th Division held their place throughout the night, all camping on the open plain, but the Light Division and their supporting cavalry remained a mile out in front, studying the growing spread of campfires that marked

Marmont's main force. What G. Anson's Cavalry and General Charles Alten's Light Division could not possibly know, in their forward position, was the news that was circulating back on the ridge. This came to the 105th when the Colonel and Majors of the 27th were sharing French brandy with Carr and O'Hare. Only these two of the 105th could they bring themselves to take drink with, which privately excluded the 105th's Colonel. Creet began the conversation, whilst pouring generous measures.

"You've not heard?"

"What?" in unison from the pair of the 105th.

"Johnny turned around at Toro, recrossed the Douro, blew up the bridge and marched back the way they'd come, then, just about all he's got crossed at Pollos and Tordesillas and marched on for us. The great most is at Nava del Rey, half a dozen miles up the road."

Both put down their glasses and stared at him, but he continued.

"Wellington's been wrong-footed, and it's us, here, that's to pull his chestnuts out of the fire! He sent too much to cover the crossing at Toro. All that were there are now force-marching back to Salamanca."

oOo

G. Anson's cavalry woke to find the Light Division marching back, already half way to the ridge, and soon orders were being shouted to mount up, patrol forward and 'do their job'. Blankets and cooking equipment were rapidly bundled up and strapped onto the rear of saddles and on forward they went, Squadrons One and Two each in two ranks, line abreast, with Three and Four in similar formation, but some 200 yards behind. The Cornets of One and Two were sent forward, with Sergeants, 400 yards before and within 20 minutes, beyond Castrejon, all came to a halt, Carr and Peterson halting together. They had no choice; the French were advancing on a two Corps front. It was a massive advance, the threat obvious and potent. They rode back immediately, to find that Anson had already been informed and Squadrons One and Two were already falling back to reform closer to Three and Four. There, holding their line, they stood watching the French come forward, but what emerged even more rapidly from the French mass were several field-gun batteries, who rapidly deployed and began sending howitzer shells in the direction of the Light Cavalry lined up before them. However, within minutes, two full six-gun Royal Artillery batteries came galloping around both flanks, to deploy equally rapidly and send round-shot back in reply. The noise was intense, batteries from both sides, plus the exploding French shells. All in the 16th did their best to calm their horses and it was with relief that the order came for Anson's Brigade to withdraw. They formed column by Regiments and a look to their right saw why retreat was so imperative, a heavy French column was marching in unison with them, almost ahead of Anson's men, creating a danger that they may be cut off.

Henry Carr was stood on the ridge, observing events. The 105th had slept in position and were now stood in battle formation. He turned at the sound of hooves to see, almost inevitably, the well mounted St. John Slade, reining in his horse.

"The Colonel wants to see you!"

Carr nodded.

"Lead on!"

Carr followed him the short way to find Brockenhurst drinking what Carr hoped was coffee.

"Sir?"

"We've been ordered to retreat."

"Yes, Sir. I'll get the Drummers to sound form up. Anything more, Sir?"

"Yes. We are to pull back to the River Guarena."

"Yes Sir."

"Who knows the way?"

"Oh, I think we can be certain that our cavalry and Commanders know that, Sir. If we just hold our place in our column, we should get there well enough. Sir."

Silence, therefore Carr saluted.

"I'll get off, then, Sir."

Carr ran to the Drum Major and soon the Drummers were beating out 'form up' and the 105th abandoned their positions to take their place within the column of the 4th Division. As they began their march O'Hare looked around and then looked at Carr.

"I don't like this!"

Carr did not need an analysis. The 4th were the right-hand column of two, the Light Division were to their left, meaning that the 4th were nearest to the flanking French infantry column making a rapid French pace. Then Carr noticed something himself.

"That's a mess!"

He drew his telescope, used it, lowered it and then used it to point.

"And, I'd say that Beresford and Wellington are in the middle of it!"

O'Hare drew his own instrument to focus himself. What he saw was a tangle of British Light Cavalry, engaged with French Hussars. In the middle were two field-guns, with Wellington and Beresford riding out of it with swords drawn, then came a charge by two Squadrons of

British Light Cavalry which saved the situation, both for the field-guns and for Wellington and Beresford. O'Hare folded his telescope.

"That does not bode at all well!"

Even within the next few minutes he was proved correct. From the very disconcertingly close French column there emerged two complete field-batteries who began to bombard the column of the 4th Division. Lowry-Cole's men could do nothing apart from lower their heads into their collars and march as fast as they could and look enviously at the Light Division to their left, whose march was wholly untroubled. Had Carr not had major concerns of his own, were he aware of his situation, he would have been very apprehensive about his brother, who was at that moment riding through Castrejon at above canter speed with French cannonballs hitting the Church tower and citizens fleeing away into the countryside. Once clear of the town came the dry river bed and Cornet Carr looked over to see the guns of Bull's battery bouncing alarmingly as the teams hurtled across at the point where the river-bed's banks sloped to be slightly more negotiable. Then the word was shouted across by Johnson.

"Cover the guns. Too many of their cavalry round about!"

The hurried order conveyed urgency, but which Squadron of the 16th were to do what, was unclear and so Oakwood led his men to the nearest guns. It was not long before Carr recognised Captain Ramsey and he cantered his horse to within hailing distance. Both had been together during Ramsey's battery's desperate escape at Fuentes de Onoro when surrounded by French cavalry at very close quarters.

"Captain Ramsey, Sir."

Ramsey looked over and grinned.

"Cornet Carr, pleased it's you!"

"Thank you, Sir. Does any of this seem familiar to you, at all?"

At that point the battery veered away and Ramsey could do no more than grin and wave, whilst Carr, or rather Baxter, kept the Troop together. All Officers looked anxiously around for any French effort at the guns it was their duty to protect, everyone now moving at a fast canter across the vast open plain.

It was the very openness of the countryside around them which was creating at least some of the anxiety amongst the 4th Division, remaining under constant, if not intense bombardment, from the very well-handled French artillery. That anxiety dwelt not least in the minds of Brockenhurst and Slade at the head of the 105th column. Carr and O'Hare were both mounted, feeling that their place was at the head of the column and that duty required them to support their Colonel, as the cannon shot buzzed, hummed, or even bounced over or between the Battalion columns. Matters became a great deal worse for Slade and

Brockenhurst when one of Lowry-Cole's ADCs, riding just ahead, was hit by a cannonball, or more accurately his horse. The ball took off the ADC's leg below the knee, but the horse was blown practically inside out by the passage of the ball. Carr saw Brockenhurst sway in his saddle, but at that moment, there was no comfort that could be given, in fact matters became worse, in the shape of Lowry-Cole himself.

"Colonel! Get your Lights out and form square with the 27th and Rifles. See what can be done to that battery. The Divisional battery will come out in support."

With that he was gone and Carr looked at O'Hare, then at Brockenhurst, who had not turned in his saddle to give any orders. Carr took it upon himself, but both shared a look of horror at what they had been ordered to do.

"I'll see to it, if you stay here and keep these two sensible!"

He turned to the Colour Company behind to see the individual that he would definitely need.

"Bates! With me."

Leaving Bates to follow, Carr galloped back to the Light Company.

"Nat! Fall out and double over towards those French batteries. Form square with the 27th Lights and our Rifles. There's too much Frog cavalry about. I'll be with you. Cole's orders."

"What!"

But Carr was gone, so Drake immediately turned to Sergeant Ellis.

"Sergeant! Fall out and double towards those guns."

Ellis was as aghast at the order as Drake, but, nevertheless, the Light Company turned from their course and began to jog away from the relative safety of the 4th Division column and out onto the flat expanse between themselves and the two French batteries. One was now limbered up and casually taking themselves up to the next position from where they could continue their work, whilst the other was in position and working their guns at battle speed. On the outside of the column, Miles was not in the slightest impressed with what was taking place as they ran, at Light Infantry pace and still in column, towards menacing French cavalry and a full battery of French field-guns.

"And what's this? Are we to be some set of Aunt Sallies, stuck up for the Frogs to fire at an' leave the rest alone?"

There was no reply. All had their own worries because they knew that Miles was right, that they were running into great danger. Meanwhile, Carr had ridden some way forward to better assess the ground and that done he returned to Drake when he came up, who had deep concerns of his own and he did not allow Carr to speak before he voiced those concerns, as Carr trotted his horse and Drake ran beside.

"Henry, this is against everything we've been taught. To stand in square against artillery. It's madness!"

"Nat, you're right, I know, but that's orders from Lowry-Cole himself. The cavalry are not too near, so get across in open order. When within range, close up into square, you at the front, and give them all the volleys you can manage. I'll see that the 27th and Bairns, to do the same. Good luck is all I can say."

Carr galloped over to the 27th Light Company, still in column and running forward. Even though the situation was fraught with peril, proprieties had to be observed as he rode up to the 27th Captain.

"Carr. 105th."

"Reardon, Sir. 27th."

"Cole's orders! Get across to that battery in open order then form square with mine and the Rifles when they arrive. We are to give those gunners as much grief as possible. Yours at the rear, I want riflemen at the front. My 105th have been told the same, I'll get onto Bairns' Rifles."

Bairns' men were already in open order and further than the 27th when Carr saw one crumb of comfort. The full field-gun battery belonging to the 4th Division were galloping out in support. The three Companies ran the distance in obedience to their General's orders, but it was not long before the French cavalry noticed them, as did the guns, but infantry in open order were too poor a target for guns and so their attention remained with the 4th Division column, best to leave scattered infantry to the cavalry. Carr was by now cantering his horse between the 105th and the 27th, both in open order. He looked towards his right, over the heads of the 105th to see French Hussars approaching at the gallop. He spoke out loud to himself, "This will need careful timing". He then galloped over to find Bates.

"Ready, Bates?"

"Sir!"

Carr looked again. The three Companies were now close, almost co-mingling, but the Hussars were merely a minute away. He could wait no longer.

"Bates. Form square."

The notes rang out and the elite Light Companies formed a square, rough and misshapen because of no previous rehearsal, but it was a defensive shape nevertheless. Carr vaulted from his horse and turned it loose.

"Bates!"

Both ran into the square and it closed behind them, just as the volleys crashed out from the side opposing the oncoming Hussars, but there was more to do. They were not yet within Baker range of the guns and a square was now a very tempting target. One French gun had already changed line and its shot carried through both the front and rear of the square, knocking men over like skittles.

"Bates! Advance."

The notes sounded out and the square moved closer to the guns, at the trot, leaving their dead and wounded behind. Carr hurried over to where his own men were and found the one he wanted, Davey, alongside a file of Riflemen.

'Davey! Can you get their Officer?"

Davey already had his sights adjusted and his Baker carefully loaded for the first shot, the ball wrapped in the thin sheet of leather.

"Sir!"

Davey cocked the hammer.

"Joe. Gives us a shoulder."

Pike stepped over and Davey rested his Baker on Pike's broad right shoulder. A second or more to sight and then he fired. Before the smoke covered all, Carr saw the Battery Captain arch backwards as though he had been punched.

"Good shot, Davey."

As Carr ran off, Davey shared a knowing look with the Rifleman beside him as he reloaded, but the Rifleman just smiled, nodded and checked his own weapon. They were still advancing forward and had now arrived at something close to 100 yards, but now all the battery guns were turned onto them. Carr gathered a huge lungful of air.

"Front rank! Full volley!"

He waited for the weapons at the front, all Bakers, to come to the horizontal.

"Fire!"

The first volley crashed out, but Carr waited but two seconds.

"Second rank. Full Volley."

Again, the volley crashed out and now Carr had to wait for a re-load, which his trained men would indicate completed by raising their weapon to the vertical, to the 'make ready'. This gave time to see the effect of their fire at easy Baker range and he could see that almost half the French gunners had been brought down, but not all and a gun fired to again wreak havoc through both sides of the square. Then came a heavier roar, which Carr hoped was from their own battery, but he decided not to wait.

"Fire when ready!"

There was an immediate response, followed by continuous firing from both ranks. The smoke hid all, but no more shot came through the square, therefore he concluded they must be doing serious damage to the gun-crews, but there were two batteries opposed to them and which of these their own Divisional battery was targeting he had no idea, the one before them or the one further on. Carr waited no more than two minutes before deciding that their position was utterly perilous, the French had more than two batteries in their own column, any of which could enter the fight and the Hussars had not given in, the sides and the rear of the square were still under attack. Bates had remained with him.

"Bates. Fall back."

As the notes sounded out, Carr ran around the small square.

"Hold your ranks, boys, hold together. We're pulling back, but don't let them in."

The 'them' which he referred to, were the French Hussars, still very much in attendance, but suddenly they were gone and the reason came from Bairns, stood closeby.

"Sir. Ours are coming over."

Carr looked left to see Heavy Cavalry, two Brigades no less, coming to them at a controlled canter. Carr gave vent to the deepest sigh of his life as the Heavy Dragoons cantered past. Their Commander stopped at the square and shouted over the heads of the still formed 105th Lights.

"Le Marchant!"

Carr came to the attention and saluted. Here was a Brigadier General of Cavalry.

"Carr, Sir. 105th."

"Well done, Major. Get yours back to the column, this isn't over yet!"

With that, Le Marchant was gone and so Carr turned to Bates for the last time.

"Well done, Bates. Now 'retreat', and that's that."

Bates grinned just before he blew the notes and the square broke up for the men to reform into their Sections and hurry back, carrying their wounded. As they began their journey, Ellis looked over at Bettridge to see what looked like a frozen expression of terror on his face, but he took some comfort in the fact that the youngster's legs were moving and so he spoke out loud to Zeke Saunders.

"Well, at least he's still upright. He didn't bloody well faint!"

Saunders knew full well who Ellis was referring to as both loped back to their column, where they were given a cheer by the rest of the Battalion. Ellis looked again at Bettridge, to see what looked like a weak smile, hopefully caused by their reception back, but he made no further comment, other than to shake his head with disbelief.

Anything spoken, would have been drowned out anyway, because Wellington had sent out a full KGL field-gun battery besides the two Brigades of Heavy Cavalry. Carr had deliberately lagged behind, wondering how the Lights of Ellis' Brigade of the 4th Division had fared against the other battery, but the noise and smoke were too great to see anything and so he left the question unanswered. Instead, he seized the reins of a French Hussar mount, quickly ascended into the saddle and was grateful that there was no French blood anywhere on the leather. He came back to the 105th just as they were crossing the Guarena, this only a shallow stream, but nevertheless men were falling out to fill their canteens with water muddied from hundreds of marching feet. However, French cannonballs began to arrive from somewhere and all canteen filling was ordered to stop by Staff ADCs

Carr rejoined the head of the 105th column and was grateful to see another whole Division waiting to support their retreat. Within minutes all serious conflict had ceased and they marched on, all pleased to now see two other infantry Divisions marching beside themselves, a whole field-gun battery and three Brigades of cavalry. Carr looked over to G. Anson's Light Dragoons hoping to see his brother, but it was impossible to distinguish who was and who was not. Soon the rest of the army came into sight, drawn up on a long, low ridge on the far side of the river Guarena. They wearily ascended the shallow gradient, for a Lowry-Cole ADC to then gallop up to Brockenhurst.

"Our Division's furthest left, Sir. There's a village over there which marks our flank on that side. A place called Castrillo, but we are placed on the ridge above it. I cannot find your General Anson, so if you would please lead the way, Sir. General Ellis' are already in that direction. You are to form beyond him. Sir."

Brockenhurst visibly puffed up at being given the nominal control of a whole Brigade and so he rode on at their head, head leaning back, his face wearing a disdainful expression. They had now arrived at the height of the ridge and so Brockenhurst and Slade turned their horses right to ride along the summit, the 105th to lead the 27th and finally the Rifles along the ridge to their position. It took but twenty minutes before they came to Ellis' Brigade halted not as far as the village of Castrillo and so Brockenhurst led Anson's Brigade on and past, to become the far left of the Allied line, 300 yards directly above the village. There all wearily slumped down, to cook what they had in their haversacks and for Surgeon Pearce to begin his mournful work on a table in the open air. However, Junior Major Carr did not rest, instead he simply ordered Bryce to save him some food. He had seen Cavalry Anson's Brigade ride to the rear behind the formed infantry and so he rode his new French mount, over to their lines. Unfortunately, the first Officer he encountered was Captain Tavender. He hoped for a cordial response after the shared dangers of the day, but he was wrong.

“Lucius! Pleased to see that you came through. I’m enquiring after my brother. Can you help?”

Tavender was releasing the buttons of his tunic after the heat of the day, and the sight of Major Carr did nothing to improve his mood.

“No. Sir. With that I cannot help you.”

Carr nodded and thought to himself, ‘No change here’, so he gave a direct order.

“Point me to his Squadron.”

Tavender looked balefully at him, but, as Senior Captain, that was something he should know. He pointed along the back side of the ridge.

“Two Squadron is next to mine. Just that way.”

There was no ‘Sir’, but Carr walked his horse on, to come upon Sergeant Baxter, who immediately recognised Carr as his Troop Leader’s brother and he sprung to attention. Men such as Sergeant of Horse, Septimus Baxter were of the type that Carr held in the highest esteem and so he felt no inclination to enforce the difference in their ranks.

“At ease, Sergeant. I’m looking for my brother. Can you help?”

“Only so far, Sir. I can say that he came through well enough, but he has taken his mount over to the Farrier, Sir. He picked up a cut getting through that village.”

Carr frowned.

“Is that some way back?”

“Probably, Sir. Couldn’t say for definite.”

Carr was well aware that he was where he should not be, he had his own important duties to attend to.

“Very good, so, if he is well, I’ll be satisfied with that. Thank you, Sergeant.”

Carr swung his horse around as Baxter came back to the attention and saluted, but Carr turned in his saddle and smiled.

“Good to know that we of the 105th have your 16th in support, Sergeant!”

Baxter came even further to the attention.

“Sir!”

Carr walked his horse back and handed him over to one of Bryce’s Corporals, before obtaining a plate of salt pork stew which he ate sat on the ground beside O’Hare. As he finished his final mouthful, the Senior Major indicated forward with his forehead.

“There’ll be doings tomorrow.”

The evidence was there before them. A whole French Infantry Corps, although much hidden in the heat haze and dust could be seen taking positions out on the plain in the last of the daylight, positions obviously preparatory for an advance. After their pork stew, plus army biscuits and several cups of water. O'Hare stood up.

"Best get around the men. A few words might help. It's all getting very serious."

Carr nodded and stood himself.

"I'll start with the Lights. That was good work today on their part."

O'Hare nodded and spent the rest of the daylight telling the same joke to each mess he came to, the one relating the tale of a Trainee Priest, who climbed over the wall of a Convent, thinking he was sneaking back into his own Seminary next door, but he blundered into the Novices dormitory and in the dark climbed into what he thought was his own bed. It was poor humour, but they expected awful stories from O'Hare. As Carr toured his Companies, not telling jokes but simply enquiring after their welfare, he passed Brockenhurst and Slade, both sat on camp stools drinking, drinking what, Carr could not tell. They both noticed Carr and so he could not pass-by ignoring a Superior Officer. He saluted as he passed.

"Making the evening rounds, Sir."

The response came not in words, but in sullen looks from both. Carr continued on, speaking softly to himself.

"All proving to be a bit of an education, is it?"

However, that was not the end of the day. The order was circulated, from Wellington himself. "Stand to before dawn".

oOo

As the sun rose on every Regiment that Wellington had, all standing waiting in a line that stretched five miles from Castrillo in the North to the Guarena fords at Olmo, it was W. Anson's Brigade of the 4th Division that could see the first evidence of a French assault. Every men could see it, a whole Brigade of what looked like Heavy Cavalry were advancing to the left of Castrillo, to cross the Guarena downstream of the village, beyond the Allied left, whilst what could only be a whole Division of French infantry were advancing with the intention of crossing the Guarena on the opposite side of the same collection of white hovels. O'Hare and Carr both had their telescopes in action as soon as the infantry mass before them did emerge from the early heat haze and could then be estimated. O'Hare spoke first.

"God! I see eight Battalions. Six in two columns, one behind the other, with two more in support, also in column and coming up behind."

Carr nodded and closed his own telescope.

"It'll be us. He's chosen us because we were the last in position here. He thinks we're the least settled. If he turns the line here, then the rest of Marmont's will come forward. We'd better get back to the Colonel and see what he wants to do."

This produced an ironic laugh from O'Hare as they hurried back, to find an ADC riding up to Brockenhurst, clearly from the Commander in Chief himself.

"Sir. General Wellington would have you meet this attack, Sir. The 27th will be on your right and two Battalions of General Stubbs' Portuguese will be in support immediately behind your left, Sir."

With that, the ADC rode on, presumably to pass on Wellington's orders to Stubbs. Brockenhurst, the deep anxiety etched across his face, turned to Slade.

"Two Battalions, against that!"

He pointed forward to the French, now around 500 yards from the river, then his arm fell.

"Supported by Portuguese!"

O'Hare had had enough.

"Sir. What are your orders? The men are already stood to."

Brockenhurst turned on him, his anger overcoming his deep unease, but his voice had a distinct quaver.

"Obey Wellington's orders, Major!"

"Yes Sir. So, do we advance in two ranks, Sir."

All that came back was a nod and so the two ran off, Carr to the Drum Major.

"Beat 'stand to' then 'make ready'."

In no time the drums beat out the orders and all in line began the process of loading their weapons. As they bit off the ends of their cartridges, Deakin spoke to his Ensign, Patrick Mulcahy, his 'wife's' son.

"Get the case off The Colours, Sir. We'll be in it soon."

The reply came back, in the same usual form that always mortified Colour Sergeant Deakin.

"Yes, Uncle Jed."

The case was removed to be thrust into Deakin's pack, giving him the chance to look despairingly, because of his Ensign's response, at Halfway. He was stood behind grinning, but now loaded, with his musket vertical, at the 'make ready'. Before moving to the 'wings' of the Battalion, five Companies each side, Carr stood with O'Hare, looking around.

"Where's Brockenhurst?"

O'Hare shook his head.

"I'd better do it. The 27th are already going down."

Whilst Carr ran out to the right wing, O'Hare ran the short distance to stand before the Colour Company in the centre, both Colours high and curling lazily in the fitful breeze.

"The Frogs are on our doorstep, boys! Time to show them the end of

the street!"

He held his sword aloft.

"105th will advance!"

The drums beat the step and the 105th moved forward. All could see that the leading French Battalions were now over the river and ascending the slope. However, the 105th had not taken a dozen steps, before Brockenhurst, his sword still in its scabbard came panting along the front of the 105th, pointing over to the left.

"French cavalry coming up. Over there and damn close!"

He gave no more detail and so O'Hare answered him.

"Yes Sir. They're not our worry, Sir. Stubbs men are over there in our support and we can safely assume that our Wellington will send some of our own cavalry down to meet them. Sir. He'll have seen them, Sir, and he'll take some action."

The cavalry support was at that moment walking slowly forward over the crest of the ridge, in the form of G. Anson's, 11th, 12th and 16th Light Dragoons. They advanced as six Squadrons abreast, two from each Regiment in the front line, each Squadron in four ranks with the remaining six Squadrons in the same formation, 100 yards behind. However, they were unseen from the slope above Castrillo where the 105th paced out their advance. Oakwood sat with Cornet Carr, watching the French Dragoons splash through the Guarena, with their own Anson sat on his horse before them, waiting for his moment, this moment predicted by Oakwood.

"He's letting them onto the slope, then we'll be down onto them with the slope to our advantage."

"Sir?'

"Yes. Let him get one or two lines onto the slope and then we smash them back into the rest. Quite simple really."

Carr took some deep breaths in the hope of inflating his confidence and checked that his sabre came free from its scabbard.

Meanwhile Colonel Brockenhurst could barely breath at all. Cavalry Brigadier Anson was allowing his opponents to advance beyond the village, then onto the slope and that would allow them to turn left in his direction. This finally broke what already shredded nerve Brockenhurst had left. He looked around for succour against his fears, but found none.

Meanwhile, in the centre Captain Heaviside was encouraging his men in his usual inspiring fashion.

"When the trumpet sounds, he says 'Aha'. He smells the battle from afar, the thunder of the Captains. Job. 39, 25."

It was Deakin, now obeying time honoured ritual, who replied as the whole line marched forward.

"Yes Sir. Sounds about right, Sir."

He could see his Colonel in his place before the Colours, but more being shepherded forward by the oncoming ranks than leading them. Brockenhurst heard nothing of Heaviside's exhortations, what he did hear was the 27th opening fire against the opposing column. At that point, Deakin, looking over at what was happening with the 27th suddenly felt someone blunder past, but O'Hare had now turned to Heaviside and Captain Bryce of Six Company, both the centre Companies.

"Heaviside. Bryce. You first."

What this meant was that the front ranks of both Companies would begin the half-Company volleys that would then run along the line from the centre, front rank then rear rank, delivering fire-power that no French column had withstood so far in all the years of the Peninsular War. The two Captains yelled "Front rank present', O'Hare dropped back into the ranks and waited, as the muskets of the front rank came down to the horizontal, but before the order came to fire, he heard drums rolling out. It took more than a few seconds for him to recognise the roll. He recognised the roll in horror.

"That's 'Fall back'!"

Immediately the line around him began to dissolve, his shouting of "Stand boys, stand", was all in vain. The whole left wing of the 105th was now a mass of running men. O'Hare ran back to the Drum Major.

"What the Hell have you done!"

The Drum Major was almost incapable of speech, knowing what he had caused, but he could say just enough.

"The Colonel, Sir. He ordered beat "Fall back". His order, Sir."

Henry Carr, stood at the right wing, before the Grenadiers, reacted with total bewilderment as he suddenly found himself alone with the Grenadiers and Two Company disappearing from behind him and also the rest of the right wing. He turned to see Carravoy, as much at a loss as himself.

"What's happening?"

Carravoy shook his head, then joined his men running back up the hill and Carr had no choice but to follow. O'Hare, meanwhile, had found Bates, at the Colour Company.

"Bates. Sound 're-form'."

The notes rang out and, hearing that, Deakin grabbed his own Ensign.

"Here! Plant the Colours here."

Colour Sergeant Bennet had done the same with his Ensign, him carrying the King's Colour and the four stood together as a rallying point. Bates was blowing for all he was worth and the men were slowly halting their flight up the slope, some now returning, but it would all be too late. Carr had sprinted over to O'Hare, who anticipated his question.

"Brockenhurst ordered the Drummers to beat 'Fall back'."

"Where is he now?"

However, before he could answer infantry Brigadier Anson had arrived, even more agitated than his horse.

"What the Devil is this?"

It was O'Hare that answered.

"Our Colonel, Sir. Brockenhurst. He ordered our drummers to beat 'Fall back'."

Anson's face did not change as he wrenched his horse's head around.

"Get back in the fight!"

The 105th were reforming, but it would be some minutes before order was restored. Meanwhile, Carr looked across to see the two Battalions of Stubbs' Portuguese, all dark blue, bar the white cross-belts, hurrying forward to fill the gap created by the 105th's retreat, the Portuguese advancing forward, led by a Brigade Officer, probably Stubbs himself. Carr could only stand in the deepest despair as his Regiment came back together, still in no shape to have any influence on events at all.

The conflict the other side of the village was progressing much as Oakwood had predicted. Their Anson, had timed their charge to perfection and now the 16th were in the Guarena, with the French Dragoons in full disarray. Their first Squadrons had been hit by a hurtling Brigade of Light Cavalry as they attempted the slope. Cornet Carr, had ridden for a gap, taking an ineffective side swipe at the Dragoon on his left, but, much more effective, Baxter and Makepeace, riding stirrup to stirrup had cannoned into the French Dragoon's Colonel, sending both him and his mount skidding down the turf to fell other Dragoon mounts behind. In such fashion their opponent French Squadron had been hammered back into the one behind and now all was confusion in the French ranks as the Light Dragoons pressed forward, sabres flashing at whichever opponent could be reached.

It was not long before French trumpets sounded and the Dragoons fell back and then their own instruments of Anson's Brigade sounded 'Re-form'. Anson was yelling to confirm the trumpet order and all could now see why. The French infantry, beyond the village were now in full flight after the attentions of the intractable 27th and the two, very capable, Portuguese Line Battalions. Every Light Dragoon now knew what was coming, a charge at the broken French infantry, and so they set themselves accordingly, even though Troops and Squadrons were now somewhat mixed, but Carr was grateful to see Baxter, Makepeace, Spivey and Nunney in close attendance. The trumpet sounded "Charge' and Cavalry Anson waved his sabre forward, now much reddened, in the direction of the advance. They galloped the short distance to arrive behind the village, to be met by desultory fire, which downed a few Light Dragoons, then they were amongst the disordered French, but many were now throwing down their arms, whilst many others threw them away to aid their flight. For Anson's men it was now merely a matter of hustling disconsolate and wounded Frenchmen back up the slope to the British lines, encouragement given by boots, sabre points and shuffling their mounts into any reluctant group. Baxter was giving good advice as his Cornet rode behind a group of prisoners.

"Best get them up, Sir. If some runs off, leave 'em. See what's arriving."

What was arriving was a fresh French Battalion, but only to give cover by standing in line to the many French fugitives. Besides, as he looked, he saw that the fresh Battalion had troubles of their own, now coming under fire from Allied batteries on the ridge. The Light Dragoons shepherded their prisoners to the top, where KGL infantry took custody, then they rode back along the ridge to their original position, Baxter noting with some satisfaction that the Colonel he and Makepeace had smashed to the ground was amongst the Dragoon prisoners being led back.

There was no such satisfaction amongst any of the 105th as they retired back to their original position atop the ridge. They had reformed and O'Hare had led them forward in support of the Portuguese, but they had not fired a shot, the French columns, assailed constantly by the pitiless Allied volleys, two every second, had stood for barely minutes before falling back themselves, leaving many dead and wounded. Back on the ridge, Carr's despair had turned to livid anger and he stalked over to Slade, who for a moment felt for his own safety. Carr with his sabre drawn.

"Where's Brockenhurst?"

Slade shook his head. He was as dazed by events as anyone. He had not thought for a moment that the 105th would retreat in such a fashion before the enemy. He was surprised and shocked at the despair he now felt within himself. As he sheathed his own sword he saw the cuff of his uniform, the lurid green of the 105th. Their shame was as much his as theirs. Carr delivered a hard, contemptuous stare and then stalked off.

Amongst Deakin and for those around him, all was a mystery. Deakin sat on the hard ground eating a biscuit and quizzing Zeke Saunders.

"What do you know?"

"Less than you. We were out on the left, you were in the centre. All of a sudden, we found ourselves on our own, with a whole Frog column coming up the slope."

At that moment Toby Halfway entered the group and spoke immediately.

"It was the Colonel. I've just come from Bill Meaker in the drums. He says the Colonel ordered him to beat 'Fall back', then disappeared."

Joe Pike then had a very relevant thought.

"He could be shot, couldn't he? For cowardice?'

Both Deakin and Halfway grinned ironically, but Deakin voiced the answer.

"That applies to thee and me! But not to the likes of Sir Ambrose Brockenhurst, Honourable Member for a flock of sheep, somewer'. They just gets sent home to write up their excuses into the paper. You and I just gets a dozen bullets and six foot, if that."

Deakin stood, stretched and voiced further thoughts.

"Whatever. The Frogs was seen off and we've a couple of dozen lads still alive or not wounded. I'll call that the bright side, but that won't be how the rest of the army sees it. We ran! It'll take summat to live that down and shut their mouths."

Unlike his usual self, Tom Miles had been sat quiet, but now he spoke up, against a man three ranks above him.

"Well I don't see it that way, your 'bright side'. We'n here to fight the Frogs and we didn't. The 27th stood the line, we didn't. Could be they've got more lads dead because we shot off! 'Tis shameful an' it falls on us!"

At that moment, the drums beat to form column and so there was no more argument as all stood up to walk slowly to the top of the ridge, where the whole of the 4th Division were forming for column of march. Anson's Brigade were to be the first in the 4th Division's column, the 105th before the Rifles with the 27th behind them. As they assembled there were no derisive shouts from the 27th, they had broken their advance slightly themselves when they heard the drums beside them, but as the 105th marched South to where Wellington now wanted the 4th to be, catcalls accompanied their march, the sad saga had been passed on throughout the army. In the absence of Brockenhurst, O'Hare and Carr rode at the front, with Slade, now feeling thoroughly misplaced, just behind. As the taunts and mockery came from all sides, O'Hare sighed and turned to Carr.

"I would that we were further back in the column, instead of leading it."

Carr's anger had barely subsided.

"Anyone who calls us cowards, I'll call them out! Damned if I don't."

O'Hare's face transformed with impatience from what he had heard.

"You will not! Facts are facts. We faced a French column and we ran. The fact that it was caused by a craven Commanding Officer is neither here nor there. He was, still is I assume, our Colonel and a member of the Regiment and he decided that we should run. That's that! We take it and carry on."

O'Hare's own mood subsided and he was pleased to see a change in Carr's face.

"We're still the same lads. You can't tell me we wouldn't have given that Johnny column a thorough mauling, if those drums hadn't rolled out. Just keep your head down and do what's asked."

Carr smiled wryly and nodded.

"So, where is our Colonel?"

Before O'Hare could answer, Carr turned to Slade, his words spoken as aggressively as he could make them.

"Brockenhurst! Any idea where?"

Slade lowered his face as he shook his head and Carr turned back round to voice his own verdict.

"On his way back to the coast and planning what he's going to say in the House. And in the press!"

O'Hare grinned.

"If so, well rid!"

Noon found the 4th Division on the South end of the ridge, above another village through which ran the Guarena, but upstream and with far less volume. Once established, the Division settled down to sleep and to cook, which included Carr and O'Hare, at least to eat. They noticed the absence of Slade as they received their Noon meal.

"Where's Slade?"

Carr swallowed a mouthful.

"Took himself off to Carravoy. Birds of a feather and all that."

At that moment their Brigadier, G. Anson rode up with an ADC. Magnanimously he waved them back down when they motioned to stand, then he dismounted himself. The topic of conversation was obvious.

"Bad business that!"

'Sir', came in unison, then Anson continued.

"Where Brockenhurst is, we don't know, but what we do know is that he will be relieved of command. Wellington's incandescent!"

He paused.

"So, we have to sort you out and that's for Lowry-Cole. Come to his Headquarters at 3.00. I'll be there."

Both saluted, but Carr had a question.

"Sir, what's that village called beneath us. For the Regimental record, Sir."

Anson frowned.

"Would have thought you'd want no entry for this day!"

Carr did not reply, so Anson continued.

"Vallesa de la Guarena."

"Yes Sir, thank you. At least we've moved from Castrillo, Sir."

Then he changed the subject.

"Do we remain in line, Sir?"

"You do. Marmont's followed us South."

The concurrent movement of both armies was confirmed when cannon-fire was exchanged across the Guarena for an hour after their meal, for it to be ended when Allied shell fire set fire to crops on the French side of the Guarena, which burned fiercely hiding all in thick smoke. At 2.30 Carr and O'Hare left their lines to walk back through the 4th Division camp to find Lowry-Cole's Headquarters. A few enquiries sent them to an isolated farmhouse with the inevitable sentries outside, the building set between two olive groves. They entered to find a Major sat at what could only have been the farmhouse table and every aspect of the surrounding room spoke of solidity, durability, tradition and age. The Major stood, soon displaying a knowing grin across his face, when he saw their green facings. The tone of his greetings said all.

"Ah, the 105th."

Carr fixed him with a challenging look before speaking, very briefly.

"Here to see the General. 3.00 o' clock."

Carr's stoney look did not change as the ADC Major walked quickly to a door and opened it, to call through.

"The 105th here to see you, Sir."

The knowing grin, now almost contemptuous, remained as he indicated that they should enter. The pair did and were greeted by warm handshakes from both Lowry-Cole and Anson. The former indicated two chairs, both of the same heavy design as the table outside and they sat. Their Divisional General sat forward, elbows on his own, smaller, table and his fingertips placed together.

"Bad business today, but no-one blames you. No-one! I want that clear, but what do we do now about the higher command for yours? A Battalion your size, needs three, you only have two. Do you have a Captain you could bring up to Brevet-Major?"

Carr looked at O'Hare.

"Heaviside?"

O'Hare nodded immediately, which brought Lowry-Cole to the next question.

"Which of you two is Senior?"

O'Hare raised his hand.

"I am Sir."

"Then you are Brevet-Colonel."

O'Hare sat back and sighed, his hands folded in his lap.

"Sir, I wish to decline. I must confess that at Badajoz I was close to resigning myself with our Colonel. I do not want that level of responsibility, Sir. You should give it to Major Carr, here. He is ready for what has passed me by."

Lowry-Cole turned to Anson who returned an equally blank look, before he returned to O'Hare.

"This is irregular. You are Senior."

"That I know, Sir, but if ordered to accept, I will resign my Commission. Sir. This is something I do not want."

Lowry-Cole looked again at Anson, who at that moment remembered Carr's handling of the square during the retreat from Castrejon. Anson's face brightened.

"I've no objection."

Lowry-Cole then turned to Carr, him sat in a state of bemusement.

"Congratulations Major. You are now a Brevet-Colonel, but of a Regiment somewhat under a cloud, I fear."

With that Carr, now recovered from his unexpected elevation, stood up alongside O'Hare, but Carr took the time to look at both Senior Officers.

"I appreciate that, Sir, and thank you, but you can count on us all in the 105th to do our best and to do our duty."

Outside, they began discussing the changes this would cause, the first from O'Hare.

"Who takes over from Heaviside with Colour?"

Carr did not hesitate.

"Slade!"

"But he's a Major!"

"Then let him Major the Colour. We've good NCOs there who can take care of him."

"Second. Carravoy will not like Heaviside moving up rather than him."

Carr simply walked on.

"You are mistaking me for someone who gives one good Goddamn about the feelings of Captain Lord Charles Carravoy!"

O'Hare grinned slightly as they made their way back to their lines. Once there, Heaviside was sent for and the reply was wholly predictable.

"Therefore encourage one another and build one another up, just as you are doing. One Thessalonians. 5. 11."

Carr nodded.

"As you say, Joshua, but the time has now come when we will be looking for more from you than quotes from the Bible."

Heaviside nodded, he well knew what would now be required of him.

"As you say, Henry. Where there is no guidance, a people falls, but in an abundance of Counsellors, there is safety. Proverbs. 11. 14."

Both Carr and O'Hare chuckled, but the latter voicing his thoughts.

"You walked into that, Henry!"

Heaviside moved to leave their small camp, but Carr bid him stay.

"Remain, please, Joshua. We need you here now, for what is to come."

Carr turned to Sergeant Bryce, now his Secretary.

"Bryce, be so good as to have Major Slade sent for."

Bryce saluted and hurried off, for Slade to arrive some minutes later. He arrived in the middle of a discussion regarding the Colour Company, which was interrupted when he arrived and he simply stood, in rather slovenly fashion, his thumbs in his waist sash. This did not endear him to Carr, who pitched straight in.

"General Lowry-Cole has made me a Brevet-Colonel, St. John, and I have moved Captain Heaviside up to Brevet Major. That means that the Colour Company is short of a Captain and we are moving you into that position. You will be in command of some very good men."

Carr's blunt speech had significant impact on Slade, his face darkened to anger and his thumbs emerged for his hands to turn into clenched fists, held at his side.

"That's a role for a Captain and I am a Major! I should be the one to take the Majority vacancy."

Carr shook his head.

"I'm afraid it doesn't follow like that. Not at all."

He paused and studied Slade carefully and what he saw was more in keeping with the demeanour of a spoilt child, but he continued.

"Regulations state, St. John, the Duke of York's that is, that no-one can be a Major on active service unless they have six years active service. You have none! A Captain's role is the very best I can do for you, but you keep your Militia rank of Major. So, I would suggest that you call for your Ensigns and Colour-Sergeants and acquaint yourself with them. They are very good men and I would have thought it a good idea for you to at least find out what they look like."

Slade was not appeased.

"I shall appeal to the General!"

Carr nodded.

"Yes Major, you may do that, but I think you will find over the next few days that he will have many and much more important things on his mind, and want no further bother stemming from the behaviour of Colonel Brockenhurst."

With that Slade stalked off, followed by immediately Heaviside.

"I feel there are some people I need to talk to."

The 'people' sprang to their feet immediately Heaviside entered their mess area, all coming to rigid attention, but, surprisingly, he shuffled uneasily, before straightening up.

"I have to tell you that I am leaving the Colour Company. For some reason I'm required to be a Major."

He turned particularly to Deakin, Bennett and Halfway, offering his hand to all, which all accepted with a look close to shock.

"I regard it as a privilege to have been your Captain, over the past four years."

Deakin came to full attention.

"We couldn't have had a better, Sir. 'T'as been an honour. Sir."

He turned to the other two.

"Right, lads?"

Bennett nodded, whilst remaining rigidly upright.

"That's the truth of it, Sir. It's been an honour, Sir. As the Lord is my witness."

The mention of the Lord brought forth the inevitable, but the three found it comforting nevertheless.

"And all who believed were together and had all things in common. Acts 2. 44."

This time it was Halfway who nodded full agreement.

"That's the way to put it, Sir. Of the best, I'd say."

The other two nodded vigorously, before Deakin had the final say.

"May we wish you good luck, Sir? As soldiers, that is, one to another?"

Heaviside smiled and nodded and, as he took his leave, all three threw up blistering salutes. With Heaviside gone, came the vital question, from Sergeant Henry Nicholls.

"So, who takes his place? Farquharson. He's Senior Lieutenant."

Deakin sat down, deep in thought, but also deep concern. He had his nasty suspicions.

"Let's hope, but we'll know come the morrow."

oOo

The morrow began early, with the soundless wakening of all in the army when the order was passed quietly around to 'stand to'. Breakfast was whatever was in their knapsacks, in the case of Davey, Pike and Miles a shared meal of army biscuit, dried beef, Spanish sausage and dried fruit, all washed down with one swallow of precious water and one swallow of even more precious French brandy. From their high point they could judge for themselves the possible events of the next hour. Across the Guarena they could see Marmont's whole army, in one long column of infantry, with a thick screen of cavalry between the infantry and the Guarena itself. Ellis was stood nearby and spoke his wisdom.

"This is a marching day, boys. At least till Noon. He'll not come up here and try his French luck with us up here!"

Thus, it proved, the French began their march, purposefully across the front of the Allied line, this having not yet moved. Observers soon concluded it to be a swift French march across to the Allied right, keeping a brook that fed the Guarena between themselves and Wellington's men. The Southward march went on through the morning, the French on their ridge beyond the brook, the Allies on their side of the insignificant stream, having crossed the Guarena at Vallesa de la Guarena. The few inhabitants of the tiny hamlet who had remained were too shocked to cheer or cry, having two huge armies marching in parallel both to the front and rear of their poor collection of dwellings. Carr, O'Hare and Heaviside, all mounted, were at the head of the 105th, with the Colour Company immediately behind. Carr turned around to discover someone who was conspicuous by his absence, one Major Slade. Carr dropped his horse back to RSM Gibney, who immediately transferred his musket to his left shoulder to make it easier to salute.

"Have you seen Major Slade?"

"No Sir."

"At all, this morning?"

"No Sir."

Carr's face darkened.

"When, or even if, you see him, inform him that he is to report to me. No delay. If he refuses, the Drum Major is to arrest him."

Behind the magnificent whiskers, Gibney's face registered shock, but he did not allow it to enter his voice.

"No delay. Yes Sir."

Carr edged his horse forward, up to O'Hare and Heaviside, the former speculating on what was happening.

"Johnny's trying to get ahead and turn our flank by turning up North when he can. That'll cut us off from retreat back to Cuidad. He's assuming he's got the coming battle won. If he manages his turn we'll have no choice but to attack him, something the Peer always tries to avoid."

Heaviside choked back an appropriate Bible quote. He had enough military knowledge to contribute to good effect.

"They march faster than us and Marmont's forcing us to protect Salamanca. However, we are on the inside of the circle. They'll have to up their usual pace to get around us."

Carr looked over at the long smudge of blue within the dust.

"That's a veteran army, he's got there, and Marmont's good. You can bet the Peer's worried. This'll be no Vimeiro."

The other two nodded and smiled at the memory of the first major battle of the Peninsular War when the 105th, along with others, had hammered four French columns into oblivion within the space of two hours, but Carr's thoughts were now elsewhere as he studied their position. He could see that Wellington had his army moving in three parallel columns and that the 4th Division was part of the left, that nearest the French, and he decided it was the strongest, comprising four Divisions. The 1st Division were in the lead, then the 4th, followed by the 5th and the Light Divisions, all this information obtained from Anson, before the march began. Inside and to his right, as far as he could tell were the 6th and 7th Divisions and two Brigades of Portuguese, the brown of Cacadores and the all dark blue of Line Battalions. There was a third column beyond the ridge and out of sight and so Carr took that on trust. Ahead and out on the left flank were both Light Cavalry Brigades, Alten's KGL and G. Anson's Light Dragoons. O'Hare was studying the scene himself.

"A magnificent spectacle, Colonel Carr! Something to tell your children and grand-children."

Carr nodded, but could not help mumble to himself.

"Indeed! If I ever have any."

Then, Carr clenched his jaw together at the thought, before uttering the single word.

"Slade!"

O'Hare's face immediately turned towards Carr.

"What about him?"

"I'd forgotten. I ordered Gibney to find him and send him to me. What does he know about firing drill and half-Company volleys? We've made him Captain of the Colour Company. We walk off the battlefield or stay on it dead, depending on the likes of him!"

O'Hare frowned. The question was valid.

"He did not attend the training we gave to the Militia that Brockenhurst brought out with him. Leave it to me, I'll see to it."

Noon came and all who predicted a battle were proved wrong. All that happened, compared to what was now thought inevitable, were three French field-gun batteries being set up to bombard the nearest column, it being the 1st Division receiving their unwelcome attentions. This prime Division of three Brigades, one of Guards, one of all British Line and the third of all KGL Battalions, altered their course out of range and the French did not cross the brook to follow and the cannonade ceased. Throughout the afternoon both armies looked at each other, the Allies more anxious as the fleeter French edged slowly ahead. The bright day drew to a close, the dying sun now in their faces, whose previous heat had caused many to use up the most of their precious water. Each column thus trudged wearily up the slope of another ridge to sleep, once more in line. As they partook of their own sparse meal, W. Anson arrived within the Seniors of the 105th, and he sat on the hard ground with them, gratefully sipping a cup of good coffee as provided by Bryce. As he took the first sip, he asked the first question.

"How are yours?"

It was Carr who answered.

"Fine, Sir. Ready for what's coming, although water is proving a bit scarce."

The reply was a mere nod and so Carr continued.

"Any news on Brockenhurst? Sir?"

"The Provosts have him. He'll be up before the Peer, if there's time and if we come out of this in one piece. It's not of the best. He'll quote Parliamentary Privilege and walk. Wouldn't be surprised if the Peer didn't give him a blistering, then let him take the first boat home and say good riddance. The Peer's concerns are very much elsewhere."

"Sir?"

"Yes. Marmont has him over a barrel. If we protect Salamanca we are cut off from Cuidad. If we secure our line of retreat to Cuidad, we lose Salamanca."

He paused.

"He's hoping for a battle, but defensive and on our terms, but Marmont will have to be desperate to bring that about and, right now, I don't think he's at all desperate."

On that depressing note and wishing to change the subject, the final question came from Heaviside, him keeping his own diary.

"Where are we now, please, Sir."

W. Anson grinned.

"You think I can pronounce the names of these damn places! Aldea Rubia is the best I can do. That's it, down there, occupied by my Lights. The inhabitants are still there, you can still see a few candles and lanterns and whatnot."

With that he stood and walked on leaving the three to stare into the gloom beyond the 'few candles and lanterns and whatnot' to the myriad French campfires which continued on as far as they could see, until the last of the fading heat haze hid them from view. It was O'Hare who rose first, remembering his promise to Carr. He hurried away and found Slade alongside Carravoy in the area of the Grenadiers. O'Hare was grateful when Binns immediately brought a camp-stool, which enabled O'Hare to sit and looked directly at Slade, and he spoke as he chose, knowing that he was Senior.

"Did Sergeant Major Gibney find you, Major? And ask you to report to Colonel Carr?"

Slade knew that Gibney had found him and would speak as such if questioned, therefore it could not be denied, but Slade had another excuse, but this wholly untrue.

"I had pressing duties and, with that, it must have slipped my mind"

O'Hare looked at him steadily, knowing that to be a wholly inadequate excuse, a summoning by his Colonel took precedence over all, but his main reason for finding Slade took precedence.

"Have you been taught 'volleys by half-Companies? We noticed your absence at training, but it will be you that controls your Company's fire."

Slade looked somewhat affronted and would not admit his ignorance.

"Each half-Company fires at once!"

O'Hare looked at him carefully, time for a test.

"One Section then Two Section?"

"Yes!"

O'Hare fixed him with a hard stare.

"Wrong! Front rank then rear rank. Your line will be each Section side by side, in two ranks, with their own Lieutenant. When should they fire?"

"When we are ordered."

"Wrong! When the smoke clears and you can see enough. That's your decision, you control their fire. Front, then rear, then front then rear, when the smoke clears so that you can see enough, and enough of your men are at the 'make ready' of course. All of yours can manage well over three a minute, they are that good. Major!"

Having been found in ignorance twice, Slade remained quiet, therefore O'Hare continued.

"Guest is the Captain of Five Company on your right, Woods the Captain of Six on your left. Both been through more set-tos than I can easily recall. If you do what they do, you cannot go far wrong. If your ears no longer work, take your lead from Colour Sergeant Deakin."

O'Hare stood up and looked down at Slade, now somewhat chastened, but burning inside.

"Our Faith is constant in thee!"

With that he departed leaving Slade fuming, especially at the idea that a mere Colour Sergeant could behave better under fire than he.

"Damn Irish peat digger! Talking to me like that, as though I were fresh from the moors and bogs myself!"

At that point, Carravoy felt the need to add some weight to what O'Hare had said.

"Well, it is pretty important, old boy! You see, continuous volleys by ranks, means you're hitting them non-stop from all along the line, but still giving their dead and wounded time to fall over and get out of the way of the next volley. There's no point putting two bullets into one of their front rank, when one will do."

Slade looked somewhat shocked at Carravoy's support for O'Hare, but he said nothing and so Carravoy re-emphasised.

"It does matter, you know. Getting it right! It's why we're still here and still alive."

With that he reached down for the bottle of Spanish red.

"Here, have some more horse linament."

The following day began brightly for the Allies, rations came up and haversacks were filled with portable food and extra was provided for their breakfast for that day. The French were close enough for their own campfires to be seen even in the good sunlight, their smoke drifting back on the soft Westerly wind. All was being closely watched by Deakin, him sat with Halfway, both munching dried meat and drinking copiously from their canteens. The water hoy was just behind for as many refills as they chose, although there was a permanent queue.

"This is going to be big, Jed. Biggest yet, I'd say."

Deakin nodded.

"You'm right there, Tobe. Could be today, or definitely tomorrow."

Then he changed the subject.

"Carr's our new Colonel! Have you heard?"

"Yes, and that could be worse. He is what he is, a King's Officer, but he knows how to handle men in a fight. I'd trust him in a pinch. If we go down, so will he, but he'll have done his best to get us out of it."

Halfway changed the subject again.

"So, who's our new Captain?"

"Search me, I've not heard. Could still be back in England!"

At that moment they heard loud shouting, but only one voice, which they recognised.

"Sounds like Carr's throwing his weight about already."

It was not long before the shouting ended and Deakin looked behind to see Major Slade heading in their direction, his face reddened and his mouth set in a grim line. The pair immediately stood, came to the attention and saluted as Slade halted before them.

"I'm looking for the Colour Company. Who are you?"

Being Senior, it was Deakin who replied.

"We belong to the Colour Company, Sir. I'm Colour Sergeant Deakin, Sir. Regimental Colour, Sir. This here's Corporal Halfway, also Colour Company, Sir."

Slade nodded, his face remaining sour and annoyed.

"Where is the rest of the Colour Company?"

"Close and roundabout, Sir. Ready to form up, as when needed, Sir."

Slade said no more, but stalked off. Deakin looked at Halfway, slowly shaking his head.

"Well ain't we drawn the short straw!"

There was no time for comment from Halfway, for the drums beat out, 'Form column of march'. No time was lost, because meanwhile the French had formed up and were already on the move, so that once again the two armies, in their constituent columns, paralleled each other towards the open fields South-east of Salamanca. At the head of the Allied column, every Light Dragoon could see that matters were very serious, because every Senior Cavalry Commander there present was riding hither and thither to try and gain a position from where more could be seen of the French advance. From one position, which was no more than a high bank, Stapleton-Cotton was seen riding back to give orders to G. Anson and soon the orders were relayed back.

"Load carbines!"

The short, cavalry carbine, almost two-foot long, was hauled out and quickly loaded throughout the Regiment and then carefully dropped back into its holster. Carr loaded his pistol and checked his sabre, finishing just in time as Anson's men began to edge leftwards to bring themselves closer to the French, led by Stapleton-Cotton himself. The order came back, "Squadrons in two ranks by Troops". Carr's Troop broke from pairs to form one line and Peterson's, now also in one line, came up behind them. Peterson edged through to join Carr, who was the first to speak, betraying his inexperience.

"What do you think?"

Peterson grinned.

"You thought you were in the cavalry. They're going to use us as infantry! If you can't take a joke, you shouldn't have joined!"

At that point they were well ahead of the leading 1st Division and they halted, whilst Stapleton-Cotton, Anson and the three Colonels rode ahead to halt on another, almost insignificant, hillock. After much pointing and arm waving, Withers came back, to wheel his horse around and face back the way he had come.

"Draw carbines and make ready!"

Their 'Pagets', as they were known, again emerged to be held in their right hand and slope back over their right shoulder, reins now in left hand only.

"Walk forward."

In one double line, Anson's whole Brigade walked forward, to crest a slight rise and there to view the object of their Senior Officer's concerns. At least a Brigade, probably more, judging by the large variety of Chasseur uniforms present, was coming their way at a good canter. Withers halted his men as did the other two Colonels.

"Fire by ranks!"

Carr's Troop brought their weapons to the horizontal and drew back the hammers, the loud 'click' sounding thunderous all along the line. The Chasseurs came on, but many Officer arms amongst their ranks were now being raised and so they slowed, but did not halt, such that they did come within range.

"Fire!"

The carbines barked out and then all was smoke.

"Second rank."

Peterson's Troop edged their horses into the intervals, enough to obtain a clear view and then be given the same order, whilst Carr's Troop reloaded. The smoke cleared for them to see the Chasseurs casually trotting away, leaving no more than a few bodies on the ground and some riderless horses following their fellows back. Peterson released the hammer on his own pistol.

"He's just feeling us out. Seeing what we've got."

Carr turned to him.

"And now he knows!"

Peterson nodded as he turned his horse to obey the order for the Brigade to fall back and return to the head of the main column, there to resume their previous protective formation for the infantry. Emotions were mixed because they were moving back alone, leaving Alten's KGL and 14th Light Dragoons to maintain the screen even further out against any more French incursions. The afternoon was punctuated by artillery exchanges, the 16th often coming up to sweating and annoyed field-gunners who, too often, had only time for one or two discharges, before being required to move on to a new position, this caused by the onward marching columns, still the same distance apart, still maintaining a parallel course.

After another night sleeping in position, the following day was little different, bar the fact that the French were now even further ahead. W. Anson was riding with Carr and his two Majors and he voiced the concern that many had.

"The Peer knows his flank is almost turned. It's either fight on Marmont's terms, us going against them, or abandon Salamanca. I don't know what he's going to do."

At Noon all found out at least what their Commander hoped, as they marched back up the heights above Moriscos to again eat and prepare to spend another night in battle lines ready for what was very likely to be the next morning's conflict. All in the 4th Division looked at that doleful village over to their right, once more with inhabitants abandoning their homes because of the arrival once again of two threatening armies, all inhabitants taking themselves away, either carrying their own burdens or leading laden carts and draught mules. O'Hare looked at Carr as their horses plodded the final yards.

"What was that you said to Brockenhurst about 'marching and manoeuvring' a while back. Well, we're back where we started. We can only hope it's all been worth it."

Carr made no reply. The one comfort was that better rations arrived and a good meal could be prepared, substantial but not exactly London restaurant standard. This was well voiced by Slade sat with Carravoy, eating what had been prepared by Carravoy's servant, Private Arthur Binns. The stew was salt-pork and peas, thickened with potato and army biscuit.

"Is this the best you get?"

Carravoy swallowed his mouthful.

"It is, yes. Some bring out their own rations, but it soon goes off in this heat."

Slade lay down his dish. Suddenly he couldn't eat.

"Do you think it will be tomorrow?"

"I wouldn't bet against it. Wellington's met his match. Expect to be back at the coast by the end of August."

Then the order came to re-form, they would be spending no night on that ridge and all quickly dismantled their cooking equipment to re-form and march down over the end of the ridge towards the River Tormes, seen occasionally sparkling between the rows of dull green trees. None of the 105th looked back to rekindle the awful memories of the debacle at Castrillo. Soon they were splashing through the fords over the Tormes at Santa Marta, this perilously threatened village almost devoid of inhabitants, with those that remained now crowded into their Church, to be led in fervent prayer for deliverance by their local Priest. However, what was even more poignant was to see their own Followers on the far bank of the Tormes as they marched downstream. Many waved and shouted, but little could be identified as to who was where or doing what. There were also many citizens of Salamanca on whichever high points were available, but there was neither shouting nor waving from any of them.

The afternoon ended with the army ascending yet another ridge, with its own villages both above and below. Shakeshaft and Heaviside abandoned any attempt at naming them, simply recording words to the effect of 'On ridge South-East of Salamanca. Two strange hills seen in the distance to the South.' That was not all that was now seen in the distance, but there was a pleasing sight now back Eastwards, because they had moved ahead of the French and once again it was W. Anson who gave the details.

"Marmont must be struggling to get his over the fords at Huerta, so we've got the choice of ground for now."

He closed his telescope.

"Which is as it may be, but Wellington's still worrying about our retreat back to Cuidad. Tonight, he's sending the 3rd Division through Salamanca and beyond, to a place called Aldea Tejada. There they can at least bar Johnny's way and perhaps give us some kind of a chance of a decent retreat. If the worst happens."

With the last of the day, the French caught up, cavalry first, then infantry and so throughout that night, with everyone duplicating Carravoy's thoughts as expressed the previous Noon about a likely retreat, tensions were ratcheted up to another level, as each man stood a two-hour picket, doubled and in a double line. Once again Deakin and Halfway stood together, muskets in the crook of their left arms, gazing out into the night, once more at the spread of the French campfires. Halfway broke the silence.

"Times like this, I'd say I miss old Bible Heaviside comin' along with one of his quotes. Sort of a comfort like!"

Deakin let out a short breath.

"Ah, I knows what you means, but you'll not get the likes from this new 'un. For all his Major's bits and pieces, I'd gamble 'ee don't know a bee from a bull's foot about infantry work."

Before Halfway could agree or otherwise, at that moment, the French campfires disappeared as though a theatre curtain was drawn across the landscape and the reason came as sheeting rain and then a violent thunderstorm, ending all hope of hot food. Within 30 minutes, the 105th suffered their first casualty of 22nd July, a panicked horse from the lines of the Light Cavalry trod on the leg of a soldier of the Fifth Company, breaking it cleanly. Consequently, the rest of the 4th Division manged little sleep throughout the night as Light Dragoons chased their horses all over the camp. Deakin and Halfway remained where they were, sat miserable, but at least wrapped in their greatcoats.

oOo

The first movement seen by the 105th, in the first of the light the following day, was all the baggage of the army being collected on the road to Salamanca and so Carr approached W. Anson, stood nearby.

"What's going on, Sir?"

Anson briefly turned towards him before turning away to observe the fate of his own personal effects.

"Wellington wants everything on the road to Cuidad. The outcome of all this, he sees as far from certain. Take it from me, he's worried."

Carr nodded, his face showing his concern.

"Yes Sir, but I'll get back, I assume we're still in column of march."

"With that you are correct, Colonel."

The final word used by Anson still came as a shock, but the drums were beating and so Carr mounted his horse and joined his men in the column of the 4th Division. Despite the rain of the night, the column soon created clouds of dust and something else besides, clouds of steam rose from each Division as the hot July sun dried their soaked uniforms, these drenched from the night just passed. The 4th Division were marching behind the 7th and soon they were through a village, which diarists were able to record as Pelabravo, and ascending the rear of yet another ridge, which had an elaborate Calvary on the road up. Albright noticed it and remarked to Sedgwicke.

"Should we not say a prayer at that place, to entreat our Lord to look favourably on our arms in the coming conflict."

Sedgwicke hurried the mules on.

"I'd say not, Sir. Best to stay with our men. If any prayers should be said this day, they should be said amongst them. It does matter to them."

Sedgwicke looked at his superior with an expression that should brook no argument, but the unworldly Albright was already in agreement.

"A good thought, Private. That is surely for the best."

However, both were not at all certain if their place should not be amongst the departing baggage, especially when sporadic shots could be heard beyond the ridge, a conflict which grew in intensity. Carr rode to the top of the ridge to look through the trees growing there, to then see a broad valley with steep cliffs on the far side. Once his telescope was focused, he could identify what looked like two whole Battalions, the red of the British and the brown of Portuguese Cacadores disputing the summits of the cliffs with blue coated French, around what looked like some kind of temple, this building held by neither side. He lowered his telescope.

"It's today, then."

He returned to the column, but little could be seen due to the fact that back there with them he was on the reverse side of the ridge from the French and there was now a continuous screen of trees, but the bickering exchange over the valley at the temple told all, that the two armies had closed. The column advanced on, almost due South, as those with a compass ascertained, all with little talk, each man with his own thoughts and fears, each often making use of their well filled canteens as the heat intensified. Then, at last, the column swung fully right to ascend the end of a ridge and see a sight none who survived the day would ever forget. To their left, as the marched along the summit, across the valley was a long hill with steep sides, set in the centre of a wide plain, seemingly to sail like a huge galleon in an undulating sea. That it was important for both sides was obvious, as their own Cacadores of Stubbs' Brigade of the 4th were now racing across the space to reach this commanding hill and so also was a strong French column, probably of Division strength. O'Hare looked across at the race, then at Carr.

"Not a chance!"

He was proven correct. Blue uniforms arrived first on the crest, then there was an exchange of fire, the smoke being seen before the sound, and the Cacadores withdrew from the unequal contest fought out just below the summit, leaving several prone, brown uniformed bodies on the slope and not long after that Divisions of blue clad troops could be seen marching into position behind the hill whilst more arrived up onto the summit. Another 20 minutes of their own marching and the 105th saw in front, their own similar hill, but not as grand; lower, shorter and rounder. Carr turned to O'Hare.

"Have we got a map? Those hills must have names."

O'Hare shook his head.

"Anson will have one."

However, the question was answered a minute later by an ADC from W. Anson.

"Sirs. General Lowry-Cole would like the 105th on the forward slope of the Lesser Arapiles just ahead. The 27th will be on the summit."

Carr nodded.

"Forward slope of the Lesser, if that's its name?"

He pointed across the valley.

"So that must be the Greater, yes?"

"Correct, Sir. And the village beyond the Lesser from us is called Arapiles."

"As you'd expect."

"Yes Sir."

The ADC rode off and Carr led the 105th down the long slope of the ridge towards the forward slope of the Lesser Arapiles, the details of which became clearer as they dropped further below; it not being steep, but covered in many large rocks and boulders.

"Sort of moorland, Padraigh, would you not agree?"

"I would. Were it not for all this skirmishing racket, I could stand here and look and imagine myself back in Ireland."

"I imagine even Ireland's going to be more peaceful than this place for the rest of the day!"

O'Hare nodded agreement.

"I'll see to our placings."

He then dismounted and jogged off, holding his sword carefully away from his feet by his left hand. Carr turned to see that the Companies of the 105th had, without orders, disposed themselves across the slope in standard order, the Grenadiers on the far right, the Light on the left, the rest in between by number, bar Three in the centre. That now settled, Carr looked up to see the top of the Lesser Arapiles covered in Redcoats, which he assumed would be the 27th, then two guns arrived at the top, their muzzles pointing menacingly towards the Greater Arapiles. Meanwhile, the rest of the army was moving into position, this observed closely by Carr. Ellis' Fusilier Brigade of the 4th Division marched smartly past to form up in front of the village of Arapiles, a good half mile beyond where the 105th were. Minutes later, Stubb's Portuguese Brigade, also of the 4th Division, marched on to fill the space between Ellis' now stationary Brigade and the 105th. There they stood for an hour and more, with no gunfire, Officers simply studying with telescopes what was happening to the South, if anything at all, beyond the empty undulating plain whilst their men sat talking and checking weapons. Eventually, Carr lost patience and, on foot, climbed to the top of the Lesser Arapiles behind him to find Creet of the 27th sat on a convenient rock, chewing on some Spanish sausage.

"What have you seen?"

Creet pointed across the valley in the direction of the Greater Arapiles.

"A lot of French, both behind and to the right of that great hill. All as static as we are. Perhaps neither of these great Commanders wants a battle!"

Carr studied the view with his own telescope, panning it to his right, to study what appeared as the French far left.

"Am I correct in thinking that Johnny's leading Divisions way over there are still marching past Salamanca, attempting a big outflank, whilst we're sat on our backsides here?"

"I'd say you are right about that, but our 3rd went through Salamanca before dawn and are over that way. So, we have got something over there."

"Yes, someplace called Tejada Aldea, so Anson told me yesterday."

Using his telescope, Carr looked again at the three leading French Divisions, seemingly crawling along the ridge almost two miles in the distance and he noted the larger gap between the first and second, compared to that between the second and third. With that knowledge absorbed and their continued progress around the Allied right flank registered as a concern, he then descended and found RSM Gibney to give a simple order.

"Let the men eat."

As Gibney hurried off, Albright scuttled up.

"Colonel Carr, Sir. Would it be permissible to move amongst the men, to offer them strength and comfort in the name of Our Lord for what is about to come?"

Carr nodded and sighed, his face wearing an exasperated expression.

"Be my guest, Reverend."

Albright beetled off and the task he had set himself was made very easy because the whole Allied army was in place and unmoving. Behind the 105th and to their right stood the 6th Division, in the valley between the Lesser Arapiles and a prominent hill immediately behind the village of Arapiles. For the 16th Light Dragoons placed even further back behind the 6th, the order came to dismount, which was generally taken as synonymous with eat and drink what you can. Cornet Carr had heeded

Baxter's advice and had supplied himself with the necessary and was now happily chewing biscuit and the ubiquitous Spanish sausage. Peterson had wandered over and Carr asked the growingly pertinent question.

"You think there'll be a battle?"

"Your guess is as good as mine. The men seem to doubt it. Seems ridiculous if we don't, having been practically holding hands with the Johnnies for the past three days, but there you are."

The same sentiment was growing amongst the 105th especially voiced by Tom Miles.

"We must have marched 50 miles since comin' back from that Tordesillas place, an' now we'n sat yer, boilin' in the sun, an' starin' at a bloody great rock!"

John Davey passed him the mess brandy flask.

"Here, take a swig of that. Sitting is always better than marching. And anything's better than fighting."

"Well, I don't go along with that and that's the feelings of most of the lads. 'Tis time we tried conclusions with this Frog crew, so let's get at it!"

Miles abandoned his studying of the distance, took the flask, then a small mouthful of brandy, but Saunders, who happened to be standing, looked across to their left.

"Well, something's happening. Over yonder."

He pointed and all stood to follow his direction and see two large bodies of troops moving purposefully towards the left end of the Greater Arapiles. It was seen also by Carr and O'Hare.

"That's the Light and the 1st Divisions moving to take the Greater! Perhaps the Ball has opened."

With Heaviside's arrival, they all watched the advance, but then they saw a rider catch up with both Divisions, the advance stopped and then they marched back. This was seen by Miles, who expressed his opinion far more vociferously than either of his three Senior Officers.

"Well ain't that just about the best of all the buggerin' about what we've seen all day. Why don't he just let us march back to Salamanca where there's good drink an' rations?"

Ellis turned and looked at him.

"Well, Lieutenant General Miles, perhaps you'd like to order a general advance in the face of the couple of dozen guns Johnny's got up on that big hill, by now."

All laughed at the sarcasm, bar Miles, but his sentiment was present throughout the army. It was shared by G. Anson's Cavalry, even when Stapleton-Cotton ordered them to mount and move further West beyond the village of Arapiles. Sullenly, they mounted and he led them over to the next village where they found almost all the Allied cavalry, both Light and Heavy. Carr and Peterson spotted Arnt Schengen, of Alten's 1st KGL Hussars, who grinned when he recognised them.

"Well met, you two."

Peterson waved in response.

"Captain Schengen, good to see you, but is there anything you can tell us?"

"Not too much, but we are commanded by Colonel Arentschildt now, Alten was wounded during that carbine exchange, the day before yesterday and Arentschildt does tell us more. That place behind is called Las Torres and our French friends are still marching along that ridge, way up there and getting around our flank, I'd say. We expect soon to be riding back to Salamanca."

At that very second he was proved wrong as firing erupted from within the village of Arapiles itself and then also came the deeper sound of cannonfire, this from beyond the village. Schengen looked over hoping to see smoke from the cannonade and he saw the first of it, easing up into the blue sky.

"Those guns are at the Lesser Arapile."

With that, each one there said no more as they looked in the direction of the village, all seeing the white smoke of the artillery conflict ascend with the heat of the day. It was Schengen who voiced the obvious.

"It would seem the French want that village as much as we do."

The cannonfire Schengen spoke of was particularly relevant to the 105th remaining in position as the French roundshot hammered into the Lesser Arapiles behind them and then was lifted enough to batter the edge of the summit and just beyond it. Any who cared to look could see that the firing came from massed batteries on top the Greater Arapiles and the only reply came from the two Allied guns that had been hauled up to the summit of the Lesser, above the 105th. These two were replying for all they were worth, then the two became one, and then none, as the final gun was withdrawn out of the very unequal contest. O'Hare spoke his judgment.

"That's more than we can cope with here. I'll bet the 27th up there, are either withdrawn back or lying down. Not a good start."

Carr nodded agreement.

"Lying down makes sense. It won't be long before their aim drops onto us with nothing else to shoot at. We're going forward."

Carr and Heaviside ran along the line and, almost immediately, the 105th ran down in open order to the depression and ditch just before the track that ran across the front of the Lesser Arapiles.

"Down! Lie down."

The order was passed along and all the 105th lay prone, whilst the ferocious French cannonade continued above their heads, battering the top of the Lesser Arapiles. This remained the French target for a good reason, four Allied guns had now been hauled forward into position and they recommenced return fire from the top. In support, a whole battery also opened fire from their right, in the space between the village and the Lesser Arapiles. Deakin looked over at his Company Commander, Major Slade, him lying on his front, but propped up on his elbows, neither his position nor his expression giving Deakin any comfort. Deakin could not help but feel a little pity,

"First time, Sir?"

Slade nodded, his face now showing a weak smile.

"'Tis only roundshot, Sir. That don't give too much to worry about. 'Tis grape as is the problem for the likes of us and there's none of that yet."

Slade did not appear to be at all reassured, but Deakin was right enough and the 105th remained safe in their dip beside the road. What did not help were the sounds of intense conflict coming from Arapiles village not far over to their right, heard despite the sound of the Allied battery above them. Carr looked over, but could see nothing. "Not our business", he spoke to himself, but it was plain that the French were making a serious effort to take the village in the centre of the Allied line.

The same conflict was being studied in much the same way by the whole cavalry arm in front of Las Torres, they also could only listen, but then the whole tenor of their position changed when Wellington himself came riding up with merely a few Staff. He went straight to Stapleton-Cotton and within two minutes, ADCs were flying around to the various Regiments and Brigades. Carr and Peterson saw one arrive at Le Marchant's Heavy Brigade who immediately began to walk their horses forward towards the French ridge almost a mile away. Then an ADC arrived at D'Urban's Portuguese Dragoons, then he came onto Arentschildt, which caused a Major of the KGL to ride up to Schengen.

"Wir bewegen uns auf Aldea Tejada zu, um in die 3 Division einzusteigen. Mit D'Urbanes Portugiesisch."

Carr and Peterson looked at Schengen.

"What's happening to you?"

Schengen grinned as he set his horse in motion.

"We are being sent across to a place called Aldea Tejada to join the 3rd Division. Us and D'Urban's Portuguese are going. They are saying that there is now a very big space between the French Division leading and the one coming second. It may mean something to Wellington. Anyhow, good luck!"

With that all were gone, leaving G. Anson's Light Dragoons, looking around in bemusement at their isolation. Even Wellington had continued on his way, accompanying Arentschildt and D'Urban. Time moved on, but not Anson's Brigade. The sound of conflict from Arapiles village ceased completely, the only sounds of battle coming from the direction of the Lesser Arapiles, this being the ongoing cannonade. However, almost an hour later, guns erupted from a point on the French occupied ridge above Arapiles village and spent shot and overshoots landed amongst them.

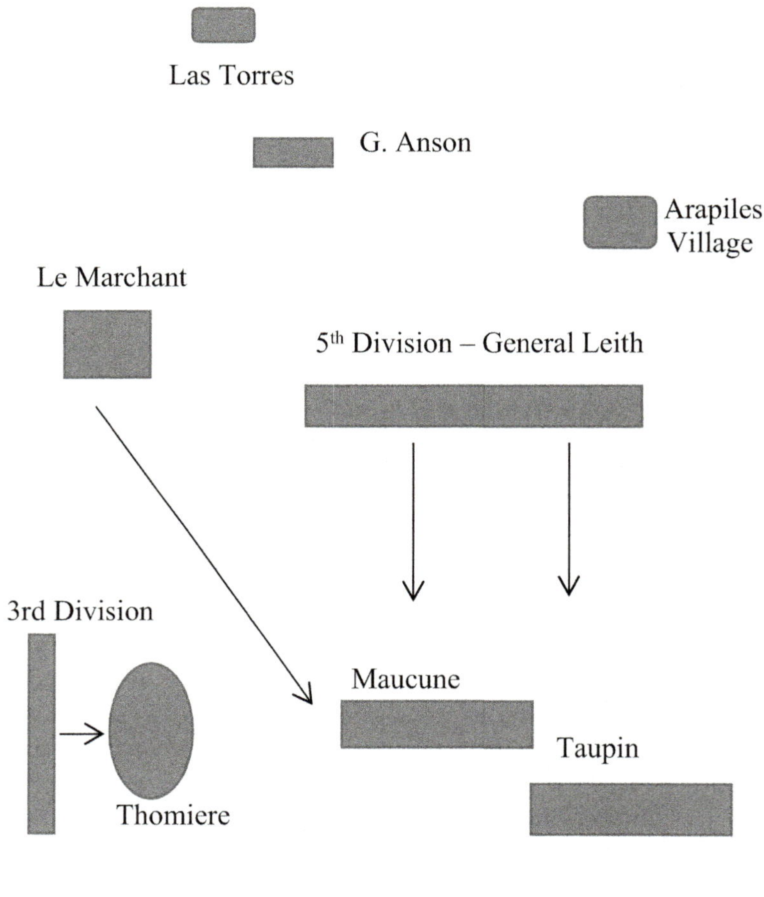

"Are they shooting at us?"

Peterson answered, somewhat indulgently.

"No Willoughby, their target is Leith's 5th, just in front of us, but a bit over the hill."

More time passed as shot, although spent, hissed and bounded past them, each man careful to move his horse out of the way. Amidst all the worry and nuisance, Carr asked Peterson a question.

"Do you have a spyglass?"

Peterson reached into his saddle-bag and produced what looked a very fine one.

"Yes, this! Got it off a dead French Officer after Talavera. Anson's had a bit of a disaster there, but we were with Cotton then and had an easy time, then fine pickings when all was done."

He handed it to Carr who decided to focus it on the ridge being traversed by the French Divisions, a good half a mile up the slope from where they were, this being the only French activity they could see.

"You know, whilst I confess my ignorance, that first French Division does seem to be a long way ahead of the second!"

He studied for merely seconds more, then ……

"Good God!"

Peterson immediately reached over to retrieve the instrument and Carr released it immediately. Once to his eye, Peterson could see the smoke of continuous volleys at the head of the leading French Division. Within a minute that Division was in retreat and running back along the ridge. He handed the glass back to Carr.

"See what you make of that!"

Carr saw what appeared to be a large blue mob, somewhat scattered, being driven back, right to left, pursued by a red mob, these in slightly better order. He looked for a long minute, seeing the conflict continue leftwards, the smoke of volleys pouring away in the wind, then he passed the telescope back to Peterson, who drew his own conclusion..

"Some of ours must've hit the front of their column and utterly smashed it backwards, so it would seem and look, Leith's 5th are going up after the rest."

Leith's magnificent 5th Division, in two lines, each line two ranks deep, were ascending the hill, their Colours bold and high as they ascended with perfect regularity, the first line comprised of his two Brigades of Redcoats, the second his single Brigade of Portuguese Line Battalions. Out in front Leith could be seen, on horseback, waving his sword, presumably admonishing anyone who failed to keep the dressing, whilst out before them, his skirmishers pushed back those of the French. Even though they were viewing from behind, the scene did not fail to seize the imagination of the young Cornets.

"I'll not forget that, not as long as I live!"

"Yes, Will. That's why we join up. We'd not see the like otherwise."

Peterson placed his telescope again to his eye.

"Johnny's pulling back the guns that were pestering us. Look!"

The instrument was handed over and through the clear lenses Carr could see French gunners man-handling their pieces back from the edge of the slope that led up to the ridge occupied by the French.

"He's no confidence of holding that. Not with Leith on his way up!"

That proved true, as the 5th Division overtopped the ridge to sweep on like a red wave. At that point the conflict itself was lost to view on what must be a plateau, but the regular ascent of separate waves of white smoke told them that controlled volleys were being poured in by one side, almost certainly their own. Whilst Cornet Carr was doing his best to make sense of events that he could not see, Peterson had noticed more movement.

"Le Marchant's going up!"

Carr lowered the telescope, he did not need it. Le Marchant's Heavy Cavalry, in two lines of two ranks, were sweeping upward and across, like a huge red and blue scythe, the ranks rising and falling as individual groups negotiated the rise and fall of the ground. Peterson took the instrument and focused it and soon he was exclaiming himself.

"Oh God!"

He could see in better detail what Carr could discern for himself as the Dragoons swept over the scattered mob that were once being chased back along the ridge and then charged still onward, their tall helmets and their heavy sabres being visible over the edge of the plateau as they rose and fell. Peterson lowered the telescope and turned to Carr, his voice in awe and shock.

"They've just wiped out maybe three French Divisions, two at least!"

Carr nodded agreement, in awe himself, because he could see, even with the naked eye, that Le Marchant's cavalrymen were still fighting their way forward and onto fresh French troops, until finally, at the far left of the slope from where they were, directly above the village of Arapiles, the last of the conflict ceased. The telescope told the story of blue uniformed French being rounded up and what was almost certainly either the 3rd or the 6th Divisions, reforming to advance further into the French positions. Then Peterson spoke the obvious.

"We'll be in that soon. They'll not keep us here, doing nothing."

Peterson was right, for at least one Regiment of the Brigade. Stapleton-Cotton arrived and led the 12th back towards Arapiles village.

"He must want them to support someone."

Carr settled into his saddle a little deeper.

"And then there were two!"

An ADC of Stapleton-Cotton came to Anson and, with the order passed on, Anson wasted no time, both his Regiments were already in 'advance' formation. He waved them forward, the 16th before the 11th. As they ascended towards the top of the ridge, the sights became worse, some British wounded and dead, but by far the most were French, all with appalling wounds. They were at the edge of a plateau, which was covered in dead and dying, some in rows where they had been hit by Leith's volleys, some scattered where they had been ridden down by Le Marchant's Dragoons. The air was filled with the cries of the wounded, even from the columns of French prisoners being marched away, because all seemed to be suffering bloody wounds. Anson had halted the 16th and 11th on the edge of the carnage, seemingly unsure of a way through. Carr looked around for someone to share his thoughts, but he found himself sharing a look with Baxter, who spoke his own thoughts.

"Battles, Sir! The bigger they are, the worse they gets."

Anson was halted with Withers, both discussing their next move, which was soon decided for them by the arrival of Stapleton-Cotton. His arm now pointing in the direction of further advance told all to everyone and so, in the same formation, two Squadrons abreast, making four rows, the 16th and 11th wheeled left and trotted further along the ridge.

Back atop the Lesser Arapiles, telescopes had not been idle either. Taking advantage of the French bombardment ceasing on so poor a target as four guns, Carr and Heaviside had climbed the height to view for themselves events over on the far French Left, their own far Right, and Carr was as much in awe as his brother at the catastrophic defeat of the French on that flank. Carr turned to Heaviside.

"That must have been close to a massacre!"

Heaviside was closing his own instrument, his face sad, his voice heavy.

"For the Lord will not cast off forever, but, though he cause grief, he will have compassion. Lamentations 3. 31. 33."

"I hope you're right, Joshua, I genuinely do."

They looked again towards the fateful ridge, but from there with the naked eye, little could be seen through the growing heat haze. Then Carr looked down, to see an ADC riding across from Arapiles village, already crossing behind Stubbs' Portuguese, who were now on their feet as were Ellis' Brigade beyond them.

"Time to get down, Joshua! What is the time?"

Heaviside pulled out his plain, very Methodist, watch.

"4.30."

"In the afternoon. Not much time to complete what needs to happen here."

They hurried down to reach the slope and the ADC rode up to meet them.

"Sir, your Division is about to advance. Lord Wellington would wish your 105th to advance in support of Brigadier Stubbs' Portuguese. Brigadier Pack's Portuguese will be on your left, attempting the Greater Arapiles. Sir."

Carr's eyebrows came together in a deep frown.

"Does that mean we are behind in reserve?"

"No Sir. To come up in support. A normal advance, all Light Companies in front in skirmish order. He leaves the where to you, Sir."

Carr nodded.

"Altogether too kind, but thank you Major."

The ADC galloped away and Carr turned to O'Hare and Heaviside.

"It's us going straight into the face of those guns on the Greater. In support of what will be to our right, Stubb's Portuguese. I'm thinking that we should be in column, but not into those guns. I want a line, two deep, intervals for open order. We're going forward not in their rear, but back and to the left of Stubbs' men."

The two ran off and Carr looked over to see Stubbs' Portuguese not moving off but all kneeling in prayer, the vivid Royal Colour and their own Standard of a plainer green clear above their double line, but held by a kneeling Ensign. Then they rose and he saw black clad Brunswick Oels run forward with Stubbs' own Cacadores out before his now advancing line of dark blue. By now O'Hare had arrived at the Light Company and went straight to Drake who rose to meet him.

"Nat, we're ordered to advance in support of those Portuguese there. Carr assumes behind and to their left. Get yours out in skirmish order."

Sergeant Ellis had overheard and he ran one way, whilst Drake ran the other.

"Right lads, on your feet, get out forward, skirmish order."

The group around Davey and Saunders levered themselves to their feet using the butts of their rifles to then trot across the front of the Battalion and form into their skirmishing files, 25 well-spaced files of three; in the case of Davey, Miles and Pike, in that order, Davey to the fore, then Miles, then Pike. Whilst Drake looked behind to see the Battalion form their line, Ellis looked at Bettridge, at least standing his place out before One Section, with his sword drawn, but there was a dark, yellowish stain widening on the inside of his right thigh. Ellis spoke softly to himself.

"Well Sir, if you comes through, you'll be the better for it, but you're on your own. Lads' lives is at stake, as matters more than yourn. Doin' it right matters more than keepin' you up together."

Drake was now waving them forward, but his eyes, as were all others, were studying the top of the Greater Arapiles, waiting for the eruption of the guns from there. Major Slade's eyes were the exception, he could only look at the ground and walk mechanically forward when Carr called the advance. He looked behind to see the Colour Party with the Standards of his Regiment curling lazily in the weak breeze, then Deakin gave him a smile and a nod, but it helped little. Just in front, Carr was studying, not the advance of Stubbs' off to his right, but that of Pack to his left, whose strong Brigade of almost 3,000 men were making their own advance directly at the Greater Arapiles, now crowded with French troops. "Good luck with that", he spoke to himself, "At least that will take some of the heat away from us." With that he was correct, the guns did open fire, but not onto his one lone Battalion in open line, but onto Pack's columns and the Brigade advances in line of Ellis and Stubbs.

Out before the 105th, Drake was stood with Ellis, closely observing some French Tirailleurs who had emerged from the side of a French column which had now come forward to oppose Stubbs, these French skirmishers operating in the hope of disturbing the left of the Portuguese advance. Drake waved his sword forward.

"Up to them lads. Hold to your drill."

The conflict began, Drake's men meticulously holding to their file drill to fire, retire and then load to move back up. Merely yards away from Davey's file, Lieutenant Bettridge was stood in a state of terror beyond imagination, as all around him vicious combat began, men firing and men falling and from behind came an urgent cry, "Sir! Keep moving, Sir" but his legs were frozen. He looked towards the French and his heart skipped a beat. A Frenchman was sighting on him, then the same Frenchman's tunic jerked back in the centre of his chest, his musket falling forward, but the dying finger pulled the trigger as the heavy weapon fell and it discharged into the ground. At this Bettridge calmed slightly to see the men, his men, firing, loading and filing forward with calm efficiency. It finally registered that the French were suffering far more than the men of his Company, all using their accurate Baker rifles. At last he felt able to move and he did, exaggerated paces sideways to his right.

The 105th Light Company were advancing steadily, protecting the left flank of the Portuguese main line, these now engaged over to their right and happily undisturbed by French marksmen from their left. By now the Portuguese line was thoroughly locked in combat with the French column and their own half Company volleys had halted the

French advance and they were now actually driving them back. Carr led his main line steadily forward in continuing support, pleased, even proud, of the performance of his Light Company operating out before him.

The advance continued, the Light Company in their regular order, dealing with the few Tirailleurs that had strayed over their way from the general French advance that was coming forward against the Portuguese and also Ellis' Fusiliers way on the far right. Ahead, Carr could see only an empty space, but he was still concerned for possible threats from his right. He turned to see Major Slade, but immediately rejected the idea, instead he called forward Colour Company Lieutenant Lionel Farquharson, who came running up.

"Lionel, get over to our right and see what the Portuguese are doing and what you think the future's going to look like."

"Sir!"

He ran off, then Carr saw what he did not like, a whole French three Battalion column was advancing, albeit slowly, around the end of the Greater Arapiles. Then came a cheer over on his right, a Portuguese cheer, meaning that Stubbs' French opponents were falling back, with the Portuguese following on and most probably, Carr feared, losing their cohesion as they pursued opponents that they had never before beaten in such a 'muzzle to muzzle' contest. Carr looked along his own line, advancing steadily forward, not shoulder to shoulder, but with a whole space interval, expecting soon to be receiving volleys from the guns atop the great hill, but now he was worried from another source. The French would have supports behind them which the dishevelled Portuguese would not defeat, then came some relief to his worries, because what must be Stubbs' Cacadores appeared across his view from the right, presumably sent there to oppose the oncoming French column he had seen. Their line significantly overlapped his own, but he shook his head.

"A few Cacadores will only hold there if Stubbs wins against that next Johnny column."

Steady volleys told him that Stubbs' men had met those French supports, but he expected the worst. Within that minute, Farquharson came running back.

"Sir, the Portuguese charged down a hill, Sir, following some French, but these rallied on some supports and the Portuguese are now falling back themselves, Sir. In no good order."

Carr raised his sword and the line halted.

"Thank you, Lionel. Back to your men."

Carr turned to see Slade immediately behind him and with this he felt he could be trusted.

"Major. Please to go forward and tell Captain Drake to support the Cacadores, but to fall back if threatened."

Consternation crossed his face, but Carr was in no sympathetic mood.

"Now, Major!"

In a state of great anxiety, Slade ran forward to find Drake over to the right of his men, all now unengaged.

"Captain. Carr says to support those Cacadores up there, but to fall back if threatened."

"Thank you, St. John. That is about to happen very soon, please tell him. Stubbs on our right is in full retreat and I can see three columns, each of three Battalions, advancing past that hill there. Those Cacadores won't hold that, but we'll support as long as we can, tell him. Then we'll fall back onto his line."

Slade hurried back to Carr, who listened to the message and was reassured by the good sense that Drake had spoken, then came deep concern again. Pack was foolishly attempting to capture the Greater Arapiles, his whole command attempting the steep slope at the centre of the hill in three lines; skirmishers, a firing line, then two Line Battalions in column. They had already been mauled by the guns above them during their advance, as shown by the bodies they were leaving behind. On top, waiting for them, were what looked like three French Battalions. Carr shook his head, he had his own concerns, as had Drake, now issuing orders to support the Cacadores.

"Close up, close up! Two deep line at half spacing. Here!"

His line would make an angle with that of the Portuguese Riflemen and from there enfilade the flank of the oncoming French column, but for the moment he would hold his line back and close on the French with an element of surprise, or so he hoped. With exceptional courage, the Cacadores formed their own two deep line at the top of a short, but significant slope. Their orders came and they stood at the 'make ready" and at 100 yards, they began their own half Company volleys into the oncoming French. The French fell in heaps, but the column was three Battalions strong and no momentum was lost and so the French closed almost to the foot of the slope, all the while sending their own fire into the Portuguese above. Drake waved his men forward to close with the flank of the column. The two lines quickly came forward and then Drake wasted no time.

"Front rank."

The Bakers came up.

"Fire!"

The volley crashed out and he repeated with the second rank, but the French mass was already ascending the slope. Bayonet work began, but for the Portuguese it was hopeless and they fell back. Drake wasted no time.

"Fall back! Back on the Regiment."

They all ran the 200 yards to see the 105th steady and motionless. Whilst Ellis led the men to their place on the far left, making sure that Bettridge followed, Drake ran up to Carr.

"There's three French columns advancing forward. One will come for us, the other two will pass us by. Stubbs is gone. They'll advance into that space and get behind us."

Carr nodded.

"Keep the men steady. We'll be falling back by ranks. And there goes Pack!"

He pointed to the centre of the Greater Arapiles to see Pack's whole Brigade falling back in the face of a huge French attack that had gone over the edge of the hill and pursued the beaten Portuguese to halfway down the slope. Many Portuguese prisoners were being pushed back up to the top, the victorious French using their buts and bayonets to hurry their ascent.

"We're pretty much on our own!"

Drake ran off to be with his men and Carr ran to O'Hare and Heaviside.

"There's a French column coming our way. We could deal with that, but there's two more that will advance past us on our right. They could cut us off. Retreat by ranks. Front to give a volley, then run back 50 yards, whilst the rear stand and deliver theirs, then they run back and through. That may get us out of this."

He looked sternly at both.

"We're fighting our way back, making them pay for every yard. No running retreat. No Brockenhurst! Not this time. Standard 50 yards."

The two shouted the orders to the Captains and Carr fell back himself to the Colour Company. There he looked at Slade, but with little sympathy. Any man in this situation was either someone whom you could trust or he was not. Slade was not. Then the advancing column came into view through the thinning smoke. Carr took it to be the standard French column of attack, about 50 yards wide, with their Eagle in the centre, the men close packed shoulder to shoulder, all perfectly in step. It looked inexorable and in the circumstances, it was. The drums further back in the column were beating out the rhythm of the advance and then came the shouts of 'Vive l'Empereur', seemingly with every five paces they advanced. Carr raised his sword and looked along his line. Everywhere muskets had come to the vertical. He would control the Colour Company himself.

"Front rank, present."

The muskets of the whole 105th front rank came down to the horizontal.

"Fire!"

The full front-rank volley crashed out and all was smoke.

"Front rank fall back!"

The men closest to him turned and disappeared, leaving the rear rank standing at the 'make ready'. He raised his sword and the line repeated the volley. There was too much smoke to see the full effect, but he could use that.

"Fall back!"

He ran back with the second line but when they passed through the waiting line, to form 50 yards back as they had been trained, he remained instead with those stood waiting. Again, he raised his sword and the muskets, all now reloaded, came to the 'make ready'. He waited but seconds before the French appeared through the smoke of the first volleys and again the muskets crashed out to his order and again his line fell back to the next line, now stood waiting. The performance had been flawless and he looked at Slade now stood with him. Carr was almost euphoric at the way the 105th had handled themselves. From what he had seen, the 105th had lost barely a man as they fell back.

Centre Repulse and Recovery

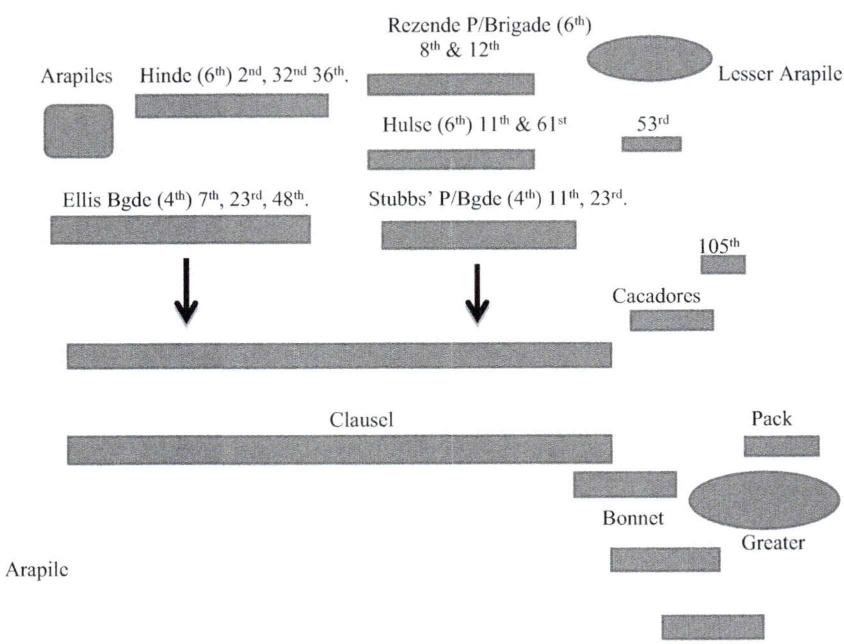

"By all the Saints, we're good! Damn good! You'd agree St. John?"

Slade seemed almost in a trance, but he did manage a slight nod of his head. The waiting line volleyed again at the approaching French, but as the 105th fell back once more, Carr felt they were now back amongst supports and therefore back far enough. A Brigade from what he took to be from the 6th Division was formed in their right rear. In addition, what seemed like massed batteries from their own side were now roaring out at any oncoming French.

"Two ranks! Two ranks. Here we stand. Back no further."

Now almost back to the track they had crossed for their first advance, the 105th stood their ground, but it was no longer drums and 'Vive l'Empereur' that they heard, perhaps the French column had halted themselves, perhaps reluctant to advance too far. However, what the 105th now heard were cavalry bugles and the thunder of hooves. Carr had no hesitation

"Square! Form square!"

The 105th, having rehearsed this innumerable times, completed a solid square within a minute, into three ranks, the first kneeling with bayonets fixed and forward, butt secure against their right knee. However, no horsemen arrived against them, instead a full charge passed across their square's right side, all famed French Cuirassiers, helmets and body armour gleaming in the sun. Carr thought for a fleeting second to fire into the passing charge, but rejected the thought, better to hold fire until they were attacked themselves. In the centre of the square stood the Honour Guard grouped around the Colours, including Deakin and Halfway, these now stood side by side.

"This looks a mess, Jed. These Frenchers is comin' over powerful strong."

Deakin said nothing, but checked the flintlock of his musket, this held at 'port-arms' across his chest. The look of deep concern on his face was reply enough.

Had Carr heard what Halfway had said he would have agreed, because the Cuirassiers had found an easier target, which he could see from inside their square and he gasped at the sight. A British Battalion was in support of Stubbs, but it was now surrounded by the French cavalry and not in square but in line. They were firing volleys, but in line it was only a matter of time before that line was rolled up by the swirling French Dragoons. The British line broke in two, one half forming a safer cluster, the other half remaining stationary, but at least the latter was firmly closed up. There was little the 105th could do, but at least they could open fire, albeit at maximum range at the Cuirassiers nearest. Carr ran to the corner of his square that was nearest the conflict.

"Independent fire on those cavalry! Now!"

Many muskets crashed out and some Cuirassiers fell, but it was all very desperate. Carr saw a fight for the Regimental Colour in the line some 150 yards away, it a glaring red. It fell and its fate Carr could not tell, but this half of the Battalion holding a line ran back and formed on the slope of the Lesser Arapiles and from there held off the Cuirassiers. However, the other group, clustered together, were still beleaguered out in the open. Then he saw a lone figure on horseback, an Officer, galloping from the group on the Lesser over to the group still surrounded. All the while those of the105th who could, were firing for all they were worth at the milling French cavalry and Carr hoped it would help and perhaps it did, because the Officer gathered up his men stood out in such peril and led them to safety, back to join their comrades holding on the slope of the Lesser Arapiles. However, now the Cuirassiers had noticed the 105th and at least a Squadron, probably two, were gathered by an Officer and he turned his men to come against the 105th. Heaviside was in command of the side they would strike first and he did not let them down.

"Be strong and courageous! Do not be afraid or dismayed before the King of Assyria and all the horde that is with him. 2 Chronicles. 32. 7."

At the sound of a Heaviside quote from behind, many grinned with determination and gripped their muskets a little tighter and set their jaws firmer. They knew Heaviside and they knew he knew his business, that being not to allow any cavalry so close that a felled horse could crash through the square, but that timed correctly, felled men and horses would provide a barrier before their ranks. 'Bible' as he was regularly known, timed it perfectly, the second and rear ranks of the square were already at the 'make ready'.

"Second rank. Present."

The muskets came down.

"Fire!"

The volley crashed out and the sound arrived of screaming horses and wounded men. Heaviside waited for the smoke to thin to see more Cuirassiers struggling through the dead and wounded that their volley had caused, but he did not waste a second.

"Rear rank. Present."

Using the shoulders and packs of the second rank as rests, the muskets came down to sight on their oncoming assailants.

"Fire!"

The result was appalling, adding to the shocking confusion. By now the second rank had reloaded and Heaviside used it, but to little extra effect. However, trumpets were sounding and the Cuirassiers were withdrawing, back up the gentle slope from where they had come. Many wounded were clinging to the pommels of their saddles, but the retreat was accompanied by shouted insults and lewd gestures from the 105th. A grinning Carr looked at O'Hare.

"I do believe we have got away with it, but what now?"

O'Hare gave an immediate answer.

"Get back into line before those guns up on the big hill see us in square."

The orders rang out and within a minute the 105th were back into a two deep, open line, but the "what now?" question still remained, until O'Hare looked towards Arapiles village.

"Looks like the 6th Division are about to give it a go!"

Carr followed his gaze to see a two-deep line of Redcoats, the nearest with their King's Colour and a Buff Regimental in the centre, and beyond them all that could be seen was another set of Colours, raised high, this a bluish green alongside the King's. What must be fugitive Portuguese from the first advance were running back to pass through the oncoming line. However, at that moment all euphoria in the performance of his men died, as an ADC Major rode past, close enough to shout an insult.

"Quit the line again, 105th?"

Carr watched him go, but absolutely livid as he was, he could do nothing and besides a Senior Officer was riding over to rein in his horse at Carr and O'Hare. He introduced himself with the utmost brevity.

"Hulse!"

The pair were in the presence of a Brigadier and peeled off a smart salute, but Hulse had other concerns.

"He's sent our 6th forward. Your 4th have fallen right back and the French have counter-attacked, they're almost at the village. Both mine are on this side, the 61st South Gloucester and the 11th Devons. I've lost the 53rd, they're back on the Lesser there, in no fit state, but we have Rezende's Portuguese in support on my right. Can I count on yours, here on my left?"

Carr was still enraged at the previous insult and his reply was brief.

"As you order, Sir."

Hulse nodded.

"Very good! As you are, in line, match my advance."

The pair saluted and Hulse rode off. Carr looked at O'Hare.

"To renew acquaintance with that column from earlier, I shouldn't wonder."

O'Hare nodded, then looked again at the menacing summit of the Greater Arapiles, still worried by the massed guns on the summit.

"As we are, then?"

Carr nodded.

"As we are!"

Still fuming, Carr jogged to the centre, the Colour Company. A good shout, to inspire his men, might help release his own feelings. He raised his sword.

"Men! We're going back up. We are the fighting 105th, the stubborn Rag and Bone Boys. A bunch of Frogs thought they had done with us but they were never more wrong. We're going back up with the Devons and the South Gloucesters, all West Country boys like us. Now we show the Frogs just what it means to tangle with the likes of us. We come from men that have stood, fought and won since the days of King Alfred. And King Arthur! And before that, they showed the Romans a thing or two!"

He took a deep breath.

"105th will advance!"

The line stepped forward, but the din was appalling. The 61st had advanced forward and had now come within long range of a French column, Allied support artillery was firing at maximum and now the French guns atop the Greater opened fire, to send cannonballs buzzing and humming overhead, but Carr gritted his teeth and led his men on. He could see that soon they would be level with the 61st, these now within mere yards of their own opposition, delivering their punishing volleys into the front ranks of the French column, which must be the one the 105th had faced earlier, it still being three Battalions strong. Carr called a halt by raising his sword. He could see the French column, but there were still many French cavalry about. To simply swing his line against the side of the column would leave his left, the Light Company, open to having their line rolled up. He called out to O'Hare.

"Into three ranks and wheel right to support the 61st. I'll have the Lights and Nine Company turn to present a flank."

As the 105th formed into three ranks, in the same order that they had formed the three ranks of their square earlier, Carr ran up to Drake and Captain Dunnidge of the 9th Company. He came to Dunnidge first.

"Michael, bring yours round to refuse a flank and face that big hill. Keep them ready for cavalry. Three ranks."

He ran on to Drake, but Drake could see what Dunnidge was sensibly doing and his own were moving to comply. Drake ran down the front of his line.

"Cavalry! We're here to stop cavalry. Keep your eyes open. There are many hidden dips in this ground."

Miles was immediately sceptical.

"Big enough to hide a horse?"

Ellis was nearby, stood with Bettridge.

"Hidden or not, Miles, you keep your eyes open. Open! If you've not swigged all the mess brandy!"

Saunders and Davey turned to look at him, their faces concerned, at which point Miles pulled out the flask and gave it a shake for all to hear the brandy inside. Then Saunders reached over for it.

"Well, seein' as it's out and handy."

He pulled out the stopper and took a pull before passing it round. Bettridge was appalled and spoke to Ellis.

"Doesn't that make them drunk on parade or something, Sergeant?"

Ellis was now replacing the stopper himself, after a good swallow.

"Well, yes Sir, it would, if this were some kind of a parade. Sir. But what it is, is some kind of God awful muzzle to muzzle. Sir."

Just then, Joe Pike, perhaps the most assiduous to his duty and no kind of a drinker, shouted across.

"Sarn't! I think we've got some trade."

They all looked left to see a Squadron of French Dragoons about to gallop across their front in the direction of the Greater Arapiles, a move that seemed wholly foolish, but the Light and Ninth Companies could only respond to what came their way, but it was Nine Company who changed the minds of the Dragoons, Dunnidge firing front rank then rear and the cavalrymen swerved right to gallop towards the end cliff of the Greater Arapiles. Meanwhile, Carr had run back to the main conflict, that which would determine the outcome in this area. He ran all the way down, almost to the Grenadiers to the end of his line, hoping to see the 61st, but when he arrived, the noise was head shattering, mostly from his own men, and he could only discern the place of both front ranks by the muzzle flash from both sides, the smoke was so thick, but it was clear from the regular crash coming from the right, that the 61st were dealing out the worse punishment. His own men were now well into the fight, the three deep line covering almost all of the right flank of the column, a volley from each rank crashing out every 20 seconds. He ran to the Colour Company, he had to do something, if only to shout encouragement and he pushed through to the front rank, where he saw that his men had closed to 20 paces.

"Serve it out to them boys! Serve it out! They can't take much more. Huzzah for the 105th!"

However, his own line was receiving fire. A soldier grunted and slumped against him, but his men were edging closing to the blue ranks and then, suddenly the French column dissolved and even through the smoke, crowds of blue shapes could be seen running back leftwards. Carr allowed only one more volley, he was concerned that the 61st may be following.

"Cease fire! Cease fire!"

The smoke cleared and they could see the pile of French dead before them, two, sometimes three deep. The French were soon gone, then arrived the 61st and both Battalions stood and cheered themselves hoarse as only men will who had achieved such a triumph against such dreadful odds. Carr saw the Colonel of the 61st running over to him, grinning like a schoolboy, which Carr soon matched.

"Wilkins. 61st South Gloucester."

Carr took the outstretched hand.

"Carr. 105th Wessex."

"A close-run business!"

Carr nodded and grinned some more, amidst the continuing cheers.

"Indeed, but what now?"

The grin disappeared.

"I'm putting mine into column and advancing. I'd advise the same for you."

"Agreed. Let the pursuit commence!"

Wilkins ran off and Carr ran up to O'Hare."

"I'm conforming with the 61st. They are going on forward in column of Companies, quarter distance."

It took three minutes for the 105th to get into order, the Grenadiers, then the Colour Company, back to Number Nine. Quarter distance meant a five-yard gap between Companies as they advanced in column. During that time, Hulse rode over and halted at Carr.

"Good support, Colonel. Well done, now I'm bringing you under my command until I hear otherwise, but I doubt Lowry-Cole will object, at least for the immediate future."

Carr saluted.

"Yes Sir, but can you tell me what happened over on the right, beyond us, Sir."

"Yes. Hinde's Brigade stopped and then pushed back the French advance. Ellis' have rallied and are in support. I think I can safely say we've won!"

The grins returned and Hulse rode off. Carr ran up the length of the column to Drake.

"Nat, we're advancing, get yours out in skirmish order. We're with the 61st and the 11th. Under Brigadier Hulse's orders. And pass the word, we've won!"

As the Light Company again ran forward into their skirmishing files, Carr turned to Carravoy, and he managed a smile, even to him.

"Lead off, please, Charles!"

Carravoy gave the order and the column moved forward, with Carr some yards in the lead, quickly joined by O'Hare and Heaviside, the former now thoroughly relieved of what had been his main concern all afternoon, especially with the 105 now in close column.

"Johnny's quitting the Greater."

They looked up in response to the simple words to see the last of the French garrison disappear beyond the top and three guns tumble down to disintegrate over the several walls and ditches.

"And abandoning his guns!"

Carr nodded.

"That's about as final as it gets!"

As they marched, they tended right to cross the slight ridge, defended earlier by the Cacadores, this still covered by the dead and wounded of both French and Portuguese and so all picked their way carefully through, but the slight rise gave enough height for them to view the whole battlefield and the sight there was enough to make them catch their breath. The whole expanse was traversed by two continuous lines, mostly the red of British Battalions, but enough dark blue to emphasise the role of the Portuguese. It was both majestic and magnificent, the regular lines sweeping forward with the Battalion Colours all high and prominent; jubilant in the bright yellow of the early evening sun.

Before the 105th, the Light Company strode forward in open order, looking for opposition, but they saw none, only fleeing Frenchmen. As they crossed the shoulder of the Greater Arapiles, they came upon several dead Frenchmen, who had managed to drag themselves only so far back. Miles immediately began to examine the nearest to be yelled at by Ellis.

"Miles! Leave it. There'll be plenty of pickings later."

The shout drew the attention of Drake, but Miles was already walking on between Davey and Pike, Davey in the lead. It was not long before they had passed the Greater Arapiles to see the last of the French occupants running away from the backslope and from beyond them there came a whole Brigade of red-coated infantry giving further urgency to the fleeing Frenchmen. They advanced on, the Allied lines and columns coming closer together as they naturally took their line towards the retreating French.

G. Anson's Light cavalry had just emerged from the scene of carnage as they rode further along the ridge which had been the scene of Leith and Le Marchant's attacks. Once clear and onto wide open ground, Cornet Carr turned to Oakwood, him trotting his horse back up their column having been called up earlier by their Colonel Withers. As

Oakwood turned his horse, Carr took the opportunity to ask about events, but first their own situation.

"Who are we following, Sir."

"That's the 3rd, who did the first damage, and down over there out to our left, are Leith's 5th, pulling themselves back together."

Oakwood took a deep breath.

"You've not heard, I take it."

"What, Sir."

"Le Marchant's been killed. He led his men against a third French Division, one too far. A great pity!"

Carr's face fell.

"Indeed, Sir. One of our best Commanders."

Oakwood took another deep breath.

"Indeed he was! However, we have not done one hand's turn this day, but I feel we may be about to be called upon. Seems we're in the best position, with what I take to be D'Urban's and Arentschildt's out and over to our right, shepherding that French Division in the right direction."

He was looking forward and from their height they could see that the wide plain that the Allied army was advancing across, terminated at a distinct ridge, the whole length of which was now covered in formed French Troops. The Greater Arapiles that rose from the plain, was now almost behind them on their left, it was the ridge in the near distance that now commanded their full attention, with even more fugitive French adding themselves along the full length. Oakwood drew the obvious conclusion.

"Too much to expect that the French would not mount some kind of rearguard."

The ridge was also growing in stature for the 105th as they advanced alongside the 61st. Once within range of his telescope, Carr studied the ridge and did not like what he saw. French soldiers were all across the forward slope, this so steep that they could form up in three, sometimes four, ranks and still see forward over the heads of their comrades. In addition, in their centre, there were at least two full batteries of field guns. He passed the instrument to O'Hare.

"Take a look. This is going to be bloody!"

They saw some Staff Officers galloping forward, whom O'Hare recognised.

"That's Packenham and Clinton. Packenham's got the 3rd, with Picton away, and Clinton's got the 6th. If we're under Hulse, we're under Clinton!"

However, it was not to be. Their own W. Anson came galloping up and reduced his horse to a walk beside them.

"The 27th are coming up behind and our Rifles too, after helping Pack get out of his scrape. Ellis' Fusiliers are coming over to us, all now back together after being pushed back. With that, the 4th have reformed under Lowry-Cole, so hold here and await orders."

Carr called a halt and the 61st passed on, all the while sharing cheers and cheery waves with the stationary 105th. When they had passed, Carr looked over to see an ADC gallop up to Packenham and Clinton, these stood together and there was a brief, but animated discussion, The result was the 6th Division advancing on alone. Carr was appalled, and turned to O'Hare.

"God, that's stupid! It was the 6th who beat the counter-attack and now they're being sent against that rearguard. Unsupported!"

They both watched as the 6th advanced forward and it was not long before the French guns on the ridge opened fire on them, men being felled with depressing regularity.

"That's the 61st and the 11th on the left of the 6th's line. They don't deserve that."

O'Hare was studying events just as closely and he was as relieved as Carr, when the advance halted, but still within range of the French guns. W. Anson was still with them both studying events and all came to the attention when Wellington himself came galloping up, to rein in his horse fiercely at their group. Whilst they expected him to be jubilant from his outstanding victory, he was not. Anxiety darkened his face and lent urgency to his words. Plainly, he saw the French rearguard as a serious obstacle.

"Anson! Ellis' Fusiliers will form on the left of Hulse's 61st up there, you form yours on the left of them. Drive back any on your front and get onto the flank of those Crapauds holding the ridge opposite Ellis. I've called over Gardiner's full battery from the 1st, they'll deploy behind you, but mostly supporting Clinton. Plainly they are the ones in need of it!"

Amidst many salutes Wellington rode off into the growing gloom. It had been well over an hour since the French had been turned back from before the village of Arapiles and the light, even that of a Spanish July, was beginning to fade. Following their Commander in Chief's orders, the Fusilier Brigade of the 4th Division were hurrying over and joined onto Clinton's left, this being Hulse's Brigade. Having seen the hurrying Fusiliers, Anson led his own quickly forward to form on their left in two ranks, the 105th alongside Ellis' 48th, with their own 27th on the 105th left. The French on the ridge could be seen, but behind sparse hedges and bushes and the growing dark added to the anxiety of the French numbers. Anson, remaining near to Carr and O'Hare looked and sighed with uncertainty.

"What's best? Skirmishers, before line, or what?"

It was Carr who replied.

"Begin as a line, Sir. Pour in a volley, front then rear, then charge. Just go straight at them!"

Anson nodded agreement, then, surprisingly, he drew his sword and stood in front of the 105th.

"105th! Make ready!"

The muskets of both ranks came to the vertical, then to Anson's orders, each rank delivered a volley into the French ranks seen in the gloom of the woodland, then, with raised sword he shouted above the cannonade.

"With me,105th! On and at them!"

He turned and ran towards the ridge and the whole of the 105th surged after him, the 27th soon following led by their Colonel Creet.

Over on the far right of the line against the French rearguard, G. Anson's Light Dragoons were held back on a slight ridge and from there they could see all that was taking place. Carr and Peterson eased their horses slightly leftwards to get a better view and what they saw made them gasp. Peterson put his thoughts into words.

"It looks as though that whole ridge is on fire!"

He was not exaggerating, the many ranks of French, back up the slope, were pouring continuous fire into the oncoming 6th Division. This non-stop fusillade, together with the French artillery, turned the whole forward face of the ridge into some kind of furious conflagration, the hundreds of points of light flaring up to be replaced by hundreds more. Cornet Carr looked forward.

"Who's that to our front?"

"Portuguese. Rezende's so I've heard and they're getting it just as bad."

The task of the Portuguese was almost impossible, these being faced with definite cliffs that could only be climbed with difficulty in good light, and only then with no opponents above. Oakwood came over to shepherd the pair back to their Squadrons.

"Get back with your men. We'll be up there soon!"

Over on the far left, the combat for the 105th was of the worst kind, more Medieval than 19th Century. Drake led his men up to the scrub and hedges to receive a volley from the French hidden there. Saunders saw his filemate, Len Bailey suddenly drop his rifle to hold his leg and hobble off to the right, then they were in amongst the French. The 105th's weapons were discharged at a range of feet and inches and then it was bayonets, boots and butts. Saunders deflected a bayonet thrust across to his left, giving him a perfect position to bring the butt of his Baker up into the side of the head of his Voltiguer assailant. With the force that Saunders could apply, the man almost cartwheeled, then it was onward, his bayonet levelled into the gloom of the woodland. Beside him were Miles, Pike, Davey, Solomon and Ellis, all fighting furiously against a strong line of French Voltiguers. The six were advancing steadily, each following their bayonet drill of using it on any who attacked the man on their left, such that Davey bayonetted a Frenchman under his left arm who was attacking Pike, but suddenly there came almost a dozen Frenchmen, at a run, led by an Officer and they were forced back, reducing the conflict to a furious melee of whirling muskets and bayonets. The French were thick between the trees and the advance had stalled.

Deakin had ordered his Ensign to hold back and now satisfied, he advanced forward with the Colour Guard of Bennet, Hill, Nicholls, Gibney and Halfway. He found himself against a French Officer who stabbed his sword forward, this Deakin deflected, but then he was barged over by a French Sergeant, then falling awkwardly into a bush. The Sergeant raised his musket to make the coup-de-grace with his bayonet, when Halfway slammed the butt of his musket into the side of the man's head. The bayonet still came down, but enough to the side to enable Deakin to roll to his right and the bayonet plunged into the ground. Halfway finished the work with his own bayonet into the man's side. There it stuck and another Frenchman came forward with levelled bayonet aimed at Halfway. Then came the bark of a pistol and the Frenchman staggered, dropping his musket. Deakin looked up to see Slade with a smoking pistol in his left hand and sword in the other, but with an 'other-worldly' expression on his face. Halfway moved to help Deakin to his feet, but not before acknowledging Slade's help.

"Obliged, Sir."

Halfway reached down.

"Get up. Jed! 'Tis safer to be standing!"

However, the British were slowly gaining the ascendancy, especially when the full 27th arrived behind the French right and rear. All along the line the French began to give way and so, following orders from their Colonel, Officers of the 27th were shouting orders to their men.

"Reload! Reload and hold. Whatever comes, open fire."

However, Carr had no intention of holding there. The French had been pushed back, however briefly and however minimally, giving time for all to reload, which he would use and then he and his men would advance, this time using fire power.

"Advance! Move forward."

The same order came was given to G. Anson's cavalry on the far right flank, only their order came from Stapleton-Cotton himself, issued to the 16th and the 11th, but the 16th were to lead. They passed Rezende's Portuguese, at this far end of the ridge, their attack now completely stalled, but they were able to cheer and shout at the encouraging sight of supporting cavalry.

"Bem feito, Ingles! E voce virar agora, sim?"

Carr looked at Baxter, riding almost alongside.

"Any idea what they're saying, Sergeant?"

"Search me, Sir, but I think they're glad to see us."

However, Johnson was now arriving with orders for Oakwood.

"We can get up over to the right, there's a possible slope up a bit of a valley, but quite narrow, Tavender's One Squadron and yours. If we get up, ride along the ridge and try to roll them up. Three and Four will go fully over, then wheel back into their rear. Good luck."

Oakwood called back.

"Column by Troops! Four ranks. Load carbines."

The attack had to be narrow if Johnson was correct about the valley and Two Squadron complied. Judging by the continuous sound, the conflict further along the ridge had not diminished as One Squadron, led by Tavender, set their horses at the slope followed by Oakwood's. From the top there came a ragged volley and, although it was weak, some Troopers and their horses slid back down, but the advance continued. Carr urged his mount at the steepening slope, then the gradient lessened and he was at the top. He heard firing, he thought from both muskets and carbines, but then this died away. He looked around, his sword erect, but there were no French to be seen, especially in the almost full darkness. Almost all of the 16th reined in their horses, Baxter beside Carr.

"Looks like this is done, Sir. Johnny's scuttled off."

Much the same was being said by the 105th as they advanced carefully through the darkness of the woodland, muskets loaded and ready, but no French were there to be seen. Soon Carr had had enough. The sounds of what had once been a ferocious conflict had died to a few desultory shots.

"Halt! Hold here."

O'Hare was beside him.

"Set pickets. We're here for the night."

Before he left, O'Hare voiced his thoughts.

"If Johnny fought all day, like he fought here, who knows?"

Carr did not answer as he sheathed his sword.

Chapter Three

"Madrid! I think I've heard of that place!"

"So, who ordered this?"

The complaint came from Captain Tavender, riding close to Captain Oakwood and Cornet Carr. It was Oakwood, being the equal, who gave the best answer he could.

"Stapleton-Cotton, would be my guess. I'd put this past our Anson, he's a bit more sense."

The cause of complaint was the fact that the 16th Light Dragoons, in open order, were walking their horses through open scrubland at the dead of night, with little but a fitful, disobliging moon to guide their way. All too frequently, they came upon dead and dying Frenchmen and all too frequently vengeful and merciless Spanish peasants who roamed the area, taking full and cruel advantage of the wounded and those incapable of resistance or flight. Tavender had more to ask.

"When do we stop?"

"At the Salamanca to Alba de Tormes road. Withers heard from Anson that our esteemed Spanish General and ally, Carlos de Espana, is holding the castle on the far side of the river at Alba de Tormes, which means that the whole French army is cut off, at least from that line of retreat. So, steady does it, we ease our way down to the road and stop."

At that point, Cornet Carr felt able to make his presence felt, although somewhat 'sotto voce'.

"Shouldn't be too hard to find a road!"

Oakwood laughed softly.

"Indeed not, Mr. Carr, so, as I say, easy does it all the way. From here, I really cannot see the point in hurrying and ending up in some ditch or even treacherous gully."

Caution was also the watchword of the 105th, now deep into the woodland, but no longer moving, with extra caution included in Carr's orders.

"Double pickets. With so many French wounded around, scavengers will be out and I don't want any of them mistaking one of ours asleep for a wounded Frenchman. So, rest and stand guard."

Heaviside and O'Hare were with him and Heaviside spoke in reply.

"I'll take first watch."

Amongst the group around Deakin and Saunders, all were taking stock of their wounds, the worst being Len Bailey with a French bullet in his right thigh. The entry point was being examined by George Fearnley, the Medical Orderly of the Light Company and trusted by them above any Surgeon, with the exception, perhaps, of Surgeon George Pearson himself, who was at that moment operating amongst the trees on the most severely wounded, working by the light of four battle lanterns. However, in the case of Len Bailey, at that moment all that was available for light was a single tallow candle and George Fearnley was shaking his head.

"Can't do a thing yet, Len. Not in this light. Tip in a drop of brandy to stop the wound going bad, and I'll give it a go come morning."

The brandy arrived and some was tipped into the wound for Bailey to wince with the pain, then seize the bottle.

"A good swig'll do me more good than any more spilled over me leg!"

He was indulged by Tom Miles, his scavenger partner, then he lay back against his backpack, hoping for some rest. Meanwhile, George Fearnley had moved on to two more wounded, Jed Deakin and John Davey, and he found Toby Halfway examining the cut in Deakin's side.

"Seems like that bayonet got a mite closer than we thought, Jed."

Deakin stretched his head over to examine the cut himself.

"Seems so, yes, but Bridie'll stitch that back up. Followers'll be out with us come morning. She'll stitch that cut and stitch my tunic."

Halfway laughed.

"Ah! Hopefully not one to t'other."

Much the same was being said by John Davey, only his cut was just below his left shoulder, therefore in his tunic's arm, both made by a flailing sword. He had only discovered the cut when he recovered his breath from the intense combat on the final ridge. For him also, Jed's Bridie was the one for the stitching, both for himself and for his uniform.

Taking first picket Zeke Saunders and Nat Solomon were some 50 yards beyond the scene of the medical examinations, weapons loaded and held in the crook of their left arms, but hammer down. They could hear the calling and movements of Spanish peasants amongst the scrub, searching for French wounded, who were unable to follow their comrades' retreat and the pairs' own position was not far beyond the area of the final conflict on the ridge. When a victim was found by the marauders there came the inevitable cries from the wounded Frenchman, who was often killed, if not also horribly abused, during the process of rob and pillage. After enduring the sounds of two or three, Saunders decided that he had had enough.

"Stay here, Nat, any that's not too far beyond, I'm dragging in. They'm soldiers, just like us, ordered out a long way from home, not wantin' to come an' dyin' badly."

Leaving his Baker with Solomon he ventured forward and within minutes he was heaving back two wounded Frenchmen, dragging them by their collars. Both had serious wounds, but both could be saved with treatment, if they were lucky. Saunders departed again, while Solomon gave each some water which met with profuse thanks

"Merci, M'sieu. Merci beaucoup!"

Saunders dragged in two more, but one would probably not last the night, nevertheless each was given a drink of water which produced the same response of thanks. Saunders went twice more until they had a row of six, at which point he resumed his picket duty.

"At least they've got a chance now. Could be they'll be picked up come morning."

It was not long before Heaviside arrived and saw the row of French wounded. Corporal Saunders immediately gave an explanation.

"Scavengin' peasants, Sir. They'm murderin' all out there that they finds. Didn't seem right, Sir, not to pull a few in, try to give 'em a chance. Like."

The response was inevitable.

"Be merciful even as your Father is merciful. Judge not and you will not be judged. Condemn not and you will not be condemned. Luke 6. 36 to 37."

Both men nodded, assuming that was a statement of approval.

"Yes Sir, as you say, Sir. We'll hold here for the next picket relief, then, Sir."

However, at that moment, the dying Frenchmen tapped Heaviside's leg.

"M'sieu, m'sieu!"

He reached from inside his collar and pulled out a Catholic cross, which, appallingly for Heaviside, included an image of Christ.

"M'sieu, m'sieu, pour l'amour de Dieu."

Saunders looked down.

"I think he wants what they call 'last rites', Sir."

Heaviside looked at Saunders, then at the man, but it was Saunders who spoke.

"He won't last long, Sir!"

Heaviside knelt beside the man, took the cross, now loose on the man's chest and held it before his eyes, the moonlight being just enough.

"Through this Holy Cross, and through the great goodness of His mercy, may God pardon thee for thy sins, those that they has committed by evil use of sight, hearing, speech or deed. May the Good Lord take thee to him and admit thee to his Heavenly House, in the certain hope at the time of resurrection on that Great Day of Judgement. Amen."

Hearing the final word, the man, with his last strength, took the cross and kissed it, before releasing his last, long breath. Saunders, knowing Heaviside's strict religious beliefs, felt moved enough to say something.

"That was a good, kind thing you did there, Sir."

Heaviside tucked the cross back inside the man's tunic and rose, his head nodding twice, but next there came something other than a quote.

"There are times, are there not?"

"Yes Sir", came simultaneously from both, followed by punctilious salutes as Heaviside departed.

It was no pleasant night for anyone in the 105th, all lying amidst the dark trees with neither moon nor starlight above and the only sounds to be heard being those of the suffering and the abused. However, dawn came early and, with plenty of wood around, good cooking fires were quickly made to brew tea and, if they had a camp kettle, some form of pottage or stew, augmented by whatever was found in dead Frenchmen's knapsacks. George Fearnley came back to extract the ball from Bailey's leg, which was accomplished quickly with Saunders and Solomon holding his leg tight and still. There was no cloth in the wound and, after the application of more brandy, this now being in good supply, four stitches were inserted and a bandage was applied. Bailey found that he could hobble well enough if unburdened of his kit and musket, and so this was spread over his messmates and a crutch fashioned from a useful branch.

With breakfast finished, the 105th formed column and marched through the scrubland to the road, along with the rest of the 4th Division, thankfully finding fewer and fewer French bodies, but all whom they came across had been badly mutilated. The 105th marched on and after little more than two miles they came to the main road that ran from Salamanca to the town of Alba de Tormes. The 4th Division were halted off the road and the 1st Division, largely unused the previous day, marched quickly past, obviously about some task. With the 105th now static beside the road, but still in column, Carr took the opportunity to call the roll. For St. John Slade this was something new, with the Colour Company paraded before him, each at 'stand easy'. As each name was called, if the name belonged to someone present, that soldier came to 'order arms' and answered. Being new to the process, Slade paused just too long if no answer came forth, adding to the inevitable melancholy of the task. Each Captain completed their totals and they were presented to O'Hare who completed his own additions and then handed it to Carr, who pulled a face to show his disappointment and then sighed.

"So many wounded, 115! Plus 5 Officers."

Then he studied the paper again.

"However, only 12 killed."

He turned again to O'Hare.

"Walking wounded?"

"Most, is my impression."

Carr nodded.

"Well, that at least is to the good."

During this, O'Hare was looking down the road in the direction of Salamanca.

"Well, here's another thing to the good."

Hurrying down the road came the 4th Division's Followers, many turning off from the road as they came to their Regiments and the cries of joy and relief were mingled with the cries of anguish as women and children discovered the fate of their men. O'Hare was impressed.

"Good Staffwork that, to get them down here, to us."

"Yes, true. So, stand the men down. Let's take the chance for some proper rest."

Mess camps were soon set up and water was set boiling to 'clean up' the cotton strips that were about to be used on wounds. It now boiled to satisfaction, the stitching of Deakin and Davey was quickly accomplished, none of this being in any way new to Bridie or Eirin and it was Eirin, now feeling better, who did the job on John Davey. That now done, the bloody clothing was carried over to a water trough, for punishing against the stones of a nearby wall. It was noticeable how close couples sat to each other throughout the morning, especially Saunders and Consuela, also Byford and Eirin with baby Jed.

Whilst the morning was spent in camp, Carr felt the urgent need to take himself over to Divisional Headquarters, hoping to see one particular Aide-de-Camp whose words of the previous day still rankled deeply. His excuse was his Regimental Report, which, when written, he carried over and delivered to Lowry-Cole's Secretary. Then he wandered through the small encampment, but much to his frustration he saw no one he recognised and, despite himself, he had to acknowledge that the ADC may not be from the 4th Division at all. Grim-faced he returned to the 105th's camp, where at least Bryce had prepared a good stew. Full rations had arrived with the Followers.

There was no such leisure for G. Anson's Cavalry Brigade, although they were about their work in a leisurely fashion, trotting at an easy gait down the road to Alba de Tormes. They were following the line of the French retreat, this marked by what was usually seen after a beaten army, discarded equipment and the occasional body of a French soldier, sometimes alive but wounded, sometimes dead, but the former hugely grateful to be gathered up into the care of their enemy as a prisoner. The journey was but a five-mile ride and all, based on the general rumour, anticipated spending the day with rounding up French prisoners trapped this side of the river Tormes. All in the column believed the retreat to be blocked by the Spanish forces of General Carlos de Espana holding the ancient castle on the far bank, this thoroughly commanding the long bridge. However, with each half mile, the feeling grew that something

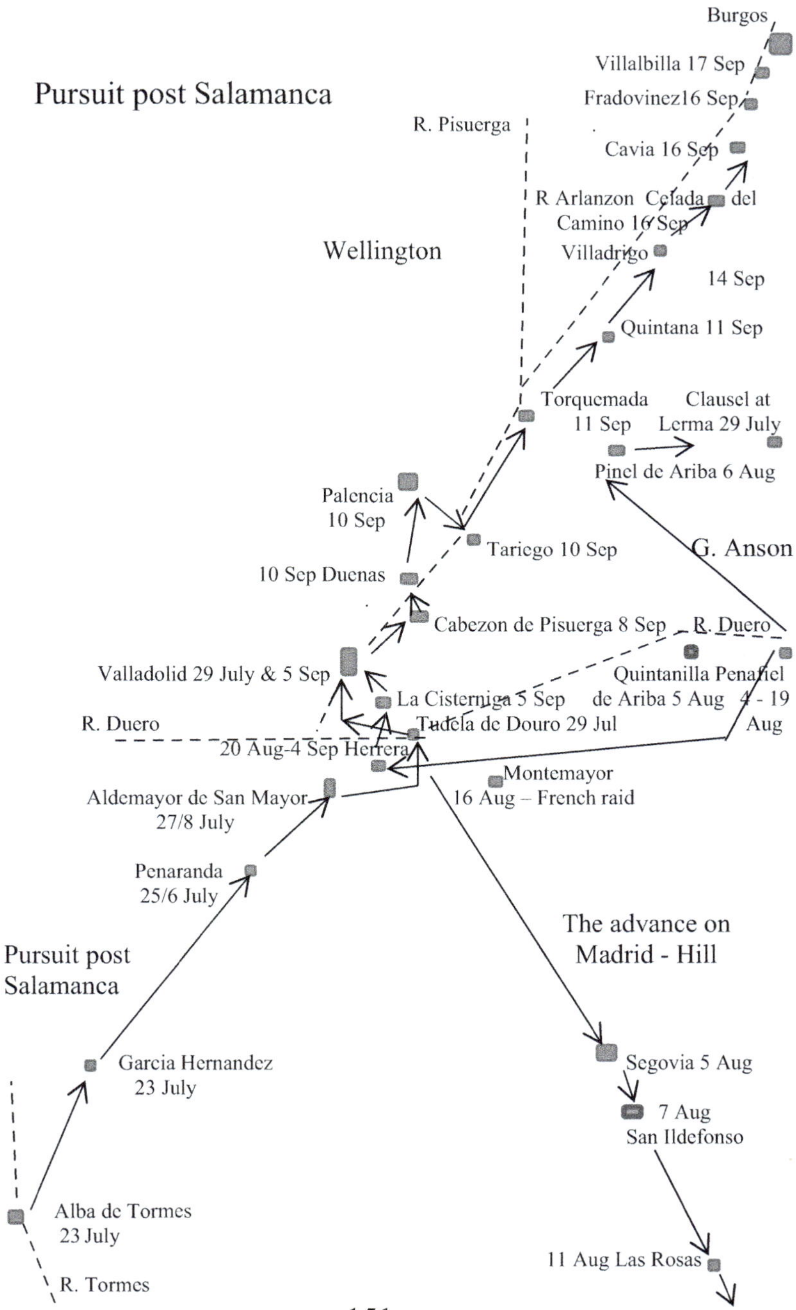

had gone wrong. The evidence of the French retreat grew more sparse and eventually the wide Tormes came within view with no trapped French army.

As they descended the long and gentle slope to the course of the river, Major Johnson came riding back along the column of the 16th.

"From Stapleton-Cotton up front. We're the first cavalry here, so we're going straight over the bridge. The first over it, so, we could be straight into combat."

As Johnson rode on, Oakwood had just enough time to call out the burning question.

"What happened to the Spanish, Sir?

The reply came over Johnson's shoulder.

"Their General pulled them out. Two days ago. Told no one."

At the bridge, there was a gathering of French prisoners, stragglers rounded up and under the guard of Bock's KGL Dragoons, but G. Anson's three Regiments swung left and began the long passage across the narrow

bridge. It was Oakwood who stated the obvious, regarding the opportunity that had been missed.

"Nothing could have forded this river and nothing could have crossed this bridge without a bloodbath."

As he spoke the last words he pointed to the square block castle at the far end which utterly dominated any passage across. They rode on, in column of fours, the 16th, then the 11th, with the 12th in the rear. Once they were on the bridge, any glance back would have seen Bock's KGL riding downstream along the river bank they had just quitted. When halfway over, Stapleton-Cotton raised a hand and the column halted. Carr could see French uniforms on the far side, but Stapleton-Cotton did not pause for long and Carr soon saw why. What had been a paltry rear-guard was now fleeing at the approach of themselves, almost 1,000 sabres. The cavalry column reached the far bank and halted, now under the walls of the Castle tower and Carr was joined by Peterson, now that they were in a moment of idleness, but both remained mounted. He had seen what Carr had not, a sight now cantering over the bridge.

"Here comes the Peer himself. In a frightful fume, I bet. We could have taken a whole French army!"

Wellington indeed looked as though he could have committed murder, especially if the throat within his fingers belonged to Carlos de Espana, but he rode to the head of the column to consult with Stapleton-Cotton and Anson. It was not long before Johnson again rode back down the line.

"Himself is taking us forward, us first, then the 11th. There will be a rearguard somewhere, count on that, and we'll have to deal with it.

Before rejoining his Squadron, Peterson voiced his discontent.

"Us and the 11th! The 12th did damn all yesterday. Stapleton-Cotton pulled them away to support some Division and spectate!"

Johnson looked blank, but Carr grinned at him.

"Well, did you not say to me some while ago, if you can't take a joke you shouldn't have joined?"

Peterson's expression did not change as he rode back to his own Troop and soon they were moving off, up through the narrow streets that contained the main road as used by the retreating French. Now there was no sign of discarded equipment and so all knew that the units they were following were now at least cohesive and probably potent. The buildings of the town finally ran out and they found themselves still riding upwards over an undulating plain with several small hills as points of interest in what would have been featureless uplands.

It was Wellington himself who led them on. The gentle ascent continued for two or three miles, before there began an equally gentle descent on a road remarkably straight, which many thought to be Roman, but few voiced the rather irrelevant opinion. After three more miles they came to a village down within the shallowest of valleys and Wellington called a halt and it was not difficult to see why. Peterson came up to join Carr and Oakwood, his excellent telescope already out of its holster. It took but a minute for its use to tell all.

"There's French infantry in the village. Looks like they're filling water bottles from the village wells. Now they've seen us, many are running over to the road. On the hills behind there's what looks like a whole Brigade of Chasseurs, put there to cover the infantry now abandoning the village."

Oakwood was using his own spyglass, but as he focused it, he spoke to Carr.

"We need to get one of these for yourself, young Carr!"

He studied the distance himself, then nodded twice; he had seen nothing to contradict Peterson. Johnson came riding up.

"It's us! He wants two Squadrons of ours and two of the 11th to put a frontal assault on those Chasseurs up there. For what it's worth,

Anson says not to worry. All Frog cavalry got a frightful mauling yesterday, so it shouldn't be too much trouble."

Oakwood grimaced and spoke his fears, even to a superior rank.

"Too much trouble! That's a Brigade, we're four Squadrons, attacking up a hill! Any reserves or support?"

"Yes! I'm assured that Bock's KGL are coming up from our left. They must have found a ford over the Tormes. They're a Brigade strong. They'll go for Johnny's right, on our left."

Oakwood sighed and his tone was thoroughly ironic.

"Yes, I suppose that does give rise to perhaps one more degree of optimism!"

Johnson smiled, but with little humour, yet he was unoffended. Oakwood's conduct since joining the Regiment had earned him enough licence and their friendship and mutual respect was growing.

"Good! So, One and Two form up in two ranks, alongside two of the 11th."

"Be nice to know the name of this damn place, where we are required to undertake such heroics."

Johnson pointed to a stone set by the roadside, the name just legible amongst the weathering.

"Garcia Hernandez."

Minutes later, under the watchful eye of Wellington, when he was not using his own telescope on the French, the four Squadrons formed line abreast in two ranks. G. Anson himself would lead them forward and he drew his sword and gave it one sweep in the direction of the hills, their summit described by a long line of horsemen, with many hues of uniform, light blue, dark blue, mauve, green and others. Now that they were off the road and slightly higher with a better view, Carr could see why the cavalry were there. It was almost as Peterson had said, not only to protect a few fugitives, but also the retreat road onward past the Chasseurs, which they could now see was covered by a long column of French infantry.

Drawing his eyes away from that, riding out in front of his Troop, Carr studied the task ahead and the first point he noticed was that the hills occupied by the Chasseurs presented no easy slope. Once at the top their horses would be blown, unless Anson exercised good care and good sense. First impressions of his handling of the four Squadrons were good, because after first negotiating a stream that was more reeds and mud than water, Anson set their mounts at the initial slope at a walk, then came the trot. The ridge was not continuous but there was a central section, defined by a shallow valley each side and this section was their objective; it was the centre of the Chasseur line, with Hussars placed either side on the ridges beyond the two defining valleys. The slope became steeper, but Anson held to the same easy pace.

"Draw sabres!"

The scrape of the steel emerging was heard above the sound of the hooves and Carr, now knowing just enough about cavalry tactics, could not help but think, "If they charge down on us now, we're lost", but nothing came and they climbed, now up a slope so steep that the Chasseurs were lost to view. One minute more and the Chasseurs were in view and Anson set his own horse into a canter on the now easier gradient, then into a gallop, which all followed, then came "Charge!", sounding from all along the line, then yells and 'huzzas'. Almost immediately the Chasseurs turned and made off, all along the ridge, riding off to the 16th's right, to a shallow valley that contained the road carrying the French infantry. Anson raised his sword and the charge slowed to a walk, the line still perfectly formed. Carr looked over and saw what may have persuaded the French Brigadier into his decision, this being Bock's two Regiments of KGL Dragoons who were just then leaving the road that ran between Garcia Hernandez and the ford of the Tormes, which they must have found.

Anson held to his walk, if only to further intimidate the French, as Bock's men took the slope of the ridge at the best speed they could. Anson ordered his Regiments into columns of Squadrons, the two of the 16th and the two of the 11th forming a front about 100 yards wide. They crossed the summit, then all in Anson's command looked left towards Bock's men, because a volley of musketry had come from their direction. The trumpeter close to Anson sounded 'Squadrons in line', the columns split out again into double lines and Anson led his men over to support Bock. A little further over the ridge height, on the backward slope that was the merest of inclines, there could be seen four Battalions of French infantry and it was one of these, in square and the nearest to Bock, that had delivered the volley. Anson halted his men to decide his own next move, thus giving them a grandstand view. The French square was now much beleaguered, because Bock's men had gone straight for the nearest side and the infantry fire was not well enough controlled, because a second volley brought down some KGL but it was delivered too late and wounded horses crashed through the square wall. Many mounted KGL leapt through the gap, several more followed and then the whole square fell apart in disorder, the great majority surrendering, but some sprinting for the steeper slopes and valleys.

Anson's men cheered lustily at the achievement, but the KGL were not done. Two more French Battalions, but in column, were running up a hill that became progressively steeper, presumably because their Colonels did not trust their men in square, but preferred to reach high ground where cavalry could not easy follow and attack. By a quirk of the air perhaps, Carr, with Oakwood, could hear orders being shouted to the running columns, "Allez vite, aller aux hauters."

"What they saying?"

"Can't say for the first, Willoughby, but the second is 'get to the height', but I don't think they are going to make it."

He was correct; a Squadron of Dragoons, bypassing the first square, galloped headlong towards the rear of the nearest column. The orders from the French Officers were lost in the thunder of hooves, but the rear ranks turned and delivered a volley into the oncoming KGL, which brought some Dragoons down, but not enough and the horsemen crashed into the first French Company and through to a second, sabring many and taking many prisoners. The surviving Companies did gain the height and joined the other Battalion in forming a square at the top. Carr and Oakwood continued to look, the latter shaking his head at what was evidently about to happen next.

"I don't believe this!"

Another KGL Squadron had gained the height and, gathering many Dragoons from the earlier conflicts, they went straight at this new square.

"That's madness!"

Oakwood, speaking his thoughts out loud, could tell for himself the significance of what they were attempting and, in addition to the risk and peril of that endeavour itself, standing nearby in support of the square was a Squadron of the Chasseurs from earlier. However, both Carr and Oakwood gasped as the Dragoons galloped headlong at the square and broke in, the square then breaking apart, the most surrendering, but many scattering and running to the French Battalions formed on the road, four in all. Both Carr and Oakwood sat shaking their heads, as the once supporting Chasseurs then rode off, pursued over the hill by more KGL. Oakwood was amazed at their timidity.

"Well I'm damned. I thought Johnny's horsemen had more backbone than that!"

However, now predicting what was clearly coming next, Oakwood's next words were of fear and horror.

"No! Don't, don't!"

The KGL, clearly intoxicated with their success and by now a mere mass of horsemen and led by Officers who should know better, if there were any present at all, charged on towards the road. The four French Battalions quickly formed square and the nearest, when approached by the charging KGL poured out fire that was disciplined and effective. The KGL swerved away, still under a pelting fire from the square, leaving many casualties on the ground and taking several riderless horses with them. All was now ended and the final resultant scene from all the conflict, spread across a half-mile of the ridge, was one of groups of French prisoners being herded back, whilst casualties of both sides, including wounded horses, were attended to, in the case of the latter often with a single shot. Oakwood had one final comment, matching the thoughts harboured by Carr.

"I hope to God, Anson doesn't ask us to do the same to what's up on that road."

However, his fears were quickly allayed. The trumpets sounded for yet another change of formation and the two Regiments formed 'Column by Squadrons', a formation that allowed them to slowly follow the four retreating French Battalions along the shallow valley that contained the road, as these quickly marched their way out of danger. Anson walked his men on, keeping the French in view, but evidence of the wreck of the French rearguard was all around and for the 16th this meant gathering up stray horses, who had joined their column for equine company, some KGL but mostly French. One took the eye of Captain Oakwood, with N13emeC on a corner of the saddle blanket and he reached over to gather the reins. The saddle was of quality and had sheepskin over the saddle-bow. He led the horse up next to Carr, enough to enable him to search the saddlebag next to him.

"Take a look in the saddlebag, Willoughby."

Carr did so and, to his huge delight his hand met something hard and round, which became a very respectable telescope and he grinned openly at Oakwood, who grinned back.

"Thought so! That had to be the mount of some Frog Officer."

At that moment the column halted, because Major Johnson, at the front with Colonel Withers, had seen a formation of Chasseurs on the skyline, their dark uniform making them highly conspicuous and, fearing an attack, he ordered 'Draw sabres'. They all anticipated the order to change formation, but the Chasseurs turned their horses and disappeared, then Carr and Oakwood saw Wellington himself, plus Staff, overtake their column, followed by two complete field batteries. Within minutes the order was passed back "Off the road" and all on horseback turned off, which allowed the Light Division to come pounding up at furious pace, led by the unmistakable and very dapper figure of Major General Charles von Alten.

Once they were past, both Light Dragoons and batteries regained the road, but Carr had spotted Major Bull and Captain Ramsey in one of the batteries, now up ahead. He turned to Oakwood.

"That's Ramsey up there. Permission to ride up and say hello? Feel I should at least ask how he is."

Oakwood nodded agreement; such a plain human gesture would not come amiss, it would provide more than a little welcome contrast to the carnage he had just witnessed.

oOo

It was the morning of two days later, when the 4th Division marched into the village of Penaranda to be immediately ordered into the fields alongside and they made camp. The Followers had marched with them and soon there was a scene of domestic good order as food was cooked and the men took stock, in a more relaxed fashion, of what had been gained after their 'examination' of French dead and wounded. Tom Miles spread all out over a blanket, mostly coins, rings, buttons and buckles, but some jewellery, such as necklaces and rosaries. Watched by Davey and Saunders he pushed to the right what would go into the group 'bank', then pointed to the collection remaining in the centre.

"That's for trade!"

Davey and Saunders nodded agreement and so Miles and Davey set off. Penaranda was a well-appointed village that seemed to have been spared the worst excesses of a French occupation, which fact was not lost on Davey, looking at the buildings, their windows and doors undamaged.

"Seems this place got away with it, although the Frogs did march through."

Miles was inclined to disagree.

"Don't take long to search and grab what they want. Get in, pull all apart, then get out. Be surprised if there'll be much to trade."

"We'll see! By now this lot of locals must be altogether used to getting their stock up into the hills when the French is about and hurrying all back down when they've gone."

They were now in the square and Davey would seem to be correct, some inhabitants had returned since the arrival of the Light Division, two days ago, their blankets spread on the ground displaying their goods. However, all was done under a gruesome sight, this now being taken down by some Provosts, the body of a French Officer that had been hanging from a balcony. Davey looked over.

"Thought that would have been gone by now!"

Miles shook his head.

"None of our business!"

His eyes were on a crate of chickens, some sausage hanging from a frame and some cuts of meat that appeared to be pork. He pulled Davey over and pointed at the chickens.

"Could ours carry a crate like that, for some way?"

'Ours' referred to their Followers and Davey thought for a moment, weighing up the choice.

"That meat will go off, we've all had enough of sausage, but carrying chickens?"

Miles had a scheming thought.

"Eirin rides in the Chaplain's cart. I'd say that he wouldn't be too much against a fresh egg now and then, for the sake of a crate like that, strapped onto the side of his cart."

Davey shook his head, amazed at his file-mate's ingenuity when it came to crafting a scheme that added to either their riches or their comfort.

"What if no!"

"Then we kills 'em all and has a good chicken stew!"

"Right!"

It was Miles who undertook the bargaining, rings, buttons and buckles being added and withdrawn as the bargaining ebbed and flowed with the farmer. Finally, a bargain was struck and they carried the wicker crate of six chickens back to their mess area. It was Deakin's eyebrows that were the first to come together in puzzlement.

"What've you done here? Do we kill this lot now, or what? Because right now we'n very well off for meat and suchlike?"

Miles stood squarely before him.

"No! These is for eggs. One's a cockerel. The way I sees it, this crate will go onto Parson's wagon an' the Chaplain can have a share of the eggs, in payment, like!"

Deakin looked at him amazed.

"An' you think that's a runner?"

"I do! I'm off to Parson. An' look! There's already an egg in thur!"

He undid the string holding the flap and pulled out the egg to give it to Bridie.

"For Eirin!"

Bridie grinned and laughed.

"Tom Miles, you amazes me!"

Miles retied the string and set off with the crate. The Ecumenical cart was not far off and Miles found Sedgwicke making Albright's meal, whilst Albright slept in the cart, this evidenced by loud snoring.

Sedgwicke was always uncertain in the presence of such as Miles and this was no different, as Miles strode up, carrying the crate.

"Parson, here's the bargain. You strap this crate to the side of your cart and you gets a share of the eggs!"

However, Sedgwicke did have some practical sense and immediately saw the flaw.

"How are they fed?"

Miles thought for a few seconds, then found a solution.

"Well, chickens eats anything and, when we stops, we'll send the childers back to fetch 'em and they can let 'em scavenge, tethered with a length of string. We feeds 'em, but you gets eggs, well some!"

Sedgwicke frowned.

"If Albright says no, what then?"

"Well, bring back the crate and we'll see what we can think up instead."

Sedgwicke was unconvinced but could not object outright.

"I will ask. I can at least do that."

Miles grinned and nodded.

"That you can, Old Parson. No harm in that!"

The following day, now marching on the road with Midday arriving, Colonel Carr, for want of different company from the usual O'Hare and Heaviside, was marching at the head of the Light Company with his friend of years standing, Nathaniel Drake. It was him who was asking most of the questions.

"Are we still pursuing or just advancing?"

The answer was immediate.

"Advancing."

"With any particular objective?"

"Yes. Valladolid."

Drake changed the subject, to the usual.

"Have you sent a letter off?"

"Yes."

"And you included your promotion!"

"Yes. Have you, got one off?"

"Yes. This morning."

"Good! So stay for the Noon meal. We've got fried eggs through some exchange between Miles and Morrison."

Carr nodded, smiled, but said nothing. The 105th were marching through another hamlet and the same was happening as they had seen in the previous collection of dwellings that morning, starving peasants and their children, and these ran forward to tug at the trouser legs of those in the column, with hands outstretched.

"Comida! Comida, Senor. Por favour, comida!"

Almost all in the ranks managed to find something from their haversacks and place it into grasping hands. It was Drake who spoke next.

"Just as well that rations have come up, generous and regular. It would be heartbreaking to just pound on, giving them nothing."

Carr's jaw set firm.

"I would that Napoleon and all his ilk could come and witness what they cause. These were once peaceful and prosperous people, living decent lives. Now look!"

Drake laughed.

"Napoleon wouldn't come here, he's given this to his brother, El Rey Joseph and Boney will soon have his own problems. Marching into Russia with Autumn, then Winter, not far away."

Way ahead, the state of the Spanish villages they rode through was of an even greater concern to Anson's Light Dragoons, each village was in a greater or lesser state of destruction and the population had either fled or were murdered. On the day of 28th July, they saw smoke rising in the distance as they came to the name sign of the next village, Aldemayor de San Martin, whereupon Oakwood made the wry comment.

"It strikes me that the longer the name of these places, the more Medieval and backward they are."

However, it was Baxter who answered, speaking under his breath.

"Or the worse we sees of what the Frogs've done, once inside."

It was Baxter who was correct, there was little humour to be seen once within the village and its square. Several buildings were on fire and there was a spread of bodies, of all ages and sexes, against one wall. The 12th were the first in and they were already gathering them up and taking them to an unburnt building. By the time the 16th rode out, after a brief halt, the building was well alight, the conflagration providing the only ceremony to the inhabitants passing. Behind Carr, Baxter made his own comment, talking to Makepeace.

"This is as bad as when we followed the Johnnies out of Santarem, afore Sabugal."

There was not reply; all in the column were too much alone with their own thoughts, their faces grim and, in that mood, they paid little heed to the mutilated bodies of Frenchmen hanging from trees, often upside down and over a still smouldering fire, the work of angry peasants, not just Spanish Guerrillas. The following day, with the 16th in the lead, the Brigade entered Tudela de Douro, the river of that name flowing in an enveloping and protective loop around that village. Inside they found the same grim scene of revenge and depravity. Tavender's One Squadron, being first in, were about the task of dealing with the dead and so, Oakwood's, next in, were approached by Colonel Withers.

"Samuel! Take yours through and up to the river. See what's on the far side, particularly over the bridge. This Duero is a serious river."

Grateful for a duty so much less unpleasant, Oakwood led his men through the town to the river, to find French manning the far side and the bridge blown, missing two arches. His men began screaming abuse across the river, at that point not 50 yards across, but Oakwood, despite appreciating the feelings of the men, turned to Baxter.

"Put a stop to that, Sergeant. It does no good."

He motioned back towards the town centre and his Squadron followed, to find Anson leading his remaining Regiments out, North-westwards and upstream . A sympathetic ADC came to Oakwood, having first told Anson.

"Arentschildt's have been told of a ford at a place called Boecillo, three miles downstream. Wellington's ordered all to cross there. Valladolid is about six miles beyond."

The journey was made at a brisk canter for Anson's to then join the end of a long column waiting to make the passage. When their turn came each Trooper and Officer found himself entering the water with two infantrymen hanging onto his stirrup, downstream of his horse. Carr found himself with two Sergeants from the 1st Division, both of the 3rd Guards. No words were spoken during the crossing, especially as, at one point, the water came up to their chins, but once over, both saluted before they ran off.

"Obliged to you, Sir. Thank you."

The army formed up on the road leading North from the ford and Arentschildt's Brigade headed the column, with Anson's Light Dragoons behind, to Valladolid which was entered during the afternoon. This was an occasion of wild celebration, which began at least a mile before the city itself, the population having heard of the arrival of the Allies at the Douro. Wellington and his Staff were riding between Anson's and Arentschildt's and he was soon in danger of being mobbed and even unhorsed and so a dozen of One Squadron were called forward to provide a barrier either side. Flowers were thrown and wine was offered, but Anson's men were not allowed to set one foot on the venerable flagstones of a city of both religion and learning. Their Brigade never came to a halt, they rode straight past the now stationery KGL, over the bridge that crossed Valladolid's own river, the Pisuerga, and out into the country beyond. Even Oakwood was somewhat put out.

"What, not even a stop to dry our boots?"

By now Johnson was riding down the column, passing on the orders that had sent them out into the bleak plain beyond, this almost a copy of that after Garcia Hernandez, only that the small hills were not quite so small.

"We're this side of the river, to patrol North-east, keeping it on our right. To find out where Johnny's gone."

This task dejected them all, they now knew only too well what they would come across if they followed in the footsteps of the French, but discovery came in an unexpected fashion. They followed the road that kept the Pisuerga in sight for some miles until they came upon several hundred refugees. They were not in a village, more accurately opposite one, it now burning on the far side of the river. The refugees had crossed the Pisuerga by the ford at the village. The 16th were in the lead and Withers called a halt when Anson himself halted, to question as best he could the thoroughly distressed people at the river bank. Carr was sat with Oakwood, studying the village burning uncontrollably and Oakwood voiced what was now almost certain.

"Looks like Johnny's over on the far bank. Not ours!"

At that moment, a woman, middle aged, but plainly now possessing nothing, because she had been able to carry nothing across the river, ran at Baxter screaming insults.

"Una maldición sobre todos

ustedes. Una maldición sobre todos los ejércitos. Que Dios los golpee a todos muertos!"

Baxter needed to thrust out his boot to prevent the woman getting so close as to do some damage, if only with her fingernails, but instead she collapsed weeping, to be led away by the village priest. Carr turned to Oakwood.

"What was that for? What did she say?"

Oakwood shook his head.

"What she said, I've no idea, but I'm sure she hates us as much as she does the French."

They quickly left the scene of such despair to ride on, using the road that followed the river, keeping the brown-green waters of the Pisuerga always to their right, whilst across the river came the regular sight of a burning village, themselves far enough distant to neither know nor see what horrors the streets contained. Johnson was riding back with them, because Tavender at the head of One Squadron was providing poor company. He looked over the waters to another collection of homes on fire.

"Arentschildt's are on that side. Nothing to envy about the task they've been given."

The day was drawing to a close and G. Anson led them to a significant hill, just as night was falling. In the distance could be seen the lights of a substantial town. He consulted his map.

"Palencia, with all the lights lit and no fires. No Frog campfires between here and there! Our job's done."

Many miles back at Valladolid, for the 105th life remained as good as it had been for the previous two days, now in a good camp with plentiful water and wood. Miles' chickens had been a great success, although the crate attached to Albright's cart was only used at night to keep them safe. During the day, the hens were led along the road, tethered by string, or they rode on soldier's backpacks, then allowed to scratch and scrape whenever there was a stop. They thrived on army biscuits, the more rotten the better, because these contained weevils. The cockerel mostly rode atop the back pack of Sally, Nellie's eldest daughter, or on that of Kevin, Bridie's second eldest. These two youngsters had grown very much closer and were at that moment, holding hands and watching the hens peck and claw at the turf, each bird on a long tether.

On the second day of their occupation of the town at least two had diverted themselves from soldiering duties, one being Miles, off conducting business, the other Byford, sat at the fire with Eirin and Jed, but reading a book, which Bridie took some exception to, this distracting him from his pregnant wife, her daughter. It was quite a thick book and somewhat old.

"Now where did that come from?"

Byford looked up.

"The University here."

Bridie's brows narrowed. She was in a bad mood, unusual for her.

"Now, what's the use of such as that, in the sort of life that we lead? With Eirin in the state she's in? You should be worryin' more about her, than the stories in some old book!"

A pained expression came over Byford's face, but his defence came from elsewhere, from Jed Deakin, knowing that Byford was of an ilk different to those around him.

"Leave him alone! Why shouldn't he read a book? Man of his education."

An instruction from Jed Deakin brooked no argument, but a frequent visitor to their fire was also there, savouring one of Bridie's dough cakes, this being Parson Sedgwicke.

"I am not surprised, Mrs. Mulcahy, that someone should take advantage of such a place as this to view what we so often do not get to see. Myself and the Reverend did so this morning, to visit the Cathedral, and well worth it, I must say!"

There was no reply and so Sedgwicke finished his doughcake, all the while thinking more of his Chaplain, but with mixed memories in his case. Albright had been in transports of delight at the opulence and treasures of the interior, whilst Sedgwicke himself, despite being High Church, had baulked at the sheer wealth of gold and precious stones in such contrast to the grinding poverty that they had seen so much of, over the past years. However, his thoughts were interrupted by Sergeant Ellis, bringing both news and warning.

"The cavalry's found the Frogs on this side of the river, but 60 miles up. We march tomorrow, rumour has it that we march on Madrid."

Joe Pike sat forward.

"Madrid! I think I've heard of that place!"

Byford lowered his book.

"Yes Joe. It's their capital."

Saunders, sat with Consuela, now chipped in.

"Well, that's got to mean something. Capturing the capital."

Now Deakin again.

"Ah, no argument there, but it's a long way across this country from where we started in Roger's Town and so comes the question of holding it!"

The day ended with a good evening meal and all fell to making their preparations for a long march. Not long after dawn and after a good breakfast, the army assembled to form a single column and they marched out on the final day of July, cheered and clapped by the grateful populace of Valladolid.

However, the following days were ones of heat, toil and the gathering of water, the last being not so great a problem as there were many villages with good wells and clear streams on the route. On the 4th August, after another day's march, the Officers of the 105th, the Senior three, plus Captain Drake were sat under an awning, enjoying the shade. Owing to the heat, Wellington had called an early halt and there was plenty of travel left in the sun before the day's end and so the heat persisted. Infantry Anson came to join them and a jug of cool water and a beaker was pushed in his direction, but he spoke before he poured.

"I've news! Captured despatches have told us that it's no longer Marmont we're up against, he was badly wounded at Salamanca. It's now Clausel. More news, El Rey Joseph has told Soult down South to send Clausel troops but Soult's taken no notice."

Now he did pour some water.

"So, Clausel's on his own and too far North, up at a no-where place called Lerma. He's so short of men that the Peer has decided he's no threat. We should get some peace for a while."

Now he took a long drink.

"Tomorrow we converge on Segovia, that's only two marches from Madrid, given a bit of a push."

Drake looked up.

"Segovia! Now, isn't that somewhere a bit special?"

oOo

On the same day, much closer to Lerma, for G. Anson's men there was no such possibility of any form of leisurely diversion, this powerfully expressed by Cornet Peterson as he and Cornet Carr, within their Squadrons, rode their route in compliance with Wellington's orders.

"If I have to look at another river, ever, I swear I'll drown myself in it!"

Carr smiled faintly, he had every sympathy. The three Dragoon Regiments of Anson's Brigade had been left up on the Douro, whilst almost all of the Allied army marched on Madrid, albeit in searing heat. Almost all, because Clinton's 6th Division was their infantry support. The one consolation was the hospitality of the locals and on this occasion they rode into the village of Quintanilla de Ariba, one of their favourites, where a glass of the local white wine and some small cakes were always brought out and offered to all 'Oficiales Ingleses'. It was the men's favourite also, but for an entirely different reason, although wine and cakes usually came their way also. Having reached the limit of their patrol zone, Withers always allowed a rest for the horses and the men, which gave ample opportunity for some intensive fishing in the well-stocked Duero. A half-hour with a crude rod and line produced a catch and Baxter, Makepeace and all knew exactly where to take their haul and the fish were quickly cooked to provide a good meal for both themselves and also for the obliging, even eager, family. On the way back to base at Penafiel, all was relaxation and bonhomie, enough to motivate even Baxter.

"Now, this is what I call soldiering! A good horse, a few good mates, decent Officers, bar one of course, a bit of good weather, an' rations is regular. Now I don't feel quite so bad towards that bastard Sergeant as chucked a shilling into my pint, some years back."

However, the next day orders came that spoilt their idyllic sojourn, in the form of Oakwood coming back from Withers

Headquarters, to pass on instructions to his two Cornets, both Carr and Peterson at that moment enjoying rolls and coffee.

"Nothing's been heard of, regarding the French. Even that Sanchez brigand hasn't been heard from, so, we must patrol North. If only as a precaution. Each Regiment takes one day and we're first."

Peterson swallowed the last of his roll.

"Today?"

"No, tomorrow."

The sun was just creating warmth after a night with some chill, as they crossed the narrow bridge of Penafiel that spanned the Duero by numerous arches, many masked by the trees and bushes that grew on the several islands that aided the ancient structure with its task, that to carry a single and important road over its shallow current. Once over, at each road junction, a Squadron of the 16th broke off to patrol in their allotted direction, until Two Squadron found itself alone and riding through the village of Pinel de Arriba, this proud title displayed above the Town Hall. Locals emerged, more from curiousity than congratulation, but the Squadron rode straight through and on for some miles, before Oakwood began to consider how far was far enough, talking as much to himself as to Carr.

"Lerma is a good 40 miles over the Duero. I'd say a ride up until Noon should do it. Then back."

Carr said nothing as they rode on. With the sun at its zenith they rode through another village, but one that did not name itself. Oakwood slowed his horse to a walk alongside a group of residents and called out two words, spoken as a question.

"Soldados Franceses?"

The reply was raised arms with open palms and a shake of the head from the nearest, his facial expression conveying total ignorance, until he spat on the ground and then spoke. He had found his way through Oakwood's tangled pronunciation.

"Soldadoes Franceses?"

He waved an arm in the direction that the Squadron was going.

"Lerma! Lerma! Creo. Un largo camino. Que Dios los guarde alli!"

Then he spat on the ground again. Oakwood nodded his thanks.

"Still Lerma!"

Ten more minutes and they were over a river with a junction just beyond, where they halted.

Oakwood was the first to dismount.

"This will do fine. We can water the horses and then depart. Nothing seen by us or anyone."

With that he pulled his own food out of his saddlebag, but he gave an order at the same time, somewhat unwelcome to those required to obey it.

"Willoughby! Someone has to do it, sorry it's you. Mount a picket half a mile up."

Carr remounted, then he looked at Baxter who nodded, then he looked in turn at Troopers Makepeace, Spivey and Nunney and all five set their horses at the trot for another ten minutes before Carr called a halt where the small river was still in reach. When all five had dismounted, Baxter climbed the bank alongside the road to look further.

"Another village some way along, Sir."

Carr was eating by now, he was very hungry.

"I'd say we're far enough, Sergeant."

Then Baxter studied the view further.

"There's a lone rider comin' this way, Sir."

Carr dropped his food onto the dry grass and joined him. In the distance, just discernible in the heat haze and framed by the village, was a lone rider. He ran back to his horse and pulled out his most recent and welcome acquisition to focus it on the oncoming horseman.

"He's alone! He looks Spanish."

Both resumed eating as the rider trotted his horse over the last half mile, then the stranger reined in his horse some ten yards before Carr and his men. Each studied the other and Carr gained the impression of a man confident in himself, slim but still muscular, dressed as a not overly prosperous Spanish farmer, in high boots with many buttons, thick canvas trousers, a wide belt, loose green shirt, with much of it covered with a leather jerkin. Above this a tanned face, but mostly in the shadow of a wide brimmed hat. Carr had no Spanish and was hoping the man would ride on, until the stranger grinned from under the brow of the hat and sat forward in his saddle. What he then said astonished everyone there in the picket.

"And what Regiment are you?"

Carr looked at Baxter, then back at the man.

"16th Light Dragoons!"

Then Carr paused.

"And who are you?"

The man sat back in his saddle, still grinning.

"Colonel John Waters. 12th Foot. East Sussex."

Carr's instinct was to salute, but he did not.

"Excuse me, Sir, but this is a bit of a strange meeting!"

Waters laughed and dismounted, leading his horse up to Carr and Baxter.

"I'll not argue with that, but your name is?"

Carr now did come to the attention.

"Cornet Carr, Sir. C Troop, Two Squadron."

"Very well, Cornet Carr, but I must ask you to escort me back to our lines. I think I have some valuable information, gathered from my roaming around these parts and we should get it to our Commander in Chief as soon as possible."

"Yes Sir, but we have no certainty as to who you are, Sir. You could be anyone, dressed like that!"

"Most perceptive, Cornet, but I'm sure you appreciate that in my line of work something proving that I am a British Officer could be rather dangerous. So, all I ask is that you do not shoot me, but allow me back to our lines, that at least."

"Yes Sir. We can do that. Perhaps now, Sir?"

Within minutes the group, now six, were trotting back the half mile, but Waters had his own questions to Baxter, alongside Carr.

"How are you finding the French? You first, Sergeant."

Baxter took a deep breath

"Well, Sir, they put up a bit of a fight at Salamanca, as just gone, but not for long. The best they put up was as a rearguard, as the day ended."

Waters turned to Carr.

"And you, Cornet?"

"As Sergeant Baxter said, Sir, but the impression I gained is that their infantry are no match for ours. During the main battle they stood for very little time, the best was put up by their rearguard. You couldn't argue with that effort."

"Anything else?"

"Well, a while back we saw four Battalions of their infantry, just dissolve before a determined cavalry assault and their own cavalry just rode off, Sir, without striking a blow. Although they greatly outnumbered us."

Waters nodded and looked thoughtful.

"Don't underestimate the French powers of recovery. I've just come from Lerma and they're coming back together. They've been resupplied. Clausel knows his business. What if he advances, what do you do then?

"Our orders are clear, Sir. We fall back on General Clinton of the 6th Division. They're South of the Duero."

He smiled at Carr.

"Good, but, talking of wider matters. Boney's invaded Russia, did you know?"

Carr shook his head.

"We did not. We have not seen any English newspapers for some time."

"Well he has. A big mistake in my opinion and one that may well have repercussions for you, down here."

At this point they had ridden up to an astonished Oakwood and Carr made the introductions.

"This is Colonel Waters, Sir. I think I can introduce him as some kind of spy! For us, that is."

oOo

For the 105th, the delights of Segovia were wearing thin. The men were confined to camp in a narrow, wooded valley and the Officers were now disinclined to make any more cultural visits. The last to return was Captain Lord Carravoy and Major Slade, the former now complaining loudly.

"The Cathedral and that Alcazar place were all very well, but the Royal Palace, now that El Rey has quit the place, is swarming with beggars and pickpockets. Some of them are children and most adept. One I saw going about his villainous business with some local, which is why I took off my tunic and folded it over my arm. At least to make it a bit more difficult."

Slade grinned weakly. He had just searched into his own pocket and found it empty of the half dozen Dollars he had begun their excursion with.

However, boredom was soon dispelled the next day, if only by marching through pleasant upland country that contained enough hills and valleys to provide interest rather than cause serious fatigue. The day's march brought them to another Spanish wonder, the San Ildefonso and in the light of the early evening, Carr and Drake, the latter on a borrowed horse, undertook the short ride from their camp. They were not alone, many more Officers from the Allied army had taken the opportunity, but Carr and Drake remained mounted, finding themselves sat at the top of a waterfall, built as a series of steps, placed before the spectacular view of the Royal Palace itself. Carr shook his head at the layer upon layer of the detailed and intricate carving rose up opposite them from an expanse of flower beds and brushed beige gravel.

"This reminds me of your wedding cake!"

Drake looked at him with mock outrage.

"I'm sure that when all this is finished you could find a job as a critic of architecture, both Medieval and Modern!"

Carr grinned.

"Another world, this! Another, for altogether different people! Come on, let's ride round. I don't fancy the inside, it'll only be furniture, suits of armour and paintings, assuming El Rey's left any on the walls, but the gardens and such do look a bit special."

They spent another hour walking their horses around the paths and roads that served the whole estate, until they turned back for their camp and within half an hour they were enjoying a light supper of dried fish, bread and the inevitable Spanish sausage. The next day saw the onward march resumed, the 105th in the centre of W. Anson's column. They had not been on the road an hour before they were overtaken by a column of guerrilla lancers, riding in twos with their leader alone at the front. All were dressed in high boots, light brown trousers and a thin green jacket. It was in no way military, but a uniform of sorts, nevertheless. Miles was not impressed and, not surprisingly, said so.

"Irregulars, be they? Is that what they'm called? Scruffy lot, strikes me!"

Ellis, marching alongside, took issue with Miles' judgement.

"Scruffy, you says. An' look at you! There's more French on you than King George's an' that's wearin' out and more hanging off than stickin' on. Their leader, this Julian Sanchez, has 1,000 Spanish dollars on his head. That's a damn sight more than you're worth! And 'sides, from what I hear, them boys does a good job, finding out all sorts as is useful. And takin' risks! If you or I gets taken we can call ourselves prisoners of war. Those boys just gets strung up, after God knows what!"

Miles settled his backpack of French design and manufacture better onto his shoulders.

"Well, that's one thing they'm useful for, I grant you, findin' out the odd thing or two, but will they stand against Frog cavalry? Or attack a square, even? That's my point."

"Well no. They does a job as is different, as you've just spoken of, but 'tis just as useful, perhaps more so, so leave it there."

Ellis then held his peace, whilst Miles marched the next few miles wearing a small smile of contentment at his small triumph. In camp that evening George Pearson came around to examine the wounds of Bailey, Davey and Deakin and pronounced their wounds healing well, which remark was pounced on by Tom Miles, him still feeling thoroughly buoyed by his minor success against Ellis.

"Does that mean we've not got to carry their gear no more?"

However, he was immediately pounced on himself by Nellie Nicholls.

"You shut your mouth, Tom Miles! Neither is full healed yet and a bit of extra carryin' and humpin' does you no harm. 'Specially if it keeps your moanin' mouth shut a bit longer and your bothersome self out of our worry!"

The vitriolic attack from Nellie shocked even Tom Miles and so he thought it best to remain subdued, but Henry, Nellie's husband, had more than an inkling about what had set his wife into such a temper.

"And just what's got up your nose? Have you had another run-in with that Betty Barker, as was?"

Nellie looked peeved and sheepish all at the same time.

"What if I have? Stupid cow that she is. Whatever I get at the ration share-out she says is better than hers. This time I went for her and Sergeant Gibney had to pull us apart. Now I'm on my best behaviour, so I am. All because of that wailin' gobshite."

Jed Deakin could not help but smile.

"From what I hear, she's on her best behaviour too. Started a fire a while back that spread and threatened to burn down Lowry-Cole's tent, or damn near close."

Hearing that, Bridie and Nellie ran over to place themselves directly in front of him, Bridie arriving first.

"What else do you know?"

oOo

The roads were mountainous, but tolerable, their feet given energy by the fact that they were marching to claim the Spanish capital of Madrid. Two days after San Ildefonso the route was still within the high plains but they camped within sight of Madrid itself, a view being studied by many telescopes, the instruments being both owned and shared. The evening camp saw W. Anson arrive at the Headquarters tent of the 105th, with the Senior three enjoying coffee, their evening meal now finished. As Anson sat, Carr looked over his shoulder.

"Bryce! A cup for the General!"

Anson pulled up a seat and watched with glee the strong liquid being poured into a metal mug. He took one sip with relish before beginning on the reason for his journey.

"From what we hear, El Rey's abandoning Madrid, so Sanchez Lancers have discovered. He's seen convoys leaving by the hour carrying all their loot, with many Spanish Afrancesados alongside, what the Spanish call collaborators,. We could be going in day after tomorrow!"

Carr raised his eyebrows and smiled at the good news.

"And French armies? Any news?"

Anson swallowed more coffee.

"Clausel's still way above the Duero and Soult's down South with Suchet, messing about in Catalonia, occupied by Bentinck's force down there. We'll be on our own for some time."

He stood up, but did not move.

"Oh, and he's allowed a rest day tomorrow, to get ourselves spruced up for a triumphant entry."

The following morning the order 'parade inspection' was circulated. On hearing the order, both Davey and Saunders held up their tunics for their own examination, each more a faded pink than red, the green of their facings now closer to the natural colour of the cloth and each garment more a patchwork of stitching and repairs.

"What am I supposed to do with this?"

Davey turned his tunic to examine the neat repair to the sword cut from Salamanca, neat, but visible nonetheless. Saunders examined his.

"Well, if nothing else, they can be clean and any new holes and whatnot patched over, I mean, what difference is an extra patch going to make? So, we starts washing."

At that moment Ellis arrived with 'parade rations', pipeclay and brick dust, packets of which he tossed in various directions.

"Buttons and belts is to be cleaned. We can do that at least."

Deakin looked up at him.

"What about hair?"

He was asking about the parade regulation of hair being pulled back tight to be smeared with candle grease and soap, then whitened with flour.

"I didn't ask and I don't intend to. Nor about stocks, neither!"

In the Light Company tent, at the back end of the day, Drake was examining the efforts of Morrison and making his own small improvements to his tunic. Hat, trousers, hose and boots had to wait their turn. Bettridge and Shakeshaft were about much the same task, then Carr walked in. Bettridge sprang to his feet but Carr waved him back down.

"Up to the best that can managed?"

Drake nodded, he knew immediately what the subject was.

"As much as can be done, has been done!"

Then he looked full at Carr.

"Much the same as going into Lisbon in the year eight? God, that seems an age ago."

"Much the same, only this will be bigger and perhaps more enthusiastic. These have been ruled by the French since the year eight."

Drake put on a thoughtful face.

"Sort of a Roman triumph. Do you think the Peer'll be in a chariot or something with a Waggoneer or somesuch stood behind? Him whispering, "You are but a man!"

Carr and Shakeshaft laughed, whilst Bettridge looked astonished that anyone could speak of their Commander in Chief in such terms, then they heard the sound of a galloping horse, followed by an unknown voice shouting the alarm.

"105th double forward. Form as you go."

The four ran outside the tent, donning tunics as they went. Luckily Anson then arrived on horseback, because Carr was as bemused as anyone.

"D'Urban's been attacked up at Las Rosas, not five miles from Madrid. A serious effort from Johnny, so we hear."

"Right Sir!"

As Anson rode off, Carr turned to the tent behind him.

"Bates! Sound form up."

The notes sounded and the 105th ran from all directions to form on the road. When Carr felt that he had around three-quarters of his command he ordered double forward. Then he found Gibney.

"Sergeant Major. We're going straight on. Send any stragglers forward to catch up."

As Gibney wheeled a salute, Carr mounted his horse and rode after his men, now two hundred yards down the road.

It was a run of five miles and the lighter 105th kept pace with Anson's Riflemen, although the heavier Irish of the 27th began to fall behind, but the nearer they came to Las Rosas the more the pace slowed, mostly because, ahead there was silence, no sounds of any conflict at all. They arrived at Las Rosas to be directed straight through by an ADC of some General, to emerge out onto what had clearly been a battlefield, albeit a small one, with dead and wounded in profusion all around, the sight stretching out and beyond towards Madrid. Carr turned to Heaviside and O'Hare.

"Off the road and rest!"

As the 105th broke formation to sit at the edge of the road, Carr felt justified in riding over to W. Anson, who was in conversation with Brigadier D'Urban. The two stopped when Carr came to them.

"Where would you like us, Sir?"

D'Urban looked weary.

"Take a rest, Colonel, then you can take your men back. Johnny made a sortie and took us by surprise, but we've now seen him off. It's all over."

Anson and Carr left D'Urban at the same time and, after allowing the men a rest, both rode together at their head back to camp, during which Anson gave some details.

"D'Urban placed his men before the village, with their horses all tied up in a picket line, but his being Portuguese they were at their siesta when the French arrived. They had enough warning to form a line of sorts, but were beaten back to Las Rosas by sheer weight of numbers and four guns were lost. The KGL saved D'Urban's bacon, these being a few KGL Dragoons and a Light Infantry Battalion, stopping the Frogs in front of the village. Even more lucky for him, the guns couldn't be carried off and they were all recovered. Sorry, but yours were the first available."

"No harm done, Sir, other than to interrupt our preparations for the grand entrance."

Very much no harm was done in the case of Miles and Bailey either, there had been no rest for them, this being too good an opportunity to miss. Taking the chance before the march back, they had scavenged out and about and returned with two pairs of French Dragoon Officers' boots, which would cut down very nicely, and also the inevitable collection of silver buttons and buckles.

The boots were in place on their feet as the 105th, with the following dawn, formed up once more on the road to Madrid and marched forward, again over the route to Las Rosas, with the 7th Division in the lead, then the 4th, with Wellington and his Staff in the lead of all. However, once through Las Rosas the situation changed markedly, because the road onwards into Madrid soon became thronged on each side with ecstatic Madrilenians and Lieutenant Shakeshaft made notes in his diary as he marched at the head of Two Section, all of which he wrote up into good prose that evening.

"Five miles out from the gates of Madrid the road was crowded with people who had come out to meet us, each bringing something, laurel boughs, flowers, bread, wine, grapes, lemonade, sweetmeats, and more. The road was like a moving forest from the multitude who carried palms, which they strewed in the road for us to march over. Young ladies presented us with laurel and even fixed it in our caps, others handed out sweetmeats and fruit. Gentlemen had hired porters to bring out wine, which they handed to us as we passed by. Every individual strived to outvie each other in good nature. We were proud of the honour paid us by the people. We entered the city with the air rent with cries of "Long Live Wellington. Long Live the English". The crowd and shouts and ringing of bells was beyond description. It was with difficulty the Lord Wellington was able to keep his seat on horseback, everyone was pressing round him. They kissed his hands, his sword, even his horse and the ground he had passed over."

For each member of the 105th, the reaction to the welcome came in different forms. Carravoy and Slade adopted their most aristocratic bearing, whilst such as Bettridge and D'Villiers grinned from ear to ear, welcoming and indulging themselves thoroughly in the attentions of each Spanish maiden who came close enough to kiss them or give either yet another laurel. For the men in the ranks, their mouths spoke their gratitude well enough, especially for the food and the wine, but strangely enough, what mattered more to them was to maintain a stolid, grim, military bearing amongst all the civilian tumult, as they marched behind their lurid Colours. They were the 'Fighting 105th', the 'Rag and Bone Boys' of an unbeaten army and to act and appear as such mattered much more, rather than to join in the extreme emotion as demonstrated by over-wrought civilians on either side. Further to that was the outrage of the soldiers of the outside ranks whom the men of the city attempted to embrace and even kiss. The Colour Party, at the head, were particularly assailed but quickly rebuffed by the bulk of Gibney, Nicholls, Hill and Halfway.

Once inside the city it was impossible for the men to disperse and so they stood in ranks for more than an hour until the crowds finally thinned enough for individual Regiments to march off into the suburbs and make the best of whatever buildings were available. Within the 105th's allocated street, each Section peeled off as they came to each doorway and all were welcomed by the inhabitants, immediately providing food and wine. Number One Section of the Light Company, and One Section of the Colour Company contrived to shuffle their way into several rooms of the same building and set up their own area, assuming that they would be there for some time. It was not long before small children, intensely curious, came to examine these huge, uniformed giants and all soon noticed how thin and hungry the children looked. Davey, Pike and Byford, fathers all, were the first to pull food from their haversacks and offer it to the watching children to see the biscuits, sausage and dried fruit quickly consumed. The most important impression was created within their watching parents and more than one spoke their thanks to the nodding, but wholly uncomprehending, soldiers, but Byford had some notion of what was being said.

"They are saying thanks. We are very different to the French."

Miles guffawed.

"Right! I should bloody well hope so!"

Ellis was stood nearby and was already thinking ahead.

"Well spoken, Miles. Now, you and Bailey get back to the road and watch for the Followers. They won't have a clue where we are. And, whilst you're there, lay off the drink and the girls. Your job is the Followers. Get them back here."

Miles and Bailey, him still limping slightly, seized their rifles and other kit and hurried out of the door. Within minutes they were back to the corner of the main road and set themselves to wait. It was not long before two girls came up to them, both regularly intoning the same words.

"Valientes soldados ingleses. Valientes soldados ingleses."

Bailey looked at Miles.

"What they sayin'?"

"Damned if I know. Something about soldiers."

"What they want? Food! All mine's gone."

Miles looked at him in amazement, the way the girls had come up swaying their hips and shoulders told him everything and all was confirmed when one of the girls spoke something new.

"Quatro reales, valientes soldados ingleses. Solo quatro reales."

"Ain't you worked it out? These is doxies."

Bailey looked shocked and studied the girls more closely, which each took to be a good sign and both sidled closer, but Bailey was appalled and looked it.

"I got one back home, same age as these, not much less. These can't be no older than Nellie's Sally."

He looked again, still shocked.

"This is terrible!"

Miles was in his pulpit.

"You says terrible and you'm right, but how else does some of these earn coin after four years of livin' under the Frogs, what with them robbin' 'em blind of every single thing as is needed to keep body and soul together?"

He turned to the girls and they could see he was angry as he waved them away.

"Go! Bugger off! Vamanos!"

The girls went, now angry themselves and one hurled some Spanish insult over her shoulder as she slunk off, before looking for more hopeful possibilities. Miles and Bailey slumped against the wall, Bailey now more depressed than appalled.

"They'm just girls! Different place, different time, could be one of mine."

"Well, Len, the best reply is what we gets from Officers when they gives us speeches, that we'm here fightin' to protect our own folks and homeland and, from what we've just seen, it's about true. We'n poundin' up an' down this messed up country, so's yours'll never have to do the such as that."

Bailey nodded with a resigned look on his face, when they heard a cry from somewhere down the road, in Bridie's voice.

"Look, there's Tom and Len!"

They both levered themselves off the wall and stood waiting whilst their womenfolk walked the final yards. Within a minute they were leading them to their billets and within five minutes the women were cooking food in the wide Spanish fireplaces while the English and Spanish children played together. The Spanish mothers were particularly taken with toddler Jed and thoroughly fussed over the heavily pregnant Eirin. Within hours they were all a solid community, determined not to allow language to be too much of a barrier at all, but it was not long before it became obvious that their welcome when they entered the city, contrasted markedly with the poverty of the families they were billeted with. This was noticed especially by Deakin, who soon concluded that very hungry children and the sacrifices of their parents were closer to the truth.

"Where they found all that provender they threw at us this morning, I don't know. It must have been just about all they had. We shares our rations, 'till things gets better. Agreed?"

No-one disagreed, in the face of such an unassailable pronouncement from Jed Deakin. However, nothing like the same level of domesticity existed in what was now the Headquarters rooms of the 105th, this containing all Senior Officers, most Captains and W. Anson himself, him with worrying news.

"El Rey has left 2,000 men in something called the Retiro, a sort of citadel. El Rey was hoping for Soult to come up, but that isn't going to happen. We got that from captured despatches; it seems Sanchez gives us better news than El Rey gets himself. Anyway, the Peer wants them out from this Retiro place, but who does that job, I know not as yet."

The word of the Retiro garrison spread throughout the billets and it was Deakin, thoroughly irritated at the news, who pronounced judgement.

"And what's the damn point of that? They won't hold out, some of they'll be killed and some of our lads too. To what gain? Damned if I knows!"

However, the following morning Anson returned, seemingly a much relieved man.

"That Retiro was taken last night. Last night, no less, but we lost ten lads killed or wounded. The 3rd and 7th Divisions did the job and, this you won't believe, inside were immense supplies of stores, enough shoes for our whole army, blue tunics for whoever the Peer chooses, gunners most likely, and enough of another type for Carlos De Espana's men and Sanchez' boys besides, And, most surprising, two French Eagles, the 51st Line and the 12th Light, the last they call Voltiguers."

The news was met with an astonished silence from his audience, but Anson did not mind when, onto the table in front of him was placed a plate of cooked ham, olives and fresh rolls. He had been very quick to appreciate in which of his Regiments he was most likely to be well fed and for this reason the 105th usually received news first, such as he was able to pass on.

The French shoes arrived for distribution the following day, by the simple method of something like enough pairs being thrown into the doorways of the 105th billets from carts touring the city. The Colour Company and the Light Company looked at their new French footwear critically, especially, Miles, Pike and Bailey, and the verdict was spoken, unsurprisingly by Miles.

"These is all very well, but cut-down cavalry boots is better. These I b'ain't using."

His verdict was almost universal amongst those who had gathered much of what they wore from French dead and therefore their French shoe ration mostly ended up on the feet of their hosts, both male and female. However, it was that day when events in the city took a different turn, this brought to them by Ellis.

"First, we're all confined to quarters because the Spanish is too likely to give us too much drink. You don't leave here unless ordered or on patrol. Second, what they calls Afrancensados, Spanish friendly to the French, is being beat up and even killed. Beaten to death or strung up. You knows how it works, such is used as an excuse to settle old scores, whether they helped the French or not. So, we've got to act like Bow Street Runners to keep the lid on and mount patrols. One Section goes out tonight, seems that it's in the dark that the wicked deeds gets done. At nine, see you've eaten and are ready to go out. Saunders, you'm in charge. Three hour stretch."

Saunders looked up from checking his Baker.

"Where?"

"Just use your sense. Wander about and show your faces, but not too far from here. There's others doin' the rounds, so look after our neighbourhood"

At nine exactly, Saunders and his trusted band of Davey, Miles, Pike, Bailey, Byford, Turner and Solomon left their billet and stood in the street outside, where he was as much at a loss as to which way to go as anyone, but Miles had a plan, of sorts.

"Well, I don't see the harm of takin' ourselves to the local square, that plaza place just round the corner, an' seein' if we can't get a drink afore we starts. On top, it'll help us get our bearings, sort of thing. It'll have a church with a name, what we can ask for, if we gets lost."

Saunders looked at him suspiciously, but a good navigation point in an entirely unfamiliar city did make sense.

"All right! Up to the main road and then on to the first plaza, as they calls 'em. But one drink! One! My stripes is worth more to me than what goes down your throat, Tom Miles."

They set off and soon came to a plaza, where Madrilenians were making full use of the carnival atmosphere, even winding it up to further heights. The seven were hailed as soon as they entered the plaza, which was a main one and of no small significance, because it did have a huge church and in the centre was a form of display, it being the two Eagles, supported by French drums, but guarded by men of the 1st Division, the Coldstream Guards. Many of Wellington's Officers were studying the prizes, including their own Drake and Carr. Whilst Saunders approached this pair of to explain their presence, Davey and Byford approached the guard, Davey asking the questions.

"What's this? A bit strong, having these out in the middle of the city, with all these Spanish?"

The Coldstream Corporal shook his head and sighed.

"You've got the truth of it there! Nosey ordered it, thought it would be good for the peoples' morale, as he put it, but we've got to keep 'em back 'cos they only wants to spit on both and, given the chance, I reckon they'd just chuck both down a sewer. Our Sergeant has gone to see our Colonel and so I reckon they'll be taken in soon, and not too soon for us."

Davey shook his own head at the unwise idea of the display, but Saunders had returned and Miles led them to a lively Estaminet. They eased their way in, being slapped and clapped all the way, to approach the counter. Miles shouted "Cognac!" and held up seven fingers. The brandy was poured and Miles pushed across two silver buttons which were pushed back by the proprietor.

"Bravo soldados Ingleses. Bien hecho en Salamanca!"

Miles turned to his companions with a huge grin on his face.

"He's heard all about us. This cove! He knows all about Salamanca."

He turned to the man and raised his glass and then he shouted for all to hear.

"Salamanca!"

The whole Estaminet must have heard because immediately glasses were being raised all over, in response to the same toast. The remaining six raised their own glasses and waved them in various directions before downing the spirit in one, then they left, steering the choking Joe Pike out before them. Miles was beaming.

"Now don't tell me that wasn't worth it!"

Saunders looked indulgently at him and led them off, towards the nearest side street. Byford had not forgotten the main reason why they had come to the Plaza and for that reason he was late leaving and had to catch them up.

"The church is called La Iglesia de la Inmaculada Concepción de Santa Teresa."

Solomon shook his head.

"Who could forget a name like that!"

However, soon they were in the back streets, a mix of houses and shops, then, even further out, what appeared to be stores and warehouses. Miles was just thinking up a good excuse to go back to the plaza for another drink when they came across an oldish man, frantically scrubbing the double doors of a warehouse. What remained to be scrubbed off was '…cesado', and he continued scrubbing as the group approached. Davey stopped and watched proceedings.

"Seems like some have got this old lad down as a friend of the French."

The man stopped on hearing Davey's words and, fearing no immediate threat, turned around to speak with evident fear and urgency, but in reasonable English.

"Yes, si, they say I help Franceses, yes, but is not true. Not true."

"You speak decent English, Senor, how come?"

The man went right up to Davey.

"I deal with English before sucio French come. I am seller, how you say, merchant in leather and wool cloth. This is my almacen, you say warehouse, si."

"That's the word, right enough, old 'un, but why have they wrote that on your door?"

He pointed at the remaining writing.

"They do this because French come here many times, but I have no choice, they come here and use. Give no choice."

He went to the door and pulled out a key.

"I show why."

He turned the key in the lock and pulled open the door and even in the light of a dying evening, they could see that the warehouse was piled high with French uniforms and clothing. Miles was the first forward to examine the stock and soon pronounced his findings.

"Some tunics, but mostly Frog greatcoats and breeches. All brand new. They must have forced this old cove to let them use his warehouse to store all this stuff."

He ran his hand over a greatcoat at the top of a pile, then turned to his companions.

"These is quality. There's coin to be made here!"

Saunders stepped forward.

"Now don't you get none of your daft ideas, Tom. Looting could mean the lash or the rope!"

"I don't mean lootin'. We can do better'n that. It just needs some thinkin' out, that's all."

Then, from Nat Solomon, words came in support for Saunders.

"Tom, leave this be, or you'll have us all on the triangle. Or somethin' higher!"

"Alright, alright. Nothin' yet, and nothing 'till I says what I finally has in mind. But first we has to put a guard on this. Anyone asks, we says it's stuff out of that Retiro place as needs guardin' and whose to question if we shows 'em it. And it's done to save the life of this old codger who is an honest merchant as sells to us back home. Speaks English and all, so must be at least half-way decent."

Of replies or objections, there came none and so Miles grinned and continued.

"Me and Joe will take first watch."

It was close to eleven when a group of men arrived, four only, whilst the church clocks struck the time of night, the first clock chimes for years. However, when Miles and Pike fixed their bayonets, all four slunk on past, muttering what neither Miles nor Pike could understand. With their three hours completed, the patrol returned to their billet and the next 105th patrol were told what to be particularly concerned about, in return for a silver button each and thus the warehouse was guarded throughout the night. The next morning Miles held court, for both mess groups, including the Followers, but it was an exclusive gathering.

"This is how I sees it. Winter is not too far away and these Madrids have had it hard, they'll be looking for something decent for the weather, 'specially if 'tis a good price. The grey beard must know some tailors as can turn the greatcoats into ordinary coats and the breeches won't need much changing at all. What we does to earn our coin is to see that the warehouse don't get done over and that the stuff gets delivered to these tailors what the old chap knows. We charges for every load that comes out of the warehouse. French kit will need an English escort or it'll get pillaged. Easy does it, takin' a bit at a time an' no-one's any the wiser. 'Cept us!"

Henry Nicholls was the first to object.

"French stuff belongs to the army and for us to do that would be the same as stealing off King George."

Deakin had been listening carefully and had thoughts of his own and he looked around the group as he spoke in his usual sagelike fashion.

"I'm not sure that applies. If this kit is in this Spaniard's warehouse, then it belongs to him. Like if some French bits and pieces was in some home, then they belongs to the family. I can't see our Provosts taking it away from this merchant, doing that'll come up the same as the French and their lootin' ways."

He paused, because he had another concern, for which he looked hard at Tom Miles.

"And so when this stuff is being carted about and we'm challenged, what then?"

Miles gave his answer of the previous night.

"We can say it just stuff from that Retiro place, what's being spread about anyway."

Henry Nicholls was not at all happy and he knew that it was Deakin that he had to argue with.

"Which won't be true, Jed, and, here's us, under King's Regulations, playing a part in some scheme to sell French uniforms to the locals. You know where that can lead."

Deakin thought for a good few seconds about his answer.

"I can't see no harm in us helping this old lad get his business back up and runnin', using what is really his. No one can call it spoils of war, like a captured cannon or purse took off a dead Frencher. None of what's in his warehouse came off a battlefield. No need for that Retiro line, I do reckon that this old boy can call this Frencher stuff his own, that's his good luck, until someone says different and, unless that comes, he can do what he likes with it."

He paused again.

"I don't see why we shouldn't give him a hand in return for a bit of coin whilst off duty. Not much different to when we dug that water ditch down Elvas way, as ended up with Zeke and Consuela spliced."

All grinned at the memory, but no argument came back, so Deakin continued.

"Well, confined to billets won't last for ever and we'll get time to ourselves to wander. They'll put Provosts on the gates and whatnot, but what we chooses to do with our own time inside the city will be up to us. If Miles here, and others, using their own time, decides to help this old Spaniard get his business back up and running, selling what the French've abandoned, well I can't see too much of a charge comin' out of that, if any."

Once more he stared hard at Miles.

"Only easy does it, like you said. Don't get carried away and draw attention to yourself. There's plenty of smart minds up at Headquarters as could think of something and you don't give 'em cause to decide that it'll be worth their while to have us hauled up afore the Provost Marshall."

He allowed that to sink in then continued further.

"And, if challenged, you tells the truth, none of this Retiro stuff. We're helping a local use French kit as was forced on him and got him called this Afran thing, to get his business going again."

The silence was palpable as Deakin continued staring at Miles, until the latter nodded and Deakin continued.

"What's happening with this stuff now?"

He turned to Saunders.

"Still under guard. We've been ordered to patrol to protect these Afran characters and this old boy is one of them, or so the locals thinks."

"Right, so we'd better keep the guard going."

The following day confinement was lifted and so Saunders, Davey, Miles and Byford went to the warehouse, which was open, with all the letters scrubbed off the doors, the wood still damp. The Spaniard was inside and grinned to see them and grinned even further when the scheme was explained. Then the fee was settled, generous to the four, so they shook hands all round with the promise to return the day after next. The Spaniard, now known as Max, short for Maximiliano Sagasta, needed time to visit his tailor contacts. Final question, did the old man have a cart? Yes, he did.

The days moved on, pursuing the end of August, and each Tuesday and Thursday a cart of uniforms was delivered to one of Max's tailors, the cart pulled by uniformed soldiers and so it was never challenged. Each Friday, Miles or Solomon went to the warehouse to receive payment in reales or even in Spanish dollars, each worth eight reales and never once did they feel that they had been unfairly paid. The guard was maintained and the pile of French uniforms gradually diminished and good coats and breeches began to appear in tailors' windows at a cheap price and so, eventually the word got around that Senor Segasta was using French uniforms to provide cheap clothes, then more and more he was welcomed wherever he went. One Friday, late August, Miles returned with eight dollars and ten reales and spoke, with a note of triumph as the coins were tipped into the mess bank.

"There, now didn't I say that this would work out fair all round! You should listen more to what I has to say."

The result was a tin mug being thrown at his head, any boasting from Miles always received such a response, but no one argued verbally.

In the 105th Headquarters, the atmosphere was nothing like so genial, the news again being provided by their W. Anson, but him being again welcomed with good coffee.

"The Yanks declared war on us, 18th June in case you didn't know, and we're having a go at Detroit. Boney's got into Smolensk. That's over half way to Moscow."

Carr sat back and sipped his own coffee, but there was no degree of shock or surprise on his face.

"Well, we can always trust our American cousins to do whatever will help France and vice versa. As for Boney, that adventure is costing him men and treasure and I cannot see it working out well, for him that is, hoping to bring the whole of Russia as far as Moscow into his cosy little Empire."

He turned to look fully at Anson.

"What for us, do you think, Sir, from that?"

Anson took a deep breath and released it as a long sigh.

"It could mean a Division from here being sent to Canada to hold the border, it could mean French troops being taken from El Rey to prop up Boney when his Russian junket goes all to Hell."

"So, it could well come out equal?"

"You could have the right of it, Colonel. Yes!"

However, Carr had his own subject.

"Sir, I want to take mine out for training. We've new recruits that we've not had a chance to work on. Can you get me some ammunition?"

Anson looked pained.

"Not King George's, but as much French as you like. There's piles of it still in the Retiro."

Carr frowned.

"Their ball is smaller than ours, more closer to half an inch, whilst ours come close to three-quarters, as you know."

"Yes Carr, but for training? You load it the same and it goes bang, just the same. As much as you like."

That evening the word went around to parade in the main street at dawn and the 105th marched out until Carr, O'Hare and Heaviside were satisfied with a reasonably flat plain, defined by the surrounding hills. They began with moving from types of column to square and then to line, sometimes two deep, sometimes three, then back to square, always overseen by the three Seniors and the pitiless hands of their pocket watches. Satisfied, Carr ordered a two deep firing line and the French ammunition was distributed, much to the concern of many, including inevitably, Miles.

"This is what?"

Ellis did not even turn.

"French, and you loads it just the same and you obeys orders, just the same. It'll go into your Baker so you do not use the special Baker stuff you've got."

During all the manoeuvring their Waggoneers, Drummers and Fifers had hammered white posts into the ground and their line was now opposite the long white row. Drake went up to Bettridge, stood out before the Light Company with Shakeshaft.

"Lionel! I will call the first volleys, then I will say that both myself and Richard are down. You take over the Company. Do you know what to do?"

"Yes Sir, but it's Luttrel Sir. As you've told me, just after Nine's front rank fires, so does ours, then it's all about seeing our targets through the smoke, Sir, for 'front rank, then rear rank."

"Yes, exactly so. Good man, Lionel, Luttrel, rather. So, keep to that and you cannot go far wrong."

Bettridge took the time to look back and was impressed by what he saw, a steady, straight line of true veterans, the rear rank 'locked on' so that their heads could be seen between those of the front rank and many heads with a kerchief wrapped around their heads, particularly over their ears, to protect from the noise, sparks and flash from so many firing-pans close to their ears and faces.

The next hour was one of continuous noise, broken only by the need to replenish ammunition pouches and clean weapons. Carr rode along the rear of his line as the half Company volleys ran up the ranks and he could see, all down his line, smoke and burning paper from the cartridges flying in the wind. His only concern was with the Colour Company, each rank were kept too long as the 'make ready', before 'present" and so he pushed through the rear rank to stand beside Major Slade. He had to shout to make himself heard.

"Major! You call fire when you can make out your target, however feint. Your Company is not matching the rate of fire of the others. I will demonstrate."

Carr took over and the frequency of the volleys increased, Carr ordering fire when the vaguest outline of the posts could be seen. Once content, Carr leaned over to Slade.

"Like that, Major. That's how it's done, that's how we've won. That's how we've got ourselves up to here."

Slade looked peeved, but the improvement came. Carr ordered a final, "Clean weapons", but all took a long drink first to ease the raging thirst caused by gunpowder in their mouths from biting cartridges. Weapons cleaned, they finished with more manoeuvres; column to line to open order and back and for Carr a special project, advancing on a narrow front with three ranks. All bar the Light Company, who were sent further into the hills to practice 'advancing by files' and 'retreating by files". Now out amongst the bare scrub, it was not long before Bettridge was given the Baker of a man pulled out by Drake.

"You'll probably have to complete a file, Lionel, and keep files in threes as casualties come. Lives depend on it."

Pained at his name again being misused, he joined in nevertheless and, although slow, he evidently enjoyed the business of 'loading and filing in" and his two 'file mates' remained indulgent at having to wait, for him to arrive at 'number two' with a loaded Baker. Eventually Carr was satisfied and the 105th reformed to march back, but this time through an audience that had arrived, clapping, cheering and shouting "Bien hecho, Ingleses." Riding at the front of his men, Carr turned to O'Hare.

"What do you think?"

O'Hare smiled slightly and nodded.

"You'll not see any better. Not in this army."

Carr smiled and set himself to admire the view and acknowledge the greetings and warmth of the people they passed. Therefore, it was not long before his men, catching the mood, now struck up with 'Brighton Camp' and the Spanish clapped to the rhythm as many walked alongside. All were in good spirits.

Much of the afternoon remained and so many young Officers, including Drake, took themselves off a bullfight, now restarted with the departure of the French. However, Drake and many others returned quickly and in no good mood.

"The only thing in that ring showing courage as we would call it, was the bull!"

Then he reached for the brandy.

"I've seen cockfights and such. And ridden to hounds, but that was from another place altogether!"

For the rest of the day, that bottle and another was heavily assaulted.

The next day, the last of August, brought more news from Anson.

"Wellington's leaving Madrid with over half the army. Off to have a go at Clausel up around Valladolid. He's now convinced that Soult and El Rey will be no bother, even though they've got 60,000 men down South."

They all turned towards him anxiously.

"No, we're not included. He's off with the 1st, 6th, 5th and 7th Divisions, the Portuguese and Bock and Ponsonby's Dragoons. We stay here with the Light, whilst the 3rd will move back to the Escorial. I'd say we've drawn the longest straw!"

Hearing that, they all reached for the brandy bottle. Then, more pertinent Regimental news came from the billets down the road, Eirin had gone into labour. Experienced Fathers grinned wryly, others accepted the news with some insouciance, but this was nothing like the situation building steadily down the road. Bridie and Nellie were at that moment shooing all men from the room, these being Solomon, Bailey and Turner.

"Out! Out! This is no place for such as youse!"

The groaning Eirin added unassailable strength to their commands and as they went Nellie turned to Trudie.

"Fetch John. He's down at the warehouse."

At that moment Pepita, their new Spanish friend and mother herself, drawn there by the uproar and hurrying men, most in a state of undress, entered the room and immediately realised what was afoot. Within a minute she was gone, but not before uttering words in Spanish which meant nothing to either Bridie or Nellie.

"Voy a buscar a nuestra comadrona."

However, within minutes she returned with a woman who obviously knew how to cope with what was taking place, being plainly the local midwife who nodded approvingly at the water now boiling on the fire and the clean cloths and towels. Byford and John Davey arrived 30 minutes later to be confronted by a locked door, but five minutes later he and Davey heard the cry of a newborn and after 10 more minutes, he was allowed into the room. Once inside, Bridie, now a Grandmother once more, presented him with a baby girl.

"Eirin's decided on Ellen, after her Aunt Nellie."

An entranced Byford was gazing wide eyed at the child and plainly he didn't much care. That evening, everyone in the house was drinking wine and brandy, drinking until all was gone.

oOo

Up on the Duero the weather conditions enjoyed may have changed little, but the situation certainly had. The earliest days of September had reduced the burdening heat, the Duero was still full of fish and the locals remained generous with bread and wine, but the threat from the North-east had increased and now occupied most minds. The 16th remained on the Duero, but had moved to Herrera, several miles downstream from Penafiel, where they had been mid-August, Herrera was closer to the key bridge at Tudela. Both Carr and Peterson, however, made no complaint, they were in a good billet. One afternoon, Peterson came in from patrol and threw his shako, sabre and tunic onto a chair, causing Carr to look up from writing his own journal.

"Any news from outside?"

Peterson poured himself a beaker of water.

"Nothing worth calling news, it's all so topsy-turvy. What's worth saying is that the Peer's at Aravalo with Clinton, keeping an eye on Valladolid. Word is he's not too worried."

Carr threw down his pen onto the table, causing a blot on the pale wood.

"Not too worried, with Clausel at Valladolid! He's advanced 40 miles, nearly, from Lerma, and he came over the Duero and gave us all a scare at Montemayor, the week before last. And he's not worried!"

Peterson grinned at him.

"I must say, Will, that your appreciation of military strategy has come on considerably since Salamanca, but from what I hear, Wellington's relying on Carlos de Espana's Castillian Army coming in behind Clausel, who may well be too far South and therefore vulnerable to such. On top, Wellington's got 28,000 men coming up from Madrid and he's waiting for them before making any serious moves."

Carr was not convinced and his face showed it.

"That's all very well, having his nose down at Aravalo, but I get goosebumps every time we're sent across the Duero from here. The men feel the same, they don't say anything, but you can see it in their faces."

Peterson grinned anew.

"You know, young Will, I do believe you are turning into something of an 'old sweat'."

Carr's face remained more than troubled, but he changed the subject.

"What's to eat?'

That evening, Withers called his Captains to his Headquarters. Cornets could attend but would not be allowed to speak and so Carr and Peterson accompanied Oakwood to the 16th's central building. They went on foot, the slope down to the Duero providing easy walking and they entered what had been the Priest's house, alongside the Church. The house could only be described as austere, compared to the ornate riches displayed in the Church next door, the walls being a lowering brown, with many religious pictures and crucifixes of various designs and sizes hanging on the walls. However, that was soon forgotten when they entered and saw Withers, stood at a table and waiting. Tavender was the last to arrive and he had to stand as all the chairs were occupied, then their Colonel began.

'I've got this from Stapleton-Cotton, as written orders. Tomorrow we are over the Douro. The foot-sloggers are nearly here and we're going after Clausel, who's drawn up for battle. Arentschildt's have found out Clausel's position, his right is on Valladolid, his left on La Cisterniga. That place we know, it's not far over from our own ford. We've been there several times, before Clausel made his jump forward, which is why we've been chosen to make this reconnaissance. That is what it is, but it is in force. We've a Division crossing behind us, the 7th. If we cross from here, we come onto his left flank, almost onto the rear of it."

He paused and looked around the room, but saw only expectant faces.

"Now, Johnny's not stupid. He's knows we're here and the threat we pose, so expect to meet a strong force of his cavalry, therefore we feel our way forward. We move forward in two columns, the 11th on the left, us and the 12th the strongest on the right. 1 and 2 Squadrons will lead our column in double line, with 3 and 4 in column side by side behind. The 12th come after them. Warn your men, tomorrow we could be in a battle. The plan is to hold Clausel here, so that D'Espana's Castillians can come in behind."

At that point Tavender levered himself off the wall.

"And Wellington has faith in this Espana? Sir?"

"I think we can safely assume that, Captain. They are our Allies and we must trust them as such."

"And the French Chasseur patrols will not have detected Espana's approach."

"As I say, Captain, the Spanish are on their way and have stated their willingness to co-operate."

Tavender sagged back against the wall, plainly unconvinced, but meanwhile Carr's pulse rate had finally subsided from the order that his Troop, C, would be part of the lead for the right-hand column. Oakwood saw the anxiety in his face as they left the building and clapped a hand onto his shoulder.

"Don't worry, young Willoughby. You and your boys will do just fine. It's only to take a look, not some hopeless charge against impossible odds! We take a look then let the infantry boys take over."

Merely to take a look or not, the following dawn, Carr was not in the most confident of moods as he led his men, in column of twos across the shallows of the Douro just outside the village. Johnson and Oakwood were alongside and, once over the dark brown river, the Brigade reformed into two wide columns each led by two Squadrons in line. Soon, when on the flat open plain, they could see the two hills that dominated La Cisterniga and caused Oakwood to break the silence between them.

"Much like Los Arapiles! Those hills, don't you think?"

Carr had barely heard, because, like almost everyone, he had been both craning his neck and straining his eyes to see any sign of the French so-called battle line. It was Oakwood who opened the obvious topic.

"I do think we should have seen something by now."

It was Baxter, riding behind and leaving the major issue of direction to the Officers, who saw the first sign of what would answer the question.

"Rider coming, Sir. Over far left."

They saw Colonel Piers of the 11th, over at the head of the left-hand column, raise his arm to halt his men to await the riders arrival and Withers soon complied. Within two minutes the rider was up with Piers and there was an obvious brief discussion, before orders were shouted from Piers and the whole formation of his Squadron line broke apart, to form columns of fours by Squadrons and gallop on, leaving Withers much perplexed, but the rider was now approaching him and he reined in his horse, both very breathless. He was a Major of the 5th Dragoon Guards, but he wasted no time on introductions.

"Clausel pulled out in the night and is retreating through Valladolid. Wellington wants all of Anson's cavalry to ride like the Devil and stop the Johnnies blowing up the bridge there. Yours are to go directly for the town, Sir."

With that he put spurs to his horse to gallop back to the 12th. Withers responded immediately.

"Two columns of fours. Full canter!"

He set off and the columns, as had that of the 11th , formed on the move, Withers leading two Squadrons, Johnson the remainder. As they neared Valladolid, once the French right flank anchor, there was no sign of any French retreat. Above the pounding hooves, Carr was able to shout over to Oakwood.

"What is the river here we're so worried about, with the bridge?"

Oakwood shouted back.

"Don't know, but it's not the Duero!"

Again staring ahead, sometimes raising themselves on their stirrups, they strained to see any sign of the French and perhaps they saw the rear of a French column entering the buildings of Valladolid. Ten more minutes they entered the buildings themselves and then, but minutes after that, they heard the sounds of a large explosion. Once they were in the town, the citizens were clapping and cheering, but, as they entered Withers had led his column down one street and Johnson down another. It was Johnson's that came to what had once been the bridge, but only one arch had gone and the good citizens were already running forward with whatever could span the gap which was about five yards wide. However, spluttering French gunfire drove them back, causing Johnson to lead his men along the riverbank, which was a paved terrace. Soon he halted his men to see Withers coming from the opposite direction, plainly they had been too late, because several French infantry columns were on the far side of the river, but moving rapidly away, even now out of range of the Light Dragoons Paget carbine. However, no time was too late for the citizens, because they came forth in their scores and dozens to greet the "Valliente Inglese caballeria" and they cavorted and danced around, clapping and singing local dancing tunes.

Withers ordered "Dismount', and the 16th led their horses away to some grazing and were happy enough to accept bread, wine and other delicacies from the grateful citizens. Two women ran up to Carr and Peterson with what looked like a flat yellow loaf on a wide wooden platter. As one held the platter, the other cut two slices and offered one to each, one in each hand.

"Tortilla, Senors. Huevos y patatas."

Carr took the portion he was offered and then a bite and his face lit up with the taste, which caused that of the lady to light up also, so she kissed him.

"Valientes jovenes Ingleses soldados. Muy valientes!"

Both Carr and Peterson bowed their thanks and the women ran on to Baxter and Makepeace, to distribute the tortilla further and Carr called out his encouragement.

"Have some, you two. It's very good."

Both took their portions and grinned their agreement in between taking bites of the Spanish delicacy, but soon Anson himself was picking his way through the crowds of rejoicing Spaniards to call out to any Officer he came to.

"Remount and get to the edge of the city. Make sure there are no French still on this bank."

Oakwood spoke their feelings as they re-formed.

"That's a disappointment! I was quite enjoying the way this had turned out,"

However, in the event is was not so bad. Just outside Valladolid there were pleasant fields, groves of olive trees and several decent buildings. Orders now having been carried out, Withers ordered 'dismount' and to make camp, which they did and then the upriver locals arrived with bread, wine and other tasty treats and a fine camp was made. At the end of their 'reconnaissance in force', which had turned into a long, leisurely afternoon and evening of eating, drinking and sleeping under the olive trees, there came orders for the morrow, brought by Johnson to Oakwood, Carr and Peterson.

"Tomorrow we patrol up our bank of the river to see what Johnny's about, further upstream. This river's called the Pisuerga, we've ridden it before and it joins the Douro a couple of miles down. It's wider than the Douro."

However, Peterson had a question.

"Any news of this Galician army, Sir?"

Johnson threw his head back and laughed half-heartedly.

"That's supposed to come in behind them? No, none, but that may explain why Wellington's delayed here a day. To push Johnny too hard may push him out of the trap!"

Thus, the following day, in columns of fours, Anson's whole Brigade trotted away from Valladolid following the left bank of the Pisuerga and as they left, many citizens waved and cheered. Johnson was correct that the Pisuerga was a major river, significantly wider that the Duero which they had known for a month. Soon, the river began to describe severe 'ox-bows' in its course and the road and the river parted company several times before they came to the village of Cabezon. With some trepidation they entered the village, their experience of villages such as Aldemayor still fresh in their minds, especially as they could see that many of the buildings were charred wrecks. It was Baxter who brought the scene back from memory, speaking to Carr.

"Do you remember, Sir, after Valladolid first time and we was sent up the other bank and came on all those poor people as had crossed the river to escape the Frogs and much of their village opposite was on fire? I reckon this is it."

Carr nodded.

"And that old lady attacked you!"

"Yes Sir, that's it, and we're in the middle of the place, but now on the other bank."

"Well, let's hope you don't meet that old lady and if you do, she doesn't recognise you. She may fancy another go!"

Anson decided to go no further and they settled for the night, many paying high prices for food the locals were reluctant to sell, which would leave so little for themselves. However, much of daylight remained when Withers came up to the fire of Oakwood and his Cornets.

"Anson's worried that we are too far forward, with no supports. There's a bridge about half a mile up. Set double pickets on the far side. One Squadron are there now, Three will take over from them. Your Two take over at Midnight, then Four. Three hour watch each Squadron."

"Mounted, Sir?"

"No, Oakwood. On foot. Let the horses graze and rest."

As Withers left, Oakwood looked at the pair.

"Picket by Troops will do it. Will, first watch, then Douglas.

Thus it was that at 11.45, Carr and Oakwood led C Troop on foot up through the village, to find Tavender at the bridge, but on their side, stood with a bottle and a glass.

"Hello, Lucius. Anything to report, that we should know about? But shouldn't you be gone?"

Even in the weak light, both Carr and Oakwood could see that Tavender was in no good mood.

"Mine are in camp here and what is there to see in this damned back of a nowhere hole? Johnny's gone, anyone could work that out, pulled himself out from what this D'Espana should be trying to do, if he's arrived at all. Damned Spanish and damned Spain!"

Oakwood eased Carr forward, by the arm.

"Right, Lucius. So, on that joyful note, we are here to take over, from Three we are told. Sorry you are finding this all so much of an irritation."

Whilst Peterson's D Troop settled in with Tavender's Squadron, Oakwood and Carr led C Troop over the bridge, to find not Captain Somers-Cocks, as they expected, him being the usual Captain of Three Squadron, but his Senior Cornet, Victor Forden, who saluted Oakwood.

"Are you taking over, Sir?"

"Yes, anything we should know?"

"No Sir, other than there seem to be a lot of cattle on this side, mooching about."

"Thanks for the warning, but where's Somers-Cocks?"

"Been seconded, Sir. He's now on Wellington's Staff. By special request and good luck to him, we all say. Which means they've bumped me up, God knows why."

"You'll do fine, but we are here now, so, Captain Forden, you can consider yourself relieved."

As Forden led his men away, Baxter placed the pickets and Oakwood spent a moment with Carr before leaving.

"Seconded! That's serious stuff. Guarantees promotion."

Carr sighed, understanding immediately.

"Which possibly explains Captain Tavender's foul mood. Did he not have ambitions such as that for himself?"

Oakwood turned to go.

"If I know Lucius, almost certainly, yes."

The following day, Anson's three Regiments were woken before dawn by the arrival of Arentschildt's KGL arriving up to them from Valladolid, followed by the 6th Division with General Clinton at their head. Both marched straight through Cabezon leaving Anson's Brigade to saddle up and follow. This they did, following the Pisuerga, in the order of 11th, 16th and then the 12th. At mid-morning they assumed a directive had come to Anson from Clinton, because the whole Light Cavalry Brigade swerved off to the right, away from the river, to patrol as detached columns with the 16th furthest out. Being so much further over, their route was flat and useless for observation, apart from some Los Arapiles style hills, one of which Carr was required to ride up with Baxter. Once on the top, they could see how the Pisuerga described violent ox-bows throughout its course, and that the 6th Division were closest to the river, with Arentschildt's KGL on their right. Carr used his telescope, but could see nothing, before handing it to Baxter who viewed everything in all directions, before deciding his opinion.

"One thing I can say, Sir, is that we are absolutely out on our own, but it looks like a German patrol coming back to the main column from further on up the main track."

Carr retrieved his telescope, then led the way down. He could see for himself what looked like a Troop of KGL joining the head of Clinton's column, but he cantered back to the 16th and reported seeing nothing. The stop for the midday meal provided a welcome break, taken at one of the small streams that fed the Pisuerga. Whilst in there, one of Clinton's ADCs came galloping the distance out to them to talk to Anson and soon the message came back to Oakwood, in the form of Tavender.

"The KGL have found the Johnnies, up at the next village. A 'heavy concentration of troops' they report. We are to come back in and take post this side of the 6th infantry, up close, us and the 12th. The KGL will place themselves between the 6th and the river. The 11th stay out wider on our flank, where we were."

"Thank you, Lucius. Things a little better compared to last night?"

There was no answer as Tavender spurred his horse a little too savagely to then canter on to Three Squadron and soon Anson's 16th and 12th were swinging left to rejoin Clinton's column, the 11th remaining in place. Once alongside the infantry, surprisingly an order came for them to canter forward and soon the main column was left behind. Carr rode alongside Oakwood, both looking over for clues regarding the French, but there were none. They skirted a small village to arrive at the beginning of a ruler straight road, with the Pisuerga remaining as huge bends, one of them bringing its waters up to the road on their left. Anson was at their head and he called a halt when Oakwood turned to Carr.

"If this is the next village, there's no Johnnies here."

He was relieved that Anson had called a halt. They were way out at the front of a column that was itself isolated, with a 'heavy concentration of troops' somewhere before them. Anson ordered 'Dismount' and so they led their horses to a small stream just ahead and settled to await events. Within an hour Clinton and his column arrived and he made the village his Headquarters, to there consult with Anson, Arentschildt and his own two Brigadiers, Hulse and Hinde. The 16th looked at what could be looked at, which was not much on the table-flat plain, mostly the odd farmer, one tending his fields, oblivious to the major events playing out not half a mile from where he urged his mules forward over the fine, brown soil.

With mid-afternoon, Wellington himself arrived and orders emerged quickly from the small settlement, arriving in the form of a Wellington ADC, this being Somers-Cocks himself, now a Brevet Major and looking for Anson, who was with the 16th. Somers-Cocks elevation did nothing to cause any inhibiting formality as he walked into the group of his old comrade Officers, grins and good-humoured comments arriving all round as he shook hands with everyone, bar Tavender, who pointedly kept his in his pockets. Eventually, Somers-Cocks turned and spoke to Anson, but all could hear.

"He wants you up to a place called Duenas, Sir, about four miles up this straight. The road crosses the river and then there's Duenas on the far side. Take no risks, Sir, but get into Duenas if you can, then stop and hold."

The arrival of such a force had persuaded the farmer to give his mules a rest and he leaned on the back of one to watch the long column of infantry and cavalry, as Anson led his men cantering down the seemingly endless treadmill of a road, until they rode onto a bridge with two pillars at each end, each of the four sporting a heraldic device at the top. Carr thought to himself, "Something Medieval there. We've gone from somewhere to somewhere else." His thoughts were accurate, for at the first houses of Duenas there was a sign, which said "Duenas. Provincia de Leon." However, no-one gave it more than the merest glance, all eyes were on Duenas and Anson led the 12th into the town to find no-one, neither military nor civilian. Anson was taking no chances and the order was shouted around the narrow streets when the 11th and 16th arrived.

"Dismount and tether. Defend the village."

Horses were secured and all drew their carbines and moved to the edge of the village to find what defensible place they could. There they sat or stood, for an hour of more staring out at a landscape, not so flat as the one before but merely the next level up. Carr and his Troop found themselves defending the buildings alongside the main road out, where it ran out and on through a shallow valley and there was a waysign, 'Palencia 3L.' Carr looked at Baxter.

"3L, Sergeant. Any idea?"

"Three leagues, Sir. About nine miles."

Carr looked across to his NCO.

"There are hidden depths to you, Sergeant!"

However, Baxter had his own thoughts, which he kept to himself, "Yes Sir, but I'd settle for someone other than you, decent as you are, if it meant less of Tavender on our backs."

He recalled their picket two nights before at Cabezon, when Tavender, on a 'wander', or perhaps for a more sinister purpose, had sent Carr and two Troopers out further to investigate a noise and a light. It had been nothing but it could have been something and he and Makepeace had been the two Troopers. Baxter came back to his fire with his companion, cursing and angry

Once his full command were into the village, it required only 30 minutes for Clinton and his two cavalry Commanders to decide their next move, the result arriving in the form of an ADC.

"Form column. We're going on to Palencia."

As Carr and his men returned to their horses, Clinton's Riflemen, one Company of the 60th, doubled forward down the straight road which eventually evolved into gentle curves running between low hills. Clinton was taking no chances and so, the 11th were out to the right and the 12th out to the left, with the 6th Division in the column on the road following the 16th in the lead. Arentschildt's Brigade brought up the rear. After almost two hours at a fast walk, Anson and Clinton entered the first of the houses that made up Palencia and, seemingly as soon as they heard the horses' hooves, the population emerged to wave, clap and cheer. Major Johnson was back with Oakwood and Carr.

"I'll wager they'd not be as cheerful as this if Johnny was still around, even with us now here. They'd be off up into the hills, away from any conflict."

Oakwood nodded agreement as he accepted a bunch of flowers from a middle-aged woman who clapped and laughed as soon as her hands were free and Oakwood reached forward to thrust the small bunch down between the bridle harness alongside his horse's head. They rode on to enter the square to find the Riflemen of the 60th lounging on benches and horse-troughs and drinking wine and eating bread, with children dancing around their feet. They were all grinning as the 16th entered and the 16th grinned back as they halted but remained mounted, Oakwood passing judgment on the spectacle of the Riflemen.

"I'd say this place has now been thoroughly recaptured! If those walked here, then they deserve a good drink."

The 60th Rifles remained very pleased with themselves, sat making the most of their sojourn, but not for the 16th, because for them the order was passed back, 'walk-on' and they had to make-do with what food and drink was handed up to them, no self-awarded relaxation for them. They trotted on and emerged from the town, with Clinton still at their head, riding through the same familiar landscape of gentle undulations. After barely two miles, One Squadron drew away from them, leaving them behind and they, Oakwood, Johnson and Carr, found themselves in the company of Clinton, Anson and Withers. Tavender's Squadron had been sent on ahead to another village which they could see half a mile further on. Soon, dust from the horses' hooves did much to obscure the progress of Tavender's men, but, through telescopes, enough could be seen of them entering the houses, lingering five minutes and then cantering back. The three could hear Tavender's report to Clinton.

"Just civilians, Sir. No French."

Clinton wanted more.

"Did you look beyond?"

A slight look of confusion passed across Tavender's face, enough to make Carr think that he had not looked, but if it was untrue, Tavender told the lie anyway.

"Yes Sir, and saw nothing."

Clinton eased himself back and forth in his saddle, his hands providing purchase on the pommel for the body movement that accompanied his turbulent thoughts and his face was full of anxiety as he turned to Anson.

"I don't like it, so far out on a limb. We've done what The Peer ordered, reconnaissance in force and found nothing. I want back over the river, at the soonest."

He turned to an ADC.

"Greatbanks! You've the map."

The ADC reached down into his saddlebag and produced the map which he unfolded and passed across to his General, who ran his finger up and down before deciding.

"No need to go back to Duenas. There's a bridge nearer, someplace called Tariego."

He allowed Anson to see the map, still unfolded.

"Yours to lead. Get to this bridge and hold it!"

Orders were shouted, the whole of Anson's Brigade turned and were soon cantering back through Palencia and down the road they had arrived on. At what seemed like halfway back to Duenas, they came to a sign; 'Tariego 1L', and they turned left to soon cross the Pisuerga using a splendid Roman bridge, but at that moment occupied by a hay cart. The old farmer grinned with the odd tooth he had left and hurried his cart horse over to the Palencia side. With the bridge clear, Anson gave his orders to his Colonels.

"Withers and Piers, yours stay here. Stockton, take your 12th over."

Anson sat forward, again leaning heavily on his saddle pommel, a tired look on his face, but now pointing across the plain to a collection of modest and apologetic buildings.

"All this has done is wear out the horses! That must be this Tariego place, not too far beyond this. Let's hope he agrees to camp there. I'll certainly recommend it."

When he arrived with the 6th Division, Clinton confirmed Anson's earlier recommendation and his command settled in the fields around the village, although there were several hours of daylight remaining. Whilst the cavalry took advantage of the good grazing and the shallows of the Pisuerga to feed and water their horses, the infantry settled into the fields and the high-ranking Officers into billets in the village, to there enjoy the decent food brought to them by their joyful hosts, happy to see so powerful a friendly force camped on their own doorstep. All had a good night's sleep bar a few of the 16th, which included Carr and Peterson, because a horse galloped close to their tent in the dead of night. Carr woke first and the most, followed by Peterson.

"What's that?"

"A galloping horse!"

"Not good!"

"Rarely is!"

The galloper was for Clinton from Wellington, with orders to advance at dawn along the Pisuerga and Wellington would be following close with the main army. To that end, the bugles blew early and, with little breakfast, Anson's men rode across open fields with the Pisuerga again describing tortuous bends on their left. Oakwood and Carr rode together, each speculating on what may happen and what their role in it may be.

"Orders are to keep the river in sight."

"So, he must have some idea where Clausel is."

Oakwood grinned.

"He has access to higher powers than you or I, young Willoughby!"

The higher powers arrived 30 minutes later in the form of a full six-gun field battery that placed itself within Anson's Brigade, behind the 16th who were leading. At the head of all were the peerless 1st Hussars KGL of Arentschildt's and it was not long before the dust from up ahead rose in denser clouds as they were ordered into a fast canter to scout further ahead. After only 30 minutes, Clinton ADCs came hurrying down the column, all passing by without a single word being imparted to minors such as Squadron Captains, but all could see the battery immediately pull out of their column and gallop ahead. Within a short while all could hear the solid crash of their firing and Oakwood spoke the obvious.

"Looks like we've caught up!"

All cavalry were ordered to deploy in line beyond the guns, so they trotted past the very active gunners and onto a slight rise, where they halted and the inevitable telescopes emerged. Carr and Oakwood followed the line of the artillery's fire to see French infantry columns crossing the Pisuerga by a long and twisting bridge, with round-shot sending up spouts of water from a wide section of the Pisuerga, which the bridge spanned. This hurried retreat was protected by a whole Brigade of Chasseurs remaining on their side, but Clinton had plainly ordered the infantry to be the target, gouts of earth being thrown up alongside the blue column. Johnson arrived and reined in his horse beside the pair, but said nothing, merely deploying his telescope but then answering a question that had not been asked.

"What happens next all depends on whether or not Johnny tries to hold that far bank and sets his guns to command that bridge."

More telescoping again.

"Well, they're all over, except those Chasseurs. Now it's up to Clinton."

The answer was the battery quickly limbering up and galloping down the road towards the bridge and halting after 500 yards further. With that the Chasseurs hurriedly followed the infantry and the so the Battery Commander ordered a further advance of about 300. Three puffs of smoke appeared beyond the river, then the sound came to them of three French guns indeed on the far end of the bridge, but their own battery had halted and deployed at a speed that won the admiration of all and they were soon in furious action against the opposing three, firing down the line of the bridge. About seven more puffs of French smoke appeared, then none, obviously their own battery ceased fire. Then an ADC arrived to stop at the Arentschildt and Anson Officer group, for the former to gallop off to his own Brigade and immediately lead them forward. Anson turned his horse towards his own men and led forward, first the 16th, followed by the 11th and the 12th. They passed the battery, now ready to move themselves, these receiving congratulations in the form of shakoes being raised in their honour, but soon, following Arentschildt's 14th Light Dragoons, they were on the bridge which was indeed far from straight, turning its deflected way across the wide channel of the Pisuerga, seemingly to jump from one useful island to the next.

Once over, the route was obvious, a right turn to follow the French retreat. Carr spoke hopeful words to himself, "We must be coming up to their infantry soon. How fast can they march?" They had crossed at a place called Torquemada, as the sign said before the bridge, and the answer to Carr's question was, frustratingly, long coming. They followed the river now on their right, with all of the Light cavalry in one long column bar two KGL Squadrons out on their left to watch for any French on that side. Within less than four miles they had crossed the Pisuerga again, its course barely visible amongst all the bushes and trees that covered the islands that aided the crossing of what was again a long and ancient bridge. With that navigated, after another ride of the same length along the river bank as before crossing, back came an ADC and all the Light cavalry pulled over to allow the artillery up from the rear to gallop on ahead. Soon came the sound of more firing, seemingly without reply and the 16th halted. Then the guns ceased and the 16th moved on to ride up behind the guns, now limbering up, and see Arentschildt's two Regiments, charging through the shallows of another river against a rearguard of Chasseurs, who soon made off without a sabre being raised in anger. The 16th continued forward to cross the river, minutes later, by a bridge of equally ancient design as that of an hour earlier, but this time it led to a village, named by its roadsign as Quintana de Puente de Arlanzon. Once across, Oakwood looked back at Carr and grinned.

"Must be a new river, that, Willoughby. Now isn't that interesting?"

Carr did not see the humour and, once over, the order to halt came back from Withers and the KGL came up from the right, having seen off the Chasseurs who were now merely a dust cloud in the distance. However, a dust cloud of equal proportions was now being raised by a column of infantry and so Carr deployed his telescope alongside Oakwood using his, but it was the latter who came first to an estimation.

"That's at least a Division on that road and there's probably more that we can't see. What will Clinton do?"

He closed his telescope.

"He'll wait for the Peer."

In that Oakwood was half right, the 6th Division came up, but no Wellington and so Clinton commandeered a house to use for his solitary deliberations, which occupied the rest of the day. Quintana had an estaminet of sorts and within two hours it had sold out of anything that could be described as alcoholic drink, especially after the 6th Division arrived, but Carr and Peterson, being amongst the first into the village, were able to secure a bottle, which they shared with Oakwood. The conversation was light, amusing and mostly of home, but Carr did ask the one pertinent question.

"Is this typical of what could be called 'strategic campaigning'? I thought all that we went through prior to Salamanca could be described as such."

Oakwood gave it some thought.

"Well, this is the game we're in. That was manoeuvring prior to a major battle. This can best be described as scuttling about before things settle down. As they will."

However, at that moment Tavender joined them, with a bottle almost empty which he seemed to be sharing only with himself. He was plainly in agitated mood and not a good one.

"Have you heard? Carlos D'Espana has failed in his march. He's not ahead of us at all, in fact some way behind. Damn Spanish, what's the point of relying on them? Utter failure from utter let-downs, I say."

He took another pull from the bottle, whilst the three regarded him, somewhat amusedly, which would have annoyed him further had he noticed, but he was now somewhat the worse for wear from the heady wine. It was Oakwood who answered.

"I take your point, Lucius, but we all know what we get from the Spanish by now. The likelihood is that they will disappoint, but I will credit them with the fact that they keep putting armies into the field. We have to bear in mind that they have a Government who couldn't agree how to run a chicken farm and so the material support they get is practically zero. It was us that put coats on their backs when we captured Madrid, remember?"

There was no answer, but Tavender emptied his bottle further, then rose to slouch off, his whole posture conveying his thoroughly black mood.

The following days saw much more of the 'scuttling', as Oakwood described it, when Stapleton-Cotton took over the leadership from Clinton, the former having consulted Wellington. Thus, there came a very pleasant week of cautious walking or trotting, never at a faster rate, through welcoming villages that provided good billets for higher Officers and good food for the ranks to supplement their rations, which were regular and plentiful. Progress was never more than six miles each day and all indulged in the leisurely wander through the Spanish countryside which never varied from low hills and shallow valleys with the occasional crag or outcrop. Also, never changing was the river Arlanzon which they had crossed at Quintana and was on their left for the first three days, then on their right after they crossed at Villadrigo, with the infantry using the bridge, which appeared so fragile and ill-maintained, that anything involving horses could not trust it at all.

As they rode their horses at a walk down a road almost identical to the one of the day before, Oakwood was not doing very much, bar dreaming of home, Carr was cleaning his pistol, whilst Peterson wrote a letter, using the stiff wood of his sabre-attache as a writing surface, both confident that their horses would follow the one in front. Peterson shouted forward to Carr.

"I think I can include in my missive home that this is hardly like being in a war at all. More like a pleasant amble between the houses of friends and acquaintances. You know, doing the social round."

Neither Carr nor Oakwood did know, such was not in their background, therefore they did not reply, both merely watched the houses of each approaching village grow in detail, each where they hoped to halt for the night, although Noon was not long past. However, they were wrong. All felt the pace pick up through the afternoon and then urgent orders came to the 16th in the lead on that day. Tavender's One Squadron hurried off left, then Anson himself came to Oakwood.

"Get yours alongside the river, down below the road. It seems Clausel is as tired of this meandering as we are."

Oakwood raised his arm right and the Squadron eased rightwards and down to the river Arlanzon. There was little room to deploy and so they remained in column, but Oakwood was worried by the number of copses and hidden areas, caused by many bushes. He turned to Carr.

"Willoughby. Get forward and take a look. Four men."

Carr turned to Baxter who nodded and so he spurred his horse on, followed by Baxter, Makepeace, Spivey and Nunney. It was Baxter who urged caution.

"Steady, Sir. Who knows what's hanging about in all these bits of scrub and whatnot."

The pace slowed and they trotted forward. Suddenly a group of Chasseurs sprang out of a clump of bushes and galloped off. Carr was as surprised as anyone and, just in case he had pursuit in mind, Baxter again urged caution.

"Just follow, Sir, at a safe distance. They may be decoys, wanting us to follow into some kind of trap. Just follow and see where they goes. A good way behind."

This they did, but not for long, because upon clearing the last of the trees, they saw what was plainly only the left flank of Clausel's line, his whole stretched away from the river, a dark blue challenge to any further Allied progress. Carr simply turned his horse.

"Job done, Sergeant. Back we go."

When they returned, they the whole of Anson's Brigade had already halted in column. They were waiting off the road in the meadows alongside the river and with good reason because D'Espana's Corps had finally arrived, two Divisions of Spanish Troops. The 16th, with a good view, looked on more with pity than with any approbation, because the whole Spanish Corps had simply slumped down, many plainly unwell, but all wholly exhausted and many had taken themselves over to the 6th Division, still on the road, to beg for food, which was given from haversacks in many occasions. Oakwood looked on, plainly moved.

"Well, Tavender has his answer now. These were either sick or starving."

The next order was not to move forward, but to make camp and so Withers moved the 16th back to find a space and create their own picket lines and encampment, because the day was indeed drawing to a close, the light fading in obedience to the lowering sun of mid-September. They were all eating when Johnson came to their Squadron camp.

"Stapleton-Cotton's decided to advance tomorrow. Our Anson's will be either side of the river, to turn M'sieu's left flank. To do that, we, being us with the 11th, will get over the river and see what can be done from there. He's keeping the 12th on this side. Ready your men. We begin before dawn."

They were woken by the last pickets of the night shaking them awake and in obedience they all wrapped their belongings into their blankets, which were then finally safely strapped behind their saddles. Withers led them down to the river, where the shallowest part had been marked, but with some difficulty, during the night. Carr's horse, as worried as any rider making the same journey into the lingering darkness, gingerly felt her way down the bank, whinnying suddenly when the bank dropped suddenly away, then she felt the bottom whilst Carr felt the water splashing over the tops of his boots. A few steps and they were over to form into two Regimental columns, the 16th nearest the river. Anson was with them and he led them at a walk along the river bank, whilst the light grew stronger. In that growing light they could see the 12th Light Dragoon's formed in four Squadron columns, walking at the same pace on the opposite bank.

Within minutes, the sun was at full strength with the disappearance of a screening cloud on the far Eastern horizon and Carr could see the Stapleton-Cotton's infantry and cavalry, the 6th Division in full assault formation of two lines, advancing forward. They were only 400 yards from the French line, with the 12th holding formation, but Anson, seeing no serious opposition, led his men on at a brisk trot and they gained on the advancing 6th Division, so that soon they were level with the French line and then beyond. Carr was sure he could see some gaudy Chasseur uniforms through the occasional breaks in the trees and bushes that thickly populated both banks of the Arlanzon and these Hussars, if enough in number, could easily hold them away from their own bank if they attempted a crossing. Then he heard cannon-fire, from behind and to the left, then movement caught his eye on the slight ridge and he saw the whole of the French line falling back, as also were the Chasseurs opposing the 12th on the far bank.

Anson halted his columns whilst Stapleton-Cotton continued his advance onto what had been the French position. Once there, he wasted no time. The infantry formed column and they continued the advance and seeing that, Anson resumed his own advance with his two Regiments alongside the Arlanzon. Carr wondered if they would recross the river, but they did not, instead walking their mounts to keep pace with the infantry. In thus fashion they advanced over the uniformly flat meadows alongside the river, passing a village on the far bank which the infantry marched straight through there being no rearguard. Someone shouted "Celada" and no-one queried how they knew the name, all were too worried about their position, all feeling exposed on their side of the river and Carr was as worried as anyone and he turned to Sergeant Baxter.

"What do you think, Sergeant."

Baxter pulled a 'thoughtful' face.

"He's falling back on something solid, Sir. He could have made a go of it back there."

Feeling marginally more comforted, Carr rose in his stirrups, looking anxiously to his right, but reassuringly seeing nothing across the dry, empty plain. Then he looked across the river to see the infantry column reach another village, but again march straight through. An ADC came down to the river and shouted orders across to Anson, such that at the next village, which identified itself as Cavia, they crossed the Arlanzon and the whole column came together, with the infantry allowed the road. Anson's Brigade, now reunited, remained between the infantry and the river, with Arentschildt's men further out and beyond, protecting their left. Anxiety grew, all knew the relative strengths of the two sides, Clausel seemingly stronger compared to themselves, even with the newly arrived Spanish, all facts adding to their worries and woes.

With the 12th now in the lead, they continued over ground that was becoming more rugged, passing between two villages, one on the road, the other on the far side of the river. Stapleton-Cotton rode up past their column and the pace increased, with the Arlanzon remaining on their right and still no sign of the French. With the increase in pace, the infantry fell some way behind and so Stapleton-Cotton called a halt when the next village came into view. All in the 16th sat their horses, not saying much, not even when the KGL galloped forward from the left to investigate the hamlet and further ahead. Within 30 minutes a galloper returned to stop at Stapleton-Cotton and his Staff, and their Commander waved his arm forward.

The advance continued, on through the village, clearly signposted at the first house as Fradovinez. Once through, another halt was called, but, even though not knowing how long they would remain there, Withers sent back the word for his men to eat, but not cook. This meant that they could dismount, but remain with their mounts, and so Carr, Oakwood and Peterson did exactly that, using their saddles as a table for their meagre meal. Sound and then movement caused them to turn around to see the sudden arrival of Pack's Portuguese Brigade, the 1st and 16th Line, who must have made almost a forced march to catch up. They appeared very much like French soldiers with their dark blue jackets and for a moment some in the British column were worried, but they were distinguished as Allies by their large and gaudy Colours flying above their marching ranks, rather than the French simple Eagle and Tricolour. With their arrival, Johnson rode back.

"Mount up, we're going forward with these newcomes."

Although smaller than before, the formation was the same, Anson's alongside the river, Pack's Battalions on the road, but now with his brown-uniformed Cacadores spread out ahead. However, the road soon described a fierce turn away from the river and the two Allied forces were forced to tramp awkwardly over ploughed fields and rough meadow if they were to maintain their direction. Anson and Pack were in the lead, but Carr and Oakwood knew nothing of their thoughts or even their orders as the slow pace continued, but presumably both Commanders wished to remain close to the river, which was why the road had been abandoned. However, after an hour the road returned from their left and they halted, the cavalry alongside the line infantry. Carr and Oakwood exercised Officers' privilege to swing their horses out of the column to enable them to see the Cacadores swarming over a bridge that spanned the Arlanzon, but Pack and Anson were there with them and they did no more than occupy the far bank close to the bridge. Oakwood shook his head.

"They'll not order us across. We're too small a force to be trapped on the far bank. This is it for the night."

The order came to dismount and an order was also given to the Portuguese Battalions to fall out and they left the road to make camp but yards from it. Soon the main force arrived, Stapleton-Cotton at their head and Oakwood had his own opinion confirmed when the word came around, "Make camp". Rations were distributed and all sat around their fires, enjoying a good meal and feeling at ease concerning their safety and welfare, because the Arlanzon was between them and the French, with a strong picket of Cacadores on the far side. Oakwood, Carr and Peterson were content to avoid conversation concerning their life over the past days, except Peterson, with one pertinent question.

"Have we any idea where we are going?"

Oakwood lounged back against a hay bale.

"Burgos is what I've heard."

With that, all slept well that night, but Anson's men were woken first and ordered to saddle-up without any breakfast. They rode to the bridge in column of fours to cross and pass through the Cacadores, all these, irritatingly, enjoying their own breakfast. Anson himself led them forward and quickly into a village naming itself 'Villabillia' and on through it to find a high point where they overlooked, from a distance, a substantial town. Telescopes were rapidly employed, Carr alongside Oakwood, who was the first to speak of what he saw.

"That must be Burgos and Johnny's pulling out."

He lowered his telescope and pointed.

"Take a look beyond, there's whole Divisions moving out from the far side."

For some time they concentrated intently on French movements, so that they did not notice a full field-gun battery deploy just behind them until it opened fire, startling their horses. They continued to watch the French withdrawal, sometimes seeing round-shot damage a building as the guns maintained rapid fire, but then the order came for the 16th to dismount, establish picket-lines, make camp and then eat a breakfast, the last most welcome. Noon came and with it no orders to move into the town and so many Officers idly continued with their telescopes, the Officers of One and Two Squadrons grouped together as they studied events. Smythe of One Squadron was stood with Carr and Peterson and he finally confirmed what his two companions thought.

"I've seen nothing on the road going out of that place for the past hour. Johnny's gone."

Then Peterson lowered his own superior instrument.

"Well, if Johnny's gone, why is there still a Tricolour flying over that castle in the middle?"

Carr and Smythe immediately tried for a better focus, before Peterson answered his own question.

"Looks like Johnny intends to hang on to that particular pile of historical stonework!"

Chapter Four

"A Thoroughly Bad Business"

"Now, who would have thought that Irish soda bread would go down so well with so many of these good Spanish people."

'Well, I don't see as it's so much of a surprise, seein' as their own bread is nothing much more than a lot of air and crackles!"

As Elie Nicholls spoke the reply to Bridie, she dropped a whole loaf of soda bread into the bag of a smiling Spanish housewife, who spoke a few encouraging words before she went on her way.

"Una vellon? Haces buen pan. A mi familia le gusta mucho."

Nellie smiled in response, but said nothing, having understood barely one word, except for the fact that a real de vellon was being dropped into her hand, but Pepita was helping at the stall and spoke in reply.

"Gracias, señora. Nos vemos mañana."

The stall had been running now for over two weeks in their Madrid suburb, starting with Nellie and Consuela dealing with the customers, whilst Bridie mostly did the baking. The idea arrived from the fact that the whole house seemed to enjoy what Bridie cooked, using army rations, which were never failing, as well as the local produce now arriving into the city. Therefore, they set up a stall in the street outside and soon customers were arriving from elsewhere in the neighbourhood. The initial finance was provided by the trade in 'amended' French uniforms, but now the stall was self-supporting. Pepita had quickly joined the enterprise and was paid wages and for good advice, particularly that their bread should not undercut that of local bakers, rather to allow their business to grow through quality, thus there was a whole range of baked niceties, mostly of Irish origin.

A patrol of the Light Company arrived back in their road and needed to thread their way in single file past the crowd there, the same patrol as had rescued Maximiliano Sagasta and, with that negotiated, Tom Miles attempted to steal a small pie from the stall for his hand to be quickly smacked by Pepita and any further ideas he had were thoroughly rebuffed by her shrivelling look, stern tone and accusing finger.

"Tú pagas, Tom Miles, como todos los demás."

This met with an approving look from Nellie Nicholls, who could certainly pick up the sentiment, if not the meaning, and Tom Miles went into the house empty handed. The rest of the patrol, laughing loudly, followed him through the door, with a comment from Solomon.

"Seems like Pepita's got your measure, Tom."

However, this did not dent Tom Miles' buoyant mood by one degree as he considered the success and benefits of his new business empire. He had noticed the Spanish money fully covering the large plate.

Some way down the street, at that moment O'Hare was entering the rooms reserved for Officers and he immediately helped himself to a cup of coffee, before grinning at those assembled, which included Carr, Heaviside, Drake and Bettridge.

"As good a billet as I've been in for a long time! I'd say this place was all at peace and settled, perhaps because Redcoat patrols are out non-stop, but that Afrancensado nonsense is all finished and city life is pretty much returned to normal."

Drake sat up, ever ready to agree.

"Entertainments too. I hear that some of the 27th, of Scots origin, are teaching the Madrids Scottish Country Dancing."

Bettridge thought he had a quip to add to the fact.

"Without the swords, one would hope. Missteps on an English dancefloor is one thing, but such as that, on swords!"

Drake clapped him on the back.

"Well spoken, Lionel! Without the swords, oh yes indeed."

Bettridge looked up and smiled wanly.

"It's Luttrel, Sir."

Drake now clapped him on the shoulder.

"Of course, dear boy. Put it down to one too many near misses past my head!"

The one dour countenance in the room was that of Carr, reading despatches passed onto him by Anson. He dropped them onto the table and his tone was more depressed than his expression.

"The Peer's laid siege to the castle at Burgos and things aren't going too well!"

oOo

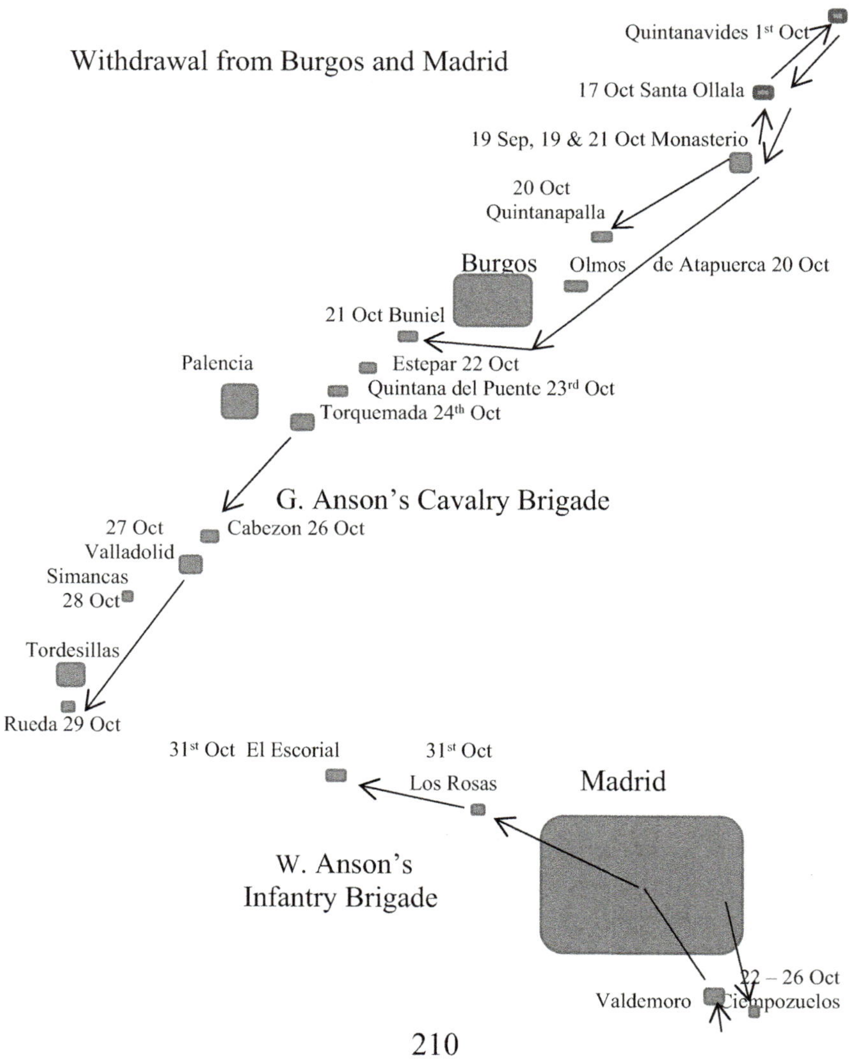

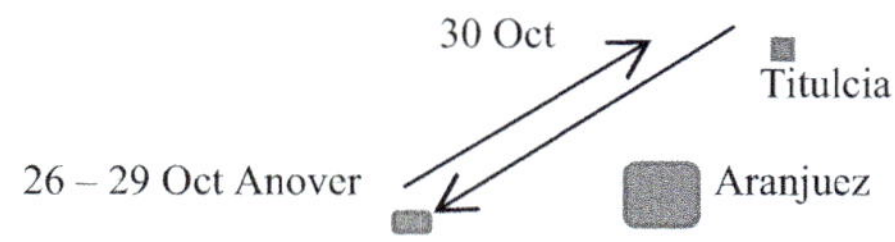

"They are French!"

Sat on his horse on the road beside the few Medieval hovels that called themselves Quintanavides and there manning a far picket for the benefit of the force that protected the siege of Burgos, Major Johnson of the 16th Light Dragoons lowered his own telescope and invited Carr and Oakwood to focus theirs.

"There! Follow the line of the road, to the far horizon, then just below it, in the gap in the woods."

His companions focused their own glasses, confirmed the sighting and then closed them shut. Whilst Cornet Carr continued to stare into the distance, Oakwood spoke his thoughts whilst looking at Johnson.

"A Squadron?"

Johnson nodded.

"At least. More probably three."

"That's the first time we've seen anything in weeks. Johnny's back. I should record it."

Oakwood pulled out a notepad from inside his tunic.

"What's the date, Willoughby?"

Carr was brought back to the present.

"Oh, um, 1st October."

"Thanks, and this is Quintanavides, or at least what they call that collection of mud and wood over there."

He gestured quickly to the small group of lowly dwellings over to his left.

"How far from Burgos?"

Now Johnson answered.

"Call it 20. Perhaps a bit more, but a nice round number."

Johnson waited until Oakwood had finished and returned the notepad to the inside of his tunic.

"Now back to Headquarters at Monasterio with the good news. On top, there's a chill wind blowing down this valley. I expected better from October in these parts."

The three cantered back the three miles to Monasterio, a village not so much bigger than the one they had just left, but at least it had a stone church, a plaza and a town hall, which now served as Anson's Headquarters. It was Johnson who entered with the report to hand it to the ADC in the hall. He studied it and looked up, somewhat alarmed, but said nothing, simply adding it to a pile for Anson's attention. Then Johnson asked the daily question.

"What's the news from Burgos?"

The ADC shook his head.

"Every battery we construct, the French blow away. They've heavier calibre guns. Nosey's now relying on mining to blow up a section of wall."

Johnson shook his head.

"And Johnny's reappeared in front of us. What a good day!"

"Perhaps not so bad. We hear that The Peer's been appointed Captain General of all Armies. Including the Spanish. Now perhaps we'll get some sort of co-ordinated effort."

Johnson sucked in a deep breath, then turned to leave, muttering to himself.

"Co-ordinated? Like mounting a siege with guns that could barely bring down a horse!"

Once outside, the three led their mounts to the stables and then entered the Officers' Mess, where most of the 16th Officer Corps were sat, reading or playing cards. They all looked up when their Major entered.

"Johnny's back! Beyond Quintanavides and in some strength."

He paused.

"Expect extra patrols, further and wider."

And so it transpired, in the form of Anson giving each of his Regiments their own area and ordering daily patrols in Squadron strength. Three days later Tavender entered the Mess having delivered his own report. He was in an even worse mood than usual and his storming around the room drew everyone's attention, including Brevet Captain Victor Forden of Three Squadron.

"Anything wrong, Lucius?"

Tavender looked up.

"Damn me, yes! Damn Spanish again. Clearly you haven't heard. Their General Ballesteros, down South, has been in open revolt against Wellington becoming Supreme Commander. Open revolt against some decent command of their half-baked armies and here we are, stuck up here, holding the French back from half their country."

"And what's happened to this Ballesteros?"

Tavender subsided markedly at the question.

"The Cortes have issued a warrant for his arrest."

Forden raised his two-week-old newspaper to continue reading.

"Well then I'd say that's that and the end of him! Be thankful for small mercies, old boy!"

He lowered the paper again, having had a further thought.

"I always had the impression, Lucius, that you were never too taken with our Commander in Chief and yet here you are berating some Spanish General for refusing to acknowledge him."

Tavender looked daggers at Forden, swallowed the glass of wine he had poured for himself and stormed out. Thus, co-operation with the Spanish was never raised again as an issue amongst the 16th, but, over the coming days, the lack of good news issuing out to them from Burgos further depressed their mood. A week later, it was Oakwood's turn to take despatches from Anson back to Burgos and he took Carr and Peterson with him. Once into Burgos, the first evidence they saw of a siege in the throes of failure were the several rows of houses that were serving as hospitals for the wounded and the fact of their being so many, spoke of the high number of casualties. They soon found Wellington's Headquarters and handed in Anson's report, which the ADC Colonel placed on a pile, but he asked them the pertinent question.

"Any news of Johnny?"

Oakwood shook his head.

"No Sir. Not since the 1st."

"Well, it's not Clausel anymore. It's someone called Souham. The guerrillas have told us that."

Oakwood saluted and left, but they tethered their horses and decided to take the opportunity to view the siege works, whilst they were there. They progressed up through the town, climbing continuously upwards, the sounds of bombardment growing louder as the buildings between them and the citadel grew fewer. They passed the final building to see a scene of wholesale devastation filling a shallow valley between two major stoneworks. The one on their left flew the French Tricolour above its highest tower, whilst that on the right had several earthworks in front of it, populated by both Redcoats and blue coated artillerymen. The trio walked towards the latter, climbed a small rise and found a Captain of Engineers, so they introduced themselves and he responded.

"Brightwood. Engineers."

Oakwood studied the view, immediately recognising that the Allied siege was being conducted from two sides; the stonework where they were and also from over from where they were, on the far side of the citadel.

"Not much happening this side?'

"No, there isn't. It's pretty much stalemate here. If we don't bother Johnny, he doesn't bother us. We both have to save our ammunition and whatever we build, and use, he soon knocks to pieces from that bastion up there."

He pointed to the Tricolour flying from what could only be the Keep of the castle and easily seen were four embrasures atop a wall much higher than themselves.

"We got this work from him quite early, on the 19th of last month, but those guns battered everything we tried to build and so now we are over there."

He pointed to the far side.

"We mined under the outside wall and got in, but the inside wall is proving impossible. This Dubreton, their Colonel, is making a real fight of it. The day before yesterday the Frogs sallied out, drove off the work parties, captured all the tools and destroyed the saps. Yet we still got up to 30 yards from the wall yesterday, but another sally by them did more damage. Then we lost a good man, who led the counter-attack and drove the Frogs back behind their walls. Somers-Cocks. He was cavalry like you."

Oakwood turned quickly towards him, shock clear on his face.

"Yes, he was one of ours, in fact a Captain in our Regiment, the 16th Light Dragoons."

He sighed again and looked at Carr and Peterson, both now equally downcast, then Oakwood sighed his obituary.

"A great loss. To us all. He was a good comrade."

Brightwood nodded, now realising the impact of the news.

"Well, all I can say is, this cannot last much longer. We just don't have the firepower and the Frogs outgun us. It's a thoroughly bad business. Over on that far side it's as big a failure as here, but we're going to try somewhere entirely new, at the Church to the South, between the wall and the river. God knows how long that will take, but we're going to blow it up as its part of the main wall and then try to get in that way. It'll take days and this is the last throw of the dice, as I see it."

He studied Oakwood intently.

"Anything at your end?"

"Yes, Johnny's stirring a bit, out in front of us."

He offered his hand.

"We should get back. So, good luck at the Church."

They all shook hands and the three worked their way back down through the town and found their horses. Still saddened at the news of Somers-Cocks they trotted the road back, saying little. After a mile it began to rain.

The following day found Two Squadron out on picket, back at Quintanavides, the only difference being rain, which reduced all visibility to a quarter. The picket was a mile further on from the village and Oakwood manned it in relays, allowing the remainder to find shelter back in the village. On this day, the far picket was manned by Baxter and his four most trusted, all five still mounted but all five holding a section of stolen tarpaulin over their heads, which at least reduced somewhat the misery of the rain. Makepeace was staring forward and was the first to see the shapes forming in the murky distance.

"Summat comin' up, Sep!"

Baxter eased his horse forward using only his knees and stared hard forward. What he did know was that French Hussars almost always had a fancy uniform and this was nothing of the kind, in fact their uniform, if it could be described as such, was so dull that, in the murk, it was hard to make out one shape from another. He made his decision.

"Get ready to ride, boys, but I'm pretty much sure these is guerrilla coves."

In that he was correct, in fact the leader of the guerrillas was not Sanchez himself, but Ignasias Mateo, him not unfamiliar with Cornet Carr's Squadron and this showed with a big grin which split several days growth of beard.

"Ah, caballería inglesa! Sargento! You I see with Teniente Carr. You are well, si? You too, Senor Macka Pees."

The sheer bonhomie of Mateo's greeting had an effect on even the dour Baxter and his companions, especially after a firm handshake and even more so after a brandy flask was passed over from Mateo and the guerrilla gestured to Baxter, after his turn, that it should be passed to the other four. The grin continued and his companions continued the good cheer which improved the mood amongst the Light Dragoons, but the respect was already there. These may not be in a smart uniform, but these were hard, tough men, who carried the fight daily to the French invaders and suffered a horrible fate if captured. As far as Baxter and his men were concerned, these were 'alright'. When the brandy flask came back, Mateo spoke his news.

"Los franceses, they come forward. Was in Miranda over Douro, now few at Briviesco. Closer. One hour, si, from here, on horse."

Baxter face registered the seriousness of the news.

"Are there any French behind you?"

Mateo shook his head, sending raindrops everywhere.

"No, no franceses this side of Briviesco. Only seis men in Briviesco."

He held up six fingers, as Baxter nodded his understanding.

"Most at Pancorbo."

"Right. I'll take that back. No need for you to go further."

However, Mateo sat forward.

"One more thing. The franceses have many men now, over Douro, this side. Pancorbo to Briviesco, many, many soldados franceses."

The seriousness of that information plainly disturbed Baxter and he turned to Makepeace, who was equally worried and showed it. They were now the only members of the Allied army who held such crucial information. However, Baxter soon settled in his mind on his own course of action and he turned and grinned at Mateo.

"Thanks for that, we'll pass it on. Now, you take care!"

Mateo turned his horse.

"You take care also, Sargento. Adios, viaje con Dios."

With that he and his men turned and cantered rapidly back down the road, soon to be swallowed in the steady rain. Baxter turned his horse in the opposite direction.

"This we have to get back to Oakwood."

Reluctantly, the tarpaulin was rolled and stowed behind their saddles, to begin a rapid ride back to 16th Headquarters at the next village back, this being Santa Olalla.

That evening, Withers called all his Officers to his own quarters at Monasterio, the next village back towards Burgos from Santa Ollala. This meant all cramming into a single room, this with but one window to accompany the door, a huge crucifix on the wall and the noise of squabbling storks on the thatch above.

"Johnny's coming forward. Seems this Souham wants to make a name for himself and is pushing forward to see what can be achieved. I suspect that he has sufficient men with him to make a bit more of a nuisance of himself than just sending out patrols."

He took a deep, weary breath.

"Things are not going at all well with the siege and now we have this Souham pushing at the door. Patrols are already at a maximum. Anson does not want to add any more, but impress upon your men that we will soon be in conflict and we must not be taken by surprise. From what I hear, today is the last effort at Burgos, involving blowing up a Church, which will endear us not to the locals, as you can imagine. The Peer knows of the French advance upon us and is sending out substantial reinforcements. This is getting serious, so we're pulling all pickets back to Santa Olalla. Keep your eyes and ears open."

Six days later, One and Two Squadrons of the 16th were riding up to take their turn at Santa Olalla, when they suddenly found two

Squadrons of the 12th riding back at them at speed and so they halted short of the village to await their arrival, with Tavender, now stationary, up at the front. Oakwood rode up to the head of the column to join Tavender, feeling justified to know what was happening, but it was not good news as the evidently disturbed Senior Captain of the 12th explained.

"Johnny's got into Olalla. A Brigade, nearly, of Chasseurs forced us out. We had no choice."

Feeling at an advantage over someone who had just run away, Tavender treated him to a withering look, which Oakwood felt to be wholly unjustified. Who would not retreat when faced with the certainty of being killed or captured? Thus, it was Oakwood who asked the pertinent questions.

"Are they advancing in force? Is this a real advance on Burgos?"

The 12th Captain shook his head.

"There was nothing behind them that I could see. You want my opinion, they're taking villages one by one for a steady advance."

Oakwood looked at Tavender, hoping for some clear directive, he was the Senior Captain of the Regiment, but nothing came, so he made his own offerings.

"Lucius. I suggest we send back word to Brigade at Monasterio while we hold here. If Johnny has no further ambitions, that's fine, but if he does, we have four Squadrons here, us and these of the 12th. We could hold any further advance."

The grave idea of four Squadrons attempting to hold back two whole Chasseur Regiments registered on Tavender's face, but the 12th's Captain spoke first.

"I agree. We do our best to stop them coming any further."

Tavender had no choice but to comply and he turned to his nearest Cornet, Harry Smythe.

"Smythe! Get back to Anson. Tell him what has happened and that we, plus the two Squadrons of the 12th, are holding here. Our side of Santa Olalla."

Smythe saluted and wheeled his horse to gallop off. Meanwhile Oakwood had had enough of waiting for Tavender to make any decision and spoke out.

"Right, Lucius. We'll make a bit of a show, yes? Four Squadrons in line, each of one rank. That may get them to think that there are more of us here, than there really are. They expect us to be usually in two ranks."

Tavender nodded surly agreement and Oakwood and the 12th Captain rode off. Soon orders were shouted and the four Squadrons formed up across the gently sloping plain that ran down to the river Arlanzon off to their right. For an hour they sat their horses, Carr making frequent use of his telescope to study Olalla, but nothing emerged on their side, but the usual bright Chasseur uniforms could be seen moving between the houses. After two hours, with no word from Tavender, Oakwood allowed his Squadron to dismount and eat, one Troop at a time and this was copied all along the line. Soon after that, Anson himself arrived with the whole of the 11th Light Dragoons and the rest of the 12th and 16th. He went straight to Tavender.

"Well done, Lucius, you did the right thing."

He drew his own telescope and used it, speaking at the same time.

"What does he have behind that village, do you know?"

"All we've been told by the 12th, Sir, is that they have no more ambition than to occupy the village with their Light Cavalry."

Anson lowered the telescope.

"And how did he know that?"

"As we were told, Sir, they came forward with only two Regiments of Chasseurs."

"Some time ago and that may have changed."

He remained studying Olalla as he folded his telescope.

"Right. We can do no more than hold here. Clinton has been informed and I expect some response from him, meanwhile we're out in the open. Hold here until dark, then set horse lines and camp."

Tardily for them the daylight did fade and so, much later, the dark closed in and swallowed the village. It was allocated to Carr and Peterson to tour the watch set on the ridge above and to the left of their camp. From the high vantage point, looking towards Olalla, points of light could be seen, obviously campfires and Peterson laughed as he spoke.

"Johnny's making himself at home."

Peterson's Troop Sergeant, Arthur Desty was with them and was never one to let his lowly military status keep his mouth closed.

"Yes Sir. As long as he stays at home! Put his feet up if he likes."

Throughout the night, peace reigned, but dawn brought a rude awakening, when their camp was over-run by all the Light Companies of the 5th and 6th Divisions. They had not been there 15 minutes before the orders came for Anson's Brigade to saddle up and mount, Oakwood bringing orders to Carr and Peterson.

"We've got the same as two Battalions, near enough, of Light Companies to go at Olalla. Someone high up wants it back. They'll be going forward in open order, so we protect them from cavalry. We're down by that river, the Arlanzon, Squadrons in line, two ranks. The 11th and 12th will be on the far side of it, we'll be this side. They're calling it a river, but it's not much more than a ditch."

The three Regiments rode out in column of fours, but soon broke out into Squadrons in double line and took their positions. Simultaneously, in open order, the Light Companies doubled forward at running pace, keeping level with the cavalry. Advancing to the right of the village, all in the 16th waited to see some resistance from the buildings, but none came.

"There goes Johnny!"

Carr heard Baxter's comment and was pleased himself to see that what was indeed two Regiments of Chasseurs were now riding hurriedly back down the road to Quintanavides. The Light Troops disappeared into the buildings and many spilled out of the far side, so small was Ollala's size. Cavalry bugles sounded and Anson's three Regiments reformed into column and, once reassembled, Withers ordered dismount to await their next orders. As they waited, they saw Clinton himself ride up to Anson, then Anson came to his Colonels and soon the word came to Oakwood, Carr and Peterson.

"Clinton's leaving the Lights here at Olalla. Us to provide cover, the 11th and 12th are pulling back to Monasterio. We're staying, so make preparations for a night in the open. Johnny's only under a mile away!"

Throughout the rest of the day and the following night, the 16th were content to wait as ordered, an infantry picket being maintained some way forward of the village, this still full of Light Troops of no less than 17 different Regiments. However, at full light all changed. Wellington himself arrived and spent a few minutes with the commander of the Lights, Brigadier Halkett, who then came to Withers after Wellington hurriedly rode off back to Burgos. After Halkett had finished, Withers called all his Officers together in the open air and gave the grim news.

"The latest attack on Burgos has failed. Preparations are now being made to retreat, but we need to hold at Burgos for at least two more days until we can get ourselves organised. It's all about numbers. We know that Souham has 50,000 men opposing us and another 60,000 led by Soult and El Rey are coming up from the South against Hill at Madrid."

He allowed the dire news to sink in.

"Here, we have 24,000 and 11,000 Spanish. At Madrid, Hill has 43,000 mixed. Even if we had taken Burgos, I doubt we could have held it. The Peer is setting up a defensive line West of Burgos, so we're giving up Ollala, but Monasterio must be held, out in front. We will be back there, along with Halkett's Lights, plus a Guards and a KGL Brigade and two Battalions of the 6th. We're all moving now, as you can see."

Behind Withers as he spoke, the Companies of Light Troops were forming columns on the road and soon the 16th were on the road behind them, for a hurried march back to Monasterio. Once there, after a day of fitting into limited space, it was a crowded night and an uneasy one, because all knew of their advanced position, intended to hold the main road. It was a subdued gathering in the cottage allocated for the 16th's Officers, almost all the talk was of retreat and how far they would have to go to escape the French and retreat was the word most often used. In C Troop, all listened to the memories of Spivey and Makepeace, the latter most able to impart the most detail concerning the last major retreat of any Allied army, that back to Coruna in 1809.

"That was when we was both back with the 18th. Retreat's one thing, starvation's another. We held 'em back well enough, keepin' the Frogs off the main column, but the army fell apart anyway from starvation."

Spivey joined in.

"That's right! There was many a cavalryman and artilleryman as ate their own horse, then tried to carry the harness, then ditched that from nothin' but weariness. And, on top, it was January!"

"Ah, yes, that's true! The cold and snow were worse than back home and we saw some terrible things on that road. The Followers got it worse, childers starvin' and freezin'. 'Twere a real bad business!"

At the back of the group, Carr was listening and then asked the obvious question.

"But later on, you won!"

"Yes Sir, that's the oddness of it. As soon as there was talk of a battle the lads came back together. At least the most. Many we never saw again."

The uneasy night in Monasterio did not last its full course. An hour before dawn the NCOs who had been on sentry duty were running through the lines of Anson's men, shouting to arms and to saddle up and form column on the road. Once dressed and ready, Carr and Peterson found Johnson stood with Oakwood.

"Souham's sending two Divisions against Wellington's centre. He's making his effort some way behind us and to the South, at a place called Olmos de Atapuerca. If they can strike North from there they'll cut the main road and that'll cut off all we've got up here. We are to screen a place called Quintanapalla on the main road and support the 7th Division who are moving out to oppose what's coming at this Olmos. Halkett's coming with us."

Oakwood was less than content.

"So, this holding business out here, didn't last but a day!"

"A day perhaps, but only if we let them cut the road."

Johnson hurried away, all had their own immediate concerns and soon they were beginning their ride just as Halkett's own men were running from their camps and billets to form up and begin their own journey back. A dour late October day was dragging itself into being as they set their horses to an easy canter back along the road to Burgos. They were not far from Quintanapalla when they passed through a heavy concentration of British troops and questions were hurled in the direction of these passive infantrymen as they passed through, to reveal that these were the 1st and 5th Divisions holding the road, which was Wellington's left centre. They cantered on to see the 7th Division all in line and moving South from the vital village of Quintanapalla, so Anson led his men in behind them, but before the buildings, to then wait and to rest their horses. Out came the telescopes and Carr could see in the not too far distance what he estimated to be two whole French Divisions, close enough to provide mutual support, advancing in the direction of the 7th, who had now split into two, seemingly weak, Brigades, each moving to oppose one French Division. Soon came the sound of heavy conflict little more than 500 yards out before the 16th, who remained stationary and awaiting orders. Wellington arrived behind them and all eyes that could, followed him, as he rode across the outskirts of Quintanapalla, but then disappeared. The conflict continued for some time with the two Brigades of the 7th holding their ground and maintaining a solid resistance and, if anything, advancing forward. Oakwood was sat with Carr, looking left and he touched Carr's sleeve.

"This'll finish it!"

Wellington must have ordered both the 1st and the 5th Divisions to advance onto the French left flank and they could both be seen across the flat plain, especially when one topped a small rise. The French General must have also seen this, because the conflict ended with a sudden drop in the sounds of musketry. The 7th, who had held their ground against odds of two to one for almost an hour, did not move forward, but what did, from behind the 16th's left, was a whole battery of field-guns, moving at high speed. Lord Paget arrived and shouted at Withers.

"Go forward with the guns!"

Then Paget was gone himself, so Withers had no choice but to follow the guns, now bouncing across the shallow ditches and lanes. He raised his sword and led Four Squadron forward, to be followed by the rest in reverse order, each forming fours as they went. Soon the 16th were passing the end of the line of the original two Brigades of the 7th Division, on ground which they still held, their own casualties on the rough turf behind them, with many more French not 100 yards before. Five more minutes and the guns unlimbered to be brought swiftly into action, but each gun managed only five or six shots and these only against the final French Battalions; they had retired so quickly out of the improvised trap that Wellington had attempted to spring on them. Within ten minutes, the 16th were following the guns back to the British lines to then camp within sight of Burgos, this now almost silent. Rumours spread that the retreat would begin the next day.

When the next day dawned, the 16th obeyed the rumours of a general retreat and began preparations for it, but the opposite was actually ordered, this reaching the Squadrons in the form of Johnson, now speaking to the three Officers of Two Squadron.

"We are ordered back out to Monasterio. Immediately. Us and Halkett's."

Oakwood frowned.

"Which means we'll be last out!"

Johnson rode on, but had time for a comment over his shoulder.

"Put a bet on it."

It took but a ride of 20 minutes to return to Monasterio to find that those who had remained to hold the village, these being the Guards, the KGL and the 61st and 11th of the 6th Division, had thoroughly fortified the village and were at the alert, with visible rotating changes to the several pickets moving out and returning over the ground beyond the village. There were at least two pickets up on the highest hill that overlooked the many low hills between their Monasterio and French held Santa Olalla. An hour later Halkett arrived and immediately gave out his orders for the retreat, these being none too reassuring for the 16th, as Oakwood passed them on.

"We go tonight. Fires must be lit to burn as long as possible wherever we are opposed by the Johnnies. They must be able to see them, which will mean up on that hill, there."

He pointed to a major hill, crowned by what must be a huge Calvary.

"Picket fires will be lit up there if he is still in Olalla or not. Whether or not he is in there, we have to find out, so that we know where a threat to our pull-out can come from. Up there, fires can be seen for miles, which will keep Johnny in the dark, whilst we use the time to get away. We keep them going until three in the morning when we can pull out. We cannot use the roads into Burgos, we have to get over the Arlanzon by a ford, then get back North of the river and away from the Castle using Burgos bridge. We will be the last to cross which calls for total silence, it's within easy range of the walls. Our footsloggers all leave come nightfall."

Carr was becoming alarmed.

"What's this 'finding out'? What will that involve?"

"We get up to Olalla, as close as we dare and take a look. We need to know where Johnny is."

Now Peterson spoke his own worry.

"And later, on our own, with no column to follow, we have to find a ford in the dark, then a bridge, under the noses of the Frogs, with them still up in the citadel."

Oakwood took a deep breath, he was as agitated as anyone.

"For the first, some of Julian Sanchez' men will guide us and for the second, that will not be a time for you to start sneezing when we're on the bridge, which you seem to be doing a lot of lately. Are you not so well?"

Peterson nodded.

"Bit of an ague, but it's passing."

Oakwood did not look convinced, but subsided

"Good! Now, us and Tavender are out to spy Olalla."

Within the hour, the two Squadrons rode out together, but soon split, Two Squadron riding to the left of the Calvary hill, One Squadron taking the road to the right of it. Oakwood led his men, in column of fours up and over the shoulder near the high summit, to find that Santa Olalla was blocked from view by other lower hills and ridges. There was no choice but to ride on but soon they came to a valley which gave a view down to the road to their right and there they saw One Squadron halted. Oakwood slowed to a walk.

"Now just what can he see?"

He continued to study One Squadron, but, being as nothing so far had been achieved by his own, he cantered on over the next ridge, which revealed nothing, then over the next which did. The telescopes of the three Officers were immediately employed, but not for long, because what was in Santa Olalla was obvious. It was full of French infantry, some even outside the village and this time two Brigades of Chasseurs were outside and deployed before it. Oakwood slammed his telescope shut.

"That will do!"

He said no more, but wheeled his horse and the Squadron followed, at a strong canter down the back of the ridge. The hills came back to them, in reverse order of their advance out, until they came within sight of the final Calvary hill, where their own pickets were. Now their ride back suddenly became very perilous and the outcome very uncertain, because at least a half Regiment of French Chasseurs were galloping up from the road across the level floor of the valley which Two Squadron were just about to enter. They were approaching from the left, which meant that Two Squadron would be at a disadvantage, being taken on their bridle hand. Oakwood needed to decide immediately, either to deploy to meet the charge, or to ride at maximum gallop to hope to escape across their path. He decided on the latter and shouted, "At the gallop", but there was little need, all had seen the Chassuers, who had every possibility of cutting them off from the Calvary hill and their fastest gallop was their only chance. The ground beneath them sped away, but seemingly not fast enough. Carr looked left, anxious about the Chasseurs, but was doubly horrified to see what must be One Squadron, trotting up the slope of the Cavalry hill, to the left of the effigy itself, and making no move to help them whatsoever, merely continuing on their own way to safety. Oakwood had also seen them and was also concluding for himself that Tavender could lead his men down into the valley and at least distract the threatening Chasseurs by threatening to attack them from the side and the rear, if they did manage to cut off and engage with Two Squadron. In that case, they should join the fight.

However, the attention of both was drawn back to their own immediate predicament. Oakwood, in order to lengthen the Chasseurs' journey was tending rightwards, but too far would take them away from the Calvary hill and then the Chasseurs would definitely cut them off. The distance was lessening between the two forces and it looked as if the Chasseurs would win, even though Two Squadron was now on the slope on the far side. Oakwood had by now drawn his sabre and all copied his action, it seemed that conflict was inevitable when suddenly, from over the top, at the run, came a column of KGL Infantry. They came in a column of twos, already a firing line, with their distinctive dark blue Regimental Colour plain above them and the King's Colour alongside. They would arrive on the flank of the Chasseurs just before these charging Frenchmen would reach Two Squadron. The KGL wheeled to confront the Chasseurs, halted within extreme range and delivered a full Battalion volley, bringing several down, then they advanced again, every step perilous because they were not in square. Another volley and the Chasseurs swerved away, it was obvious that, if a cavalry action began with Two Squadron, the Chasseurs would have this infantry on their flank, pouring in volleys. If they attacked the infantry, vulnerable in line but adroit at forming square, as these Rosbifs always were, then the English Light Dragoons would attack them.

Two Squadron, now at a canter, rode past the end of the KGL line, each cheering the other, cavalry to infantry and vice versa. Oakwood dropped back to Carr.

"Lead them back. I must offer my thanks to that KGL Colonel. If you see Captain Tavender, tell him I would very much like to see him!"

Carr cantered on and entered the village to ride to their camping ground where his men and Peterson's dismounted, as exhausted as their mounts. Carr was as incensed as anyone by the inaction of One Squadron and he led his horse up to Sergeant Baxter,

"Sergeant, please see to my horse. I must find Captain Tavender. Our Captain Oakwood needs to ask him some questions."

Baxter grinned as he took the reins

"Yes Sir. There's one or two I'd like to ask him myself!"

Baxter led Carr's horse to the tethering lines, looking up knowingly at Makepeace and Spivey as he did so.

"Tavender again. And we all know bloody well why!"

Meanwhile, Carr had reached the lines of One Squadron and could see Tavender remaining stood by his horse, examining the head harness. Carr immediately strode up.

"Captain Tavender, Sir. If I may?"

Tavender turned towards him an irritated expression on his face, but he said nothing and so Carr continued.

"May I ask, Sir, that you make yourself available for Captain Oakwood? He will not be long in arriving, he held back to thank the KGL Officer who led his men to our aid, back then, when we were in such severe danger of being cut off by French cavalry. I would have thought that you could not have failed to have seen the affair for yourself, Sir."

Tavender's expression did not change.

"If your Captain Oakwood has an issue with me, you may tell him that I will be in my tent."

He pointed with his thumb over his shoulder, but he had no chance to move, because Oakwood, having been delayed merely long enough to shake hands with the German Colonel, came thundering up at the gallop and then leapt out of the saddle. Carr thought that Oakwood was about to jump on Tavender, but he halted merely inches from his chest. He was clearly utterly livid and shouted, rather than spoke.

"Captain Tavender. Can you explain to me why you did not come to our aid just now, when you were in a perfect position to do so?"

Tavender was shocked at the vehemence of Oakwood's assault, almost physical, certainly at maximum verbal, and he said nothing for that moment and so Oakwood continued.

"Was there any good military reason why you chose not to risk your command in coming to the aid of mine? Captain!"

Tavender had now recovered somewhat and stared back, straight at Oakwood.

"I judged that you were in little danger, Captain Oakwood, and saw no reason why I should risk casualties in my Squadron, when your own was riding safely out of danger."

Oakwood thrust his face forward to but inches from that of Tavender.

"Safely out of danger, Captain? So safely out of danger were we, that a whole Battalion of KGL infantry felt the need to run from their own secure position to aid us in getting safely out of danger, as you put it. They saw the need, why not you? You are of our own Regiment. Aren't the words comradeship and support ones you use too often? Could you not at least have ridden down and seen us home, even of you decided that we were 'getting ourselves safely out of danger'? A genuine threat from you and those Chasseurs would then have given up completely."

Tavender was now feeling wholly uncomfortable. An audience of Troopers was gathering and Oakwood's arguments were powerful and plainly called into question Tavender's judgement and even his courage. He stepped back.

"If you have any problems with my conduct, Captain Oakwood, I suggest that you take them up with the Colonel. I am perfectly willing to answer questions from him, but no more from you!"

With that he turned and stalked off, the audience making way for him, but the disdain and suspicion on their faces was not lost to him. His Senior Sergeant was amongst the crowd and Tavender fixed him with a look.

"Shelby! Take care of my horse."

There came no salute from Shelby as Tavender passed him by, instead the veteran Sergeant spat on the ground before collecting his Captain's horse.

oOo

The darkness had deepened with each passing hour and the French campfires in the distance had faded throughout the night just as stars fade with the dawn. Nevertheless, wood was regularly piled onto the campfires around which stood Cornet Carr and his Sergeants and

Corporals. There was little by way of conversation as the minutes ticked by. His whole Troop was responsible for the upkeep of the picket fires until 3 o' clock and so his men stood and warmed their hands and bodies against the comforting flames, some dozing but all needing no orders to keep the fires burning, all noticeable as beacons, even from the far distance. Nothing could be seen of Santa Olalla, but Carr was certain that there were French pickets on the intervening ridges and hills which lent purpose and necessity to what they had been tasked to do. Carr consulted his watch in the light of the fire and all heads turned towards him, hopeful that this would make an end to this tedious watch on a bleak hill under the eerie and overly large effigy of a writhing Christ nailed to a cross. This time Carr nodded.

"2.55! Pile on the last of the wood and let's take our leave."

The wood was duly added and they led their horses down the steep back slope, walking, all fearing to ride over the treacherous surface of the steep gradient down. Once back in Monasterio, all was uncannily quiet, now that the infantry were long gone, all that could be heard when they entered was the snorting of the horses, the jingle of harness and the occasional crack of a burning log from the fires in the square. Colonel Withers was waiting at the head of the column already formed and ready to leave as Carr's Troop arrived.

"All done, Willoughby?"

"Sir."

"Fires stoked up?"

"With all that was left of the wood, Sir."

"Very good. Well done. Take your position, we leave immediately."

The column moved out, leaving the comforting light in the square behind them and then out onto the inky blackness of the Burgos road. Within seconds they were swallowed in the enveloping dark and there came the surreal sensation of riding on a treadmill and no progress being made. This impression was only broken by the sound of their horses' hooves and the passing of the occasional tree or building, these revealing their presence only by their silhouette set against the paltry light of clouds that faintly denoted the sky, these reluctantly allowing light through from an obscured half-moon. They sensed, as much as saw, the guerrillas arriving alongside, these so necessary to guide them to the ford over the Arlanzon. If they missed it, they would blunder straight on, to come under the very walls of the citadel. Carr heard the Guerrillas close by in the darkness talking and one spoke the name 'Mateo' and so Carr softly called out.

"Mateo! Is that you?"

A voice replied as a mounted figure drew near.

"Ah, Teniente Carr, is you. You still alive. Is good, I think!"

Laughter came from the ranks behind Carr as he answered.

"Yes, is good I also think. Are we far from the Arlanzon ford?"

"No, Teniente, not far now, but mucho is not good for you, I think. Many franceses they come to Burgos and many, we hear, come up from Andalusia against Madrid. Is not good for you. You go back to Cuidad Rodrigo, si?"

Carr nodded in the darkness.

"It could be, Mateo. We hope not, but could be."

"Will not be good, Teniente, to go so far, pero Dios decidira!"

A pause before he spurred his horse on.

"River is near. Viajar con Dios, Teniente."

Then he shouted into the darkness

"You also Sargento Baxter and to you, Senor Maka Pees!"

Laughter and cheerful replies came out of the darkness, then Mateo was gone. However, one minute later all changed. A cannon fired and soon after burning carcasses, bundles of rags soaked in oil, came tumbling down from the citadel walls. The column halted and Mateo himself came hurrying back to Anson, just ahead with Withers and Johnson.

"The French are awake, can fire at bridge and us. One fool of my men gallop over with no, how you say, cloth, rags, on horse's hooves. The noise bring French to walls. Cannot use bridge to get back. We must use another way over Arlanzon, not bridge, another after bridge. Is not too far, is not too bad. My men will show place."

The anger in Anson's voice was plain, but his question was civil.

"Are the rest of the army over?"

"Si, Senor. You are last. Pero, is not too bad we at our ford."

"You lead the way."

Anson saw no further need for secrecy, all could see the light from the burning carcasses illuminating their comrades in the column and Anson began a brisk canter along the road to soon be led by Mateo off left and down. Two more guns fired and the solid shot, probably speculative, hummed past them, well wide, but then they were swallowed again by the night as the light of the carcasses died. The descent they could only feel as their horses leant forward. They passed a guerrilla on horseback, there to mark the way and soon they heard the rush of water over the shallows of what for them would now be the first ford. Carr's horse was reluctant to step out from the bank, but a kick from his heels sent her in and immediately he felt the chill of the cold water almost to his knees, then the rush of the central current against his leg and his horse's flank. A half minute of wading through the rapid flow and his mount began to climb and the far bank was gained, but there was no stopping. The column continued on and Carr took the opportunity to pull off his boots and at least pour out the water. The fast-flowing Arlanzon, now on their right, could still be heard as they walked their horses on, with the highest tower of the Burgos citadel now silhouetted against the sky as the darkness receded. Thanks were given by all, that so far there had been no reaction from the French, as Anson's whole Brigade, the last of the retreating army, passed by very much less than half a mile from their very walls and well within range of their highly potent artillery. They crossed the road that led down from the bridge which they should have used and all hunched a little lower, then they were grateful when their mounts had crossed the road, because then the drumming of the hooves fell silent as once more they were on soft pasture. The second ford to regain the North bank of the Arlanzon was less onerous than the first and with each half mile cantered after the crossing the tension fell away. With the dawn they rode into the main encampment of Wellington's army, around Buniel and all in Anson's column, unsaddled their horses, unbuckled their blankets and fell fast asleep beside their own horse-lines.

The same dawn was also warming the streets of Madrid, much further South, but this day was to be very different from those of the previous nine weeks of occupation and it began with Lowry-Cole calling all his Senior Officers to the local Church. Once again the assembly contained, uninvited, an obstructive Priest, very irritated at so large a congregation crowding his Holy House, but not one prayer, hymn, nor praise to His Lord was being offered, the use was to be wholly secular and, what's more, military. His ire increased even more when he was hustled from the building by Lowry-Cole's Provosts, him requiring secrecy. Carr and O'Hare were there with W. Anson and Creet, his other Colonel, but Cole wasted no time.

"We have confirmation that Soult and El Rey are on their way up to us with something like 60,000 men. We, that being those under General Hill, have only 43,000, which includes 10,000 Spanish. The Peer is in a bad fix up at Burgos. The siege has failed and he has Souham and Caffarelli coming at him with 50,000 when he has only 35,000 mixed. Hill has received orders to delay Soult and El Rey, without engaging in battle, which means that we march South, seemingly to meet the pair, or at least to create that impression. We march to Aranjuez, 40 miles South of here, at first light tomorrow."

The passing on of these orders eventually caused Bridie to be lamenting in no uncertain terms to Jed Deakin, him having just broken the news.

"It's a crying shame, Jed, is it not, to have to be leaving so good a crib as this, what with a baby now and the stall doing so well."

Deakin's first reaction was to reply in sharp manner, but he curbed his instinct. The past weeks had been one of comfort and contentment, something that the Followers had precious little of during their years with the army. He relented and sighed.

"I know, love, I know, but it was never going to be forever. We've had a good few weeks of good times. The war's come back and we have to go. Some place called Aranjuez. It sounds well enough."

However, she was not fully appeased.

"Well, 'tis still a shame to be leaving the likes of Pepita and all hers, good people that they are."

Deakin smiled.

"Well, we're not leaving them with nothing. That stall does a roaring trade and she knows now how to make what you make, doesn't she? The soda bread and all? Us being here has done that family some good, and that's a fact."

Bridie frowned a little at the strength of his words, but she did nod agreement.

"Well, there's truth in what you're saying, but do you think we may ever be back this way?"

Deakin kissed her.

"Who can say, love, we can only hope so. I'd say we'll be marchin' back through here, after we've marched South to this Aranjuez place. There's too many Frenchers on their way, we have to pull back some ways."

The following morning, whilst the 4th Division was marching out of Madrid, Nellie and Bridie were arranging their final batch of soda bread on the trestle table in the street below their billet. Firm and sincere handshakes had been exchanged much earlier by the men before they left, but now there were hugs and kisses all round, especially for Eirin and baby Ellen, between all the families, both Followers and Spanish. When the former departed, the last thing they saw when they turned to give a final wave to Pepita was her serving from the baked niceties displayed on the table. A final wave back from Pepita and they were gone, following Hill's army, now fully out of the city, watched by many mournful citizens, far fewer than had welcomed their incoming, their departure almost certainly presaging the return of the French. In the event, the march for the 4th Division was not the full 30 miles, they stopped short of Aranjuez, this beginning with Carr standing at the road sign, making a tortured attempt at pronunciation.

"Chee empo zoo elos", although the sign said Ciempozuelos, O'Hare felt the need to offer some praise.

"Your Spanish is improving. Couldn't have done it better myself!"

Carr was unamused.

"Orders take little notice of the impossibility of pronouncing some of these names, but we're back here in reserve to oversee a ford, crossing the River Jarama, South-East of here, at a place called Titulcia. Anson gave me the 'up and down', for all the use it is."

He pulled a paper out of his pocket and read from it.

"Now this will make you feel better, if I can read it right."

He pulled the paper more fully open.

"Hill's dispositions – each a Division. The 2nd Division is over the river at Aranjuez and at Colemar de Oreja. Some Spanish are far over to the East and to left of them on the Tagus, with Slade's cavalry behind them at Morata. We are here at Chee empo, Skerrett's Brigade of Anson's is at Toledo and Anover. The 3rd is close to us at Valdemoro, the Light at Arganda behind us, D'Espana's Spanish with them and Portuguese at Chinchon behind us. Portuguese cavalry are in Aranjuez, Alten's at Getafe on the edge of Madrid. Finally, Ballesteros has been ordered to support our right with his army from the West."

He lowered the paper in triumph.

"Now I feel like a General, but I'll need a map."

O'Hare remained sceptical.

"It'll take more than that, but meanwhile we follow our men into this Chee-empo place we've arrived at and then get down to this possible crossing we may find ourselves defending. That's a lot of men which Hill's got for this job, but it feels spread out."

Two hours later they were stood at the river Jarama with Heaviside, Carr making judgement first.

"That is some river, with this Titulcia on the far side."

His two companions did not disagree, the Jarama was indeed wide and the red roofs of the village beyond the river confirmed his second statement. Neither did they disagree with what came next.

"Johnny will not cross here, I don't think there is a crossing. It's Aranjuez that matters."

O'Hare continued gazing at the dark, fast flowing waters.

"Your map told you that, did it?

Carr began the walk back to their camp.

"That's what maps are for. Little chance of crossing here. You'd agree, Joshua."

"These waters shall not part. No Red Sea here."

"Nor will there be any kind of French Moses, one would hope."

They walked back through Ciempozuelos, pleased to see that the Followers had caught up and the 105th were settling into their allotted billets, even though crowded, because they shared the village with the 27th and their Company of the 60th Rifles. Soon there was the aroma of cooking, laughter and songs, which pleased O'Hare.

"Not too great a contrast with the delights of Madrid. I'll settle for a week or so here."

There was no settling comforts further North. The 16th Light Dragoons were drawn up in battle line on the ridge at Buniel, overlooking Burgos. They were part of the rearguard for the bridge behind them over the Arlanzon, with Anson's the furthest forward, apart from Julian Sanchez' guerrillas who were placed the closest to the now triumphant citadel, it still proudly displaying its Tricolour above its highest tower. Behind the 16th and nearest to the bridge were deployed General Hope's 7th Division, and alongside them were Brigadier Bock's KGL Dragoons. Many of the cavalry were wearing their cloaks, the weather was turning cold, the scudding wind carrying sheets of drizzle. The rest of the army had crossed some time before and their Noon meal had been eaten, but cold and unsustaining. The afternoon wore into evening and still no movement, but when Stapleton-Cotton came back over Buniel bridge and spoke to Anson, Bock and General Hope, the result was that they did no more than all move into the woods nearby, as the rain increased. Carr heard Baxter state what was now fairly obvious.

"Looks like we're here for the night."

It was an utterly miserable night. The rain increased and the damp wood created no fire hot enough to cook, not even a hot drink and it was a miserable cavalcade that finally moved back to Buniel bridge come the light of the dawn, when the 7th crossed first, then Bock's KGL, then finally the 16th as part of Anson's Brigade. From their wet and equally miserable mounts, as they finally crossed, they were able to look down on the now substantially increased Arlanzon, compared with their experience at the fords two nights' previous. The guerrillas sped off along the original river bank, deciding not to cross but to conduct their own affairs to the South. Then, the whole day was spent slithering along muddy roads, many men dozing in their saddles, woken only by the jolting of their mounts and the ingress of rainwater down the backs of their collars, despite the black tarpaulin cover that many lowered from the backs of their shakoes. From time to time they were ordered to halt and watch, all sat miserable in the rain, too disconsolate to even speak to each other. The day blessedly ended when they reached the village of Estepar, which Anson's had all to themselves, the rest of the army, including the 7th and Bock's Dragoons, having passed through. It ended on a sour note, this from Tavender, as the Officers of the 16th sat around a fire half made up from the dwelling's furniture.

"Have you heard? Ballesteros has been arrested by his own Generals."

Johnson looked up, puzzled.

"But we knew a warrant had been issued by his own Cortes?"

"Yes, but down South of Madrid to hold back El Rey, he refused to move his army, in rebellion to the Peer's appointment and in disobedience to his clear orders to cover Hill's flank from the West. Now Hill is badly exposed because of that. Both him and us will soon be in retreat."

He took a deep breath, released it and slammed his right fist into his left palm.

"Damn Spanish and their damn idiot Generals."

"And you know this, how?"

"One of Hope's ADC's is an acquaintance of mine. They were the last out of here, before we came."

"Well, never mind Lucius. A retreat on our own or with Hill is still a retreat. We obey orders and make the best of it, as always. Same with Myers' Four Squadron. They didn't want to go, but they've been called up to the main column. That's orders, it takes us down to three Squadrons, but we get on with it."

He held up a bottle.

"Try some of this spirit, if that's what it is. It may be the household's lamp-oil, but it does the trick."

Tavender took a pull from the bottle, pulled a face and then left, slamming the bottle down on the table. No-one paid this too much attention. Something was always bothering Tavender, no-one knew what it was and no-one particularly cared.

The following day, Anson's remained stationary as rear-guard in Estepar, this during a slightly better morning only as much from the fact that it was not raining and, when finally allowed to leave, they were on a marginally better road that had not been churned into a quagmire by the passage of a whole retreating army. Carr rode on as the morning drew to a close, thinking of the Noon Meal, until cries of alarm could be heard from behind, the rearguard pickets of the 11th had galloped up to the rear of the column and were shouting their alarm, many in clear panic.

"Johnny cavalry! Thousands of them, coming up at the gallop."

In response, the order came back down the column, "At the canter!"

The immediate use of spurs increased their horses' pace and Carr, now alone before his Troop, looked around and was puzzled that they did not stand then and there, but his question was answered when they rode over a bridge that spanned a deep water-course, probably a man-made drainage ditch, which drained down into the Arlanzon, 200 yards below the bridge. Once over, Stapleton-Cotton himself directed them up the slope behind the ditch onto a slight ridge, the watercourse itself now manned by two Light Battalions of KGL using the trees and bushes on the bank as cover. Julian Sanchez Lancers did not cross and, when the 16th formed line, these Guerrillas could be seen stationary off to the right, their line stretching down to the Arlanzon.

However, riding off to the left, these having crossed the river, was another Guerrilla band that soon disappeared over the ridge's shoulder. Anson's men had not stood in position for a minute, before the first French cavalry arrived, the usual mixture of Chasseur uniforms but all with the high narrow feather plume above their shako or busby. An immediate disciplined volley from the KGL Battalions brought them to a confused halt and they withdrew, whilst their Commanders consulted on their next move. Meanwhile, more and more French cavalry were arriving, more Chasseurs and now also Lancers and Dragoons. From their higher point on the ridge, Carr could see all this happening and yet more French horse were visible far off, coming to join the already overwhelming numbers on the far side of the watercourse. He became seriously worried and turned to look at Baxter, who himself seemed far from at ease, but a half smile and an upwards tilt of his head did something to ease Carr's fears. The original Chasseurs came forward again and the two Battalions of KGL opened fire again, this time independent but no less furious, then Withers arrived alongside Carr and he motioned Oakwood over. Withers had to shout above the endless musketry of the KGL.

"From Stapleton-Cotton. We must hold these back for the rest of the day, as best we can. Anson has eight Squadrons. Our Myers' being taken off reduces us to three, but we have two of the 12th and three of the 11th. We must hold the bridge, attacking from two sides any that cross, one squadron from each side, so our three will stay on this side, with one of the 12th. The second of the 12th takes the far side with the three of the 11th. That's four each side. Stapleton-Cotton commands our four on the left, Anson will hold the right between the bridge and the Arlanzon. We move now."

The 16th turned their mounts leftwards and rode a short distance to command the exit from the bridge, from their side, to enable them to charge into the flank of any cavalry that emerged. The KGL fire had slackened for want of targets along the bank, but it did seem that the French were now going to make their main effort at the bridge. There the 16th waited, but not for long, before a French attack arrived, grey uniformed Chasseurs. Oakwood drew his sabre, he had already made the count.

"That's a Brigade. Two Regiments. Eight Squadrons."

However, Stapleton-Cotton did not arrive at them, he came instead to Tavender's One Squadron placing himself at their head and he timed his move forward perfectly. He gave no shout, instead he led his men forward by simply waving his sabre forward and spurring his horse into an immediate fast canter and then a gallop. Anson was leading a Squadron from the other side and they hit the Chasseurs just as their first Squadron were almost off the bridge. Hit from two sides the French were crushed into a solid mass, no further progress possible and the bridge became a jam of men and horses. Many KGL, led by enterprising Officers, ran to the bridge and began pouring fire into the Chasseurs motionless upon it, all now a helpless target. It lasted but minutes before the trapped Chasseurs spun or reversed their mounts and rapidly quit the bridge, leaving many dead and wounded both on the bridge and on the Allied side. The two victorious Squadrons turned and rode back to their original line, but of Julian Sanchez Lancers nothing could now be seen, they had been on the French side of the watercourse, but had escaped, somehow. Stapleton-Cotton cantered up to rein in his horse at Number Two and spoke to Oakwood.

"You're next Captain. No change of tactics. Hit them in the same way."

With that he rode off, leaving Oakwood and Carr to examine the bridge, it's surface now almost covered with dead and wounded, mostly the latter. Carr was horrified.

"What of the wounded, down there. Some are ours!"

Those who could were crawling off the bridge, they knew that remaining there under the hooves of another conflict would mean their end. Oakwood shook his head.

"Fortunes of war, but those KGL lads are doing what they can."
As he spoke, many KGL were dragging wounded out of the area of any possible future combat and leaving them on the bank. The pair had little time to examine events any further before another French attack approached, this time eight Squadrons of light blue uniformed Chasseurs, only now they were coming on at full gallop. Oakwood raised his sabre

and the eerie scrape of nearly 70 leaving their scabbards was heard, but then Oakwood spurred his horse forward and Carr did the same. They gained speed down the slope and all fixed their eyes on the Chasseurs, their Colonel now onto the bridge. Carr's senses were filled with thundering hooves, the shouts of his men and the wind on his face from the speed of their ride. The Chasseurs' first Squadron were almost clear of the bridge, but were given no chance to deploy. Oakwood screamed "16th!" at the top of his lungs before crashing his horse into that of the Chasseur Colonel, sending it spinning in a tangle of legs and rider into the two behind, also bringing them down. Then Carr was in the melee himself, his own horse hitting an opponent sideways, an English Light Cavalry horse being almost the equivalent of a French Dragoon's and the extra weight told, but it was almost impossible to reach anyone with a sabre, the crush was so great.

The most that took place was ineffective long-range fencing in which Carr was briefly engaged, the jar of the determined blows reaching up to his shoulder, but nothing more. The damage was done by the KGL, these now equal on both sides of the bridge, pouring fire into those stuck on the narrow passageway that was the bridge. As before, feeling themselves helpless and in great danger of being felled by a KGL musket ball, those who were not in the sabre conflict turned and fled, followed soon by those who had managed to cross. Suddenly, for Carr and his men there was empty space before them, where once there had been French Chasseurs, these now all making off in some disorder, back the way they had come. Carr, both bemused and intoxicated at the same time, turned to Baxter.

"But I didn't hit anyone!"

Baxter grinned, so did Makepeace.

"Well, don't worry about that Sir. We've seen 'em off, that's all that counts. Those German boys did the damage."

Baxter was correct and the same had now gelled in the mind of Stapleton-Cotton, to hold the French on the bridge and provide the KGL with easy targets. Thus, it continued for over two hours, each time the French being held on or just over the bridge, but each time it was a little more difficult as the French employed fresh cavalry and Anson's men were called upon to repel each attack three, even four, times, therefore, it could not go on. Riding back from another conflict that was the most desperate so far, Johnson came up to Oakwood and Carr, but they had seen for themselves what he was about to point out. Johnson pointed back over his shoulder as he spoke.

"This is ending. The Frogs have got over the Arlanzon on their side of the ditch and it looks as though they'll make an effort to come back across the river and get onto our flank or even behind. We cannot hold both, the river and the bridge. Our four on this side will take the bridge, the other four take the river. We hold as long as we can and give the KGL time to get away."

With no further orders, Johnson, soon joined by Withers, led the line down the slope to form 50 yards from the bridge, it and the area before them a charnel house of dead and dying. However, no more French efforts came in their direction, seemingly the French Commander was relying on the force now beyond the Arlanzon, but Anson's men now manning the river bank proved too menacing, especially when they dismounted and sent effective carbine shots across the river. However, other French cavalry forces were moving even further downstream where they would be unopposed, it was only a matter of time before they came over and got behind the hard pressed cavalry. When the KGL were safely away and far enough away, a bugle sounded and Anson's formed on the road to canter quickly after them, but any Trooper looking back could see more fresh French cavalry already approaching the bridge they had just abandoned. At a jogging run the KGL were far down the road, but their pace was no match for men on horses and Anson's men soon caught them up. The KGL had fought for almost three hours and were as exhausted as Anson's men, but their ordeal was far from over. Within half an hour the French had their full cavalry force over the watercourse and deployed across the full, wide valley of the Arlanzon. The Allied column was still retreating, when Withers came from Stapleton-Cotton to consult with Oakwood, all the while taking anxious glances over his shoulder.

"We must protect the infantry. Soon we'll have to form and make a stand."

"Do we still have eight Squadrons, Sir?"

"Yes. Just! So, it's the same as before. Anson with four on the right, us four under Stapleton-Cotton on the left. Further left still are some Guerrilla cavalry, but not Sanchez'. Let's hope they can stand for more than a minute. They'll need to."

Anson's Brigade continued in column for merely a few minutes more, before the bugle sounded to deploy into lines of two ranks. This they did, but the retreat continued, the eight Squadrons spread across the flat valley in a line stretching over half a mile wide, but the French more than matched them, especially on their own right where they were not constrained by the Arlanzon. The French line soon broke into a canter and the gap began to close and so, again, a bugle sounded and the British line halted to turn and face their oncoming pursuers. Johnson rode down the 16th line, repeating the same mantra.

"Hold them up. Hold them up. We'll not beat them, but we can stop them. It's for us to make time for the infantry.

Carr turned to look and he saw that the KGL were now a good half-mile beyond and so, buoyed by that, he faced his front once more. Stapleton-Cotton was leading his wing forward, a tall, broad figure on a huge horse, his straight, Dragoon sabre hanging loosely from his right hand. When he increased to a trot, so did his line, he was not going to meet the French at a standstill, as though it would make any difference, Carr thought, his apprehension growing, because the French were in their thousands. The gap was now closing rapidly and Stapleton-Cotton spurred his horse into a gallop and he was into the French line, his sabre swinging high. The Chasseurs were not in a solid line, as were the British Light Dragoons, and Carr chose a gap and spurred his horse for it, fixing the Chasseur on his right with as fierce a look as he was receiving in return. The Chasseur swung first and too early and Carr took the blade on his own so that it slid down to meet the bell guard, then Carr made his own swing rightwards and back, the end of the blade connecting with the back of the Chasseur's neck. The point bit deep and Carr saw the blood flow before he was past, then opponents oddly fell away from before him, the French seemingly content to draw the British out but not engage too closely, or perhaps they were now too wary after their experience at the bridge. He was amazed as they turned and drew off, then British bugles sounded and Anson's cavalry, all eight Squadrons, halted on the ground they had gained. The bugles blew again and they turned to resume their retreat, but still maintaining their combat line. As they rode back, Carr saw the Chasseur he had engaged now dead on the dry ground, a deep red stain next to his neck. Then it struck him that he had just made his first kill and he felt his gorge rising so that he leant rightwards in case he vomited, but Baxter came up to him and patted him on the back.

"Steady Sir. It was him or you and there'll be a lot more of that before we're out of this!"

Another half mile found the French closing again and so the Brigade turned again to face the oncoming horde. Stapleton-Cotton employed the same tactic and again the 16th closed, but again the French held off somewhat, leaving the 16th to whirl their horses in the midst of the melee. Carr again engaged a Chasseur in fencing, ultimately ineffective for both, but the French had been halted and were forced back. Showing great discipline, Anson's whole Brigade halted, held their line and did not pursue, with many French cavalry lying at the feet of their horses, but also with some of their own dead. However, their own wounded were being helped back onto their horses and held there when they again resumed their retreat. The same happened three, perhaps four times more, Carr could not be sure, but Oakwood, angry and tired shouted his thoughts.

"This is more like a damn quadrille than any kind of battle! They dance around us and we around them."

Another half mile and they were required to turn again to halt the oncoming French, the 16th remaining on the left of the Brigade line. Once more they stood and waited as the French line approached, details growing as they did so, but this time their opponents would be Dragoons, no tall plume on any busby this time, instead a steel helmet and a broad white cross-belt. Once more, Stapleton-Cotton led his four Squadrons forward, a trot into a canter then a full gallop to meet the oncoming and solid line. This time, after the impact, the French Dragoons stood their ground and this time the conflict was fierce and brutal, a melee of whirling sabres, men and horses, all accompanied by the shouts and screams of both men and their mounts. Carr held a tight line with Baxter, Makepeace and the others, their solid line pushing back individual Dragoons, such that at least three opponents, Carr was too preoccupied to count whilst trying to push forward, were caught in the gaps between the men of the 16th and immediately punched or sabred to the ground. One was despatched by Baxter as Carr took the Dragoon's backhand swing, leaving the Dragoon exposed to Baxter's cut into his neck, but suddenly, as the Dragoon fell, everything changed.

One Squadron, from the far left, were without any warning driven across and into Two. Carr felt the whole contest heave sideways as Tavender's men crashed into them. All was confusion as the shout went up, "Back boys, pull back!" The reason quickly became all too clear, the 16th's line was now completely mixed up with Spanish guerrillas who were being driven into the flank of the British line by yet more French, this time Cuirassiers. These had worked their way around the British left flank and had driven back the Spanish guerrillas from their position, then further back again into their British allies. Soon the whole was a mixture of Spanish, French and British and a bugle sounded 'Fall back' and the 16th turned their horses and fled, their line now broken. A Cuirassier angled in from Carr's right and seemed intent on crashing his horse into Carr's own mount, but a sword thrust into the animal's face reduced its speed, causing a swerve, and Carr was merely knocked sideways, not enough to halt his own flight and the Cuirassier fell away behind. Stapleton-Cotton's left was now broken and falling back, therefore his right, Anson's, once stubbornly holding their ground, were now forced to comply with the 16th's retreat and so, in groups of six or up to a dozen, they galloped back in a full retreat of their own. Content with their victory over the only cavalry rearguard opposed to them, the Cuirassiers and Dragoons did not follow closely and Anson's gallop soon slowed to a canter, then a trot and the Squadrons came back together. With that, Johnson arrived, to ride alongside Carr and Oakwood and before he spoke, they could see that he was a bringer of bad news.

"Withers has been captured! Or killed! I don't know. He led a dozen men into those Cuirassiers and must have been surrounded and taken. I've looked, but I cannot see him. He's gone."

The retreat continued, but many Troopers' mounts could now manage merely a walk, they were so exhausted, as were their riders and these fell back, unable to maintain the general retreat. Oakwood looked behind at the sad sight and shouted over to Carr, Peterson and also, Tavender who was near.

"Hold back! Hold back. As much as we dare. Give those a chance."

His own Squadron, plus Smythe's Troop of Tavender's dropped back to cover those nearest, but yet more fresh enemy cavalry were pursuing forward, at a good canter. Baxter hauled a wounded man, who was dismounted, onto his own horse, whilst Spivey gathered the reins of the man's loose and exhausted mount and urged it into a trot. However, they were not charged again, the French Commander was presumably content that he had broken the British cavalry, now he was intent on catching up with the infantry who had done so much damage at the first bridge. However, succour to Anson's defeated men came in the form of another watercourse that also drained into the Arlanzon, but behind it were Bock's 1st and 2nd KGL Dragoons, almost 800 sabres and Major Bull's whole field-gun battery, this drawn up to dominate the bridge over. The KGL Dragoons were to the left of the guns, protecting the watercourse on that side, the road from the bridge running between them. However, towards the River Arlanzon, to the right of the bridge, there was no cavalry, only the guns. In any order, as they arrived, Anson's men crossed the bridge to safety but, exhausted, sat their horses on the road, or close.

Once over and past the guns, their Officers began the task of pulling their Squadrons back together, whilst Bull's gunners delivered their first salvo into the oncoming French. At the sound, Carr turned his mount to look back and see that the French, still in overwhelming masses, had halted to reform themselves. It took barely ten minutes, before the ranks of the French recently engaged, parted to allow through yet more fresh cavalry and these came on at a fast canter, most converging on the bridge, but what looked like a whole Brigade of

Dragoons detached themselves from the mass and swung to the Allied left to ride off to the flank and along the new watercourse

Stapleton-Cotton, hatless and with one sleeve in shreds, was riding up and down before what was left of Anson's Brigade, remaining in a loose column, screaming at them to reform. The exhausted look on the men's faces added to his own anxiety, but his orders still rang out clear, "By Squadrons! Two ranks! Now, damn you, now!" Bull's first salvo had served as a warning which halted the French, but they had fired no more, instead his Gunners stood silent and ready beside their reloaded pieces. Oakwood was now beside Carr, his own shako cut through the brim at the side and blood trickling down, which he wiped away with his cuff. He was looking back at the departing French Dragoons.

"They're off to find a crossing, just like those damn Cuirassiers back earlier."

However, Carr had no time to reply, Stapleton-Cotton was issuing his orders, not to Withers, he must indeed be lost, nor Johnson who was elsewhere, but to Tavender, him now as Senior Captain nominally Second in Command. One Squadron, now reformed, found themselves at the head of the Brigade. The order could be overheard by most, including Carr and Oakwood.

"Lead your Squadron over left and form to the right of Bull. Fill that gap between them and river to cover the watercourse on that side between the bridge and the river. The rest will follow"

As Tavender led off his Squadron, which would show the way for the whole of Anson's Brigade. the leading French were almost at the bridge and would be there within less than two minutes, but now Stapleton-Cotton was screaming at the top of his voice, Johnson was galloping up the line and Oakwood was stood up in his stirrups, adding his voice to the general uproar.

"What the Hell is he doing! He's riding across the front of the guns! They can't fire!"

Anson's Brigade, led by Tavender, were now indeed masking Bull's guns and they very much now needed to fire at the oncoming French. Stapleton-Cotton was shouting "Gallop, gallop!" at the Light Dragoons, as often as breath would allow and within a short, but seemingly endless while, Anson's tired men and mounts cleared the guns and Bull ordered a volley. Then, more disaster. The guns were not depressed far enough and their charges sailed over the heads of the French who were now over the bridge and deploying. A second salvo, rapidly loaded did more damage, but not enough. The French, moving almost at the gallop, were over the bridge in force and arranging their line.

Stapleton-Cotton galloped over to Bock's KGL, to then stand up in his stirrups and raise his already bloodied sword. He led the charge down the slight slope and gained some success. The KGL were fresh and the French were beaten back to the edge of the stream, but eventually the superior French numbers told as more came over the bridge and the conflict became more equal, the strident sounds of fierce combat emitting again as they had all afternoon of steel on steel and the shouts and screams of men and horses. Anson, now back in charge of his whole Brigade, had no choice, but to lead his men into another charge, before the French on his side captured the battery and then rolled up the KGL Dragoons. Anson placed himself before his men, stood up in his stirrups and waved his sword forward. Carr now studied their opponents closer, in the centre were Lancers. For him this was new and his heart missed a beat, but he pulled his chinstrap tighter and followed.

Aware of the state of his men, Anson began with a walk and then broke into a gallop at the very last moment, taking advantage of the fact that the French received the assault standing. Nevertheless, the impact had little serious affect, instead degenerating into a melee of whirling horses, rising and falling sabres and the shouts and screams of combat. For Carr, his arms as weary as anyone's in Anson's Brigade, his work was more defensive, wheeling his horse to hold off any French and countering any sabre stroke or lance thrust that came near enough. Lances, he found were not so terrible if you only had one to deal with, you deflected the point and this he did, to bore in on one Lancer, but then he defended himself with the shaft. When Carr had two against him, Baxter beat down one point and then rode in to thrust the point of his sabre into the man's chest, and he reeled back, badly wounded. However, it was a desperate effort on the part of all, with little hope of any genuine success. Inevitably, they were forced back, then there came, almost as a relief, a bugle call for full retreat, a rapid withdrawal. All of Anson's men turned at the sound and urged their mounts into one more gallop. Bull's battery was already off and over the plain and so Carr looked over to see what had become of Bock's KGL and the reason for retreat was laid out before him. They had been overwhelmed on their side and were fighting off, whilst still retreating, their own French cavalry opponents, who, to the relief of all, soon fell behind, content to have gained the ground fought over.

However, it was not the end. Stapleton-Cotton must have obtained his own personal bugler who blew the notes of 'form line". The KGL Dragoons heard, although some way ahead, but they did halt and turn and Anson's, in no way reformed, simply halted where they were and made a two-deep line as best they could to the right of the KGL.

Their French pursuers came on steadily, but Stapleton-Cotton's defensive effort was quickly abandoned when a mass of French, a whole Brigade came charging for their left flank. Carr, holding his mount steady could only answer his own question inside his own head, "Here's the Brigade that rode off at the second watercourse. They've found a way over." Stapleton-Cotton now saw the hopelessness of his position and the bugle sounded again for full retreat and so it began. The KGL mounts, still fresh, soon outpaced those of Anson, but the desperation in Anson's men subsided somewhat when they saw the two KGL Light Infantry Battalions now waiting and drawn up in square, one further back in echelon, but both steady, regular and well-formed into three ranks, the first kneeling with bayonets thrust forward, the second and third ranks with muskets at the 'make ready'. They were drawn up where the plain finally narrowed, an escarpment now thrust itself from the hills on the right to close with the river, now severely constraining any cavalry manoeuvres. Bull's Battery had not quit the fight and were deployed and ready in the remaining gap.

Carr looked behind and again became more relieved to see that the French were not pursuing so closely as to present any immediate danger to him and so within a few short minutes Carr and his Troop rode past the very solid square of KGL Light Infantry who gave them a very hearty cheer as they did so. They fully appreciated the effort that had been made to hold the French cavalry from them for so long and now it was their turn. They did not have long to wait. The leading French cavalry soon arrived and enveloped the square, but, now having arrived beyond the second square, Carr and Oakwood could hear the continuous and disciplined volleys of the KGL Light Infantry. Anson's and Bock's both turned and faced back, all still mixed together and in uneven groups, but now they could see that the French cavalry, almost as mixed as themselves, had been beaten off by the KGL square, with many dead and wounded French Dragoons lying around the edge. Bull's battery opened fire on any French cavalry in range and therefore, now unassailed, the KGL square marched back, still holding their formation, back the 150 yards to stop beside the second square and hold there. Soon more French cavalry arrived and were dealt with and beaten off in the same way, this time the two squares together causing even more casualties. Whilst the squares held off the French cavalry, the indefatigable Stapleton-Cotton rode through his men and he came to Carr and Oakwood, there to repeat what he had said to all before.

"Well done boys! Well done. We've got away, but now we must back up those infantry there. Get in line, show a front."

In response and utterly weary, the men of Bock and Anson shuffled their horses into line to at least present the appearance of a front, but it was not needed. The light of the late October day had finally succumbed to darkness and the French drew back and were lost from sight. Stapleton-Cotton ordered his command into column, Anson's, then his infantry, then Bull, finally Bock's bringing up the rear. It was a limb sapping trudge back to the next town, identified as Quintana del Puente as they passed the sign. Once in and past the pickets on the outskirts, the column halted and many of Anson's men had to be pulled from their horses, they had fallen asleep across their mounts. Somehow all horses were cared for and then both Heavy and Light Dragoons of Stapleton-Cotton's gallant band sank to the ground and slept, whilst for the wounded, stupor and exhaustion provided the anaesthetic to the treatment of their cuts and stab wounds.

However, with the French so near, they were not allowed a full night's rest and, for the vital pickets, even less. They were saddled and ready in the full dark, such that dawn found them on the road to Torquemada and they arrived at just after Noon, where they knew they would be able to cook a decent, if hasty meal. However, at Torquemada, Baxter was amongst the first to shake his head at the sight of Redcoat drunks rolling around the streets all with wine bottles in their hands, or sharing one with a drunken companion, each clinging to the other for mutual support. However, it was Makepeace who spoke.

"This is how it starts, Seb. Just like Coruna. And no Provosts bothering to stop 'em. They're all way off down the road, leavin' these for the Frogs."

Makepeace put his boot to the shoulder of one drunk, him with the number 68 on his collar, who had lurched against his horse and gave him a kick that sent him sprawling into a doorway, from which he did not rise, he merely flopped an arm over his chest and began singing. Johnson came riding up in an evident hurry.

"Baxter. Makepeace. Keep a tight rein on the men as they arrive. Allow none to wander off further into the town, get them to the outskirts. We must stop to rest the horses, or we would move straight through. Keep a close watch."

Both saluted and then directed those of the 16th who arrived up to them into and through the narrow streets and alleyways to the right, where open grassland gave their horses some hope of feed and rest. Orders executed and now joined by Spivey and Nunney the pair returned to the main street to drag the drunk out of the doorway and make use themselves of the room within, setting Spivey to take the first turn on watch. They searched and found a sack of flour, some apples and some salt fish. Within an hour, the 16th were riding again, between the 11th in front and the 12th in the rear. Carr looked with more curiosity than disapproval at the sprawling soldiery until Baxter put him right.

"Them's for a French prison, Sir, as few comes out of, what with the hunger and disease."

Makepeace had something to add.

"True, but if 'tis French Cuirassiers as picks 'em up, they'll lay on a few cuts first, like we saw at a place called Bembibre, on the way back to Coruna. I know they was drunks, but that was plain cruel."

However, soon the questions of drunks and the conduct of a past retreat were left behind. Orders came for Plasencia where Wellington was reported to be forming a line, with the intention of offering battle.

oOo

O'Hare's hopes of a gratifying week of rest and relaxation were about to be severely curtailed by three days when, on 25th October, Carr and O'Hare were called to W. Anson's Headquarters, the largest building in Ciempozuelos, but the meeting was in no way social, instead brief, business-like and thoroughly military. Carr was pleased to see that his Brigadier at least looked rested and moderately cheerful, despite the news he had been ordered to impart.

"We have to march tomorrow down to a place called Anover, just this side of the Tagus, us and Stubbs' Portuguese of our Division, that is. The French are up to us, Soult and El Rey. You know the figures as well as I do, 60,000 men, but how many are close up to the Tagus, we do not yet know. There is a bridge at Anover and that's our task, to deny that, if any Johnnies arrive. Skerrett's Brigade of ours are already there but are ordered to move up the Tagus and hold the bridge at Aranjuez, the important one. They are closer to it than us, so we take over the Anover bridge. The Followers must move back to Valdemoro. When we retreat, it will be through there and we can pick them back up."

Carr frowned immediately.

"When we retreat, Sir? Not if?"

Anson looked at him steadily.

"It's when, Colonel, definitely. Wellington's failed at Burgos, as you know, and he's pulling back, because he's outnumbered, just as we are. The whole task is to keep apart our El Rey and Wellington's Souham as long as possible, so that we can get ourselves back into some kind of shape."

Carr returned the steady look, him now much motivated by the talk of retreat to speak his mind, but he choose his words carefully, nevertheless.

"It would seem that the optimism after Salamanca was somewhat misplaced. Sir."

Anson returned the steady gaze, but his eyes were somewhat darker.

"That's the game we're in, Colonel. Events can conspire, and this time they have."

He stood and motioned all his Senior Officers of the 105th, 27th and 60th to consider the map on the wall, his voice remaining hard.

"This is what worries me. Anover is way down here."

He ran his finger down the course of the Tagus from Titulcea along to Anover. It took several seconds.

"About 15 miles from here."

Then his finger moved back to the mid-point of its original track and stopped at Aranjuez.

"Johnny will be aiming for here, Aranjuez, we are certain, where there are bridges and fords aplenty over the Tagus. If he gets over there, us down at Anover will be out on a limb and certainly cut off. So, when we get down there, maintain a constant readiness to march back. Quickly! One way or the other, we will be marching back."

The order that they would be moving was circulated by mid-afternoon, but what depressed spirits more than moving away from what had proved to be very acceptable billets was the fact that they would be parting company with their Followers at the coming dawn, the first time for months. However, despite the bad news, life in the two mess camps progressed along its usual course, which included Bridie and Nellie returning from the post-Noon ration share out. Nellie was in exceedingly good spirits, such that, she threw a bag of army biscuits into the lap of Tom Miles, the bag itself showing no age at all.

"There, Tom. Them's for you to share around. All new baked."

Anyone looking at the expression on Tom Miles' face would have thought that he had been given a bag of gold, he was so astonished and the look did not disappear when he looked inside to see the biscuits to actually be fresh and pristine, but it was Nellie's husband, Henry, who spoke first, looking at her as puzzled as anyone.

"And just what is it that's put a fizz into you, this drear afternoon?"

She turned to him grinning, her good, white teeth contrasting to the red of her full cheeks.

"That Betty Barker, God rot her! I've not seen for some time, good thing, but we've heard that she didn't get out of Madrid. Ran off with some Spaniard, so she did!"

She grinned around the camp, before turning to her dear friend.

"Isn't that what you heard, now, Bridie?"

Bridie's comely face broke into her own grin.

"That's the truth of it. Ran off with some kind of local waggoneer or some such and didn't get out, so she did not."

Deakin could not help but laugh.

"Then that Corporal in Number Four must be countin' his blessings, to get shot of her. Now there's a man with a load off his mind!"

Thus, their last meal was cheerful enough, despite what must happen on the morrow, but all were well used to such enforced partings, with Deakin imparting his cheery wisdom to his beloved Bridie.

"Now, don't be too vexed that you'm leavin' here. We passed through that Valdemoro on our way here and I remembers it as a place well set. On top, if rumours be true, we'll soon be on our way out of here and on back to Madrid."

Her face brightened.

"Oh Madrid again, Jed. That would be grand, so it would."

However, Deakin on shook his head.

"Now don't get your hopes up, love. If we goes back there, 'twill only be to march straight through. Things be gettin' serious, but you'm not to worry. The army's in good shape."

A last hug and kiss from all men to all Followers, including even an acknowledging nod between Miles and Nellie, the 105th formed their column and began their march, soon to merge with the 27th and the 60th, followed by Stubb's Portuguese, and thus the whole of W. Anson's Brigade began their journey. The march was made in one day, the 15 miles to Anover being well within the compass of infantry such as those of the 4th Division. However, for the Light Companies of W. Anson's Brigade, settling comfortably into their billets within a sizeable village would have to wait for the next morning, explained by Carr himself when he came to the camp ground of the Light Company and found Drake.

"Anson's Lights have been given picket over the river, for the night. The 60th and the 27th have already gone."

It was Ellis who spread the word throughout the Company, with simple words, spoken without a break in stride as he walked through their area.

"Get kitted up. Fall in on the road!"

Already tired and immediately grumpy, the Light Company formed and then they marched the mile to the River Tagus, crossed the ancient bridge and took their directions, these decided by Anson himself and delivered to Carr.

"The 60th are on the road, the 27th to their right, you set up a line to their left. If it eases your mind at all, with us being so far down here, the bridge at Aranjuez will soon be blown, if not already."

He turned, but then had an afterthought.

"And the river's now too high for the fords."

With that, he departed, four 105th Officers staring into the growing darkness, with no defensible feature evident anywhere at all. As Ellis chose the picket groups, Carr, Drake, Bettridge and Shakeshaft walked forward a few hundred yards across the flat fields. There was just enough light remaining to see the utterly flat horizon. The only words were spoken by Drake.

"Ever felt so far out on a limb?"

His companions could only shake their heads in the growing darkness, before they took themselves back over the Tagus to Anover, passing the first picket from Stubb's Cacadores who were now walking up to the desolate point that they had just quitted.

The 25th October had been in no way more cheerful for the 16th Light Dragoons of G. Anson's Brigade, at that moment making a night march on the road out of Plasencia, Brevet Major Tavender riding alongside Brevet Colonel Johnson, the former in his element regarding the Spanish performance at Plasencia, which had scotched Wellington's plans.

"Damn Dons! Couldn't hold a barn door closed. We had a good line where we could hold up the Johnnies, but those incompetent cowards couldn't even hold Plasencia bridge. Now we've had to abandon the whole thing. The Peer should just send them off and we conduct our own affairs. They can't be trusted and that's that."

Johnson felt disinclined to argue, Tavender was too correct, if too ready with the insults, but he did make one comment, before returning to doze in his saddle.

"Tomorrow or the day after, we'd have pulled out of there anyway. All that can be said is that we're just a bit quicker to the next defensive position and the sooner Johnny gets fed up with pushing us Westwards, the sooner we can all rest and billet up for the winter."

For Cornet Carr, the length of a squadron back, no kind of sleep came easily as his horse plodded and squelched along the disintegrating highway. He could only ponder what the next days would bring, he could ask Baxter, but he was asleep on his horse and so he pulled his cloak closer against the banks of fine rain that descended from the utter blackness above and wait until dawn. He allowed himself one biscuit at the top of each hour and, five biscuits later, the shape of the backs of the final four Troopers of One Squadron began to emerge from the damp gloom before him. He stood in his saddle to ease the cramp in his chill limbs and settled back once more, to soon find himself on a bridge that looked very familiar, apart from this time the centre was being packed with gunpowder, then the clear memory came to him, and he spoke, half out loud. "This is where Tavender got so annoyed about Somers-Cocks getting seconded. That puts us back to Valladolid." He turned to Baxter, now awake.

"This is Cabezon, Sergeant, on the Pisuerga, where that old lady tried to kick you off your horse! Better keep a wary eye!"

The comment produced but a half grin from the veteran Sergeant and they rode on over the bridge, but the order came to halt and dismount. With orders relayed from Johnson, Tavender came back to Oakwood and Carr.

"Set picket lines, draw rations and cook. We're here with the 51st and a Battery as rearguard."

"Any sign of Johnny?"

"No, Captain, so make the most of it. He'll not be far behind, so we hold this bridge."

Oakwood looked at the bridge.

"Not all of it, it would seem!"

Tavender briefly looked over his shoulder at the road, where more barrels of gunpowder were being added to those already stacked in the centre of the bridge, the waggons that brought them, now being driven back. Tavender, did not reply to that comment, instead he issued further orders.

"Pickets on the far side. Carr, you're first!"

Oakwood looked at Tavender's now disappearing back, him now moving on to Three Squadron, then he turned to Carr. Oakwood had made his own decisions.

"Two hours for you, then two for Peterson. Tavender didn't say how long. Lose no chance to sleep, but get fed first. No point starting pickets now, there's still some of the army yet to cross."

Oakwood was correct, the first Battalion of the final Division of the column had just marched onto the bridge and, plus any cavalry, would take at least a half hour before all coming over. However, the day passed peacefully, with Anson's men able to eat and sleep in the shelter of the trees and farm buildings, whilst Troopers of the 16th took turns over the river to sit their horses and stare back down the road. It was during the following night that events became more tense and troubled. The 51st were manning pickets immediately beyond the bridge, with Three Squadron providing the pickets further out, when an hour before dawn and still very dark, gunshots were heard and the picket of twenty Troopers of Three Squadron came galloping back into the 16th camp. "Mount and stand-to", could be heard everywhere and an alarm throughout the camp of the 51st soon sent that whole Battalion running across the bridge to join their pickets. Anson himself followed and the 16th, now mounted and ready, could only watch from their side. Within minutes they heard the order from Anson to the 51st, 'Open fire!', and musketry spat out into the night. This continued for five minutes and then the infantry ran back, this time past Bull's full battery, now in place and able to command the whole bridge, with the 51st to their left, the 16th Light Dragoons to their right.

The darkness receded further and the scene beyond became gradually revealed, this being French cavalry some three or four hundred yards beyond. The single howitzer in Bull's battery sent a shell in their direction which exploded several yards before them, but the point had been made, 'No further!' As the daylight grew, so did the French forces until they included their own field-gun battery which began an exchange between themselves and Bull. As the shells and cannonballs began to arrive, Anson rode up to Johnson.

"Pull back beyond effective range. The 51st will do the same. Let the artillery conduct their own argument. They don't need us."

The exchange continued for an hour with little harm done, at least to the Allied side, until both sides regarded the exchange as pointless and a ceasefire reigned for the rest of the day, the only exchange between the two sides being conducted through telescopes. Stapleton-Cotton himself came back to the bridge and made his own pronouncement.

"They'll give no trouble today. He's just building up his forces. Tomorrow will be more lively!"

The day wore on towards evening, with the 16th still resting, cooking and sleeping under the trees in the quarter mile between Cabezon and its bridge. Carr was amazed at how easily his men fell into sleep, one wrap of their cavalry cloak and they were quickly into sub-consciousness, whilst he could not quell his own roiling mind sufficiently to drift into the sleep that he knew he would need over the following 24 hours. With the last of the day, orders came, "Light fires and withdraw at 3.00am. Cross Valladolid bridge and take post on the outskirts." With full dark, Bull and the 51st withdrew, leaving Anson's cavalry to tend all fires, but Johnson toured the camps of his men, giving orders to Oakwood.

'Draw lots or something for who tends the fires. No need for the whole damn Regiment to stand about waiting to pile on wood!"

Oakwood chose at random, depending on whom he encountered, but it did not include any Officer, only NCOs, and so Carr slept in the quiet of the enveloping darkness. With three in the morning well passed, Anson's three Regiments walked their horses quietly away and through the village of Cabezon and down the road to Valladolid, the weak moonlight revealing the vaguely familiar buildings and those wrecked by fire and still unrepaired. Behind them they heard the roar of Cabezon's bridge being blown. All was eerily quiet and totally dark, as was Valladolid, which they entered half an hour later with the river Pisuerga on their right, all in marked contrast, even allowing for the dead of night, to the last time they were there, remembering being given tortilla by the ecstatic citizens. At the bridge, beside an enormous fire, stood a group of Provosts who directed them across, but first they were required to negotiate a stack of gunpowder barrels piled at the near end, then into the suburb at the far end, at the edge of which they found a Regiment of Portuguese Cacadores, all making preparations to defend the buildings that side of the river. There was still no sign of dawn, when Anson came to Johnson with orders, although they did not include anything onerous for the 16th. Johnson immediately passed them on, moving through his Squadrons, first to Oakwood, informing him of where Anson's men were.

"The 12th are on picket upriver from here, on this side, the 11th remain on picket at Cabezon. We hold here. Stand your men down for the moment, I suspect that Johnny will be coming down on this side, he'll not try through Cabezon, he'll not get over the river with the bridge gone."

"Which means, if you're right, he'll leave those poor Devils in that village alone. There was destruction enough."

Johnson made no reply as he moved on, leaving Oakwood to find his own comfort in the abandoned houses and villas on that side of the Pisuerga, but first Oakwood, for his own peace of mind, took himself to the edge of the buildings to find that Johnson had already placed pickets there from Four Squadron, these alongside sentries from the Cacadores. Oakwood smiled as he noticed the cavalrymen and infantry already exchanging brandy, food and tobacco, and he muttered softly to himself as he walked back.

"Let's hope you still have such to exchange in two weeks' time!"

The 16th were woken from sleep by the clattering of the 12th riding back through the suburb, raising the alarm. Plainly they had been driven in. Oakwood stopped a Captain of one of their Squadrons.

"What've you seen?"

The Captain stilled his horse.

"Johnny's come down our bank in force. Infantry on the road, guns next to them and cavalry in the fields. Do you know what we've got over the river?"

"No, but there'll be something. Are you crossing?"

"Yes. Now!"

The 16th were all by completely saddled and mounted, when came Tavender with some unwelcome orders.

"Get yours to the edge and see if the Portuguese need any support."

Oakwood's first response was a puzzled look.

"I don't think cavalry will be much use for street-fighting, Sir."

Tavender wrestled angrily with his reins.

"Do it anyway. Johnny may send in cavalry first."

Two Squadron was already formed on the road ready to ride back to the bridge, but Oakwood's first order to them was 'About turn' and so they trotted to the outskirts to find the Cacadores Colonel, who was English.

"Littlejohn. 7th Cacadores."

Oakwood saluted.

"Oakwood, Sir. 16th Light Dragoons. Do you need us?"

Littlejohn threw back his head in puzzlement.

"No! Nice of you to come up and ask, but no, not now. If we couldn't see them, I'd ask you to ride out and take a look, but no. Their skirmishers are already up to mine. Get back over, we won't be long in following."

To support his words came the crackle of musketry, as the French closed and began their efforts to push into the town. Oakwood rode back down his column, calling for another 'About turn' and cursing Tavender for a nonsense order. Simultaneously Baxter was uttering curses for the benefit of his own Troopers and no-one was in any way amused. Two Squadron, the last of the 16th, crossed the bridge to find the whole of the 51st drawn up at the bridge exit, one wing each side and Bull's whole battery placed to completely command the bridge and the approaches on the far side. Oakwood's men joined the rest of their own 16th with the 12th and 11th of Anson's Brigade, where all three were placed behind the guns and infantry. There they waited, watching the gunners check their bags of grape-shot and their elevations and it was not long before they began to sight their pieces in earnest. The Cacadores, hugely outnumbered, were retiring back through the houses, but in good order, Carr noticed, each man pausing not for a second after firing before running back down the main street under the protection of his comrades. The reason was obvious, the French Light Troops were advancing in numbers and probably not only down the main road, but also in from the side streets. Soon, the Cacadores were arriving at the bridge from all directions to sprint over, but Littlejohn was not pulling them completely out of the fight, instead, once across, they were directed down the bank close to the water, from where they could send accurate rifle-fire back over the Pisuerga, without masking the line of the 51st above them.

With the last of the Portuguese across, Bull's men opened fire, sending charges of destructive grapeshot hissing down the main street, causing the French skirmishers to scurry for cover. However, it was not long before a French battery unlimbered many yards up river on the edge of the houses, but their position was such that they could only train on the nearest wing of the 51st and their Colonel soon ordered them to lie down. The French battery continued their ineffective fire, whilst Bull's ceased fire for want of targets. As so often, Johnson came to Oakwood for discussion, as a kindred spirit and level-headed consultant.

"Stalemate! He'll not try here."

Oakwood laughed ironically.

"More fires then, up till midnight?"

Johnson laughed.

"Don't bet against it!"

"Here's the one to ask!"

Johnson followed Oakwood's gaze to Wellington, who had arrived behind Bull's battery, with Stapleton-Cotton. His right arm pointed across the bridge, then pointed up river in the direction of the still active French battery, then he rode off. Stalemate continued for another half an hour, then came the roar of a full battery volley from just upstream, plainly from the Allied side. Oakwood looked at Johnson.

"Seems the Peer has taken exception to those annoying Frog guns up there."

The belligerent sound continued for some minutes, then ceased, but nothing came from the French side either. Johnson nodded.

"Seems that Johnny's seen sense!"

Then a Stapleton-Cotton ADC arrived to rein in his horse beside Johnson.

"Orders are to pull out, now, and head for Tordesillas. Infantry, then guns, then you, Sir."

At that moment came the loud, if distant sound, of a large explosion. Johnson looked at the ADC.

"Can you explain that?"

"Yes Sir. That would be the bridge at Simancas downstream. It must be under threat, but is now a pile of rubble in the riverbed. We're falling back on a line based on the Duero from here to Tordesillas. This bridge will not be far behind."

"Blown, you mean?"

"Yes Sir. Blown."

With that, he spurred his horse on to ride up to the new Allied battery further upstream and give them the order to retire. Johnson shrugged his shoulders and order "Form column". When the infantry and the guns had passed across their line, the 16th, the last of Anson's, trotted unmolested onto the road to Tordesillas. Then the weather worsened, driving rain on a bullying North wind, with nothing in its belligerent path across a bleak and seemingly endless plain. Cloaks were quickly employed and the tarpaulin back-flap of their shakoes pulled down, then each Trooper hunched into his cloak and tried to ignore the trickling water that gradually soaked the knees of their breeches. The day and its light finished quickly, but no orders came to require any change of any kind and so Anson continued his men on through the darkness, following the decent road. They came to a village, now deserted, and there Anson decided that he had had enough, he was well aware of the burden placed on his men at the bridge of Cabezon. With no orders to the contrary he allowed his men to eat and sleep in the buildings, a welcome break from the grim weather. Many of Two Company piled into the nearest building, caring little about any distinction between Officers and men. Peterson made a bee line for the furthest corner, his cavalry cloak already around him.

"Is there a roof over my head?"

He did not look up, nor wait for any answer, but sank to the floor and was instantly asleep. For all it was a night undisturbed, but not a complete one, the first disturbance manifesting itself with an invasion of German speaking soldiers at around 5am. The noise and the light from a lantern woke everyone in the room and then someone calling out, when they saw that much of the room was covered in sleeping cavalry.

"Entschuldigen Sie, meine Herren. Wir wussten nicht, dass das Z immer voll war."

Carr had first wakened, when the door opened and he sat up, immediately to recognise who they were.

"You're KGL Foot from that fight back to Quintana. Come in, we'll make room. Come in."

He pushed Peterson awake.

"Move over, it's those KGL from that horrible retreat some days back. Make room."

The KGL were only four Officers and they picked their way across the room to sit and rest against the wall. One spoke passable English and, after introductions, he explained, before he dozed off himself, aiming to take advantage of the brief time he was now likely to get.

"It was us that blew up the bridge at Simancas. With some of them on it. Then we lit fires for half the night and marched. Now we are here."

Carr nodded in the lantern light before pulling his cloak closer.

"Lighting fires for half the night. We know all about that, don't we Douglas?"

However, Peterson was back to sleep and all soon joined him. The second disturbance was much more official and serious, an ADC arriving with the last of the darkness from the opposite direction to the KGL, with both news and orders, such that Oakwood was called to Johnson's building, to return within ten minutes.

"Johnny's got over the Duero at Tordesillas. The whole line's compromised. The Peer's ordered all bridges to be blown and we, that's all of Anson's, are to ride on to somewhere called Rueda, just South of Tordesillas where we meet the 1st, 6th and 7th Divisions. There to put a stopper in the bottle!"

oOo

With the arrival of the same dawn, Carr, Drake and Bettridge were supervising the changing of the pickets, Carr in particular, for the benefit of Bettridge, confining his instructions to the arc of countryside each Section of the Light Company should be responsible for. All was conducted with wide sweeps of his arms, whilst Bettridge listened intently.

"The night, Luttrel, is when changes are made by the enemy. With the arrival of daylight you write down what you can see and compare that with the observations of the previous afternoon, to identify any changes that may have occurred."

Bettridge nodded furiously, not sure whether to look at his Colonel or at the landscape in question, but then O'Hare arrived, mounted.

"Message from Anson. Johnny's in Aranjuez, and something's gone wrong with blowing the bridge. If he gets over in force, we're cut off, but we've no orders, one way or another, so Lowry-Cole's remaining here!"

Carr was horrified.

"I've heard of the maxim 'obey the last order given', but that's insane."

That said, Carr's face then changed to one of intense annoyance.

"The only order that can come is to march out of here, so get all ready and packed. This will be our last day here, I'm sure of it."

Then he looked up, down, sideways, then back to O'Hare, his disturbed thinking complete.

"So, what's Anson saying? There's no change, or pull back to our side of the river?"

O'Hare shrugged.

"No orders! No change!"

Carr's jaw clamped together whilst he thought for a second, then he spoke his exasperated thoughts.

"This would be damned ignominious and utterly tragic if we were taken down here for want of orders!"

The rumour that the French had crossed at Aranjuez and were repairing a bridge to enable a full crossing of the Tagus had rapidly spread throughout the Battalions of the 4th Division and was being discussed forthrightly in many places, none more so than amongst Major St. John Slade, Captain Lord Charles Carravoy and Lieutenant The Honourable Royston D'Villiers, whilst taking their Noon meal. Lord Carravoy was the most vociferous, this time the subject of his polemic being their Commander, Lord Hill.

"As if Wellington were not bad enough, now we have the usually reliable Hill catching the disease. We were sent down here for the paltriest of reasons, now we're forgotten. Some Staff Officer's mislaid his piece of paper."

D'Villiers, generally the more reluctant to speak in such superior company, was, nevertheless, the most anxious.

"Do you really think we've been forgotten? I mean we are a whole Division! Hill would not just leave us hanging around down here, surely, for want of some attention?"

Carravoy turned on him.

"Who knows?"

Slade at last managed to finish the huge mouthful he had been vigorously chewing.

"Can't we just march North or something and get back to Madrid another way?"

Carravoy looked at him as though he were a fool.

"Have you not noticed the state of Spanish roads? Ours back home are bad enough, but us, wandering North over Spanish hillsides! We would soon be ridden down and held by Frog cavalry and that would be the end when their infantry and guns came up. We are horribly outnumbered."

"Well, I put it down to breeding!"

The other two turned towards him, both equally bemused at the utterly unrelated statement and so Slade expanded on his thought.

"Hill, yes. He's nothing more than minor gentry, not much more than Squire stock. No experience, you see, of carrying the responsibility, of taking the big decisions. It's not bred in. They get overwhelmed and such as this is the result. You'll see!"

Carravoy and D'Villiers, remaining equally nonplussed, looked briefly at each other, before resuming their meal, this being of very good local pork. D'Villiers ended the subject by pouring some more wine for both himself and his two companions.

Whatever the reason for no orders and their not moving, either Hill's incompetence or that of his Staff, anxiety grew throughout the 4th Division, knowing that each hour's passing meant that the very competent and efficient French Engineers could further advance their repair of the bridge over the mighty Tagus at Aranjuez. Carr paced around like a tiger in a cage, questioning both Officers and NCOs several times regarding their state of readiness. Finally, having exhausted the questioning of his own men, he took himself over to the 27th and found Colonel Daniel Creet, him stood anxiously outside his own tent.

"Have you heard anything?"

Creet shook his head.

"No, nothing!"

Creet stood shaking his head, his jaw working furiously, before actually speaking again.

"But Hell's Bells, Cole's got enough clout in this damn army to take his own decisions. The Peer would back him, that's for certain. I mean, are we holding any of El Rey's army down here, opposite us, do you know?"

Carr shook his own head.

"Without Light Cavalry, there's no way of finding out and I'm not risking any of my Lights on a job such as that. Johnny is overly supplied with cavalry and any infantry scouts out on that table-top wouldn't have a chance. We're at the river, just over and that's that."

However, at that moment a horseman did appear, an ADC probably from Cole, they judged by his high rank, this being a Colonel. What he said answered the argument just passed.

"We march at dusk! Ready your men."

It was Carr that replied.

"They have been, this last half day, but march to where?"

"Valdemoro. Back the way we came."

"That's a night march on roads we've only used once. We could get lost!"

The ADC turned his horse preparatory to leaving.

"Cole's employed a local guide, so fear not."

With that he was gone in a flurry of cloak and horse-tail, when Carr looked at Creet.

"We employ our own. Agreed? One we can trust, paid out of Regimental funds. One guide in the pay of the French could lead us right into Johnny's arms. Can you furnish that, one we can trust?"

Creet nodded.

"I can. My Senior Major has a Spanish servant who'll not want to be captured by the Frogs whilst in our service and not on the Roll. He'll see to it that we get someone trustworthy."

Dusk arrived and, without the need for further orders, the 4th Division assembled on the road, Anson's Brigade at the head and Stubb's Portuguese in the rear. The 105th were behind the 27th and the column began their march. Carr could not bring himself to remain with his own men and so he placed himself up at the head of the Brigade with Creet and Anson, because up with them was their own guide, accompanied by Creet's Major's servant. Re-assured by both this and the pace they were setting, Carr, now calmer, placed his horse beside the other two Senior Officers. Once there, Carr heard extra news, both good and bad, from Anson.

"Skerrett's holding at Aranjuez, holding what Johnny has at the bridge there. He's been ordered to hold at all costs, because the bridge was only half blown, half a width remains. We must march behind Skerrett's position to get onto the Madrid road. There's good and bad in that, Skerrett won't let us down, but the 'at all costs' bit sounds somewhat desperate. It shouldn't have come to this and that's the truth."

"Nothing for it but a forced march, then, Sir."

"That's the truth of it, Carr, there's no arguing with that."

After the darkness fully closed in and the moon rose, the road passed as though on a blacked-out treadmill, as it always did for a night march, all following the grey blanket roll of the man in front, this barely seen by the light of a quarter moon. After two hours, the 105th Light Company took their turn as scouts at the head of the column, accompanied by a Section of their own Brigade Rifles. Carr went with them, taking their Spanish guide. The man had been interrogated every hour by the 27th's servant, him up with them.

"Es este el camino correcto para Valdemoro?"

The answer always came back, "Si, este camino es bueno."

At the head of the column the sound gradually came to them, a sound they all recognised. Lowry-Cole was at the head of the column with his own guide.

"What do you make of that, Carr?"

"I'd say that General Skerrett is still doing his job, Sir, and following orders."

The sound was unmistakable, not that of a full battle, but regular cannonfire and this a deeper sound.

"That's French twelves, Sir, but a night action always favours the defenders, so that's something."

Half a mile more and they were further surprised. They had reached the Valdemoro to Aranjuez road where it intersected their own and in the half light of dawn, they heard rather than saw, one of Skerrett's Battalions already marching across, on their way to Valdemoro. Lowry-Cole called a halt to allow the Battalion to pass and their Colonel came across to his stationary and waiting Divisional General. Skerrett's Colonel wasted no time.

"Langley, Sir. 20th. We've stopped them crossing the bridge, Sir, and as soon as we heard that you were on your way, we stuffed some greatcoats full of straw, lit some fires and took our leave. The rest of the Brigade is following on."

"How far back?"

"Not more than two miles, Sir. It's no further distance to the bridge."

"What were the forces opposing you?"

"Significant, Sir, I'd say. A whole Corps"

"And can they cross the bridge?"

"Only one arch was damaged, Sir, leaving half a causeway. Their attempting to cross that cost them a lot of men."

"Very good, Langley. Carry on."

The salute was delivered as Langley turned his horse, but Lowry-Cole turned to Anson.

"Hold yours here, Anson. Cover the rest of Skerrett's when they retreat. We don't know what Johnny will manage to get across that bridge, or when but if he does give them a stop. I'll leave you the Cacadores of Stubbs'."

"Hold for how long for Sir."

"I want you into Valdemoro with the dawn. Conduct yourselves accordingly."

With that said, Carr and Anson rode back down the column and, within minutes, Stubbs' Portuguese Brigade had turned left at the crossroads, whilst the 105th marched straight on to form up on the far side of the Aranjuez to Valdemoro road and the 27th merely marched up to halt at it. Stubb's Cacadores, these plainly not at all happy at the task given them, were led by their Officer down towards Aranjuez to act as pickets. Creet soon came up to Carr.

"I'm not at all happy with that lot as my pickets. I'm sending my Lights out as a screen between us and them. I'd advise you to do the same."

"It'll do no harm, but when the last of Skerrett's comes through, we wait 15 minutes, then go?"

"Agreed, leaving fires."

"Leaving fires."

The order from Carr eventually led to Ellis passing along the double rank of the Light Company, all sat waiting.

"Up off your arses, we're out as a picket screen, 'tween us and them Portugee."

Miles was incensed.

"Then what's they Cacadorey brown-jobs goin' out for? Can't they do that well enough? All the rest back here is lighting fires!"

Ellis white teeth showed in the dark as he grinned sarcastically.

"Well, you can ask your Colonel, Private Miles. As I understands it, he'll be coming with us."

Thus it was, that, whilst Ellis disposed of the pairs into a picket line, Carr, Drake, Shakeshaft and Bettridge stared out into the darkness and studied the silence, as did the well-disciplined Cacadores maintaining their own silent watch towards Aranjuez, this now thoroughly quiet. It was not long before they heard a challenge and then the final Battalions of Skerrett's Brigade came marching rapidly up the road, the last followed by their own Cacadores in rear, whose Officer saw no point in their remaining so far behind a force that was soon retreating anyway and so he hurried his men along to the end of their column. Carr ran over to the final Battalion and secured an Officer, a Captain.

"Are you being followed?"

"No Sir. Of that I'm certain. My Company and those Portuguese was the last away, leaving the fires and the straw dummies, Sir. He won't come over until light."

"Thank you. Very good, well done."

With that, Carr returned to his own men, sent a message to Creet, which turned out to be superfluous, because his full 27th were already formed on the road and moving off, then he sent a message to O'Hare to march the 105th on as quickly as possible. As the sound of the tramping feet died away, Carr stood silent with his own Light Company, until the silence was complete.

"That'll do. We're out of here."

An hour later, the Church at Valdemoro was picked out by the weak rays of the rising sun to the East, emerging over an almost ruler straight horizon, as the 105th descended the gentle slope into the town. It was not long before Carr and O'Hare heard the unmistakeable sounds that they had heard so often before on the retreat to Coruna and Carr quickly made his decision.

"Creet's made a mistake here, allowed his men a stop and a rest, and they've found the drink. We march straight through. Pick up the pace and put men you can trust down the flanks. You and Gibney. We can only hope that Skerrett sent his straight through."

Whilst a drummer beat out the extra pace, Gibney and O'Hare pulled the Senior Sergeants and Corporals out of the line, where they were soon employed fending off the drunken Irish of the 27th, all too eager to encourage their worthy comrades of the 105th to join them in a 'good drink'. Blessedly, it was only the 27th, there was no sign of Skerrett's. This time it was Ellis who did the swearing as he fended off a drunken 27th Corporal.

"Bloody Diddykites! We could've stopped here and had a good rest and a bite to eat. Now it's full of these muckrake drunks and wasters. Bastards all!"

Standing nearby, Bettridge heard every word and it did nothing to allay the shock of seeing drunken Redcoats now beyond their Officers' control, but what did impress him and cause no small swelling of pride, was to see, because he was at the rear with his Light Company, the accentuated swing of the right arms of the 105th in column, the movement accentuated by the green on their cuffs. All had now transferred their weapon to their left shoulder and the regular step and pace of every man exuded quality. It was at that moment, more than any other so far, that convinced him that the Regiment he was part of, was indeed elite and of the highest rank, as they strode imperiously through the chaos around them.

A different kind of chaos then ensued when they met their Followers waiting on the Northern edge of the town and the column, as they marched on, was enveloped in a rank of anxious women and children, all peering into the ranks and calling to their menfolk, the sentence invariably terminating with the words, "Are you alright?" A mile out of the town a furious Major-General Lowry-Cole galloped back down their column, presumably on his way to back Valdemoro, but the 105th soon came to another village where the order came back from Carr to cook and rest. The village's water-well was soon very busy and cooking fires sprang up all over, the Redcoats smiling at their Spanish audience, mostly small children, all soon eating army biscuit. With food taken, came two hours sleep and then they marched on to reach Madrid within the hour, where they halted at the outskirts. The 27th had caught up, no rest for them, they were marched straight on, but the still incandescent Lowry-Cole now issued his orders, which again came down through the ranks to once again reach Sergeant Ellis causing him to tour his Company, Baker Rifle subconsciously cradled in the crook of his left arm, but this time he had more understanding for the men of his Company.

"Get what rest you can. We're the Rearguard, all the Lights of the 4th Division. The rest'll be forming soon and takin' off to Madrid. Orders've come for one hour's rest, then we're out on the line. If nothin' else, we'll give a chance for the women to get away. And them!"

He pointed with his thumb over his shoulder to where Skerrett's most badly wounded were being helped or loaded into local farm carts, ready for what all expected to be a long retreat, back to 'Where? Who knows?' The word 'rest' had a different meaning to veterans such as Davey, Miles and Saunders, for they were on their feet immediately to get out early and secure a building that would be incorporated into any rearguard position, where they could sleep, eat and keep watch in turns. Thus, with swift kisses and hugs to their 'wives', the 105th Light Company made off to some likely farm buildings that gave a good view, all knowing that it would require a very fastidious Officer to move them if they were already well established into a good defensible position.

Back with the main body of the 105th, Bridie was sat alongside Jed Deakin, the question she asked long anxious in her mind, the warning that they would be marching soon heavy on her mind.

"Do you think we'll be spendin' any time back in that Madrid, Jed?"

Deakin shook his head.

"No, I don't. The whole army, includin' those up North, is pullin' back. Soonest! The Frogs is closin' in, two to one over us, is what I've heard. We'll be straight through and back to Salamanca, easy! Further still, I shouldn't wonder."

Bridie's shoulders sank and her hands came together in her lap.

"Well, a shame that. To see Pepita again would be grand, would it not?"

Deakin put his arm around her and kissed her sun-tanned cheek.

"Well, don't take it so hard. You said you liked Salamancee and when we marches though Madrid, who's to say you can't sneak off for a mo', you and Nell, to see how things are with them. But don't you get left behind! There's not one Officer in this Division as it not in the worst of moods."

On that point Deakin was absolutely correct, this borne out by the arrival of Major Slade.

"Colour Sergeant! What the Devil are you doing still sat on your backside? Get the men up and formed on the road."

Deakin leapt to his feet, his face showing his anger at the sheer unreasonableness of Slade's statement, but Slade was an Officer of King George and if one of those told you that black was blue, then there was only one answer, "Yes Sir". Nevertheless, faced with such as Slade, he felt justified to murmur under his breath and if Slade heard, he didn't much care.

"That needs an order first, afore I sends lads up to stand idle, blocking a military road!"

However, Slade had some justification on his side, despite being immediately fixed by Bridie's deepest, blackest stare, and he quickly took himself away to take his place because the 105th were already assembling. The march through Madrid was dour and sombre, each man in the 4th Division feeling deeply the contrast to their triumphal entry of the August past, after which all the inhabitants had relied on them to keep the hated Franceses away from their beloved city, but now the victors of Salamanca were marching in their own retreat to allow their former oppressors back in. The pace was quick, such as to not allow too deep a study of the faces of the citizens they passed, some sorrowful, some accusing, but none sympathetic. Bridie and Nellie, once the camp was packed up, which delayed their own entry into Madrid, were part of the Battalion sized group of 4th Division Followers that came through on the end of Stubb's Portuguese Brigade and when they came to it, they ran off down the side-road that had been their home for some months. However, what came next was disappointment, all the houses were boarded up and there was no bustling and busy stall outside the home of Pepita and her family. Worried about spending too much time there, they nevertheless banged on the door, but an upstairs window of the house next door was opened and a woman's head appeared, angry and dishevelled.

"Qué quieres?"

It was Nellie who answered with a question of her own, even though she understood not at all what had been asked of her.

"Pepita?"

An arm came out of the window to wave in the direction of the town outskirts.

"Se fue! Antes de que los franceses vengan, y su vil sapo de un Rey."

After that tirade, from which only the tone of its delivery gave either women any sense of what had been said, the window closed with a thump and Bridie looked at Nellie.

"Well, may the Saints preserve them, wherever they are."

Both women crossed themselves and hurried back to the column.

The Rearguard was commanded by W. Anson and, being as assiduous as he was, he toured his lines of the eleven Light Companies and three of Rifles of the 4th Division, but he quickly passed over the position of the 105th Light Company. Miles and the others had gambled correctly that a well-placed and well-fortified Light Company need not be moved. As the last of the day passed and the cold began to assert itself, so Drake took Bettridge and Ellis a half-mile forward to top a slight rise from which they could see further. It was Drake who spoke first, whilst using his telescope.

"There they are!"

He passed the instrument to Bettridge.

"Right down the road, opposite us."

Bettridge, unused to such instruments, struggled to focus it for his own eyesight, but eventually he did, yet said nothing and so Drake answered for him.

"French Hussars! They've crossed the river and have got up to us."

He passed the telescope to Ellis.

"You'd agree Sergeant?"

Ellis had no problem focussing the telescope and lowered it after merely a few seconds.

"French cavalry alright, Sir. Nothin' civilian about them, not no herd of cows, neither!"

Drake grinned as he turned to begin the walk back. Once at their lines, Bettridge was sent to find Anson, whilst Drake returned to his own billet which was at least warm, having a fire grate at the opposite end to what must have been a cow byre at the other. Morrison had prepared a decent meal from the most common and usual ingredients of Spanish sausage and beans, thickened with army biscuit and so he ate and then slept until someone would come to wake him up. This came in the form of one of Anson's Majors, who at least politely shook him awake, to give the simple order.

"Form up, we're leaving. The main body's way ahead."

Drake shook the sleep from his head.

"Light fires, Sir?"

"No! No point. They know we're here, but they'll just let us go. They know we'll give up Madrid and they don't like street fighting any more than we do."

Drake was by now stood and donning his greatcoat.

"Very good, Sir. At our best speed."

It was, indeed, at Light infantry pace that they marched through the streets of Madrid, with not a soul at that time of night to note or mark their passing. The dawn found them still marching, but Anson allowed a rest at Las Rosas. Miles questioned Ellis as he passed on to them the welcome order halt.

"For how long?"

"Count on an hour. Enough to make a drink."

Then Saunders joined in.

"The Followers? Can you say?"

"Nothin' definite, but they can't be too far up. We'll be with 'em come nightfall, shouldn't wonder."

Ellis was completely correct. After the rest, with late afternoon, they were at San Lorenzo de El Escorial, but this time there was no sightseeing, the occasion too serious and the weather for the last day of October too dismal. There, Hill had assembled his whole force and the mood was now lighter, all now knew that they had escaped the clutches of Soult and El Rey, even though they had lost the prize of Madrid. The 105th sat around good fires and discussed what was to come and how they would cope and get through. It was Deakin who first imparted his wisdom to all in both messes and their Followers.

"There's a retreat comin' and in bad weather. So, 'tis boots that matters. If you can walk you can finish the day and get to food. If your feet is cut and bleedin' so's you can't walk, each step takes more out of you than if you was well shod. There'll be lads fallin' out, be sure, either drunk or exhausted and if they'm dead but still has boots, get 'em as spare. B'ain't no shame in that, if it gets you to the end."

He allowed his blunt, even brutal words to sink in before continuing.

"An' we sticks together. Like as not this army will fall apart, as they did at Coruna, so keepin' together and holdin' what we've got will get us through. This won't be nothin' easy."

Having finished his speech on survival, he looked at Miles, as veteran as himself.

"Anythin' you want to say, Tom?"

Miles folded his arms, then unfolded one to rub his unshaven chin.

"Rain can be worse than snow. Rain soaks in and adds to the weight on thee, no good thing if you'm already cold and tired and hungry. Fact, it adds to the cold, does wet. While the whole army is yer, wagons and all, try to get a piece of tarpaulin. That over thee will shed the water, givin' less weight and helpin' with the warmth. I'd say we've got two days here and then we'm marchin'. Right, Jed?"

Deakin merely nodded, his face grave and worried, and so all finished the good meal, but during the dead of night the space around their mess fires was deserted of men and the dawn found all with useful pieces of the precious tarpaulin, all stolen, bartered or bought from the Wagonneers in the transport park. The best piece was fashioned as both a cloak and a hood for Eirin to cover both her and baby Ellen, a back-cradle soon constructed for carrying her and another made for Jedediah, him little more than a toddler. All were cut and lashed together by Davey, Miles and Pike, the former the handiest with the bending and binding of thin, pliable whips. All followed an Ellis' design, this from memory, him having served in the Americas and seen how many Indian women carried their children on long journeys. Each was crafted very carefully, all expected each to have long employment.

The chickens were allowed to wander off. Sally would not countenance the ending of their lives, when rations were regular and plentiful.

oOo

Chapter Five

"This be worse than Coruna!"

"We look more like a column of fleeing peasants and refugees than any kind of army worthy of the name!"

Carravoy and D'Villiers looked across at St. John Slade, him frowning out from below the brim of his fully lowered shako at the sight on the road before him. The Followers were mixed into the column, as per Hill's orders and, in truth, it was difficult to tell soldier from Follower as they began the trudge out of El Escorial, the November weather, cold and bleak, with rain greatly shortening the view either way, both to the front and to the rear. All those on the road were bundled up against the weather, the Followers in army cast-offs, often from past battlefields and the soldiers swaddled in any garb of a similar nature, thus was achieved the appearance that had so irritated Major Slade, that of a gathering of similar souls all about to flee from some great danger or catastrophe. Carravoy hitched his pack a little higher, spreading the load of the straps better across his chest and his shoulders, all the while looking at Slade.

"This is what a long Winter march looks like, no surprise to anyone, I would have thought, but take my advice and get yourself a backpack for your own essentials. With that, you can keep near what matters to you. This is a Winter retreat and all kinds of things can go wrong."

Slade's frown intensified.

"But surely we have servants to carry that sort of thing?"

Carravoy sighed indulgently.

"Yes, normally, yes, but we've seen an army fall apart from what may be awaiting us over the coming weeks and if that includes your servant, you're in trouble. When things become particularly grim he may choose to simply abandon your items as unwanted extra weight and preserve his own well-being. Or he gets robbed, that possibly being more likely."

He did not turn towards him, but he spoke the question anyway.

"You'd agree, D'Villiers?"

"I would. This could be another Coruna. I hope not, but with that discipline went to blazes. We were hardly an army at all, save the rearguard, they held together."

Slade leaned forward to look at him.

"But surely the rope and the lash? The Provosts?"

Carravoy laughed as he walked forward to mount his horse, held by their servant Binns, him also thoroughly loaded, bound around himself and ready for the march.

"Not if they've joined in the general collapse as well. Those Worthies can desert as well as any others, but perhaps less likely I grant you."

D'Villiers had remained static alongside Slade, anxious to correct any poor impression that Slade may have gathered.

"But we didn't fall apart! Not us, not the 105th. We're better than that. We began the march as a Battalion and we held together all the way through. After the retreat, we got ourselves up onto Elvina ridge at Coruna, Colours flying and marching. Properly, as though we were parading in front of the King!"

With that he left the shelter of the doorway they were standing in, to join his Section of Grenadiers at the head of the 105th column. This left Slade wrestling with conflicting thoughts concerning backpacks, the possibility of a disintegrating army and the evident pride that D'Villiers had in the 105th of which he, Slade, was a major part. He noticed that few Officers were riding, almost all horses were being used for baggage, but he mounted his own horse anyway.

The route was upward, ever steeper and ever more winding. Carr, O'Hare and Heaviside preferred to march. The exercise created warmth and conversation was easier, which helped to take their minds from the wet and the fatigue. It was Carr who began, him looking straight ahead, although the view was greatly curtailed by the sheets of rain that descended from the mountain range that he could not see, but he knew they had to cross and so was the subject of his opening enquiry.

"So, we have to cross something called the Guadarrama?"

O'Hare's posture as he marched stolidly along did not change one inch as he answered.

"That's what I've heard it called. This mountain range which lies ahead."

"Bad as the Sierra de Gata?"

O'Hare grinned ruefully at the thought of the mountain range they had crossed three times between Ciudad Rodrigo and Badajoz during the years of campaign past.

"One can only hope not, and this isn't the middle of Winter."

He paused.

"Do I recall spending Christmas Day up on one of those passes?"

Carr shook his head.

"Can't say I do, but I do remember spending one Christmas Day marching to begin the Coruna retreat. What is today?"

"First November, but, ah, well, we can only hope that things hang together a bit better this time. Particularly if rations get back to us. That's what counts. You'd agree Joshua?"

"Eat, that thou mayest have strength, when thou goest on thy way. I Samuel 28. Verse 22."

"Perfectly put Joshua. I could not have expressed it better myself, indeed I could not."

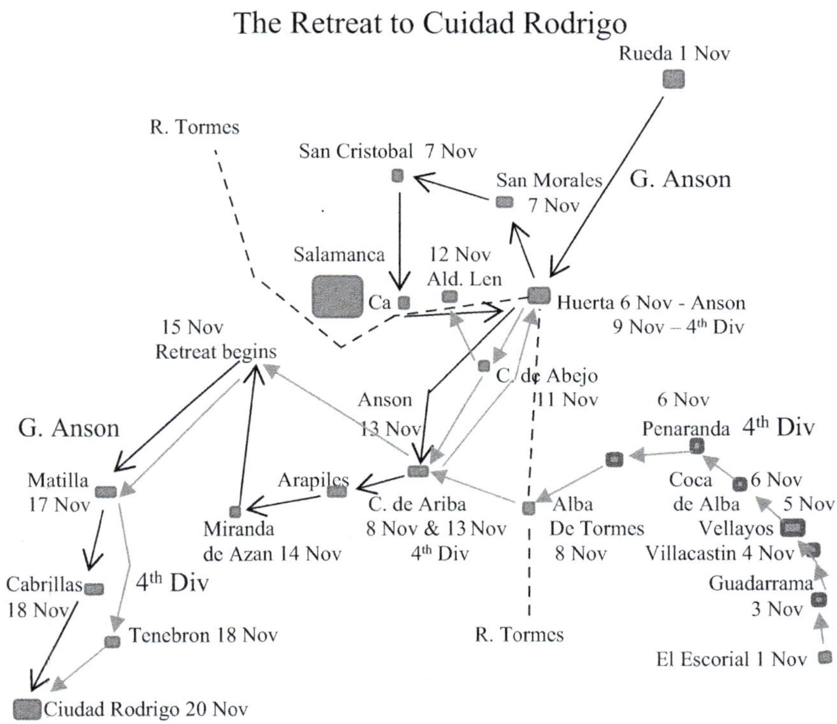

Carr chuckled and produced a brandy flask which he passed first in the direction of his companions, beginning with O'Hare.

Behind, in the ranks behind, the atmosphere was simply one of dour determination. All knew that a Winter retreat was their fate for the coming weeks and so the mood was simply to cower down, to present as least of themselves to the wind as possible and tramp on through it. Little was said, because that meant exposing your face and so the only sound was that of army boots hitting the gravel of the good road out of Escorial. Deakin, as Senior Sergeant, had taken Hill's directive to the full and Three Company marched as five columns, the Followers and the children in the centre, protected by two ranks of taller soldiers either side. Deakin could not see Slade, but he could be certain that Farquharson, their Lieutenant, would certainly turn a blind eye to the odd combination. He, amongst many Officers of the 105th, knew how important the Followers were to the men and that their safety and comfort greatly affected morale. Deakin was correct in his conclusion; his Lieutenant had no concerns over the illegal formation whatsoever. In addition, Deakin had worked out a scheme whereby the two outer ranks were rotated so that all took turns to act as a screen against the wind and the driving rain. After one rotation, Tom Miles found himself alongside Nellie Nicholls, but, after exchanging a look of bitter animosity, nevertheless, the two moved closer, the better to give warmth and shelter to the other.

The day ended with the climb complete, but all expected a night to be spent on the summit with the unrelenting wind and rain, but there came a complete and welcome surprise, a substantial village existed close to the summit with the same name as the hills it surmounted, Guadarrama. Therefore, sheltered in doorways, arches and narrow alleys, each man produced from his pack his share of dry kindling and the resultant fires produced enough heat for a decent stew and a hot drink, this added to by the locals providing extra bread, fruit and apples. All had by now learnt to say 'gracias', but the reply was too often no more than a sad nod of a Spanish head. All knew that the Franceses were on their way back, but at least there was a good chance that these 'peleando soldados Ingleses, 'fighting English soldiers' so Byford thought, would come back and free their land and so some appreciation needed to be shown. A better night's sleep was had by all than had been expected, albeit not so dry, because the rain did not stop, but a check under baby Ellen's back-cradle made Eirin and Byford smile and briefly embrace. She was warm and well, something that Nellie, Bridie, Consuela and Deakin also felt the need to investigate and establish for themselves.

The following day was all downward, but the wind and the rain did not relent, if anything it was worse because they were now all the more exposed on a Northern slope, with a North-east wind sending the slanting rain full into their exposed right cheek and ears. However, Hill, or his Staff, had organised the Commissariat and, at day's end, they marched into Villacastin where rations awaited their arrival and were duly served out. Firewood was gathered, legally from the surrounding forests, or illegally from domestic woodpiles and a good meal was enjoyed by all. Again, the locals were sympathetic and, despite the obvious retreat, one woman entered their billet, this being the woman's own stable, bringing bread and milk, arriving soon after Ellen began to cry, which she must have heard.

"Pan y leche para los niños."

She pointed to the children as she spoke then the good lady, wrapped all in Spanish black, beamed at the sight of the baby in her cradle and, as she left she placed her hand on Deakin's right chest.

"Peleas con los franceses. Usted volvera."

Deakin looked at Byford, already digging out his 'Treatise on the Spanish Language' and soon thumbing the pages.

"First bit is that we fight the French, I already knew that. Next is ………"

He found the necessary page.

"We come back."

Saunders, sat close to Consuela, nodded his head.

"Let's hope so. Wouldn't want to let that old dear down!"

That gift was not the last over the coming half day, given this time in the form of words from Ellis, passing on the order from the concerned and sympathetic Hill.

"He's given us twelve hours here. Must mean no sign of the Crapauds being anyway near. So rest up and make sure of your kit. We could be weeks on this pull back."

Orders now having been passed down, he went over to the two carrying frames and looked down, one still occupied by Ellen and, for some reason she smiled up at him, which caused a profound emotional reaction in this hardest of soldiers, such that he needed to take a very deep breath, more than one, to regain control of himself. However, Nellie noticed and, always having some regard for Senior Company Sergeant Ellis, she patted his right arm, twice, and then offered an empty cup to him, to emphasise her question.

"You'll take a drop of tea with us, Ethan, will you not?"

Ellis' face registered his pleasure and surprise, so he set his rifle against the wall, took off his back-pack and sat on it. The tea duly arrived and Ellis took his first sip.

"Them carrying frames is working out well?"

It was Bridie who answered.

"Indeed they are Ethan, thanks to you."

"Good! I saw 'em workin' well enough when I was in the Americas."

All the while, Nellie was staring daggers at Tom Miles, daring him to say one thing that could start any kind of argument. He held his peace.

The full twelve hours were granted, but, when the need to leave finally came, it was urgent, with Ellis back to his old self, pacing the sitting column of the Light Company impatiently.

"First up. We've got to move!"

He was correct. Carr had received his orders from Anson, their Brigadier now knowing from Hill that Wellington was withdrawing from the Duero at Rueda, uncovering the bridge over the river at Tordesillas. With a hard march, the French could come down and cut them off, splitting Hill from his Commander-in-Chief. The pace was set and it was a tired column that entered Velayos, only 15 miles beyond Villacastin, where they would be fairly safe, but to get there they were forced to use dreadful mountain tracks and paths. It was there that Lowry-Cole called all his Colonels together to give one blunt message.

"Wellington wants us at Alba de Tormes on the 8th. You'll remember it as the long bridge we crossed the day after fighting Salamanca, that I'm sure. Today is the 5th. It'll be better roads after this, but it's still 80 miles in three days. We push on hard and if it costs us stragglers, then so be it. He wants us within a march of Salamanca on that day. The 8th."

As they filed out, Creet came up to Carr.

"No fireworks nor bonfires for us, this night, then?"

Carr could only turn to him, smile weakly and then shake his head.

"Nor penny for the Guy. We've got too many that look like one of them already!"

Over the next days the pace was set and, with each day, with the rain unrelenting, more and more 'fall-outs' could be seen at the side of the road, but very few wearing the green of the 105th and almost all caught back up with the column during the night. By the time they reached Penaranda, with one day's march ahead of them to Alba de Tormes, strong and tireless men such as Gibney, Hill and Saunders were carrying four muskets each and thus the column held together with minimal loss. The cradles and often the younger children were passed around the Company to be carried in whatever fashion, when the pace began to tell on both the youngsters and the carriers, but no-one complained, each wordlessly accepting the additional burden. However, the burden of their rider, plus poor food and the cold, wet weather proved to be too much for the mounts of Carravoy and Slade. Over the last 15 miles to get to the long Alba de Tormes bridge, they staggered too often from fatigue and want of good food, therefore both gentry Officers found themselves on foot marching to the same rhythm as the men in the ranks, whilst leading by the reins their failing mounts themselves.

oOo

Almost 60 miles to the North, Cornets Carr and Peterson rode side by side as they set their mounts to walk up the slope that would gain another stop at another observation point. It was their Squadron's turn as rearguard.

"Is this better than being in the main column, do you think?"

Douglas Peterson looked across at his less experienced comrade and smiled knowingly.

"Yes and no! In the main column you will find yourself slogging along over churned up roads, whilst we can choose our own path. On the other hand, for them rations are more certain. So, from that you can take your choice. Then again, we don't get shouted at by irate Spaniards who think we've given in and given up."

Carr had no answer and, besides, they had reached the hilltop and Oakwood was already using his telescope to study the view back on what was one of the better weather days of their retreat from Rueda. The two Cornets sat their horses beside him in respectful silence as he panned the instrument across all the distance available. Finally, he closed the instrument shut.

"Nothing!"

The telescope went into his saddle-bag.

"Dismount on the back slope. Allow the men to light fires and cook. We'll be here until three, allowing us enough daylight to catch up with the rest of the Rearguard."

It was Peterson who asked the obvious question.

"Do you think Johnny's missing a trick here?"

Oakwood nodded as he sat back in his saddle and brought up one leg to rub the inside of his thigh. The leather there was wearing thin.

"I do! He's got endless cavalry, that we saw during that business some days back, and he must have enough fresh infantry to make a push and halt our retreat."

He then dismounted.

"But, why should we care? I don't call this a forced march of any shape, more like a gentle amble back, were it not for the weather. I hear that Hill's the one required to do the push on, but only because of what Johnny could perhaps do from up here, where we are, but he's not doing it."

He led his horse back into the leafless trees that topped the hill.

"Douglas you do the first two hours, I'll do the next, then you, Willoughby. Six hours will see us out of here, duty done."

Carr was leading his horse alongside Oakwood.

"But a retreat's still a retreat, isn't it?"

Oakwood threw back his head at so obvious a question.

"Yeees!"

"Not good!"

"Noooo!"

"Were you at Coruna?"

"No I was not, but I'll tell you one thing, young Willoughby, which you may be driving at, even though you don't know it. The men don't like a retreat. It feels as though we're giving best to Johnny, whereas the men fancy their chances against the Frogs at any time, under any circumstances, even outnumbered, and here we are walking away from them. They get angry, despite what their leaders say and they see no reason why they shouldn't get drunk, whenever they can."

He turned to Carr, his face now serious.

"You saw it at Torquemada."

It was now Carr's turn to be worried.

"So, are we going to fall apart?"

Oakwood shook his head.

"No! But we'll lose some, we already have, and be prepared to see some inglorious sights on the road back to wherever. Rumour has it that Wellington wants to offer battle to Souham and El Rey at Salamanca again. Let's hope, but if we have to go back further, having been pushed back yet again even from there, then I expect, shall we say, that discipline will be less than assiduously observed."

"What of ours?"

Oakwood shook his head as though unsure.

"I've faith in Johnson, he knows what the dangers are for us. As long as we have our horses, we'll keep together and get through."

They were now in the trees and Oakwood tethered his horse.

"So, it's the horses that matter. Right, I want this obeyed throughout the Squadron. Break out the fodder nets and each man gathers a net full of grass or whatever's around to feed his horse at the end of each day. Rations will come up for us, but nothing for the horses, of that you can be sure and this wet and cold does for them as much as it does for us."

Thus were spent the following days, Cavalry Anson's Squadrons in rotation watching back for any sign of pursuit, but none was seen and on the 7th November, as part of the Anson Rearguard, the 16th came trotting into the village of Huerta with its many fords over the River Tormes, each rider looking not exactly fit for a Full-Dress Parade, with faded cloaks and breeches and half-full fodder bags bouncing behind each saddle. The 16th counted themselves lucky, they had seen the 11th swing off right to mount a high hill from which to watch for pursuit and the 12th had swung off left to occupy an insignificant village, isolated and lonely on the wide bleak plain. Whilst his men dismounted and tended to their horses, Johnson took Tavender and Oakwood to examine the fords. At Huerta, the River Tormes split into two channels with a significant island between the two, but the main ford was the first they came to and they did not need to see, because they could hear, that the fords were surely impassable. The sight that did greet them where the road entered the water was that of a surly, powerful current, armed with a variety of logs and branches, even domestic and farm items. The level was merely feet below the very edge of the bank and it took only a minute of observation for Johnson to walk back. He spoke more to Oakwood than to Tavender.

"Pointless remaining here, trapped against that. Get the men mounted, I'm moving North, up to the main road, which will take us straight to Salamanca, if ordered."

Then he did turn to Tavender.

"Lucius, send one of yours over to Anson. He's with the 11th up on that hill. Tell him we've moved up to the main road and why. In fact, from where he is, he'll probably be able to see it for himself, but I want it explained."

However, Tavender was not content, to leave such shelter with the rain still falling.

"But we have the 11th and 12th out before us on watch. If any Johnnies arrive, they'll give warning."

"Your faith in our brother Regiments does you credit, Lucius, but I prefer to have our future in our own hands. Things don't always happen as they should. We move!"

Tavender's face darkened, but the two left him there and walked on, to soon part and Oakwood then arrived at his own Squadron, some with saddles already removed. He spoke first to Carr.

"Remount, we're moving. There's no crossing the Tormes here, so we get up to the main chausee to Salamanca where our retreat will be open and down a good road. Within two days we'll be back there anyway. May as well get up to where we best should be, before the roads flood!"

The end of the march to the main trunk road coincided with the arrival of nightfall. Soon after their sparse camp was made, Makepeace and Spivey came into their camp beside it, each with barely an armful of firewood. Baxter raised his head as the small pile was allowed to fall on the ground.

"Is that the best you can do?"

Makepeace had spent the last hour rummaging around in ditches and on tracks and was not in the best of moods.

"We must have gone more'n a mile lookin' for even this! If you think you know a better place to look, feel free!"

Even though him a Sergeant and Makepeace a Corporal, Baxter knew better than to respond in any way and he put his own initial comment down to his own misery and ill temper. The wood did provide enough heat for hot tea, but after that came a night of misery, the rain too persistent to sleep, with no shelter anywhere on the open plain and so all in the 16th sat huddled in their cloaks, amongst their horses for warmth and shelter, listening to the falling rain or the hacking cough which so many of their comrades were now afflicted by. With the following dawn came some measure of relief, orders came for the whole of Anson's Brigade to pull back and hold the Southernmost part of the San Cristobal ridge, where the ridge descended down to the river Tormes. Being closest to their objective, the 16th gained the village of San Morales, just to the North, for themselves and many gave silent thanks to Johnson's wariness and caution, which had given them that advantage. There he allowed a period of rest and food in good billets, whilst the 11th and 12th caught up, then all three proceeded onward over the two mile ride needed to take them up to their own station on the now November bleak and very exposed upland.

As the 16th Light Dragoons rode away from San Morales, so the 105th walked into a tinier village that named itself as Coca de Alba. Carr was back with the Light Company when they arrived and was almost as dismayed as Drake at the very few buildings of any use, but his thoughts soon moved elsewhere, unlike his companion.

"Coca de Alba! I've seen bigger farms, in fact this is what it must be. Someone's farm. Hardly a place to mark the end of what has been a sterling effort of a forced march!"

Carr was unimpressed by his friend's verdict.

"Close your eyes, count to ten and you'll see it no more."

"Five is all that's needed!"

Carr let out a sharp breath in dismissal.

"What concerns me is where we go now. The whole of Hill's Corps halts here. We've arrived, but at a different kind of Alba! Not the one that includes Tormes."

As they arrived, so Hill's army claimed their ground and set up their camps to rest and examine their much abused kit. Typical of Hill, rations arrived, in plentiful quantity and hedges and copses were soon hewn down to provide fuel including more than one dilapidated fence, one condemned by Tom Miles discerning eye and therefore quickly demolished. Jed Deakin took the opportunity to take stock of his command and so first he examined the clothing and footwear of the children and anything he disapproved of was passed to Halfway and Bailey for repair, as best they could. For this they used discarded horses' harness, which they had picked up as 'will be useful', along the march. Most of the children wore cut down army clogs held on with leather straps and Deakin smiled to see his Kevin Mulcahey doing his best to repair the footwear of Nellie's Sally. Inspection and requirements completed, he slumped back against his own pack, grateful for the empty sky and the crackle of the flames in the cooking fires. Then he began to worry. They were not out of the woods yet, either there would be a battle or another retreat back, each containing its own perils. However, it was not long before his soldier's subconscious took over and he fell fast asleep.

As that day ended, Lowry-Cole called his Divisions Brigadiers and Colonels to a barn in the village and he was again brief, but this time not so brutal.

"Our Division is now under Wellington's command and tomorrow we march for Calvarissa de Ariba and to get to it we must cross the river at Alba de Tormes We're back onto the Salamanca battlefield, at the place where the first shots were exchanged, if you remember."

Their own W. Anson felt the need for more detail than he was being given.

"What's the news of Johnny?"

Lowry-Cole looked at him sternly, but he did not fail to notice the other expectant faces alongside Anson.

"Two days away, with a substantial force. And it's Soult now, not Souham, so our guerrilla friends tell us. The chances are that he'll try first to cross the Tormes, either at Alba de Tormes or at Huerta. The Peer wants us all ready and in the right place."

The following day, in obedience to orders and after a leisurely start, they had been on the road to Alba de Tormes for no more than an hour before Drake's eyebrows came together in recognition and he turned to Shakeshaft.

"Wasn't there a cavalry set-to here, day after Salamanca?"

Shakeshaft nodded.

"Yes, there was and if you took the trouble to keep some kind of record or diary yourself, you would have noted it and had no need to enquire. It's Garcia Hernandez."

However, Drake did not hear the last words, pangs of both regret and full realisation had forced themselves into his mind.

"God, I haven't written! The last one was Madrid, I got two away from there!"

Then he calculated the weeks and did not feel so neglectful.

"Last one was on leaving Madrid. That's not so bad, then that Anover place, then this. That's not so bad, but I must try to get one off."

He paced on for half a minute more, before mumbling more to himself than anyone near.

"And Henry, our Colonel. I doubt he got off one from Madrid. I must give him a bit of a nag."

Half an hour more and another thought.

"Give a shout for Lieutenant Bettridge."

The call went out to be immediately answered. He was marching merely yards behind.

"Sir?"

"How are you doing, Lionel? Not too fatigued I hope? Kit holding up and such forth."

Bettridge nodded furiously.

"It's Luttrel, Sir, still Luttrel, but yes Sir, all quite well, thank you. Sergeant Ellis has been giving me a few pointers. You said I should listen to his advice, if you remember, Sir."

Ellis was also marching just behind. Drake turned to look at him and there was no change in the flinty exterior whatsoever, but Drake grinned anyway.

"Well, that's a good thing Luttrel. We seem to be making a good Section Commander out of you, despite everything."

Gruff noises came from Ellis behind and Drake grinned knowingly and did not expand on the 'despite everything', but by now they were descending the streets of Alba de Tormes and soon onto the almost quarter mile of bridge that crossed a wide expanse of the Tormes, this now deep and surging around the many buttresses.

"The last time we were on this thing, we were marching the other way."

It was Shakeshaft who replied.

"After a notable triumph."

"Yes Richard. How things can change and what awaits us in this place we're being sent to, named Calvarissa de Alba? The French had it for most of the day of Salamanca."

The road climbed and then levelled, the landscape now familiar from the march that followed the triumphant day of Salamanca. However, this was not a day of high Summer, as that had been, this was a day of showers that ambushed their column, causing the rapid employment of cloaks and top buttons, either off or open, the mild weather causing many to overheat, until the rain returned once more. Yet the road was good and rapid progress was made, the wagons and carts matching easily the pace of the marching men. One of the carts carried the two spiritual worthies, Sedgwicke and Albright, each broadly content within the shelter of the canvas cover of their wagon and three of the Nicholls family, Sally, Trudie and Violet, with the eldest, Sally, reading religious stories to her sisters, this much to the pleasure of Chaplain Albright. The six miles from the bridge passed easily and, once in Calvarissa de Alba, the 105th were directed left off the main road to their allotted area. With the three sisters back with their mother, Albright directed Sedgwicke to continue on further than the 105th camping ground, to just beyond, and after two hours all of their own affairs were completed, a meal had been eaten, Sedgwicke was busy with the mules' harness and Albright was reading from the Bible. However, both were caused to suddenly look up; a small group was coming towards them along the track out of the village, led by a Priest, him swinging a heavily smoking incense censer, whilst chanting in a shrill tenor voice. Almost two dozen of his flock followed with heads bowed. Albright looked at Sedgwicke.

"Do you think this is what the Catholics called Vespers?"

Sedgwicke nodded.

"What else, Sir, at this time of day? But where?"

"Should we follow, do you think? Perhaps add ourselves to the congregation?"

Sedgwicke vigorously shook his head.

"I think not, Sir. They are very devout where their own Faith is concerned, so I feel that we, as English and somewhat removed, however slight, from the strict doctrine of their Catholic Church, may cause some offence, as heretics, in their eyes.

Albright watched them go on their way, somewhat reluctantly and when they had disappeared over the slight hill, he once again picked up his Bible.

"I would suppose there is a risk and therefore some sense in what you say. However, tomorrow we will follow in their direction and discover their place of worship, if there is one."

The following day with breakfast inside them they walked the path. It was not long before they came to a small building, almost cubic in its dimensions, but clearly of some religious significance. The pair went around to the front, which overlooked the broad valley where the first exchanges of the battle of Salamanca had taken place, and they stood before the surprisingly small door. They were too late to go inside, it was already occupied for a service as the sounds from within informed them, but the pair studied the frontage and Sedgwicke gave his opinion.

"I'd say this was once a Roman temple, converted into a Catholic place of worship. Thereby 'Roman Catholic'!"

The humour in the juxtaposition of the two words was lost on Albright, instead he brought his hands together and beamed with pleasure.

"I would say that you were correct, Private, and are you not uplifted that such a place of heathen ritual has now been brought within the Christian fold to now be used for the praise of our own Lord Jesus?"

Sedgwicke nodded, but the door remained shut and the sounds of the service continued. He turned to his superior Officer.

"Perhaps we should take a bit of a stroll, Sir, and not be present when they emerge. We may cause some unpleasantness."

Albright's answer was positive, this shown by beginning the walk along the cliff edge, but it was not long before they came upon unpleasantness of a much more severe nature than anything concerned with differences between Religious doctrine. Some 50 yards along the cliff edge, between the cliff and the nearest field, on the path, was a row of bodies, over a dozen, obviously French soldiers killed during the exchanges there during the battle of Salamanca. All were from the day of the battle, little more than three months earlier and all still had a blue French tunic and white, but now dirty grey, breeches, but no boots nor hose. Each body had sunk from decomposition and the activity of scavenging animals, but there was still flesh on the skulls and hair, but the eyes were deep sunk. Albright was appalled.

"Why have these not been buried? All ours were. This is utterly unChristian! These men were baptized, of that I can be certain."

Albright knew why.

"Yes Sir, we bury our own, but we gather the French dead, such as this and leave them for the locals. Sometimes they do the right thing, sometimes not, as here. The French are much hated, Sir."

"Hated or not, all were baptised, as I said, and should be buried. Properly! We should do something about it."

He hurried back to the Church, just as the Congregation was emerging and he went straight up to the Priest who was in the act of locking the doors.

"Senor Priest."

The man turned to fix Albright with his fierce brown eyes, set back in a thin, sallow face. He was dressed all in black, a deep black frock coat and the typical Catholic Priest's black, four-cornered hat, but he said nothing in reply and so Albright continued.

"Do you speak any English, Senor?"

The answer was a curt nod, but no change of expression. Albright continued and pointed.

"There are bodies of Christian men, over there. They should be given proper burial."

The answer proved that the Priest's English was fairly good, but he quickly proved that he had no sympathy with this Englishman's sentiments.

"They are French. They come from the Devil. If you want them buried, then you bury them. I have forbidden my people to touch them!"

With that he spun on his heel so fast that his skirts flared outwards, then he hurried away. Sedgwicke, not usual to condemn anyone, could not stop himself from making a comment to the man's receding back.

"Nevertheless they took their boots!"

There was no reaction from the Priest who continued to hurry away. Somewhat stunned, the pair stood for a minute and then set themselves to the path upwards to reach their own encampment.

"We should tell Colonel Carr."

"Yes Sir, we should. At least make an attempt at our Christian duty."

However, at that moment a missive from Colonel Carr was coming to them, as carried by Brevet Major Heaviside, who had no wish to spend long in the company of any Anglican cleric.

"Chaplain Albright. Good morning. I fear that you must break camp. Immediately. Our Division has been ordered up to the fords of Huerta to arrive this day. Please make all speed."

Albright looked at him in some consternation.

"Major, I must appeal to you to allow me some men to bury some French soldiers, who lie unburied, casualties of the recent battle. Just over there."

Heaviside shook his head.

"No time, Chaplain. None at all, we must be away. That thou doest, do quickly. John 13, verse 27."

With that he hurried away and Albright remained standing, looking worried and frustrated, but Sedgwicke was already dismantling their cooking tripod.

After a ride of only an hour from Calvarissa de Alba for the mounted Senior Command of the 4th Division, his Brigadiers, were all sat watching one of Lowry-Cole's ADCs attempt the ford across the Tormes to Huerta. Carr was sat mounted with Creet and O'Hare watching the ADC, him now well into the water, the tension showing on their faces as the Tormes came up to the horse's stomach, then almost to the saddle blanket, but no more and the ADC was across. Creet gave a sigh of relief.

"So that's one male heir we won't have to fish out to save the family estate!"

Creet's gaze followed the soaking horse as he climbed the far bank.

"That was the easy part. It's the next on the far side of this island that matters. Yes or no!"

Carr now chimed in.

"What happens if he doesn't come back?"

His two companions spoke almost in unison.

"Then we can't cross!"

Both laughed and then settled to wait. Thankfully, the ADC reappeared and once more set his horse to the perilous ford he had just negotiated. The animal, memory very clear, was reluctant to enter and required a heavy kick to persuade him to continue forward, but the crossing was begun. Once he was halfway across, Lowry-Cole became impatient and shouted for an answer.

"Well?"

The ADC did not answer immediately, concentrating on controlling his mount, his tail swishing with discontent, but once the water had subsided to his fetlocks, the ADC gave an answer, needing to shout above the sound of the surging waters.

"It's not passable, Sir. I got only a quarter of the way before being almost carried away. Not really possible for cavalry, for infantry absolutely out of the question. Sir."

Lowry-Cole looked first at Skerrett, then Anson, then at another ADC.

"Get that back to Wellington. Huerta fords impassable."

The ADC sped off, just as the force that was the 4th Division infantry arrived and peeled off the road to the fields either side, after a march that had lasted for them for little more than an hour. Lowry-Cole then looked at the one Brigadier who had not been subject to his gaze; Stubbs of the Portuguese.

"Yours to keep watch, Stubbs. I'll give you the Divisional battery. Keep a good watch, night and day."

With that, all returned to whichever campfire they called home, which for such worthies as Officers meant tents. Carr arrived at his just as the final peg was being driven in and he was not in a good mood.

"Out of good billets in that Ariba place to come out here and find that the fords are impassable. Surprise, surprise!"

O'Hare poked the fire to improve its chance of quickly achieving enough heat for some tea.

"True, we could've done without this after that stretch from Madrid, but sure as sure, we'll be back out tomorrow and into somewhere better. We've just got to cope, what say you Joshua?"

Both Carr and O'Hare laughed together expecting the inevitable quote, but Heaviside laughed with them and replied in plain English.

"Make the best and hope for better!"

O'Hare laughed some more.

"So, who said that?"

"My wife!"

O'Hare returned to encouraging the fire.

"No possibility of any counter argument to be made there, then."

Thus, it was a cheerful trio that sat around their fire waiting for the stew to heat and so also it was throughout the 105th, they had had one good rest and the march out to Huerta had barely warmed their backs. The night was not cold, nor wet and with the dawn came the order that they would be marching back, this time to Calvarissa de Abajo, but it would be on the morrow. Carr broke the news to his fellow Officers.

"We are to be a reserve, at this other Calvarissa. This one called Abajo. I hear the 3rd have already arrived, but we have an extra day here, out of the way."

"Is Picton still with the 3rd?"

It was Heaviside who answered.

"As far as I know. He's come back out and replaced Packenham."

Carr nodded.

"A step back for Packenham. Still, he won glory at Salamanca, the way his 3rd hit that leading French Division."

He paused, then continued.

"That seems a long time ago, but this situation's building. Rumour says that it's Soult we're against and he'll probably try Alba de Tormes first."

O'Hare laughed.

"Which keeps him off our backs and wastes his boot leather. He'll never get over that bridge! There are two Brigades down there plus Divisional artillery, so I've heard."

Thus was the day spent in idleness, many Officers walking to the bank of the Tormes to check the fords, but finding no change, the current was impassable, but perhaps less deep.

The march back with an unseasonable sun shining on their backs was shorter, therefore quicker than the march out and on better roads, but when they approached Calvarissa de Abajo, the word was passed back through the ranks that Picton was sat with Lowry-Cole who was reviewing the 4th Division as they marched up to join the 3rd.

"Picton! Picton's up ahead!"

It required nothing more to bring the performance of the 105th up to parade standard, there was no love lost between that Major-General and the 105th Wessex and that included the Officer Corps. Carr grinned as he turned to see all weapons transferred to left shoulders and he heard his Battalion pick up the step and his Sergeants screaming admonishments about where heads, shoulders and backs should be. Sure enough, at the side of the road at the edge of the village on their horses sat Picton, Lowry-Cole with him. Picton was, as usual, all in civilian black, including a black top hat, his inevitable umbrella hanging down from the rear of his saddle. At the sight of the lurid green of the 105th, his face darkened to match that of his hat, but Carr had briefed Heaviside, riding with O'Hare as a pair behind. In time with the beat of the march Heaviside called out.

"One, two, hup!"

The three arms came up together and their heads turned to regard the highly irritated Picton. Then a count of four foot-steps.

"Down!"

Their hands returned to their reins and their faces to the front, for Picton to then endure an exhibition of precision marching, Colour Guard in place and each Captain saluting with his sword, even including St. John Slade, who had made fruitful enquiries of Deakin as to what all the fuss was about. Strangely, even he enjoyed the impressive march past. Certainly Lowry-Cole did, smiling and returning the salute of Carr, O'Hare and Heaviside. Picton just glowered, as though nursing a tooth-ache.

oOo

In Calvarissa de Abajo, the 105th were allocated some buildings, but the Light Company were not allowed to enjoy the breakfast of the next day, the reason why arriving in the form of Heaviside, hurrying up to Drake.

"All the Light Companies of both Divisions are to march up to opposite Aldea Lengua, now, to watch the fords there. Find Major Archer of the 45th. He will be in command."

"Do you know where the road to the ford is, Sir?"

Heaviside pointed back.

"It must be that one there."

Drake led the Light Company on himself, across a field to join the road Heaviside had indicated and he was reassured that it was correct, because several Light Companies were already using it, with more arriving. It was not long before they found themselves waiting to ford the Tormes themselves, Drake immediately very concerned, remembering the state of the river at Huerta. However, the river had subsided somewhat, enough to cross, and at Aldea Lengua the riverbed was broad and the water therefore more shallow. Nevertheless, he could see the men of the Light Company in front of them manfully wading onwards, with the water up to their ribs. The cold was a shock and he heard his own men gasp, but he forced himself onwards and soon, but not soon enough, the water became more shallow. Once over, he looked for Major Archer and almost immediately identified him by the number of Captains walking up to him and saluting. Once he was certain that his Company were assembled, he did the same.

"Captain Drake, Sir. 105th."

Archer took a brief look at his plan.

"Right, Drake. I want yours out with the Rifles and Cacadores, making a strong picket. Pack's Portuguese were already here and they, with the rest of the Lights, will remain in the village itself. I'll be out with you. Get yourselves out there now. Reports state that the French are building on this side of the river and so I expect contact. We have cavalry up on San Cristobal ridge over to our left, but I expect no support from them."

"Beg your pardon, Sir, but what matters most if the Johnnies do show up. Holding the village, or holding the ford?"

"The ford. We contest the village and hold it if we can. It'll be a nuisance to Soult us remaining in here, but, in extremis, we hold the ford."

"Sir!"

Drake came back to his Company and gave the order himself to form column and march on. Not far beyond the village he found two Companies of Rifles, one commanded by their own Rifles Captain Tom Bairns of Anson's Brigade, and also two Companies of Cacadores. The ground was open for miles beyond the village and the picket was formed atop a slight rise that gave a panoramic view. Drake went straight up to Bairns.

"What does Archer want? Do you know?"

"A line, semi-circling the village. Now then, your red coats can be seen for miles, so what say you get yourselves into the smallholdings just upstream of the village? There's both cover and shelter. No one's there yet, so you may as well take it."

Drake smiled and nodded vigorously.

"No time to lose!"

He called out to Ellis and led his Company at the trot around to the outskirts of the village, where there were indeed many hedgerows, stone walls, stores and small byres. They had been followed by a Cacadores Company and both settled into their positions, many taking the chance to light fires, all easily out of sight behind the walls and buildings. Nevertheless, Miles was less than content, even as his breeches and socks steamed from the heat of their fire. He held out his Baker Rifle, the stock on the soil.

"Do you want to know why we be yer? Way out front?"

Davey was holding up his own socks to the flames.

"No really, but you're going to tell me."

"We be yer, because we've been given this fancy bundook, same as our Rifles, which means we operates, same as our Rifles, way out the front, where all be very chancey."

At that moment, Pike was reversing out of a chicken hutch, but he had heard all and he held out six fresh eggs.

"We wouldn't have got these!"

Davey accepted his pair and cracked them open to pour each raw into his mouth, then he spoke, seriously.

"I hear what you says about our Baker, Tom, but 'tis a sharp weapon as've kept the Frogs back away from us many a time before now. I'll take that smooth along with the rough!"

Miles was swallowing his own eggs, when Ellis appeared, his face serious, his body crouching.

"Stand to, we've got some trade."

He joined them as they took position behind their bank and its surmounting hedge, but Davey was ignoring the view for the moment, now studying their hedge, it thick and concealing atop the bank.

"Whoever laid this hedge knew what he was about. He should come to Gloucester, we've competitions for such as ...."

Ellis brutally interrupted.

"Sod your competitions! That's Frogs only part way off, get up and take post."

Davey needed to do no more than to ease the barrel of his weapon through a gap in the almost horizontal branches and peer through a gap above that. His eyesight was above perfect and he used Miles' standard term.

"Tassel swinging bastards!"

At that moment, Drake arrived, with Lieutenant Bettridge.

"Now, Lionel. Those out there are Voltiguers, skirmishers like us. Most of them have a tassel alongside their shako. Often they come with sharpshooters called Tirailleurs. They have red shoulder tabs and collars and have a more accurate musket, not as good as our Baker, but better than the standard French Charleville. Definitely better than our Brown Bess."

He handed Bettridge his telescope.

"Here Lionel, take a look!"

Bettridge took the telescope and pulled open the sections.

"It's Luttrel, Sir."

"Of course! Now, take a look."

Bettridge knelt on the bank and used the telescope to see a thick screen of Frenchmen advancing cautiously from 300 yards and the distinctive yellow tassel could indeed be seen. He stood back up.

"Yes Sir. Voltiguers, as you say."

"Right. The idea is to keep them back and not allow them to mount a rush. So, when should we open fire, do you think?"

"At maximum accurate range, Sir!"

Drake grinned and looked at Ellis.

"Have you been imparting your knowledge, Sergeant?"

Ellis gritted his teeth, highly impatient that an occasion as serious as this, when a whole Battalion of Voltiguers was advancing towards them, was now being used as a tutorial for the novice Bettridge,.

"Yes Sir, but what are your orders, Sir?"

"Why, as your Section Lieutenant has stated, Sergeant."

"Yes Sir. Best men on the Officers, Sir?"

"Of course. Now, Lieutenant, you have command."

Ellis let out a deep breath, still impatient, then he looked at Bettridge.

"Sir, your best marksmen here are Davey, Miles and Saunders.

"Can't they identify Officers for themselves?"

"They can, Sir."

Now doubly impatient, Ellis inclined his head in the direction of the French and Miles and Saunders joined Davey in a firing position. He was the best marksman of the three, having carefully loaded his Baker and he fired first, at just under 200 yards. His target doubled almost in two, as though he had been kicked by a horse, dropping his sword, and then folding down to the tilled earth, his shako now covering his face. Within seconds, Miles and Saunders fired and also found their targets, but the Voltiguers still came on. At 150 yards, Drake gave the order.

"Fire!"

80 Bakers barked out and above 50 Frenchmen toppled to the ground. Their surviving comrades immediately opened fire and French musket balls slapped into the bank and the hedge branches, whilst others buzzed overhead. Faced with such potent opposition, the Voltiguers went down into cover, in their own hedgerows and ditches and a sporadic exchange of fire began. Conflict was now general across the whole of the picket screen around the village and the 105th had some support from across the river from Redcoats sent along the bank. The exchange continued for almost half an hour, the 105th sending careful shots into the Voltiguer positions whilst their own casualties were merely two, both wounds. Then Bettridge arrived at Saunders' position.

"Captain Drake says we are to pull back."

Saunders was in the middle of reloading.

"Any reason, Sir?"

"The French are sending heavy columns into our centre. Three, in fact. One will affect us, so we may be cut off if we do not retire now."

Saunders completed his reload and stood, to a half crouch.

"Very good Sir, but if we fall back only to those buildings behind, we can get a few more as they struggle through this hedge. We'll still be close to the road, Sir."

"Yes Saunders. Very good. We fall back as you say."

All around had heard and they sent a last shot out through the hedge and ran back across the plots of vines and vegetables, Saunders shouting Drake's orders across to Shakeshaft's Section, then they were into the first buildings of the village. Once there, all set themselves to await the French and it was not long before Saunders looked again at Bettridge.

"Independent fire as they come through the hedge, Sir?"

Unsure as to the correct answer, nevertheless, what Saunders had said made sense.

"Yes, Saunders, as you say."

Zeke Saunders took a deep breath to shout.

"Independent!"

The first Voltiguers were struggling through the compact hedge and the first were soon hit by the carefully aimed shots as also were those who followed. When twenty or more lay dead or wounded at the hedge, no more came through, instead those remaining returned fire. At that point Drake arrived.

"Well done men! Well done all! Now back to the main road."

They ran back further, to a road that was already busy with retreating men of all types, but there was no sign of Archer and so Drake called out to his men.

"Get reloaded. We'll hold here until we know better."

That knowledge was not long in coming when a Company of Cacadores ran back to them, down the main road that led to the river. The most senior that Drake could see was a Sergeant and so he stopped him.

"French?"

"Sim, Senor. Many. All to go, Senor. Over river."

The Cacadores ran on and past, so Drake found Ellis.

"We're being thrown out of this village, which means everyone has to get back over that ford. I'm taking us back to man the far bank. The last to come back and into the water will need whatever cover we can give. It could be Bairns' men."

Ellis gave no reply, but ran off to shout for everyone to get onto their feet and follow him down to the ford. Drake looked back up the road to see green-jacketed Rifles now making an orderly retreat back down towards him. Seeing that, he ran off and was soon in the water with the last of his Company, the nearest man being Bettridge, so then they waded together through the deepest area of the ford.

"Thought I'd better wait and see you back over, Sir."

Drake clapped him on the shoulder.

"Good of you, Lionel!"

"It's Luttrel, Sir."

"Of course. Now position your men to cover this ford. The Rifles will be back shortly and will need our support when they are in the water and Johnny arrives on the bank. Without us covering them, they won't have a chance."

On hands and knees, they climbed the now wet and slippery bank and then turned left, Cacadores were manning the immediate right. What Drake took to be Packs' Portuguese Brigade were assembled back towards the main road, but in close support if needed. His own 105th Light Company, as ordered by Ellis and Shakeshaft, were already positioned, their Baker Rifles dry and loaded but water running down from everywhere from their soaked clothing. Bettridge noticed that the Company were in three ranks, but did not ask why and he had no time, because the last of their force, the Rifles, were now entering the water. Drake took full command.

"Make ready!"

All Bakers came to the vertical and by now the final members of the Rifles were in the water and struggling to cross at their best speed. In less than a minute French Voltiguers arrived, in clear view, and Drake did not give these any time to set themselves.

"Front rank, present. Fire!"

The front rank fired and many of the newly arrived French were downed, then Drake ordered the second rank to fire, then the third and then back to the first. Continuous fire was sent across the river, also from the Cacadores downstream, giving the Riflemen the protection they needed, many still helpless in the water and struggling over. However, only a few were even wounded and only two green clad bodies were now floating on down the Tormes. Then, to Drake's utter amazement, a French column arrived and descended straight into the ford, a whole Battalion, on what seemed to be a Company frontage. Pack's Portuguese had been ordered back up to the river and, now positioned along the Allied bank, they all immediately opened fire, frantically reloading to prevent the enemy crossing.

Some Voltiguers manned the far bank to give supporting fire to their assaulting column, but it was nothing like as effective as what was coming from the opposite bank. The head of the column was being continuously swept away and they struggled barely to the middle of the ford, before the column broke and all turned to wade as best they could back to safety, some throwing away their muskets. The contest had now become a slaughter, the Allies pouring fire into the backs of the struggling French, the water of the Tormes now running red and many blue coated bodies were now floating away in the strong current, some, badly wounded, vainly attempting to keep their faces above the water. Joe Pike was amongst the first to pass a judgement on what he saw and he did not mince his words, turning to Drake, just behind him.

"Sir! This is murder!"

The word tipped Drake away from his own determination to disable as many in the blue uniformed enemy as possible and the realisation hit him that he was looking only at French backs, all doing their best to escape. Pike was correct.

"Cease fire! Cease fire!"

His men quickly stopped, but not so the Cacadores nor Pack's men further along the bank, they continued at their best rate, killing all the French they could, until a Senior Officer, perhaps Archer himself, ordered them to stop. With that, within a very short space of time, the only sound to be heard was the rushing waters carrying away the dead and the breeze through the leaves above carrying away the smoke of the combat. Ellis turned around at the sound of Bettridge vomiting behind a tree, the sight still vivid in the youngster's mind of bullets jerking the blue cloth covering the backs of helpless French soldiers, for them to pitch forward into the chill waters. Ellis went over and placed his hand on his back and he pulled out his own small flask of brandy.

"Ease up, Sir. 'Tis the game we're in. I can't see the Frogs holding off like we did, we can say that for ourselves, at least. Sometimes this is a rough old game, Sir. The like happens. Here, take a pull on this."

Bettridge took the small flask and then a swallow from its contents, to cough twice and then stand upright, but breathing heavily. Ellis retrieved his flask, nodded in his Officer's direction and then walked off. There was no other sound, the French had broken off the contest, taking their wounded with them. Within a minute the river and the breeze had carried away all signs of combat and many in the Allied force simply stood staring at what was now a peaceful scene, then Archer arrived and found Drake.

"Pull back! We've orders to return to Calvarissa, back to Division."

Quickly away they soon did, ignoring the parting shots from Voltiguers who had now returned to claim the river bank.

oOo

Johnson had bid them accompany him and they had ridden forward from their position on the ridge to obtain a useful, telescope view of Aldea Lengua from where they watched the conflict just finished. His companions were Oakwood, Carr and Peterson, called upon to join him as soon as Johnson heard the sounds coming from the village merely half a mile to their front.

"We'd best take a look."

From their ridge they saw almost the whole saga, three French Brigades, both Voltiguers and Line advancing inexorably towards the thinly held Allied positions around the village, then the Allies falling back followed by the French, who then entered the village to fully occupy it as their own. Next, they saw the Allied defending force retreating quickly back to Calvarissa de Abajo to the South of the river. Finally, and much more alarming, they saw coming from the East at least three Brigades of French cavalry, cantering as though intent on using the ford.

"We've given up the Aldea ford. There must be some retreat on. The Frogs are piling in cavalry after their infantry. Best get back to Anson."

Once back on the main ridge, a messenger was sent to Brigade Headquarters and one soon returned, with orders for the whole of Anson's Brigade, but these came from Stapleton Cotton himself. Johnson himself carried the word to his four Squadrons.

"We're abandoning this ridge and everything is to cross at the next ford down from Aldea, that being at Cabrerizos. We've used it before, but get yours into column, at your best speed."

It was a long cavalry column that descended the end of the ridge to enter Cabrerizos, the cavalcade anxiously observed by worried local citizens, but no words nor questions were exchanged. Anson's was the first Brigade into the fords and crossed without too much difficulty, the ford beds had been heightened with stone between the two islands in the river. Once over, they were met by an ADC who rode up to Anson, the result of which exchange caused them to turn left, upstream, much to the dismay of all three Regiments. As Johnson rode up to the head of his column, Oakwood took the opportunity.

"What's this all about? Going back up river?"

Johnson barely slowed his horse.

"We're to watch the Aldea ford. The one we just saw abandoned and, with Johnny cavalry riding to use it, we have to keep it covered."

"For how long?"

Johnson waved both hands in the air to demonstrate his own ignorance and perhaps those of his superiors, and he rode on. It took merely minutes to arrive where ordered and much to their relief within the 16th, it was a Squadron of the 12th who were ordered to dismount and take their carbines into the trees at the ford to watch and wait. The rest of Anson's Brigade also did exactly that, to wait, but further back. They were all well rested and fed from their spell on the ridge and so fires were lit and they contentedly brewed tea and occupied themselves with kit and their horses. There was even some November sunshine, not unusual in Spain. Thoughts were not so languid with Anson, stood in a group with Johnson, Piers of the 11th and Stockton of the 12th.

"The 3rd and 4th Divisions are back at Abajo, a mile and some. Should Johnny try to come over, we must give ample warning and hold off any cavalry for as long as possible."

Stockton was not impressed.

"We saw three Brigades of cavalry arrive opposite here earlier today and we are only one."

Anson was not impressed either, but in this case with Stockton.

"You think I don't know this is a bad business? If we keep our wits about us, we'll get out of it. Rumour is Wellington's pulling back to Salamanca and will offer battle there. Our standing here should not be too long."

It was soon nightime and the Troopers of Anson's Brigade were lulled into a long sleep by the sound of the rushing Tormes through the ford of Aldea Lengua. However, an hour before dawn, Baxter came to shake Cornet Carr awake. Only when he could see open eyes looking back up at him, did he speak.

"Sir, it's our turn to take a watch."

Carr rubbed his face and then his hair, before pulling on his shako."

"No chance for a shave, then?"

Baxter laughed at the irony.

"No shaving for anyone for some time, Sir, is my guess."

Carr sat up, reached for his boots and then pulled them, disappointed to find them still damp.

"Very good, Sergeant. Is my horse saddled?"

"She is, Sir. The picket point is a mite upstream. There's a better view, around the village over, sort of."

Carr walked to his horse, she being held by Makepeace, him in the company of Spivey and Nunney. He mounted and they all walked their horses to the picket point to there relieve those of the 12th sat their horses waiting. Carr passed their Officer now going in the opposite direction.

"Anything?"

"Just a few French songs from some way off."

"Perhaps they're more cheerful than us!"

"They've reason to be!"

With that, Carr's group sat their horses to await the full dawn. They were well above the ford, so where they were, the river ran silent and it was Nunney who spoke first.

"I think I can hear something, Sir."

Carr turned to him, concerned.

"Can you say what it is?"

"Well, if I had to bet, I'd say it was marching men, Sir."

Carr thought for a few seconds.

"Who's at the ford? Do you know?"

"Ned Shelby, Sir. Captain Tavender's Squadron."

"Spivey. Get back to there and tell him to be fully on his guard. Then tell Colonel Johnson that you've heard marching men."

As Spivey rode off and Baxter nodded his approval of Carr's response, Carr pulled out his telescope to spend a frustrating 20 minutes waiting for the light of a dull dawn to improve. He turned to Spivey.

"I can hear something, now. Can you, still?"

Spivey nodded.

"Sir! Clear now."

Carr tried his telescope again and now there was enough light to see what must be a whole French Division entering the village, with two more following over the slight rise. He closed the telescope.

"That's it! Seen enough. They're coming at the ford, a whole Corps. We go back to Abajo."

The journey was made at the canter, for Carr to speed himself on to enter Anson's Headquarters and find Lowry-Cole of the 4th Division there with him. Carr sprang to the attention and saluted.

"Sir. There's a heavy infantry column marching into Aldea Lengua. I've just come from there."

It was Lowry-Cole who spoke.

"Any cavalry?"

"None I could see, Sir, but there's some already in there, Sir. We saw them go in yesterday."

Lowry-Cole turned to Anson.

"So, he's coming forward. Picton and myself can hold here, but what about Huerta? He could also be coming over there, in addition to what he's sent across those two fords upstream of Alba de Tormes. That's the threat. Two whole Corps have been seen coming over those and now there's a third making to cross here.

The two stared at each other, realisation dawning on Anson.

"Cavalry job, Sir?"

"Yes, 'fraid so. Go and take a look, but take no risks. Whatever's coming over here, we can hold back, but go and take a look at Huerta. Come back to here when you know, but if we're gone, make for Calvarissa de Ariba. That's practically on the old Salamanca battlefield. The Peer is hoping to make a stand there, but the news about two whole Corps crossing upstream of Alba de Tormes has now made that less likely, but that's where the army will be found."

Anson rose, somewhat resignedly, Carr noticed, to gather his pelisse, sword and shako.

"Lead on, Cornet. We've some riding to do today!"

The one consolation was that their own camp was astride the Huerta road, just North of Calvarissa de Abajo and, from there, the journey was made at a canter. Once within half a mile of the fords, Anson halted his Brigade and then rode forward with his Colonels and two Captains from the 12th, these required for possible messages. Using the best vantage point which that side of the Tormes offered, Anson rose in his stirrups, the better to gain advantage for his telescope, but he used it for less than a minute.

"Nothing!"

He pushed the sections shut and then looked at each of his Colonels.

"We get back, now. This far forward we could be cut off by those trying to get over at Lengua. I feel as though my head's inside a lion's mouth. We get back, there's no sign of any Crapaud over this ford, anywhere, neither in the village nor beyond."

The 'about turn' was made in very quick time and a lively canter took them back to Calvarissa de Abajo. The road from the ford was reassuringly deserted and the last of the 3rd and 4th Divisions' column could still be seen marching away in the distance. Oakwood and Carr were looking across the fields towards the Aldea Lengua ford in the distance, but Carr saw them first.

"French! Coming our way up from the ford."

Oakwood took out his telescope and used it for half a minute.

"Not cavalry, infantry, but we'll need to move."

His wish was immediately answered, Anson had also seen them and the column began to move, but not to follow the 3rd and 4th Divisions, instead Anson tended left, South, off the road and over the flat plain. Again, at a lively canter, they covered the distance and Anson's instinct had been true. Soon, they could see the sister Calvarissa, that called Ariba, and beyond that the very distinctive twin Arapiles hills. Once in the village, Anson was called to Stapleton-Cotton and so the order came to dismount, when all did their best to give their horses water, either from the many troughs or a nearby large pond. Whilst stood with their horses at the latter, Carr and Peterson pondered their fate, the conversation begun by Peterson.

"We're in trouble!"

Carr looked over from examining his horse's neck.

"How so?"

"He's been caught with his trousers down. Horribly outflanked upstream of Alba de Tormes where the Frogs've got two thirds of their army over the Tormes and we've just allowed the other third over at Aldea Lengua. The only good thing is that we're not too spread out, but we've lost Salamanca, unless we can win another battle here."

"That gloomy?"

"I'm afraid so."

Anson's Brigade were allowed a night in Calvarissa de Ariba, but, post breakfast, all heard the bugle notes ordering mount and the column soon reformed to ride out of Calvarissa on a good track that led to Los Arapiles, and thus the two huge hills grew in size the further they rode on. The track led them along the foot of the Lesser Arapiles, the area still littered, but not overly so, with the detritus of the battle, mostly items of uniform. Once in the village itself, anxious locals emerged from their houses, worried looks on their faces at the obvious return of the two mighty warring armies that had tracked and fought their way across their part of Spain for the past year. However, there was no stopping. Anson led his men onto the ridge that had been the scene of the first and most vital engagement of the battle and there, on its summit, they came to the most gruesome evidence so far of a major battle having taken place there. The ridge was too high for cultivation and in too many places too dry and rocky for grazing and so the more they progressed to the area that had seen the initial clash and the fiercest fighting, the more the evidence grew that the French dead had been left to the elements and scavenging animals. It was worse where the 3rd Division had first clashed with the leading French Division and on that hill, above the village of Miranda de Azan, was where the bones and skulls were most thick on the ground, many still shrouded in the remnants of French uniforms, many with flesh still attached, not yet gnawed off by such as rats and foxes. Most disturbing were the horses' hooves playing football with the numerous skulls. At the head of his Troop, Carr rode his horse, shaking his head.

"This is shocking!"

It was only Baxter who heard and he voiced his own opinion.

"I've not seen the like, Sir, and that's the truth."

At that moment, Oakwood turned his horse back to accompany Carr.

"We're to hold this ridge. Johnny Frog, if he comes, will come up from the South. We hold here to keep the way open to the Ciudad road. It's a retreat, probably back to there, but for the moment we hold here. And camp."

Carr turned rapidly towards him, his whole body pivoting in the saddle.

"Camp? Here? It's the stuff of nightmares!"

"Then close your eyes and occupy your mind with something pleasant. There must have been some nice girl you were sweet on, back home. If Johnny comes, he must see this hill occupied. Grit your teeth and put up with it. You think I like it?"

There was a definite edge to Oakwood's voice and so Carr said no more, instead he dismounted when they came to a stop and he found Peterson, who, wordlessly, helped to clear a space where they could at least lie down.

oOo

As G. Anson's cavalry were making their ghoulish way along the ridge to Miranda de Azan, the 4th Division, with the 3rd following, were themselves entering Calvarissa de Ariba, after a rapid march from Abajo starting at dawn, but the 3rd marched on, towards the two great hills. The 4th were ordered to halt and fall out off the road to allow the 3rd to pass on and O'Hare took one look as he dismounted.

"Well, that's Picton gone. One blessing, at least!"

With all in his Brigade now taking their ease, Anson himself rode up to Carr, O'Hare and Heaviside and the three rose to their feet.

"Carr! We the 4th are Wellington's far left and we are the centre Brigade, Skerrett on our left, Stubbs on our right. Yours hold the village."

"What are the prospects, Sir?"

"A battle if Johnny wants it. Himself rode out with the whole of the 2nd Division to try and hold the two Corps that came across the Tormes upstream of Alba, but there were too many. So, he's drawn us up here, with a cavalry screen way far out to give warning. We've got a good position right around from here to the Ciudad road, including both of those damn great hills. We're here for some days, so make the most of it. If there's no battle, we're back to Ciudad. Stores in Salamanca are already being destroyed, those that we cannot load onto carts, that is. Baggage to go back now and the Followers tomorrow. If there's to be a battle it will be the day after, at the earliest."

With that he rode on and Carr looked at his two companions, the implications of what had just been said still circling in his head, but he pulled himself back to the immediate.

"Right! I'll place the Companies. Padraigh, if you could warn the Followers and you, Joshua, please organise a baggage convoy. Anything that's a cart and can carry provisions. Followers walk."

The first to get their orders were Drake's Light Company and they were not unwelcome, as Carr pointed down the slope from the village.

"Nat! Get yours into those buildings on the outskirts. Charles' Grenadiers will be on your left. That barn is your link with them. You'll be in it."

The idea of occupying good buildings altogether exceeded expectations and Drake's face showed it.

"Those down over there, Henry? Fine, yes, consider it done."

"If the Frogs look likely to push you out, you know what to do?"

Drake grinned and nodded.

"Oh yes indeed!"

The conversation with Charles Carravoy was nothing like so understanding nor convivial, but Carr was now two ranks above Captain Carravoy and so there could be no argument regarding his orders.

"Charles! I want yours extending the line of the Light Company."

He raised his arm to point.

"From that barn occupied by Drake, over to what looks like a cowshed. That substantial farm will be in your centre."

However, Carravoy could not allow all to pass without some comment.

"Out before the main line?"

"Yes Charles, and if they come, they do not gain those buildings without a cost. And when you quit them, if you have to, you set them alight, otherwise Johnny will turn them into a very useful gunline that will do us much harm. That must be denied. Clear?"

There was no answer.

"Charles! Clear?"

First came a nod, then the answer.

"Yes. Clear."

Carr strode back into the village, on the way answering with both his hand and a grin, the salute from Lieutenant Simon Ameshurst. Heaviside was the next to achieve his mission, quickly reaching the 105th's handful of carts and wagons and issuing orders for them to be loaded and move further up the road to Salamanca. The word 'cart' of course included that of the 'High Church' Reverend Albright and any contact with him would be highly distasteful, but Heaviside knew his duty and he found their cart deserted, but the pair could be seen walking back from the Church that was once a Roman Temple. It was Albright who spoke first and from a distance, his voice cheery and welcoming.

"Ah, Major Heaviside. Good day to you and God's Blessing also!"

Heaviside clenched his jaw, then released it to reply.

"Good day to you Chaplain. I fear I come with bad news. This day, you are to take yourselves back to Salamanca, preparatory for a general retreat. To go back this day."

Albright leaned forward, his hands together with his face both puzzled and anxious at the same time.

"A general retreat? Surely our force of arms is sufficient to preclude so drastic a measure, Major?"

"It is more than likely, I fear. Therefore, we must make all sensible dispositions to prevent any possible harmful, even disastrous, consequences."

Albright drew himself back, his face now simply worried, his eyes now anxiously regarding the soil beneath, then he looked up again at Heaviside.

"But will you not join us both in prayer, Major, to beseech the Good Lord that our efforts will nevertheless prevail?"

Sedgwicke was aghast at Albright's suggestion, being well aware of Heaviside's deeply held non-Conformist convictions and he felt deeply embarrassed himself at such a suggestion.

"Yes Sir, but I'm sure the Major has very important business to attend to, Sir. We could say a prayer together, Sir, to that effect, with the sunset. Back in the Church, Sir."

The answer from Heaviside stunned Sedgwicke.

"We will pray together. Here."

Albright grinned mightily and indicated with his hand the track he had just used.

"There is a well-appointed Place of Worship just down over the hill."

Albright's crass answer, to a man with beliefs such as Heaviside's, again set Sedgwicke writhing inwardly with embarrassment. However, Heaviside was already kneeling.

"We can pray here, kneeling together on God's good earth."

Somewhat bemused, Albright and Sedgwicke joined him and, to the latter's relief, Albright made no effort to lead the Prayer, as Heaviside placed his hand atop the cartwheel and leant his forehead against his forearm.

"Oh Lord, our guide and wellspring of courage and fortitude, support us with your strength over the days to come, sustain us with thy mighty hand. Let thy strength be our own, that we may be held up through the hardships and endure the trials to come, but above all, that we do thy will and live in thy glorious Light. Amen."

The repeat came from both and Albright crossed himself, but Heaviside had already risen to his feet.

"Now, Chaplain, you must make all preparations. These are anxious times. I can do all things through him who strengthens me. Philippians 4, verse 13."

With that he turned and departed, leaving the pair more than somewhat stunned by the conviction and authority with which Heaviside had led their brief devotions. Of the two, Albright looked to be the most dazed by what had happened and so Sedgwicke abandoned him to his own recovery and began to pack their cart.

Meanwhile, on his rounds amongst the Followers, O'Hare had arrived at the campfire of Bridie and Nellie and with his appearance both had sprung to their feet and curtsied, Bridie finding the right words.

"Good day to you now, Major O'Hare, your Honour, Sir. 'Tis pleased that we are that you've taken the trouble to come amongst us and tell us both of what we're needin' to know. There's all sorts as are flying about."

O'Hare bowed in the direction of both.

"You are all well, yes? Yourselves, Eirin and Consuela? What about the children? All well?"

Bridie continued to answer.

"They are all well, your Honour and thank you for asking."

"Yes, I do have some news for you. May I sit?"

There was consternation from the pair at the idea of their Senior Major wanting to sit amongst them and share their fire and so Nellie hurriedly found a blanket with which to cover the nearest box that O'Hare could use. That done, O'Hare sat and the women looked at him anxiously, this time Nellie asking her question.

"You've bad news, your Honour, have you not?"

O'Hare shook his head.

"Not necessarily, Mrs. Nicholls, but both possibilities are not good. There will either be a major battle or a retreat. A retreat back to Ciudad Rodrigo, which will be some way and not in good weather."

Bridie and Nellie looked at each other, their thoughts similar, but not spoken. Battles put their men in danger, retreats not so much, but it meant hardship for themselves and their children. Bridie turned first to him.

"Which, do you think, Sir?"

"I cannot tell, Mrs. Mulcahey, but all Followers must begin the journey back. It's for the best, just in case. You must leave tomorrow, but it's best that you get yourselves someways up the road to Salamanca before this nightfall, after our evening meal. And during tomorrow, it's best that you get yourselves some way along the road that leads to Ciudad. So, you must all make a start back to Salamanca, with the last of today's light."

"Will it be as bad as that for Coruna, do you think?"

O'Hare smiled and shook his head.

"I would say not. We are not so far North, so I do not expect snow, and there is plenty of food in Salamanca which will come with us on our retreat. It may be November, but I hope for a better journey than then."

He smiled, hoping that his words had gone some way to allay their fears, then he continued.

"If you are at Salamanca for the early morning, I feel certain that you will be issued with substantial rations. What we cannot take with us is being destroyed, so I'm sure our Commissary would prefer to give it to you than to burn it or tip it into the river."

His face became thoughtful.

"On the other hand, there may be a battle, which we're sure to win, and you'll only need to march back!"

Bridie and Nellie both turned to each other and nodded in the other's direction, then Nellie turned and grinned.

"Well, truth to tell, we do feel better for those kind words, Major O'Hare, Sir. So, now, will you not take a drop of tea with us, Sir, and perhaps a dough-cake that Bridie's just baked?"

O'Hare looked at each in turn and grinned himself.

"Mrs. Nicholls, Mrs. Mulcahy, it would be an honour."

The tea and cake rapidly appeared and for the next half-hour there was no other conversation than reminiscences of younger days in Ireland, which went some way, at least, to banish into the background the worries of all three. All three soon adopted their own Gaelic Mother Tongue for the ensuing conversation.

That evening all Followers said their farewells to their men as they returned in ones and twos from the front line to receive their evening meal, then they began the five mile walk to cross the Tormes using the city's main Roman bridge and spend the remaining hours of the night under the walls of the Cathedral. The following dawn found them waiting on the road out of Salamanca, this crowded with the Followers of all the Allied Regiments that were within walkable distance. Also, as the light grew, there waiting with them were the carts of the Commissariat, liberally doling out barrels of salt meat, cuts of fresh meat, and sacks of flour and biscuit. Sedgwicke and Albright had managed to find their own 105th Followers and it was Sedgwicke himself, now with a veteran's experience, who began to apply some forethought, remembering the hideous trials of the Coruna retreat.

"Sir, we should avail ourselves of the food which is being issued. As much as we dare, without overloading the cart."

Albright looked puzzled, but not unresponsive.

"Do you really think so, Private? Do you think it wise?"

"I do, Sir. I think it very wise."

"Then do so."

So, with the help of Bridie, Nellie and Consuela, extra was begged for and readily given, especially to such beguiling women as

Bridie and Consuela, the result being that three barrels each of salt pork and salt beef were loaded into the cart, along with five sacks of flour and six of biscuit. Sedgwicke studied Albright's small, but heavy chest, full of religious books and texts, memories of the retreat to Coruna suddenly clear and fresh. When Albright was elsewhere, he dragged it out of the back of the cart and then hauled it down the bank of the Tormes. In its place he loaded two more barrels of salt pork, topped with a sack of biscuit.

As the convoy moved off, the younger children, these being Eirin's Jedediah, supervised by Nellie's Violet, made themselves comfortable on the flour sacks, whilst the remainder of their families walked behind, at this point in time Eirin herself now carrying baby Ellen in the back cradle. The Commissariat convoy had departed first, after much food had been simply dumped into the Tormes and it was not so far ahead. Nellie and Bridie were, as usual walking alongside the cart on Sedgwicke's side and, after but a few miles, Nellie pointed off to the right, where the Commissariat vehicles could now be seen, no longer on the main Ciudad road but taking one that clearly took a different direction to their own.

"Parson! Why do you think, now, that all them wagons with the food, is off on a different road to that of our own? Is there any sense in that?"

Sedgwicke could only stare and wonder at such an oddity, but Albright, now regarding himself as a man with some degree of military knowledge, offered his opinion.

"I would suspect, my good woman, that they are taking that route because of the superior quality of the roads. That does make a difference, you understand."

Nellie crossed her arms and looked less than convinced, even grumpy.

"Well, that may well make sense, your Honour, but we can all hope that their better road takes them not too far from ours. We'll all be needin' some of that food."

Sedgwicke, despite hearing all, still held his peace, but his thoughts asked the question, what could be a better road than the main chausee between Salamanca and Cuidad Rodrigo?

Meanwhile, serious events were taking place in Miranda de Azan, which began with Johnson shouting at all with any authority to get the Regiment mounted and into column. Whilst fitting the bridle and bit to his mare, Carr called over.

"What's afoot?"

Oakwood was by now mounted and impatient.

"Wellington's in the village and has called all of Anson's down off this ridge for a scouting job. I can only assume that he wants to take a look at something. We are the escort and it doesn't pay to keep him waiting."

The waiting was indeed minimised and it was not long before Wellington was at the head of the 11th's column, with that of the 16th and 12th out on either side, by several hundred yards. There was a slight rise out of the village of Miranda de Azan and, once surmounted, they were on high ground covered in scrub and stunted trees. It was Wellington with the 11th who halted first and the 16th and 12th soon followed. The reason was plain, on the far ridge could be seen a continuous column of French Divisions. Oakwood, Carr and Peterson came together and used their telescopes to examine the formations, Oakwood speaking first.

"That's one, or both, of those Corps that got over the Tormes upstream and are now marching to get onto our flank and there's no useful gap for us between any of them, which lost them Salamanca."

Peterson was examining more to the right.

"Covered by what must be a whole Division of cavalry on the slopes below."

Carr, in contrast, had been studying the hills to the left, one feature had seized his attention and through his telescope he identified it.

"There's a French flag on that hill they are marching from."

Oakwood focused his own instrument.

"That's a Tricolour that will be marking redoubts and what-have-you. Johnny's got enough men to both march around our flank and man earthworks."

He closed his telescope carefully.

"You remember Ciudad? We're going to see it again and that's not all that's on our plate. Remember that third lot coming over at Aldea."

Plainly, Wellington had seen enough, because the 11th were wheeling around and so Johnson did the same with the 16th. Soon they were back in Miranda and the orders rang out, whilst Wellington's ADC's and some additional messengers from Anson's Brigade began to ride off in three directions, West, North and East. Now back on the ridge, the 16th began to strap onto their saddles all that they had left behind in their camp and within minutes the three columns of the Brigade began to form. As they parted company to lead their own Troops, Peterson felt moved sufficiently to shout over to Carr.

"Can't say I'm sorry to quit this open graveyard. I'll not forget this, not ever."

Almost immediately they were riding down the backslope of the ridge and, at last, there was no sound of either bones or skulls being kicked or crushed by their horses cantering hooves.

The message was delivered to the 4th Division at Calvarissa de Ariba at the gallop, an ADC of Wellington came thundering in, his horse now exhausted and blown from the four-mile ride. Many turned to see him dismount at Lowry-Cole's Headquarters but what did surprise them was how soon messengers came running out of the building, going in all directions, but one ran over to Carr.

"Colonel. We are to retreat immediately. The French are threatening the Ciudad road. There is not a moment to lose!"

Carr ran off, shouting for Bugle Bates and as soon as men could respond to his urgent notes and gather their belongings, they formed into columns between the buildings of the village. Thus, with men still joining the ranks, the 4th Division began its rapid march up the road into Salamanca. In the Light Company, there was much conjecture concerning what was going on, begun inevitably, by Miles.

"This is all a bit of a rush, b'ain't it? Have the Frogs got near the Officers' wives, or summat?"

Ellis was marching alongside and he was also concerned over the hurry, but wholly in the dark as to why.

"Them's well gone, Private Miles. Gone back with the baggage, nice and safe and all arranged so as not be too hard on their feet, shouldn't wonder."

"So you knows no more'n we?"

"Only what I can work out for myself, that we're in some kind of trouble and we've got to march long and hard to get out of it."

The twin towers of one of the largest Cathedrals in Spain grew larger and clearer, but there was no marching through the city, instead the 4th Division skirted the walls and buildings alongside the Tormes to arrive at the far side of the city, where Wellington himself was seen surrounded by his Staff. However, the 4th Division were not called upon to halt, instead they continued straight on, along the good, straight Ciudad chausee. The roads were occupied with refugees from the city being shepherded aside by mounted Provosts and Deakin and Halfway looked sympathetically at the narrow stream of distraught humanity alongside them, all failing to keep pace with the marching soldiers, all burdened with the few possessions which they could carry, some with no possessions, these carrying children instead, some pushing handcarts, some towing reluctant animals. Halfway, shaking his head as he spoke, felt moved to comment.

"Back in the Summer, these was welcoming us, like we was Christ the Saviour himself."

"We was, back then, Tobe, but 'tis all very different now. The Frogs have brought all their armies together, so I've heard. More'n we can cope with, so back we goes."

As the distance increased, so the refugees dispersed off the road to whatever villages and shelter they could find. The soldiers of the 4th Division envied them, because the rain which had been threatening all day, now came down in torrents, soon creating deep puddles in the road, its once firm soil soon churned into clinging and slippery mud. The column slogged on, the only sound that of the rain on their backpacks and the tarpaulin that many now used, if only the flap at the back of their shakoes. The rain pounded the road, turning ordinary puddles into the hissing ponds, which they could sometimes avoid, but just as often they had no choice but to march through. The cold and the weight of their clinging, wet breeches soon began to tell, but there was no halt. As darkness fell, Miles began to object.

"When do we get a stop? Get a rest?"

As usual it was Ellis who answered.

"You want to stop and try to sleep in this? Better to keep moving. Hope for better."

'Better', when it came, barely justified the description. With the arrival of daylight, after an exhausting night march through unrelenting rain, they at least had a better idea of their surroundings and the rain eased, but did not stop. However, a halt was permitted and all fell out to the side of the road and lit their fires with the dry kindling they always carried, but nothing by way of sustenance arrived. Saunders stood and looked down the road to see it empty, then he sat down.

"No rations!"

Davey looked at him.

"Nothing from our wagons?"

It was Bailey who answered.

"They went yesterday. Ordered away early."

"And we got no issue before we left that Calvarissa place!"

"No time! We had to shake a leg out. And quick."

Corporal Saunders went over to their cooking pot with his own haversack.

"We all puts something in. Everyone!"

Of water to cook there was plenty, but it was a very thin gruel that was divided to sustain them for the coming day's march. That began in the continuing rain and continued on until Midday, which saw another meagre meal prepared from whatever remained in their haversacks. The biggest trial of the day came at the first river, this was swollen and could only be crossed by a ford. The crossing was made in files of four with the men linking arms and with Carr, O'Hare and Heaviside holding their horses in the strong current just upstream of the wading men. When any mounted Officer of the 105th came up they were required to take their turn and prevent any loss. Carr saw the disgruntlement on the faces of Carravoy and Slade but ignored it. He was as wet, hungry and tired as anyone. The light was fading as they crossed another river, mercifully this time by a wide bridge and the rain stopped, but a cold wind sprang up and so all sat in the open fields beyond the river, huddled together around paltry fires that barely provided light in the growing darkness, let alone any heat. Many lay down to achieve whatever shallow sleep they could in the desperately trying conditions.

Carr was sat in their portable canvas shelter, no more than a canvas sheet supported by four poles, sat with O'Hare and Heaviside, drinking coffee, miraculously provided by Sergeant Bryce, and eating army biscuits. Carr looked at O'Hare.

"What have you heard?"

"Who from? The men?"

"Yes."

"Very annoyed, as usual. Why aren't we taking the Frogs on? They've never beat us yet. Why are we doing this just because of a few blue uniforms?"

Carr sighed.

"They said that at Coruna. But now there's no rations, unlike then. Have you heard anything about that, Joshua?"

"Yes, I'm afraid so. The Commisary is far to the North. Presumably the Quartermaster General opted for the route furthest, thereby safest, from the French."

Carr looked at him shocked.

"You got that from whom?"

"One of Lowry-Cole's ADCs. A Member of the Brethren, as am I."

"The QMG being James Gordon?"

"The same."

Carr folded his arms and clenched his jaw, his face livid.

"God rot him, not his first blunder, so I've heard. If we cannot issue rations, especially in this weather, then the army falls apart. From starvation, it's as simple as that!"

O'Hare nodded.

"This we know, Henry. We can only hope that ours hold together. They did before, after Talavera and with Coruna. Nine in ten are veteran soldiers, the 105th matters to them, you know, possibly more than it does to us. Have faith."

Carr remained stern.

"Faith is one thing, leadership is another. I remember what Lacey said on the way back to Coruna. First chance I get, I'll say the same."

It was a sullen army that came together at Noon, forming on the road, this more disagreeable to stand on than the fields they had just quitted, the road now being liquid mud. From the ranks, even from those of the 105th, the question was called out to Officers, "Any rations today, Sir?" The answer was always a shake of their head. The march began, the rain fell and the rumour spread, coming back to the 105th Light Company, via Len Bailey.

"You heard?"

From many places came the one word answer.

"What?"

"About rations. They're on the wrong road. Way up North. They'll not be near us for days."

Miles, unsurprisingly, was the most incensed.

"Days! So what happens? How do we get fed, 'specially in this? How can they expect us to not go off scavengin'? 'Tis that or march 'till you falls over!"

Ellis was close alongside and had heard all.

"You go out maraudin', Miles and you'll be answering to me. There's plenty of lads as'll feel just as bad as you, but they'll stick. We've all marched hungry before and got through, this b'ain't so very different."

Miles was in no way subdued.

"In this? I'd rather have cold than this!"

He shook some water out of the right sleeve of his greatcoat.

"At least at Coruna they got some grub back, even when we was in the Rearguard. This time some fool of an Officer've made off with all the rations and we've got not a biscuit to keep us goin'. There's got to be something from somewer'. Even you knows that!"

Saunders was marching just behind.

"Never mind, Tom. Next woodland we'll get you some nice acorns."

However, everything was too bleak to accommodate any humour and each, with their own thoughts and empty stomach, slogged on.

True to his word, on the outskirts of the next village, a sizeable one called Matilla, Carr called his Officers to what was little more than a large stable, where, once they were assembled, he climbed the first three steps of the stairs up to the loft and he wasted no time with explanations.

"Many of you were on the Coruna retreat and so, to many of you, my words will be familiar. I can only repeat what was spoken then by our Colonel Lacey. His maxim was, 'First, your men!' This will be as bad as Coruna, perhaps worse, because this time there is no food at all. If we are to hold together, whilst other Regiments fall apart, and they will, it will take leadership on the part of you, me and anyone who holds any measure of authority. It comes through example, what they endure so do you, but most importantly you look first to their welfare before you look to your own. I do not want to see any Officer looking first to themselves, then sitting miserable on his own. Sit with your men, they will want to know what is happening and it is up to you to give them hope. Added to that, what you have, you share, because of one thing you can be certain, they will be sharing out what they have amongst themselves, to get their comrades through this and so, therefore, should you. We are the Officers and men of the 105th together, so this is the time to sit by their fires and pass the spirit flask if you have any. If they feel that you are doing your best to get everyone through this, sharing with them what they have and listening, then they'll follow you and we'll hold together.

Before Carr descended, Ameshurst raised his hand.

"Any idea how long, Sir."

"Before we reach Ciudad? My guess is four days. Tell them that and say that at Ciudad there is food and shelter. And then into Winter Quarters, I shouldn't wonder."

With that he looked at O'Hare.

"Major! Our worse cases of fatigue and illness spend the night in here."

O'Hare came to the attention and saluted, as Carr walked out, followed by Officers all in different shades of humour. For such as Ameshurst and even D'Villiers there was no need for any request to join their men, or even hesitation, because on their approach their men simply shuffled up before their fires and made room. For others, at the opposite end of the spectrum, Carravoy and especially St. John Slade, to sit amongst such as their men in convivial sociality was practically alien. However, Slade knew Carr's order and the wrath that he could then visit on anyone who failed in what Carr saw as their duty and so he hovered just outside the small camp that was Deakin, Halfway, Nicholls, Gibney, Hill and Bennet. It was Deakin who saw him first and moved sideways himself.

"Come and have a warm, Sir. One thing, we can get a good fire going."

Slade sat himself into the space now available on the narrow seat of branches, but he stared awkwardly ahead. Then he remembered Carr's instruction and he pulled out his silver spirit flask and he offered it to Deakin, but he held up his hand.

"Best you hang onto that, Sir. You have plenty of ours. 'Tis French. Try some."

Slade took the flask offered and drank to find that it was of a very good quality, better than his own, but his face remained puzzled, this noticed by Deakin.

"Yes Sir, French. Got by trading."

Slade's face became even more puzzled.

"Trading?"

"Yes Sir. It goes on a lot between us and the Johnnies, between the lines, like, between pickets. They can't get tobacco and we can't get brandy. A sort of obvious need that we both can help each other out with, if I've explained it right."

"But isn't that consorting with the enemy?"

"Well, Sir, yes, there's some strict Officers as would see it that way, but it does no harm and, man to man, we gets on quite well with the Frogs, prob'ly because of such as the trading. We tries to be decent an' so does they, generally in the main. An' the world goes round like that. Sir."

With that topic now well developed, memories came back of other significant 'trading' occasions to each of the gathering, each giving their own descriptions of memorable deals struck during extraordinary circumstances. All had a story of the exchanges whilst obtaining water at the Portina brook between the two French attacks at Talavera. Gradually Slade felt more at ease as the stories came out from the six veterans, as they described a world that Slade had no idea even existed.

There was no rain that night and, despite the ground being sodden, all were able to get some kind of rest, but at first light there was again no issue of rations. Saunders took Solomon and Bailey into the nearby wood to look for acorns, to find it partly occupied by men of the 27th and soon their search found them both on the same territory. A 27th Corporal soon took umbrage as he scooped up old and dirty acorns for himself.

"These is ours. You take yourselves off to your own patch!"

Saunders and Solomon were both big men and they stood together, but Saunders looked around and saw an area that had not yet been searched. He looked at the 27th Corporal and nodded.

"You can have this and good luck."

Then he turned, pulling Solomon with him.

"Some bloody state we're in, fighting over acorns!"

It was an angry and disgruntled army that assembled on the road, in some quarters there was even talk of betrayal by Officers looking first to themselves. Nevertheless, the march began and before Noon they came up to the Followers and a halt was called. They all gathered together and the first question asked was to Nellie and Bridie, by Deakin.

"What food have you got? We've had no rations for the best part of three days."

It was Bridie that answered.

"We got some extra, but only what we could carry on our backs. Enough for a good meal this Noon, but Parson got extra loaded into his cart, before we quit the city."

Deakin nodded.

"God Bless Old Parson! So, a decent meal now, but we've three days to get through and no issue on its way."

The statement 'no issue' was not accurate, because Grenadier Guardsmen arrived carrying buckets, of what looked like meat, of some kind. One walked up to Nellie.

"Hold out your apron!"

She did so and the contents of the bucket were tipped out onto the open canvas. The description of 'meat' was altogether too flattering.

"What's this?"

The Grenadier went on his way.

"All the transport bullocks have been slaughtered. That's the result."

The contents of the apron were appalling, some of the meat still had the hide attached and at least half was offal of the worst kind, there was even an eyeball. Nellie continued to stare.

"Seems to me that everything on them poor animals has been cut off as isn't pure bone. What do we do with this?"

Deakin came over to examine.

"You make the best! This we eat now before it goes bad, saving what we've got for days comin'."

Nellie looked at him, more than a little irritated.

"Well, the best will be next to nothin', but 'twill fill a hole, I do suppose."

No more than a third of the issue was fit enough to go into the pot, but with peas and biscuits it was a meal that they all ate with relish. Then Ellis arrived.

"Form up. We move, Frog cavalry's been sighted. Far off, but they'm come up to us."

Bridie looked at him, somewhat anxiously.

"Did you get anything to eat, Ethan? Did you now?"

Ellis face remained blank.

"No more than you got, and poor commons that was, but get packed up now, we have to move. His cavalry's caught us up."

However, he did tarry long enough to scrape out the pot offered to him by Nellie.

Within the retreat column next over to the North, this called the centre column, equally threatening French cavalry were being viewed through the telescopes of Two Squadron, 16th Light Dragoons, along with many others from G. Anson's Brigade, Peterson being the most anxious and thereby the most curious.

"What will they do?"

Oakwood lowered his own telescope.

"There's a lot of them, but not enough for a serious assault and they've neither infantry, nor guns. They'll just follow, pick up stragglers and perhaps test us out."

Then it began to rain again, heavily.

"This'll keep them back! They no more like fighting in the rain than we do, especially with their doubly fancy uniforms."

The 11th and 12th of Anson's Brigade were beginning to move and so Oakwood wheeled his horse to follow.

"They'll stay out there and we'll stay as a screen."

The afternoon wore on and the rain did not cease. What was noteworthy for the 16th were the increasing number of stragglers and marauders out and away from the road and running across the fields to escape, often in groups of five or six. Baxter shook his head and spoke his thoughts out loud, to no-one in particular.

"This is how it starts!"

With the column in the South, regarded as being nearest to the French, it was the same, the cavalry continuing the retreat out in the fields, whilst the infantry did their best on the road, but all casting frequent glances over their left shoulders to the hills where the French cavalry followed. Now that the Followers were with them, the formation that had got them over the Guadaramma mountains was adopted, the Followers protected in the centre of the 105th column. Evening meal, taken mid-afternoon and mercifully in a dark, sheltering conifer wood, was no more than hot tea and one biscuit, but even that was interrupted, this time by Drake, running through the area of the 105th Light Company.

"Get your weapons and follow me!"

Then he was gone, but the direction was obvious and they all ran from their camps, donning backpacks and belts as they ran. Drake had continued on, because the several Regiments of French cavalry, who had been following their column, were now much closer. However, a line was being formed of all the Light Companies of the 3rd and 4th Divisions and Alten's Light Cavalry Brigade was further out. Drake, Shakeshaft and Ellis indicated their place in the defensive line and all stood to watch as at least a Brigade of Chasseurs come advancing down from the hills at a canter. Drake saw Alten's Cavalry Brigade, three Regiments, draw sabres, the dull flash of almost a thousand weapons clear even in the poor November light. Alten's were in the direct line of the French advance and he led his Regiments forward at the canter to meet them, but no contact was made. The French opposed by Alten suddenly wheeled away, apart from at least three Squadrons who were able to ride on, being as they overlapped Alten's line. These, however, did not get far, because they soon met the line of Light Troops and the volleys rang out, not just of muskets, but also two field-guns that were now present and these added their weight. Soon, all French cavalry were in retreat and so Drake, along with all other Officers and the cavalry, sheathed his sword. Bettridge was alongside him, but it was Drake who passed judgement.

"Well, that wasn't worth leaving our fires for!"

"No, Sir. Bit of a fuss about nothing."

"Yes Luttrel, as it turned out, but it could have been something, were they more than just cavalry."

As the rain fell again from a darkening sky, Carr, O'Hare and Heaviside, were again sat under the meagre canvas screen that served as Headquarters, but at least they were able to drink hot coffee. Carr asking the most anxious question.

"How many have we lost?"

O'Hare answered first.

"Three! All had to fall out from exhaustion."

Then Heaviside.

"Two from me. Same reason."

Carr nodded, now reasonably content.

"That we can live with and they may catch up. We're spending the night here and I'd say that little pantomime before dark will be Johnny's one and only effort, at least with our column and we're the nearest. What happens to the other two on roads up to the North, I know not, but I'd say that was it. He knows we're back to Portugal and he will get himself out of this weather. They must be suffering too, so our only enemy now is cold and hunger, but Johnny's now got back for himself just about the whole of Spain."

Cold and hunger were the sole topics around the fires of Jed Deakin and Zeke Saunders, all sat hungry, but at least they were warm from the good fire, but food was the discussion. 'Parson' Sedgwicke was present and Deakin asked him the first question.

"Good of you to tell us about your extra, Parson, so, what've you got on that cart? What's left, I mean?"

"Two and a half barrels of salt pork and the same of beef. Four sacks of flour and five of biscuit."

"What does the Chaplain know of it?"

"Everything. I needed to get his permission to load it in the first place."

'And he's feeding himself from it?"

"He is, but small portions."

Deakin nodded.

"Small portions!"

He drew a deep breath.

"Would he, do you think, give from what he has in his cart for the childers? And the women, and all them with small 'uns? Across all 105th Followers? Not that there's so very many."

Miles answered first.

"Be a cold-hearted sod if he didn't!"

Deakin silenced him with a look, then he turned to Sedgwicke.

"Parson?"

"I cannot see him saying no. He is a most unworldly man, but the Spirit and the Word of the Scriptures dwell strongly within him. I will ask and I expect a positive reply."

Sedgwicke stood up, Deakin with him, for him then to speak the warmest words that Sedgwicke had heard since being sent to the 105th as a common criminal and a defrocked Priest.

"You're a good comrade, Parson. Standing with us all as you do. We're all thankful that we can count you as one amongst us."

Sedgwicke was so embarrassed that he almost blushed as Deakin shook his hand, but Nellie had her own words.

"You're a Saint of a man, so you are, Parson darlin'. A true Saint, as to try your best with that oddity as calls himself a Chaplain."

With words such as those still ringing in his ears, Sedgwicke left the circle, but now doubly determined not to disappoint those who had called him "a good comrade", as he now also regarded them. He found Albright reading the Bible, his final session of the day, by the light of a candle.

"Sir!"

Albright lowered the book.

"Sir, you are aware that over the next days, food will be very scarce. You remember seeing the rations convoy taking a different road to us after leaving Salamanca?

Albright nodded.

"Well, Sir, it was not only a different road, it was very much the wrong road and because of that the army will have no food for the next three, perhaps four days."

He paused.

"Well, Sir, we have extra in our cart and I propose that we use it to sustain the women and children of our Regiment, Sir."

Sedgwicke emphasised the final four words of his sentence.

"As both a Christian and a comradely act. Sir."

Albright's head moved from side to side.

"But we will go hungry!"

"Yes Sir, but we will keep the women and children, especially the children, alive and well, Sir. Or at least very much increase their chances of reaching food and safety."

He held back from saying that which would be most damning, which being, "What would the men think if their children die of cold and hunger, whilst we feed ourselves well?", but Albright was beginning to nod his head, slowly, then more definitely.

"Do it, Private! Indeed, yes, do it, for does not the Good Book say, Luke 6, verse 38. Give, and it will be given to you. Good measure, pressed down, shaken together, running over, will be put into your lap. For with the measure you use, it will be measured back to you."

Sedgwicke nodded his head in thanks.

"That is a great kindness, Sir. The men will know you for it."

Albright nodded quickly and blew out the candle, then he climbed into the cart to sleep.

oOo

"What were you saying? About Johnny's last throw?"

Carr looked across at O'Hare, a wry grin on his face.

"Perhaps, yes, a slight exaggeration, brought on by cold, hunger and wishful thinking."

O'Hare grinned slightly and studied the distance, looking back the way they had come. Furthest from them was the village of Matilla, they had passed from it not an hour since, whilst in the middle distance, could be seen at least three Brigades of French cavalry. Both sides were stock still, simply regarding each other, the only movement came from horses tossing their heads or reaching for grass. Carr continued with his analysis.

"He's weighing up his options, him now confronted by the whole of the 4th Division, us stood as Rearguard."

He then had a further thought.

"Do you think that this may be an actual tactic? To keep us stood here, in the cold and wet, thus stretching out the days before we make shelter in Ciudad?"

O'Hare smiled again.

"I would not put it past them. Using the weather against us, rather than their weapons. They know that we cannot move away, or at least, not so easily, but they're no more immune than we are."

In the ranks of the 105th, the conversation was much the same, only involving much more colourful language and much of it directed at their Commanding Officers. Saunders was now highly incensed and finding a ready audience and kindred spirit in Miles.

"We should be pulling back. 'Tis the cavalry's job to be holding off such as these. Hold them off and then catch us back up. They're on horses!"

"Ask me, this lot of Commanding Officers that we has over us here, don't know their arse from their elbow. First off, they lost the rations, second, you'm right, they'm usin' us infantry for a stand-off with Frog cavalry. I don't see the sense, but yer we be!"

Saunders was anxious for more than the reason out there before him. The Followers had been sent on ahead and no one could say when they would be reunited and Consuela was suffering in the cold. He had fashioned a poncho from a discarded horse blanket which seemed to help but they had to part company before he could find out if she was any better. They were all worried about the Followers and now, the fact of simply standing 400 yards away from French cavalry with no movement anywhere, was trying Saunders patience severely. He turned to Davey.

"We didn't hear back from Parson. Do you think that extra will come their way, for the women and children?"

Davey patted him on the shoulder, a significant reach up.

"I do! Parson will find the words. That's what they do, Devil Dodgers, find words!"

At that moment the answer to their first concern sounded out, a volley from twelve field-guns, the Divisional Batteries of both the 3rd and 4th Divisions. The aim of the first volley was off, but the point had been made; "Charge and see what you can do, or sit and be cannonaded to pieces." The French cavalry did neither, but made a rapid about turn and rode back into Matilla.

When all French horses were out of sight, the order came to form column and this was achieved at the run to be followed by a rapid march, or as rapid as could be achieved over a road that again was no more than liquid mud that sucked off boots not lashed on with any handy material, discarded horse-harness being preferred. For an hour they slithered on with the rain falling, each occasionally losing their balance and lurching into their neighbour, but always the nagging hunger which acorn porridge did nothing to alleviate, only, in many cases, inflicting severe stomach cramps causing men to fall out beside the road to ease themselves and then run to catch up.

As the daylight faded the results of the hunger and cold became only too obvious, not just the scavengers out in the fields, these now in larger bands, but also those who could walk on no more, because now both soldiers and Followers could be seen collapsed at the side of the road. The rain, the mud and fording the swollen streams that were now rivers, had placed demands upon their starving bodies that they could no longer sustain. Some lay still from death or sheer exhaustion, some were able to raise a feeble hand in supplication, but the 4th Division marched on, yet with notable exceptions. Grenadiers from Ameshurst's Section picked up two Follower children and carried them onward, taking turns to carry, despite their own hunger and exhaustion. In the darkness they caught up with their own Followers and many anxious questions were exchanged, but so far no one had fallen out. Saunders had immediately embraced Consuela, she at least sat above the sodden earth on a 'bench' made from fallen branches, wrapped in her horse-blanket.

"Are you all right? Did Parson get you some food?"

She nodded.

"Sim! But I eat not all, some I give to Eirin. She must make milk for baby."

He could do no more other than wrap his arms tighter around her.

The night was the most miserable so far. The rain had ceased but that brought on the cold and as the warming fires died in the night, so did many in the column. With the dawn could be heard screaming from the Followers as they discovered both women and children who would never rise again, also the cries of soldiers who found comrades who would never waken again, all succumbed to the cold and hunger. However, there were none from the Light and Colour Companies of the 105th, because the veterans' advice of Deakin and Miles, plus Sedgwicke's extra food were keeping them alive. The next dawn, sustained by nothing more than a hot drink from pots suspended over rekindled fires, the 4th Division again formed column to plod and stumble along the now indistinguishable road, this now merely a broad width of churned mud from the wheels, hooves and feet of the Divisions gone before. At the rear of the 105th column, suddenly Davey raised up his head lowered against the rain, which had returned with the progress of the morning.

"What the Hell is that?'

It was a noise of intense squealing and grunting, a noise unknown to all of them, bar two, one being Bill Turner, him of wide and varied experience.

"That's pigs!"

The single word came back from many directions, this supported by Nellie, the second with the knowledge, she deep within the Light Company column.

"Pigs, yes. That's the sound of 'em, right enough."

At that confirmation, all then looked up to see a whole herd of the animals, hundreds, as they charged down the slope, left to right, for what seemed like the gap between the 3rd and the 4th Divisions. Up ahead, Stubb's Portuguese immediately broke ranks, as did the whole of the 3rd Division and soon shots rang out. The pig herd, their route now blocked, split into several groups which ran along the whole line, looking for escape, but still in their original direction. Many inevitably ran along to the 105th and the whole column fell apart as each starving man dived and tackled whichever panicked animal came within reach, bayonets now drawn and stabbing at the captured animals. There was uproar, of squealing animals and shouting men. All Officers were taken completely by surprise at the collapse of discipline, but Carr, O'Hare and Heaviside saved their voices, any attempt to restore any order was completely hopeless. An animal was secured by the most athletic, such as Joe Pike, and the most agriculturally experienced, such as Toby Halfway. After as many animals had escaped as their nimbleness allowed, or were instead captured and killed, the final result was a whole pig on the shoulders of both Saunders and Solomon and one on the shoulders of Henry Nicholls, none caring for the blood that ran down and restored the colour of their uniforms. The column soon reformed and the burden of the slaughtered animals was shared in turn, adding to the burden of carrying the children.

The Noon stop began with fierce and rapid butchery, whatever came off first being immediately thrown into the cooking pot with a good fire beneath, it quickly bringing the water to the boil. All looked anxiously at the stewing meat, Nellie blocking Miles' approach when she felt he was too close. There was no need for any calls to come as all presented their pannikins and Nellie relented, even though the meat was not fully cooked and it was quickly shared out, a decent portion for each. Zeke Saunders smiled contentedly to see his Consuela at last enjoying a good meal of boiled pork, crushed acorns and biscuit.

Anson and Lowry-Cole came back and rode straight up to Carr, Lowry-Cole appearing the most concerned.

"What happened here?"

Carr was unmoved.

"The men obtained a meal, Sir."

"It was undisciplined chaos!"

"Yes Sir. I suspect that tends to happen when the need arises to capture a herd of pigs! The men could not resist a meal on the hoof, you might say."

Lowry-Cole's face darkened, but Carr cared little. Through appalling staff-work his peerless 105th had fallen apart from starvation, not the cold, that they could cope with if fed. He was in no mood to choose his words carefully, but his Divisional General was far from satisfied.

"I expect you to take action."

He then rode off, leaving an embarrassed and even confused Anson remaining with Carr and O'Hare, then Anson pulled a wry face and rode off himself. O'Hare watched both ride on to the 27th, then he turned to Carr.

"He'll get little better from the 27th, but what are you going to do?"

"What I am going to do, is go back to Bryce at our tent and if he hasn't obtained a decent portion, then he's back down to Corporal!"

O'Hare grinned and joined him in the short walk. Then, after a meal of pork and biscuits, at the end of which the bones were sucked clean, Carr issued a Colonel's order, which was read with some indignation by Carravoy in conjunction with Slade, them reading one copy together, and Carravoy was the first to burst.

"All horses to be used for the wounded, the sick and the infirm!"

At that moment, Heaviside passed by and Carravoy turned to him, waving the paper.

"Is this true?"

Heaviside halted beside the pair.

"Is what true?"

"That we can no longer ride our horses? They are to be used only for those unable to walk?"

Heaviside looked at both in turn.

"It is indeed wholly true. Thou shalt not harden thine heart, nor shut thine hand from thy poor brother. Deuteronomy 15, verse 7. Pray and give thanks that you can fulfil the Word of the Lord."

With that Heaviside walked off, leaving the pair to await the arrival of whichever of the infirm was most in need of a ride on their horse during the afternoon march. It was Heaviside who returned with one of the most needy, arriving at Slade and the man needed to be hoisted up, but he spoke his thanks, in between fits of coughing.

"My thanks, Sir. Just a couple of hours and give the ride to another. I'll be good for a couple of miles after that."

Deakin, standing by, then looked at Slade, but the response was that Deakin was given the reins. Slade would not be the one to lead the horse.

That day, in the centre column, no one was riding in G. Anson's Brigade either. Cornets Carr and Peterson were walking together, both leading their horses and, after a silent hour, Peterson spoke first.

"Makes sense, that order."

Carr knew immediately what Peterson was referring to, the order to lead their horses and walk. Carr turned to look at his own mount, her head low, her mouth open.

"Yes. One cannot argue. If we don't get some fodder into them soon, then we'll be infantry."

Peterson took a deep breath and sighed.

"Things have come to a pretty pass. Take this morning when that damn
fool Gordon sent us off before the Light Infantry had moved out ahead of us, so that we left them behind and alone to cope with whatever came up. There was no cavalry cover for them. Have you heard what happened?"

"Not in the detail."

"Well, I got it off a Lieutenant in the 51st, part of the 7th Division. Whilst we were out South, on Gordon's orders, Johnny Dragoons got around the Lights, no surprise there, and up to the column and plundered the 7th's baggage. Then they captured Paget. Utter shambles."

"Paget's gone!"

"That's what he said."

"Damn! I thought our job was to support the Lights. To be there at hand, sort of, or so I thought."

"So did everybody else. Except Gordon!"

"Where are the Lights now?"

"Just behind. That's the 7th, just in front."

"Shouldn't we be absolutely last?"

"You may be right, but with the state of our horses?"

The question remained unanswered as they emerged from some woodland and the road took a sudden dip into a deep valley containing a fast running river. The 7th Division in front were at that moment using three fords to cross, the three Brigades merging again on the far side into one column when they re-gained the road. The 16th arrived at the river just as the last of the infantry were entering the fords and Peterson looked around for superior Officers.

"I'm riding through this! What's the point of getting wet feet, when I've a horse to carry me over."

He mounted and walked his horse on, but he need not have worried, the order came to mount and all in the 16th kept their feet dry, but, on the far side, all were again ordered to dismount and walk their horses up the steep slope. They had achieved the level ground above and were walking on when there came from behind the clear sounds of combat and the call came along their column, "Mount up! Mount up!" and all did so, to see Anson riding back to the valley, with the 12th following behind. Johnson led the 16th to follow and they rode back to the edge of the valley to see almost all of the Light Division still over on the far side of the river. Many were waiting to cross at the fords, but the great remainder were in fierce combat with French infantry, the sounds of the continuous skirmishing coming to them across the wide space of the valley. The far side was being held by a thick skirmishing line of what looked like three Companies of Redcoats and one of green-jacketed Rifles, these doing their best to hold back an even thicker line of French skirmishers, whilst the rest of the Division hurried across the fords as best they could. What could only be a Senior Officer of the Light Division galloped up the slope and stopped at Anson, then the order came for his three Regiments to form two lines along the crest. This was done in minutes and then many in the Brigade looked over their left shoulders to see the three Brigades of the 7th Division, hurrying back to give support, which meant descending half-way down the slope to take their positions, each Battalion part of a four-man deep Brigade line, the three Brigades one behind the other.

Meanwhile, the Companies of the Light Division which had safely crossed were now formed along the river bank, some Companies placing themselves further up the slope from where they could fire over the heads of their comrades below, these now formed up along the river's edge. As the rearguard Companies remaining beyond the river now ran down to cross it themselves, those already formed and waiting, opened fire on the French Voltiguers who were following, bringing down many but several of the fleeing British were also now spread across the bleak hillside, running for their lives to cross the river at any point. Carr was sat beside Oakwood and, from their vantage point, they could see clearly the size of the French force on the far side. Carr turned to Oakwood.

"Do you think he means to cross?"

Oakwood nodded.

"He will if he can. That's a whole Corps over there, as far as I can see."

As if to emphasise his words, a battery of French field-guns emerged from the tree line on the far side and opened fire on the lines of the 7th Division.

"Have we got a charge in us?"

Oakwood nodded.

"One that goes down, but we'll not get back up here for another!"

The conflict had settled into a lively exchange across the river. The final British rearguard Companies were now all over and the whole of the Light Division was holding the bank against the now outnumbered Voltiguers, who began to suffer heavily, but more were arriving from the crest above. Carr looked along the valley.

"I'm glad those guns are not on us!"

Oakwood looked in the same direction, leaning forward.

"The same from me, but their shot seems to be doing little damage, just ploughing into the mud. I can't see many casualties."

Carr looked more closely to see that Oakwood was correct. The solid shot was simply sending up showers of mud from the soft earth over the steady lines of the 7th.

"So what happens now?"

"We stay here, until Johnny gets fed up!"

Carr grinned.

"Well, talking of feeding, at least the horses have a chance to get some grass into themselves, with us just standing here."

Carr's reins were being continuously jerked by his mount's head as she went searching for grass, which was more brown than green, but at least more than half plentiful atop the slope.

It was the short November day that brought a halt to the conflict. Once the gloom had thoroughly settled in and targets could no longer be identified, all firing ceased. The Light Division climbed the slope and the order came to Anson's to dismount and make camp. Ample firewood was obtained from the nearby woodland and the 16th sat around good fires, but with nothing to eat. Carr was sat with Peterson.

"When did you eat last?"

"Shut up!"

With that, Peterson rolled into his cavalry cloak and fell asleep, leaving Carr to his own thoughts, which were brief, before he did the same, "Well, at least it's not raining!"

Just before dawn, in the first light, both were shaken awake by their Sergeants, Baxter speaking for both.

"Sirs, we have to form up. Johnny's still there."

The two Cornet's found their horses, still cropping the short winter grass, but they mounted and joined their Troops on the valley crest. The two infantry Divisions, the 7th and Light, were already there. What they saw were many French Battalions, what they heard were French drums sounding across the valley. Oakwood then decided what that signified.

"That's the advance. He's giving it a go!"

They waited and waited but no French movement came. The waiting continued until French cavalry descended to the river, but they did not look in any way menacing, especially when they rode gently into the fords to allow their horses to drink. Then they rode back up to continue in the same direction, away, following their retiring infantry. From the top of the slope, what they took to be an Officer of Chasseurs turned and saluted with his sword. Oakwood spoke again.

"That's it then. That's that for 1812. All we have to fight now is the cold and the hunger!"

How desperate that fight was going to be was revealed when they rode into the next village, that being named Cabrillas, the namesign being all that remained from before the time when the centre column marched in. The 7th and the Light Divisions had obviously been ordered to march quickly straight through, because there was no sign of them when the 16th rode in at the head of Anson's Brigade. Even from the outskirts, every house, most likely built in the Middle Ages, has been pulled apart for fuel, nothing remaining to mark their place but their brick foundations and the stone chimney above the gaping and desolate stone hearth. Carr gasped at the destruction, but the scene was worse further in, drunken soldiers lay in the road or staggered along it. There were many butchered horses and harness lay in many places amongst the detritus of an army that had given up. Cavalrymen lurched and sagged amongst the drunks. Most gruesome to the senses, two bodies hung from a central tree, neither in uniform, presumably hung by the Provosts for looting, but evidently these military enforcers had been overwhelmed by the indiscipline and riot that came with the following Divisions of the centre column. With their cold hands the 16th gripped their reins and their horses tighter with their knees, so that in stony silence and with no glances either side, G. Anson's Brigade rode on through.

With midday came the rain and W. Anson's Brigade marched up to their own scene of riot and outrage, in their case the village of Tenebron, but, just outside, the order came to halt. The rain was again teeming down, but even through that insistent sound there could be heard the sounds of uproar and rampage. Anson himself rode back to Carr.

"Keep yours together. There's enough to man a Division in there, but not one that's not drunk and wound up enough for murder. We're going through the fields alongside, there's a track that should serve. If you've NCOs that you trust, get them out as a screen. This is the worst yet!"

Carr turned to O'Hare.

"You and Gibney. Get them out, the ones we've used before. Ours are as hungry as any in that village, so we get past as quick as we can and keep those marauders away. Remind them we wear the green, we are the Fighting 105th and as good as any Guards and better. We've proved it often enough. Hold to the Colours! No disgrace to the Regiment. What would Lacey say?"

During the pause, the trusted were selected and sent to the side of the column that would face the village, much of which was now burning, the flames adding their mournful sound to the screams and shouts. Then the column moved forward, at a quick pace. Behind the Light Company, who were the last in the 105th column, came the cart of Albright and Sedgwicke, with Sally, Trudie and Violet in the back. Sedgwicke was now desperately anxious, the peril that they were in was now all too obvious and very serious. As the Light Company, with the Followers sandwiched in the centre, moved forward, so did Sedgwicke urge forward the mules. On leaving the road, the cart slipped and slithered in the ruts and holes of the track, which deteriorated the further they progressed. As they passed the ends of the side streets that marked the edge of the village, they could see crowds of Redcoats staggering and cavorting within the interior, all drunk and oblivious to the falling rain. Sedgwicke's anxiety grew as many at the far end of the streets they passed, stopped their antics and noticed the passing column, but also their cart, these inebriants waving their arms and pointing in their direction. He was indeed fearful, remembering what had happened on the Coruna retreat when drunks and marauders had slaughtered his mules for food and the cart had been pulled apart for fuel. However, they progressed on, even though the cart lurched and stopped in alarming fashion, but the good mules pulled them onwards. Then came a worried shout from Sally in the back.

"Parson Sedgwicke! There's a lot of men following us!"

Sedgwicke glanced backwards through the rear opening of the canvas cover to see a growing crowd of dirty and dishevelled but plainly determined Redcoats following them, some now running. Sedgwicke whipped the reins onto the mules' backs, but over that rough track they could go no faster. Then some men overtook the mules and then the girls screamed. Sedgwicke heard Albright calling down to the Redcoats, now with hands on the cart, that they were Men of God and about God's work, but Sedgwicke turned to see at least two drunken Redcoats now wrestling with the girls and then one stopped whilst holding down Trudie to shout from the back of the cart. Sedgwicke heard only one of his shouted words, but that word was 'food.' Then the cart stopped, the Recoats at the side had halted the mules and were slashing at the harness. One mule began to kick and buck, but it was stabbed in the throat and quickly subsided. The Light Company had progressed on, several more yards and Sedgwicke was now desperate and filled his lungs with air.

"Help! Help! Saunders, Davey! Help!"

It was only the final rank of the column that heard, but one man turned and then nudged another for the word to quickly spread that the cart was in trouble and many now turned to run back. Saunders, Nicholls, Hill, Davey and Ellis were amongst the chosen to guard the column and they arrived amongst the first. They ignored those Redcoats with the mules, both now dead, and clambered quickly into the cart. Albright had been pulled to the ground and was in a heap but now rising. Sedgwicke was in the back, close to succumbing in his fight with a soldier in Grenadier uniform, but Saunders landed a heavy blow into the Grenadier's face and then kicked another out the back of the cart.

"The girls! Get the girls out!:

Sedgwicke and Davey pulled the almost hysterical girls to the front of the cart and propelled them down to waiting men of the Light Company, these distinguished from the rabble by their green cuffs and collars and holding their line. Meanwhile, Ellis and Saunders were defending the rear of the cart, Saunders yelling between bouts of combat, Henry Nicholls was back in the cart pounding senseless the Grenadier who had overcome Sedgwicke.

"Food! Get the food!"

However, Ellis knew it could not be done. Many more drunken and desperate Redcoats were now arriving and climbing into the cart, even from under the canvas cover at the sides.

"Zeke! Zeke! Leave it. It's hopeless. We've got the girls out."

He swung a salt-pork barrel into the head of another assailant.

"Time to get ourselves out!"

He threw out into the road another barrel and a sack of biscuit which served as an effective distraction, then they retreated to leave the cart from the front and jump down beside the cart yoke to run back to the waiting column. Saunders had seized a sack of biscuit on his way and this was noticed by a wild-eyed Redcoat, but Saunders shoulder charged him into the mud. By now men were cutting lumps of flesh from the mules and intent on chewing the raw meat, others were converging to obtain a share for themselves and so both men regained the ranks of their comrades unscathed. Before moving on they looked back at the cart and the mules but little could be seen of either, other than the canvas awning that was now being shredded by many bayonets. The cart was covered in red jacketed men pulling and cutting at every single part and feature. Seeing the anger and frustration on Saunder's face, Ellis put his hand on his shoulder and turned him back towards the road.

"Come on, Zeke. No more we could do. No one's hurt, that's what matters."

The remains of the day were of deep depression, deepened no only by the rain and the mud and many considered the foremost question, when does hope turn to desperation and then into despair? However, through no other reason than solidarity the 105th held together and set themselves to continue to place one foot in front of the other. If their comrades held to the Regiment, so would they. If their comrades put the Followers and children first, then so would they. All thoughts were now only on survival not only for themselves but for those they called mess-mates and family, thus those on the horses were rotated and children were carried, baby Ellen on Byford's back, regularly checked by Eirin, the toddler Jed rotating around the backs of Saunders and Solomon. During a mid-afternoon stop, Jed Deakin stood and waved a finger in all directions.

"We don't lose no-one! Whoever has to be carried, gets carried. Clear! We'll get 'em time on the horses. This be worse than Coruna for my money, but from what I hear come tomorrow we'll not be too far from Roger's Town and could be they'll get some food out to us. There's a good chance of that, I'm certain. Not even our Staff could cock this up again!"

Determination now somewhat higher they trudged on, but the signs of an army falling apart increased with every mile. Between villages there were fewer drunks but many more whom simple exhaustion had claimed, their figures stretched out beside the road, where their bodies had been hauled clear and now pounded by the piteous rain. That night was spent wherever the rain had not flooded, because what could have been a sheltering ditch or even a shallow valley was either a deep pond or a raging stream. To attempt to light a fire in the open was hopeless and so all simply sat huddled together against the slanting rain to await the dawn when at least there was the relief of movement and the knowledge that they were moving closer to the succour they so desperately needed.

The following dawn, Bryce, carrying three cups of lukewarm coffee, came into their canvas awning and found Carr, O'Hare and

Heaviside slumped together on their stools with their backs to each other as though a stand of muskets. Water was running between their feet. Bryce gently nudged Carr first.

"Sir! Sir!"

Carr awoke, but that was an exaggeration, his head rolled from side to side as his senses began to register. As Carr sat up, so did he awaken his companions, as he accepted the coffee.

"Well done, Bryce. Thank you."

The coffee helped, but the first words Carr spoke to his companions were not inspirational.

"Two days! Two days from Ciudad. Seems like a century."

O'Hare sipped his coffee, carefully, relishing each drop across his tongue.

"Anything to eat?"

"No!"

With that blunt reply, Carr stood up, but he turned to his two companions.

"Are we hanging together? That's what matters."

O'Hare nodded.

"I'd say we are. I wouldn't fancy us for a Sovereign's Day parade, but I'd say we are."

Carr nodded and buckled on his sword.

"Right then. One day at a time!"

The 105th formed quickly on the road, wishing to leave all memories of the miserable night behind. As they stood, awaiting their time to move off, Carr, O'Hare and Heaviside walked down the column giving what encouragement they could. Whilst Heaviside regaled all with uplifting quotes from the Bible, O'Hare tortured all with awful jokes. Each Bible quote did at least as much to cheer those who heard it as did O'Hare's awful jests, the quotes probably more, but even each sorry parcel of humour from O'Hare did at least induce a wry grin from those who heard. Carr simply sang the praises of all, then the march began, but now came the Winter cold to replace the Autumn rain. All through the column, whatever could be employed to deflect the scouring wind was used, even musket butts were hoisted next to red raw faces. Noon was merely a rest, but at least fires could be lit, using the remains of olive groves that had been cut down by Divisions passing ahead. Deakin was sat, warming his hands at the more than halfway decent fire, worrying about his grandson and grandaughter and studying those around whom he cared for. How was Eirin, how were Nellie's girls, even his precious Bridie? Nothing he saw gave him comfort. He threw some more sticks on the fire, and mournfully studied the resultant flames, then he heard drums beating. His head jerked up and he looked at Toby Halfway, who was now looking at him.

"That's 'turn out for biscuit'!"

"I'll go!"

Halfway rose and began to run along the column, him and Henry Nicholls joining the line of the strongest, those most able to run and carry. Saunders and Solomon then came up to a grinning Deakin.

"Biscuit!"

Both grinned back at him and soon they were running in the right direction and came to a queue of wagons where sacks of biscuit and peas were being dropped down to welcoming and receiving hands. Each man was given two and these were carried back joyfully to their own mess areas. Saunders and Solomon hurried back, to immediately kneel in the centre of their group, then hand out two biscuits each, which were quickly consumed, but a third was then able to be given. With distribution still taking place, Anson, stood chewing biscuit himself along with the three Senior Officers of the 105th doing the same, now spoke what was fairly obvious.

"I think the post-Noon march will be somewhat delayed."

Throughout every mess of the 105th a potage was prepared of biscuit and peas, each spoonful soon wolfed down. However, with all consumed, it was not too long before the column was formed and O'Hare, once again, with Carr and Heaviside, took advantage of the moment to encourage all once again, O'Hare perhaps the most cheerful.

"Come on now, boys! March on some more. There'll be more like that and the better we march the sooner we gets to it."

The road was now drier and firmer, most often frozen and so better progress was made. As the day faded and the ground for night camp was gained, so their faces were uplifted once more to see a long queue of Commissariat wagons and the drums beat again, this time for a double ration which became simply all they could eat. With all settled Deakin went over to Byford and Eirin to check on baby Ellen and little Jed. A broad grin spread across his face to see Ellen being suckled and Jed chewing on a biscuit, sat on Consuela's lap, both wrapped within the horse blanket. Deakin sat and hung his head from all forms of exhaustion, the burden he had shouldered for the past five days now removed. Bridie came and sat with him, kissed him and arranged a blanket around the shoulders of both. Sleep came better with full stomachs and good fires, so that it was a more cheerful and animated 105th that formed on the road after another issue of biscuit, peas and salt-pork so that, for the first time for days, cooking pots were full for a good breakfast. They marched on and, as their column swung right to follow a bend in the road, Halfway nudged Deakin, having studied the far distance.

"That's Roger's Town!"

Deakin nodded and managed a wry smile.

"Never thought I'd be glad to see that place again, but 'tis the Pearly Gates as far as I be concerned!"

oOo

Carr marched into the winter quarters of the Light Company without knocking and Shakeshaft and Bettridge sprang to their feet, but he waved them back down. It was Drake that he had come to see.

"Have you seen this?"

"What?"

"A letter from the Peer. Sent to all Colonels and above."

Drake dropped his spoon into the bowl of stew he was eating and looked indulgently at his Regimental Colonel.

"Well, being the mere Captain of an unfashionable Line Regiment with a number the wrong side of a hundred, I'm not too surprised that I'm off the circulation list."

He pointed to the stew.

"Have some of this bean stew. It's very good, I think Morrison's put some fish in it."

"He's blaming us!"

"The Peer? Us? For events on that horrendous retreat?"

"Yes!"

"And what does he say that has stretched your equable temper to such a pass?"

Carr gave Drake a stony look, then he held up the page, to then lower it. He could speak from memory.

"It's full of it! We suffered no disaster, nor any privations. There was no reason for what happened, we suffered no hardships, except being exposed to the........"

He looked again.

"Inclemencies of the weather. He attributes all to the inattention of the Officers of the Regiments to their duty. We were little pressed by the enemy. We did not enforce the order of the army. I could go on. It's a damned cheek! Did he write as such to Gordon, that dullard, who wandered off with all the rations?"

Drake sat back and nodded sagely.

"I did hear that he had the Colonel of the 82nd arrested because he lost so many men, but such as that from Wellington surprises me not at all. He worries over our lives in battle, but our general welfare when out of it, is another world to him. He simply expects us to be there when needed. His surprise and even indignation at what happened between Salamanca and Ciudad gives me no astonishment at all."

He sighed, then pointed again to the stew.

"Have some and forget about Wellington venting his spleen on the likes of us! We must get our own letters off, now that we are back here in Garda. We can tell them that it is a very pleasant town. Tell them more about that, than what we've just been through. And where's your brother? You must write to him as well.

"Somewhere near Oporto, place called Aviedo."

"On the coast! Lucky dog! Rather me than him.

The words were now unheeded, Carr had finally succumbed to the idea of eating instead of fulminating about the injustices of Wellington's letter and so he was now spooning out for himself a large portion of the aromatic stew.

oOo

Chapter Six

"All Lies and Subterfuge!"

Making full use of the privileges of rank, General Sir Henry Livermore sat in the reserved seats in the Strangers' Gallery of the House of Lords, very much in plain clothes and equipped for the winter weather, listening to an impassioned statement from Lord Sellick of Ffynes. The good Lord was building to a crescendo, stating that the Colonists, as they were still referred to, "Needed to be taught a lesson, that the British Lion, though wounded, was not to be trifled with, and that, after their thorough trouncing at both Queenston Heights and more recently at Frenchman's Creek by our heroic Redcoats, a punitive expedition should be undertaken into the Colonies. This would both secure the Niagara isthmus and ward off further Colonial incursions, but it would also provide a base for further incursions of our own into the Northern areas of this so called 'United States' with its rebellious and aggressive people."

Livermore flexed his hand on the top of his walking cane, satisfied with what he had heard and then he grinned slightly to himself at the thought that the worthy Sellick of Ffynes had now earned the position he had been promised in the Office for War and the Colonies and the promise would be kept, such that he would soon be offered a minor Ministerial position within the Department that oversees the Navy. Then, as replies and arguments from the floor were heard and debated, Livermore looked around the gallery, at the many faces; bored, fascinated or simply blank, and he wondered to himself, "How many of you are agents of our enemies, both real and potential? Well, you've just heard something to chew on today!" The motion was duly passed with a large majority and so Livermore rose and departed the House to stand at the gate and signal for his carriage, which was waiting up in Whitehall. Once seated and his hands now being warmed by the small charcoal-burner, he sat back, but he was still worried. Radipole's scheme was now set in train and it was now crucially important. Wellington had been thrown out of Spain and was back on the border, mainly because the French had concentrated their armies against him, something which, in theory, they could do at any time. Anything that had the potential to reduce those forces was worth pursuing and the one bright spot was that the timing was good. Napoleon, so intelligence revealed, was now back in Paris, having left almost 500,000 men behind him in the snows of Russia. In addition, the American Continental Army's second invasion that had been repulsed at Frenchman's Creek, which could make the

'Colonists', as Sellick still referred to them, now feel somewhat nervous, even vulnerable.

The carriage crunched onto the frozen gravel of Horse Guards Parade and he quickly descended from his carriage to enter the wide doors within the portico, first acknowledging the 'present arms' of the two Grenadier Guards there on duty. He hurried further into the warmth, unbuttoning his greatcoat as he went, to finally enter the December gloom of Secretary Wilson's own domain, the office that provided a bulwark to his own. The grandest of grandfather clocks, boomed out the eleventh hour, but Wilson was holding out his skeletal hand, the pure white of his cuff very prominent, but in the hand was the letter that Livermore had been expecting. He took the letter, nodded his thanks towards Wilson and then entered his own office to break the seal and read the letter even before he sat. It was as he had expected, Sellick's motion had been whipped, its assent certain, as had indeed transpired, and the letter, written before the vote, was from the Minister for War himself, Lord Bathurst, instructing Livermore to arrange for a strong Division of three Brigades to be transported to Hamilton at the Western end of Lake Ontario. This with a view to mounting a punitive expedition across the isthmus and securing the town of Rochester, which could be used as a military base, supplied from the Port of Kingston. The letter continued, stating that monies would be made available for the augmentation of St. Catherine's Dock and Fort Erie, the former being able to support the latter. He read the letter again, then he left his office to lay the paper on Wilson's desk.

"Get that copied to Royal Ordnance at Woolwich, the Commissariat at the War Office and the Military Governor at Hamilton. You'll need to discover his name. All stamped 'received' and acknowledged by me. Last, a letter to Fortifications. I want a plan drawn up for how they would substantially augment Fort Erie in Canada. Two copies of that and another two of a plan of how St. Catherine's Dock can be improved, within reason, of course."

He then looked quizzically at Wilson.

"And those Letters of Authorisation I warned you about."

Wilson swung his deep brown cadaverous eyes up towards Livermore, a questioning expression on his face, the question being "How could you possibly doubt that they are not already prepared and waiting?", then the lugubrious gaze descended to guide his hand to the handle of a drawer from which he extracted two letters, one in an open cover addressed to the Governor General of Hamilton, the other in an open cover but with no address. He handed both to Livermore, who took them and then smacked both into the arch of his thumb and left forefinger, whilst stood thinking.

"We need someone who knows the territory to take the Bathurst copy to Hamilton."

He thought for no more than a second.

"Get hold of Bertram Lacey. He was in the first business on that border and not doing much these days. We'll promote him to Brigadier and send him. He can take Radipole. We'll dress him up as a Major."

He then took both Authorisations into his office for his signature.

"Here we go!"

oOo

Both fast frigates had parted company the previous day, having made good passage across the Atlantic, both propelled by a chill and muscular North-east wind that sent a steady, but not stormy, thrust across the starboard quarter of both. Thus, together they had held station, but when the Noon sight of the 31st December stated 46.57 Latitude and 58.57 Longitude, with St. Pierre Island off to starboard, the two frigates slowly drew apart, Sirius for the St. Lawrence seaway, Ariadne more Southerly for Bathurst Bay, New Brunswick. Easing slowly in with the last of the day, Ariadne anchored for the night within sight of the coast, such that dawn found the ship's longboat crunching into the shingle of the steep beach. The North-east wind that had carried them across the Atlantic now piled a significant surf onto the shingle, such that their passenger had to be carried from the boat to the dry of the shore and lowered safely down, him wearing plain Colonial clothes and with a small satchel over his shoulder, this held by a broad leather strap. The seaman knuckled his forehead as he handed over a carpet portmanteau.

"Good luck, Sir."

Jean Dulongue nodded his thanks and began his ascent of the beach, the loose shingle not making for easy progress, but he found enough time to turn and wave at the longboat, that now, with backed oars, was leaving the beach. The summit was gained, then the road and then he saw the only house in the landscape, not very far off and on the opposite side of the road. He walked to the front door and lifted the heavy knocker to use it three times. A teenage boy opened the door, but said nothing, but Dulongue had his question.

"This is Nash Creek?"

The boy nodded.

"I hope I have found the house of Mr. Macbrennan."

The boy nodded again.

"Could you please tell him that Mr. Du Lac is here to see him?"

The boy turned, leaving the door open and soon Macbrennan arrived, but he stepped outside, motioning Dulongue to follow him. Without a word they walked the short distance to the stable and once inside Macbrennan turned to him and stood, plainly waiting. Dulongue reached into the satchel and pulled out one of Livermore's Letters of Authorisation, which Macbrennan read, but it was brief and he soon looked up, speaking in a clear Aberdeen accent.

"Ye'll need a horse and a special saddle?"

"Yes, and some food. Enough to get me to La Pocatiere. You know it?"

Macbrennan nodded.

"I do. On the coast, but spend the night at Edmundston, the Sheep's Fleece. The Innkeeper is one of ours, he knows to ask no questions."

"What about La Pocatiere?"

Macbrennan shook his head.

"There ye're on your own, so be careful. There, ye canna know where anyone's sympathies lie, French, English or American."

With that warning he then went to the back of the stable to fetch a well-made saddle from the rack and carry it to a sturdy mare and begin the process of securing the saddle and bridle. With all in place, Macbrennan lifted the top leather of the saddle away from the layer beneath to reveal a hidden compartment and Dulongue inserted two pieces of artist's paper, each folded four times, pushing the stiff documents well inside. The portmanteau was secured over.

"What will ye tell them your business is? They'll ask, your being a stranger and I guess ye'll need some excuse to be there."

"Salt fish! To set up a factory. My family were involved in that, back in Nantes, a long time ago."

"In that case go on to Saint Jean Port Joli. That makes more sense. It has a quayside."

Dulongue nodded agreement, so Macbrennan, now satisfied, led the horse to the front door of the farm and, once there, he handed the reins to Dulongue.

"Wait here. I'll bring out some food."

Within minutes he returned with a bag bulging with bread, cheese and apples, which he handed up to the already mounted Dulongue, who smiled down at Macbrennan.

"Happy New Year! It's the first today."

Macbrennan smiled slightly, this accompanied by the faintest nod of his head, then Dulongue pulled the mare's head over and began his journey along the coast to pass quickly through a small fishing village and then follow a clear road sign for Edmundston which steered him onto a good road that took him through gentle hills covered with woodland. He patted his horse's neck.

"I'm going to call you Fabienne. I have a sister of that name."

The following day, whilst Dulongue was settling himself into lodgings in Saint Jean Port Joli, after proclaiming himself intent on setting up in a salt fish business somewhere on that coast, HMS Sirius had penetrated as far down the St. Lawrence seaway as her Captain dared, close to Quebec City, and her two passengers were being transferred into a small Royal Navy sloop that could navigate the narrow waters of the St. Lawrence and past Montreal, which was to be their journey onwards into Lake Ontario and then to Hamilton at the far end. Brigadier Bernard Lacey, in full uniform, and Major Redeemed Radipole, equally splendid in his lower rank, climbed carefully down the steep tumblehome of the frigate whilst their sparse luggage was being lowered by rope. All was soon done and the two vessels parted, with cries of "Good luck' from the higher deck of the frigate. Thus, over the next three days, whilst Dulongue made himself very familiar with Saint-Jean Port Joli, the two Army Officers allowed themselves to be steadily carried up the St. Lawrence to finally enter the ocean-like expanse of Lake Ontario, where the good sloop stretched her wings to undertake the passage across to the port of Hamilton.

Thus, on the fourth day of their arrival, when Dulongue was leaving Saint Jean Port Joli, having been wined and dined the previous evening by the Mayor who constantly regaled him with how perfect his village would be for a salt-fishery, Brigadier Lacey and Major Radipole were approaching the Military Headquarters across from the quayside of Hamilton. The two men, despite the huge difference in their age and experience had struck up a more than workable relationship, both being keen chess players and across the Atlantic this had whiled away many an hour, Radipole usually being the victor, but the discussion after the game brought the two further together.

The Headquarters at Hamilton was of high colonial style, the frontage topped with the common elongated Roman style triangle, the windows Italian Renaissance. Altogether it spoke of power, wealth and authority. What did not please Lacey was the very much less than perfect 'present arms' from the two Militia sentries at the door, but they passed on through to the reception desk, where the man behind the desk greeted them with a look of astonishment, even alarm, at the sight of a Brigadier General and his Major ADC striding purposefully into his domain. With no easement of his expression he stood to receive the pair, but Lacey's manner did much to put him at his ease.

"Good morning. I am Brigadier-General Lacey, this is my ADC, Major Radipole. We hope you can help. We are here to see the Governor, General Tallwood, we believe. Here is our Letter of Authorisation."

He placed Livermore's letter onto the redwood counter, the receptionist noting the large, Ministry for War seal and the state of alarm returned. He picked up the letter as though it were a religious relic and examined the seal as he held it in both hands. He then walked around the counter and his voice trembled slightly as he spoke.

"If you would both be so good as to wait here. I will take this to the General now. I'm sure he will want to see you directly."

Lacey nodded his thanks and agreement, but remained standing.

"Is there somewhere that we could sit, whilst waiting?"

Confusion intensified further within the receptionist and he sidled over towards a door off the hall, indicating the entrance with his left hand whilst still holding the venerated letter in his right.

"Yes, of course. If you would be so good as to wait in here. I'm sure you will be comfortable."

Lacey nodded once again in his direction, for the pair to enter the room and sink into deep, dark-tanned and studded armchairs, probably French from before the time of Wolfe. However, the luxury lasted but two minutes before Tallwood himself entered the room, as eager and as anxious as his receptionist to convey to the pair both their welcome and his efficiency. He was evidently not much younger that Lacey, his uniform was very much old-style late Eighteenth Century, but he was not corpulent and he was easy on his feet. He went first to Lacey, extending his hand with a broad smile on his weather-beaten face.

"Welcome, General Lacey."

Then he turned to Radipole, who saluted, very smartly, this being returned. Then Tallwood turned to his receptionist.

"Metcalf! Have these gentlemen been offered any refreshment?"

Metcalf's shoulders fell three inches.

"No Sir, they have not."

"Then bring coffee to my office at your best speed."

Leaving Metcalf in the room, Tallwood led the way down the hall to an imposing door, already open to permit entrance to a large office, the major feature being a huge desk, its expanse of green leather dominating the room, competing successfully with the dull varnish of several pictures of battles, both of land and sea, but there was one portrait, that of George II. Tallwood sat behind the desk, this occupied solely by Livermore's now opened letter and he smacked his palms on its surface.

"French! Left behind for us."

By now Lacey and Radipole had seated themselves on two equally elaborate chairs, these missing only the arms of Tallwood's, who then sat forward, studying Lacey.

"You name is familiar General. Were you at Quebec when we held it against the Continentals in 75?"

Lacey shook his head.

"No, I was not, but I served here for many years after, from Lieutenant to Colonel, staring across the border, waiting for their next effort, which seems to have arrived with your tenure here."

Tallwood nodded, then grinned.

"But we've sent them packing! And made then sorry. We got Detroit back in August and gave them a bloody nose at Queenston Heights and Frenchman's Creek. They'll not try again for some time, I'll wager!"

Lacey smiled and nodded, then he slid the Livermore copy of Bathurst's letter across the desk. Tallwood managed the distance with his own arm to pick up the letter, break the imposing seal with a loud crack and then begin to read. The further his eyes went down the page, the further his eyebrows went upward. Having read all, he dropped the thick paper onto the desk and looked hard at Lacey.

"We are going to invade!"

The first word was heavily emphasised, but Lacey had his reply ready.

"We wish to secure the neck of land between Lake Ontario and Lake Erie to block off any further efforts across there. Both those invasions you mentioned came across there. As you have read, we wish to augment Fort Erie and capture Rochester, from which we can meet any further invasions immediately. Monies will be available to expand St. Catherine's Dock around the coast from here, from which Fort Erie can be supported. Rochester can be supported from Port Hope and Cobourg, both immediately across the lake."

He paused to regard Tallwood steadily.

"But that you have just read for yourself, so, for any of those requirements, do you anticipate a problem? Any that cannot be overcome from your good offices here?"

Tallwood sat back, struggling to take everything in. Soon he would be in the middle of a small war which would dwarf everything that had gone before. He shook his head, before answering weakly.

"No, none."

Lacey sat back and grinned.

"Good! Now your role in this is threefold. First, in the Spring a strong Division will arrive, three Brigades. They will need accommodation both for themselves and their materiel. Secondly, you need to gather your Militia to both here and up the coast at Mississauga, for embarkation at Port Hope and Cobourg, when the time comes. For the third, Major Radipole here has some drawings."

Radipole slid his hand into his satchel and pulled out two folded drawings and passed them across.

"These, Sir, are our proposals for the strengthening of Fort Erie and the improvements at St. Catherine's Dock."

Tallwood gathered both, but did not open either, then Lacey spoke.

"Those are to help you make the necessary contracts to complete both works shown in those plans. I trust you have someone with experience of military engineering?"

Tallwood nodded.

"Yes, we have two Engineers who can oversee such as that."

"Good! They will obviously be required for the improvements of Fort Erie. For St. Catherine's Dock, we must leave that to your civilian contacts."

Lacey sat back, arms folded and smiling.

"When can you start? Very soon, I hope."

Tallwood nodded again.

"Yes! Yes, I will get my people onto it immediately."

"Good! Now, both Major Radipole and myself will remain here for perhaps a month. We need to make a report, you understand, which will describe all the satisfactory progress as it arrives, we are sure."

He leaned forward, conspiratorially.

"This is an important affair, Tallwood. International affairs, you understand. If all goes well, and it's in your neck of the woods, then, who knows? A return home and a knighthood for the man who oversaw preparations and made it all possible. Men have felt the touch of the sword on their shoulders for a lot less!"

With that, Lacey stood and bowed, Radipole saluted and both left the room, passing by the belated coffee and leaving Tallwood to read Bathurst's letter once more and then begin writing many letters of his own.

Sometime later that day, having ridden the forty miles to Quebec and now being secure in comfortable lodgings with his horse stabled, both paid for in advance, Dulongue set out in the first dark of the evening, to find what he had been told was the 'French Quarter'. In reply to the question to his landlord, "Where do they speak French?", he had received the reply, "Cross on the ferry, get behind the Cathedral." He was now on the ferry and, looking ahead as the ferryman sculled his craft efficiently across the running tide, he could see the tower and the spire of the building he sought. He decided to check with the ferryman.

"Où sont les bars Français?"

The reply was immediate.

"Derrière la cathédrale."

He gave the man a shilling as he stepped out of the boat, which seemed to please him greatly and then Dulongue set out, using the lights within the tower of the Cathedral as an aiming point. He entered several bars and inns, ordered a glass of wine in each and listened. It was when he heard nothing around him but French, that he waved the landlord over and spoke in English.

"I am new here, from London. Is it all French here?"

The landlord nodded, but his face remained grim as he spoke.

"Was New France. It still is!"

Dulongue grinned.

"So, you have no love of the English?"

He pulled a face and shrugged. Dulongue knew why, the British would have spies out to test the sympathies of men such as this landlord, but the man did speak his mind, as though wishing to unburden his hidden feelings.

"We speak French, but we do not live as French. The English, they attack, but is not the right word. How you say?"

"Come down."

"Yes, they come down on us any time we ask for more ……… Francais?"

"Frenchness."

"Yes, in our lives, but we live and work and get along. We are different, but the British are happy to rule us and not try to change too much. Is not so bad, I think."

"What extra 'Frenchness' would you want?"

"To keep our festivals and to have our people elected to the Council."

"Bastille Day?"

"Banned!"

"And a French Quebecian standing for the Council?"

"Banned!"

Dulongue nodded resignedly.

"Where I come from only those with property can vote. Any efforts to change that is clubbed to the ground. It is not so very different from here."

He took off his hat and showed the scar behind his ear, the result of a narrow escape from France, but a wound was a wound. The landlord studied the mark and then responded.

"So, you come to Canada? You are right, it is little better here, as you will soon understand."

"So you say, but not in the new country South of here."

The landlord froze, but Dulongue continued, leaning forward, his voice low.

"Can I get there? Is it possible? French parents, but British I was born, yet I have no love for their King, nor their Parliament. You stand as a free man in their country and still they give you this."

He pointed again to the scar, before replacing his hat.

"There must be some who try to get down South."

The landlord finished cleaning a glass and stared hard at Dulongue.

"You wish to move South? Well, that is your own affair."

"I do, yes, but can you help?"

There was no reply and so Dulongue reached into his pocket and produced a gold guinea, which he slid across the bar in the landlord's direction. It was quickly seized and taken from sight. The Landlord then leaned forward and spoke quietly.

"I have heard, only heard, this is rumour, you understand, that there may be some people in an Inn called the 'Fighting Cocks', in Montreal."

"Have you known people who have gone there?'

"Yes."

"Did you ever see them again?"

"No, but I know no more. This is rumour, no more than talk I hear in my bar. If true, I do not know."

Dulongue nodded, smiled and pushed across tuppence for his drink and left. He was not required to wait for a ferry, the same oarsman was there to row him across and receive another shilling. Late that evening Dulongue packed his portmanteau and at dawn he was on the already busy road along the South bank of the St. Lawrence to complete the 150 miles to Montreal.

oOo

Whilst Dulongue was easing his mount over the four-day journey, Lacey and Radipole were making their presence felt at various meetings, imposing themselves if only by the fact that they were often the only wearers of the scarlet uniform. Inwardly Lacey was pleased,

Tallwood had set about his tasks with some vigour and all three of his duties towards his orders were addressed by many assemblies of worthies that Tallwood made them aware of and also ensured that they were invited to.

Whilst their tasks that were part of the deception progressed satisfactorily, and in plain sight, on the ninth day of the New Year Dulongue rode Fabienne into Southbank Montreal. There was no need to remain on that side, the St. Lawrence was completely frozen, the way over well marked and so, once over, he sought the way to the Inn called the Fighting Cocks. His first enquiries were met with blank looks, until someone said "Ville Marie" and pointed. He rode in that direction and made more enquiries until he found himself looking up at an Inn sign that showed two cockerels in close combat and the two words new painted, but over a much wider background, that also of new paint. Dulongue understood the significance of all and why so much empty space remained either side of the simple two words and he spoke softly to himself, with a deep sense of understanding

"They were forced to paint out the French and make the sign English. There's more suppression here than in Quebec."

He tied Fabienne to the hitching ring and entered, carrying his portmanteau. The barman, or more possibly the landlord, because he looked authoritative, was polishing a glass and he immediately gave Dulongue an inquisitive, even suspicious stare, but Dulongue advanced confidently up to the bar.

"Can I get lodgings here and stabling for my horse?"

"Shilling a day for you. A shilling for the horse. Food all found. How long do you expect to stay?"

"One week. Perhaps more."

"Pay the week in advance."

Dulongue nodded, felt for his purse and found fourteen shillings in the form of two crowns and two florins, all relatively new and above suspicion, but nothing close to freshly minted, Waters had been very careful over that. The landlord picked up a crown and tapped it several times onto the copper-sheathed bar before scooping all up, then pocketing all. Then he took a deep breath.

"Jules! Marie!"

A boy and a young lady came running in, through an entrance behind the bar.

"Jules. Stable this gentleman's horse, from out front. Marie, show him to Six."

Jules disappeared through the same door behind the bar, whilst Marie came around to the front. She attempted to pick up the portmanteau, but Dulongue seized the handle first.

"That's fine! I'll carry it, if you could just show me the way."

The result was a coquettish smile and a firm look upwards from brown eyes, before she walked to a door at the far end of the bar-room, which opened onto stairs upwards. He followed her swaying hips up the short flight, then onto a corridor.

"I see your sign outside is newly painted."

She turned and nodded, but said nothing, so he continued.

"Did it once say Lutte Contre les Coqs?"

She then turned fully towards him.

"It did. How would you know that?"

He smiled.

"I speak French. I was born in France."

"And now you speak English and work for the English."

"Right for the first. Wrong for the second."

"So what do you do, if not work for the English?"

"I come from Hamilton. I work there, translating. English to French. French to English. A useful thing to be able to do."

"And what are you doing here?"

He pulled wry expression.

"Ah! In these times it is usually best for a man to keep his business to himself."

By now they were in the room and Marie was throwing open the curtains, whilst Dulongue threw the portmanteau onto the bed. The curtains now drawn back, she turned to him

"I could light a fire, but that would be tuppence extra."

"Do it. Do I pay you? Now?"

The smile of the bar-room returned.

"You do."

Two penny coins were found and handed to her, then a thruppence.

"C'est pour vous, Marie. Merci."

Again, the smile.

"Merci beaucoup, M'sieu, but do not speak too much French. In Montreal it can get you arrested!"

With that, she left the room, giving him a smile and a final look, with her left hand on the door jam. With Marie now departed, Dulongue unpacked the few items that he had in his portmanteau, the spare clothes and toiletries were removed, but the quality duelling pistol remained in. Then he sat to ponder his next move. There was clearly British suppression here and that bred resentment, but he must tread carefully, there was always suspicion of strangers and strangers asking questions doubled any suspicion. He could be taken as an 'Agent Provocateur', but Marie could be useful, already she was probably spreading the word that he came from Hamilton, was French and spoke French. That was a good start. He rose and took himself downstairs to the bar, hoping for a good meal of quality French cooking.

He spent the next three days, frequenting the bar and spending time elsewhere, in the town or riding Fabienne South of the river, familiarising himself with the roads that led South. He may need to use one, if he was to meet anyone of any significance from the new Republic. Each evening he sat in the bar and Marie brought him bottles of the local ale, which he found very acceptable. All around him in the bar he could hear only French spoken but there was one group who were always gathered in the same corner and always the same men. One evening Dulongue sat as close to them as he dared in order to overhear their conversation and often he heard, "Le mal Anglais', and often one of them was describing some slight, insult, or plain frustration inflicted on them by anyone British, from common soldiers to Montreal officialdom. The next evening he sat further away and Marie brought him his customary bottle of ale, so he indicated with his head the men sat in the corner.

"Who are those men? They seem to have little regard for the English."

She gave a quick look over her shoulder, then turned back.

"They all hate the English. Be careful of them, the English know of them. They do things, but I'm not sure what."

Dulongue smiled and looked up at her.

"Be careful of them? They are dangerous, yes, because they wish to get rid of the English, just as the Americans did? Am I right?"

Her face became serious, even worried.

"Something like that. I have heard their talk."

"What talk?"

"Anything that damns the English!"

With that she wiped the table.

"Be careful!"

As she left to return to the bar, Dulongue looked over at the men, five of them, even the oldest could not be much over forty. If he was going to make contact with Free Quebec sympathisers, they were the most likely that he had found so far. The next evening he decided to act and he went to the bar to buy a bottle of wine, which came from the landlord's dwindling stock and it cost eleven shillings. He took the wine to the men's table and placed the bottle in the centre.

"I'd like to buy you men a drink. I believe we have some sympathies in common."

The largest and the most bewhiskered looked up, then at the wine, then back to Dulongue.

"We speak French here!"

Dulongue nodded.

"So it would seem. Nothing but French, but what I have to say is best said in English. The fewer that understand, the better."

No reply came, but the men all shared suspicious or anxious looks between themselves.

"Do I get to sit down?"

The hirsute leader indicated to the two opposite, these sat on a bench, that they should move up to make room, they did so and Dulongue sat down. Marie brought over some glasses, her face showing her deep concern, then Dulongue poured the wine and he raised his own glass.

"To freedom and our own country!"

Dismissively and showing little enthusiasm, all raised their glass and drank, then the leader looked at Dulongue.

"You can call me Jean."

Dulongue smiled and drank from his own glass again.

"That is my name! Jean Du Lac."

"In which case mine is Michel."

He sat forward aggressively, right forearm on the table, his left hand on the table edge, the forearm vertical.

"Now just what sympathies are these that you talk of?"

"To rule ourselves as Free French."

Michel sat back, releasing a dismissive gasp.

"There is nothing special in that! All here who count themselves in any way French think that. Such thoughts are nothing special."

Dulongue returned his gaze impassively.

"If so many of you here think it, what do you do about it? Is it not something you also would want? They managed it down South!"

Michel did not move, but he studied Dulongue for some seconds.

"We do not know you! We are just men who live and work here and speak French, because this was once a French colony. I think it best that you leave us to our drink and our talk. Thank you for the wine."

Dulongue sat forward and returned Michel's hard stare.

"You know as well as I, that the Americans would wish to take the lands this side of the river and the lakes, but first they must defeat the

English, but they have now lost. Twice! But there are things happening now, up in Hamilton, which point to an English invasion. If that invasion were defeated, the Americans would be more likely to try again and this time win. Would you like to be part of a Republic or stay in an English colony?"

Michel sat back.

"Goodnight M'sieu Du Lac. We wish you a good night's sleep!"

Dulongue finished his wine in one swallow, stood and bowed in the direction of the men, but there was no response. He returned to his room, loaded the pistol and waited. The hours passed into almost dawn, but nothing happened and no-one came. With the city now silent, he slept through what remained of the night, enjoyed a late breakfast and then spent that day wandering in the city, continuously checking that he was not being followed and he was not. At the day's end, his hopes had begun to sink, perhaps those men were just discontents who did nothing. Marie served him an evening meal, saying nothing but the accusing look she gave him spoke her strong disapproval; nothing needed to be said, but her thoughts were obvious, "What are you doing? You could be arrested or killed. You're being stupid." The men came to sit in their corner, but Dulongue made no contact, instead going early to his room, where he pondered his next move, should this one fail, as now seemed very possible. After more than an hour, there came a knock on the door. He approached and placed his ear close to the wood.

"Who's there?"

"Marie!"

The answer was more like a shout than any kind of greeting, but it was her voice and so he opened the door. Immediately he saw a terrified Marie with a pistol against her neck, then the pistol came from there to slam against his forehead. Marie was thrust aside for men to enter the room, then all went black as a bag was thrust over his head and he was pulled forward. He was aware of being frogmarched along the corridor then to stumble down some stairs, supported on two sides then finally pushed into what he took to be a coach, this confirmed when it began to move, jolting and swaying. He rose from the floor but he was thrust back down and so he decided to keep quiet. After several minutes, enough for a journey out of the city, the coach halted and he was pulled onto a seat and the bag removed. There were three men in the coach, two were pointing pistols at him, the third was sat immediately opposite, but none were those of the Inn. The interior was lit by the light of tallow candles in two lamps and the yellow light made all inside look much less than healthy, but the unhealthiest aspect came from the savage look the man opposite gave Dulongue.

"Do you know what we do to English agents?"

Dulongue took a deep breath.

"I can imagine, but I'm not one of those. I come from Hamilton where the English are making preparations, almost certainly for an invasion of their own into the United States."

The stark revelation changed the man's expression to what could be described as mild shock and so Dulongue seized the moment and sat forward, showing aggression of his own and the two pistols came nearer, but he spoke harshly, all the same.

"And I don't know you! This could be a English trap. Why should I trust you, just because you dragged me from my room to here? You could be hoping I would reveal something, but I tell you now that I have news from Hamilton and documents to back that up. It will prove what I say about the Yengees!"

The contemptuous word, meaning foreign invaders and oppressors and most often used by Native Indians, caused the man to sit back.

"What documents?"

"They're back in the Inn. Had you come to my room with no violence, I would have shown them to you."

"So what's happening in Hamilton?"

"Preparations to receive a lot of soldiers, amongst other things. In places like Mississaugua and Port Hope."

"What other things?"

"Why should I trust you? Revealing more could betray my comrades back in Hamilton."

The man raised both hands and lowered them, motioning for the pistols to be lowered and they were.

"We learn that you were born in France, but we do not like it that you speak English so well. Why?"

"I was raised in France, but my family were successful merchants and we had to flee to England in '93, from the guillotine. My family came to Canada in 1805, forced out when there was such a strong threat of a French invasion, a French hating crowd wrecked our home and business."

"Where did you live after you came?"

"Just outside Saint Jean Port Joli."

"Doing what?"

"Salting fish, there's plenty around there that do that. We did that in Nantes before the Citizens' Councils started condemning all and any merchant 'Aristos' to death."

"Why did you end up in Hamilton?"

"My parents died of the fever in the year Nine. I sold the business and moved. I wanted something better. There I translate, I hope to teach, but the children of Free Quebecians!"

The man sat back.

"We must see these documents."

"You will, if you take me back, but I will speak all that I know only to an American Officer. That way I know that my information has reached the correct ears. It is vital that they know what I know. That you can arrange?"

The man nodded.

"Remain at the Inn and you will be contacted. Be patient."

He turned to one of the guards.

"Retour a Montreal."

The man exited through the door and soon Dulongue heard shouts in French and felt the coach turning. The return journey was occupied by questions on Nantes, how fish were salted and the charms of Saint Jean Port Joli. Dulongue knew that this was all a test and all questions were fielded, until the last.

"Are you Catholic?"

"No, Huguenot."

"And you hope to teach! All schools in Quebec are Catholic."

"Not all, I believe and let's say I hope for more enlightened times. Such as exist in the new Republic!"

The following morning, Dulongue walked casually from the Inn, now content that the documents shown to the men the previous evening had convinced them of his authenticity. After ensuring that he was not being followed, he purchased some clothes and a large satchel, went to an Inn and there he disguised himself in the privy, his own clothes going into the satchel. He then walked casually to the Military Headquarters of Montreal, but he hurried inside, not caring to look up at the huge Union flag suspended above him. His first action was to extract Livermore's Letter of Authorisation from the lining of his boot and his own short report on progress so far, which he had written immediately prior to leaving his room. The receptionist appeared annoyed when approached by this civilian dressed in Quebec fashions, but his face immediately changed when Dulongue placed Livermore's letter before him for it to be read and the man immediately became subservient.

"How can I help?"

"I need to see your Military Governor immediately. Take that letter with you."

The man rose, picking up the letter carefully. He disappeared down a corridor and Dulongue went to a window beside the door and looked for anyone stood watching. There was no one, at least not opposite. He returned to the desk to see the receptionist and also a middle-aged man in a Colonel's uniform hurrying in his direction, his hand held out in welcome, his face beaming, but his eyes betraying his anxiety.

"Mr. Du Lac. I am Colonel Feltwood, the Military Governor. You have some business you need our help with?"

Dulongue nodded.

"I do and it must be done quickly. Not here, but in the privacy of your office."

Feltwood gestured with his hand back along the corridor.

"Of course! Please come this way."

After another look backwards, Dulongue followed him, into a modest and dingy office whose sole decoration was a portrait of King George III. Dulongue sat down before Feltwood had arrived at his own chair and he leaned forward.

"Colonel. You have read General Livermore's letter?"

There came enthusiastic nodding.

"I have, yes."

"And noted that it says all help must be afforded to myself?"

More nodding.

Dulongue then produced his report.

"This must get back to England as soon as possible."

He slid the report across the desk. Feltwood reached out for it, and turned back the top fold, as though to read it, but Dulongue's own hand coming down over prevented any further movement.

"You do not read it, you only seal it. I will need a cover, also to be sealed."

Feltwood produced the thick paper for the cover, but Dulongue first indicated the report.

"Sealed. Please."

Feltwood did so, with the red sealing wax and using his own stamp. Dulongue then wrote the address on the cover, which enveloped the report, which was also then sealed closed. He then stood up, with the document now in his hand.

"This will get back as quickly as possible, I hope, which means military escort to Quebec and a trusted Officer placing it into the hands of the Captain of one of His Majesty's warships. Nothing less."

Still standing, he pushed the document forward, for it to finally arrive before Feltwood, who now stood himself and held out his hand. Dulongue took it and nodded his thanks, but Feltwood beamed out what he hoped would be thorough reassurance.

"Have no doubt, Mr. Du Lac, all will happen as you request and you will mention my name and the help we gave to General Livermore, I hope?"

Dulongue merely smiled.

"I will, if I get back. But that letter must! Now, do you have a back entrance?"

oOo

His room was not empty when he returned, sat waiting was his main interrogator from the coach. Dulongue studied him carefully, before speaking.

"Things have moved?"

The man nodded, but his face remained stern.

"They have. Here are your directions, with a map to direct you."

He held out a sheet of paper which Dulongue stepped forward to take. The paper now delivered, the man stood and walked to the door.

"If you are not genuine, Du Lac, this will be the end of you!"

Dulongue ignored the comment.

"There will be an American Officer waiting for me? If not, what I have will be torn up and scattered to the wind!"

The man turned and paused on his way.

"That is what we have arranged, or at least asked for. It's up to the Americans how to respond."

With that he finally departed and Dulongue closed the door. He read and studied what he had been given. The meeting was for the morning of the following day, in the early light, 8 o' clock. The instructions were to ride through a place called Hemmingford, after which there was a crossroads where he would find a coach waiting. The first of the villages listed to guide him was familiar from his explorations of the previous days, but he did not wish to trust a journey in the dark and so the only alternative was to leave now and spend the night out on the plain or in the forest. The cold weather did not make that sound attractive, but there seemed no other way to be sure of making the time. He immediately left the Inn, bought a blanket and the heaviest boat-cloak he could find, returned and packed both satchels and his portmanteau, then he went to the bar and, luckily found Marie there.

"Marie! I have to make a journey. Do you think you could pack me some food?"

He placed his newly purchased large satchel on the bar. She took it, but the same accusing look was on her face. Within a minute she returned with the satchel now containing bread, cheese, apples and a bottle of ale. The most inviting was some kind of pastry.

"What are you going to do?"

"Best you don't know."

"Will you come back?"

"I expect to."

He slid a full guinea coin across the bar but did not remove his hand until she had covered his and the coin could be taken back without being seen.

"I'm sorry about what happened to you last night. Buy yourself something nice!"

With that he dragged the satchel off the bar and went around to the stable where he saddled and bridled Fabienne himself, first checking that the papers were still in its place within the saddle. Then he left, to cross the St. Lawrence by the ice-bridge, grateful for the warmth of the boat-cloak. The road-sign, this now known to him, clearly stated 'St. Mathieu', which marked his route South and he set Fabienne to an easy trot. The light remained good as the villages were gained and passed through, but the cold increased with the dying of the light. In the last of the day, he came to Hemmingford, which proved to be no more than a few houses and a church on a straight road across an bleak, empty plain, but the road beyond disappeared into thick forest. Hemmingford offered no shelter and so he walked Fabienne forward into the trees. He had no deep concerns over spending a night in the open, this was nothing new, but some shelter would be preferable and the chance to light a fire. Luck was with him, he came to a grassy clearing with a stone-built store at the far edge. This he shared with Fabienne, she could keep him warm almost as well as any fire, but he kindled one anyway and settled to eat Marie's food. Inside the satchel he found a hastily written note, "Be careful. These are bad times with many bad men. Trust no one." He smiled, surprised that she could write, but also at the sentiment the note conveyed. He had liked her and he was pleased that she liked him, but that was as nothing compared to what he had to achieve on the morrow. He restoked the fire, rolled himself in the blanket, then the cloak and set his watch against the wall, hoping that the light of dawn would waken him.

In the event it was Fabienne that woke him, snorting and whinnying when she eyed the grass her tether did not allow her to reach and so he hobbled her and allowed her out of the store. His watch stated 7 o' clock and so he ate the last of his food, pulled Fabienne in, to then fasten the saddle and bridle and re-gain the road. The trees closed over above him, re-establishing the gloom of the dawn, but it was a matter of minutes before he came to the crossroads, where he saw a coach, but much more significant was what he took to be a whole Company of

United States Rangers, just visible in their buckskins but, nevertheless, plentiful on both sides, all with their weapons at the ready. Plainly, his threat to tear his document to pieces in the event of betrayal was useless, he would be shot at the first gesture. One Ranger ran to the coach and so Dulongue walked Fabienne further, dismounted and led her the final yards, when a man, well-dressed, came out of the coach and stood waiting. Dulongue casually hitched Fabienne to the wheel of the coach and stood silent himself. The man then spoke.

"You would be M'sieu Du Lac and you have some information for us."

"If the 'us' is who I want it to be, then yes."

"Meaning?"

"There must be a United States Officer in that coach or I say nothing and give you nothing. I'm tired of playing games! I had to spend a night out in the forest to be here at the time you chose."

At that point there came a voice from within the coach, a deep Southern drawl.

"Rest assured, Sir, I am an American Officer and we appreciate the trouble you have taken. Please to come inside."

At this, Dulongue went to Fabienne's saddle and pulled out the papers. He held them up for the man to see and then walked to the coach door and entered. Inside was an elegant man, probably in his thirties, wearing an immaculate Republican uniform, the bright red of the deep lapels contrasting with the dark blue of the coat, all set off by white shirt, breeches and hose. The other man joined them and closed the door and it was he who spoke first.

"So, you have something for us?"

Dulongue sat back, smiling slightly.

"You have the advantage of me, Sirs!"

The Officer sat forward.

"My apologies. I am Captain Pierre Brassard and this is Mr. James McMichael."

Dulongue bowed in their direction with his head.

"Your servant, Sirs!"

He then unfolded one of the documents to show it to be the plan of a fortification, one-part a cross-section showing the construction, the other a full plan, including the Niagara estuary. Dulongue pointed to the latter.

"This is a plan of how the British plan to improve Fort Erie with these gun emplacements. They want to do it quickly, with earthworks fronted by stone. A simple and quick addition, shown by the section."

McMichael took the plan and studied it, counting the new embrasures. He came to twelve.

"And this proves what?"

"That the British wish to secure the neck of land between Lake Ontario and Lake Erie. That fort, strengthened, at the entrance to the Niagara River would prevent you sending anything down that river to support what you have further in. That is part of the scheme they have, which includes to invade across there."

Brassard undid the buckle on a satchel besides him and pulled out a map of the area. He spread it out, so that all could see and Dulongue noticed that Fort Erie was already shown. McMichael was plainly the most suspicious, speaking with a clear Irish accent.

"How did you come by this?"

Dulongue looked at him directly, smiling openly.

"A clerk in the Military Engineers department is a rather lonely man and he was befriended, shall we say, by an attractive woman who spoke of the rumours now abounding about Fort Erie and St. Catherine's Dock. She told him that her brother ran a coastal fleet and would wish to bid for the contract to transport the stone for the fort. To see the plan and estimate quantities would help his bid to be successful, so she said to him, and so we had the use of it for a night."

McMichael nodded, but was clearly not fully convinced.

"Very clever!"

DuLongue then casually tossed across the plan to augment St. Catherine's Dock.

"There's the plan for the docks, so that Fort Erie can be better supported. Coming by that was easy, you only needed to ask for copy to help you make a bid."

However, McMichael gave it barely a glance, because Brassard had now turned his attention from the map.

"If they are planning an invasion, what else makes you think that?"

Dulongue now treated him to a direct look.

"The military in Hamilton are buying up warehouse space. All they can get. On top, farmers' fields are being sequestered, obviously for camps, because Militia are being called up all over and arriving now, as we speak. Every day, vessels and barges arrive in Mississauga and the small port of Cobourg."

Both opposite returned to the map to find the latter fishing village. McMichael looked up.

"Why there, do you know?"

Dulongue released a deep breath.

"Well, I'm no military man, but you look across the lake and you see Rochester. If they gain that and, with Fort Erie strengthened, that neck of land will be secure for them. From there, they can come further South and do who knows what? With respect, Captain, you know what it means to meet British Redcoats in the open field, muzzle to muzzle."

Brassard nodded slightly, but it was McMichael who spoke again.

"We've heard it was spoken in their Parliament that a Division should be sent to do this work."

Dulongue shrugged.

"That's for you to interpret."

McMichael's eyes narrowed.

"What do you hope for, from this?"

Dulongue's face hardened.

"If the reinforced British secure a hold on that side of the lakes, what chance is there for a Free Quebec? Only a successful American invasion can do that and these plans makes the chances of that so much more remote."

"You could be a British agent!"

The bold accusation surprised Dulongue, but he reacted immediately with a prepared reply.

"Doing what? An agent taking a risk like this would be trying to persuade you to do God knows what! I'm not persuading you to do anything, this is information, no more. You can react to it as you choose. You could do nothing! Not move one gun or one soldier. No risk! I am telling you what I know and what my comrades in Hamilton have gathered. Were I an agent, would I be doing all that I have done, with all the risk, just to give you a mere warning? I'm here to warn you to keep watch. To be on your guard."

McMichael then sat forward and jabbed his finger even further.

"You could be trying to get us to move troops there, whilst the damn British attack elsewhere!"

Dulongue sat forward, his face merely inches from that of McMichael. His voice then rose a few decibels.

"I can't answer that. The whole damn thing that they're up to may be a ruse to disguise some move elsewhere! What I'm telling you is what I know, the British are making preparations for an invasion. It may be ruse or not, but it's happening on the ground."

He paused, staring straight at McMichael.

"So! There's the plan for the fort."

He waved it at him.

"For the rest, you can use your own contacts in Hamilton to see what's happening and it's more than obvious. I'm giving you a warning, that's all. There's no risk to you, but, if you've any brains at all, you'll get someone over there to Hamilton and you'll find out what I have said is true! Or not bother!"

He sat back, obviously exasperated.

"I've had enough. There's no more I can tell you. I took a risk, taking myself up to Montreal to make contact with those who could bring this meeting about. There are none in Hamilton that we could trust. That is a very British town."

He sat forward almost on his feet.

"There is no more I can tell you. What you do with it now, lies in your own hands. I wish to take myself back to safety. I wish you good day and good luck."

His face showed exasperation as he left the coach, with no more words and he closed the door himself. Outside was a Ranger Officer and Dulongue went up to him.

"Anything to eat? I used up all mine last night!"

The Captain grinned and indicated towards two of his men stood nearby. They both reached into their haversacks and drew out biscuits, dried fruit and some strips of dried meat, all then being dropped into the satchel hanging from Fabienne's saddle. Dulongue pulled out a strip of the dried meat and held it up.

"Beef or buffalo?"

The Ranger grinned.

"Buffalo!"

Dulongue grinned and took a bite.

"The best!"

He then mounted and turned her back North.

"Good luck, Captain. Maybe we'll meet again someday. In Quebec, I hope!"

He set Fabienne to a good canter and the further North he went, the more he felt at ease, but soon he was tending as much West as North. His destination was Quebec and then home. He would take no more risks in Montreal.

oOo

General Livermore looked at the calendar on the wall. The squares showed that this was the final day of January and, that simple fact once more confirmed, for it was not the first time he had carefully studied the simple matrix, his thoughts moved to the Peninsula. Wellington was in Winter Quarters, having been forced back over the

Portuguese border, but in less than two months, he would be advancing again. Ten days previously he and Waters had been at Wellington's Headquarters at Freineda, not a dozen miles West of Cuidad Rodrigo, where he had learned of Wellington's plans for the Spring and also of reports from Spanish agents which indicated that El Rey was refusing Napoleon's request to send troops back to France. He now looked at the clock on the wall showing 11 am. Waters and Radipole should have arrived by now, but there was no time for him to become in any way irritated because at that moment Wilson knocked on the door and opened it to allow in the pair and also the booming chimes of the grandfather clock.

"Colonel Waters and Mr. Radipole are here to see you, Sir."

"Send them in."

Both entered and Livermore waved at the chairs before his desk, indicating that they should sit, and Livermore wasted no time on greetings.

"I've received word from Dulongue saying that he is to meet the Americans. That dated 17th January, got it today, which is why I've asked you here. Nothing more than that, so the result I do not know, but the seed has been sown, that I think we can safely assume. Where he is, I do not know, he could even be back in the country as we speak, but whatever, two of our three deceptions are in place; the statement in the House of Lords and Dulongue's efforts over in Canada."

Then, somewhat anxiously, he looked at Radipole.

"And you and Lacey. You are just returned and it went well, you think, with your part in all this?"

Radipole's pale eyes opened a little wider and his delicate hands came together on his knee.

"I'd say so, Sir, yes, very much so. General Tallwood in Hamilton, I must say set about his orders with the utmost celerity. As we left, Militia were arriving, arrangements for stores and accommodation were completed, boats had been sequestered and plans were being drawn up for the fort. Finally, money is being spent on St. Catherine's Dock and the fort, in one form or another. All the signs were there for anyone to see. Or discover, with the minimum of questioning."

Livermore nodded.

"Right, so Dulongue's message is thoroughly supported."

He chuckled.

"Knew I could count on Lacey to carry it off! And you, of course, Radipole. Job well done."

He sat back and looked at each in turn, Waters last.

“So, the last prong of the trident! Waters, have you your villainous forger and other men of the hood ready in place?”

Waters grinned.

“Events proceed at Weymouth. They ride at anchor as we speak, under more than one watchful eye. From within a hood!”

Livermore nodded, his voice resigned, as though he wanted no part in the dishonourable business that was to come.

“I can leave that particular piece of skulduggery to you.”

It was not a question, more a statement of fact and with that, he drew open the bottom drawer of his desk to bring up three fine-cut glasses and a bottle of even finer Scotch whisky, from which he poured three generous measures and pushed two glasses across his desk. Waters looked on eagerly, Radipole not so certain, but Livermore took no notice, even if he had realised Radipole’s disquiet and he raised his glass.

“Confusion to the Frogs!”

They all drank, Waters looking into his glass appreciatively before swallowing all, Radipole wondering how he would manage what remained after a tentative sip.

The ‘events’ then taking place, which Waters was referring to, were nothing as Livermore imagined, but he would have been pleased nevertheless. French agent Raymond Ballinger was staring through his spyglass, set up on a frame at the window of his rented rooms at the top of a building in the long rank that overlooked Weymouth bay. He could see out at anchor four transports and two warships, one a powerful frigate, the other a very useful brigantine. They had arrived two days previously. He knew that two more transports were moored at the harbour quayside, but for the whole picture he must find out more and get a report across the Channel. Small supply craft were plying back and forth to the six vessels in the bay and so he knew that he would not have much more time to discover just what was afoot. He allowed the telescope to drop forward and then he stood to put on his greatcoat and leave the building to walk unhurriedly to the quay. The walk was but a short distance, but he knew not that he was being followed, there being a goodly crowd walking the promenade. His ‘tail’ was one Jane Reakes, she carefully dressed so as not to give the impression of wealth, but that of a respectable girl, not moneyed, but from a well-to-do family. Behind her came her ‘support’, ex-Marine Luke Kettle, him following several yards behind. Ballinger had grown in the suspicions of the local Government Intelligence agents, who watched over the minor, but nevertheless important, Naval base at Weymouth. Just too often Ballinger had taken himself to the quayside, especially when any Royal Navy vessel was at the quay or anchored just outside, asking questions, "for a book", was his usual excuse. No-one could say how he was supported, but he lived in good lodgings that gave him two meals a day. Always comfortably dressed, here he was again, making off to the quayside.

Miss Reakes followed carefully, stopping several times, waiting and watching, waiting until Ballinger stood studying one of the transports. A sailor was working in the bows and Ballinger called across.

"That's a fine vessel! Coaster?"

The sailor briefly looked up.

"Nah! She can do all. High seas, anything."

"Any chance of a berth?"

The sailor looked up.

"If you've done the time!"

"Ten years, nor more, in the Merchant. Indiamen, East and West."

'Could be then. Come back in a couple of hours. The Lieutenant'll be around then."

"Where bound? With what?"

The sailor shrugged.

"What do they tell us? Told off to prepare for cold weather though, and cleared for passengers."

"When do you sail?"

"High tide tomorrow. We're sailing empty, so we take on ballast, We're the last, and ours is expected soon."

"You're cleared for passengers, but none aboard yet?"

"That's what I said. That's why the ballast!"

Ballinger waved his thanks and turned to leave, but Miss Reakes was now stood close by.

"Sir! Sir! Please do excuse my interruption, but do I have it right that you are a sailing man?"

Ballinger saw first the comely face within the bonnet, then the anxious expression. He removed his own hat and then bowed.

"I am, Miss, yes, of many years."

She treated him to her most winning smile, then her face dissolved once more into anxiety.

"My fiancé is on one of those warships out in the bay, an Officer. He tells me not to worry, he'll be home in but a few weeks, he says, but would you know the time it would take for a voyage to Portugal, then onto Canada, then back? I fear he has told me less than the truth, to prevent me from worry."

Ballinger's mind reeled. This was luck indeed, but he reacted well to the moment.

"Your fiancé has told you what, Miss?"

"Eight weeks."

"That would be a long passage, Miss. You could expect to see him back in six, given fair winds."

She beamed back at him and curtsied.

"My thanks to you, Sir, and good-day.'

He swung his hat across his stomach and bowed as she left. Ballinger then churned over what he had learned; cleared for passengers, but empty to Portugal, hence the ballast and then Canada. Four transports and cold weather clothing. He did the additions, estimating using six merchant vessels. That could mean around 2,000 passengers, assuming over 300 each, not a high number but right for a long passage. He decided to wait, loading ballast meant that such as Ship's Bosuns would be on the quayside and they would know more. He did not have long to wait before the carts arrived with sacks of stone, to pull up alongside both moored vessels and soon, in groups of four, the heavy sacks were being winched aboard each vessel, all under the watchful eye of the Ship's Bosun. He walked up to the second vessel and approached the intently concentrating Warrant Officer.

"I'm told you may have a berth?'

The Bosun did not lessen his concentration for a second.

"Aye, always, for the right man."

"I've done ten years on Indiamen. East and West as a Master's Mate."

Now the Bosun did give him more than a glance, finding Ballinger's physique acceptable, as was his maritime status, almost the equal of his own.

"We sail on tomorrow's tide. You come back before then, you've got a berth."

"What's the cargo?"

"Passengers!"

"Needing six ships!"

"Aye. The worst kind of passengers, Redcoats! Bloodybacks! Hundreds of 'em."

"But not from here."

"No. Portugal to Canada. As if carrying such weren't bad enough, we're then takin' 'em down the St. Lawrence. Chance we'll get iced in and find ourselves over the side with pick-axes for a month nor more."

His attention had returned to the sacks of stone, or at least the straining rope that now disappeared down into the bowels of the ship.

"So, by tomorrow's tide."

Ballinger felt himself dismissed and was grateful to hurry off. His place with the Bosun was now taken by John Wallbridge, ex-Bow Street Runner and one of Waters most trusted operatives in the British homeland, sent there by Waters to oversee this most crucial operation. He first showed the Bosun his brass badge of Office, the impressive Coat of Arms of King George III, with the etched words 'John Wallbridge. Government Agent' clear beneath, the whole affixed to stiff black leather. The Bosun looked worried, but Wallbridge soon put him at his ease.

"It's alright! What did he want?'

"A berth."

"Anything else?"

"Where to and what with."

"And you told him."

"I did. Told him what he wanted to know."

The return of the anxious look, but for a very different reason.

"Did I do wrong?"

"No! You did exactly what we wanted, but if he comes again, you've not seen me. This didn't happen. Right?"

The Bosun nodded vigorously, then Wallbridge nodded himself.

"Rule Britannia!"

With that, Wallbridge turned and hurried through the streets to Ballinger's lodgings. Ballinger was hurrying also, he could waste no time in forming his letter to Napoleon's own Intelligence Service. He was studied by many eyes, as he entered his lodgings, one pair in particular lodged in the head of Government Agent Henry Beale, him only in his early thirties and new to the Service. Wallbridge soon joined him.

"Is he in?"

Beale nodded, as did Wallbridge, in response.

"Right M'sieu Ballinger. Let's see what you do now!"

A watch was kept throughout the night and Wallbridge arrived with the dawn to find that, nevertheless, he was late for the major event, as Henry Beale, told him.

"He's out already to meet the Postboy. He must think he has something worth hurrying over."

Wallbridge nodded, well satisfied.

"Right. Your horse is handy?"

"Tied around the corner."

"You have some paper?"

"Yes, for my own report."

"Never mind that! Fold it up, scribble some address on it, then go and stand alongside our Ballinger. Mark what he hands up, then come back and follow the Postboy. Out of town, get Ballinger's letter off him."

Beale quickly did as he was bid and was soon standing next to Ballinger at the post point. The Postboy was on time and Beale saw the heavy letter handed up with an overlarge seal. Minutes later he was on horseback and following the Postboy, so that on the steep hill North of the town, he overtook him, seizing the Postboy's reins. In fear of his life, him having been robbed more than once before, the Postboy threw up his hands.

"Take the lot! I don't care."

Beale displayed his own brass badge for the Postboy to examine.

"King's business! I just want one."

He held out his hand and received the bag. Ballinger's letter was not far down and prominent by the size of the seal. Beale returned the bag to the now merely astonished Postboy, who now felt that his official role should be asserted. This character was only Government.

"These go on the Royal Mail coach out of Dorchester! That's what should happen to that one."

Beale ignored him.

"What's your name and don't lie. We have ways of finding such out."

"Len Muxford."

"Well, Len Muxford. This never happened, so there's no need to tell anyone, anything, now is there? Bad things happens to those as spreads about the doings of Government Agents."

Muxford nodded, now plainly very intimidated. Satisfied, Beale gathered his reins.

"God speed, Len Muxford! Safe journey."

After the Postboy rode on, Beale waited on the road, but not for too long, as Wallbridge, Jane Reakes and Luke Kettle all rode up to him. Wallbridge examined the letter and the address, but did not break the seal, being more concerned for the weight. He nodded his appreciation.

"Good quality paper! Addressed to some road in the Elephant and Castle. Right, let's get this delivered and see who lives there."

Three days later the quartet walked into Charing Cross Square, leading their horses. Wallbridge collared the first Postboy he came to and showed him his brass badge.

"Postboy for the Elephant and Castle. Where?"

The young lad, much intimidated, pointed to a group not far off.

"Jimmy Doidge's one of 'em. The tall one."

Wallbridge gave him a shilling and walked off, leaving the beaming Postboy to examine the coin in the weak daylight. The four surrounded the group and then Wallbridge approached, first showing his badge to the lad pointed out.

"Jimmy Doidge. You're needed!"

Doidge immediately ran in the opposite direction, but straight into the much less than gentle embrace of ex-Marine Kettle, who held him fast as Wallbridge came over.

"What you running for Jimmy? What you afraid of? You been up to wickedness?"

The answer was a frantic shaking of his head, but all was pacified when Wallbridge held up another shilling.

"We need you to take great care with the delivery of a certain letter."

He waved Ballinger's rather superior document in front of him.

"Now! Delivered now and you make sure it goes into the hand of who it's for, a Mr. Duncan. Him only, clear?"

The boy, now immensely puzzled, looked from Wallbridge to the letter and back.

"What about my others?"

"After. This shilling now, another when you get Duncan to the door, so's we can see him. Mr. Duncan it must be, then you earns your extra money. I'll make it a florin."

The shilling was held out and taken. He looked again at Wallbridge and then at the grim and very disapproving face of Luke Kettle.

"My horse is just there."

The letter was given special place in his coat pocket and the journey began, Wallbridge and his trio following someway behind. The Thames was crossed using Blackfriars Bridge and then the Postboy followed the road due South. They could see him study the address, then he turned to his followers and pointed down a road off to the right. They spurred on their horses and saw the Postboy dismount to approach the door of a well-appointed house not far down the side road. The Postboy stopped for a minute, not certain of which house, which was helpful as it gave the four time enough to spread themselves along the road, each with a clear view of the door, but Wallbridge placed himself right opposite. He waved the Postboy forward and he used the large, black knocker. Then he waited, but not for long, when a tall, swarthy and well-built man opened the door. They saw the Postboy ask his question and the man nodded. He then turned back into the building, but soon returned with the payment. The letter was handed over and the door closed. Wallbridge walked up the road, following the Postboy, sufficient enough to be out of sight from any of the windows of the house. He caught up with him and glowered down at the lad, who was grinning in anticipation.

"That was Duncan?"

The Postboy nodded.

"You're sure?"

"I am! He said he was, straight off!"

The florin was handed over and the Postboy rode off, at a good canter. Wallbridge looked at his companions.

"Right. Another wait. Let's see what this one does. Cove that big'll not be too hard to spot when he does it. So, we keep watch."

For the wait, they occupied a room opposite. A full crown and the brass badge gaining them access to a family home, with a meal available if paid for. Luke Kettle took the first watch, whilst the others rested, either eating or sleeping. The afternoon turned to evening and then night, so that in the dark they could watch the door closer from the shadows in the street outside. A single candle was lit in an upstairs window of Duncan's building, to remain for almost two hours before being extinguished. The watch continued and with the dawn, as with Ballinger, the man left the house to stand at the Post Stop and the Weymouth routine was again applied to secure the letter. That done, Wallbridge weighed the new package in his hand.

"Now heavier by some way, with an Alfriston address, that down in Kent, if I recall right."

He smiled, although it was more of a grimace in his case.

"Right! Back to barracks."

'Barracks' in their case, was the floor under Waters' office in Great Smith Street. Once safely within, Wallbridge very carefully broke the seal of Duncan's package cover, ensuring but one chism. Inside were two more documents, all unsealed, which Wallbridge ignored. Ballinger's seal was broken, presumably by Duncan, and Wallbridge took a minute to read this third document.

"It's all in there, what he found out at Weymouth."

Then he read Duncan's covering letter for the package, nodding his head more and more with each sentence.

"Good! Just what we want. Ballinger's is to 'go over' with no delay, so it says, but not by who or in what. So, job's now to get this put back together with a few helpful additions."

He looked at ex-Marine Kettle.

"Time to get Jimmy the Glass down here, with all his gear."

Kettle seized his hat and left, but by now Wallbridge was shaking his head.

"It can't be this simple. Frog Intelligence is better than this. Send a few letters down to the coast and get 'em put in some handy boat. Too simple! They uses Postboys to move the stuff to London, then the coast. All done in plain sight, but what then, after that? Payment has to happen somewhere, they all can't be diehard Buonapartists. Coin has to come in somewhere. And why not in code? All that moves around Spain is in code!"

Jane Reakes was sat just along the table reading one of the accompanying letters.

"Why complicate matters with code? Having a code book can incriminate. They use code in Spain because of the high chance of capture. Here, who waylays Postboys for national advantage, hoping to find a useful Government letter? What robbers take, they burn, getting rid of evidence. After finding the money."

"So, these take the risk of Postboys being robbed and the message not arriving."

"The post is getting better and nowadays it's all paper, nothing valuable. Money doesn't move that way so much now and robbing a Postboy means the rope. The post is worth the risk, it attracts no suspicion and it keeps Ballinger on watch, instead of a week way on a London trip to deliver.

Wallbridge sighed, she was almost making sense. He looked again at Duncan's package cover, particularly the address and the addressee.

"The Occupier. Watchwell Cottage. Alfriston."

He turned to their map on the wall.

"Alfriston, down in Kent. What's on the coast, near there?"

Henry Beale was first to the map and ran his finger down to the coast.

"Cuckmere Haven. About three miles down. Seaford and Newhaven just over, Westwards."

Wallbridge nodded.

"This is beginning to make some sense, but the only sense so far."

Wallbridge continued shaking his head, or scratching it, or rubbing his chin, but his worried thoughts were interrupted when Jimmy the Glass arrived, by Hackney carriage. The undersized, wizened and unshaven man was hurried into the agents' rooms, propelled by Luke Kettle. Jimmy was dressed in a good coat, but of some age, carrying a bundle that shook and rattled when he placed it on the table. Wallbridge looked up, still studying the documents and still worried.

"Jimmy! We've a job for you, for top coin."

Jimmy's brows furrowed.

"You mean I b'ain't arrested? This ugly cove 'ere ain't told I nuthin'!"

"No Jimmy, not arrested. Not 'till the next time you tries to forge the King's own image. Now sit down. We've two jobs. It'll earn you three guineas, if done well."

Wallbridge pushed Duncan's package cover towards him.

"First, you repair that seal, so's no one even suspects it's been broken. Next."

He then pushed across Duncan's covering letter.

"You copy that, word for word, with a few extra sentences added on."

Jimmy pushed Duncan's cover to one side. The seal was easy, but to reproduce a whole letter! He picked it up and held it to the light in the window.

"This is good paper! Koops most like, if you've 'eard of 'im."

He studied further.

"An' there's a watermark. I'll need some more. Bond Street sells this, most like."

Wallbridge turned to Jane Reakes.

"Do your best. If not we'll have to make do with what Duncan's already written. Take a look at that watermark, before you go."

Jimmy showed her the distinctive design and then she left with an accurate, if rough, likeness quickly sketched out by Jimmy. He then extracted his tools, including the powerful magnifying glass from which he obtained his sobriquet and set to work, first heating the wax on Wallbridge's own desk. The seal was soon repaired and the seal design carefully reconfigured under the glass, using delicate chisels and knives. Within two hours, a grinning Jane Reakes returned with a package of paper. Jimmy took a sheet, held it to the light, compared it to Duncan's and nodded. Then Wallbridge slid a final piece of paper across.

"Right then, Jimmy. For your next two guineas, you add that sentence on the end, then do the signature."

Jimmy studied it carefully, but pointed to a word.

"What's that?"

Wallbridge leaned forward.

"Jimmy, I'll tell you, please follow the words."

He began to read, from upside down, but he now knew the words off by heart, although given to him by Waters.

"Our agent in Royal Ordnance reports that, late December, they were ordered to arrange transport for a strong Division of three Brigades including weapons, ammunition, clothing and food supplies to be transported to Hamilton at the Western end of Lake Ontario, with a view to mounting a punitive expedition across the isthmus and securing and fortifying the town of Rochester.

The tricky word is isthmus, Jimmy. Isthmus! A narrow neck of land between two lakes. Is all now well with you?"

Jimmy nodded vigorously, now smiling.

"All's well, Mr. Wallbridge. By the end of the day. Can I work 'ere?"

"By all means, Jimmy, with good commons thrown in."

However, Wallbridge then sat forward, his voice threatening.

"King's business, this, Jimmy. King's business! Us against the Frogs, so not a word. Hoike this about and I'll see you in lavender. It'll be the rope.

Jimmy was wholly unfazed as the details of his possible execution and funeral were spelt out, instead he arranged his pens and ink.

"Not a word, Mr. Wallbridge. Not a word. Patriotic as the next man, me. On me muvver's grave, I swear!"

The result was subdued laughter around the room, then silence for the wait, plus rest and food, until Jimmy had finished his work. They could all be on the road throughout the night.

oOo

Their prediction had been correct, because for that night they rode South, all four, with the re-sealed and augmented package safe in Wallbridge's inside pocket. Daylight had broken when they arrived at Alfriston, but Wallbridge took them to woodland, just outside. With the day's village activity beginning, he sent forward Henry Beale to await the Postboy. In the event the young lad came out of the village to him, not in from the next village beyond, but Beale placed his horse in front the Postboy's to halt his exit, showing first his brass badge.

"King's business!"

The Postboy reined in his horse, but, unlike those previously, he appeared wholly unfazed by so imperious a statement, after all he was still within a village and no pistols were being pointed at him.

"What's that to me?"

Beale ignored the question, instead showing him the re-assembled package, address foremost.

"You know that address?"

A nod.

"Do they get much mail?"

"Some, not much."

"Regular?"

Now a shake of the weather-beaten head, despite his young age.

"I'd say, yes. Most is quality."

By now Beale's companions had ridden down to them, but the Postboy remained unmoved.

"You want that delivered, you give it 'ere and I'll do it now, but it's extra. I've done the village already, so it'll cost you a shilling!"

Wallbridge found a florin and tossed it over.

"Another if you do exactly like we say."

Now a beaming smile.

"Whatever you say, Sir. Just as you wants it."

"How far?"

"Around the next corner."

"Down a lane?"

"Yes, but short."

Now numbered five, they walked their horses to the lane and Wallbridge and Jane Reakes dismounted, leaving their horses with the remaining two. With the Postboy, they walked up the lane, but Wallbridge and Reakes stopped someway short and did not walk forward until the Postboy brought the occupier to the door. Then they walked past, appearing merely as passers-by, father and daughter, but both were astonished that the occupier turned out to be a woman. She paid the Postboy for the package, then quickly closed the door. The pair did not retrace their steps, but found a back lane that came around to the main road, where they rejoined Beale and Kettle. The Postboy was long gone and Wallbridge set his men to their positions.

"Luke! First watch from those trees back over. Keep out of sight from everyone. Four hours on. Next watch, Henry and Jane, at 1 o' clock. If anyone comes, you're a courting couple. I'll come back at four. Luke, when you come off, get yourself down to this Cuckmere and get lodgings in any likely place. Have a snoop around there. Henry and Jane, when you come off, get lodgings in Seaford, next down the coast. See if there's anything that berths there as can cross The Channel."

He paused, thinking further on his arrangements, then he continued.

"There's Runners coming down for the night watch, they'll be staying at the Revenuer's barracks in Newhaven. I'll lodge in this Alfriston at the Inn. Anything that you think looks lively today, that's where I'll be. Anything not, at the barracks 6 of the afternoon day after tomorrow. Keep awake and keep alert. This is close and it's a smuggler, better than evens, carrying letters for extra coin, not some handy French cutter taking the chance to close with the coast."

In the event, it was 'not anything' and four days passed. Two women came and went to the cottage, but, when followed and watched, nothing happened that was in any way suspicious. At their second meeting in Newhaven, Wallbridge was distinctly worried that no one who had visited the cottage went anywhere near the coast, all who came to the cottage returned to their own homes. The woman of the house never ventured out of the village. Jane Reakes tried to remonstrate with her superior.

"Sir, does it matter? The package is at the coast. Sooner or later they will get it over the Channel which is what we want. Does it matter that we don't see it?"

Wallbridge shook his head.

"It does! It's our job to see that package into the hands of French intelligence. Then we can be certain. Until then we carry on, watching and waiting."

However, he then sat back and sighed, depression and even defeat clear by the set of his mouth.

"A woman took it in, but we saw no man go into that cottage."

Then realisation lit his face.

"Why? Because her man's at sea! 'Tis a smuggler, that we can say, as spends days away on legal trade, then does a run across to get the brandy or whatever when business says yes, but, we can't stay here for ever, nor the Runners, especially. It may end up like you say, but we've not run out of time altogether yet.

However, each passing day spoke louder of failure, no more so than to ex-Marine Luke Kettle, watching and waiting at the hamlet located at the bridge over the Cuckmere River, where he lodged in the Inn. Each day he counted the fishing boats in and out of the Haven with the tide, all the while acting out his cover story as a ship's outfitter, giving enough excuse to talk to the fishermen. This gained him nothing and so, almost in desperation, pursuing the smuggler idea and on a day when the wind brought the rain up from a cold Channel, he leant on the bar of the Inn. He and the Innkeeper had made a good acquaintance and so Kettle felt able to take the chance.

"What's the chance of a drop of French? I'll pay the extra. Worth it on a day like this."

The Innkeeper looked at him for three long seconds, then he reached down behind him for a plain bottle and poured Kettle a measure. He took a sip and nodded.

"No Spanish, this!"

He took another sip.

"No need to tell me how you come by this!"

The Innkeeper smiled and tapped his finger twice on the side his nose. Kettle finished the brandy, laying on the performance of savouring every drop, but with the last swallow, he was out of the door, on his horse and making for Alfriston at a good canter. He went straight to Wallbridge in his room, to find Jane Reakes and Henry Beale with him, all poring over maps and papers, but these soon lost their importance when Kettle spoke.

"The Inn at Cuckmere gets French brandy."

Wallbridge sat back and thought.

"So! He has connections, but how close to our smuggler?"

More thinking.

"Who can mock an Irish accent?"

Jane Reakes spoke first.

"No need to pretend. One of the Runners is Irish. Michael Rourke."

Wallbridge smiled.

"And you know that, sort of how?"

She blushed, but Wallbridge continued.

"Get him over here. This is a long shot, but what's left? You, Jane! I want you into Brighton and you come back with a bolt of linen. Irish for preference, but any will do."

The following evening, Bow Street Runner Michael Rourke, looking prosperous in civilian clothes, was sat at the bar of the Cuckmere Inn, waiting his moment and drinking French brandy, happily paying double the price. When the Innkeeper was closing for the night, Rourke leaned over the bar.

"Can we have a word, you and I. I've something in mind which could do us both some good."

With all other customers now gone, Rourke was motioned down to the cellar, where he wasted no time.

"I'm hoping you can steer me to the right people. I've been pushed along the coast to here by the Revenuers. Linen is my trade, Irish linen, getting it across The Channel for the French ladies. Belgian and Dutch too. There'll be coin for you, if it comes off, fair's fair. Coin for us all!"

The Innkeeper looked at him steadily.

"Why me?"

Rourke grinned knowledgeably.

"That brandy didn't come from Scotland!"

The Innkeeper's brows came together.

"Coin! How much?"

"More than you make in many a month running this place! Have you any idea of the price that good linen fetches over the water, four times what it fetches here. Four times! I just need a lad with a boat as can handle a dozen bolts of the stuff."

Rourke remained silent, allowing his words to hang in the air and giving the Innkeeper time to think and ponder, but after almost half a minute he did speak.

"You didn't get this from me. In fact, you were never here and you pay me now for what I know."

Rourke dipped his hand into his right-hand coat pocket, pulled out a guinea coin and threw them onto a nearby barrel. Silence. He found two more and the Innkeeper scooped them up.

"Get yourself to Newhaven Hard. Ned Goodhind's the man you want. He's a yawl as plies up and down the coast here. Portsmouth round to Ramsgate. He's your man. Knows his way over, if you take my meaning."

Rourke looked at him steadily, his face stern.

"Now, you'd not be trying to gull me, would you? Now you've got payment. There's coin to be made for all from this, much of which could well flow across your counter, but there's chastisement for those as bears false witness!"

The Innkeeper stared straight back.

"Ned's the one you want."

"And you're a customer!"

A nod of the Innkeeper's head, nothing more.

"So, who shall I say sent me?"

"Ben Lofthouse."

The following morning Wallbridge was at the cottage in Alfriston, hammering on the door. The woman answered, to immediately have Wallbridge's badge thrust in her face.

"King's business! We'll know your name!"

The woman almost fainted with terror.

"Daisy Goodhind!"

At the sound of the two words, she was rushed back into the cottage and pushed into a chair, to be held by two Bow Street Runners. Wallbridge bent down and stared hard into her face.

“That package you got, three days back. Where is it?” And don’t lie, or it’s the rope, which I can save you from, if you tell us now what we need to know.”

Wild-eyed with terror, she stared at the accusing faces filling her parlour.

“Me husband has it!”

“Still! Not gone across yet?”

“No.”

“At Newhaven?”

Furious nodding at all in sight.

“It’s ‘im! Me husband. He made me do it, for the money.”

Wallbridge turned to the Runner Sergeant and pointed to the distraught woman.

“Under lock and key.”

The four Agents and four Bow Street Runners, all out of uniform, made quite a stir as they galloped out of the village and onto the Newhaven road. An hour at a good canter brought them to the entrance of Newhaven Hard, little more than a sloping quayside, where Rourke was waiting, a bolt of cloth, wrapped in rough canvas across his shoulder. Wallbridge nodded and Rourke walked the few yards to the warehouse, above the entrance to which was the prominent sign,‘Ned Goodhind. Coastal Trade’. Behind him, bobbing gently with the waves, in plain and prominent sight, was a well-appointed and well-maintained medium sized coaster, yawl rig, both masts with neatly furled red sails. Rourke entered the warehouse, the bolt still on his shoulder and he stood waiting until the four men inside turned to look at him.

“I’m looking for Ned Goodhind.”

One man, standing right centre, planted his feet more securely and folded his arms.

“Who’s doing the looking?”

“Someone who can do him a lot of good, if what Ben Lofthouse told me about him is true.”

There was no change in his stance, but, uninvited, Rourke had moved to a table and unwrapped the bolt of linen, to then, with great flourish and drama, unroll two yards. He then gestured towards it with his left hand.

“You know what this is? Irish linen. Worth a fortune across the Channel. I’ve a dozen of these to get across, there’ll be a buyer over there and all I need is a handy boat with handy lads as can take it there. How’s a guinea a bolt sound?”

The man studied the cloth.

“Fifteen the lot sounds better.”

Rourke nodded and grinned.

"Fifteen it is. So, where do you go and when?"

"Dieppe. Tonight, with the ebb tide."

"Dieppe would be just the place, I've a contact there already, with Belgium and the Dutch not far off."

Rourke then found guineas in his pocket, selected three and threw them on the table.

"Those for taking me over tonight, with this sample, for good favour. And you'd be Ned Goodhind!"

The man nodded as he picked up each coin, his face still blank, but Rourke was still smiling.

"There's good trade here and coin for all. Every two weeks, if I can get the cloth."

He looked at each of the other three, as though they were already good comrades.

"Come the night, then!"

With that he turned and left the warehouse, to walk back to Wallbridge.

"Goodhind's there. The one in the leather jerkin. With three others."

Wallbridge nodded and reached inside his own coat, to pull out a quality duelling pistol.

"Check pistols."

All did, then Wallbridge led them forward. They entered the warehouse at a rush, pistols prominent and pointing menacingly. All there immediately threw up their hands, but one was incensed enough to shout a challenge.

"Who the Devil are you? There's too many sailors close-by and handy if you think you'll get away with what you robs from here."

Wallbridge looked at him, smiling slightly.

"And what might we want, in this cave of yours?"

"Honest goods belonging to honest men!"

Wallbridge sniggered, placed his pistol on the nearby table and walked up to the indignant and angry man.

"You'd be Ned Goodhind!"

No reply.

"You've got a boat, that one out there, as is going across to Dieppe. Tonight."

The blank look changed to one of deep anxiety.

"You a Revenuer?"

"Oh no, Ned, worse than that. I'm here because a package was delivered to your home some days back that you are about to take across to France and give to some Frenchman. For payment!"

A sinister pause.

"That makes you a traitor!"

"What proof?"

"We delivered the package ourselves to your home and your wife tells us that you still have it. And we read it before it got to you. Best you hand it over, Ned, then I'll tell you what I can do for you, because, right now, it's the gallows dance for you, and your missus and these others here! The rope's already round your necks, but I can loosen it some, perhaps altogether, if you give me that package and then you and your boys here do something for us."

Another pause, whilst he grinned menacingly at the other three. One immediately broke down.

"Ned! Give it him. Let's hear what he has to say."

Goodhind stood for no more than a second, before turning to go to a cupboard at the back of the warehouse and extract Duncan's package which he handed to Wallbridge, who immediately held it up before Goodhind's face.

"This is a communication from French spies in this country to their masters in France, which you are about to deliver into the hands of said masters. Can you still feel the rope?"

He then felt inside his own coat and pulled out a parchment, which he also held before Goodhind's face.

"But this, Edward, God help me, is a King's Pardon! There's no names at the top saying who's been pardoned, but all I've got to do is write in whoever I choose."

His face dissolved into an evil leer.

"Could be Edward and Daisy Goodhind."

Goodhind's jaw fell at the same time as his eyebrows swept upward and his eyes bulged. Wallbridge then continued.

"You help us out, and this is yours, with your names written in and then all your past transgressions of smuggling and acting the Postboy will be wiped off the slate!"

Goodhind was breathing rapidly.

"Help you out, how?"

"You take the package, you deliver it and you get your coin off the Crapauds. But, there will be two extra added to your crew."

He turned to indicate Luke Kettle.

"Ex-Marine Luke Kettle here, will come with you to see the package handed over. You can call him your new bodyguard. You will also take the Irish linen seller, with his cloth. Tells a good tale, does he not? That's for extra security on the boat and to add to the overall picture of smugglers about their trade. It'll draw attention away from you and Kettle. We want nothing unusual about you to see, if you take my meaning. Any problem with any of that?"

Goodhind shook his head.

"Good. Do as I've asked, then you will be acting in the service of the King against the King's enemies and this pardon will be yours."

He spread it out on the table, the Royal crest prominent and gaudy at the top.

"Do you have pen and ink?"

One of the three rushed to provide what was asked for from another cupboard and both were placed near at hand for Wallbridge. He dipped in the quill, shook off the excess and then looked at Goodhind, a pleasant but disturbing look on his face.

"It is Edward and Daisy, is it not?"

Goodhind nodded quickly, but furiously, his face remaining deeply troubled. Wallbridge wrote in the words, blew on the ink to make it dry, then he refolded the document and returned it to his inside pocket.

"That will be yours upon completion of what we agreed and a report from my two men confirming as such. You'll be earning this by executing the King's business!"

Another reptilian smile as he finally handed over the package.

"Now! The tide's on the make. Perhaps you should ready your vessel. What are you taking over?"

"Tobacco!"

"And bringing back?"

"Brandy!"

Wallbridge nodded.

"I should have worked that out for myself!"

oOo

Ex-Marine Luke Kettle looked with both sympathy and amusement as his Bow Street Runner companion ran again to the side of the boat. After the unpleasant sounds of vomiting, Rourke returned to their place in the waist of the boat, amidships, both sat on the hatch cover, where the pitch and send of the boat was at its least, but not enough for the land-locked Rourke. Still grinning, Kettle studied him further.

"You get used to it. You'll have your sea-legs for the trip home."

Even in the poor light from the half-moon, Kettle could see Rourke sag down with misery.

"If anyone sends me onto a ship again, I'm away off to Ireland. On a big ferry from Liverpool."

Kettle clapped him on his shoulder.

"Not long now. This is a decent barky and I'll give these their due, they handles her well."

With no light on board, save that of the merest candle lantern that illuminated the compass binnacle, the yawl had maintained a heading of Sou-sou East, with a good driving South-west wind beam on to fill all five sails set over both masts. A cry came from the bows.

"Ship ahead! Three points to larboard."

Kettle stood and craned his neck, to see a large vessel, judging by the lights in her rigging and from within her hull. He studied and thought.

"Big 64, but she'll be across us. He'll not change course, our Ned. No need."

Kettle was correct and the spirited yawl surged on, for another hour, before the lights of Dieppe blinked on the horizon, these becoming fainter with the growing dawn. One more half hour and Goodhind, with a consummate skill that Kettle could not fail to admire, eased his vessel, powered by a reefed mainsail, up to the jetty, close enough to where ropes then snaked back and forth, for the vessel to be hauled close up to the quay and secured. Two gangplanks were swung over and lashed in place, one for cargo, the other for personnel, which Goodhind, Kettle and Rourke crossed together, the latter carrying his bolt of linen. Goodhind's crew were already hauling up the bales of tobacco and the three men had not reached the end of the jetty before barrels of brandy began to emerge from a nearby warehouse. Two Gendarme sentries approached and seemed more interested in Rourke with his bolt of cloth, but Goodhind immediately pacified both with a welcome in French, a quick "Il est avec moi", in the direction of Rourke. Then both were distracted much more powerfully by a large, bulging pouch of tobacco for each, which immediately occupied their attention when they pulled them open and savoured the rich aroma.

Kettle looked at Goodhind as the bales of tobacco were hurried back along the quay and the brandy barrels hurried forward.

"A quick turnaround?"

Goodhind scowled and did no more than nod, but Kettle continued.

"You got the package?"

Another nod from Goodhind, then Kettle questioned him again.

"And you know where to go?"

"Done this a few times!"

Kettle looked hard at Goodhind.

"A few! All to help the Frogs against us for a bit of extra coin! Seems that Pardon was too easy gained."

Goodhind scowled again and indicated a side street. Rourke now left them for the main street where the town's commerce took place and Kettle followed Goodhind. Nothing was heard other than their footfalls between the high walls in the narrow, cobbled street and they met no one that early in the morning. Kettle kept pace, then Goodhind pointed to a particular door, but Kettle now gave his instruction.

"No mention of Marines. I'm just one of your crew, a bit more handy than the others, here to see you come to no harm in this lively seaport, what's no different to any other. The less fuss the better. Get this handed over, get your coin and we gets back to the barky."

By now Goodhind was pulling on an iron lever and Kettle could hear the sound of a bell from within the building. A shutter in the centre of the top half of the door opened and a face appeared, the eyes within it studying Goodhind, but no words were said. Then came the sound of bolts being withdrawn and the door opened. Goodhind walked forward with Kettle following, but a hand came across his chest, then words in a thick French accent.

"Who is he?"

Goodhind turned.

"My Guardian Angel. These is rough times. Too many places these days is no place to be for a man on his own! 'Specially if he looks like he may well have a bit of coin. Beaucoup d'argent!"

Kettle pushed the hand down, then followed Goodhind down the passage into the building. At the end was a door, which Goodhind himself opened, to then enter and see a sparse figure of early middle-age, sat at a table, but incongruously wrapped in a heavily brocaded dressing gown, with thin, artistic hands protruding from elaborately embroidered cuffs. He was evidently sat waiting, staring steadily forward from a head crowned by a plain, round, russet cap.

"Ah, M'sieu Goodhind. We saw your good vessel enter the harbour. You have something for me?"

Goodhind walked forward, leaving Kettle stood by the door.

"Seems like I got you out of bed!"

"The tide controls us all, M'sieu Goodhind, you would agree? The tide of events also, it would seem."

The obscure prose was lost on Goodhind as he dropped the package onto the table and the man picked it up to examine the seal, not carefully, but too much so for Goodhind.

"There's still water enough for me to quit your harbour. I'm loaded by now. That's what came to me for delivering and now it's with you. I'll take my payment and take my leave."

The man looked up and ceased his examination of the seal, which he then broke. Four documents fell out, but he selected first Duncan's covering letter and he broke that seal. He took two minutes to read the contents, all the while nodding slowly. Then he read the letter from Ballinger. Goodhind had grown more impatient with every second.

"You read that in your own time. That was given to me, it's now delivered and I've a boat to get past the Revenuers. Is all good enough?"

The man nodded, lapsing into French with his enthusiasm.

"Oui! Tout cela est tres important. You have our thanks."

With that he opened the drawer in front of him and produced a leather purse which he tossed towards Goodhind and it landed on the edge of the table, but Goodhind's hands were ready and soon one was inside the purse to extract three of the many coins within.

"Yankee dollars! Good enough."

He weighed the purse with one hand.

"Do I need to count it?"

"Non, M'sieu Goodhind, you do not. So, until the next time."

The purse was tied to Goodhind's belt and his coat buttoned over. With no more than a nod, they left the room and then the building to hurry back to the quay and the boat, where Rourke was waiting, sat aboard on the hatchway. There were many French watching and so both chose their words carefully when Kettle went immediately up to him.

"All's well?"

Rourke nodded.

"Three gold Napoleons for that linen, off some woman in a dress shop. Fancy stuff was there in the window and I got her to open up, saw her there inside. When this war's done, there's coin to be made for someone with the connections and the right know-how. There'll come a time when there'll be no need for smugglers."

Kettle's expression did not change.

"Perhaps, but meanwhile that's just what you are and we've got to get this off the quay, then out and away where there's plenty of searoom. So, on your feet and lend a hand."

The gangplanks were already swung back, one to the ship and one to the quay, leaving the task of poling the boat away with the long sweeps normally lodged under the main spar. The breeze was still strong and so Goodhind set the headsail only, which moved the bows smartly around, then the sternsail only, which completed the turn. Then, with all sails set, Goodhind's smart yawl sailed majestically out of the harbour, to soon dip and curtsy with the waves of the open sea.

oOo

Merely three days later, Jean-Jacques Regis de Cambaceres reached across to the corner of his desk to retrieve a pale blue heavy paper cover, embellished with the black silhouette of Napoleon Buonaparte. He turned back the cover to reveal two documents pinned together, the top a translation, its companion a letter from George Clinton, Vice President of the United States, requesting aid in the form of munitions and warships to help repel an expected well-resourced British invasion between Lakes Erie and Ontario. He added two more, each with a translation, one being Ballinger's letter, the second being that of Duncan and he read again the translation of all three, then he closed the folder and stood to depart his own office. It was but a short walk to the administration offices of Napoleon himself. They were adjacent, Cambaceres being the Second Consul, second only to First Consul Emperor Napoleon. His authority unassailable, he swept through the outer Offices to find Napoleon stood in the centre of the final room, him dictating to six Secretaries all at once, but Napoleon ceased when Cambaceres entered. He looked at his Emperor, seeing the sunken eyes, the thin mouth and the drooping shoulders, remarking to himself that this man was now very different from the one who had swept the Austrians and Russians aside at Ulm and Austerlitz, but he said nothing. Whilst Napoleon looked at him quizzically, Cambaceres raised the folder to eye level before placing it on the huge mahogany desk.

"C'est tres important, Sire. Il s'agit de l'Espagne."

One week later, in the Spanish Spring of late February, El Rey Joseph, Napoleon's brother and the King of Spain, stood angry and anxious beside a window of his Madrid palace, looking down into the street below. Watched by scowling Madrilenians, a long column of blue coated French infantry were marching past to begin their march Eastwards, back into France. These were from his own Army of the Centre and he recalled vividly the clear orders he had received, whilst at the same time identical orders were arriving elsewhere in Spain, all ordering French Divisions to march East, just as his now were. His and the other French armies in the Peninsula, five in number, these being the Armies of Portugal, the North, the South, Aragon and Catalonia, were all to provide units to reconstruct a new Grande Armee. The command was for 40,000 men in total, leaving El Rey with less than 200,000 across the whole of Spain, but these troop movements were not the only distressing orders. El Rey must move his palace to Valladolid and the army of the Centre and that of the South, were now to be based around Salamanca and would be sufficient to contain the 'a reduire' Allied army now in Portugal. The remaining four French armies were to be scattered, deployed to maintain a hold on existing French territory. French forces there in Spain were now to be deployed on the defensive, there were to be no more offensive operations to regain territory. Still anxious for the security of his Spanish Fiefdom, El Rey turned away from the window to both distract and console himself with his favourite indulgence; what to take with him as loot and plunder out of this premier Palace of Spain for his move to Valladolid.

As El Rey had read his orders, so did Wellington read a captured copy and 'a reduire' was translated with relish, 'to be reduced'. Clearly, this was a useful and welcome French belief.

oOo

Chapter Seven

Across the full reach of Spain

The Officers of the 105th Wessex filed in through the front door of their Battalion Headquarters, which trebled, not only as Headquarters, but also as the Officer's Mess and their Dormitory. It had been raining all day and many were relieved to shed their sodden greatcoats and hang them up on whichever hook or protuberance was free and available. All were weary, the day's exercise had not only involved musket drill, but also manoeuvring at speed and an entirely new drill appropriate for a space where manoeuvre was limited. Some had found the whole day's training more strenuous than others, the three most to suffer being Carravoy, D'Villiers and Slade, the former being the first to voice his dissatisfaction at the removal of a certain comfort afforded only to Officers, as he slumped down in a chair.

"Running around and firing off muskets in one formation or another is one thing, but not allowing us to take our horses for the journey to and from is quite another."

Nathaniel Drake turned around and grinned.

"Ah, yes, Charles, but what if we were called upon to eat your horse, as we had to, on our way back to here! Last November."

Drake's unrepressed cheerfulness always irritated Captain Lord Charles Carravoy and he merely glowered briefly in Drake's direction as he pulled off his boots, damp and muddy almost up to the brown turn-down at the top. However, Reginald Charters, Captain of Two Company, was in a far lighter mood.

"Well, I think the men did most admirably today with the first, a long run into position and then four shots with three reloads well inside a minute. And in this weather. Top drawer, I'd say!"

Drake spoke in agreement.

"I'd go along with that! It was polished, proficient and most heartening to see! Seems to me the men enjoy it. Damn fine soldiers, ours, and I'll say that to anyone."

He turned to the last of the least athletic three.

"You'd agree, St. John."

Slade was examining his own socks for damp and pleased to find that his highest quality boots had protected his feet, but this did not lighten his mood as he very briefly glanced up at Drake.

"If you say so!"

Slade then looked over at Ameshurst, him stood at the notice-board, where was pinned a sheet of paper, showing orders for the rest of the week.

"Ameshurst. What's tomorrow?"

Simon Ameshurst turned to run his finger down the sheet, to carefully read out the words.

"Tomorrow is; volley, charge, fall back in good order, re-load, volley and charge forward again."

Carravoy shook his head.

"Oh joy! And what did he call that business of today and was the same as yesterday and the day before?"

"Attacking over a narrow front with four firing lines. The Romans did something similar, you know. The Centurion blew a whistle and the front rank fell back for the second to go up and take their place. Fresh men to the fore, you see."

"Right. Fine. So that's what we've been doing, aping the Romans. It is so reassuring that it has a military description and now with its own special bugle-call, as composed by him and our Drum-Major."

Ameshurst felt somewhat aggrieved at his superior's condemnation of something that made perfect sense to him.

"Well, if we have to hold or attack on a front of five Companies, he wants some way of bringing the back two ranks into the fight. Firing from behind a hedge of bayonets is what he called it."

Carravoy snorted before replying.

"And how long would that last in the confusion of a battle?"

The question concerned Carr's new drill of engaging on a limited five Company front. One wing formed the first two ranks, the other the rear two ranks. As explained to all Officers by O'Hare out on the moors, if there was no room for a full, two-rank firing line, it was vital to still make full use of the 105th's ability to fire up to four rounds a minute. The third and fourth ranks must be brought into the action by firing through the first two at close range.

Charters lowered his month-old newspaper. Like many, he was no admirer of Captain Lord Charles Carravoy.

"And just how did yours cope with all the to-ing and fro-ing, Charles?"

The reply was weak.

"Well enough!"

Charters grinned and returned to his newspaper, reading reports about Napoleon rebuilding his forces in Eastern Europe to oppose the now advancing Russians and Prussians, therefore, engaged in that, from then on he held his peace. He had himself observed, because his own

Two Company had been standing adjacent to the Grenadiers, the awful confusion in D'Villiers Section, whilst Ameshurst's performed well first time. Eventually, D'Villiers had to leave the drill to his Sergeants. With that memory now rekindled within himself, Carravoy turned away to find an empty arm-chair by the wall, but at that point, Shakeshaft had found a subject much more diverting on the table in the centre of the room.

"I say, look, a newspaper, not even two weeks' old."

He held up the front page of The Times for all to see and the headlines there were wholly lurid, on a topic that all knew only too well. It was Drake who walked up to share the front page and, out of character, he spoke sternly as he read out the headline for all now listening.

"Willoughby-Gordon recalled from the Peninsula."

The steady and level-headed Surgeon George Pearson, sitting in the corner, looked up from his own papers.

"What else does it say?"

Drake returned his gaze to the page and began to read.

"The Military Secretary at the Horse Guards, General Sir Henry Livermore, has recalled Colonel James Willoughby-Gordon, Lord Wellington's Quartermaster in the Peninsula, to England. The official reason given is that Colonel Gordon 'does not turn his mind to the duties to be performed by the Quartermaster-General', but this newspaper is of the strong opinion that the true reason is Colonel Willoughby-Gordon's outright spying for the Morning Chronicle whilst on Wellington's Staff. It is clear that what too often appears in this insidious Whig newspaper could only be known by someone in Wellington's confidence, the only other being Wellington's Secretary, Lord Fitzroy Somerset, a man of such integrity and loyalty as to completely exonerate him of any suspicion towards such underhand practices."

The normally accommodating Charters, his own newspaper now crumpled on his lap, also took a stern view.

"Damn good riddance! It was him that sent all the supplies off on the wrong road during the retreat back to here. A thousand plagues on him! Does it say we'll get Murray back instead?"

Drake ran his gaze down the column.

"Yes, but there's more and no surprise. Our wholly unesteemed ex-Colonel, Sir Ambrose Brockenhurst, it reports, has spoken up in the House in support of Willoughby-Gordon as 'a praiseworthy exposer of the true situation regarding Lord Wellington and the Spanish campaign in general."

Charters clenched his jaw, before speaking.

"Has anyone told the truth about Brockenhurst? It was his cowardice that brought shame on us all that we still haven't lived down. I've heard us called the 'Run and Roam Boys'!"

Pearson had been listening and spoke before returning to his papers.

"Chances will come, be sure of that, you noble Hectors, of once more advancing bravely forward against bayonets and cannonfire! That French raid against the 50th at Bejar shows that things are moving once again, both for them and very probably us. I've not conducted my last operation on shattered limbs or to probe for French musket-balls, of that I'm certain."

Ameshurst, all the while, had remained at the notice-board.

"Well, here's something new. Two things. First, all about kit. All Officers are now to wear stove-pipe style shakoes, that great-coats are to be left behind, a single blanket now to be carried, light six-man tents are to be used and each man is to have his own small camp-kettle."

Carravoy stood up, appalled. His greatcoat was of the highest quality and to him invaluable.

"What! No greatcoats? That's ridiculous, does he think this Winter just gone is our last?"

Ameshurst shrugged his shoulders.

"Well, far be it for me to speak in support of our revered Commander-in-Chief, but presumably he thinks the tents and blankets are sufficient."

Drake nodded, but not in agreement.

"Greatcoats keep us warm, I'll grant you, but they are heavy, especially when wet. They slow our pace on the march. The Frogs always march faster than us, we have to try to get that back, a bit."

Ameshurst now turned to face his audience again.

"Which brings me to the second thing. On the 3rd March we leave here for a place called Moimentina de Beira. Does a name like that tell us anything?"

Drake immediately answered.

"In my experience, the longer the name the more backward and inhospitable."

However, three Officers had immediately rose, hurried over to their map of the Peninsula and it was Farquharson of the Colour Company who found it.

"North, and more West than East. Do you think it means anything?'

Charters spoke again.

"He's assembling columns of advance, dear boy. The game's on!"

D'Villiers, now seated, but equally as puzzled as before, only for a different reason, now looked up.

"Today's the 27th Feb. So that means five days from now!"

Charters applied the correction.

"No Simon, blood of my heart, four! 1813 is not a Leap Year! 28th and 1, 2, 3. Four!"

Meanwhile, Shakeshaft was still devouring the newspaper.

"Oh, here's something else. There's some trouble in Holland and they want the Prince of Orange back, but he's going to stay on Wellington's Staff."

Carravoy, still very irritated and furiously wearing out the fabric of his chair arm with his fingertips, spoke up from the side.

"Well now, doesn't that surely mean that we can all sleep easier in our beds!"

On the morning of the 3rd March, the Light Company were busy readying themselves for the move North, all inside their billet and not yet out in the street. On arriving in Garda they had immediately secured for themselves, as much by the muscle of Saunders and Solomon, the billet that they had used in the days prior to Sabugal and good relations with the Portuguese residents had been quickly re-established throughout the Winter. Now they were about to depart again and the final business was being concluded. Stood with the Head of the House, John Davey was checking over the fence panels of the animal pen he had constructed, Pike was examining the joints of the rockers on the cradle he had made. Examining in the company of the Father of the baby who would now be the new occupant, now that Ellen was about to leave. The Mother and the daughters of the house were all busy fussing around Eirin and Ellen and pressing food and dried fruit upon all within reach. At this point, Jed Deakin was looking sternly at Tom Miles.

"What have you got that we can leave for these people?"

Miles's face creased into an annoyed frown.

"What?"

However, such a retort had no impact on Colour Sergeant Jedediah Deakin.

"What? Something we can leave as a gift, for memory, for their putting up with us, that's you what's most included, an' don't tell me you've not got spare. And more spare than most!"

Pay was deducted for any part of a uniform lost and so whatever spares that could be stowed in their backpacks were always present, especially badges and buttons. Still scowling, Miles unbuckled the flap of his backpack and reached down to the bottom to pull out a cross-belt badge, the brass still bright and showing the Roman numerals 'CV' below the crown. Deakin took the oval object that was normally affixed where the belts for the ammunition pouch and bayonet scabbard crossed over. He gave it a polish on the tail of his tunic and walked over to the Head of the House, him now inside the room with Davey. He held out the badge, which the man took and then Deakin offered his hand which the man seized with appalling ferocity. Deakin returned the grip, all the while smiling and nodding.

"Good luck, Franco.

The man released his hand at last.

"Boa sorte, Jed. Nós nunca esqueceremos você soldados ingleses!"

Deakin looked at Consuela, now well able to translate, there being such a crossover between Portuguese and Spanish.

"Good luck, they'll never forget you English soldiers!"

Deakin turned to the man again and once more smiled and nodded, before turning to pick up his own back-pack, musket, and haversack.

"Right, you lot! Outside! All is forming up, don't pay to be the last."

With the final handshakes between the men and kisses and hugs between the women, they all took themselves out the front-door where the 105th were already filling the main road.

Whilst the 105th and the rest of the 4th Division were preparing to leave Garda, G. Anson's Cavalry Brigade, now down to two Regiments, the 12th and the 16th, had been on the road for three days, marching up the coast through Oporto during the previous day to reach the town of Braga, 40 miles North of Oporto. The coast roads had been good and the weather reasonable, but spirits amongst the Officer Corps of the 16th were somewhat dampened. They had received a new Colonel, a Scot named Alexander Collins, a man not overly dour, but professional and cheerless when it came to executing his own duties and inspecting that of others. It was noticed on his arrival that he had passed over greeting Tavender, refusing the offered hand, before moving on to Oakwood. This was the cause of some speculation but not sympathy for Tavender, because during their time in their Winter quarters, Tavender had set up a card school and now many of the Regiments Cornets were heavily in his debt. This did not include Cornet Carr, who hated cards, but it did Cornet Douglas Peterson, if only to a minor extent.

The doings of Tavender and the discussions of such, placed a cloud over the spirits of most Captains and Cornets, which was intensified when they reached the town of Braga. G. Anson's had entered the village to find Grant's Brigade already there and occupying the best billets, so they had to make do with what was left available, mostly agricultural in function. Nevertheless, Carr and Peterson made the best of a barn and then wandered into the town centre to find a very busy and packed estaminet. Peterson looked at Carr.

"Better than walking around the rest of this place!"

Therefore, they entered and, after much shouting at passing Portuguese waiters, they received a bottle of wine and two wooden beakers. No sooner had the wine been poured, when a Captain of the 18th Hussars, one of Grant's Regiments, came to sit at their table, bringing his own bottle. He waved them back into their seats and offered his hand to both.

"Leonard Wakefield, 18th Hussars. At your service!"

They introduced themselves, but Wakefield launched immediately into what he wanted to say.

"Did I see Lucius Tavender at the head of one of your Companies?"

Peterson nodded.

"You did! Now Captain of One Squadron. He used to be a temporary Major, but that now we've Alexander Collins as Colonel, Tavender's been pushed back down to plain Captain."

Wakefield sat back and grinned.

"And how are relations between the two? Your Colonel and he? I have experience of both. They were with me in the 18th, back in the year five."

Peterson and Carr looked at each other, before Peterson managed a diplomatic answer.

"Let's just say, not as they should be."

Wakefield pursed his lips and nodded.

"Alex Collins is now your Colonel."

It was spoken more as a statement than as a question, then he continued.

"Tavender been playing cards lately, has he?"

Both Carr and Peterson looked at each other again and both simultaneously nodded agreement, but Peterson had something to add.

"But this is the first Winter quarters where it has become so regular."

Wakefield paused to consider the statement, then continued.

"I was a mere Cornet then, myself, present company acknowledged and Tavender was a Captain and most adroit, or lucky, or whatever, at cards and many built up a debt in his favour. One of our Cornets, a Ben

Douglas was certain that he was cheating and challenged him over it. Tavender had choice of weapons and chose pistols. Tavender got his shot off first and Douglas was hit, not fatally, but failed with his own, no surprise. When they dug out the ball they found that Tavender had loaded a ball made from hunting lead, you know, softer lead so that it spreads on impact and does more damage. He must have had some ready made in his duelling case. Douglas was damn lucky; the ball went into his waistline. Nothing too vital there, but he was down. He managed to fire his shot, but wide."

Carr's expression became concerned.

"Duelling gets you cashiered!"

"Not back then, but Tavender did a bunk anyway! Rumour has it that he ended up in some backwater Yeomanry, Somerset was mentioned."

"And Douglas?"

"Had to turn it in. Too much muscle damage, so he couldn't use a sword."

Peterson then had a thought.

"So where does Collins come into all this?"

Wakefield sat back and took a deep breath.

"Douglas was Collins' brother-in-law. Married to his youngest sister. Collins was a Senior Captain then."

"And you were all together in the 18th?'

Wakefield poured some of his own wine into the pair's now empty beakers.

"We were and, well, I know that one should not speak ill of a brother Officer, but let's say, no tears were shed at Tavender's departure, not the least from many a Cornet owing Tavender a large Note of Credit."

Peterson took a drink from his beaker.

"And this cheating thing. Anything ever proved?"

Wakefield shook his head.

"No! But Tavender had the luck of the Devil! When the stakes were high it always seemed to be him that prevailed. You can draw your own conclusions from that, one way or the other."

He then took a drink himself.

"So! If you take that and the hunting ball he used against Ben Douglas, Tavender has no stock whatsoever with any in the 18th."

There was a pause whilst all thought, then Wakefield sat forward, grinning.

"So, enough of all that. We'll be moving East soon, so what do you think of the Frog cavalry you've met so far?"

With relieved grins and another drink, the two gave their answers and opinions, which took them through a pleasant evening until the Innkeeper closed his bar, his stocks now much depleted.

Moimentina de Beira revealed little of interest for the Officers of the 105th and to the rank and file it was a town like any other, providing billets dry or wet, cold or warm. The day after their arrival, O'Hare was sat with Heaviside mulling over billet allocation and requirements for supplies, when O'Hare finally completed a request for estimates of salt pork and looked across at Heaviside.

"When did he say he'll be back?"

Heaviside was busy adding his own columns of numbers for new boots and did not look up.

"He's with Lowry-Cole and all other Colonels and Brigadiers of the 4th Division."

O'Hare poured some more coffee from the jug on the table, this just arrived and then he returned to his paperwork, but it was not long before Carr did arrive back. Seeing the coffee, he poured some for himself, whilst the pair in the room looked at him in anticipation and they had to wait until he had taken at least two sips.

"Plans are laid! He's going back into Spain as four columns, the most Northern will be the Spanish under Giron, next South will be Scotch Graham's, next down what's called the Centre, himself in charge, and the

most Southerly, Daddy Hill. We're in the Centre and we are to be in Miranda do Douro the 20th May. First stop Villa Nova de Foz Coa, about two day's march East from here on our way to this Miranda."

O'Hare put down his coffee cup in astonishment.

"20th May! It's only the 6th March."

Carr nodded, but was unmoved.

"Orders are for training and more training, which gives six weeks, about. Assume two for marching to this Miranda place, so four more weeks to hone and improve. Extra cartridges will be provided."

He looked at the pair, one to the other.

"So! We start with the Officers. Who needs bringing up to scratch?"

O'Hare gave a sigh, whilst he thought.

"No one stands out, not even Slade. Farquharson, Howarth and Deakin are pushing him along. There is the likes of D'Villiers. For him we have to trust Carravoy and Ameshurst."

"Would I not like to swop those two around! Ameshurst is a first class Officer, but a Lord's a Lord and how do you set a Lieutenant over such as that?"

Carr sighed himself.

He sighed again.

"So, what about the men?"

"I've not seen better and I doubt there's any better in Portugal. You'd agree Joshua?"

Heaviside rose up in his chair with his hands together on the table.

"For if the readiness is there, it is acceptable according to what a person has. Two Corinthians, Eight, Verse 12." O'Hare nodded, his face serious.

"The men are getting into fights. Not with each other, but with other Regiments. That debacle at Castrillo before Salamanca when Brockenhurst ordered the Drummers to beat recall, is still fresh in many memories and you know how merciless Regimental rivalry can be. There's nothing that comes under the heading of 'understanding' in what they are saying."

Carr's face became grim.

"That's both good and bad, but try to keep them away from other Regiments. We don't want to lose men to the triangle, so the sooner we're on the road to this Villa Nova whatnot, the better. Meanwhile we keep them busy, tire them out and thereby out of the concerns of the Provosts."

"Let your eyes look directly forward and your gaze be straight before you. Ponder the path of your feet, then all your ways will be sure. Proverbs, Four, Verses 25 to 27."

"Yes, Joshua, I'll sure that's the way, but was there anything else?"

Heaviside nodded.

"Chaplain Albright lost his cart in the retreat and cannot find another. At least one that he can afford."

Carr's shoulders sagged.

"Blast the man, but we must help. He means well, the men like him and they think the world of that odd cove Sedgwicke, his servant. Help him out from funds, will you?"

Heaviside nodded and both expected another quote, but none came and so Carr jumped up before Heaviside changed his mind.

oOo

The 105th were parading in the bright, warm sunshine of a Portuguese late Spring day in the first week of May, but their spirits were anything but uplifted. They were at 'stand easy' by the roadside, waiting for the other Battalions of W. Anson's Brigade to come up, which meant that they were required to endure the comments of Skerret's Brigade marching by, these also of the 4th Division. The most enthusiastic with their comments were the 7th Royal Fusiliers and most comments were variants on, "The French are up this way, so you'll be going back the other way." It was all that Saunders could do to hold back Tom Miles, who would, if released, have sprung into their ranks and laid about all and sundry, but Miles had to content himself with screaming threats, whilst holding up his own cuff.

"You ran back quick enough at Salamanca, you done-up-pretty bastards! Better watch out for anyone with this green, 'cos if I sees any of you soppy girlies with your half-arsed busbies, you'll not forget your time with Tom Miles!"

Ethan Ellis was stood nearby and was as angry as Miles, but rank and discipline required silence from him, also, therefore, from the men in his Company.

"Miles! That's enough. Hold your place and hold your tongue!"

Miles clenched his jaw together, but his anger was plain and remained at boiling point, but it greatly subsided when the 20th East Devons of Skerret's Brigade marched past and warm greetings were then exchanged. Both Battalions remembered the desperate fight at Maida in Italy, in the Summer of 1807 where they had fought side by side to hold Lowry-Cole's left flank against immense French pressure and so the contrast with relations with the 7th Royal Fusiliers was both total and immediate, grins and shouts of welcome now filling the space between them. When the three Battalions of W. Anson's did finally arrive, these being the 27th, the 48th and the Provisional Battalion made up from the remains of the 31st and 66th, the 105th marched onto the road and followed behind, forming ranks of four on the march. Carr, on horseback at the front had gained a flavour of what had just taken place and he turned to O'Hare.

"Let's hope Skerret's march straight through this Villa Nova de Foz Coa, our first destination. It won't be simple, keeping a lid on all this!"

In the event the march was uneventful and W. Anson ordered Skerrett to keep the 7th beyond Villa Nova de Foz Coa and also the 23rd Fusiliers of his Brigade, so when the 105th did arrive the town was occupied by the 20th and so throughout the two days spent there, both Rankers and Followers of both Battalions were in and out of each other's camps, indulging in trading and yarning during the day, singing and dancing during the evening.

The following week, far away up in the furthest reaches of North-west Portugal, Oakwood entered the billet of Two Squadron's Officers and looked at his two lounging Cornets as he poured himself some water.

"Sojourns over. We leave Braga tomorrow to get to Braganza on the 20th May. There we await orders for the advance into Spain."

Peterson sat upright.

"So this is it then? We're going back!"

Oakwood looked at him steadily.

"Don't get carried away. A look on the map, and I've done that, shows damn all good roads to this Braganza, instead there's at least three ridges and four rivers. So, get yourselves ready for a hard ride!"

The Advance across Spain

First Advance

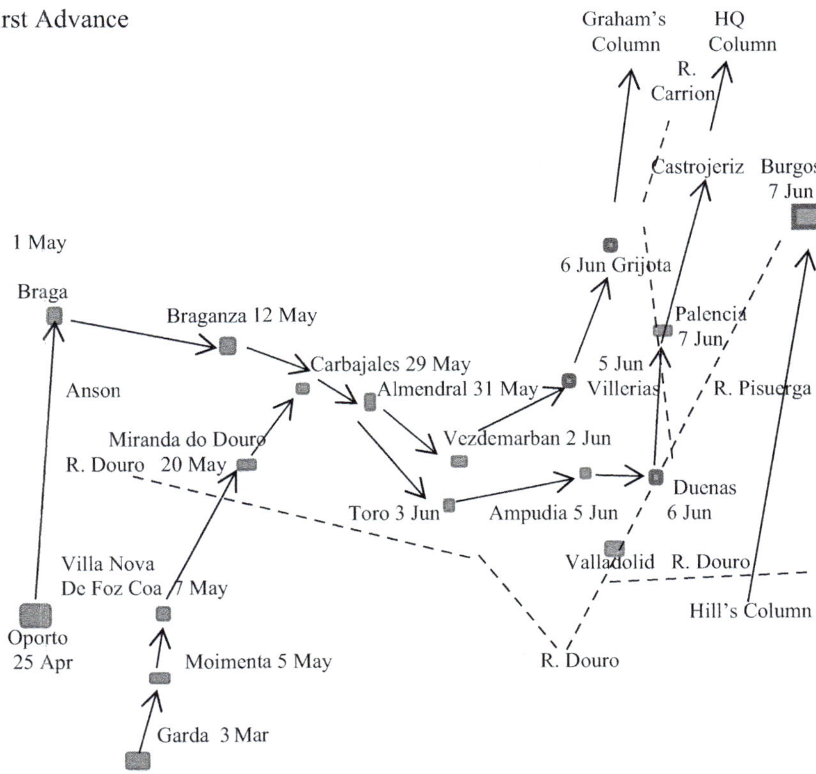

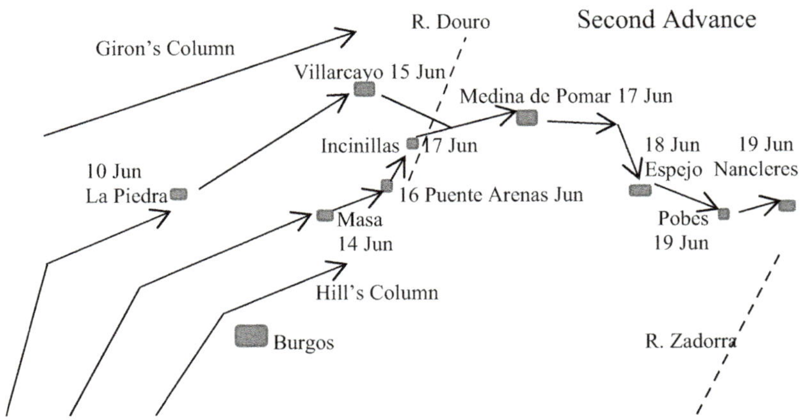

It was not long into the first day when Carr and Peterson found Oakwood's prediction to be horribly accurate. Only five miles out of Braga, their way climbed steeply, becoming more a track than any kind of road and they were forced to allow their horses to pick their own way, the column soon losing all formation. At Noon, Oakwood, Carr and Peterson arrived up to Major Johnson, him waiting at the side of the track, but he soon sent them back down the hill.

"Sam! Drop yours back. The supply wagons are falling badly behind. Each Squadron will take a turn. Protect them from marauding bandits and give whatever help you feel is needed or asked for."

Oakwood pulled his Squadron off the track and allowed Squadrons Three and Four to ride on past and upwards. With the passing of the last file of Four Squadron, they could see the supply wagons, some way behind, lurching and rocking over the rough ground. Oakwood turned to Carr.

"Willoughby take yours back and do what you can to speed them up. We'll wait here and take our turn."

Carr led his men back down the track and he could soon see the distress, even suffering, that was inflicted on their Waggoneers. Carr rode up to the Sergeant on the lead wagon.

"What can we do?"

"Attach ropes, Sir, to the wagons. That'll keep us stable and you can give the extra pull when needed."

Carr nodded.

"As you advise Sergeant. We are here to help."

The ropes were attached and the four Squadrons of the Regiment rotated on the task throughout the day, such that the four wagons were hauled safely intact and upright into the first collection of houses, these called Salamonde, an extraordinary hamlet, existing in an incongruous scoop taken out of the mountainside, the only safe perch being occupied by the small church. The place was far too small to accommodate even one Regiment and so the night was spent in the new six-man bell tents, these all pitched within the steep fields. The morning came and Carr awoke to find that both Peterson and Oakwood had rolled down the slope into him, such that all three were almost on top of each other. Carr pushed Peterson off.

"No wonder I was having a strange dream. As though I was in some kind of rugby scrum."

Peterson pushed back.

"Surprised it wasn't something more to do with that girl you've been seeing in Braga."

"Unfortunately not, but it would have been a damn sight more agreeable than this tangle!"

The day's march began and soon it became obvious that the wagons could not keep up without the extra ropes and aid as afforded by each Squadron and so the rotation continued, each Trooper taking a turn with a rope fixed to his saddle with the other end on some strategic point on a supply wagon. The following night was spent on a bleak hillside and the following after that, after another very arduous day, in Chaves, a place more sensible in its location, such that it even had a castle to defend any incursion from the North, down the valley of its major river. The castle provided accommodation for all Officers, but it was the following days that tested all endurance to the limit. The weather turned against them, but nothing so hindering as the terrain. The mountains between Chaves and the next town, Vinhais, were the highest of the journey. Now seven days into their exertions , Collins was riding constantly up and down his column, his normal, dour Scots demeanour descending deeper into concern, anxiety and ill-temper. G. Anson also was often present and both could often be seen in consultation, as their men picked their way across the hillside, often needing to be many yards apart to find their way, as though a band of irregulars. On that day, Collins himself came to Oakwood.

"Two more wagon horses have died, more like had to be shot and we've used up all the spares. Dismount two of yours and get their horses into the harness."

Oakwood was astonished.

"So the help didn't help enough, Sir!"

"No! And now one of the wagons cannot move at all!"

"How do I choose, Sir. Draw lots?"

Collins exploded.

"What the damn do I care how ye do it! Ye're as good a judge of horses for the job as well as I."

Oakwood immediately turned his horse down the line and chose two that looked the least athletic and the most sturdy. Their riders were most disgruntled at now having to walk, but their mounts were put into harness and the column laboured on. However, it was the following day when matters became even worse. The rain fell in torrents and the track became so bad that the wagons could make no more progress, even with ten ropes attached to ten horses. Collins rode back to the Waggoneer Sergeant who stood to salute but was deeply worried by what he had to say to his Colonel.

"Sir. If we try to roll over this, we'll smash a wheel, Sir."

However, Collins was wholly understanding.

"What d'ye suggest, Sergeant?"

"We'll have to unload, Sir and see what that does. We may even have to pick up and carry. That can be done with enough men, with all unloaded."

Collins nodded and rode back to his men, speaking instructions to each Squadron Captain. At Oakwood, he repeated his words.

"The wagons can go no further. They must be unloaded and manhandled forward. Your Squadron to take the second. Every able-bodied man, Oakwood, y'hear? Officers and men. The wagons come with us, or we're useless. Every man to do his share. Rank counts not!"

With that he rode further up to find Tavender at One Squadron and pass on the message to him. Oakwood signalled his Squadron to follow him back and the hard labour began. Peterson's Troop unloaded the second wagon and Carr's pushed and pulled. At one point, the cart, now empty, had to be manhandled up onto a shelf despite the pulling effort of many horses. Peterson's men carried their burdens or strapped them to horses as best they could to follow on, but they spent more time stood still waiting for the cart to make progress, than following. When another lift was required, Carr found himself at the back with Baxter and his three particular friends, all with hands and shoulders to the cart. Baxter gave the call to lift.

"Two. Six. Up!"

The cart was hoisted and continued on. Spivey looked at Baxter.

"Two six! You must have been in the Navy!"

Carr was walking close by.

"Yes. Press-ganged!"

Subdued laughter came all round, but it did not last long. One Squadron's wagon was stuck again and needed lifting. Carr's men walked forward to help and Collins soon arrived because of the delay.

Men placed themselves all around wherever they could, but Collins Scots temper exploded once more, not at the men, but at Tavender, who was still on his horse.

"Captain Tavender! I ordered every able-bodied man tae do his share. Officers and men. Now dismount, Sir, and get your shoulder under that wagon an' gi' your men a hand. I want to see your hands dirty and your back sore, just like these guid lads here!"

Tavender was so astonished at such an order being delivered by such words that he dismounted without thinking, but soon his own aristocratic temper surfaced and his mouth set into a grim line as his men made room for him alongside the cart. The cart was lifted and pulled onto the next shelf and progress was made. The day continued, one of unrelenting labour in the rain, the water running in sheets down the track making their footing treacherous as they struggled to achieve purchase underfoot to haul their precious transport up the never-ending height. It was only darkness that brought respite and all slept out on the mountain, finding whatever shelter they could. From their supplies, so jealously harboured, they made a good breakfast and relief did come when they were at last over the watershed and draught-teams could manage on their own but ropes were still required, this time as brakes. At Noon they entered Vinhais, another village nestling content in its own valley, but Anson only allowed a meal before ordering his Brigade to march on, march being the word, all were ordered to walk their horses. The three Officers of Two Squadron were walking together, but saying little, Collins' tirade served up to Tavender, an Officer of the Regiment, when all was said and done, remained clear, stark and alarming in their minds, their feelings on the matter not reduced by their own mental and physical exhaustion.

Carr had debated within himself whether to pass onto Oakwood what he had learned in the estaminet in Braga, but he decided against. His two years, almost, of military service had matured him greatly, but even more they had made him appreciate the value of Regimental cohesion and so he held his peace and was encouraged in his decision by the fact that Peterson had also said nothing. Anson gave no order to halt at day's end and so it was in full darkness when they finally entered Braganza, to find the town already occupied by D'Urban's Portuguese Dragoons, but it did not matter. Anson's men and their mounts were so exhausted that they slept in the streets, men and their mounts both, wrapped in whatever cloaks and blankets came most easily to hand.

oOo

In far better physical shape than his brother, and on the same day, Brevet Lieutenant Colonel Henry Carr, led his men into Miranda do Douro. He had paced his men over the journey, seeing no point in arriving early, content with an easy march on the good road that gently ascended the valley containing the upper reaches of the Douro, all the way cheered and clapped by jubilant Portuguese. In the event, the decision regarding the pace of march was made for him, because ahead on the road were both the 6th and 7th Divisions, their commanders seemingly of the same mind as Carr, but these were all Major-Generals and their decisions far outranked his own. W. Anson's followed Skerret's Brigade into Miranda do Douro, for Carr to be immediately approached by a Provost Captain as they followed the 48th into the town. The Captain came to the attention and saluted.

"Sir. Would you be the 105th? Colonel Carr in command?'

Carr returned the respectful salute.

"Yes to both."

"Welcome to Miranda do Douro, Sir. If you would care to follow that Trooper there, he will lead you to your place of holding."

The Captain pointed to a mounted Provost, who immediately saluted when Carr looked at him after the Captain had finished. The Provost then spoke his part.

"You are further up the other Miranda river, Sir, the Fresno, but I think you will find it to be most serviceable."

Carr and O'Hare both saluted and marched on.

"Do you get the feeling that this campaign may be somewhat better organised than those that have gone before and we've been part of?"

O'Hare smiled wryly.

"First impressions, all to the good. I'll grant you that."

The camp was flat and spacious, with clear water from the nearby Fresno. In the bright May sunlight the myriad white bell-tents of all the other Brigades of the three Divisions stood out in the new Spring green of the good pasture that were the fields to the North of Miranda. Deakin, Davey and Saunders immediately took themselves over to the Fresno to try their luck with the fishing and it was not long before all three had a collection of a species that they could not name, but the plump flanks of each were all that concerned them. That sentiment was shared by Nellie and Bridie when they saw what had almost become a shoal that was spilled out next to the cooking pot, this now illegal for the ranks, but no one cared too much where the Followers were concerned and so a communal fish stew was quickly embarked upon.

As was their wont, Deakin sat with Halfway preparing tobacco pipes
whilst Eirin cared for baby Nelly and they also watched over Jed's namesake, Eirin's eldest, then busying himself with exploring rabbit holes.

"Here we go again Jed. What's this, fourth time in?"

Deakin ceased the activity with his pipe. He needed to think.

"I'd say. There's Coruna, the first, then Talavera, then Salamanca, just gone, and now this. You'm right, Tobe. Fourth!"

"Be this goin' to be different?"

"Well, you've heard the rumour. Lots of Johnnies bein' took back to France and I hear the Dons've won at last, over East Spain somewhere. So perhaps this'll be different."

"The lads look good, right up to the mark."

"You'm right there. Sharp as a packet of needles, as my old Father would say, but the lads is rankled still, about that Brockenhurst mess just afore Salamanca. An' gettin' stick over it."

Halfway nodded

"Could be a good thing, that, Jed."

"Could be good, Tobe, I grant you, but if 'tis still a stone in Carr's shoe, being a man like him, it could mean us gettin' stood up in some tight pinches."

"Only time can tell with that one, but the lads are good. I'd trust us, in most common face-offs. The Frogs fell away easy enough at Salamanca. Don't seem to have the stomach for it."

Deakin nodded.

"But that wer' well across Spain. The closer we gets to France, the more they'n defendin' their own hearths and homes. 'Twould make a difference to you an' me!"

At that moment, Nelly was deposited on Jed's lap, whilst Eirin was called to help with the fish stew. The pipes were immediately discarded and no more military conversation took place, all attention now being on the gurgling Nelly, sat content with her Grandfather and fascinated by his tunic buttons.

Contentment was prevalent in the Headquarters room of the 105th, Carr, O'Hare and Heaviside all sat drinking coffee. Carr laid his cup on the table.

"How many did we lose on the march?"

O'Hare answered immediately.

"Two."

Carr became concerned.

"Desertions?"

"No. One just dropped dead; he was wounded at Salamanca, the other is with the Provosts. Assaulting one of their Corporals."

Carr nodded, content.

"That's a flogging and return to the ranks. I'll settle for that!"

"Any news on the advance?"

Carr poured some more coffee.

"What I know is that himself has left his favourite Headquarters at Freineda, close to Cuidad, and has moved up closer to us, at our favourite Villa Nova de Foz Coa, but he's got four columns to worry about. The last date I heard for an advance was 29th this April. Hill's Southern column will be moving first, then Graham's from Braganza, he's left centre. We're the last to move, being right centre and we're under The Peer himself. Giron's Spaniards way up North have been moving for some time. This is the big effort and it seems that much may be in our favour. What say you, Joshua? Something military this time, perhaps?"

Heaviside's face became blank and thereby into pulpit mode and Carr knew that his request had been in vain.

"For I know the plans I have for you, declares the Lord, plans for welfare and not for evil, to give you a future and a hope. Jeremiah 29, verse 11."

O'Hare chuckled at Carr being ignored and reached behind him for the whisky, a bottle of good Irish.

oOo

General Graham was sat on his horse, his mount unmoving on the riverbank, but Graham himself was animated enough, grinning whilst he toasted each Battalion from a large whisky flask, acknowledging both Foot and Horse as they entered the fords over the river Manzanas, the minor river that marked the boundary between Portugal and Spain. Lieutenant General Thomas Graham, the Hero of Barossa, was immensely popular with the men and each Regiment returned his toast with waves and shouts. It was well known that at that battle he had personally led the victorious charge of the Guards Brigade on his right, before riding across the battlefield to lead the decisive charge of his Brigade on the left. Many hoisted their shakoes onto the muzzle of their muskets, or simply waved their shako in reply before they entered the water to wade across, obeying the marker flags placed by their peasant guides. The 16th Light Dragoons, upstream of Graham, but within earshot of all the celebrations, sat their horses, awaiting their turn. All were intently studying the fate of the 12th of Anson's Brigade, who had entered first and all could see that the water came up to the riders' knees and above, showing that the river at their ford was narrow, but deep. The four Squadrons of the 16th were in column, to enter in order; One, Two, Three and Four and Captain Tavender, now well aware of the depth of the water, began to pull off his boots, this noticed by Colonel Collins.

"Captain Tavender! So, if the French are over there waiting for us, you'll be fighting them off in your stockinged feet!"

Tavender, his face immediately puce with anger, pulled his boots back up to their full height, but, on entering the water he pulled up his knees to an undignified angle and allowed no water over the top of his expensive and elegant footwear.

For the 105th, as part of Wellington's column and not yet required to move, the days that followed the departure of Graham's column from Miranda and into Spain were days of chores and tedium. Lowry-Cole insisted on inspecting all his Battalions, but whilst Carr expected some comment on how the 105th had saved the day for him at Maida, but all that came was a brief salute at the end of the inspection and him then riding off. Carr allowed a rest day for a general 'make and mend', but it worked out as more one of yarning, smoking and predictions for the future. The latter was given a boost of accuracy when Drake entered the Officer's mess, with a despatch sent to all Battalions of Wellington's column. Drake took great joy in reading it out loud, certain that it superseded all other topics of conversation then in progress.

"Listen! Hill has taken Salamanca. Three days ago, and Madrid has been abandoned by the Frogs."

The news quickly spread throughout the ranks of all Battalions and, when she heard it, Nellie looked anxiously at Bridie.

"I hope Pepita and her family are safe and back in their home."

Bridie nodded and crossed herself.

"With The Blessing, they will be."

However, at that moment events were moving apace, this beginning with Lieutenant-General Stapleton-Cotton riding up to the 105th Headquarters cottage and doing no more than putting his head around the door.

"Carr! Yours are the nearest. Get your Lights and come with me. At the double."

The next voice to be raised was that of Carr, shouting into the next room.

"Bryce! Find Captain Drake and tell him to bring his Company to Headquarters at the double."

Within ten minutes, Carr, Drake and the Light Company were following an Aide de Camp Major of Stapleton-Cotton's Staff to soon find themselves at the bank of the Douro where it flowed with some considerable force through a deep chasm alongside Miranda. There was no bridge over the Douro there, because access down to the river bank was impossible and both Drake and Carr now stood at the edge, looking across the deep chasm that confined the powerful and fast flowing Douro. After one minute of studying the angry river, they turned to each other in astonishment, because they could see Wellington himself with half a dozen Staff plus Hussar escort, perched on the far bank at the point where a windlass contrivance had been constructed by Engineers. Several stout ropes spanned the chasm over to an identical contrivance on their side. Stapleton-Cotton came over to Carr.

"Lord Wellington has ridden up fast from Salamanca. Now he needs to come across to us. His direct ride has placed him on the wrong side of the river."

"Yes Sir, so what do you require of my men?"

"Send two over. Firstly, to ensure that all is still safe, second, to work the windlass on the far side. The escort will be busy keeping watch, they are on the French side, after all. Also, for safety's sake, the windlass on our side needs manpower also, so two more."

He turned to the Light Company, formed up in Fours.

"Those two will do to go over!"

The two he pointed at were Zeke Saunders and Tom Miles. Carr's gaze followed Stapleton-Cotton's pointing arm and so he gave his orders.

"Miles and Saunders, into that basket. Pike and Solomon, get onto that windlass and get them across."

The surprise on Saunder's face was much over-matched by the alarm on Tom Miles' and a tug on Miles' sleeve from Saunders was required to get him to move. There was a platform to aid entry into the basket, which was at least deep and robust, but Saunders examined the ropes and pulley above on the spanning rope and was reassured to see it to be of good ship's cable. Meanwhile, Miles was closing his eyes as the basket lurched out over the chasm, powered by the windlass on their side and soon also by that on the far bank. Whilst Saunders kept a watchful eye on the straining ropes, Miles stood gripping the side of the basket, shaking in every limb. The sound of the rushing waters over a cataract just downstream of Miranda was now very audible and a large bird flew under the basket. Saunders followed its flight.

"I think that was an eagle!"

Miles still had his eyes tight closed.

"Bugger and sod your eagle! 'Tis a bloody Angel I needs."

The basket was swinging alarmingly as the cable bobbed with the strain of the two men, but they were nearing the far side, a little quicker than before, because Wellington had ordered two extra of his Dragoon escorts to man the windlass on that side. Not soon enough for Miles, the basket bumped against the rocks next to the platform and Saunders shook his shoulder.

"We're here."

Miles opened his eyes, saw the platform and almost leapt out of the basket, but they were not allowed to quit the platform, because a tall figure, with an overly long face, in a dark green uniform was stood alongside.

"You two. Hold the basket steady for his Lordship."

Saunders and Miles dropped off the platform and held the basket whilst Wellington climbed in alone. He was winched across very rapidly and the basket was then worked to and fro for the rest of Wellington's Staff, one at a time. When the last was on his way, only Miles, Saunders and the escort remained, Saunders now helping with the windlass.

"Who's the toff in green?"

The Dragoon grinned.

"Slender Billy! The Prince of Orange."

Saunders nodded and guffawed.

"One at a time for them, I see."

The Hussar laughed.

"Where's the surprise in that. Got any baccy?"

"If you works the windlass from this side to get us back over."

The Hussar nodded and so Saunders and Miles pulled out their full pouches and each dropped a good handful into the open pouch. By the now the basket was empty and on its way back, so the Hussar called down one of his comrades to the windlass. When Miles and Saunders were in the basket and then beyond the platform, the Hussar called out to them.

"Well, good luck boys. We're back to Salamanca. May see you again."

By now Miles had his eyes tight shut as the basket again began to swing and dip with the weight of two passengers. Saunders pulled at his shoulder.

"Open your eyes and take a look, Tom. You'll not see the likes of this back home."

Miles' eyes did not open, but his mouth did.

"I have got the likes of this back home and 'tis called the Avon gorge, but I never wants to cross'n like this, not ever, an' that's a fact!"

It was little more than a minute before the basket bumped against the rocks on the Miranda side and the pair climbed out. Wellington and his Staff had long gone and so Miles and Saunders rejoined the ranks of their grinning comrades.

"Never thought you'd reach such heights, Tom! Sharing a basket with Nosey. Never did."

This came from somewhere but Miles had by now returned to his old self, wholly disgruntled.

"They ordered us into that contraption to see that it wer' safe and what did we get for'n? Not a shilling, nor nuthin' lower. Bloody Staff! Bloody toffs!"

However, once back to their camp, they found no camp at all. Puzzled, Carr hurried to O'Hare.

"Orders just arrived, we march over the top of the big Douro bend to Carbajales de Alba. Orders from the Peer himself, just arrived.'

Carr became mildly annoyed.

"Just arrived! He didn't waste any time. We've just winched him over the Douro and immediately he sends us on our way to somewhere different."

The Brigades formed and the pace was set. Although the roads were generally good, no one was under any illusions that they would be there before nightfall, but the pace was 'tactical', all the same. Following the 4th Division, the Followers began to feel the strain of the rapid march. Bridie looked at her and Nellie's children, then at Eirin.

"This is goin' to bust us, so it is. Sure, they've not stopped since we left that Miranda place!"

At that moment a Troop of Provosts galloped up.

"Off the road! Get off the road. The 6th Division is close behind!"

Nellie stood with arms akimbo.

"An' just who's goin' to be lookin' after us, with all these knife wieldin' Spanish Devils roamin' these hills?"

The Provost Sergeant reined in his horse and grinned.

"Not to worry, Ma! There's plenty of us Provosts on this road up to Carbajales. The whole army's on the move."

Hearing the commotion, Albright and Sedgwicke, riding in their new cart, pulled their new mules and cart to a halt and Albright leaned down.

"Fear not, my good woman. I feel your welfare is high in the concerns of those who guide us and we must have Faith in the Good Lord."

Nellie's sour face betrayed her faith in the former, but she said nothing on that subject, more on one concerning the latter.

"Well, thank you for that Reverend, but a ride for the children in your cart, surely now, would that not be serving the Will of the Good Lord?"

By now the 6th Division were pounding by and Nellie could only see, not hear, that Sedgwicke was saying something to Albright, then a welcoming arm came from Sedgwicke pointing to the back and the tired children were allowed to climb in. With the 6th Division now past, the Followers resumed their own march and Nellie and Bridie were pleased that the Provost's words were indeed true. Much of the army remained on the road, Provosts included, as had been promised, but also a great deal of transports and artillery. When, in full darkness, they all dragged into Carbajales, they found their men with tents set up and rations cooked and Ellis with less than comforting news.

"We're here for just one night. Pontoons are coming up from Miranda, the way we've just come, but they're to get down past us to a river called the Esla, at somewhere called Almendral and then set up."

"Who for?"

"Not for you, Miles! Artillery and wagons'll be my bet. They'll find other ways of getting the likes of us across. Or in your case a straw basket on a piece of string!

No one laughed. Relations were always too raw between Tom Miles and Ethan Ellis, but it was the Sergeant who was the closest with his prediction. The whole of the 4th Division were ordered to march Eastward to the River Esla, to a point opposite the village of Almendral, but they were ahead of the pontoons and found themselves confronted by the mighty Esla, surging its way onwards to join with the even mightier Douro. Carr and O'Hare stood with their Brigadier W. Anson, who told them of Wellington's intentions.

"He wants over quickly, to take the Johnnies by surprise, but luck to the lads that've got to try that."

Carr noted that the valley of the Esla there was nothing like as deep and sharp as that of the Douro at Miranda, but it was deep and sharp enough to build the current into something substantial. His eye was caught by movement just upstream, a long column of Hussars and infantry were approaching the edge of the swirling water, the foot soldiers downstream of the cavalry. O'Hare folded his arms, a gesture of deep concern in his case.

"I've seen this before and it'll cost."

However, it was Anson who responded.

"These are the only fords available in this area. We have to see if they are passable."

The first into the water were the horses and plainly they were soon in distress and it required all the skill of their riders to quell them, although the water was not at its most powerful at that point. O'Hare gave his judgment.

"Not good footing. Not a good start."

Each Hussar had an infantryman holding onto his stirrup, hoping that the body of the horse would take much of the force from the powerful current. With much stumbling and frantic recovery from many, the column edged across, both Hussars and infantry together, anxiety building within all the watchers on the Allied bank. All knew that the effort could turn into complete disaster. Carr turned to Anson.

"Is this the only place where this is being tried, Sir."

Anson did not take his eyes from the struggling column.

"No! It's being tried upstream as well, four miles up, with D'Urban's Portuguese and Bock's KGL. These are Grant's Hussars."

At that point Anson took a sharp intake of breath. In the centre of the river three horses had collapsed, sending the riders into the water and also their soldiers. Two of the soldiers lost their hold on their stirrup and were carried away, as was one Hussar. The other two Hussars and one soldier each held onto their mounts but were carried downstream. Anxious and annoyed Carr watched, as, with the horse providing most of the power and swimming, they managed to gain the far bank, but other foot soldiers had stumbled into holes or against rocks, sending them deep into the current and then, in some cases, the stirrup was torn from their hands by the force of the water. Some managed to regain their footing and struggle out to one bank or the other, but several were carried downstream and away. Two more horses went down with more infantry and the cries of both animals and men could be heard above the noise of the surging water, as their feet found purchase, only for them to be swept away again. Some, the lucky, found enough ground beneath their feet to reach the bank on either side, but others were carried away, until even the red of their uniforms could not be seen within the curling brown waves.

High on a promontory, Carr could see Wellington and his Staff, all using their telescopes, but Carr had mixed feelings and thoughts. There was anger within him.

"Was that worth the risk? Sir?"

Anson was now using his own telescope.

"Him up there would say so. Look, bar their few casualties, Grant's Brigade are over, with two Battalions of infantry. He'll call that a success, us now on the far bank in force. How many would we lose if we had to force a bridge? Johnny's now got a Brigade of cavalry behind his flank with a two Battalion Brigade of infantry in support."

He closed his telescope with a snap and walked away. Carr and O'Hare remained to see that ropes were already being pulled across to aid the fixing of the pontoons, expected that day, to safely span the still treacherous water.

Further North, G. Anson's Light Dragoon Brigade were at their own Esla ford, but now looking back at what had been their third attempt, having now failed at two crossing points, the river being too strong and too deep. Peterson was riding alongside Carr.

"Well, that's put a spanner in the works! We were the lead for Graham's whole column. The word is that we march down to a place called Almendral where some pontoons are waiting for us. We'll be following in the footsteps of Wellington's men."

"Not as planned then?"

"No, but it's usually rivers that upset the applecart, almost more than the doings of Johnny himself."

"How far then, this Almendral?"

"A day, should do it, for us. Two for the infantry."

Two for the infantry also applied to the 4th Division, but not from speed of marching, but for days remaining idle. They did not cross the day of the Hussars and infantry, instead those with the rank had the privilege to sit and watch the pontoons being levered across the river, which had now fallen substantially. The next day they did cross, to march rapidly and unopposed, forward on straight roads that bisected gently rolling countryside, the full opposite of what had been endured West of the Douro. They halted mid-afternoon, no reason being given other than it made no sense to advance too far until the whole of Wellington's column was across and deployed. Camp was made and the Followers began to prepare a meal. The weather was dry and balmy and all sat in contented mood, then RSM Gibney arrived.

"Any of you ever been slaughtermen?"

Davey and Solomon raised their hands.

"Come wi' me!"

"What's this about Sar' Major?"

"The Brigade's bought a flock of sheep. Paid top price, shouldn't wonder, an' now all's got to be killed off, an' t'meat distributed round. Calls gone out for lads as've done such before an' that includes thee!"

As the light was finally fading, Davey returned with half a sheep and Solomon with two fleeces, which Bridie and Nellie immediately began to scrape and wash in a nearby stream. The next day both were drying on Davey's and Solomon's backpacks as they marched forward, the road signs pointing to Zamora. One fleece would serve as lining for baby Ellen's back-cradle, to ease any chaffing and when it was dry Tom

Miles did the shaping. All was content and at peace as they marched forward, even Miles and Nellie exchanging a civil word when it was found that the fleece fitted perfectly down inside the back-cradle. The second was turned into a sleeveless jacket for young Jed, but put aside for the next Winter.

The following day was the 1st June and, having crossed the Esla at Almendral from the necessity of Graham's fords being impassable, Wellington and Graham's columns were advancing across the open countryside almost side by side. The two major columns were required by Wellington to pass through the streets of Zamora at rapid pace and for the first ten minutes this was almost maintained, but Zamora was a major local town and all from within and without came and thronged the streets. The noise of the cheering was deafening and the slaps and handshakes equally wearying. The columns slowed to a crawl and the jaws of those who saw it clamped together with emotion as a small girl came up and seized Gibney's hand, to hold it all the way to the edge of the town. Luckily, her brother remained with her and when the column halted and broke up, the giant Regimental Sergeant Major knelt before her, speaking words that many in his own Battalion could barely understand.

"Nah then, lass, that's th'brother there, he'll guide thee back to tha's ain folks, where th'Mother'll be attending on thee, of that ah'm sure."

He looked up at Bridie and Nellie, both fighting to hold back tears, and both took the cue to give the girl and her brother two doughcakes each. Gibney then guided both on their way back into the town buildings, but plainly he was wholly overcome and both women patted his arm as they left him to his own thoughts and overwhelming emotions. The whole army then camped outside and those near enough listened to the sounds of music, dancing and celebration emanating from what seemed to be every street in the town. The celebrations continued with Spanish dancers touring many of the camps to give much appreciated exhibitions of the many forms of Spanish dance, which all drew large and appreciative audiences. However, the Scottish and even the Irish Battalions, not to be outdone, replied with exhibitions of Gaelic dancing which drew loud cheers and applause from the Spanish. Wellington was not best pleased with the late hour of retiring, but within the town the celebrations continued throughout the night.

Despite the activities of the late evening, both columns marched away from their camping grounds on time. The weather was seasonably warm and, for the Officers of the 16th Light Dragoons the whole affair seemed more like a holiday mounted trek than any form of serious campaign. When the two columns came close enough for identification, Cornet Carr looked across and saw a column of infantry distinguished by the bright green of their facings. In his place in the 16th column, back at Two Squadron, Carr could not gain the permission he needed and so he rode up to Collins at the head.

"Sir. My brother's Regiment is just over there. May I take a moment to visit?"

Collins looked across to judge the distance and found it to be no more than a two minute ride.

"Very well. Five minutes, nae more. Ye understand? Then ah'll need tae see your ugly snout back here!"

Collins was clearly in a better mood and so Carr grinned, saluted and rode off. Within the 105th, O'Hare was the first to notice.

"Some kind of Light Dragoon coming our way."

Carr looked over and grinned.

"Not some kind, a particular kind. That's my brother!"

The two Carrs dismounted and embraced before walking together, leading their horses. Soon, the Elder pointed up at Major O'Hare.

"You remember Padraigh O'Hare?"

Young Carr reached up and shook O'Hare's offered hand.

"Indeed I do. Pleased to see you again, Sir."

O'Hare grinned widely and nodded.

"And to see you again also, Willoughby."

Carr began the questioning.

"Any action?"

"No, not since the retreat. Just the business of crossing rivers to get to here. That was desperate enough. We couldn't cross the Elsa North of you and had to follow you over the pontoons."

"Same here, desperate business for us as well until they got those pontoons in place."

"Yes, but that's past now and isn't this simply wonderful country. No problem with fodder here, endless fields of growing corn.

Carr nodded and smiled indulgently, then he looked at his younger brother carefully.

"Any news from home?"

Young Carr nodded.

"I got this when we left Braga."

He pulled out a letter from his tunic pocket.

"You can keep it for a while."

Carr shook his head.

“No, you keep it. Father will expect you to have all the letters safe when you get home. If I keep it and anything happens to me, you’ll be one short.”

“This one’s from Beatrice. You’re now an uncle! Uncle Henry to Niece Maud.”

A pang of sadness overcame Carr.

“How old?’

“Fourteen months.”

Carr nodded sadly, to have not been made aware directly, regarding such an event, but his Father was obdurate. Carr had entered the army having been totally forbidden.

“Did you reply?”

“I did.”

“Did you tell them about me? They may at least be vaguely interested that I am now a Lieutenant-Colonel, albeit probably temporary.”

“I did, sent one back to Beatrice after receiving this one. But what about Jane? Is she well?”

Carr nodded, smiled and the gloom lifted.

“Got a letter when we were in Garda. All’s well, living with her Aunt, Lady Constance. She did not mention her Father, so I can assume there are still no major concerns from that direction.”

Both grinned at each other, but young Carr was now conscious of the time.

“Five minutes our Colonel said and he’s a Scots stickler. I’d best get back.”

He re-mounted his horse, but Carr had a suggestion.

“Nat Drake’s at the back with the Lights. Ride past and say hello.”

Cornet Carr swung his horse’s head around and with a last wave to O’Hare, he cantered off. He waved hello at Nat Drake, him at the head of his men, in relaxed mood, his shako swinging from the pommel of his sword. However, when he returned to the 16th, it was just in time. Anson’s Brigade was leaving the column at the canter. Carr placed himself alongside Oakwood.

“What’s going on?”

Oakwood gave him but a brief glance.

“We’re off to a place called Vezdemarban, there to meet some Guerrillas. I’ve probably tangled the Spanish way of saying it, but it’s North of Toro, which is our next big town after Zamora. Giron’s column will pass through that area and it’s our job to make contact. Anson with the 12th will try to find Giron, while we've been ordered to this Vezdemarban place for a chat with the Guerrillas. See what they know."

It required but half a day, across totally featureless countryside that made but small demands on their horses. Vezdemarban proved to be a place of minor significance, apart from the fact that it was possibly on the route of Giron's column and was home to about 400 Spanish souls who, so the 16th found having made their winding way to the centre, were entertaining Giron's 'roaming eyes', these being the Guerrillas of Julian Sanchez. They were led as usual by Ignacius Mateo and this carnival figure, upon seeing them enter the Plaza, strode towards them with a bottle of wine in one hand and half a long loaf in the other.

"Ah, Senors Dragoons, you have found us! Is good, I think!"

He was plainly more than a little intoxicated and Collins looked at Johnson.

"Who the Hell is this?"

"Guerrillas, Sir. This one we meet frequently. One Ignacius Mateo, who operates around us. You may have heard of them, Sir. Tough fighters and they do us a lot of good with what they find out. They give the French a headache too."

Collins' face still bore a frown.

"Heard of them, aye, but never seen."

He dismounted, as did Johnson.

"Tough fighters, ye say?"

Johnson frowned deeply as he spoke the appropriate reply.

"Yes Sir, and if the French capture any of them they are put to death on the spot and not overly quick!"

This seemed to have a beneficial effect on Collins, who advanced towards Mateo extending his hand. The Guerrilla took it, then offered the bottle to Collins, who grinned and took a long pull at the bottle, much to Mateo's delight. Collins then returned the bottle.

"I am Colonel Alexander Collins. 16th Light Dragoons. Pleased to meet you."

Mateo's white teeth beamed across the Plaza.

"Alexandro, I am pleased to meet you. You have someone I know well with you, Teniente Carr. I know well from past. He is well, si?"

Collins pointed back to Carr, who had remained in the column and Carr raised his hand in greeting.

"Ah, Teniente! You are well I see and there is Sargento Baxter and Senor Maka Pees. Hola!"

He waved the bread as though it was a sword and drank from the bottle again. The whole column of the 16th was now laughing openly with amusement, but somehow, at this point, Mateo had brought himself back together.

"Come, I have things to tell, from my Generalissimo Giron."

He waved them over to some dilapidated tables which were at that time occupied by his Guerrillas, all drinking with the locals, but they soon made way on Mateo's approach. On seeing this, Oakwood looked at Carr.

"Let's go and listen. Why not?"

They dismounted and hurried over to hear Mateo begin, him sat at a table with his Lieutenant, a fiercesome looking man, with Collins and Johnson on the other side. The Lieutenant filled up four large cow horn beakers with red wine as Mateo began.

"My Generalissimo is soon at Villalpando, five leagues to North. We see no French past days, they fall back before us."

He clinked his beaker with his Lieutenant, then with Collins and Johnson, before drinking and then continuing.

"The news I have is that the Usurpador de Titeres Joseph….."

He spat on the ground, as did his Lieutenant.

"…… has left Madrid. He has many wagons with, how you say…. robbery, what he has robbed......... and many, many Afracensados."

Again, both spat on the floor.

"He has Regiment of soldados Espanoles, who have joined his army. Traidores all!"

All listening in the 16th were surprised that those words did not motivate any more spitting on the ground, but Collins had his own question.

"Have you any knowledge of where the French are now?"

"We are hearing from our camaradas that they go to Valladolid. All! They take what they have robbed and Afrancensados with them go."

"French soldados?"

Mateo emptied his glass.

"Valladolid! Joseph there with all men, we believe."

Collins stood and held out his hand, to both men, to receive two solid handshakes in reply.

"We are grateful, Senor Mateo. What you have said is very useful to us. We must now ride back and tell General Wellington what you have found out for us."

Mateo immediately stood up himself, seizing the bottle again.

"Vayan con Dios, mis amigos!"

He then waved at the whole of the 16th, all still mounted and looking on.

"You also, muchachos!"

The Light Dragoons laughed openly and waved back, as Collins and Johnson saluted and returned to their mounts, as did their Officer audience. Collins spoke rapidly to Johnson as they moved.

"We knew that Madrid had been abandoned, but not that he's moved to Valladolid. Also, we've found Giron. Let the men replenish their water canteens, water the horses and then we get back. We must pass this on at our best speed."

oOo

The atmosphere in the room was as before a comedy play that had been well reviewed and so all sat in anticipation of an enjoyable hour as the performance opened with Lowry-Cole entering the room with one Aide-de-Camp. All immediately stood, Brigadiers and Colonels, to be immediately bidden to sit. The venue could well have been some kind of theatre, but more recently had plainly been some kind of French barracks or even a stable. Lowry-Cole got straight to the point.

"Two columns are concentrating here in Toro, ours and General Graham's. General Hill has crossed the Douro and will soon join us. Giron's up to the North and, having moved through Villalpando, he may well be more to the East than we are. Our four columns have pushed Johnny 60 miles back across Spain from the border. All his picket Brigades, placed to hinder our advance, have fallen back for fear of being outflanked by one column or another. For the same reason he abandoned Salamanca and even Madrid. Reports have him and his army at Valladolid, which is in some way confirmed by the combat at Morales on the 2nd this month where Grant routed some French Dragoons. Morales is five miles East of here."

He leaned forward, his knuckles supporting him on the table.

"The feeling is that El Rey will have to offer battle sooner rather than later or be pushed back across the whole of Spain. If he's going to make a stand, sense would suggest that he defends the line of the Pisuerga, with the Douro securing his left flank. So, prepare your men, could be tomorrow or the next day, assuming he has it in him to try conclusions."

Carr hurried from the building and summoned his own command structure, Majors, Captains and Lieutenants, to a nearby barn to pass on Lowry-Cole's warnings. Thus, within ten minutes, such as RSM Sirus Gibney, Ethan Ellis and Jedediah Deakin were moving amongst their Companies spreading the warning themselves. All then paraded and Jed Deakin standing before the Colour Company was typical, with Slade, Farquharson and Howarth observing nearby.

"Now listen! There could be a set-to tomorrow, or the day after. Check everything, the kit that gets you there, then your bundook and cartridges. Your musket clean with a new flint, any cartridges as don't look right, perhaps damp, throw away and get new. The outcome of what could be comin' up will matter, we get beat, we'n back into Portugal, so make sure that all is as should be."

He turned to Major Slade.

"Have I missed anything out, Sir? Anything you'd like to add?"

Slade took two paces forward and ran his gaze along the rank of tanned, but blank faces. He felt slightly intimidated, knowing that each was a thorough veteran, which he was not, but he had commanded them at Salamanca and he felt more secure for that.

"No Sergeant, other than to emphasise that all must be right, but I can add one thing that I have learnt, that anything that is possibly worn out and could cause a problem, can now be replaced, free of charge, such as boots or backpacks. On this occasion."

Slade returned Deakin's salute and then walked away, leaving Deakin to dismiss the Company. For the rest of the day, the 105th took literally the granting of replacements and long queues were formed at Brigade Quartermasters wagons. Tom Miles soon became engaged in a vehement argument with a Quartermaster Corporal over whether or not his boots were sufficiently worn to merit replacement, an argument which the Corporal won. However, no-one in the Light Company asked for a replacement English backpack, all were too content and trusting of their existing, looted from the French.

The following dawn found Wellington's centre column formed on the road, his being the largest and most powerful, therefore the longest, with the Light Division in the lead, then the 7th, 6th and 4th Divisions with the 3rd at the rear. Although formed on time, it was some time before they actually marched out of Toro and onto the Valladolid road, the delay being caused by waiting for the route to become clear after Graham's column had moved off, these now departing to again resume their own route Northwards. When the march actually did begin, for the 4th Division, being the fourth in the column's order, the dust was thick, all raised by the three Divisions in front and the weather was warm, growing hotter by the hour. However, the 105th Light Company, marching at the rear of the Battalion were in good spirits, which an observation from Tom Miles did nothing to dispel as he studied a Calvary that they were passing, this one unusual for its particular tiled roof.

"I swear we passed that on the retreat. We'n on the same road as we was on when goin' back to Roger's Town."

It was usually Saunders who responded to any Tom Miles' comment and this was no different.

"Surprised you had your head up, with all that rain."

"Well I did, an' that we passed, after this Valladolid place, what we'n all headin' for now. That means we'n back up nearly to where that retreat started and that without firin' a shot."

Now Ellis joined in, marching alongside.

"You complainin'? Not enough battlefields to go roamin' about on, pickin' up swag!"

Miles took immediate umbrage, more so as the criticism came from Ellis.

"I don't know where you gets that from! Makes no sense! I don't like battles no more'n you! I likes my head on my shoulders and don't much take to the riskin' of'n. You can speak for yourself."

John Davey looked over at Ellis.

"He's got a point, S'arnt! Last Summer we had to fight our way all up to here and now 'tis no more than a hard march."

Now Joe Pike spoke up from behind.

"Until now. They tell us there could be a battle, tomorrow, even today."

This thought ended the conversation and they marched on, at what Senior Commanders would describe as 'tactical pace'.

Were any of the 105th Light Company with the 16th Light Dragoons, at that moment riding far to the North as part of Graham's scouting cavalry, their minds would have been quickly set at rest. Plainly there would be no battle for some time, this now obvious to the Officers of the 16th, all sat their horses, panning their telescopes from their front left where was seen Palencia in the furthest distance, then their far right at Valladolid, somewhat nearer. However, what occupied their attention were long columns of French infantry, easily seen in the bright sunshine, all moving North-east. Cavalry Brigadier G. Anson was with Collins and Johnson, observing with most of the Officers of the 16th nearby. Anson pushed the sections of his telescope closed. He had seen enough.

"He's abandoning Valladolid and the line of the Pisuerga. So, unless he fancies making a stand on the Carrion, based on Palencia, I'd say there's not much left where to offer battle for a good hundred miles."

He turned to Collins.

"We must get this back to Wellington. He's on the Valladolid road. Who do you trust to take the message?"

At this Johnson spoke up.

"I'll go myself."

The answer was a simple nod from Anson and so Johnson turned in his saddle to One Squadron, just behind.

"Sarn't Shelby. You and six others. 30 mile ride. Ready in five minutes."

G. Anson studied the horizon again, but with sight unaided.

"I'll tell Graham. I'd say we've now turned Johnny's right flank."

Collins was staring ahead himself.

"Aye Sir, especially with Giron coming around even further tae the North."

Anson released a sharp breath, a sort of ironic laugh.

'You can forget them. At least for now. They're just bluff. Their Government have given them too little ammunition. Until we can get some to them, they're just back in reserve."

However, he did not appear overly concerned, the reason being revealed by what he said next.

"Back until we get some to them, which may not be too long. Things have changed, our advance has been so rapid that we can now be supplied from Coruna and Gijon on the Biscay Coast. Perhaps even Santander fairly soon. The Frogs have lost Spain, Collins, mark my words. There'll be one final set-piece on Spanish soil and I wouldn't bet against us."

With that, he turned his horse, but not fully, because he had final instructions.

"Hold here and keep watch. Graham will be up with you tomorrow with new orders. Take care and keep watch. Johnny will have his own Chasseurs out covering his retreat."

For the 105th Wessex the day ended, not in conflict, but as a thoroughly bucolic scene in a field next to a river. Carr was patrolling the bank alone, concerned over the placing of pickets, when he met Nat Drake, equally concerned over the pickets from his own Company. Drake saw Carr first.

"Where are we?"

"We are at a place called Ampudia, North of Valladolid and that bit of road over there alongside this river runs straight into Palencia. Considered by many to be Johnny's last chance to make a stand."

"Well, it has to happen sometime, but we're up to Valladolid you say? North of it? Wasn't that supposed to be El Rey's new capital?"

"Well he's off to find another now. Perhaps he fancies Burgos."

"From what I hear, he's welcome to it."

Carr removed his shako and rubbed his hand over his forehead.

"Are your Followers up?"

Drake shook his head.

"No, nor are they likely to be, nor are rations, the speed we're pushing on. Not until Johnny decides to stop running. Was it not supposed to be here that he turned at bay? But that's gone, so, is Palencia the next possibility?"

"I know no more than you and Anson doesn't know much either. I get the impression that, with Johnny having wings on his heels, the Peer is having to make things up as we go along. Each day requires a different scheme."

"Juggling four plates in the air, so it would seem."

Carr laughed. He could always rely on Nat Drake to at least make him smile.

"Are yours set?"

"Pickets you mean?"

"The same, but keep watch. We are in the presence of the enemy, as the phrase goes, over that river. Oh, and I'm sure this matters to you, but we are now part of what's to be called the 'Headquarters column'!".

"Promotion! We must mention that in our next letter. I place the emphasis on 'we'."

Carr waved his hand and walked on, into a camp falling increasingly silent. They had been marching hard for five days with only a minimal stop at Toro. Carr could only wonder to himself, "If he gives up Palencia, two more days and we'll be in Burgos. El Rey has to make a stand somewhere or allow himself to have been pushed right back across Spain."

With that thought he came to his own tent and within five minutes he was fast asleep.

The following day, with the light full grown, Graham himself came into the camp of the 16th Light Dragoons, these still on their perch above the Pisuerga valley. As soon as he arrived his telescope appeared and was focused on the distance. He called Collins over and two Scottish accents filled the air.

"Did ye see any movement this morn, Colonel?"

"Nae, Sir, none. All we saw was during yesterday's eve."

"Campfires?"

"Aye, where ye can see Palencia now, Sir."

Graham closed his telescope.

"Reet! We'll move on, but easy does it. Ah've a feeling he fancies Palencia, now he's takken his tripes oot o' Valladolid!"

Collins and all within earshot did not try to stifle a laugh, but Collins had to reply.

"Aye, Sir. Easy does it, that's the word. Are ye staying with us, Sir?"

"Aye, ah will. The sooner ah know what yon festie beastie's set his mind to, the better."

"Is the column following, Sir?"

"Oh aye, but an hour behind. Maybe less."

They descended from the hill and found a road that led East. It was not long before they came to a village that had the appearance of being little more than a collection of medieval stables, but there was a clear stream and Graham ordered a halt to water the horses. Peterson looked around.

"Do you think this place is big enough to have a name?"

"Thought I saw what looked like Villerias painted on a bit of wood some way back."

When they dismounted, locals suddenly appeared with bread and wine which they pressed onto the Light Dragoons. Peterson took his bread and then a drink of wine from an elderly lady.

"Gracias, Senora. Muchas gracias."

However, she then pulled him by the sleeve to the back of her hovel and pointed at three graves, each marked with a name, two male and one female. The soil was relatively fresh. She pointed to each as she spoke.

"Mi hijo, su esposa y su hermano. Disparado por los franceses."

Tears came as she then wrung her apron.

Carr looked at Peterson.

"I think it's pretty obvious what happened here!"

He turned to the old lady and bowed his head. He could only speak in English.

"I am so very sorry, Senora."

Then he waved and pointed to the far horizon.

"Franceses, no more! There!"

She looked up at him.

"Desaparacido? Se fue de aqui?"

"Si. Franceses no more!"

Astonishingly, she took his hand and held it up to her forehead, close to tears.

"Gracias Ingleses. Gracias."

Carr was utterly moved by the old lady and gently extricated his hand.

"Adios, Senora. Gracias por el pan y el vino."

She smiled, her mouth almost toothless.

"Adios, Ingleses. Vayan con Dios!"

They both nodded, smiled and left her staring at the graves, both grim faced, but the Regiment was moving on and so more villages came and went, each with their own fresh graves.

For the 105th, now marching hard Eastwards with Ampudia now behind them, they knew not what lay ahead. Atrocities were now seen, plainly perpetrated by their own side, both guerrilla and civilian, all being the bodies of French stragglers, naked and mutilated, spread often at the roadside or strung from trees, often pecked at by birds and gnawed by rodents. As they rode past, the faces of Carr, O'Hare and Heaviside were etched with grim lines but the experience turned into complete contrast when they entered the outskirts of a neat, well-appointed and well cared for village, seemingly where nothing so unsavoury as what they had seen all morning, could ever happen. As they marched in, the third Battalion in the column of the Fourth Division, the local population were still alongside the road, cheering and clapping, despite the entry parade now being several minutes old. O'Hare did his best to smile and wave.

"No murder here, then! At least not on their own roads and streets."

Carr had been looking far ahead.

"Perhaps what's coming up gives us the answer."

Rising above all other buildings was an elaborate church, its gleaming white frontage comprised of several arches and alcoves, each of the latter holding the statue of a benevolent Saint, him, mostly, beaming down beatifically on the Faithful below. This detail became clear as they came closer, revealing yet another feature, this being white, crenelated walls that surrounded all, pierced by a black, elaborate, wrought-iron gate which began a path that led up to the welcoming, wide-arched entrance to the Church. O'Hare quickly summed up what he saw.

"Monastery, this!"

Carr laughed sarcastically, as he released one breath.

"Really! You think so?"

What made the conclusion so obvious was that the Monks were all outside, congregated close to the gate, where the Senior Brothers stood out before the minor ranks, these repeatedly chanting hymns. The Senior Brothers were also chanting but one was swinging a smoking thurible, from which the incense wafted away in the direction of their march. Four of the Seniors threw Holy Water over the passing ranks, whilst he who was most probably the Abbot, genuflected in their direction with one hand, whilst holding up a picture of a Saint with the other, all the while intoning his own prayer. Heaviside immediately steered his horse to the far side of the road to avoid being hit by any of the Holy Water, but O'Hare turned to note that many in their ranks, Irish Catholics such as himself, genuflected in response and held their thumbs to their lips. "There!' he thought, "No harm done, probably a lot of good."

The march continued, at the same 'tactical pace' until they passed a road sign that clearly stated 'Duenas'. This, a typical Spanish town, was quickly marched through, but the road was constricted on both sides by cheering crowds, such that those on the outside ranks had to use their shoulders in order to maintain their place in the ranks and Sergeants were forced to use the spaces between Companies to avoid serious collision. However, it was all good natured, so that all on the outside ranks and most of the centre emerged from the town with flowers stuck between themselves and their backpacks and a few small cakes and sweetmeats secreted into their pockets. Once through and now outside, Carr consulted his map and O'Hare came alongside.

"And this is?"

"Duenas, just passed through, as you read for yourself on that sign and that…."

He indicated forward with the map.

"……. is the River Pisuerga, with Duenas bridge over it, a bit downstream."

He studied the map further.

"Upstream, a bit, the River Carrion flows in and, if I've got it right, we'll be crossing this Pisuerga here. Assuming Johnny won't be holding the far bank, although he probably is, if we re-cross the Pisuerga upstream of the Carrion junction, then we're past Palencia. The Carrion flows through there. If he lets us beyond the Carrion, Palencia's gone. He can't give us it so easy, so my money says Johnny's making a stand here, just ahead, or he's got to fall back for miles. From what I hear, even Burgos won't be tenable."

O'Hare studied the river.

"I hope you're wrong and I'll be happy to take your money. Call me a bit of a funk if you choose, but I would rather march than fight battles any day of the week, especially when one here would mean fighting our way across a river."

Had he been privy to the sight that greeted the 16th Light Dragoons, acting as Graham's escort, O'Hare would have pressed Carr to take the bet. Once again from a lofty point, in this case the village of Grijota, high on its hill, Graham, Anson and Collins were in a group again using their telescopes, whilst ADCs politely accepted the offers of bread and wine that were being brought to them from all directions.

Many locals, using eyesight alone, could see the many French columns moving East, abandoning the line of the Carrion and quitting the crossing point at Palencia. Some, unlike their military guests, were studying the country to the North, where red-coated British columns could be seen hurrying East. Anson permitted himself a brief glance.

"He's being outflanked everywhere. By us up here and Hill down South, with the Peer right in his teeth!"

Graham at last accepted some wine and turned to Anson after drinking.

"Aye, George. He hasnae the men. Four columns coming at him speaks for itself."

Waiting at Duenas, Colonel Carr had nothing to study or occupy his mind for a good hour after arriving. Bored but curious, he crossed the River Pisuerga by Duenas' Medieval Bridge and a ride on alone some half a mile had revealed nothing, but he had no sooner returned back over the river, when Anson rode up, pleased to find him so easily.

"He's pulled out, from Palencia and away from the Carrion. Orders from the Peer, the whole 4th Division is to get up to Palencia bridge and get over the Carrion that way. We stay our side of the river to get there, the Peer doesn't want a whole Division isolated and trapped against any river. The whole Headquarters column is going through Palencia, Graham's circling from the North, Hill from the South."

Anson's order was quickly spread throughout the Battalion and within 15 minutes, in Company order, parading on open fields, the 105th were ready to march. They were behind the 27th and the 48th, the requirements of seniority had to be applied for such an occasion and so the 2nd Provisionals brought up the rear with the 60th Rifles. The fields were a mixture of pasture, ploughed fields and scrubland, the river to their right soon became the Carrion when it flowed into the Pisuerga, but also to their right front the buildings of Palencia grew larger and more distinct. Another Brigade, of which Division of the Headquarters column it was impossible to tell, were already onto the bridge, each Battalion marching across with Colours flying. Carr turned in his saddle and shouted back.

"Deakin! Colours!"

Deakin immediately pulled the leather case up from his vivid green Regimental Colour and Harry Bennet did the same to his King's, then each handed the Colour to their Ensign marching alongside. From somewhere a band was playing and the 27th and 48th wheeled right onto the bridge road, their own Colours bright and prominent, the distinct buff Regimental of the 48th behind the paler buff of the 27th. However, soon the colour that these provided was entirely subsumed into the colour provided by the crowds, these first encountered thronging the walkway over the bridge, some even standing on the parapet. The great majority were waving something colourful, from the Spanish Royal Standard or the red and white quartered Banner of Castille and Leon, down to a simple handful of coloured ribbons. On into the streets where the echoes from the high walls redoubled the sounds of the cheering and clapping, the noise was incessant, as the Redcoats were passed on from one band to another. Flowers showered down from the high balconies above, even out of the barred windows of a Convent, where a huge statue of the Madonna above the forbidding door beamed serenely down on Wellington's Redcoats, one Battalion after another marching smartly through. Gifts and food of all kinds were pressed on the soldiers, all quickly stuffed into pockets or haversacks. The column marched straight through and yet further still, to the other side, where many pulled out flowers that had been thrust down behind backpacks and even into collars and cuffs. Deakin was quite moved as he gathered his own floral tributes and then turned to his Ensign, this being his step-son, of sorts, Ensign Mulcahey, him at the moment pulling a flower from between his tunic and The Colour sash.

"Hang on to those, Sir. Good memories comes from such as this. This tells us that we'n doing some good in this place, in this war, though war it be."

"Yes, Uncle Jed. I was thinking much the same myself."

Deakin nodded and forgot rank for that moment.

"Good lad. Give them to your Mother."

Then Deakin looked over at Gibney.

"Some show that, Sar' Major. Makes you think."

Gibney was strangely moved.

"Aye, Deakin, tha's the raht of it. Ah'd say them seein' us means the end of them being under th'weight of th'Johnnies and 'tis us as've caused that to come about, raht enough."

Deakin said no more and kept the step. There was no break in the pace, the Headquarters column pounded forward, Colours being furled and stored whilst on the march and the River Carrion and Palencia fell far behind. At the front of the column, Carr looked over at O'Hare.

"Next decision concerns Burgos. What's he going to do about that?"

"The Peer or El Rey?"

"Both."

"The Peer'll take his four columns North and just leave the place behind, you'll see! El Rey will have to get into his carriage again and take off, just like he did here and at Valladolid."

At that moment an ADC of Lowry-Cole came galloping down the column to rein in somewhat fiercely at the head of the 105th.

"Johnny may be making a stand. Wellington's convinced they're going to dispute the River Hormaza in front of a place called Castrojeriz. From Hill's column, which is nearby to our right, he's sending forward the 2nd Division plus a Portuguese Brigade and a Spanish as well. From the Headquarters column, Alten's and Ponsonby's cavalry Brigades will be in support of the Light Division, who will advance from us. Our 4th is in reserve. We're moving up now."

Before issuing orders, as the ADC continued down the column, Carr looked at O'Hare.

"You should have offered a bet!"

"I still will. A guinea? Johnny pulls back."

"Done!"

Carr turned in his saddle to see his first Senior Officer, Charles Carravoy.

"Charles! We are in reserve for an assault, possibly over a river. Pass the word back, 'Ready for engaging the enemy'!".

When the word reached the Colour Company, both Deakin and Halfway, swung their muskets from their shoulders to silently check flints and the touch-hole in the priming pan, this done with a narrow quill, but they did not load, instead they re-slung their muskets. If they did indeed enter into combat, they could load in seconds. The pace of the 4th Division increased, all listening for the sounds of combat up ahead. After a half hour of marching, some cannonfire could be heard, but it soon died away. The 105th marched on, holding their place within the 4th Division and soon Carr looked over to the right and saw the attack column from Hill's Corps, then to the front as far as he could, to see a line of trees.

"I'd say that's a river!"

O'Hare grinned.

"If we cross it, you owe me a guinea."

His smile grew wider as they approached what was indeed a river and they marched straight across a substantial bridge.

"I'd say that settles it. We're over the River Hormaza. Johnny was outflanked yet again and pulled out."

Another fifteen minutes and the order came to clear the road. The 105th moved to the side as did the whole of the 4th Division and it was not long before two cavalry Regiments trotted past, going to the rear, the first Regiment towing a field-gun. O'Hare studied it carefully.

"That's a French Twelve. A serious piece of fire-power. Obviously captured, so there must have been some kind of action somewhere."

Carr pulled out a guinea and passed it over.

"Just where, we'll leave to the Historians, but a captured gun is just that and a serious trophy."

oOo

Far away in London the atmosphere in Waters' office was much more subdued, but nevertheless workmanlike, a mildly satisfied mood of 'progress made'. Sunlight streamed in through the windows, emphasising motes of dust that floated on the mild air currents, but no-one was considering a Summer stroll in the park. The three sat, contemplating the latest news from Spain and Europe and it was Livermore who moved the discussion on.

"So, Wellington's crossing Spain as if on wheels and El Rey's lost some men, but what of Boney and this Treaty of Pleischwitz he's signed with the Austrians and the Prussians? What do we think? Bathurst's in a funk!"

Of the three, the one with the shrewdest and most detailed analysis was Radipole, who read from his own report.

"It's true that Buonaparte has given both the Austrians and Prussians a bloody nose at Lutzen and Bautzen, back in May, but as I see it, this Treaty is but a temporary cessation. At both battles, he lost more than he could afford and, as we speak, he sits with his men on the Elbe. The initial terms weren't as good as Napoleon wanted. He accepted an armistice of just under seven weeks to 20th July, with six days' notice to end it at any time. The French remain in occupation of Saxony between the Oder and the Elbe, based at Wittenberg on the Elbe. They hold all of Germany to the west of the Elbe, as well as the islands in the Elbe. The Eastern Allies have agreed to provide supplies for the besieged French garrisons of Danzig, Mödlin, Zamosc, Stettin and Küstrin every five days.

Radipole lowered his paper and took a deep breath before continuing, this time giving his own thoughts.

"This armistice is generally considered to be one of Napoleon's most serious mistakes. On 1 June he was well positioned to the north of the Allies, and was about to cut their lines of retreat to the east. The Allies would either have had to risk a third battle, in a weaker position than before, or retreat further East away from Prussia. It is possible that the Prussians and Russians would have split, with the Russians retreating towards Poland and the Prussians making a last stand in Silesia. In either case the Austrians weren't ready to intervene, so Napoleon probably missed the chance for a major victory against those two."

He sat back, his face blank. Any reaction should come from his audience and it came from Livermore.

"What are your sources?"

It was Waters who answered.

"We have agents on the Elbe and direct communications with Prussia, Austria and Russia."

Livermore looked at Waters.

"And they are reliable, both sources?"

"I trust them, but what of the three Allies, are they reliable? Do we need to send any more bribes in the direction of Austria?"

Livermore sat back and began to nod his head.

"Negotiations have begun with all three. One million sterling each to Russia and Prussia, if they will break the Pleischwitz Armistice and half a million to Austria, if they will re-enter. Count Von Merveldt has assured us that they will."

Waters shook his head, sadly.

"Well, if that's what it takes, that's what it takes! All three have had their armies kicked around for the past 15 years, but we need them back in the field."

He sat back, then turned to his scholarly assistant.

"So what's Boney's situation?"

Radipole pursed his lips in thought before answering.

"His army is not in the best of shapes. Always short of food and he is very weak in cavalry. So many men and horses were left behind in Russia!"

Livermore slapped his hands onto the edge of the desk and held them there.

"Right! So what of ours in Spain. Will this make any difference?"

Waters looked at Radipole, but he decided to answer himself.

"No, neither one way or the other. As our Radipole here has said, it is but an Armistice. The Russians and Prussians have not been knocked out of the war and Austria is poised to re-enter, all financed with our money, which they'll take. Boney can send no reinforcements to Spain and no more from there can reach him in time to make much difference when it all starts again on the Elbe. Also, if he takes any more from El Rey, then his glorious brother will have no chance of holding ours in Spain. Fact is, it looks very much as though he will fail in that anyway."

Livermore thought for a moment.

"Could he abandon Spain and hold the Pyrenees?"

Waters nodded.

"It's possible, but it's wholly against Boney's nature to give up anything."

"Right!"

Livermore stood up.

"No need to worry then, at least not for the present. Now, both of you, with me. Lunch at my club."

oOo

"So what about Burgos?"

"It's back over your right shoulder!"

Nat Drake turned his head slightly before realising the absurdity of what he was doing.

"How far?"

"About 20 miles."

"Given up?"

"Yes, given up and not even blown up. At least not thoroughly."

"How do you know?"

Carr was on foot, but he now pulled his horse up to his right side, preparatory to mounting and riding back up to the head of his Regiment. In the cause of more trivial and diverting conversation, he had been walking alongside Nat Drake for the past hour.

"Lowry-Cole keeps us appraised as much as he can. He doesn't have to and Picton certainly doesn't, but our own Divisional General, our Gally Cole as the men call him, does."

He gathered the reins together.

"You know I feel that our Lowry-Cole is somewhat more uplifted in his spirits than when we first joined his Division back in Garda."

"Aren't we all, the way this is going? What's Johnny doing, do you know?"

By now Carr was mounted, but he paused to speak one last time with his friend.

"He's got our four powerful columns marching North East against him, all rounding his flank, all in parallel. We're pushing against weak opposition, like that damp squib of a caper yesterday at Castrojeriz, that we were held in reserve for, but didn't even come up to a skirmish. However, be not deceived by such; reports say that he's gathering together every French soldier within reach across Spain to make a stand. Sooner or later there's going to be the Mother of a battle between us, with all we've got, against El Rey, with all he's got or can easily get together. It'll be the decider, in my view. If we win, we'll be home next Summer, if we lose, expect another three years."

"Well, speaking for the moment, that would be quite welcome, rather than slogging along this endless, straight, flat, featureless road, so much so that my feet keep telling me to get off the treadmill."

Carr gave one final laugh before spurring his horse forward.

Further North, Cornet Carr and Peterson would have agreed with Drake, bar one thing, this remarked on by Peterson.

"I do believe my horse has got fat!"

Carr laughed.

"And you put that down to what? Mine is already."

"All this green corn he's been feeding on since we crossed the Douro."

Carr smiled and looked around, what he saw confirmed Peterson's statement. Endless, open fields, all bathed in warm sunshine, stretched away to the horizon, all covered in cereal crops half grown and deep green at this stage of their growth. He reached for his water bottle and took a drink, then another, his spirits raised by the uplifting sight of the brightly uniformed Troopers of Anson's Brigade column, both before and behind, walking their horses forward and raising a feint dust that drifted away in the currents of heated air.

The bucolic mood ended when they entered the hamlet La Piedra with daylight fading. The order to halt and dismount was passed back and Two Squadron obeyed, but Carr and Peterson, once dismounted, stood and looked at each other, Peterson the most puzzled.

"To where? This place has been ravaged, not just once."

No building had any doors or window shutters or even frames and several had no roofs. Between the buildings was scattered the detritus of a marching army, empty sacks that once contained food, but, more poignant, the personal contents of each house, plundered, but then abandoned to be scattered far and wide. Carr led his horse to what had probably been a stable, but now it was hard to make the distinction between such and a dwelling.

"Well, at least it's not raining!"

The ration wagons arrived and food was cooked, using what wood was available to make fires, which unfortunately included broken furniture. As darkness settled, Carr and Peterson, sitting amongst their Squadron, began to hear challenges from the 16th's pickets and all immediately stood to reach for swords and pistols, but nothing more was heard. However, what did appear into the light of their fires were the ragged inhabitants of the village, returned to reclaim at least the ground their houses stood on. There were many children and they tentatively approached the men sat eating around their campfires. Baxter took one look at the group regarding at him, then he turned to Makepeace.

"You're not hungry!"

Makepeace lowered his spoon.

"I'm not?"

"No! Nor you Perce, nor you Len."

With that he motioned two children to come towards him and he then fed both, in turn, with his own spoon. His three companions did the same, whilst their adult parents came and sat or lay by the fire, saying little, waiting for the dawn in which they could attempt to reconstruct their shattered lives. When the 16th rode out the following dawn it was to the sound of cursing men, distraught women and timber and shattered furniture being moved from one place to another, perhaps one more hopeful than the other.

In the days that followed, the pace of the Headquarters column slackened and the Followers caught up during one long afternoon halt. Jed Deakin sprang to his feet at the first sight and ran to greet Bridie and he took her in his arms.

"Are you alright? Has rations been got to you?"

She placed her hand on his unshaven cheek and kissed him.

"They have, and, sure, has it not been too bad at all, once we gave up the ghost of chasin' you lot. And Parson's been a Saint, so he has, making sure the young ones got a lift in that cart when they got a bit fagged."

Deakin stroked her chestnut hair just once.

"Well, as long as you're here and all in one piece. I'll have to thank Parson, good, kindly soul that he is."

Meanwhile, Nellie had immediately started preparing the evening meal from the rations issued when they entered camp and it was not long before the aroma of a Bridie stew began to pervade the area around their part of the camp. The tents were set up, kit divested of and so John Davey lounged back against his back-pack.

"As soldiering comes, I can't see it getting much better than this. Easy marchin', an' regular rations."

Joe Pike was sat nearby.

"I'd agree with that and now that Aunt Nellie and Bridie are up, there's good cooking with good rations."

Tom Miles lifted himself up from his own reclining position.

"Meaning what?"

"Meaning that what we get now could well be a mite tastier and perhaps even a bit more tender then what we've had to eat lately."

Miles now sat fully upright.

"You complainin' about my cookin'?"

At this point, as usual, Zeke Saunders intervened.

"Now just how big a surprise is it, that Nellie and Bridie are better cooks than you!"

Tom Miles subsided into a sulk.

"I does my best with what we gets."

"No one's arguing that and there's plenty as comes out of the pot you cooks in and nothing wasted. Credit to you for that, but Joe's got a point and don't tell me you can't taste the difference."

Within himself, Miles had to agree and so he changed the subject, this aimed at Joe Pike.

"And what's all this Auntie business? Them two's no more your Aunt than I am!"

Joe Pike looked at him sternly.

"Well. I like to be polite. No harm in that. And appreciative!"

Davey was now returned supine on the ground.

"Oh, now there's a special word. You've been spending too much time with Byford."

That particular was sat just over from the three, with baby Nelly on his knee and Eirin at his side.

"You keep me out of this!"

However, Nellie Nicholls had overheard all.

"You leave Joe alone, Tom Miles! He can call me Aunty if he likes, that being a whole sight better than what I gets from the likes of you!"

The camp subsided into laughter and good humour, so that eventually all, even Tom Miles, sat quietly discussing and telling tales until Nellie called them to their cooking pot and a good meal of beef stew and doughcakes was enjoyed. For the next three days the mood persisted, the pace of each day's march no longer so taxing and Officers turned a blind eye to toddler Jed and baby Nelly being carried on the backs of those within the ranks. On the fourth day, 14th June, the three Commanding Officers of the 105th were sat in their allocated room in the hamlet of Masa, the other rooms being occupied by fellow Officers of the 4th Division, whilst the men camped all around. There was one serious question, put to Carr by O'Hare, the former had just returned from a briefing with Lowry-Cole.

"Is Johnny going to defend the Ebro? We'll reach it tomorrow at a place called Puente Arenas. Presumably that name means there's a bridge there?"

Carr took off his shako, sat and poured himself some coffee, which he drank whilst eating a fresh baked biscuit.

"If he does defend the Ebro, it won't be for long. Graham's got around the headwaters, to a place called Villarcayo. If he spends too much time holding us, Graham will come down behind him. Expect a token resistance, perhaps, but that will be all. And, yes, there is a bridge there."

The following day, the 4th Division, leading the Headquarters column, marched out of Masa in full combat order, all Followers well to the rear. The road now ran through mountains and it twisted and turned for most of the day, but soon the way became consistently downwards, yet it did not emerge from valleys and gorges until well through the afternoon. Then the column halted and the call went out for all Light Companies of the 4th to advance forward to investigate the river and the bridge, the news brought back by O'Hare.

"Nat. Get yours forward and look for Major Pildon. He'll have specific orders."

Drake led his men forward and soon ran up to Pildon as he gathered his command.

"Sir. Captain Drake, Light Company 105th."

"Drake! Yes, I remember you and your men from that business at Aldea Lengua, back in November. Pleased you're with us again."

"Thank you, Sir. What do you wish of us?"

"The Lights of our Anson's will try the bridge. The Lights of Skerret's are going for a ford upstream. Stubb's Portuguese Lights and his Cacadores are divided in reserve for us both. Anson's Rifles cross first on the right parapet, with yours in support. The Lights of the 27th and the 48th will be on the left in that order."

"How far to the bridge, Sir?"

"Not half a mile. Get your men ready."

Drake saluted and ran back to find his men in two ranks patrolled by Sergeant Ellis, him making last minute inspections. Drake then passed on the details.

"We are going over the bridge just up ahead over the Ebro. We go along the right parapet, following our Rifles, the 27th and 48th will be on the left. We may find Brigadier Skerret's Lights coming down from our left once we're over. They are attempting a ford up there. We'll have Portuguese in reserve"

As they turned 'right face', Miles made his inevitable comment.

"Just so long as they 'half-arsed' busby bastards of the 7th in Skerrett's is kept away from me, that's all!"

Ellis turned on him.

"Enough from you Miles!"

They marched on in two lines, following Pildon's orders. It was not long before they heard the rushing waters of the Ebro, but no houses came into view when they reached the river, because the road, for some distance, ran along beside the river bank. There were many anxious examinations of the far side, Shakeshaft as often as anyone, hurrying forward with Luttrel Bettridge.

"I don't want to worry you, Luttrel, but us bouncing along here makes us horribly exposed to artillery from the far side. If you hear anything, either run or fall flat!"

Bettridge was somewhat bemused by the advice, which should he choose and why, but the two files of Light infantry hurried on. The Rifles came to the bridge and began their drill of filing across, each man moving whilst always under the cover of two poised Baker rifles. The Riflemen crossed the bridge and began to issue down the right bank, with the 105th Lights following, when movement on the far side of the road, caught Davey's eye.

"Sir! Mr. Bettridge, Sir. Over the road."

Bettridge looked over the road, to find himself immediately charged and then embraced by a matronly figure, from whom he could not escape. More civilians appeared from the doorways and alleyways and the celebrations began, with the Light troops of the W. Anson's Brigade being the first to enjoy the bread, wine, cheese and cakes that were being thrust upon them. It was some time before the tearful and ecstatic lady could be prised away from Bettridge, much to the amusement of his Section, and even then he was dragged into a nearby house. Ellis found Drake, busy eating some fresh bread.

"I'd say this place was clear, Sir. So what now?"

Drake swallowed some bread to empty his mouth.

"The best order I can give is that we wait here for the main column and show ourselves appreciative of this heartfelt welcome. So, carry on Sergeant!"

Ellis grinned and soon he also was feasting on bread, cheese and wine. It required half an hour before the main column came over the bridge, led by Wellington himself, who was clapped and cheered all the way along the main street, until greeted with wine and bread by one whom everyone took to be the Town Mayor. The military routine for the 105th asserted itself in the shape of Anson arriving to pass on Lowry-Cole's orders to Carr.

"We're up into hills behind here. Up as a precaution. I fear these hills will have to be crossed in the worst way, if we're to maintain direction North-east."

Therefore, in obedience, the 4th Division spread itself up and across the slopes behind Puente Arenas, not envious of the Rifles and Cacadores who had been ordered to climb up even further, to the summit to create a strong picket line. The night was spent in their bell-tents and Tom Miles did the cooking which no-one commented on, then came relief in the form of Anson himself, riding up the slope, to halt at Carr.

"We're following the Ebro upstream, using the road. Get yours down. The other four Divisions are already on the road and moving, Picton's in the lead."

Officers' shouts for Sergeants soon echoed across the slopes and Anson rode on upwards to bring down his Rifles and the Cacadores. Within an hour, the 4th Division were hurrying North, with the Ebro slowly diminishing in its deep gully on their left, as they progressed further upstream, but the road was taxing for them all, always upwards and always between high bluffs and cliffs that often hid them from the sun. However, it was an endurance of only four miles before they came to a village that gave them a right turn, this indicated by a Provost stood with his horse tethered to a sign saying, 'Incinillas', and their march came to a halt on the far side of the village buildings. There the rest of the Headquarters column were resting, surprisingly for the night, although there was much daylight remaining. The reason was brought by Carr to 105th Headquarters, this lodged in the one room they had been allocated in a sizeable farmhouse.

"He's pulling his army together to face the Frogs, who are gathering in a place called Vitoria. Our marching days are down to but a few."

The response was silence for some seconds, but the next words spoken came from Simon Ameshurst.

"Well, the men are up for it. They're as fed up with these constant marches as we are."

The same concerns were occupying the experienced minds of Deakin and Halfway, who were, as was usual on such occasions, enjoying their pipes whilst sat on a wall in the warm evening sunshine.

"Another big 'un comin' up, Jed."

Deakin examined the contents of his pipe for quality of smoulder, before answering.

"That's what we'm hearin'. The Frogs is pullin' theirselves together for a final settlin' of accounts, one way or the other. On our side, there's four columns, all strong, and all comin' together and Nosey's not doin' that for no reason. I d'reckon 'tis because the Frogs is doin' the same and that means a big 'un, and not too far forward. There's us, the Portugee and the Dons, and we've pushed the Frogs full across Spain, ‘till they’ve only but a small patch left. That El Rey, he’ll not give best and just walk out without makin’ some kind of effort to knock us back.”

“Bigger that t’others? Salamancee? Talavera?”

Deakin nodded.

“That’s my feelin’, an’ this stop here’s not come amiss neither. I ain’t never done marchin’ like this, not never! Followers is often way back, sometimes a day behind.”

All the while Halfway had been looking down the road and he eventually stood.

“Talkin’ of Dons. What’s this comin’ onward?”

Deakin now stood to observe for himself and soon he saw the head of a column of Spanish infantry headed by Officers in the most magnificent of uniforms, all topped off with a bi-corn hat worn ‘athwartships’, this topped by either a collection of feathers or one tall, single plume.

“Looks like some kind of Mayday parade, Tobe! Must be Dons, like you say.”

However, what followed set both back from their prejudgement. Each following Battalion marched behind their Colours, each a variation of a diagonal red cross on a white background, but the bearing of the men following drew grudging admiration. Each was in full Spanish uniform and each marched as though following their Colours and wearing that uniform now counted for something. The stern faces, the upright bearing, the matched step and the full swing of each arm caused Deakin to slowly nod his head.

“Well, these boys’ve come up a grade or two. A long chalk off the usual starvin’ and diseased crews we’ve seen in the past.”

Halfway was nodding in agreement himself.

“Well, if they can fight and stand as well as they looks and marches, then I’ll be happy enough to see these next over in the line to me.”

Deakin looked at his good friend and smiled.

“Could well come to that, Tobe. These is now a full part of what we’m goin’ forward with.”

At this point, Tom Miles sauntered up.

“Dons! Will they trade for baccy?”

Deakin looked over at him, his expression significantly lacking in any degree of warmth or greeting.

“Dons will already have some.”

“Sugar?”

“They’ll have that too.”

“What about boots?”

"These you'm lookin' at have got them too."

Miles gave a scowl and a grunt and shuffled off.

"Hope they fights better than they gives chance for trade!"

There was little chance for trade over the days that followed for anyone, this fully observed by the 16th Light Dragoons, patrolling the hills above the single road now used by all three columns, bar Giron's Spanish, who remained to the North. As they walked their horses along a goat track above the road, Cornet Carr could not help but comment as he studied the spectacle on the road below. There, it ran through a shallow valley and on it was every Allied uniform, all filling the road, so that both before them and behind, the head and tail of the endless column could not be seen.

"It's like a whole city on the move!"

Baxter was much more sanguine.

"Tens of thousands, Sir, aye! An end to all the marching, some is saying, but like others say, 'Be careful what you wish for.' There's thousands down there as won't see the end of the day of battle that's on its way."

Carr looked at him somewhat surprised.

"You'd rather delay meeting the French?"

"I'm not saying that, Sir. All I'm saying about battles is, the bigger they are, the bloodier they are."

When that day ended, the 4th Division, part of all that was on the road, counted themselves lucky that the long column's halt coincided for them with a small town, where the Officers of the 105th had been given two rooms. Carr entered and dropped his shako onto the table being used by Shakeshaft to write up his diary. Carr peered over his shoulder and read.

"17th June. Entered Medina de Pomar."

He stepped back from the table.

"Will any of these place names matter when all this is written up, when we get back home?"

Shakeshaft, unmoved continued writing.

"The truth is the truth, Sir. Some historian, sometime, will be grateful. Our march across Spain will, without doubt, be considered historic in the annals of military history."

O'Hare laughed and slid a dish across the table towards Carr.

"Here, have some of this."

He then pushed across some bread whilst Carr looked at the substance in the dish, his face both delighted and puzzled at the same time.

"Am I mistaken?"

“No you are not. That’s butter. Obtained back in Puente Arenas. There is more, but we are coming to the end, so help yourself whilst you can.”

Shakeshaft’s annals now forgotten, Carr drew up a chair to the table and reached for the knife, this also slid across by O’Hare.

The following day, Hill’s and the Headquarters’ columns remained together, but were ordered to take a different route from Graham’s, each column being sent along roads that twisted and turned through a tangle of hills. The 16th were riding forward after the Noon halt, to provide advance guard for Graham and, to that end, they found themselves riding up to a very senior group of Officers, their own G. Anson being the most Junior. Soon Major Johnson was riding down the column with orders for the whole 16th, stopping at each Squadron Captain, Carr and Peterson were close beside Oakwood and thereby able to overhear.

“Graham’s up front with Stapleton-Cotton. Says he can see what he thinks is Reille’s Corps, from intelligence, marching across us to join with El Rey in Vitoria. They’ve stopped and appear to be offering battle, setting themselves up on a hillside about half a mile down the road. We’re to escort Ramsey’s Battery to a position on the right, in case there’s some Frog cavalry out that way.”

As Johnson moved on to inform Three Squadron, it was evident that the 16th should not move until the guns arrived. However, there was no time to ask the obvious question of ‘How long?’, when Ramsey’s Battery arrived at some speed, to canter on past. Carr, to his disappointment, was unable to greet Ramsey in any way and soon they were following the battery across the gentle slope that formed the side of the valley. Ahead, the valley floor rose up to form a ridge, the valley road climbing to cross it, and it was not long before they could see at least six French Battalions drawn up on the slopes, with probably more behind. They rode on, the guns bouncing over the rough moorland, but Ramsey soon chose his ground and his men unlimbered their pieces to form a gun line, then they sat to wait for Graham’s infantry to begin to make their presence felt. Collins led the 16th further to the right, on to the slopes from where they could protect Ramsey from any French cavalry and, once there, they sat to watch events as they unfolded. Oakwood looked at the French, lower than where he was, but at the head of the valley.

“They won’t stand, the Frogs. Look, Graham’s sending his whole column against them.”

Oakwood’s conclusion was borne out by what could be seen back down the road, where Graham’s three Divisions were pounding forward and also what was now in the valley immediately beneath. In the fields either side of the road, two KGL Light Battalions were advancing in skirmish order. At that point, Ramsey's single howitzer began dropping shells down onto the French position, his men reloading with smooth precision, such that the white smoke of the explosions burst over the French at least once a minute. Oakwood watched the first five explode, but the French did not move, so he turned to Cornet Carr.

"Willoughby! Take a dozen higher up, to where you can see off to our flank. He's staying there. He's either brave, stupid, simply cannot discern what's going on, or there's a whole French Corps marching to his aid."

Carr called forward the first three files of his Troop and led them upwards. After ten minutes, with their horses breathing heavily, they reached a vantage point and Carr immediately felt the need to turn to Sergeant Baxter, having looked far over to the right.

"Sergeant! Get back down and tell Colonel Collins that there's a whole Division of ours just arrived from the right and are marching for the end of the French line."

Baxter had seen for himself and was soon on his way, leaving Carr and his companions to study events. The newly arrived Division was the Fourth, with W. Anson's Brigade in the lead, the 105th behind the 48th, the 27th behind the 105th. Henry Carr turned to O'Hare riding alongside.

"My experience tells me that we can hear a howitzer!"

O'Hare peered forward, but the slope of the ridge prevented him seeing anything worthwhile.

"I'd say your experience has the right of it, but at what and by whom remains a mystery."

However, soon they heard the order for all Light Companies to come forward and soon after that, Drake led his Company forward at the double. Carr dismounted and handed the reins to Sergeant Bryce.

"I'm going with them."

He ran on, following 2nd Section of the Light Company. It was not long before they were able to see into the valley; the strong French position, the KGL Lights, the field-gun battery, the 16th Light Dragoons and Graham's advancing Divisions. The Rifles of Anson's Brigade were already working towards the heights further to the right and onto the end of the French line, but the Light Company of the 48th had halted before it, at long range. There was no Senior Officer and so Carr took command, running first to the Captain of the 48th Light.

"Captain! Work right with your men and support the Rifles. Close skirmish order. The 105th Lights will be on your left, advancing from here."

Soon the Lights of the 27th arrived and Carr went up to their Officer, a Lieutenant.

"Form in reserve of me."

Then he came to Drake.

"Nat. In files, we're going straight at the left of that Frog line."

In files of three, at a width of 26 files, Drake's men advanced forward. Carr came over to Davey, in the lead of the file of Miles and Pike.

"Davey! Tell me when you have the chance of a shot."

"Sir. It'll not be long now."

50 more yards and Davey called across.

"Sir."

Carr called out.

"First in file! Pick your targets and fire when ready."

Davey was the first to fire and a French Officer fell, then others, as the bullets from the accurate Bakers found their mark, but the French Corps Commander had now realised his peril and he sent out his own Light Troops to hold back the newcome threat on his left, whilst his main line fell back, still under howitzer fire. As the French Battalions broke formation, the Lights of the 4th Division eased cautiously forward, but this was soon exposed as overly cautious as the whole field-gun battery of Bull galloped forward and past, with Light Dragoons as escort. Then their own W. Anson arrived, on horseback.

"Double forward, Carr. See what can be done."

Carr led the line of Light Companies forward at the run, to find Ramsey's battery unlimbered and opening fire at the retreating French Battalions, all six guns practically on the original French position, but they were now being harassed there themselves by the remaining French skirmishers. Carr pointed upwards to their position.

"Nat! Drive those off."

Carr then waved the 27th to come forward and strengthen the skirmish line as Drake led his men forward, himself carrying a Baker rifle so as not to distinguish his rank when facing marksmen. His Company advanced, filing forward, with Miles now taking aim, using a boulder to steady his weapon, with Davey reloading beside him. Joe Pike was coming forward, ready and reloaded, but Davey held up his hand, whilst Miles fired, bringing down a French Tirailleur.

"Easy does it, Joe. These will be gone soon. B'ain't worth it to take any risks to hurry on what's going to happen anyway. These'll be gone no matter what you does or doesn't do."

Davey peered up over the boulder.

"Look! They'm all on their way off and out of it."

Joe Pike could see that Davey was right, all the French Light Troops were now retreating away over the hillside, all at the run to catch up with their own Brigades. They were being further pressed by the KGL advancing by the road and at that point Carr sheathed his sword.

"Re-form and wait."

Within half an hour, the 4th Division were down on the main road and soon up to the French position, marching on past wounded and dying Frenchmen. Following Graham's orders, the 4th Division fell in after Graham's 1st Division but before his 3rd and soon they saw a road sign for Espejo and they marched straight through, with no more sign of the French. Riding alongside, O'Hare cocked his ear over to the right.

"Do you hear that? I'd say there are some serious goings on, over in those hills beyond."

Carr nodded agreement.

"That's a major engagement. I'd say that Johnny's resolve to prevent further progress is stiffening up."

At that point they came to a crossroads with a clear sign, pointing left, and stating Vitoria 8 Ligas.

To the right of Graham's column, remaining in the hills, Officers of the 16th were at a loss as to where to look to make any sense of what was happening. What was clear were several columns of Allied infantry occupying all major roads that led East, but above them in the hills, were bands of Guerrillas and Squadrons of regular Allied cavalry all riding hither and thither. However, for their Brigade life was much more clear cut, because Graham had issued Anson with clear orders, these being to remain on Graham's flank and keep watch as he led his men East. All were grateful that Anson was not one to keep his Officers in the dark and at mid-afternoon he rode up to them on an advantageous ridgeline. At once he called his two Colonels and their Majors to him and soon after Anson's advice was passing down both columns, their directions usually aided by a pointing arm, in the case of Two Squadron, belonging to Johnson

"We're for a place called Subijana-Morillas, an important crossroads. If you get diverted for any reason, head for that prominent hill, the one that looks a bit like a sphinx, without a head. Subijana's to the left."

With that, he rode on and the three Officers of Two Squadron immediately deployed their telescopes onto the headless sphinx, to see a large village just to the left. However, no-one became detached and, with the last of the light, Anson's entered the town, to the usual enthusiastic welcome, but much had already been expended on a large Guerrilla band that were already there to hold the cross-roads. It was commanded by El

Charro himself, Julian Sanchez, but the 16th were not surprised to find that Ignacius Mateo was amongst them and, on seeing them he quickly came over to Two Squadron and all were pleased to see that on this occasion he was completely sober and eating the meat of what could be any animal, ripping flesh from the bone with his strong teeth.

"Hola, Senores. You are alive and all well, is good, I think."

Mateo had become hugely popular with Two Squadron and the bonhomie began as he stood before them waving his meat bone to emphasise his words.

"This is day, I never thought to see, all Spain, there, is free of los piojos franceses and soon we drive them that way, over the mountains and back to their agujeros sucios......"

He turned to a studious, bespectacled man standing close by, enough to hear what was being said, and the translation arrived.

"Filthy holes!"

"Si, filthy holes they come from."

He waved his arms in the air in triumph.

"And they take the afrancensados scum with them. There is no place for them in free Spain."

He took a deep breath, enough to give energy to the wonderful thought, before continuing.

"Vitoria is full of them. Them and all the saqueo robado......"

The translation came immediately.

"Stolen plunder."

"Si, all that they have taken with their filthy hands from the people of Spain."

Oakwood leaned forward in the saddle, grinning openly.

"We'll get it back. They'll not get it all back over the mountains. We'll get it back."

"Si, si, Capitan, is good, but my men in Vitoria tell me the franceses say they win this time, but I say they talk as donkeys. This time we drive them to the river, the sagrado Bidassoa, there into their own country and then we follow!"

Mateo was clearly becoming intoxicated with his own rhetoric, but Oakwood was indulgent.

"What you say will come true, Mateo, the days of the French in Spain are indeed numbered. The next days will show that, there can be no future for them in Spain."

Mateo beamed an incandescent smile and his voice rose a few octaves.

"No future for them in Spain! Si, only Spanish and you as our guests. You stay here tonight, si? Then we drink, si?"

Oakwood dismounted, as did Carr and Peterson.

"Alright, Mateo. Just the one."

"Si, one and then one more, si?"

He then looked inevitably for Baxter and Makepeace.

"And I get some wine to you, Sargente Baxter and to you too, Senor Makka Pees. And your muchachos."

By now, Two Squadron could not contain their laughter and it was a cheerful Two Squadron of the 16th Light Dragoons who dismounted to walk their horses to their billets.

The night for the 4th Division was nothing like so cheerful, nor so restful. Graham ordered them to rejoin the Headquarters column which meant marching to the town of Pobes, through the dark, but with a local guide. When they arrived they were just in time for a meeting called by Lowry-Cole for all his Colonels and Senior Majors and so there was no immediate rest for Carr and O'Hare. Instead they found themselves sat on rough pews in the local Church, enduring the smell of several oil-lamps, the light from which fell first on a sorrowful Madonna. However, more so onto the polished brass of the Altar furniture with the large crucifix suspended above, with its tortured Christ, whose bejewelled halo picked up the yellow light most of all. As usual Lowry-Cole wasted no words on greetings or any form of congratulations.

"Tomorrow we will be in battle formation. Behind this wall, believe it or not, is the river Bayas with what we believe to be the whole of Reille's Corps on the far side. Wellington believes that they will defend it stiffly to give French infantry, still on their way, the time and space to get into Vitoria and join El Rey. This could be the opening of the major battle that's been coming now for a long time, so, at dawn, make sure your men are up to the mark. My Aides have your orders."

With that he walked up the aisle, this signalling that the meeting was over. Carr rose from his pew and waited for an Aide to find him, he spoke the 105th number and the paper was handed over, for Carr to hold it up into the better light of one of the lamps.

"Anson's on the right, downstream of Skerret's. They go over the river from here, so we go over downstream of them. Stubbs Portuguese in reserve."

He passed the paper to O'Hare.

"Anson's take position from where Skerret's line ends. Us in the left centre, 48th, 105th, 27th, Provisionals."

The dawn of the 19th June was merely an almost indiscernible lightening of the clouds to the East as the 105th marched South, their boots squelching over the mud of a ploughed field, this now wet and slippery from the persistent heavy rainfall which had fallen all night, but was mercifully easing. The Light Company all carried their Baker rifle wrapped in their blanket, head down against the tumbling layers of light rain that fell from the still black sky. Bettridge was marching alongside Sergeant Ellis, although with not quite so martial a footfall, the ground underfoot being so treacherous.

"Do you think we could be lost, Sergeant?"

Ellis drew in a deep breath, which he released as a sigh.

"No Sir. It'll be something new if a whole Division gets lost over a walk of half a mile. As I understands it, we has some river on our left, and the Rifles has the job to scout out the route beyond and get us there, if there's no local as can do the job. All we has to do is to keep goin'. Sir."

There were human shapes to their left, already in position and when there were no more it was only another 200 yards before they came to a halt themselves. Then Major Heaviside arrived.

"Light Company get to the front. Skirmish order. You will find our 60th out further in front. Be ye doers of the Word and not hearers only. James, One, verse 22."

Bettridge, now crouching alongside Drake, whispered as Heaviside disappeared into the gloom.

"Does he always say things like that? The religious things, I mean?"

"Yes, Lionel. He does and the men will follow him anywhere!"

"It's Luttrel, Sir. Still Luttrel."

"Of course, yes. But fear not! I'll get there."

They were easing their way forward, the field now sloping gently to the river. The rain did not stop and so Drake delayed the order to load, but the light was growing rapidly, such that Drake could use his own telescope to study the far side of the river. The Riflemen of the 60th were crouching behind the reeds at the river bank some 50 yards ahead, but Drake could see a French battery up a slope not 500 yards beyond the river. If Drake could see the battery, so could the French gunners see them and the battery immediately opened fire, but not at them, the balls were aimed elsewhere. From their side, their own batteries began their reply, a deeper more incessant roar, plainly of many more guns and it was not long before one of the guns in the French battery was hit and flew back several yards, minus one wheel, the barrel pointing absurdly, almost despairingly, up at the sky. After that, it was not long before the French gunners pulled all their guns back over the ridge behind, plainly the contest was far too unequal, and the order came forward for Drake to advance. The rain had mercifully stopped some time ago and, already in their files of three, they followed the Rifles of the 60th to see almost all over the River Bayas at the moment when Drake's Light Company entered the water themselves. It was fast running and shallow, but the river bed treacherous, with many boulders and rocks and so several stumbled and fell, but always onto one knee, keeping their precious Baker above the swirling current.

Soon Drake's men were amongst the 60th, these crouching down amongst the dense reeds of the far bank. Drake found Captain Tom Bairns, him down amongst the reeds unsure of when he should move forward.

"Tom! What've you seen?'

"Nothing beyond what you can, but I'm moving mine forward now, up to the edge of these damn reeds, but to stay in and see what's what from there."

"Right! But what would you rather, mine file in with yours or we follow in support?"

"In support, but close."

"As you choose."

Bairns ploughed on through the reeds, passing on the order for his men to do the same. When all the 60th had disappeared, Drake shouted over to Ellis.

"Ease forward, but stay behind the 60th."

Drake drew his pistol and checked the priming. Bettridge was beside him.

"Come on, Lionel. Time for some Light Infantry work."

"It's Luttrel, Sir."

"Of course, but we're still Light Infantry."

Pushing through the reeds was arduous, but upon reaching the edge, they saw that the 60th were out and crossing a wide-open field of rough pasture, with a hedge bank on the far side. Drake was straining his eyes to see movement through the gaps in the hedge as he led his own Company forward in support.

"This I don't like!"

Ten more steps and he was proved correct, musket fire erupted from the hedge-row. All the 60th dropped to the ground and began to return fire. The French fire from the hedge must have been a full volley because at that moment nothing above the odd shot was being sent their way. So, from a crouch, Drake stood up; the 60th needed their support.

"105th!"

He began to run forward and his men followed, to dive down onto the rough turf just as the next French volley arrived and the bullets sang overhead. Davey and Pike found themselves prone between two Riflemen, with Miles on the far side of the one on their left. Davey brought his rifle forward but could see little of their enemy. He turned to the Rifleman.

"What can you see?"

"Damn all! All we can do is skim the top of the bank below the hedge. Best chance then of hitting something."

What the Rifleman said made sense and so the line of 105th and 60th soon adopted the same and sent a steady stream of accurate fire skimming over the top of the bank. Drake was alongside Bairns and he rose up just enough to look either side, beyond their two Companies, to see nothing there.

"Tom, we can do no more than hold here. Looks like the other Lights of Anson's are pinned down back at the reeds, just as we are here. Advancing against that, we'd lose too many."

"Agreed, but waiting here will do it. Either they get outflanked by Skerret's or they don't like the look of our four Battalions coming on in support."

Drake rolled onto his back and lifted his head, to see behind him many rows of black shakoes above the reeds. His own 105th were over the river. He watched and waited to see the Battalion emerge, form into columns of Companies, the Colour Company immediately in line with him, both Colours uncased. He rolled back to look at the hedgerow and within seconds there was no gun smoke issuing from it. Drake waited another 30 seconds.

"Tom! Time to move forward."

Both Officers rose and ran forward, their men taking their cue. At the hedgerow and once through, they found several dead and wounded Voltiguers and both Companies pressed on, but not before Drake had picked up a Voltiguer shako and pulled off the twin yellow tassels that hung down alongside.

"Here you are Lionel. Your first souvenir."

Bettridge's face was pained at the misuse of his name, yet again, but he had the manners to thank his Captain.

"Thank you, Sir. These are something special I'm sure."

"Indeed they are! The Voltiguers badge of office, you might say. Voltiguers! French elite troops."

The 105th columns were hurrying forward faster than Drake's Lights were advancing and soon Carr caught up with Drake.

"You got through some of their skirmishers, I see. Anything else?"

"They pulled back a battery, but I expect you saw that. What we were against you can see scurrying about 300 yards or so up in front. It doesn't look as though there's any serious line up ahead."

Carr looked forward and could only agree. They had just crossed another hedgeless bank to see another wide, open field with nothing to be seen that could mark its far boundary.

"Right. Get yours further ahead. Say the same to Bairns. You will either chase them on, or they'll stand and then we can give them a volley or two when we're formed up, but if there are any formed units up there, we will need to know."

Drake thrust his pistol into his belt and unslung his Baker rifle, to then run forward at a fast trot. Soon the whole skirmish line was moving forward just as rapidly, looking intently across the field, but seeing nothing that threatened. They passed a small hamlet, but saw no-one, however, what they had not realised was that they were going slowly upwards and eventually the incline changed to downward and so did the situation they faced, completely. They had topped a ridge that overlooked another river, but from their height, they could see at least two bridges, each with their own hamlet and on each bridge was a dense column of French infantry, all retreating rapidly over to the far bank. Drake and Bairns both raised their arms for their men to halt, but almost immediately there occurred a better reason to halt. Two French field-gun batteries were on the far side and they immediately opened fire on seeing Drake's and Bairns' men.

"Fall back! Fall back!"

Both shouted simultaneously and they retired behind the ridge, for Drake to continue on to Carr.

"There's another river just over. What must be Reille's are retreating back over it using two bridges, at least. They'll be over by now and supported by artillery."

"I need to see."

They both returned to the ridgeline and knelt to see over. It was as Drake had described, but Carr looked in both directions and then at the fields beyond, now full of French troops.

"Right, Nat. If memory serves, that village front left is Nancleres and that river is the Zadorra. It protects Vitoria, so our marching's done. Johnny's drawn a line in the sand. It's hard knocks from now on."

Chapter Eight

Vitoria

"You hear that, Jed?"

Deakin nodded, but all that Halfway could see was the peak of Deakin's bobbing shako, the sky just grey enough to contrast with the black.

"I do, and so I have, this past hour, nor more."

The sounds that they could hear were of rumbling wheels, marching feet and whinnying horses, as they sat in the field on one side of a road that led down into Nancleres. The sounds of an assembling army came from both near and far as the 105th sat in the damp of the morning despite the late June weather, some wiping away any possible moisture from the flint and priming pans of their muskets. Chaplain Albright and Sedgwicke moved amongst the sitting men, but many stood to receive the Chaplain's blessing and good wishes and to give their own thanks and good wishes in return. Sat with Deakin on the low bank was Bridie, she saying little, her arm through his, her head against his shoulder. Next to Halfway was another Follower who had attached herself to him, the 'widow' of the soldier who had dropped dead during the march to Palencia. Halfway had made no objection, for she, Esme, had joined the Regiment as a Follower back in Taunton before Maida in 1806, but now, unattached and with no man and therefore in some jeopardy, she had simply been absorbed into their group, nothing said nor objected to. Esme now regarded Halfway as her 'army husband', herself as Halfway's 'army wife'. To Halfway, and his group, the union was a natural as the sun rising each morning.

There was little talk amongst the men of the 105th, each kept to their own thoughts, dwelling on the fact that this would be a battle that surpassed all others and they well knew what this day would probably bring; the Hell of the firing line. Amidst the din and carnage caused by standing merely yards from the enemy, they would be required to stand their ground and fire off more than three rounds a minute, to calmly re-load their muskets, biting open black-powder cartridges that would parch their throats, always obeying orders, suffering the worst that the French could throw at them, but always holding their place in the line, a Sergeant's halberd in their backs if they did not.

Whilst their Brigade sat in the folds of Monte Arrato, this a feature above and behind Nancleres, all their Officer Corps stood above on higher ground, waiting for better light. Amongst them, in contrast to the rank and file, conversation was brisk, where Brigadier Anson was doing his best to describe their role in the day's events, as the June early dawn threw more light onto the surrounding features. He began by pointing over to the right, across the defile through which ran the river Zadorra and also on its Southern bank, opposite to them, the main trunk road from Madrid to France, this transport artery making good use of the very convenient river gap in the high hills around.

"We don't move until we see Hill making some progress along those heights beyond the river."

All followed his direction to see, in the better light, what was more than just a 'height', it was a very significant ridge that ran all the way Eastwards, dominating the valley and finally overbearing the town of Vitoria itself. Carr studied the ridge, by now much more than just a silhouette on the skyline.

"And what of the columns to the North, Sir? Do they influence us at all?"

Anson shook his head.

"Not at the start. The Peer wants us to advance up the valley towards Vitoria only when Hill has got beyond the French flank. North of our column are Picton and Dalhousie, what difference they make to us remains to be seen. Beyond them is Graham and further than him is Giron, both ordered to hook around Johnny's right flank, but all of us have to cross the Zadorra, except Hill, up there on his ridge."

W. Anson's simple description did not translate into the experience of the Light Dragoon Brigade commanded by G. Anson, which at that very hour sat unmoving in a village called Etxabarri-Ibina. They were as far from the centre of Vitoria as was Nancleres, but with nothing like as good a road forward and with a village name which no-one had so far made any attempt to pronounce. All of the Brigade were sat dozing in the saddle, they had been riding for most of the night of the 20th, after precious little sleep for that of the 19th. Little rest had been allowed them over the last miles to the Basque-named village, Anson being required to move his Brigade as and when Graham required, often immediately and often by night. Cornet Carr, dozing on his horse alongside Oakwood, was brought back to consciousness by a group of Staff galloping by, but his eyes did not open soon enough for him to identify who they were or where they were going, yet it did mean that something would soon be happening. He could only turn to Oakwood.

"What do we know, Sir?

"What we know, Willoughby, is not much more than we knew yesterday. That our job is to get over the river at two places, one called Gamarra Mayor and another named Abechuco. For now, my guess is that Graham is getting his column in order. Tedious perhaps, but if Graham thinks it worthwhile, then my guess is that we can take him on trust."

At that moment, their Brigadier, G. Anson himself, rode down their column with a rolled map conspicuous in his left hand, this not unnoticed by Oakwood.

"I think something's about to happen, Willoughby. Seems like Graham's satisfied. Best get back to your Troop.

Carr turned his horse and trotted back, but in the event his Troop came up to him, because Anson had immediately ordered his Brigade forward. They left the unpronounceable village to enter a wide, flat plain and soon the orders came back, 16th to lead. Collins interpreted this into Tavender taking his One Squadron off to the right to scout for any French and Oakwood to undertake the same, but to the left, whilst Three and Four remained on the road. Two Squadron accelerated into a canter, feeling the slight down slope of the Zadorra valley under their horses' hooves. Collins remained with Three and Four and he led them into the next village, whilst Oakwood halted his own Squadron some way outside and to the left, but level with the sparse collection of white buildings, all grouped around their Church. Oakwood arranged his two Troops in line abreast and so Carr and Peterson came together with Oakwood, Carr pointing to the village.

Battle of Vitoria

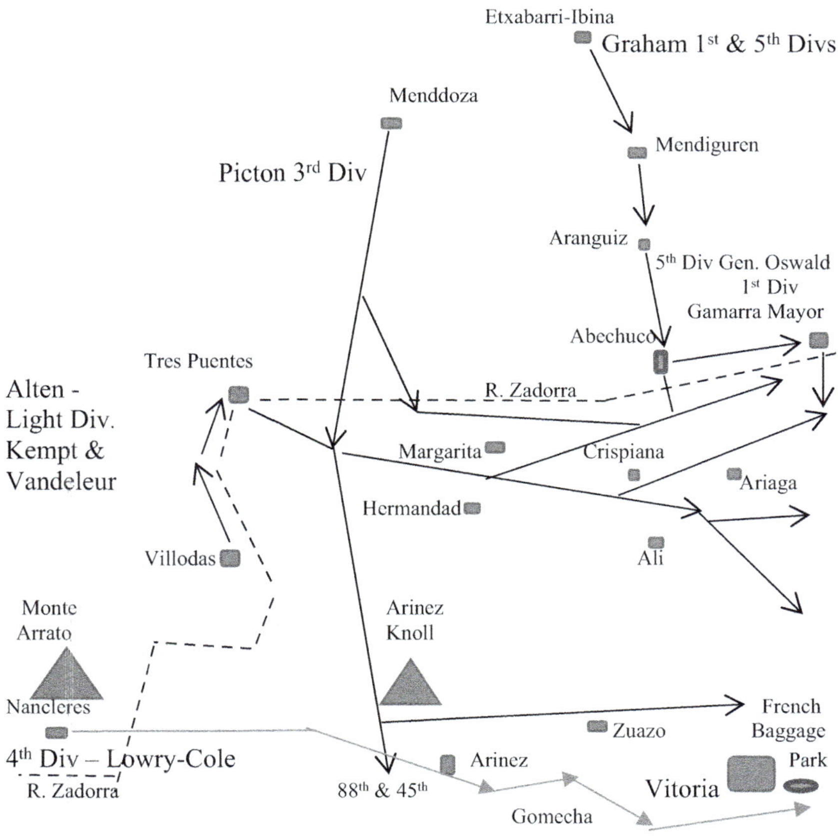

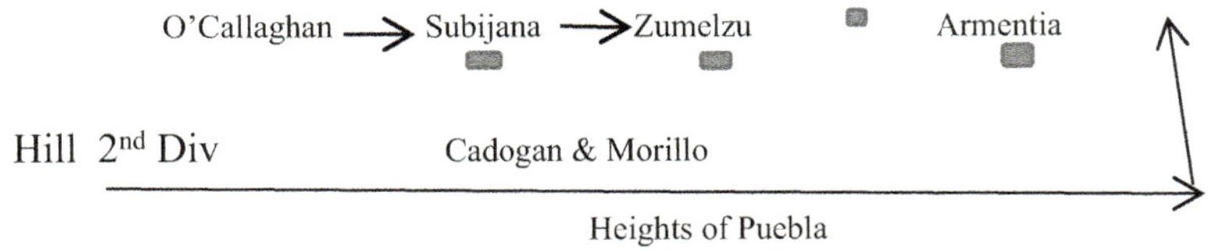

"Not a sound out of there! Johnny's pulled out."

Peterson had been taking a drink from his water-bottle.

"No surprise. Johnny's all on the far side of the river. Bar a few skirmishers and whatnot to detect our coming."

Oakwood had a rough map, copied from that given to Major Johnson.

"That's Mendiguren, by my reckoning. It being pronounceable."

His words fell on deaf ears, because both Cornets had lifted their heads. The faint sounds of musket-fire, then louder cannon-fire were coming to them from their far right, over some distance.

"Sounds like the Ball's begun!"

Carr did not reply, nor Oakwood, instead both subconsciously checked their sabres in their scabbard for easy drawing above the twentieth time.

The gunfire was far more audible on Monte Arrato and whilst the men of the 105th could see nothing, sat in their clefts and dells, their Officers still on their height looked immediately to the ridge, all using their telescopes. Events were clear to be seen, mostly because the white uniforms of the Spanish infantry of Hill's column, all stood out so prominently amongst the bushes and the scrub. They were atop the ridge in strength, albeit at the very beginning of the feature immediately above the defile, but now pushing forward rapidly against a very outnumbered screen of French skirmishers. Not one British Officer lowered their telescope, but Middlemore, commanding the 48th, soon made a comment.

"That won't last!"

Several minutes later, he was proved correct. A strong Brigade of French had advanced along the ridge to oppose the Spanish and the advance turned into a static firefight, ferocious, as evidenced by the volumes of gun-smoke and the accompanying sounds that came to them across the valley. However, it was W. Anson, now nodding with satisfaction, who replied.

"That'll do! That worked! Did you not see where those French came from? Up from the valley where they were waiting for us, but no more. The more that Johnny needs to send up from there, the better for us."

Creet of the 27th was grinning as much as anyone and, seeing a whole British Brigade joining the Spanish and begin to push the French backwards once again, he added his own comment.

"There'll be more sent up soon. If we get along that ridge in any strength, then Johnny's done for!"

His words were coming true, the Spanish and the Redcoats were once more advancing forward, a steady, seemingly inexorable, advance. In addition, another Redcoat Brigade had now entered through the defile itself, below the combat above, and were spreading themselves across the slopes below the ridgeline, between the river and the steep ridge slope. Anson closed his telescope.

"It'll be us soon. The Peer'll be happy with that!"

Carr had been using his own telescope on events further along the valley, then he spoke with deep satisfaction.

"Indeed he will, Sir. There's yet another French Brigade going up. All the less for us to deal with!"

The first that the men of the 105th knew about the 'Peer's happiness', was Heaviside and O'Hare coming to walk amongst them, O'Hare coming to the Colour and Light Companies.

"On your feet now boys! We've arranged a nice pleasant stroll for you up into town!"

Failing to rise to O'Hare's humour, nor Heaviside's Methodist blandishments, the 105th formed into column of companies, behind the 48th, but ahead of the 27th and the Provisional Battalion of Anson's Brigade. As the gunfire to their right continued, heard but unseen, everyone for the last time checked their weapons, took a deep breath and followed the order to march forward.

For the men belonging to the Cavalry Brigade of G. Anson, the advance continued. What proved indeed to be the hamlet of Mendiguren was passed through and left behind, with the Light Dragoons of the 16th in the lead and the 12th in support. Graham himself was up with Collins on the road beyond the deserted village, all now staring hard at the next as it came into view. From their place out on the left of the advance, Oakwood, now joined by Johnson, had been studying both Senior Officers even more closely than his own way ahead and when he saw them halt, he halted his own Squadron and drew out his telescope. It needed but a moment's study.

"Next bunch of hovels down there. Full of French and named Aranguiz!"

Johnson turned to him smiling.

"Why so keen to name each of these villages?"

Oakwood's expression became a slight frown, but one of irony, rather than annoyance.

"I do believe anyone has the right to know the name of the place where he may find himself breathing his last!"

Johnson made no reply, but merely grinned.

The next activity came on the main road, one of Graham's ADCs riding back towards the rest of Graham's column, now mostly infantry and Oakwood spoke again.

"This is where it starts! But first we wait."

Neither Carr nor Peterson felt inclined to argue with their Captain's prediction, for each felt the knot in their stomachs grow a little tighter. Even from where they were, both could now see that this battle was going to be huge, for each could see, even with the naked eye, the thick gun smoke issuing from the high ridge in the far distance. It took a while for Graham to bring up his Battalions and arrange them as he chose, deciding on Portuguese Cacadores as skirmishers, then Pack's Portuguese in the van, Longa's Spaniards on the right and Anson's Light Dragoons remained deployed on the left. However, even with deployment completed, there was no movement forward towards Aranguiz, easily 300 yards before the furthest advanced Cacadores and so Johnson turned to Oakwood.

"I've no idea what he's waiting for!"

For some time they remained waiting, hearing much, but seeing nothing to comment on.

oOo

Not so the Fourth Division, far over from them in the right centre. At that moment they were marching down the high street of Nancleres, this a major road leading down to the bridge over the Zadorra, the windows of the dwellings either side more often than not, containing a pale, terrified face. The hurried pace through the buildings soon slowed and then came to a complete halt. The word came quickly back, Ellis hearing from a Corporal at the rear of Nine Company.

"Lowry-Cole's stopped the whole Division. The Frogs have got the whole bridge closed up. Guns and infantry."

Ellis turned to Davey and Saunders.

"That'll be our cue!"

He was not wrong, soon the call came for all Light Infantry of the Fourth Division to advance and Drake's men quit the column to run forward down the road. The three Brigades of the 4th Division; Anson's, Skerret's and Stubb's Portuguese, had been held back behind a bend in the road out of the French line of fire and this bend had to be passed around before Drake could see anything, as he and his men ran forward with all other Light Companies. Ellis ran up to Drake, who could now see very clearly what they were about to face.

"Sir! What's our purpose?"

The ferocity of the reply came as a shock to the normally unshakeable Ellis, it coming from his usually cheerful and sanguine Captain.

"To kill the French, Sergeant! What you can see down there, you shoot at! This battle may be decided elsewhere, but we have opponents here, so we give those all the fight we can!"

Such a fervent outburst did worry the veteran Sergeant. Was Drake seriously roused up? Would he lead them into a situation more perilous than needed? He took his own decision and stood still as his men passed by, shouting at his Corporals and Chosen Men.

"When we get there, holding drill, nothing more!"

Drake led them towards the trees that lined the river bank and the 105th Lights settled in, each taking a tree-trunk for cover, but always firing obliquely, never directly over. Davey was first to a sturdy oak, where he loaded and looked up river, to his left. Fifty yards up, there was a Tirailleur using his own tree for cover, but exposed to anyone downstream of him. Davey sighted and fired. He did not wait for the smoke to clear, but he dropped back for Miles to take his place. Miles needed to wait for over a minute, this time looking downstream, but he saw a target and downed the man, in this case a Voltiguer. Before Pike took Miles' place, he had a question.

"They've cannon here, why are they not using them?"

However, Ellis was nearby.

"They're waiting for the columns. A better target. That's the threat, not us, but it could be, just as much, that they're saving ammunition. This is a day-long job."

Carr had gone forward far enough to see his Light Company in place and was pleased to see how his men settled to their drill, but then Anson arrived, out of breath and plainly worried.

"Johnny's got both bridges covered tight. Ours here and the next upstream, a place called Villodas, but there's a third a good half mile above that, some place called Tres Puentes. Seems some peasant has told the Peer that there's no Frogs there and he's sent a Brigade of the Light Division, Kempt's I think, upstream to see if they can get across there. If that fails, then getting over here and at Villodas will be one damn bloody business! So send the word down the line, get at their gunners, skirmishers can wait."

Carr saluted but decided to go himself. As he ran down, his breath caught in his throat to see a whole Company of French Voltiguers charging over the bridge, but his breathing was restored when the advance was brought to a bloody halt by the fire of the Light infantry Companies placed at both sides of the bridge and so, reassured, he ran on to come first to Lieutenant Shakeshaft.

"Richard! Spread the word, go for their gunners. We may need to force a crossing here, so reduce their gun-crews."

Carr came next to Ellis to receive a less than encouraging reply.

"Would if we could see any guns, Sir. Strikes me they're upstream of the bridge. Up on that bit of a hill. There's none I've seen on t'other side from us."

Carr rose up and quickly peered through the trees on the far side, but he saw enough to tell him that Ellis was correct, there were no guns directly opposite.

"Right. Sergeant. Disengage. We're going the other side of the road."

Then Drake arrived, concerned to see his men abandoning their positions.

"Something new?"

"Yes. We're for those guns on the hill above the bridge. They matter more."

The word was passed and the 105th Lights fell back and ran upstream to find the Light Company of Skerret's 7th Fusiliers ineffectively using muskets against a target well over 100 yards away. As they arrived, Shakeshaft and Bettridge shouted instructions.

"The gunners on the hill."

That was all the instruction needed, but, as he closed to the riverbank, Miles instantly recognised the distinctive headgear of the 7th and was none too gentle with his words as he joined the 7th Lights firing line and took his position, knowing exactly what was required.

"Shift over, shite-auk! The Rag and Bone Boys is here, and we're the lads for this job. You keep the 'eads down of they tassle-swingin' bastards just over. Leave the gunners to us!"

The Fusilier was too astonished to reply quickly and decided not to anyway as Miles brought up his Baker, set the sights, set himself into a firing position and then fired. As Miles reloaded he looked at the man, him still not sure how to react.

"What! You on holiday? You ain't but fired one shot! Them just over, make 'em worried, assuming you knows how to use that spruced up bundook you carries! 'Tain't just for parade, theece know!"

Miles' harsh words brought the man back to reality and he raised the very well cared for musket and fired. By now Miles had reloaded.

"Good boy! So between the two of us, we just might keep both our 'eads on our shoulders."

oOo

Much further upstream along the Zadorra, the leading Battalions of Graham's column were at last going forward, when Oakwood looked at his watch.

"Noon! Good job it's a June day with plenty of daylight left!"

Johnson just shook his head, but from out on their position, Two Squadron watched the Cacadores advance forward at the run towards Aranguiz before them, supported by the blue tunicked Portuguese, distinguished from the French by the wide width of their crossbelts, but also and mostly by the lurid pattern of their Colours, deep red and blue with a multi-coloured patterned circle in the centre. The 16th with the 12th behind kept pace at the trot, all intent on the Cacadores, but Oakwood had his telescope fixed firmly on the far side of the houses.

"Johnny's off! Giving us this place as well."

Now with the naked eye, Carr could see blue-uniformed French running back from the village to the next back, a large one, but Oakwood had seen more.

"That's a line of trees either side of that place. We're at the river. It's now this gets serious."

"Yes, Sir, but he's not quite gone from here."

Carr's words were supported by the fact of the Cacadores and their Line Battalions were still hurrying forward, but not at the village, rather a distinctive hill off to the right. However, this also was not long defended, after one volley from the French defenders, the Cacadores were onto the rough slopes and then on the summit, many then seen waving and cheering, their shakoes on the muzzles of their muskets. Oakwood released a sceptical sigh.

"Would that were all this takes!"

With Aranguiz taken, Graham began re-grouping his force and soon the ADC arrived with new orders to Collins, which sent Johnson riding along their line to halt at Oakwood.

"We're having a major go at that place."

His right arm was now pointing upstream to 'that place', a village someway off, then he continued.

"That's Gamarra Mayor. The one behind me is called Abechuco. They've both got bridges that we have to cross."

No more was said on the subject of objectives, there was plainly no need, what needed further explanation was who would be attempting what. For that, Johnson was thoroughly brief.

"Yours are for Gamarra, with a Squadron of the 12th. You support the Fifth Division and three field-guns. Good luck!"

Oakwood grinned, but more from sympathy than humour.

"You're for that Abechuco then?"

"I am."

"Then good luck to you, also!"

Johnson grinned as he rode off, but Oakwood was by now turning to his own men to place them in column alongside a Squadron of the 12th. Introductions were shouted across.

"Oakwood! 16th"

"Meredith! 12th. Are we the lucky ones?"

Oakwood just threw up his hands as the Squadrons trotted on, to soon be overtaken by the three, hurrying field-guns, eager to set up before the arrival of the whole 5th Division, who were now jogging forward, but some way behind, with their Major General Oswald riding at their head. Advancing as three units; guns, cavalry and infantry, the whole force continued to cross the open fields, trampling beans and corn, as the buildings of Gamarra Mayor grew larger. The three Officers of Two Squadron were riding together and as they slowed, it was not long before they saw a Brigade from the 5th Division draw ahead, now at the run, but the Brigade's three Battalions remained in column as they ran forward. Their Light Companies were soon far out in front, accompanied by a Company of Brunswick Oels, their all black uniform with the high black plume atop their shako, standing out distinctly amongst the faded pink of the Redcoats. Oakwood was looking across and forward.

"First in! Good luck to them, that village is barricaded and well defended."

As if to emphasise his words regarding the French determination to hold the village, French field-guns opened fire from across the river, one ball causing casualties in the column of the leading Battalion still coming up behind the Light Companies. When these Light troops came up to the barricades and engaged the defenders, the smoke and noise from their combat became incessant and ferocious, many Redcoats and Brunswick Oels falling back from the barricades, killed, dying or badly wounded. Then, when the whole column of the Brigade arrived, three French guns in the village began continuous fire, causing more casualties and soon, on the outskirts of the village, lay many more, all wearing Allied uniforms, either prone or writhing with pain. Oakwood turned to Peterson and Carr.

"Best get back with your Troops. We may end up having to charge through this village!"

Carr needed to merely drop his horse back a few yards, where Baxter sat his horse, both his arms folded over the saddle-pommel, him not having failed to notice the immediate serious casualties before the village.

"Nothing much different about today, Sir."

By itself the remark was wholly vague, but placed alongside Baxter's earlier comment about big battles, it made perfect sense. However, Carr could only observe, as did the rest of the Squadron, the efforts of the Brigade of the 5th Division attempting to force an entry into the village. Even from a distance of over 300 yards, the shouts and other sounds of desperate combat came to them clearly and, at first, it seemed as though the attack had broken, as a wave against a cliff on the sea-shore. However, all the while, the Brunswick Oels had been hammering at the barricaded windows of buildings to the left of one of the blocked off roads, the main one, and two gave in at the same time. The German Riflemen were immediately in and through, soon in some force, with many Redcoats following. An enterprising Officer then led them to the first floor, or perhaps from their own initiative, so that in no time they were firing down from the windows onto the backs and shoulders of the defenders of the barricade alongside them. The defence immediately crumbled and the Redcoats swarmed over, pulling the barricade apart as they climbed over and through. Probably now taken from behind as the Brigade swarmed through other buildings, the defences of the remaining two entrances on that side quickly succumbed and the 5th Division were into Gamarra Mayor.

They saw Oswald himself riding into the village, following his first Brigade, who were already in and clearing the village. His Portuguese Brigade, these being Sprys', were ordered up to the river to line the bank between Oakwood's Squadron and the first houses, whilst Oswald's third Brigade remained in reserve. Carr turned his attention to Gamarra bridge, to see fugitive French swarming across, a continuous stream fleeing to the opposite bank, then he heard Baxter's next comment from behind, spoken perhaps for Carr's benefit or perhaps not.

"This is where it gets very bloody!"

By now Gamarra Mayor bridge was empty, all living French now over, but Carr knew what would come next and both his stomach and throat tightened. One, two and then three Redcoat Companies emerged from the village onto the bridge and charged across, but the leading files did not even reach the centre, before several French cannon opened fire, many plainly trained perfectly down the line of the bridge.

Whole groups of Redcoats were swept away, as if by a giant broom. Survivors behind ran on, for those behind to receive another devastating discharge of French grape-shot and musket shot. Barely a handful actually crossed the bridge and they ran around the side of the bridge to find safety down the bank, but French Voltiguers ran forward and shot each one, bar two that threw themselves into the water and scrambled under the bridge. From their bank, Spry's Portuguese opened fire on the Voltiguers and they were forced back, but no more Redcoats made any effort to cross the bridge. Swallowing hard, Carr turned to look downstream and could just make out Abechuco bridge, just under a mile further down. There were no soldiers on it at all, either red, blue or brown and the conclusion was inescapable, Graham's force was held at the river and could not cross without dreadful casualties.

oOo

At Nancleres bridge there was no change either. For more than an hour, almost two, a hot exchange of fire had been maintained between only skirmishers, the French gun-crews having been pulled back out of harm's way, leaving their guns silent and stationary, but still obviously potent should the main columns appear and attempt to force the bridge. Carr had returned to the main column of the 105th, there to await orders, but impatience took hold and he climbed the steep 200 yards above the road to a vantage point that gave a view beyond the river. The clearest feature was a large, high knoll, which he estimated to be about three-quarters of a mile from their own high point. He drew out his telescope and focused it, for a large collection of mounted French Officers to swim into view, the whole topped with plumes and feathers, their uniforms, obvious even at that distance, ostentatiously florid and decorous. Carr called to O'Hare.

"See those on top that hill, right opposite. I'd say that was El Rey himself, with all his magnificent retinue."

O'Hare looked at the knoll and then focused his own instrument.

"I'd say you were right, but something seems to have stirred them up, as we speak!"

Carr used his own telescope again and, indeed, many of the group were pointing and several were now riding across to Carr's left. He studied the movement for some minutes, then he turned to O'Hare.

"Any ideas?"

O'Hare was busy with his own telescope, but instead of the knoll, he was focusing further up the valley of the Zadorra, beyond the slopes of the prominent knoll.

"Plenty! We're over the Zadorra upstream. Kempt must have got over at that Tres Puentes and he's helping out what I'd take to be Picton or could be Dalhousie at their bridge. My money's on Picton and I can just make out what must be his men on the far side, but what matters is that Kempt is driving off the guns covering Picton's bridge. They must have come up from behind them. Looks like only three of the six are getting away."

Carr's telescope came immediately to his eye and he could make out for himself, green coated Riflemen, now taking possession of three French field-guns and several horses. Next, several Companies of green uniformed Riflemen plus a Battalion of redcoats gathered at the guns, with still more running up from the Zadorra on the left. Five minutes more and Battalion after Battalion of Redcoats and Portuguese Line infantry from Picton's Third Division were sprinting over the Zadorra bridge. Then came their Major-General, whom Carr identified as indeed being Picton and the various Regiments began to form themselves into some kind of order, Picton riding up and down, plainly taking both his own Division and Kempt's triumphant Brigade under his own command. Another Brigade came from the same direction as Kempt's had previously and someone with the knowledge made the comment, "That'll be Vandeleur. So all of the Light Division are over."

Anson and then Lowry-Cole arrived beside Carr and O'Hare and studied developments through their own telescopes, events which evolved into Vandeleur advancing towards Vitoria along the bank of the Zadorra and Picton's whole Division, two British and one Portuguese Brigades, all now over the bridge, advancing to cross the face of The Knoll, followed by Kempt's Brigade, all advancing down to pass behind the bridges of Villodas and Nancleres. A single French field-gun battery opened fire on them, but their advance was unstoppable. The final use that Carr made of his own telescope was to study the top of the knoll, to see El Rey and his Senior Officer Corps turning their horses away from their vantage point, plumes and feathers the last to disappear from view behind the crest. Carr turned his telescope on the fields below and he grinned for the first time that day.

"What he put there to cover Villodas bridge is pulling back. Ours here at Nancleres will not long follow."

In plain sight crossing the empty fields was a French six-gun field battery and a single Battalion of infantry, these running hard to escape being cut off by Picton's inexorable advance. He continued watching for one more joyful minute before closing his telescope.

"Padraigh, we must get back down. We'll be over ourselves soon, so get down to Drake and as soon as he sees those French guns pull back, tell him to get a messenger back to Anson or even the General."

O'Hare soon split away from Carr as they both descended and he ran to find Drake, him with his Light Company, shouting instructions and encouragement in equal measure.

"Nat. Picton's Third are over the river and coming up behind those guns opposite. When they pull back, as they must, get a message back. We need to know soonest."

Drake nodded and ran off to the place where the guns could best be viewed, where he found Davey and Saunders, but he looked first at the guns up on their hill. Saunders fired at a Tirailleur and then spoke to Drake as he reloaded.

"Sir! Any change?"

"Picton's over and going to cut these off. They won't be able to stay there, so, Davey, when they go I want you to take back the message."

Saunders had by now reloaded.

"Happening already, Sir."

Drake looked up to see the French gunners now back with their pieces and manoeuvring them backwards.

"Davey, go!"

Then he took a deep breath to shout for the benefit of his Company all around.

"On the gunners, men. On the gunners. The more we get now, the less they'll get of us later."

All on the bank obeyed, but the French gunners were well practiced and it took little more than a minute before the hillock that had been their position became empty. Meanwhile, Davey was running back up the road to find Lowry-Cole at the head of Stubb's Portuguese. He ran up, came to the attention and saluted.

"Sir! Beg to report, Sir, that the French battery on t'other side of the bridge has pulled back, Sir. Gone!"

Lowry-Cole looked at him intently.

"So what's left?"

"Nothing formed up that we could see, Sir. Just skirmishers as've been up against us for the past hour, nor more. Sir."

Lowry-Cole turned immediately to Stubb's

"We go over, in echelon. Yours first and when you get over, tend left and link with Picton. Anson's will go straight on, just behind and in the centre, but in support of yours. Skerret's last and will tend right to link with Hill's on the ridge."

Then he turned to Davey, remaining at attention.

"Well done, Corporal. Back to your Company."

Davey saluted and ran back, to a skirmish across the river as intense as it had ever been, where he found Drake.

"They're coming down to us, Sir. The columns. I told the General and then I heard him give the order."

Drake looked back up the road to see the head of the Portuguese column, the brilliant colours of their Standard clear and stark in the strong sunshine. Then he looked across the river, then at the bridge. Ellis was stood nearby and he knew exactly what Drake was thinking and he had no qualms about voicing his anxiety.

"Best hold back some, Sir. Best to move when they Frogs over the river gets their sight of what's coming down the road at them."

Drake was plainly angry, for what reason, Ellis did not know, but Drake was enough of a professional to know that Ellis made sense. Nevertheless, he was determined that the 105th Lights would be the first over and Stubb's men were now in plain sight and would soon arrive.

"105th! To me."

Drake ran back to the road, to halt merely yards from the bridge. Miles heard and turned away from the river, but not before delivering a passing shot to his 7th Fusilier companion.

"Looks like we're to be first onto the bridge, Sir Royal, so next time you fancies mouthin' off at the 105th, just you remember what you saw yer today. What we did an' you didn't!"

Miles ran to join his Company, but other Captains of other Light Companies there plainly had the same idea, certainly those of Anson's 27th and 48th, but the 105th were first there in strength and Drake drew his sword and held it aloft.

"We've had our fill of this boys! Now, forward! Over the river!"

He ran forward, first onto the bridge, still covered by dead and badly wounded Voltiguers from their foolish attempt to cross over themselves much earlier. Ellis was up behind Drake, leaving Bettridge and Shakeshaft to command their own Sections. Drake was in the lead and now halfway over the bridge. At that point, a ragged volley came from the banks on both sides and Ellis heard the buzz and hiss of musket-balls, both above and between, then he saw Drake drop his sword, for it to hang from his wrist by its cord. Drake staggered over to the parapet and Ellis followed to hold him up and then came Saunders.

"Zeke! Get him off the bridge."

Between the two of them they dragged him over to lay him down in the ditch alongside the road on the far side. Ellis quickly looked him over to see the hole in his tunic just above his waist on his right side. He undid Drake's buttons to see blood now soaking his shirt, which he ripped open. The wound was plain, but whether the ball was inside, or had glanced off his ribs, he could not tell. Now Drake was breathing rapidly, in short breaths. Ellis looked at Saunders.

"Can't tell how bad, but we must get on."

He bent over Drake.

"Sir. Just lie here quiet now and the Followers will pick you up. Do you have a cloth, or something?"

Drake pointed to his pocket and Ellis pulled out a clean, cotton handkerchief. He made a pad, then pulled out Drake's belt from the breeches loops, passed the belt around Drake's body and tightened the pad hard against the wound.

"You'll be alright, Sir. Certain you will. The Followers and Surgeon Pearce will see you on the mend in no time."

A weak nod came from Drake.

"Right, Sir, now you stay here, Sir. They'll soon be along to pick you up."

Both men rose and ran on to follow the advance, most of Stubb's Brigade now being over the bridge. Ellis and Saunders ran up the slight rise of the road from the bridge to find themselves on a wide-open expanse that rose slowly up towards some kind of scrub covered knoll. However, he was looking for his own Company and saw them, identified by the green of their cuffs and collars. He and Saunders ran to catch them up, but they had now halted, complying with the other Light Companies of the 4th Division. Ellis ran up to Shakeshaft.

"Sir! Mr Drake is down. You are in command."

Shakeshaft looked horrified, then very worried.

"Down! As in dead?"

"Badly wounded, Sir, but alive when we left him. You have to take command, Sir."

Shakeshaft looked at Ellis, then at the line of Light Companies either side, then straight ahead which was well populated with retreating French infantry and their supporting field-guns. He then looked behind and it was with great relief that he saw the columns of Anson's Battalions advancing up the slope towards them. They were clearly visible, with Stubb's Portuguese in the lead and now passing through the line of 4th Division Lights. Ellis remained there, staring at him.

"Sir?'

"Hold here for now, Sergeant. We'll see what comes next. We've crossed the river, there's bound to be some changes."

However, Shakeshaft soon changed his mind and gave new orders on seeing all other Light Companies run in whichever was the right direction to rejoin their Battalions.

"Sergeant! Gather the men, we are rejoining our Battalion."

Shakeshaft led his men over to the 105th, who were in column and still advancing. Shakeshaft ran up to Carr, whose face showed a deeper and deeper level of concern, but he allowed Shakeshaft to come up to him first and Shakeshaft spoke first.

"Sir. I thought it best to rejoin the Battalion, Sir."

"Where's Captain Drake?"

"Wounded, Sir. Crossing the bridge. Quite badly from what I hear, but alive when Sergeant Ellis left him."

Carr's face then wore a deep and worried frown, then he took a deep breath and brought himself back to the present.

"Very good. Thank you. You are now in command of the Light Company, so get them out ahead but remain in touch."

They marched on, Anson's Battalions in tight columns, the whole Division's Brigades in echelon following Stubb's Portuguese Brigade. Carr managed to clear his mind of worry about Drake as he led his men on, looking first over to the right at the main ridge where the battle had begun, to see Redcoats now some way along its length. They were now in an obvious firefight up there, judging by the amount of gun smoke, but they were way past what must be the main French position in the Zadorra valley. The Brigade below them, also from Hill's Corps, were advancing across the ridge slopes and were now contending a large village, which was also some way beyond the main French position and Carr consulted his map to identify the village as Subijana. Then he heard many voices around him, breaking his train of thought, "There's the Peer," and he looked over to see Wellington himself, bringing forward and arranging all the field-guns of all the Divisions from Nancleres and Villodas and soon all were roaring out, an incessant crash from a massed battery. Then Wellington disappeared in the direction of Picton and it was Picton himself who appeared next from over the skyline of the slope of Arinez Knoll and soon there was a conference between him and Lowry-Cole. The 3rd Division then appeared behind Picton, marching on, whilst the 4th began to move and march on beside them, and on, for some significant time, with the guns behind never ceasing their bombardment of the retreating French. The slope flattened and Lowry-Cole called a halt, just below the summit of the ridge they had been climbing. From there they could see no further ahead, Stubbs' had halted, as had themselves, only Skerret's Brigade could be seen moving, now over by the main trunk road and continuing to move forward.

Next, two Brigades of Picton's marched up onto the skyline, following what looked like at least three Companies of green-jacketed Rifles. The second Brigade were Portuguese and these halted on the skyline almost immediately, whilst the leading Brigade continued on. Plainly these were going to be the troops who would continue the advance, whilst the stationary two Brigades of Lowry-Cole's 4th Division remained standing in reserve. The Rifles soon disappeared forward over the skyline and the first Brigade, still marching, shed its last Battalion, this being Scottish and they halted above the 105th and to the right of the waiting Portuguese. The remaining two Battalions continued to hurry on over to the right, across the view of Deakin and Halfway, these stood in the front rank of the 105th column as the Colour Guard. Deakin turned to Halfway.

"Look, part of that lot movin' right. Bloody Diddykites!"

There was no mistaking the bright yellow of the 88th facings, nor the almost complete yellow of their Regimental Colour, now prominent alongside the King's Colour. Halfway made no comment, mostly because he was not sure if he would be heard above the incessant din of the guns on the ridge down to his right, the largest concentration of field-guns he had ever seen. From over the ridge before them, barely heard, came the additional sounds of combat; rifles and muskets, this for around ten minutes and then, again barely heard, came the bagpipes of the Scottish Regiment beginning their skirl as the Scots advanced forward, their bonnets finally disappearing beneath the ridge. The Portuguese Brigade advanced alongside them. With that Picton rode up to Anson.

"Who are you?"

"Brigadier Anson, Sir."

"I'm taking one of yours as reserve for my 74th Highland, just gone over."

He pointed to the 105th.

"Those! They were with me once. Good as any!"

Without waiting for any reply from Anson, Picton turned his horse in the direction of the 105th.

"Carr! Get yours up over that ridge and support my 74th going for the village. Your best support, mind, not that half-baked effort before Salamanca!"

Carr's face reddened, but he reeled off a clean salute with no words, then he drew his sword and turned to his men.

"One Hundred and Fifth!"

With nothing more, he led his Regiment forward, to soon cross the ridge, the slope rapidly falling away, to show the small village of what he took to be Arinez with its own church, this with a distinctive tower and cupola roof rising high above all else. The nearest streets and alleyways of the village were crowded with French infantry and Picton's Riflemen of earlier were all outside in the fields, unable to progress further but the oncoming 74th Scots would soon enter the fight for the village. The Portuguese were halted and contesting with a French Brigade to the left of the village. With the advance of Picton's men, the cannonade had ceased and the guns were now limbering up, but O'Hare was now looking directly rightwards, towards the main trunk road and the fields beyond.

"That's where the job will be done. If at all! The 88th and the 45th Nottinghams, if I've got that right."

Picton's two Battalions had marched on, down the slope to reach the main trunk road, the 88th halting astride it, the leading 45th continuing some way beyond, their oddly shaded blue/green Colours prominent in their centre. Both were in columns of Companies, with no skirmishers out before and what had worried O'Hare was that the 88th were opposed by a whole Brigade of French infantry, three Battalions, whilst the 45th beyond was opposed to another, but in their case only two Battalions. The Colonel of the 88th could be seen out, on foot, before his men.

"That's Wallace, doing that on his own. We should be down there with them, not backing up Picton's Scots for some scrawdeen village!"

Carr could only shake his head. Picton's two Battalions were overmatched by five and the French had the advantage of the slope, but then he saw Wallace lead his men forward, remaining in ten individual Company columns. The 45th soon followed in the same formation and the leading French Battalions marched down to meet them, in their three-deep firing line. Still advancing, the 88th soon broke column formation and smoothly formed their own two-deep firing line, but they had not taken ten paces in this new formation before the French fired a full volley, albeit at maximum range. The Connaughts suffered casualties, but closed their ranks and advanced on, breaking into a run, Wallace taking his men up to less than 30 yards of the French line, this now at a standstill. Then the 88th half-Company volleys began, the orange fire and smoke rippling down their line from the centre outwards. Hit non-stop, the French line began to dissolve. Wallace's rapid advance had given them no time to reload and within a minute the French Battalion had suffered appalling casualties, the first line all gone, most of the second and with gaps even now in the third. The survivors broke and ran, to run either side of the second French Battalion, now advancing forward in column, two Companies wide.

Under Wallace's orders the 88th ceased fire and reloaded to advance forward in line once more. Once within range, the head of the advancing second French column gave what fire they could, but the 88th closed their ranks and advanced on, to wrap their line around the head of the column, the outside Companies, right and left, almost forming parallel to the sides of the French column. Then the half-Company volleys began again and those of the 105th, on their ridge, could see in all its stark horror, just what happened when a column met a firing line. Within seconds, the column was being flensed, the outside ranks, front and sides, being peeled away by the incessant musketry. The column held their ground for mere minutes before it also dissolved and the survivors poured to the rear, again around the sides of the third Battalion, but this was now covered with a mass of panicked fugitives. Carr and O'Hare could see desperate French Officers shouting and waving their swords, frantically attempting to form some kind of firing line from their own command and the wreckage of the two Battalions once before them. Then the 88th arrived, now all reloaded and the punishment began again, but this time not for so long. Wallace ceased fire and the pair could see the 88th fix bayonets. Wallace raised his sword and the 88th advanced again, and from somewhere, perhaps on the wind, came their eerie moan, as the 88th charged forward. However, not one bayonet was used, the French mass turned and fled, soon to break apart and become a spread of fugitives running back to Vitoria. The 88th gained the top of the ridge that their opponents had first advanced from and stood to cheer, shakos on the ends of their bayonets. Behind them, on the ground lay many of their comrades but surrounding them was the wreck of a three Battalion French Regiment. Beyond them, the 45th had been performing similar heroics, albeit against a lesser enemy, but that enemy had broken as soon as their three Battalion neighbours had begun their headlong retreat. O'Hare looked at Carr and shook his head in wonder.

"Wallace! I'd make him a General."

Carr could only nod his head and think, but these particular thoughts he kept to himself, that a huge hole had just been torn in the French left-centre and with Hill as far along the ridge as he now was, the result of the battle was now a foregone conclusion. Behind him, in the Colour Guard, Deakin had his own thoughts, different, but unlike Carr he was moved to voice them out loud, to Halfway, him stood just behind.

"I never had much time for they Diddykites, nor ever will; lyin', twistin', shysters the bloody lot, but when it comes to puttin' up a fight, well, that down there was as good, probably better, than any you'll see, anywhere, in any army. Even I've got to give 'em credit for that!"

The 88th and 45th now remained in position on the ridge just captured, their own Brigadier riding down the slope of Arinez Knoll towards them. Carr and O'Hare were now looking ahead, down at the village, which was now in the possession of the 3rd Division and full of Scots and Rifles infantry. In addition, the Portuguese Brigade of the 3rd were now advancing even beyond the village, to the left, pushing back their French Brigade. Picton had remained on the ridge, overseeing all, and was just about to depart, when Anson came up to him.

"Sir. Will you still be needing my 105th?"

Picton looked down with his best scowl.

"Seems not, Anson."

Then he looked across at Carr and raised his voice.

"Seems not. And just as well!"

With that, he and his Staff cantered down the long slope towards the village and Anson then turned to Carr.

"Wellington will be reorganising before we move forward, which will put us, yours in particular, back in the 4th. Look, he's making changes already. Dickson's guns are going forward as we speak."

Carr had heard of Dickson as the Artillery General and the whole massed battery was now on the move with all their guns, drawing them carefully, but steadily, forward to the next position, with Wellington and he who must be Dickson, overseeing all. Then Wellington began riding in the direction of Lowry-Cole, already shouting new orders. These were soon delivered by ADCs and executed, whilst their Commander in Chief, remained stationary on the slope of Arinez Knoll, above the village of Arinez, which was now a base for further advance.

In obedience to Wellington's orders, the new lines came together and, from their elevated position, the 105th could see fully the magnificent and intimidating display now spread in all directions and drawn up for the next advance. Two-deep, the 105th were in the centre of the second line, whilst the first line before them comprised 16 full Battalions, Carr taking the trouble to count the sets of Colours. In their own line were 14 more and behind was a third line comprising Stubbs' Portuguese Division and all of the cavalry of the Allied centre. As the font of all such Battalion knowledge, O'Hare decided, using their Colours, that the 105th were behind the 74th and the 88th of Picton's Division with their own 27th of W. Anson's on their right and the 43rd of the Light Division on their left. Before them, Dickson's guns were already in a long firing line, duelling with an almost equal French gunline in the far distance. The first line began their advance, each Battalion with their Colours high and prominent above their marching ranks, weapons at 'Shoulder arms'. As they went forward themselves,

Carr, O'Hare and Heaviside were together before the Colours, each marching with their swords sloped over their right shoulders. Carr turned to O'Hare, both observing the detail of the wide panoply that was the battle on their side of the field. Redcoats and Spanish had by now pushed far along the high ridge, some now even descending from the heights to menace the next French defensive line including their new gunline. Meanwhile, on the slopes below, the Redcoats were on to the next village after Subijana, which meant that the French line was close to being completely outflanked on this side, yet again.

"How much longer would you give this?"

O'Hare pulled out his watch.

"4 o' clock. This'll be done by six."

"And what have we done?"

O'Hare shook his head.

"Not much!"

"You know that Drake is down."

"I did. It was passed along the ranks. How bad, do you know?"

Carr pulled a worried face.

"Bad, but still living was the best I got."

"We can only hope!"

Heaviside was close beside them, black-jowled and by this time in need of another shave.

"Faith is the assurance of things hoped for, the conviction of things not seen. Hebrews 11, verse 1."

Mildly impatient at the fate of Drake being acknowledged with yet another Bible quote, O'Hare leaned forward to look at Heaviside.

"Now that is one I know, spoken by the Brothers when we were having the living daylights waled out of us. I didn't understand it then and I'm not much better now."

Heaviside made no reply.

oOo

Back at Nancleres' bridge, for Nathaniel Drake, the subject of their concern, hope came in smaller doses than did despair and both of these only during brief periods of consciousness. When one bout of sentience arrived, his main worry were Spanish peasants, because now that the conflict had moved on, all that remained around him were the dead, the dying and the seriously wounded, the source of rich pickings for the scavengers who would soon arrive. The noise of battle was now distant, the major sounds heard all came from close range, these now issuing from the parched throats of the wounded who lay around him, both French and Redcoat. He knew that these scavengers cared little for nationality, all that mattered was coin, personal jewellery, any silver on uniforms and then often the clothes they lay in, if not too damaged by combat. He could only breathe in short breaths, the pain in his side was too agonising and he knew that he was continuously losing blood. Despair came often from the thought of dying in a Spanish roadside ditch and never again to see his beloved Cecily, nor their child, Henrietta. He tried to roll over and rise, but the pain was too great and his head swooned, such that he fainted, falling back onto his stomach. Then, suddenly, the pain returned, not from anything that he was doing, but because he was being roughly turned over by two Spanish peasants, their breath hot and sour as he was searched, first his pockets, then the buttons of his tunic examined for silver, then his throat for any necklace. One scowled and swore, then his face brightened when he found Drake's left hand with his wedding ring and a knife was produced.

Then something swung through the air to connect with the side of the man's head and he fell sideways, but not senseless, for him to scramble backwards and then to his feet. Then came a tirade of unmistakably Irish insults.

"You gombeen Spanish gobshites! Be off with you before we puts a bayonet through your filthy peasant gizzards."

The 'weapon' that had felled the man was a heavy iron ladle, wielded by Nelly Nicholls herself and the bayonets were on the ends of muskets picked up and held menacingly by Consuela and Esme, whilst Bridie was now kneeling over him.

"Mr. Drake, Sir. You're wounded!"

Drake looked up into the kindly face and managed a weak smile at the obvious comment, but gratitude came next.

"I'm grateful for what you just did."

That was all he could manage and his head slumped back down.

"The least, your Honour. Spalpeens, the lot of them, and are we not doing what we always do anyway during a fight such as this, but we must get you back or somewhere. The bandsmen will be here soon, we saw them picking up just now. Parson's with them."

Drake knew what 'picking up' meant, being loaded into a cart and transported somewhere, perhaps a long or short journey, but agonising nevertheless, but Bridie continued.

"Well, there's not too many of ours as've fallen, Sir, not above a handful."

Meanwhile, Nellie had been scouring the vicinity for any more battlefield scavengers and, finding none, she turned her attention to Captain Drake.

"You should let us take a look, Mr. Drake, Sir. At least to change whatever has been put upon it."

Drake winced as he was rolled onto his back by Esme and Consuela and then Bridie undid his tunic and then pulled up his torn shirt to reveal the dressing applied by Saunders, this now blood soaked. "Well, we can change that at least."

She undid the belt and eased away the padding to reveal the wound, but little could be seen due to clotted blood. Bridie held out her hand to Nellie.

"That good water, what we took from the village well."

Nellie handed it down.

"Now we need a clean piece of cloth."

This was obtained by ripping off the shirt of a dead French Officer nearby and the wound was cleaned, then Esme spoke up.

"Let me. I've worked in an army hospital many a time."

She knelt beside Drake and gently pulled the wound open, but despite her care, Drake gasped in pain, then Esme spoke further.

"It depends if the ball is still in, Sir, I'd have to say it is. A French ball is smaller than ours and your thick tunic and shirt will have helped, but perhaps it's still in, but not too deep. Whatever, you'll have sore ribs, at least cracked, maybe broken, but I can see bone and the ball must've hit that first."

Drake took as deep a breath as he dared.

"Well, I'll settle for sore ribs and that's the truth."

At that moment a cart drew up, driven by Sedgwicke, with a bandsman alongside, who quickly examined the wound.

"It's not bleeding too bad now, Sir, but we'll get another pad on there. Clean! The last thing we want is some infection."

More French Officer shirt was obtained, Bridie certain that it was silk and the wound was again washed and covered. Then Nellie and the bandsman hauled Drake to his feet, his face a picture of agony as he was eased around to the back of the cart and lifted upwards. The cartbed was thick with straw on which lay another member of the 105th Light Company, but Bridie rolled up two French jackets to place under his head.

"Sure, that will ease the journey, Mr. Drake. Parson here thought of that."

"I'm very grateful to you all."

Sedgwicke now turned in the driver seat.

"I feel we should follow the Regiment, Sir. It is most likely that Surgeon Pearson will set up at the end of any advance, which in all likelihood will be some way forward from here. Probably at the site of tonight's camp."

Sedgwicke waited for no reply, instead he whipped the mules into motion. The cart jolted over the rough track and both Drake and the soldier winced with pain, but then grinned at each other.

"Corporal Pawlet, is it not? Mr Shakeshaft's Section?"

"Yes Sir, it is. Sorry to see you here, Sir,"

"How many did we lose?"

"Five, Sir. Me and you, two that can walk and one dead."

Drake lay back.

"Let's hope that last number remains unchanged!"

oOo

Far over to the North-east, for the Light Dragoon Cornets Carr and Peterson, there had been no change during the last four hours, such that G. Anson had ordered them to dismount and pull back from any danger, leaving the Portuguese Infantry Brigade to exchange desultory fire across the Zadorra. The major confrontation was by cannonfire, both Allied and French gun-crews frantically working their pieces to reduce the fire of the other. Plainly there were many more French field-guns on the far side of the river, but they had more targets to concern them, not least any group of Redcoats that showed themselves at the far side of the bridge, threatening another attempt at crossing. The three guns with the 16th had twice to send for more ammunition and finally the Captain had to acknowledge that his men were exhausted and so he ran over to Oakwood.

"Can any of your men relieve some of mine at the guns?"

Oakwood knew that it was useless to call for volunteers and so he turned to the first ranks of Carr's Troop.

"Baxter! First three ranks. Dismount and go and help with the guns. Do what you can."

Baxter's face registered intense annoyance at such an order, but he dismounted and motioned for the first three ranks, twelve men, to follow him. The Artillery Captain pointed four towards each gun and they found themselves alongside very tired and sweating gun-crews. Baxter looked at the gunner with the most stripes.

"What for us, Mate?"

"After firing, wheel her back up and if one of you could bring forward the ball. And helping with the ramming won't come amiss."

Baxter nodded and gave his orders for who was to do what and then they began the hard, physical labour of hauling the gun back into position by turning the wheels and then loading for the next discharge. Meanwhile, Carr and Peterson, overcome by curiousity, were up at the riverbank, looking downstream at Abechuco bridge.

"Correct me if I am wrong, but I have the distinct impression that Abechuco remains in French hands!"

Peterson nodded agreement.

"I fear you are correct and also that no one of ours will be going over any of these bridges until some of ours arrive up alongside that far bank and dislodge the Johnnies that way."

At that moment Carr and Peterson heard the sounds of very heavy fighting, but still too far away to fulfil their own hopes. The sounds were arriving from the plain after Arinez Knoll, where the first line of the advance from Arinez was heavily engaged with the next French line. For those actually within the advance, the noise was appalling for all inside a quarter-mile, within that space the sounds of musketry competed very well with the incessant cannonade from both directions that was sending solid shot humming and buzzing just above their heads. The second line, containing the 105th, had halted and so Carr and O'Hare were given time to look ahead and try to make some sense of what they could see, O'Hare being the first to comment.

"Looks like the usual jumble. One can only hope that it's clear in someone's mind."

"If it's clear in El Rey's mind, he'll be pulling his men out and saving what he can. Look, ours are pouring down off that ridge now and from the slopes just below as well, getting onto their flank and even into their rear."

O'Hare had given that the merest glance; he was looking ahead and he saw their first line divide, left and right, one Brigade to a village on the left, the other to a village on the opposite side. Even with the naked eye he could see, through the gap created, that there were no French opposing them. There was a yawning gap in the French new defensive line.

"We'll be moving soon!"

He began checking his weapons, both pistol and sabre, but Carr, the tedious pedant, was busy consulting his map again, identifying the villages as Zuazo on the left and Gomecha on the right. O'Hare was soon proved correct when Wellington himself arrived at Lowry-Cole and they could hear the simple order given to him, emphasised by a pointing arm.

"General! Get your Division into columns and advance into that gap."

Wellington remained to watch, as Lowry-Cole issued his orders and ADCs quickly came back to the 4th Division Brigadiers. Carr and

O'Hare listened intently to what was said to their own W. Anson by the ADC.

"Your 105th and the Provisionals to lead, Sir, in column side by side. The 27th and 48th will follow, placed the same. You will be supported by Brigadier Stubbs, then Brigadier Skerret. Good luck, Sir."

He saluted and then rode off. Anson then turned to Carr.

"You heard that?"

Carr nodded, saluted and then turned to Heaviside, just behind.

"Column of closed companies, Joshua."

Heaviside ran back and within minutes the drums were beating out the order and the 105th line broke as the ten Companies reformed into a column, closed up at quarter distance, a four yard gap between each Company, each in two ranks,. The Provisional Battalion came up on their left, the four Colours of the 31st Huntingdon and 66th Berkshire prominent at the fore. Lowry-Cole was sat his horse out front, the animal seemingly as impatient as he was, but it was not long before he waved his Division forward, seeing Anson's now fully formed and ready to lead. The advance was only a little slower than a quick march, but the 105th gave Wellington a cheer as they passed, which he acknowledged with a smile and the raising of his riding crop to the peak of his bi-corn. It was not long before they found themselves advancing between the conflict around the two contested villages, but there were practically no French forces in view ahead. What seemed to be a ceiling of cannonballs passed overhead, but jaw and stomach muscles clenched a little tighter when one ball hit the column of the Provisionals and casualties began to scream in agony, but both columns pressed on, Carr remarking his worries to O'Hare.

"Seems that Johnny's gunners have turned their attention to us."

"If they have, it won't be for long. Ours are coming off that ridge in Brigade strength and off the slopes below. The Johnnies'll be pulling back soon, or they'll get themselves cut off."

Carr looked ahead and thought, perhaps, that there was less gun smoke to be seen on the French gunline, but this was not borne out by the buzz and hiss just above. Then his attention was drawn to a small ridge to their left front, in line with the Provisionals' advance, now being occupied by French troops, as many as three Battalions, he estimated. They formed a firing line three deep back up the slope and awaited the inevitable onslaught, which would come from the Provisionals, certainly supported by the 27th coming on behind. The Provisional Colonel was already extending his line, his Companies breaking out from their column and running forward to form a two-deep firing line, but, so Carr estimated, the French line of three Battalions would more than match them, even if they were in their customary two ranks. Carr made an immediate decision.

"Padraigh, lead them on. I'm taking two Companies onto the flank of that hill."

He turned and ran back, past the Colour Company to the Grenadiers.

"Charles. Fall out and get ready to advance onto the flank of that hill. Three deep line."

He registered Carravoy's slightly astonished expression, but did not wait for an answer, instead he ran on to Two Company and Captain Charters.

"Reginald. See Charles moving out and forming a three-deep line, get yours onto his left. We're going to flank that hill."

Trusting Captain Charters to comply, Carr ran back to Carravoy and as he did so, he could see a ferocious firefight on the slopes of the hill, which had halted the advance of the Provisionals.

"Right, Charles. Fix bayonets! It'll be one volley and charge!"

Two Company were now arriving and Carr repeated the order, to then draw his sword and stand before the newly formed line. He held the weapon aloft, waved it forward and both Companies marched forward, Officers out front. The distance came down to barely over hundred yards and the French Commander soon noticed their advance and sent out two Companies of his own to oppose them. Carr waved his sword forward again and their advance quickened. The French had managed a line of sorts and their volley came first, ragged, but complete and Carr felt a blow to his shako and another to his left arm. Grunts and cries of pain came from behind and Carr glanced behind both ways to gratefully see all Officers still in place. He led his Companies to well under 50 yards, then he raised his sword to halt.

"Full volley. Make ready. Present. Fire!"

However, only the front rank of the three fired, both Companies holding to their training. Obeying their drill both the second and third ranks counted their three seconds before firing and both delivered their controlled volley. Through the thinning smoke, Carr saw that the two French Companies were now a wreck. He raised his sword.

"Charge boys, charge! Hurrah for the King. Hurrah for the 105th!"

The line surged forward, Carr soon finding himself overtaken by Simon Ameshurst and his inevitable bodyguard. Within seconds, they were at the French line where the dead and wounded from their volleys were unheedingly trampled underfoot. A French Officer stood his ground, virtually alone and Carr parried two blows from him, before a

Grenadier dealt a heavy blow to the side of the Frenchman's head with his musket butt. Only a few more steps forward and Carr saw that their attack had been effective. The French were running down the back of the ridge and the Redcoat uniforms of the Provisionals were appearing on the summit. A Major came running down the slope to Carr.

"Thank you, Sir, for that. Things were getting a mite awkward!"

Carr took the offered hand, but he was worried that they were now behind their own advance.

"I'll leave this to you. Must get back to my own."

He began calling out to reform but he did not wait for tidy ranks, instead he began to run and the two Companies followed. Anson's Brigade were easily identified, if only by the lurid green of their own 105th Colour and it needed only five minutes of running to overtake the head of the 4th Division, which was still his own 105th, with the two Battalions on their left now being a Brigade of Stubb's Portuguese, these having moved up to replace the Provisionals and the 27th. Carr took position alongside O'Hare, who turned and grinned.

"Enjoy your little excursion?"

Carr took off his shako.

"My hat didn't!"

Then he looked at the rent in his left sleeve and then rubbed his arm.

"And I'll have one stiff arm in the morning."

He replaced his shako.

"How much longer would you give this? The fighting bit, I mean."

"Oh, another hour, he's pulling back everywhere."

oOo

Beyond the Zadorra, his Colonel's brother would have disputed that in every way. He and Peterson could now hear conflict in Abechuco, which at least signified progress of sorts, but there was not one Redcoat over the Zadorra, bar the two cowering survivors of the first catastrophic attempt over Gamarra Mayor bridge. Carr stood up on the bank of the river.

"Does something happening in Abechuco mean that some of ours are at last getting up on the far side? That we've actually entered the benighted place?"

Peterson pulled at his friend's sleeve.

"Perhaps, but you are too good a target up there on that bank. We'll know soon enough, one way or the other. For now, back to our Troops. We could be in action ourselves within minutes."

They walked back to see that Oakwood had been in a similar mind and that he had recalled his Troopers back from the guns, these all still firing at the best rate possible with their original crews, as also were their French opponents. Then a Major ADC for Brigadier Oswald came up to Oakwood.

"We're trying again with our bridge, hoping to have silenced their guns, somewhat."

"Doesn't sound like it, Sir."

"Perhaps, Captain, but now we're in Abechuco, we have to give it another go up here. Ready your men, you may be called upon."

With that, the ADC trotted his horse back into the village and Oakwood looked back to see his own Squadron in column of fours, but dismounted. However, content with that, he walked his own horse over to Captain Meredith of the 12th.

"Did you get that? They're trying the bridge again. They may want us."

"To do what? Charge those guns! Over a bridge!"

Oakwood shook his head and turned his horse away.

"We must be ready. Or pray for a miracle!"

The Squadron of the 16th heard rather than saw the assault across the bridge and when the firing quickly subsided, Oakwood drew his own conclusion, turning to Carr and Peterson.

"I think we're here for a little while longer!"

Then a thought.

"Willoughby. As we are in Abechuco, take yourself back to the river and keep watch on that bridge. If we get over there, we'll soon be over here. Go on foot. Take Baxter."

Carr motioned for his Sergeant to follow and the pair walked again to the riverbank, to find cover and for Carr to look downriver at Abechuco bridge and again be disappointed. It was deserted, but Baxter had been making his own study and he asked with hope, more than fact.

"What can you see on the far bank, Sir, some ways down below, with your telescope? Are there any of ours on their way up?"

Carr had brought the instrument with him and extended it to focus on the point where Peterson had studied earlier and was now on the same point indicated by Baxter, the furthest possible with their instrument.

"Not much down there, Sergeant, other than French."

Then came an uncertain thought, regarding what he had seen. He looked again. Perhaps some in green, but he did not voice the possibility. Meanwhile, Baxter's attention was drawn upstream to Gamarra and he spoke with a weary voice.

"What's that saying, Sir? If at first you don't succeed!"

Carr turned his attention upstream to Gamarra Mayor bridge and saw, to his horror, that a third assault was going across, to be met by another storm of fire from the French side. The only measure of extra success was that a significant body of Redcoats got further across the bridge than previously, but once on the French half that also was destroyed by intense French cannonfire and musketry. Whilst Carr clenched his jaw and Baxter shook his head, the survivors fell back, dragging as many wounded with them as they could, whilst French fire on them was fully maintained. Baxter recovered first.

"Abechuco, Sir. It's getting over there, or nowhere, for us. After some of ours gets up to the Frog side of that bridge, then there might be some useful doings for us up here, but not before."

For the next half-hour, Carr used his telescope to study what he could see of the far bank at Abechuco bridge, each time unsure if he saw the green of Allied Riflemen. At the sixth or perhaps seventh time, perhaps a different colour and he handed the telescope to his Sergeant.

"I can no longer trust my own eyes, Sergeant, but can you see what I think I saw, some of ours, Redcoats, down beyond that bridge?"

Baxter looked at him, his expression showing mild astonishment at being asked for an opinion by a superior Officer, even such a relative novice as Carr, but he took the telescope to use it for less than a minute.

"They're here, Sir, up to us on the far side. We'll soon be over that bridge and then things'll change."

Carr took back the telescope, used it for a minute himself, then closed it whilst watching the bridge with a naked eye, to see, sooner than Baxter supposed, a whole Battalion of Redcoats charge onto Abechuco bridge and reach the other side, almost unopposed. He watched as another crossed and then a Regiment of cavalry. He used his telescope again.

"I think that's our own Regiment, just gone over. Back we go!"

They ran back to their Squadron, calling out their message as soon as they were within hearing distance.

"We're over at Abechuco and a force has got up to its bridge from downstream!"

Oakwood turned in his saddle and called out.

"Mount!"

The Squadron obeyed as Carr arrived.

"I'm almost sure that I saw our own 16th go over the bridge after the infantry."

Oakwood did no more than nod, then turn his attention to the village, to await any orders. However, what did happen was an almost immediate cessation of French cannonfire from the far bank. Oakwood turned to Carr.

"That's it. Johnny's pulling out!"

Minutes later, the same ADC as before came riding out to Oakwood and Meredith trotted his horse across to hear.

"Ours are coming up on the far side, either some of the Light or the 3rd. We'll be going over soon, yours following the first of the infantry. Best you follow me."

The Major turned his horse and Oakwood followed, with Meredith's of the 12th following immediately. The Major was correct in his prediction, but first they had to negotiate streets that had been virtually knocked to pieces by four hours of cannonfire. They followed a Battalion of Redcoats onto the bridge and Carr had to close his eyes and allow his horse to find its own way, such were the appalling sights spread over the surface of the bridge, the aftermath of three failed attempts to carry an attack to the far side. He felt his horse jerk and lurch as she picked her way across, then they were over and onto the main chausee that ran along the South bank of the Zadorra. There were many French casualties there and even some abandoned guns, but they were over, yet no-one seemed to know what to do next as there were no French to be seen. Oakwood looked around for a superior Officer and one did come running up, off the bridge, a Major, the number 9 on the front plate of his shako, leading a large group of Redcoats and Brunswick Oels, but he wasted no time on introductions.

"Captain. Take your two Squadrons downstream of the bridge and hold there along the riverbank. There will be more of the 5th coming over and some more of ours will be arriving up to here from downstream. I'm sure the rest of your Anson's will soon be up from Abechuco."

In obedience, both Squadrons lined the riverbank, two ranks deep, but the first to reach them were some filthy and hard-eyed Riflemen, supported by Redcoats of the 43rd and 52nd. However, a look beyond them revealed that their own 16th were now approaching, their uniform distinctive on the wide road; broad, red facings highlighted by the white of their single crossbelt.

oOo

Three miles away to the South, Carr and the 105th were receiving their own orders, these from Lowry-Cole, him riding hither and thither across the front of his Division, but halting briefly before the 105th and the order was quickly delivered, this time using a telescope to indicate direction.

"Carr! Get yours into that village and clear it. The 48th will be in support on your right, the 27th on the left and Provisionals following. The place is called Armentia!"

The 105th had remained in column and so Carr made the necessary slight turn to the right and he led is men over the fields and onto the main road into Vitoria and then over it to see Armentia. There he halted and turned to Slade, leading the Colour Company.

"Pass the word back for the Light Company to come forward."

The word came to Shakeshaft via a Lieutenant of Nine Company.

"Sir. Orders from the Colonel. Yours are to come forward and lead into a village. Sir."

Some part of Shakeshaft jumped upwards in his lower stomach and his pulse rate increased, but Ellis was already calling out orders.

"Double forward. When out front, in files!"

The Light Company swung out from the 105th column and doubled forward to then spread out into their files of three and jog forward towards the village of Armentia, the files of Shakeshaft's own Section on the left, those of Bettridge on the right. Shakeshaft placed himself some way in front, staring intently ahead for any sign of French occupation, especially the squat tower of the village church, rising above the surrounding lower buildings. The hills behind and above were alive with retreating French, whilst any Redcoats that he could see were descending from the ridge to his right, but they would arrive behind them, not into Armentia. He turned to Ellis.

"Sergeant! You're with Lieutenant Bettridge."

"Sir!"

"Do you think they'd leave a rearguard in there?"

"It would make sense, Sir!"

"Voltiguers?"

"Who else? Sir."

The idea of elite French troops, almost certainly strengthened by sharpshooting Tirailleurs, did not ease his fears nor apprehensions to any comforting extent, but the sooner they were over the open approaches and in the village's streets and houses, the better.

"At the run!"

Shakeshaft began his own sprint forward and, from under 100 yards, musket fire spluttered from the windows facing him and the belfry of the Church tower. He heard grunts and cries from behind and two bullets buzzed uncomfortably close to himself, but he ran on to soon gain the first houses. The men of his own Section were soon battering their way in, through doors and windows, but he heard no sounds of conflict. However, the six that comprised the files of Davey and Saunders, having gained entry through smashed window shutters, were not surprised to find the lower rooms of their house empty, Saunders speaking the obvious.

"Fire a volley and then get off to a better position, further back. From now, we're in files, they'll be waiting."

Wasting no more time, Davey ran to the back door and trained his Baker to any likely French firing position. He saw none, so then he nodded. Miles ran out and took position at the corner of the back alley to peer forward up the main road. When he was satisfied, Pike ran out into the road to kneel in a doorway, taking cover just as a French bullet smacked into the porch wall behind him. Miles fired at the window from where the smoke issued forth, then he reloaded, kneeling, whilst Davey came to the corner and, standing above him, fired into the same window. When both were reloaded, Davey called across the street.

"Joe?"

The reply came across.

"Clear."

Covered by Pike, both ran forward together to find their own cover, Davey a porch, Miles a plain doorway which he had to kick in. Then all three trained their weapons down the street. A hundred yards up, two Frenchmen emerged running from a doorway, their red Tirailleur epaulettes bouncing as they ran. All three fired and one fell to lie still and the other stumbled, to then limp on and disappear. The three reloaded and then, during that, Saunders, Byford and Bailey continued the advance, filing carefully on, each, when exposed out in the open, always under the protection of the other two.

Meanwhile, Ellis and Bettridge were at the Church, kneeling in the road beneath a house wall that was part of a street into the Church Square.

"Why just us sent in, Sergeant? Why not the whole Battalion?"

"Because the Frogs, just like any other army, will have cannon further back in the village and a whole Battalion, crowded in a street, is a perfect target. Sir. A few skirmishers, like us, b'ain't worth it."

"So, what do you think, Sergeant?"

Ellis only had eyes for the single opening at the top of the belfry, but there was a row of six open windows below the roof line of the main structure, with another seven below on the next floor down. There were two open windows at ground level and two shut doors.

"What I think, Sir, is that there could be one, maybe two of 'em, in each of those windows and as soon as we cross this square, they loose off, bringing down as many of us as possible, then shin down the stairs and make off."

He looked up to the upper storey of the house to his right, the windows open and he knew who was in there.

"George! Anything?"

The reply came down from George Fearnley, Sergeant of Two Company.

"Nothing! But that don't mean nothing."

Bettridge was stood just behind.

"What choice do we have, Sergeant, but to charge across."

Ellis turned angrily back to him.

"If it's like I say, Sir, and likely, you charge across that space and you stand to lose half the Section."

Bettridge could only reply weakly.

"It's our duty."

Ellis was now angrier than ever and exhaustion and impatience got the better of him.

"You can charge across, Sir, the rest of us will do this like we've been trained! These lads is too quality and valuable to be wasted on a mad caper like that!"

Ellis again looked up at the upper windows of the house to his right.

"George. How many you got up there?"

"Dozen! More down below."

"Get some fire through those windows! Make 'em think we're coming over."

As Fearnley's men opened fire, Ellis turned to Bettridge, him totally at a loss, now that what he had taken to be a direct order had been ignored.

"What do you know about Catholic Churches, Sir? Where's the door most likely to be in these churches of theirs? Sometimes at the side?"

Bettridge stared back puzzled, but Ellis repeated the question, but in a different form.

"Where's the door? Far end or side?"

"Far end, Sergeant, almost certainly. Opposite the Altar"

"And where's that, here, Sir?"

Bettridge thought for a second.

"Well, on the right, the back wall's a curve. That for the altar, I would imagine."

"Right, Sir, then I take it that your orders are that we drop back down this road, get left and come at the Church from the left. Sir! Where there's likely to be a door."

Bettridge nodded and Ellis turned and then ran back down the street.

"You lot, with me!"

Over 20 men of the Section followed, Bettridge with them and they found a long alleyway, took it, then into a space between two houses which brought them to a street, from the end of which they could see a door into the Church. Fearnley's men were still sending accurate fire through the windows of the side they could no longer see, as Ellis peered around the corner.

"There's still windows on this side, but a shorter run to that door, which looks like the main one. In there, they'll know we ran back and they'll be worried and, with a decent Officer, they'll have put two and two together and decided a way to make life difficult."

He peered around the left corner, to see a house with windows that overlooked the space they now had to cross. He reached behind for the crossbelts of the nearest man and pulled him up, a Chosen Man.

"Brigstock! See that house? Get in there and clear any Johnnies from the windows."

He turned again and pointed to three more.

"Thomas, Evans, Hamlin. Go with him."

The four turned the corner, ran and crashed into the house. Musket fire spluttered from the church windows around the door, but the four ran on, so that, within a minute, they heard three shots, then Brigstock was waving from an upstairs window, which Ellis acknowledged.

"All clear to our left. So! What are your orders, Sir?"

Bettridge swallowed hard.

"Are the men loaded?"

"They are, Sir."

Bettridge raised his sword to his shoulder.

"Then over we go!"

He led the run across what was only a wide road. Shots came from the same Church windows as before and one man stumbled, then they were at the door. It opened easily and Ellis knew why.

"Open for an easy get-out."

As Bettridge took a step forward, Ellis put his arm across to bar his entry and he turned to the nearest three men.

"Barnes! Dunnidge! Michaels! You at the door. Barnes you stood, Dunnidge crouched, Michaels kneeling. Soon as this door opens, fire. If you sees a Crapaud, fire at him, if not fire anyway. Get some smoke in there."

The three took position, Ellis pushed open the door and the three fired, for the rest to rush in through the smoke. Inside were a dozen French stood on the galleries at the windows and the Baker rifles spoke and most were felled, two quickly throwing down their weapons. Ellis then looked at a small doorway to their left, through which could be seen some stairs.

"Right, Sir. Now for the Tower."

Ellis turned to his three.

"You reloaded?"

Two nodded as the third returned his ramrod to the guides.

"Right!"

He crept forward, followed by Bettridge and the three, to enter the door and look up. All that could be seen was the next landing, the view up the tower blocked by the ongoing flights of stairs. Bettridge felt he should contribute in some way.

"Fix bayonets?"

"No Sir, just cocked and ready!"

"As you say. So go on."

"Sir. You are the Officer. Go on don't sit well. Come on is better!"

Apprehension crossed Bettridge's face, but, nevertheless, he stepped around Ellis and began to climb the stairs.

"Sir. Your pistol. Check it first."

Bettridge pulled out the pistol from his waistband, a high-quality duelling pistol, and checked the priming, before fully pulling back the hammer. He then resumed his climb, Ellis' Baker rifle at his shoulder. The climb required three flights of stairs before they came to the fourth and last, which led back and up to their left. Bettridge turned the corner onto the small landing and looked up to see a moustachioed face and a shako with a yellow tassel, but he saw the face before he saw the musket pointing at him. Ellis, however, had seen the weapon first and he shoved Bettridge over against the wall with his Baker rifle, just as the Voltiguer fired, the noise deafening in the narrow stairway. The ball smacked into the plaster wall behind, then Ellis fired and, beyond the smoke, they heard a body slump down. Another Voltiguer came hurtling down through the smoke, bayonet extended, mouth wide. Bettridge lifted his pistol and fired, and the man, now hit, lost his footing and crashed into the same plaster wall. Bettridge looked down, saw the man choke up two gouts of blood and then fully slump down. He stared at him, the first man he had killed, but now Ellis was up the stairs, followed by Barnes and Dunnidge. Michaels stopped and looked at Bettridge.

"Sir? You alright, Sir?"

Bettridge nodded, although he was near to swooning and so Michaels remained there with him.

"Him or you, Sir!"

Michaels expected Bettridge to lead and he did manage to move, placing a foot on the first step to

then hear shouts from above,

"Je me rends! Je me rends!"

Then came Ellis' harsh tones.

"Surrender do you? Frog bastard! And how many did you hope to get

before you turned it in? Murderin' Crapaud shite-auk!"

Bettridge and Michaels had no chance to climb further before a Voltiguer was hauled out of the doorway above by Ellis, his shako knocked off and then hurled down the stairs to collide painfully with the plaster wall. As he tried to raise himself, pushing down on the body of his dead comrade, Ellis had by now fixed his bayonet and was advancing down the stairs, his face a picture of fury. The Voltiguer finally got to his feet and raised his hands in supplication, convinced he was going to be bayoneted.

"Non! Non! Ne me tuez pas! Je me suis rendu. S'il vous plait, j'ai des enfants."

However, Ellis used his bayonet to indicate that he should move downstairs and the man gratefully began his descent, as rapid as he could, whilst taking anxious looks behind him at the point of Ellis' bayonet, either threateningly close or reassuringly pointing at the ceiling. Once back down in the Knave of the Church, the two Frenchmen who had earlier surrendered were stood forlorn, having been stripped of everything except their uniform. The brandy and food they did have was being shared out between some members of Two Section. Bettridge and Ellis immediately stepped outside the Church to see Shakeshaft and One Section emerging from the streets and alleyways nearby and Shakeshaft went immediately up to Bettridge.

"All's well, Luttrel?"

Bettridge nodded, as then did Shakeshaft, before replying.

"We hold here. This is the edge of the village. We wait for the Brigade and there's the 48th anyway."

The 48th Light Company were entering the village from the right and they were not long waiting before Carr, O'Hare and Heaviside appeared around the Church corner, Carr smiling when he saw the pair stood safe and sound.

"Village cleared and no cannon?"

Both nodded.

"Right! Back in column and forward. We've seen the last act, at least on our side of this affair."

oOo

The last act was beginning elsewhere, alongside the Zadorra to the North of Vitoria and it promised to play out as a prolonged and very bloody affair, the reason being given by Cavalry G. Anson himself, speaking to Collins and Johnson, just downstream of the bridge.

"The Frogs are desperate to keep the main road open out of Vitoria and onto San Sebastian and France. By all accounts there's any amount of booty and treasure on the far side of Vitoria that they want to get away."

The evidence of desperate resistance was not far away. The French Battalions that had defended the bridge to hold Oswald over in Gamara Mayor were, with the river on their right, conducting a controlled and effective withdrawal against the increasing numbers of Allied troops crossing over from Gamarra Mayor. At that moment, Graham himself arrived, having ridden straight up from the bridge at Abechuco.

"Anson get yours down right, towards the city. Colville, Grant an' Vandeleur are all comin' forward and they'll need cavalry support. Johnny's nae finished in these parts. For one, there's plenty left in thone village over yonder, Ariaga's the name and Howards 1st will soon be pushing at it from the Abechuco side, closin' the gap between it and the bridge."

He pointed to a substantial village immediately in line with Abechuco bridge, but half a mile to the South. The smoke and noise around it spoke of fierce fighting, so plainly the French were determined to hold the village for as long as possible, this to allow substantial groups of French troops to retreat up past it to the South, that way still open. With no more than that, Graham turned his horse to ride back over Gamarra Major bridge, leaving Anson and Collins to look for Colville's men plus any other Allied Infantry Brigades and what to do to obey

Graham's orders. Tavender was nearby and what he saw added to the confusion, him looking in the direction of Vitoria, this being South and to the left.

"Sir! French cavalry!"

Both Anson and Collins looked to where Tavender was pointing and in that direction they saw a massed front of at least four Regiments, supported by a full battery of field-artillery. Anson rose in his stirrups to look both ways several times, both to the French cavalry and to Ariaga. Then he used his telescope, to soon snap it shut, a worried look now on his face.

"Heavy Dragoons, sent to cover his infantry as they retreat, with artillery in support."

Johnson, meanwhile, was studying the infantry hurrying out of Ariaga and not only infantrymen.

"Sir, they're leaving and abandoning their artillery around the village."

Now both Anson and Johnson turned to see French gunners riding off on team horses, leaving their guns abandoned, alone and forlorn on the level plain. Anson turned back to the French cavalry.

"Well, that's one problem done with. At least on that side."

Anson then resumed his studying of present events, all the while considering what the possibilities were for the future. Having made up his mind, he turned to Collins.

"I'll not take on all that cavalry in a straight contest. Not with their artillery ready to enfilade any advance we make before we even get there. If Graham's right and there's three Brigades coming at that Ariaga place, those Dragoons will come forward to help their infantry get away. That'll be our chance to make a nuisance of ourselves, then the guns can't hit us without hitting their own. If you do go, Collins, you hit and pull back. If those Dragoons know we're here on their flank, they can't ignore it, some will come to oppose us, so there'll be less on our infantry. That's all to the good! Our worry is that after taking that Ariaga, ours'll be broken up when they come out and easy meat for Dragoons! If that looks likely, we go forward."

He then turned and fixed Collins with a fierce stare.

"I want your men under total control, Collins, you hear me? Total control and two Squadrons at a time. Get involved when the French are all broken up. I'll say the same to Stockton for his 12th."

With that, he rode over to the 12th Light Dragoons nearby, leaving Collins and Johnson to ponder how and when to carry out their orders. Naming names was a start, so Collins turned to his Captains nearby.

"Tavender and Oakwood, yours first. Myers, Forden, in support."

He turned to regard the Dragoons.

"If we go at all!"

As he spoke, the French Dragoons came forward, one long line, but with the ground to the far side of Ariaga as their objective. Collins then used his telescope.

"There's many of our infantry on the far side of that village, where those Johnnies are going. Whoever's running this for them, he sees that as a bigger threat than anything up here. 1st Division's pushing forward from Abechuco across the river and there's more of ours coming up from further downstream to join them. There's no way past Ariaga on this side, but if Colville or whatever can get past that village on the far side, the Johnnies in there will be cut off. That's the job for those heavy Dragoons, to stop that."

At that moment, Tavender spoke out, clearly impatient and very unhappy with what was proposed.

"Sir, should we not simply charge the French right? Two whole Regiments, us and the 12th, onto their flank would see the thing done, Sir. We could be accused of rank cowardice!"

Collins did not even trouble to lower his telescope.

"That's a big word, Captain, but you heard Anson's orders and I believe he has the right of it. We are outnumbered perhaps five to one by heavy cavalry and exposed to a whole field-battery if we move from here. If in trouble, the infantry can take care of themselves by forming square and when those Dragoons retire from trying that, broken up, then we do what we can do. We'll at least be partially masked from those damn guns by scattered Dragoons. It makes more sense to worry them from their flank, than mount some idiot charge,"

Collins closed his telescope and turned to Johnson.

"Right, as I've said. One and Two first, Three and Four Second. Each Squadron in two ranks, one Troop behind the other."

Each Captain then turned his horse to organise his men, but Tavender plainly remained annoyed and frustrated. Once in formation, it was Anson himself who led them forward, the 12th adopting the same formation as the 16th on their left As they walked their horses forward, the scene to the South of Ariaga came more into view, but then a single French round-shot bounced several times across the turf before them, meaning they were still out of range and their ranks opened up to allow it through. However, Allied infantry columns were now advancing forward on the far side of Ariaga, so then at least two of the French Dragoon Regiments accelerated into a charge. Carr, out before Three Troop, had just enough time to see the leading Redcoat Battalion form square, then all was just a picture of smoke, dust and confusion. Carr looked across and saw that Tavender was still in a state of high agitation, rising frequently in his stirrups, his right hand opening and closing as he held his reins. Carr now looked forward to see the French Dragoons falling back from a square still intact, but other Dragoon Squadrons came charging in, plainly against infantry, but these he could not see because of the dust and swirling horsemen.

The French cavalry Brigadier had by now seen Anson's two Regiments approaching and had detached two of his own to swing to their right, halt and confront Anson's, who then held up his sword for his own men to halt. Another French roundshot hit the turf and, at the first bounce, sailed over their heads off the hard ground. Carr saw the impact, then turned to Oakwood.

"Will Anson charge?"

Oakwood continued to look forward.

"It's a nice decision, but were I him, I would not. There's that artillery and we've pulled two Regiments away and the infantry can take care of themselves. There's too many of ours coming up past that village and, in squares if needs be, they'll give that cavalry a mauling then advance on. The Johnnies'll pull back soon, they'll have to."

However, Anson was now pointing his sword forward, continuing only at a walk to slowly close the gap between his own Brigade and the waiting and potent French Dragoons. A third roundshot now hummed above their heads, but within two minutes Oakwood was proved correct. All French Dragoon Battalions began to pull back from Ariaga and finally the two opposing Anson used their right reins to turn and match the retreat, riding back to their guns, which were now being limbered up to their horse-teams. Further action by these French 'heavies' was now unnecessary; all French infantry were out of Ariaga and hurrying along within their own protective cavalry. Anson now rode across to Collins for a better view and, close to Oakwood and Carr, he used his telescope, his face now bearing a deep frown.

"There's something daft happening on the far side!"

Collins drew his own telescope, as did Carr and Oakwood and what they saw was a mere two Squadrons of their own Light Cavalry galloping up from Vitoria to attack the combined mass of French Dragoons and infantry. Within a minute, one of the two Regiments of Dragoons that had been opposed to Anson's Brigade, had swung right and charged the two Squadrons, four against two. Anson raised his sword.

"Collins!"

Anson spurred his horse into a canter and the 16th followed. Carr saw the Dragoons hit the Light cavalry and soon it was apparent that the conflict was moving in their favour, the British Light Cavalry were being driven backwards. Anson spurred his horse into a gallop and within seconds they had hit the rear ranks of the Dragoons, but they had faced about and met the charge. The two lines met with shouts and yells from the men, the clash of steel on steel and the screams of the horses. Carr's mount crashed into the shoulder of a Dragoon's and their blades met to slide up to the hand-guard. Their faces came together, merely inches apart, the unshaven face of the Dragoon showing bared teeth and narrowed eyes under the dull brass of his helmet. Then their horses continued past each other and Carr could only take a swing at the Dragoon's back, but it was a poor connection as they continued apart. With that, he was onto the Dragoons assaulting the Light Cavalry and he came up behind one, stood up in his stirrups and brought his sabre down heavily on the Dragoon's neck, cutting into the cloth of the collar beneath the helmet. Then he was past and amongst the Light Cavalry they were there to rescue, but all was a melee of whirling horses and slashing sabres. A trumpet sounded and all Dragoons turned away, many sending a final sabre slash at any who thought to pursue, then all was quiet, save panting horses and some groaning men. They had come to the aid, perhaps even rescued, two Squadrons of the 15th Hussars, cavalry wholly unsuited to a combat with Heavy Dragoons. Many 15th Hussars were sat on their horses in a state of shock, they had lost several men, but Carr was not able to wait for any verbal exchange, Baxter was calling out to him.

"Sir! That's recall."

Carr had not heard the notes of the bugle, but the 16th were now disengaging from the Hussars and forming up to return to where the 12th were, these some way behind, but they had come forward in support as soon as the 16th charged forward. The Brigade quickly reformed and followed the French, the 16th and the 12th now riding side by side in column of Squadrons. Soon Gamarra Mayor bridge came back into view over on their left, Oswald's men now fully across the river and advancing, their erstwhile opponents now matching the retreat of the whole French army and moving Eastwards. Anson continued to lead his cavalry Brigade in that direction, at a gentle trot, observing Oswald's men pushing forward into any gap in the French loose and therefore very ineffective defensive line. At that moment Graham came riding up to halt at Anson and many 16th Officers trotted across to hear, including Collins, Johnson and Oakwood.

"Ah'm pulling Oswald's out, they've takken a beatin'. You take over an' push those Johnnies on, as best ye can. Howard's First is coming up from Abechuco, two Brigades; Stopford's Guards and Halkett's KGL. If any afore ye stand, they'll soon be up tae support!"

Oakwood looked over to see that Oswald's men were, indeed, disengaging, so he looked behind to see a Redcoat column in the distance, advancing menacingly up from Abechuco bridge, then both he and Johnson rode back to the 16th, their position now on the far right of Anson's line, where Carr and Peterson were waiting at Two Squadron. Johnson rode on to Three, leaving Oakwood to pass on what he knew, speaking of what he had heard and then from what he could see, now up ahead.

"We're now the pursuit, with a Division following, but this lot are still together. Not beaten, not by a long chalk."

The French, formed into loose columns, having now moved away from the bank of the Zadorra, had entered the space between two areas of woodland and Anson had no choice but to follow and so they entered the clearing, now marked by many badly wounded Frenchmen who could go no further. They rode past many scattered and despairing men, several of whom managed to haul themselves over the ground to avoid the oncoming cavalry. The Brigade emerged into the open and Peterson called out to Oakwood, putting into words the concern that they all thought.

"You've the right of it, Sir. This isn't over!"

The thought was obvious, because the French Heavy Dragoons of earlier, were now forming up across Anson's path, plainly to cover the retreating French infantry. In response, Anson led forward the 12th to form a line of four Squadrons and Collins ordered his own 16th into two columns of two squadrons each. As the 16th maintained a walk forward behind the 12th, Anson led the 12th into a strong canter, then a full charge. The clash as the two lines met along the full length was almost sickening, fierce and brutal, the screams of horses and then men, the clash of steel on steel, then the continuous rise and fall of swords and sabres. The 16th continued to walk forward, but the conflict before them remained on the same ground, plainly the heavier French Dragoons had held the charge and, in some places, were forcing the 12th back. Collins raised his sword and, at that signal, all his Regiment drew theirs, the eerie scrape heard above the noise of the conflict some 200 yards before them. He pointed his sword forward and the walk soon became a trot, then a strong canter. In two columns, the 16th were more of a wedge and they rode into any gaps between the horses of the 12th and pushed others forward with the impetus of their charge. The result had more in common with a rugby field, because the extra weight of the 16th against the centre of the Dragoon line began to tell and there they were forced back. The 16th, with the now reinforced 12th, urged their horses forward, with furious but ineffective sword blows being exchanged at the point of contact. However, eventually the horses of the Dragoons gave way and the line was broken, but French bugles were already sounding and the hard-pressed French horsemen turned all along the line and sped away.

It was plain that they had performed the task given them, because two, steady French infantry squares were revealed, formed up to cover the ongoing retreat, one behind the other. Now without opponents, the 12th and 16th halted on the ground just won, staring at the solid French infantry, the nearest square with the Regimental Eagle in the centre. Anson was nowhere to be seen, nor Collins, Stockton of the 12th, nor Johnson, each Captain now needing to control the men around them. This gave Tavender the licence he sought, especially when some Cacadores arrived, a Section at least, and they began exchanging fire with the first square. Convinced that this square would soon break and fall back, Tavender raised his sword.

"One Squadron! With me!"

He spurred his horse forward and many followed, both 12th and 16th, all heady with their success against the Dragoons. Baxter was close by to Carr, plainly aghast at what he was seeing.

"Oh God. Ned! Do something."

The Ned he referred to was One Squadron's Sergeant Shelby and they saw him ride across the path of three men, but that was the limit of what he could do. The square, in the standard three ranks, were plainly veteran and remained steady and waiting, the front ranks kneeling with bayonets outstretched, the two behind with muskets at the 'make ready". Soon those of the second rank came down to level and they heard the order, "Deuxieme rang. Tirez!". The volley was delivered with perfect timing and many horses and men fell, merely yards from the square. The charge was halted by the one volley and those still alive and still mounted were shocked back into their senses and turned away. More Cacadores were now arriving, having run to maintain contact with the retreating enemy and French soldiers began to fall more regularly, so at that point, the squares began to move, holding formation but retiring back. Then they broke into a hollow column to enable them to march quicker, but still holding a strong formation, almost as formidable as a square. Anson finally emerged, but remained stationary on his horse. Baxter had watched all and felt no need to hold back his admiration for the French.

"Tidy lads, those. Credit to them for that!"

However, Ned Shelby had dismounted and was walking amongst the Light Dragoon casualties, most of whom were from his own Squadron. He came to one body, turned it over and then looked back at Collins.

"Captain Tavender, Sir. He's dead!"

Collins did no more than shake his head twice, then half turn in his saddle.

"Smythe! Are you still alive?"

An answer came from the disordered ranks.

"Yes Sir. Still alive."

"One Squadron's yours."

With no more words, Anson led his Brigade forward, all Squadrons from both Regiments forming as they rode, following the retreating French. They rode on for almost four miles, each yard showing the signs of a beaten army, wounded, dead and dying, and abandoned equipment. At the first village they came to, Anson halted his men, as daylight failed he decided that he and his men had had enough, the French had passed on and gone, there would be no more action that day. As usual, the citizens came out of the trees and hills and did their best to be hospitable to the 600 and more Light Dragoons, all weary and many battered and wounded, but most simply slept whilst the citizens gave thanks for returning to an intact village, not one that had just been fought over. However, there was one last act performed by some of those of Two Squadron as led by Sergeant Baxter and augmented by French brandy. Baxter raised his beaker to his three comrades, Makepeace, Spivey and Nunney.

"Here's to the memory of Captain Lucius Tavender. Him now no more than that! A bad memory and that soon forgotten!"

oOo

In the same dying light, South of Vitoria, the 105th were marching through a scene that swung from high farce pantomime to drunken riot. The centre Divisions of the Allied army, plus many from the ridge above, plus cavalry now dismounted, had come up to the French baggage park, almost all of which had failed to escape and remained stranded across many acres. In places there were soldiers dancing with joy at the riches they were now able to stuff into knapsacks and backpacks, whilst elsewhere others fought over barrels of brandy or plate and goblets of precious metal. The whole scene was one of cavorting tumult, soldiers throwing anywhere all that did not meet their ambitions for drink and gold and in any direction. All accompanied by angry shouts of warning and challenge as they scrambled over and into every kind of cart and transport, from the meanest farm cart to the best-appointed carriage. Amidst the confusion of pillaging Allied soldiers, Spanish civilians were garnering their share, but also there were trapped and abandoned French Followers, some well-dressed Officers wives and their families. Many others also making most of the chance of pillage were Allied Followers of one quality or another. The noise was tremendous, the shouts of triumph and anger, amid the screams of the frantic women. Men such as Byford were reminded of early Medieval paintings showing Heaven or Hell, but here there was no order as for a conceived and carefully composed painting, all was an uncontrolled and frantic scramble of crowded soldiery and civilians, all fighting and searching to make the most of the chance for riches they could only dream of.

To such as Gibney, Ellis, Nicholls and Hill, the threat to the 105th was obvious and with their Officers, they strode up and down the marching ranks of the 105th, fixing with malevolent stares any man whose eyes dwelt too long on the free-for-all for loot that existed but yards away, RSM Gibney's voice prominent amongst many.

"If any of thee fancies tha' chances in that lot, there, tha' can get that clean out of tha' brains and remember who tha' belongs to. Tha's 105th! An' there's none better! Tha' wears the green an' that counts. Tha' saw the Guards holding all out of Vitoria, back there, so they can be trusted not to fall apart, and so can thee! Hold tha' ranks an' march on!"

At the rear, in the final Company, Tom Miles and Len Bailey could barely contain themselves, but Ethan Ellis had fixed both with a baleful stare and continued to do so as they marched on. However, John Byford was in a different state of agitation as he looked across at the chaos of pillage and destruction and so he broke ranks and ran up to Lieutenant Shakeshaft at the head of the Company.

"Sir! There's paintings, works of art, being thrown around like, like, bits of old carpet! Many are priceless, Sir. By great painters!"

Shakeshaft turned to look at him and saw the desperate concern in his face, but Byford had more to say.

"Sir! We should rescue what we can, otherwise they'll just be destroyed, burnt, used on campfires, trampled to nothing. Sir!"

Shakeshaft then moved out of the column and looked back. He was a literary man himself and had more than a little sympathy for Byford's anxiety.

"Sarn't Ellis! Take Byford here and twelve men and rescue the paintings that's worrying him. Paintings only! Get what you can."

Ellis was appalled. He and all other Sergeants had been doing their utmost to prevent their 105th from falling apart into a looting mob and here was Shakeshaft ordering exactly that, to allow some to enter the madness, albeit to rescue paintings, not to gather plunder, but to enter that sea of temptation! By now Shakeshaft was back within the column and so Ellis turned on the cause of his own anxiety.

"Byford! What's all this?"

"Paintings, Sarn't, back there. Works by great artists, centuries old, being thrown around and trodden into nothing."

Ellis' expression became an uncomprehending frown, and so Byford continued.

"Looted from Spanish palaces and whatever, many back there and being damaged, even destroyed! Trampled into the dirt! We should do what we can and get them to safety, as many as we can. It's up to us, if we are not to be condemned by those coming after us, instead of being praised for the effort and trouble we took. We had the chance, yet we did nothing!"

Such high-flown sentiments had but a minor impact on Ellis, but an order was an order, yet Ellis was staring daggers at Byford.

"Right, you with me! Saunders! Follow me and Byford with a dozen. Orders! To go back and sort him out, him and his paintings. Then we've got find the Regiment after that, God help us."

Saunders had heard all and was as bemused as Ellis, but he called out the next three files of the Section. Miles and Bailey were not in the last three, but they sidled out anyway as Byford hurried off, with Ellis alongside. It was Byford who led the way, running to the point where he had seen the paintings scattered onto the ground. It was not long before they arrived and Byford picked up the first stack he came to and propped them against a cart, brushing off the dirt and examining them for damage. It needed no deduction to realise that they had come out of that particular sturdy cart, such as was used for moving furniture and he climbed in to find several more stacks, each of perhaps a dozen paintings. Saunders, Davey, Pike and Solomon climbed in with him, Solomon hurling back a first, then a second Scotsman, both of whom had a deep interest in what such a large and well-appointed vehicle could contain. Davey took one look at Byford, who was busy examining the collection, all stood on edge at the back of the wagon.

"John! Forget all your mooning over how wonderful they are! Get them off this cart, then we'll have to find something smaller to get them out."

There was another similar wagon behind and Ellis had led more men over the side to himself pick up a painting, to then study the subject and become increasingly puzzled as to its worth, but this one and the many others in the wagon were then carefully passed over the side to waiting hands.

Meanwhile, Miles and Bailey had taken themselves elsewhere.

"Tom! What about Byford and his paintings? Ellis might see we're gone!"

"Forget that! There's enough worrying over them as don't need our help. We ain't got much time. I'm for that carriage there, the one with the fancy painting on the door."

The 'fancy painting', as described, was the crest of a titled French General, Eugene Casimir-Villatte. Miles bounded over to the carriage and pulled open the door, which opened easily. The door opposite was closed, all to the good he thought, but his attention was soon drawn to a bound chest and an open box full of silver plate and religious chalices. He quickly rejected these as being too big to carry and conceal, so he concentrated on the chest, which was frustratingly padlocked, the flats bolted to the wood.

"Len! Look around for something heavy, or some tools in the back of this thing!"

Bailey, right behind him, scuttled off to see what could be found, meanwhile Miles examined the box of plate again, but scowled as he was forced to reject all as being too big. He then worked the padlock angrily, but alongside the box with the chalices he had noticed that there were two or three of exactly what he needed to save his neck, or more likely his back, from Ellis. Then Bailey came back with an iron bar and a small mallet. It needed a very frustrating pair of minutes to hammer away the plate under the lock, but then it was done and the lock was prised away and the lid opened. The chest was full of Spanish doubloons, 'pieces of eight', a large, heavy coin, but coin all the same and the gold still bright. No more words were needed as both scooped handfuls of coins into pockets and knapsacks, many spilling onto the floor of the coach. Then the far doorway opened and a face appeared, its chin framed in the pale-yellow facings of the 88th and speaking in a heavy Irish accent.

"And just what would you have here then, boys? Would you be thinking of keeping such as this all to yourselves, now?"

Miles stared back with pure hatred, but sense prevailed in the urgency of the moment.

"Paddy! There's no time nor need to fight over this. There's enough for all. You take what you can and so shall we. Agreed?"

The Connaught Ranger smiled, revealing yellow teeth and so Miles dwelt not at all on the sincerity of the grin, but, along with Bailey, he finished filling to the absolute his own pockets, knapsack and many into his backpack. Then Miles found a dead Frenchman, pulled off his backpack, went back into the carriage and filled that, until the weight of that was too great. Bailey did the same with a French knapsack. That done, Miles gave the Ranger a swift glance as he continued to gather handfuls for himself, then he backed out of the carriage, Bailey with him. The others, now in possession of a small cart, were about to leave, pushing and pulling at the vehicle, this now containing too many paintings to count. Miles and Bailey followed, but soon it was clear that the heavy coins in their pockets and elsewhere were very obvious, bulging and swinging whilst they walked. Miles came up to the rear of the cart.

"John! Joe! Zeke! Drop back."

They did and Miles immediately opened the pockets and knapsacks of both and began transferring coins, whilst they continued to move the cart. Bailey called back Solomon and Turner and began to do the same with them, spreading the burden to avoid Ellis' suspicions, who was at the front pushing all miscreants out of the way with his rifle. Joe Pike was not at all happy to be a part of retaining stolen money.

"Tom, this is robbery!"

"Shut up! Even the Officers is joining in. If we don't have it, somebody else will and we'll still be poor and they'll be rich. I wants it the other way around!"

The coins were ladled out from the pockets and knapsacks and spread around as best they were able. The French backpack and knapsack were secreted under the stacked paintings. Just in time, because Ellis had noticed the commotion at the rear of the cart and hurried back.

"Miles! Bailey! Where you bin?"

Miles immediately, and in triumph, pulled out of his tunic the rolls he had found in the coach alongside the plate box; paintings cut from their frames and rolled up.

"Rescuin' these! Not all is still in their frames. I'd say these is worth the trouble, too!"

Ellis could only scowl and fume, but the rolls were, indeed, works of art.

"Right, now get your backs onto this cart. We've a Battalion to catch up to."

The cart proved to be a useful vehicle and the road was clear, very much due to the temptations that existed on either side and they sped along, all in buoyant mood, Byford because of the rescue of so much artistic heritage and the rest from the weight of the Spanish 'pieces of eight' in their pockets, haversacks and in the cart itself. Their speed was such that they caught up with another vehicle, the contents of which were much more mournful. It contained several of the 105th wounded, all gathered up and driven by Chaplain's Assistant Sedgwicke, who had followed the 105th on its progress across the battlefield. Ellis and Saunders caught up with it and looked at those inside, Saunders seeing him first.

"Captain Drake! Sergeant, there's Captain Drake."

Ellis climbed up the outside of the cart using one of the many horizontal bracing-struts along the side.

"Sir! Sir! Can you hear me?"

Drake managed a quarter turn of his body and a half turn of his head.

"Ellis? Saunders?"

"Sir, we thought you'd been right knocked over when we crossed that bridge. The Battalion is just up ahead, so we'll get George Fearnley back, Sir. He's as good with bullets as any Surgeon and he'll get to you quicker. You just hang on, Sir, and we'll get you seen to."

The athlete Pike was sent running after the Battalion and minutes later George Fearnley was climbing into the cart, to open Drake's tunic and ease away the dressings. He made an examination, then looked up at Drake and his face wore a frown.

"I'd say the bullet was still in there, Sir, judging by the size of the wound. Had it glanced off, there'd be more bruising. Sorry Sir."

Drake managed a weak smile.

"Nothing to be sorry for, Sergeant. My own silly fault for being so far out in front."

"Well, Sir, if you'll allow me, Sir, I'll give it a try. To get the ball out."

Saunders was close alongside.

"He's done plenty, Sir. He got a ball out of Mr. Rushby's shoulder after Maida and one out of Tom Miles' leg after Talavera and one out of Byford's shoulder after Foo-Entez, Sir. And others besides!"

Drake was too weak to weigh the good or bad in the choice between Fearnley and the 105th's Surgeon and so he nodded, then slumped back.

When both carts arrived at the 105th's area, after not too many enquiries as to where, on both sides of the way in they found fires lit and cooking in progress. Sedgwicke steered the cart to the camps of Deakin and Halfway and then Drake was carefully lifted out of the cart by at least eight willing hands and laid out beside the fire on a blanket. Nellie and Bridie immediately hurried over, Nellie the first and she wiped his face from dirt and perspiration

"Mr. Drake, your Honour, 'tis The Blessing that you're still alive. We'll get you some water and then some broth, so we will, then off to the Surgeon, where I'm sure you'll be taken well care of and soon up and about and right as rain!"

Zeke Saunders was kneeling close by.

"No, Nellie. He stays here and George is going to try to get out the bullet. He'll be at it quicker than the Surgeon and I don't see as there'll be too much difference between what George can do and Surgeon Pearce."

He looked up.

"George?"

Fearnley now knelt down beside Drake and examined the wound again.

"It's got to come out now, Sir. 'T'as been in there some time, perhaps with cloth took in and so we're now in the time for infection."

In between sips of water, given by Nellie, Drake lifted his head.

"I'm in your hands, Sergeant."

Fearnley then looked up, looking for Tom Miles, him at that moment tipping his coins into what had become known as the 'mess chest'.

"Tom, you remember when John took a bullet at Foo-Entez. You got two reverse-clamps. I needs two now."

Miles tipped in the last from his tunic pocket and ran off to the centre of the 105th's ground, where the Headquarters and, more importantly, the Surgeon's tent was, in which Surgeon Pearce was already working and expected to be working throughout the night. He ran inside, looked for the rack of instruments, saw what he needed and seized two from the array. A Surgeon's Assistant moved to bar his way, but Miles went right up to him and thrust the clamps up to his face.

"These is for Captain Drake. If anyone objects, see the Colonel!"

With that he sprinted out of the tent doorway. Meanwhile, Fearnley was cleaning the wound with brandy, which Drake soon detected by the aroma.

"Can I have some of that?"

Fearnley gave him the flask.

"As much as you like, Sir."

Drake swallowed three good mouthfuls, but the next object to arrive at his lips was the wooden gag.

"We have to put this in, Sir, to stop you swallowing your tongue, but I'm sure you knows that well enough."

"Yes, Sergeant, but I'll have another pull at that brandy first."

With all in place, Fearnley reached across for his knife and Bridie handed it to him from the boiling water on the fire.

"Sir. I'm going to have to cut between the ribs, so's I can prise them open."

A curt nod from Drake and the cut was made either side of the entrance wound. Drake's fists clamped together, but his body did not move, being pinned down by Saunders and Solomon. With the cut made, Fearnley eased open the sides of the wound, then Esme arrived.

"I can help. I was an Orderly in a hospital."

She had brought clean, damp cloths with her and she wiped away the blood, then Fearnley looked again.

"Your top rib is cracked, Sir, but not broke. No bad thing when the clamps go in, it'll ease over a bit further."

At that point the two clamps arrived, handed down to Fearnley immediately by a breathless Tom Miles and the clamps were inserted, the screws turned and both ribs prised apart, Fearnley watching the cracked rib intently should it break completely. Whilst Solomon and Saunders held Drake down as the agony returned, Nellie mopped his perspiring brow.

"There now, your Honour Captain Drake, Sir, 'twill soon be over, so it will, and George here will have that nasty ball out of you in a trice."

Fearnley now had a probe in his hand which terminated with a small hook.

"That was the worst of it, Sir. This will sting, but not be too bad."

Saunders looked at Drake, then at Fearnley.

"I think he's fainted!"

"All to the good!"

Fearnley eased in the probe and pulled it down from one end of the cut to the other, an inch down which revealed nothing so then he searched deeper . The probe stopped midway, so Fearnley took his forceps and eased them down alongside the probe, closed them and grinned as they did not close fully. He eased all up and out to see the ball between the ends of the forceps. Deakin was a keen observer and he was not the last to slap Fearnley on the back.

"Well done, George. Neat and proper job!"

Fearnley smiled and dropped the ball onto some cloth..

"Not quite over yet!"

Whilst Esme wiped away more blood, he reinserted the probe with the hook turned in the direction of movement. Once, twice and for a third time he searched the wound, the third time bringing out a sliver of wool and he stared at it, as though it were an offending recruit.

"I'd say that's now done!"

He tipped more brandy into the wound and Drake groaned and opened his eyes. Nellie picked up the ball.

"There now, Sir. George got that out of youse, just like I said. That's for you to keep, now, to show your Grandchildren."

She dropped it onto his chest and Drake picked it up, then he winced in pain, which Fearnley realised.

"Just stitching you up now, Sir. All's out as far as I can tell and the wound's clean."

Fearnley began the stitching, but then he looked up.

"It's getting dark. I need a lantern. Tom?"

He handed up the clamps to Miles, who again sprinted over to the Surgeon's tent and then up to the same Assistant, Miles oblivious to the screaming from the operating table.

"There you are, mate. All back safe and sound, but needin' a bit of a clean. Now we needs a lamp, so I'll take one of those from the door."

oOo

The uproar in the French baggage park continued throughout the night. By bribing some sentries and by-passing others, Miles and Bailey made two more excursions into the scene of wreckage and despoliation and returned each time with pockets full of various coins, small valuables and some silver cutlery, but nothing to equal the worth of the Spanish doubloons. They had returned first to the carriage of General Villatte, but all was gone, even the wooden chest and the boxes of plate. However, their haul included many flasks of brandy and a good drink was enjoyed by all in their mess area and one flask was propped up beside Captain Drake, him now sleeping, covered in a horse blanket.

Early the next morning Colonel Henry Carr was woken by his Sergeant Clerk, William Bryce, with coffee and fresh baked rolls.

"Sir. General Lowry-Cole is here. In a bit of a temper, Sir."

Carr immediately swung his legs off his cot and pulled on his breeches, then his shirt. He was buttoning his tunic as he went outside, to find Lowry-Cole gazing around him.

"Sir? You wish to see me?"

Lowry-Cole turned around to see Carr still working on his buttons.

“Wellington’s apoplectic! No surprise. He expected the army to be ready to continue the pursuit and half of it hasn’t yet gone to bed!”

For some moments, Carr stood still and silent, not sure how to respond, then he realised that he had to make some reply.

“Sorry to hear that, Sir.”

“This has been almost as bad as that near mutiny after Badajoz!”

“Sir, but, begging your pardon Sir, why have you come to me? Surely, General Anson can give you more information.”

“I’m here to see for myself, because most of my Division and almost all of General Anson’s have fallen apart! Gone missing!”

Carr bridled at the implication and drew himself up to his full height.

“Well, that does not apply to your Hundred and Fifth, Sir. We can be ready to march in half an hour, should you so order. Sir.”

The silence between them was palpable, but Lowry-Cole seemed the more discomfited and so Carr broke the silence.

“Can I offer you some coffee, Sir. We’ve just baked some bread, in addition.”

Lowry-Cole bowed his head in thanks.

“Thank you, but no. I have other Regiments I need to visit. However, plainly, all praise to you and to your men for holding together in the face of such temptation.”

Carr resumed his full height and peeled off a salute.

“Thank you, Sir.”

As Lowry-Cole mounted his horse to depart, Carr returned to his tent to be followed in by O’Hare.

“We’ve called the Roll.”

Carr took the paper to him, but O’Hare spoke the figures first.

“Five men killed, three Officers wounded, 34 men wounded.”

Carr looked at the figures, then at O’Hare.

“Is that all? That’s the least of any battle we’ve ever been in! And this was the biggest!”

“It is and that’s the truth, but the wounded Officers include Captain Drake, as you know. The last we heard it was somewhat serious. He got it leading the Lights across Nancleres bridge.”

Carr dropped the paper, a look of deep concern overcoming his face.

“Yes! Yes! I must go to him.”

“Indeed you must, yes, but he’s not with the Surgeon, he’s being cared for by the Followers and men of his own Company. They operated on him last night and took out a bullet!”

“His own Company! They operated! Not Surgeon Pearce?”

"Yes for his Company, no for Pearce! Sergeant Fearnley, their medical chap worked the necessary. When I looked at Drake, he was asleep, but being thoroughly fussed over."

Carr seized his shako.

"The Light Company?"

He did not wait for an answer, but hurried out of the tent to both walk and trot to where he knew the Light Company were. All the while he had Cecily and Henrietta on his mind and the low proportion of men who survived operations. It was not hard to find the correct place within the Light Company area, Drake was the only figure prone on the ground, being fussed over and he recognised Bridie and Nellie. When Carr approached all sprang to their feet and saluted, but Carr gave the most perfunctory return of salute and halted now beside Drake, who opened his eyes and looked up.

"Henry. Sir. Good of you to trickle by."

A box suddenly appeared beside Carr and he nodded his thanks before using it to sit down.

"So, how are you?"

"Not up to a 20 miles march, but better now than I thought I would be yesterday."

"What've you been told?"

"A bullet hole, a cracked rib and eight stitches so that they could get at it."

"As conducted by Sergeant Fearnley?"

"Yes, and I'd like to say, now and for the record, that I have no complaints. Not one!"

"Surgeon Pearson said what?"

"Nothing! He took one look, neither frowned nor smiled, then just beetled off."

Carr looked around at the staring and anxious faces, then back to Drake.

"And you are being well cared for?"

"As though I were a new-born babe!"

Carr was immediately conscious of the nodding heads and now smiling faces of the audience all round. He fixed on Bridie, who answered what she thought was the obvious question, even though not spoken.

"He's eating well, so he is, your Honour, Sir, what with rations coming up so regular. I'd take that as a good sign, should we not, now, Sir?"

For the first time, Carr himself smiled and nodded.

"I should think that it is, Mrs. Mulcahey, and I myself have good memories of your cooking."

Bridie curtsied.

"That's kind of your Honour to remember that time, so it is. Was it not just before that dreadful march back from that place when we was up near Roger's Town?"

"Yes, Mrs Mulcahey, that's my recollection also. The place was called Alfayates. Not a place I'll forget, not only for the reason of your cooking!"

Bridie smiled but Carr had returned to Drake.

"So what's this tale about you leading the charge over Nancleres bridge?"

Drake arched his eyebrows.

"Someone had to be first. Why not the 105th?"

Carr nodded and sighed.

"Right! So ! Plainly you are in very good hands. Being well fed and well cared for, medically that is."

Bridie felt now a very good time to mention Esme.

"Medically's the word, so it is, your Honour. Esme, here, used to work in a Hospital, so she did."

Carr was able to identify Esme as the woman who curtsied at that point, but said nothing as she stared at the ground. Carr returned his attention to Drake.

"Well, when we move, which will be soon, we'll get you into one of the wagons."

Bridie again.

"No need to trouble yourself with that, Mr. Carr, Sir. Parson and the Reverend Albright have said they'll take him into their cart. Sure, in there he can be lying on a good bed, so he will."

Carr nodded in her direction, patted Drake on the shoulder, stood, properly returned the salutes of all soldiers there present and then walked off, much relieved at the state of his good friend.

At that moment, the very pair of magnanimous Clerics were on their way to an auction that was about to take place, this of all that was saleable and had been gathered from the wreckage of the French baggage park, including animals. Albright was eager to attend, but harbouring a serious concern, stemming from his own inadequacies and also that of his Assistant.

"I do feel, Private, that we should be looking for two superior draught animals, superior to the two that we have at present, these being more of the donkey species than the mule, notwithstanding the fact that it was of their kind that carried our Dear Lord into Jerusalem, but for drawing a wagon I do judge them as inferior, but, I myself, am no judge of what would be superior."

Sedgwicke could not, in any way, ease the anxieties of his Officer by speaking of his own capacities, but he knew someone who could.

"I do know someone who could help, Sir, and it will take but a moment to ask him."

With that, Sedgwicke trotted off and soon returned with John Davey, whom Albright immediately began to question.

"Am I correct in thinking, Private, that you may be a good judge of draught animals, suitable for our Ecumenical transport?"

"Well Sir, no real expert in what you might call bloodstock, but I can tell which animal from another as would be best for pulling a wagon such as yours. Sir."

"Very good, Private. We will rely upon your expertise and the guidance as sent to us by our Good Lord."

Davey's face remained expressionless.

"Yes Sir."

The auction was merely a few yards away and already beginning. The vast majority of the bidding was for the carts and vehicles, but most were claimed by the Commissariat before any bid could be made and with so many animals, the bidding was low. One Guards Officer stood nearby was delighted with his triumph, exclaiming such to his companion.

"Stap me! A stallion like that for nine guineas! When we get him back, he'll be out to stud."

His companion laughed.

"A General's mount for certain. Pity it didn't include the saddle, but such as that may well be coming up later. Harness and tack and what have you."

Sedgwicke returned his attention to the ring, where, all the horses now having been sold, mules were being led in, four at a time. He leaned towards Davey.

"Any of these?"

Davey nodded.

"There's two. Not old, well-muscled and matched for your cart. I'll give you a nudge."

The nudges arrived for the second and fourth, the first bought for two guineas, the second for one and a half. Albright was delighted.

"A bargain indeed, for two such sturdy animals."

He watched as Sedgwicke walked into the ring and led the pair away, then he turned to Davey.

"A good purchase, Private. A most gratifying outcome. Were not our actions guided by the Good Lord this day?"

Davey nodded and smiled.

"No doubt, Sir. I'd say you've a bargain there, Sir. They'll see you over many a mile."

Davey remained standing expectantly for a moment, but Albright had turned and hurried away with Sedgwicke behind, leading mules. More than a little aggrieved, Davey spoke his thoughts aloud, but only to himself.

"And a shilling wouldn't of come amiss, you tightwad skinflint, by some way of thanks, looking at what you could've bought instead, you not knowing any better!"

With that he hurried back to their camp, where Deakin was the first to see him.

"What was all that about?"

"Albright wanted help choosing mules at the auction."

Miles then became interested.

"Did you get a coin?"

Davey shook his head.

"From that cheap skate Chaplain, I'd say not, but I helped out Parson. That's worth doing."

Many heads around nodded agreement. Nothing more need be said.

Later that morning, on the pretext of foraging for bedding for Captain Drake, Colour-Sergeant Deakin led Davey and Saunders, all three being NCOs, back to the French baggage park, it still being well populated, but only now with citizens from Vitoria. Many were carrying back items useful for their homes, but the three were looking for a small cart for their own Followers, not least to enable them to transport the now very valuable and now very heavy 'mess chest'. Sanders soon found something and pulled it out of a pile of wreckage and abandoned clothing. Deakin studied it.

"Looks like what they calls a dog-cart. More like a toy for the childers, pulled by the family dog, but this one's a decent size."

They returned with their find just as the bugles were sounding, 'Prepare for march' and camps were being rapidly dismantled. Whatever loot and booty had been gained over the past 24 hours, was stuffed into back-packs or, if now condemned as too heavy, finally lodged with Quartermasters and Commissaries, for a very generous commission. The road was filled both forward and back with all the Divisions it could hold, all formed up and ready to march, with many held off and waiting in the fields beside. All Wellington's army was assembled, Divisions,

Brigades and Battalions, with Generals, Brigadiers and ADCs riding up and down, their hooves unable to drown out the screaming Sergeants, all incensed at the sight of their hung-over rabble, slouching in their files, prior to the order to march. The order came and all started on the main Pamplona road, but soon they saw Graham take a main road away to their left, him taking a force that included G. Anson's Brigade as cavalry, at that moment these were all that could be seen. Carr looked across hoping to see his brother, but the cavalry were on the far side of the column. None had marched more than a mile before it began to rain, a steady, soaking downpour that did nothing to ease aching heads or leaden feet. However, in the days that followed, with brighter weather, the 105th took on another nickname, once the story of their rescue of the paintings had spread. Lowry-Cole himself had seen them transported on their way to safety, two of the paintings being identified as by Velasquez. Although it did not last for long, the 105th acquired a new title, 'The Rembrandts', but few in the army appreciated the connection and their name soon reverted back to the 'Rag and Bone Boys'. Nevertheless, two months later a letter of thanks and appreciation for the rescue of so many works of art arrived from the Royal Society of Arts to Colonel Carr. It was passed on to Shakeshaft for safe-keeping amongst the Regimental records.

oOo

Chapter Nine

"Over there, Willoughby. That's France!"

Carr reached across and pushed Peterson awake.

"I think we should get up."

He removed the blanket that was protecting his own face and immediately felt the depressing and steady impact of serious rain.

"If only to get out of this."

"What time is it?"

"Past the time when we should be on our feet."

Peterson rose to the sitting position and pushed up the blanket that had been sheltering his own head from the rain. Then he looked around.

"Seems like we've all been allowed a bit of a lie in!"

The statement was evidenced by the sight of many of the 16th Light Dragoons remaining under their blankets, their shakoes and equipment beside them, themselves still fast asleep. At that moment a young boy, not yet a teenager, arrived with two bowls and a pot of bean stew. He offered each a bowl, which they accepted, then he ladled out some of the hot stew. Peterson immediately began to eat, but Carr remembered his manners.

"Mucho gracias, Senor."

The boy bowed in his direction.

"De nada, Senor. Mi Madre le envia las gracias."

Then he went on his way to offer the same to Oakwood and Smythe, both lying nearby, but Carr was grateful for the hot food and now concentrated on eating. However, the extra sleep allowed by Anson was now brusquely terminated by Collins, him striding purposefully through his reclining Regiment.

"On the road in 30 minutes. Graham's on his way."

Graham himself arrived within 15 minutes and rode directly to the house in the village that Anson was using as Brigade Headquarters. Another ten minutes and out came one of Anson's ADCs to give orders to Collins, who immediately ordered, "Mount and form up." Soon after, both cavalry Regiments were waiting on the road used by the French the previous day and the word came back down the column, Johnson informing Oakwood and Carr of their purpose, at least for the morning.

"Were out in front of Graham's Corps. He's been sent after all the Johnnies who escaped this way, supposedly up North-East, towards the border. Could be that whoever their General is, he'll gather a decent force from all the fugitives that we pushed on through here yesterday. These and Clausel's are the only French left in Spain worth a damn."

Baxter, sat his horse behind them and overhearing, turned his head towards Spivey.

"Back to the war, then!"

Spivey chuckled.

"Least we've been fed. Once by our own and once by them Spanish. Blessings to be counted!"

The column moved off, Graham in the lead with Anson, him leading the 16th with the 12th following behind. As they moved off, Carr turned to Peterson.

"Any idea about the name of this place?"

Peterson looked uncertain, but managed a reply.

"El Burgo is what I've heard."

"El Burgo?"

He spoke no more, the subject not worth pursuing, and so the buildings of that name fell behind. However, the pursuit was conducted at a walking pace, which puzzled all in the Brigade, the reason only arriving via evening chatter around their campfires, in the case of Two Squadron the reason for the leisurely pace being conveyed by Major Johnson, as usual sat with Oakwood, Carr and Peterson.

"This morning was a God-awful shambles. We thought that the Divisions the Peer had given Graham were coming up close behind, but not at all. They were all on the road to Pamplona, going East and had to be turned around, counter-marched and then sent after us. They won't reach us until Noon tomorrow and then only if we halt and wait."

The response was blank looks from the Two Squadron trio, but Johnson had more.

"Worse, he's had Norman Ramsey arrested!"

The three came bolt upright, Oakwood the first to reply.

"He' being Wellington?"

Johnson nodded.

"Yes. All from a mix up of orders and not at all Ramsey's fault. Wellington told him that his battery had been assigned to Graham, but everyone thought that Graham was part of what was moving East to Pamplona, including a late arriving ADC. This 'whoever' actually told Ramsey to get going, along the Pamplona road and catch up, the numbskull of an ADC believing we were on our way there. Wellington came up in a dreadful fume and, instead of taking it out on his lumpen Staff, took it out on Ramsey for disobeying orders! Can you believe it! The disobedience, through no fault of his own, being that he wasn't with us, up here, where Wellington thought he should be. Wellington found him on the road doing his best to get to us, thinking we were half way to Pamplona. No disobedience at all!"

Carr, knowing Ramsey so well, became the most incensed.

"How can he be arrested for attempting to conform to a false order?"

Johnson shook his head.

"You've got it there, young Willoughby. The whole army's incensed, we all know about Ramsey at Fuentes d'Onoro. You, more than most!"

Oakwood was equally angry.

"It's plain damn wrong!"

The expression on his face turned to anger.

"Wellington's jumping up and down on the men who did all the fighting yesterday, when the whole of today's mess is all down to lousy Staffwork by those preening aristos who have attached themselves to his personal retinue because of family connections."

Oakwood's jaw clamped together for a few seconds, before he continued. No-one felt inclined to interrupt.

"Damn wrong! Stuff like that can happen after a battle. Ramsey may have been wrong, although it doesn't sound like it, but you give a man like Ramsey the benefit of the doubt in situations like that! Of which there are plenty, especially after a set-piece the size of yesterday's!"

When the order came for 'lights out', many Officers of Anson's Brigade rolled themselves into their blankets with thoughts on the popular and well-respected Royal Artillery Captain, thoughts which were rekindled the next morning when, riding out of yet another rainstorm, his Battery arrived minus Ramsey and the question put to the Battery Lieutenant in command regarding where he was, received a brusque answer, "Still in gaol!" The surly gunners took position in the column between the 12th and the 16th and the pursuit continued, but at the same leisurely pace, this being remarked on by Carr, riding alongside Peterson, Carr still angry over the treatment of a man he looked upon as a personal friend.

"The French can march faster than this! We're giving chase like some old woman!"

However, it was Oakwood who answered.

"Keep a lid on it, Willoughby! You know as well as I, we've no infantry. Perhaps today we will get some, perhaps not."

Carr scowled beneath his shako, this the only protection he had from the teeming rain, the run-off from the top entering his collar, which lowered his spirits even further.

'Perhaps today' was the accurate prediction and it came in the form of two KGL Light Infantry Battalions, Pack's Portuguese Brigade of two Line Battalions, a Cacadores Battalion and, finally. Bradford's Portuguese Brigade of two Line. They arrived in the late afternoon, two hours after Anson's force had entered the village of Segura and Graham, sat up on his horse, inspected the new arrivals as the eight Battalions squelched by in the rain. When he looked forlornly down the road for more, none came. Anson's Officers, part of the audience, turned away and hurried off to the comfort of their pair of well-appointed houses in the town. They had divided themselves between these two, in a locality that was not too ravaged from the attentions of a rapidly retreating French army and one reason why the town had been spared was in

Pursuit after Vitoria

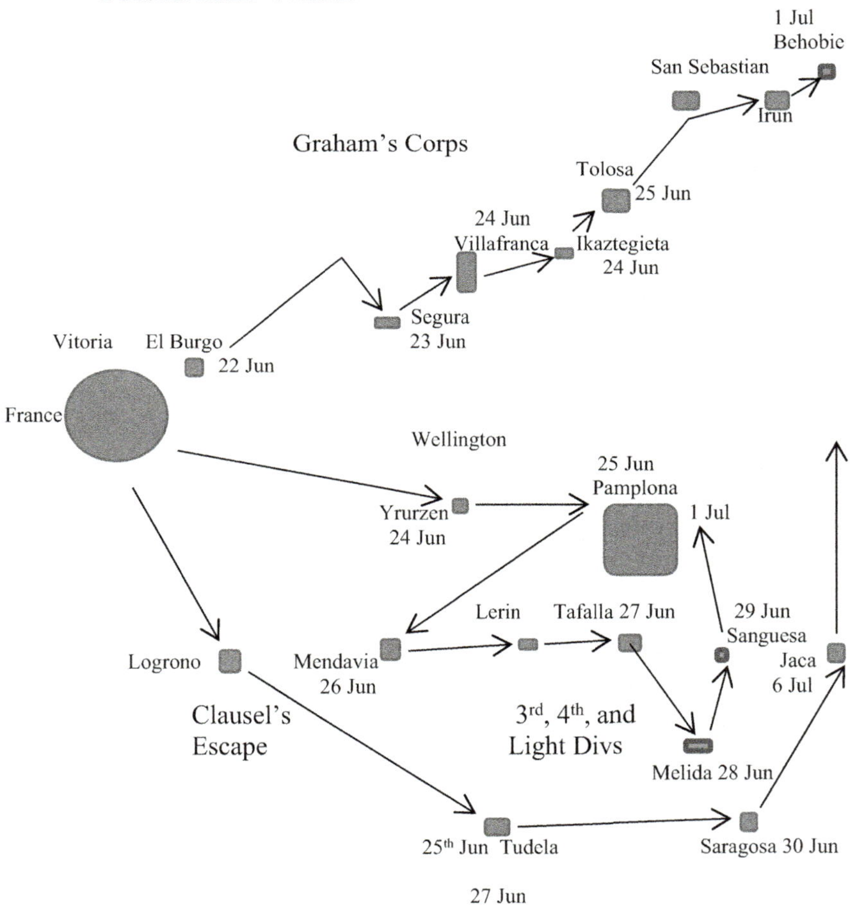

the square. In and around the cantina a full Company of Spanish guerrillas sat drinking wine, all very much in triumphant mood and from a tree in the centre swung the bodies of at least five French soldiers. Carr took a moment to study the group, but he could not see Ignacias Mateo and he was in too black a mood himself to join him anyway, had he seen him there. Instead, he hurried inside to brood on his own thoughts.

A night's sleep in the dry did restore his mood somewhat, even when Baxter shook him awake, with the early June dawn barely complete.

"Sir! Our Squadron's needed. For reconnaissance, Sir."

Carr sat up and was soon wide awake.

"Just ours?"

"No Sir. One from the 12th as well."

"To go where, do you know?"

"No Sir, I'm not told such as that. Just to fetch you. Sir."

Carr dressed and left the house to find both Squadrons on the road, the all blue uniform of the 12th contrasting starkly with the red front-pieces of his own 16th. His horse was ready, so he mounted to see Graham himself at the head of the column along with Anson and they immediately trotted off, which soon built to a canter. Carr shouted ahead to Oakwood.

"Somewhat more urgent, this time!"

Oakwood turned to him, but briefly.

"The Frogs are in Villafranca, just up ahead."

The distance spoken of was little more than a mile and, before that was achieved, Graham halted the column to study a small village off to the right and every telescope paralleled his to see that the village was occupied by French troops. Graham led them further on, for the road to climb a hill and then descend into the river valley which held Villafranca itself, now seen clearly, but they halted at the top where the view was even more alarming. The whole French force which they had been following, as many as three Brigades, were arranged to defend Villafranca. Also, the small village they had examined minutes earlier plainly formed the far left of this defensive line. What added to the urgency of the moment for both sides was the reason why Graham was being denied entry to Villafranca. Down a valley in the mountains opposite and to the left of the town, marched what appeared to be a whole French Division, these approaching the town from the far side of a river that flowed past the far end of Villafranca. If Graham could capture the town, then this Division would be cut off. Within a minute, one of Graham's ADCs was galloping back down the road, obviously with the task of hurrying on the infantry which had just joined Graham's command and were now urgently needed, but had not yet caught up. The two Squadrons with Graham could do no more than sit and wait, the tension and impatience palpable, as they watched the French column in the distance seemingly inch themselves out of their high valley and down into the river valley of Villafranca. Oakwood spoke what was a fairly obvious conclusion.

"This isn't going to work."

The first to arrive were the rest of the 12th and 16th Light Dragoons with the field-gun battery behind and, with their arrival, the two Squadrons immediately re-joined their Regiments. It was not long before an ADC cantered down the road, ordering all the cavalry to the side so that the artillery could ride up to a hill from which they could bombard the French centre close to Villafranca, albeit from a distance. The artillery soon unlimbered and opened fire, the noise echoing around the tight hills, the smoke drifting Eastwards towards the French. It was 30 minutes before any infantry arrived, first the Cacadores Battalion, at the run, who were immediately sent to support the artillery, whose fire had not slackened at all over the intervening quarter-hour. Next came Bradford's two Portuguese Line Battalions and almost frantic ADCs ordered them to attack the French left at the outlying village. Graham's plan to hold the French left and centre, while crossing the river to cut off the approaching French Division, soon became clear to all who sat and watched the battalions deploy immediately as they arrived. The two KGL Light Battalions were ordered to attack the French right, which involved crossing the river being approached by the hurrying French Division and the KGL would be supported by the Battalions of Pack's Brigade arriving soon after. Following their orders, the many Battalions hurried off to cover the half-mile or so to their positions, whilst Bradford's single Cacadores Battalion remained stationary in the centre with the artillery.

Orders then arrived for the 12th and 16th, that they move to form line either side of the Cacadores. Of Graham's force, these were the first to move forward, alone, despite the Allies on both flanks being some time away from beginning their own assault. The Cacadores advanced in 'open order', with the field-guns sending grape-shot above their heads at maximum range, but many amongst the Light Dragoons were soon shaking their heads at what they thought to now be inevitable. The French Colonel of the centre Regiment, two Battalions strong, knowing he was under cannonfire and that only Light Troops were coming at his centre, ordered his men opposite the Portuguese out into open order and they spread across the hillside to double their width and advance forward. When they closed with their opponents, the Cacadores, outnumbered, were halted by superior firepower and then pushed back by weight of numbers. An ADC then rode up to Collins.

"Sir, from General Graham, get forward against those French. If nothing more, hold them there."

Oakwood and Carr could see the puzzlement on Collins' face at so vague an order, but he soon sent back his own, 'check and load'. With this, all carbines came out of their holsters and were, as ordered, checked and loaded. With the artillery roaring away at any solid French formations on the hillside opposite, Collins led his men forward, four Squadrons riding together, all in a single, two-deep line, the 12th beyond the guns on their left conforming to the same. The French Colonel, with his men still in open formation and now menaced by cavalry, called them back into line and the Cacadores edged forward once more. It was not long before the 16th came up alongside the Portuguese skirmishers, many now being treated for wounds behind their own open firing line. Once there, Collins ordered "Halt and dismount" but, remaining in the saddle himself, he turned around to face his own men.

"Every fourth man!"

All knew what that meant, that one Trooper would hold the mounts of three others, who would dismount and fight as infantry. Carr handed his horse to the nearest Trooper, already holding two and he accompanied his men forward, all now with their 'Paget' carbine at the ready. Carr checked his own carbine at the same time as Oakwood, but his Captain walked on, plainly very much less than convinced by what they were about to undertake. Even less certain regarding the benefit of what they were about to attempt was Sergeant Baxter and he immediately made his feelings known to Corporal Jim Makepeace.

"Just for show, this! Are we expected to do any damage with this Paget? They Portugee has Bakers, twice the range of this."

He briefly held up his carbine and continued on. 'For show' it may be, as many thought, but artillery fire continued to hiss over their heads and the Cacadores, feeling reinforced were closing to effective Baker range. With that, Makepeace turned to Baxter.

"These Frogs got any cavalry? I don't feel too good so far from my horse."

Baxter looked left and right.

"Ain't seen none!

"All to the good then! Perhaps we should open fire! At least we can put up a bit of a show, cause a few bangs!"

With that, the order to open fire came from Collins and the 16th kept up a brisk fusillade at what was well over effective range, but the Battalions forming the French centre remained in place, moving neither forward nor sideways. Johnson looked over to Oakwood as he used his ramrod to complete a reload.

"We're holding them here. All to the good and that's the point, they can't move anywhere to reinforce any flank."

Oakwood grinned.

"No Sir. Not even the Crapauds would allow a whole Brigade of Dragoons, a field-gun battery and a skirmisher Battalion to advance happily through their centre."

"Pleased that you appreciate the finer points of all this!"

At that moment a musket ball buzzed uncomfortably close to Johnson's shoulder.

"All is not without risk, though."

At that moment Oakwood had brought his carbine to his shoulder, but he decided to hold fire.

"They're pulling back, Sir. Some of ours must've got around a flank somewhere. Perhaps both."

Colonel Collins had seen the same and was calling for the horses to be brought forward and soon, accompanied by the field-guns and the Cacadores, the 16th were walking cautiously forward, picking their way through the dead and wounded of both sides. The ground continued to rise for some 200 yards, then they were at the crest that had been held by the French and they could gauge for themselves what had happened, because all was in clear view beneath, looking down into the valley that held the main buildings of the town. The French centre, including the Brigade once opposite them, were retreating into Villafranca itself, using the three bridges over Villafranca's own river, whilst on the Allied right a French rearguard was delaying Bradford's Portuguese, these now issuing carefully from the recently captured village that had been the French left flank. To the Allied left, however, the French Division was now hurrying along the road beside the river with the KGL and Pack's Portuguese held back on the Allied side. Their opponents, who had succeeded in keeping the Allies at bay, appeared to be, with the use of telescopes, a full Battalion of French Voltiguers, judging by the amount of yellow that could be made out on their shakoes, these probably deployed down from the escaping Division.

The 16th were now halted in line of Squadrons, with the artillery between themselves and the 12th. Carr and Peterson now sat their horses together.

"Well, we did what we could!"

"Indeed yes, Willoughby, but plainly the French have made good their exit."

At that moment any conversation was rendered impossible by the first salvo from the guns, all six sending solid shot across the valley, the black dots being easy to follow, at least for half their journey over to the new French line, this now crowning the heights on the far side of Villafranca.

"Last act?"

Peterson was pointing to the right, where the Portuguese on the right had finally crossed the river above the town and were advancing in full Brigade strength up the slope and onto the French left flank. He was correct, because on their own left, the French Division had now escaped and the French Commander, with that achieved, had decided that they had held back the Allies for long enough and therefore their final line atop the ridge was now pulling back also. He plainly saw no point in being held there any longer to no good purpose, whilst other Allied troops manoeuvred around his other flank or even got behind him. Within seconds the French line had gone but the Portuguese on the right continued upward to gain the crest. Peterson now took a welcome drink of water and spoke as he hammered in the stopper, this for emphasis.

"All done, then!"

Carr made no answer as the Regiment formed column of fours by Squadrons and walked their horses down to the nearest bridge, leaving the Royal Artillery battery to limber up and follow the 16th and the 12th across the river. Once into Villafranca, citizens came out of cellars and what could only described as holes in the hillside to clap and cheer. However, for Anson's Brigade there was no stopping, only stooping from the saddle to hurriedly drink a beaker of wine handed up by many citizens, the wine slopping everywhere as it was hurriedly poured, consumed and the beaker handed back. Once on the road out of the town they found Bradford's Portuguese Brigade coming down from the right, off the ridge they had just taken possession of as the French withdrew and now Graham himself was up ahead with an eye assessing all. A conversation ensued between Anson and two other Senior Officers, with much arm pointing from Graham, but the result was that their Regiment of Cacadores from earlier, hurried on up the road, with Bradford's two Line Regiments following, then both of Anson's followed in the rear of the Portuguese. Carr looked at the roadsign as they passed the final buildings of the town and spoke out loud to no-one in particular.

"Tolosa 3L"

However, Sergeant Baxter had overheard.

"About nine miles, Sir."

"Thank you, Sergeant. Grateful for the information!"

For Anson's Brigade what followed was merely a ride up the road, but accompanied by the sound of occasional fierce fighting, which usually died away almost as soon as it had flared up and also they passed many dead and wounded at the roadside, both Portuguese and French, the latter almost always in Voltiguer uniform. With the ending of the day, even before the daylight had truly begun to fade, the sounds of fighting faded and then died away completely. With the last of the daylight, Anson's men entered the village of Ikaztegieta, where Carr saw another waysign, this one reading as Tolosa 1L, and this time he had no need of any instruction.

oOo

"Do you think he's paying us out for, shall we say, the disobedience of the evening before last?"

O'Hare did no more than re-hitch his backpack without breaking stride on the main chausee from Vitoria to Pamplona.

"According to my assessment of our Wellington, I doubt it. He's not one to waste his men in anything but a good cause, neither their lives nor their energy. He's got high hopes of us catching up with El Rey before he gets to Pamplona."

Carr could only think of his tired limbs, now more so from the second day of forced march, but a thought did occur.

"Perhaps El Rey will put up a rearguard. That'll slow things up a bit."

He then had another thought.

"But if there's one cove I do not feel sorry for, it's that scut Nat Drake, riding comfortably in Albright's cart, with some of the Mulcahy and Nicholls girls entertaining him by reading from Robinson Crusoe, that provided by his Company intellectual, Private Byford."

O'Hare grinned and settled his pack once again as they pounded on at Light Infantry pace, the roads now thankfully firm and dry. Combat with a French Rearguard did occur, but it coincided with the Noon halt and so no extra rest was gained. Cannonfire echoed back down the road, but nothing that sounded like a musketry exchange. Carr was sat at the roadside with O'Hare and Heaviside, with only two of the three eating the inevitable Spanish sausage, because Heaviside was eating new army biscuits and English cheese, a real luxury. All were listening to the distant sounds of combat, O'Hare providing the judgment.

"Doesn't sound like much. Nothing more than a bit of exchange between artillery."

However, when they did arrive at the areas of combat, the first being seen before the town of Yrurzun and the rest at intervals over several miles, the frequent rows of dead of both armies spoke of a serious attempt to hold back the Allies advance. Finally, at what was the last place of action, a nameless hamlet, they saw a captured cannon, an unmistakable French 12 pounder, this adorned by triumphant Riflemen of the 95th. The long column pressed on, the 4th Division before the 3rd and the 7th, all following the Light Division in the lead. Finally, Pamplona came in sight, the horizon appearing unspectacularly uniform, devoid of any significant buildings for so important a city, even allowing for the growing darkness. Anticipating the ending of the day's march, all three of the Senior Officers of the 105th, had finally unslung their packs from their shoulders as, onward and yet further, they passed through the first and well-appointed suburbs of the Spanish capital of the North-East. It was Carr who spoke the obvious.

"Looks like we've lost the race, El Rey's taken his parade off into the mountains."

There was no reply, because all three had seen another issue to occupy their thoughts. All felt a moment of anxiety when they caught sight of Pamplona citadel, illuminated by the last clear rays of the sun, the French tricolour flying prominently above the highest tower. Now it was O'Hare who voiced the thoughts of all three.

"Now that I do not like the look of!"

Carr and Heaviside could only agree, seeing the strength of the defences, walls inside more walls, increasing in height towards the interior, such that three rows of gun embrasures could be seen clearly, potent, menacing and almost impossible to advance against.

"We'll never get in there, not without casualties 10 to 1 against."

This from Heaviside, but Carr had drawn his own conclusion regarding how Pamplona citadel would be dealt with.

"We'll by-pass it! El Rey will have left a garrison and hope to push us back and relieve it, sometime in the future, but for now his armies are scattered and in no fit state to provide any resistance. Low on morale and even lower on materiel. He'll not be worrying us for a good while."

All three spoke no more, pausing to study the formidable walls, thankfully beyond the river from where they were, but still well within range of the larger field-guns. However, soon the major buildings of the city blocked their view and the four Divisions were directed to their camping grounds, where all slumped to the ground utterly worn down. Then the Followers arrived, Nelly being the first to arrive amongst her men, all stretched out on the Pamplona turf and still festooned with all their kit.

"You lazy lot! Get the tent up, whilst we gets the fire goin'. Sure, isn't there enough to be doin' just with the business of getting' the all of youse fed, without having to put up tents and the like?"

The tent had been carried by Nat Solomon for the last part of the march and all, having now shed their own packs, hauled themselves to their feet and made short work of its erection. Food was prepared and the evening wore on, but somehow, through some channels, the more enterprising of the city realised that this army was rich with coin and booty and many itinerant sellers wandered through the camps, festooned with all types of luxury displayed on trays and hanging from poles secured to their backs. One was waved away by Tom Miles with some choice words, but Deakin called him back and he stood to examine the wares on show from all kinds of levels and angles, such were the surfaces and perches on which the niceties were displayed. John Byford joined him, then Bridie and Eirin joined both, to pick over what the Spanish tinker had. Bridie picked out a head scarf and Eirin a waist shawl and a small kerchief for Ellen, to keep off the sun. Then the bargaining started, via fingers, the man holding up ten for ten Escudos, whilst Deakin held up three. A bargain was struck at six, Deakin seeing no point in bargaining further, they had Escudos in plenty, some doubloons having been exchanged at the Quartermaster's, albeit at a usurious rate, and anyway, both wives were highly delighted at the purchase. Consuela tried to push Zeke Saunders awake, but he was too exhausted and too fast asleep and so Byford bought her three wrist bracelets from another seller, determined to recover the debt in the morning.

With darkness now complete, Carr took himself to Reverend Albright's cart. At his approach, both Albright and Sedgwicke stood, Albright somewhat lost for words, whilst Sedgwicke, following the mores as taught by his higher social background, knew exactly what to do and say.

"Sir, good evening. We've just made some tea; can we offer you some? Do please make use of my stool, here."

Carr fully appreciated the graceful welcome and bowed his head in response, but politely declined.

"Thank you, but no. I have come to see your patient, whom you are so kindly caring for. I trust he is inside?"

Carr pointed to the cart, whilst Sedgwicke answered.

"Yes Sir, he is, having just taken food with us, but I would nevertheless wish to provide you both with some kind of refreshment, Sir."

Carr smiled as he began his climb up into the darkness of the interior.

"Well, that would be most kind. The tea you spoke of earlier would be perfectly sufficient."

Carr fully entered the cart to find Drake lying down, propping himself up on one elbow. Carr spoke first, dispensing with any greeting.

"You seem better!"

"I am!"

Then he fully raised his head to shout, enough to be heard by the pair outside.

"Sorry to be troublesome, but any chance of a lantern? If you'd be so kind."

The reply came from outside, Sedgwicke's voice.

"Of course, Sir. Directly."

Within a minute a candle lantern was passed in and Carr set it between them.

"You must be better if you worry about the amount of light available to you. Is it your appearance or something of that nature giving you some concern? I wouldn't worry too much about shaving."

Drake ignored the dig.

"I'm out of here, tomorrow or the day after, at most. It's not the boredom, the girls read to me and that's well enough, but……."

He dropped his voice to a whisper.

"…… it's Albright! Always jumping in and wanting to discuss some religious notion or other. Some bit of the Bible!"

He took a deep breath, but the whisper continued.

"And, anything we eat has to be blessed and have grace said over, then the Sermons begin, all the while as we eat. Lord!"

At that point the cart awning parted and two china mugs of tea were placed on the floor of the cart.

"Thank you, Sedgwicke. That's kind."

Sedgwicke's face and hands disappeared and the two began to drink their tea. Then the premier subject arose, as usual from Drake.

"Have you written?"

A guilty look came over Carr's face, giving Drake all the answer he needed.

"Well, I have and so should you. Especially after a set-piece like we've just been through. They'll have heard about it and that it was a big one and important. So, after you leave me, a few lines at least! They'll want to know that we both came out the other side."

Carr nodded, then he studied his friend in the yellow light.

"You nearly didn't! Were it not for Fearnley and the Followers you could be in some cart on your way back to Santander and not likely to survive. That was a mad-cap stroke leading the charge across that bridge, all out in front on your own."

Drake took a long drink and then set the mug down on the boards of the cart. His face now became very serious, matching the new subject.

"It doesn't happen to you! You're a Colonel, they wouldn't dare, but to us Captains we get it too often, from any group of Officers. We are greeted as the 'Run and Roam Boys'. Never mind Heroes of Maida, or Vimeiro, Talavera and the rest. That damn Brockenhurst sent our standing down into the dirt, and many wish to rub it in. So, us first over that bridge would do our reputation no harm at all, or so I thought."

The outburst completely dispelled any mood within Carr to remain light-hearted or jocular. This now concerned pride of Regiment, it was deadly serious and so he nodded in both sympathy and agreement.

"I see that, I do. I feel it also, but our time will come. This I know, there's none in this army as can put up a fight better than us and that we'll show. I don't know when, but it'll come. Then we'll see! Run and Roam Boys! There's plenty of the more fashionable Regiments that resent the reputation that we've built for ourselves, us just being common old Line, a number over a hundred. That's where it comes from. We were one of the Regiments he trusted to clear Badajoz. Remember? That will rankle with many. The "Rag and Bone Boys" don't crumble to nothing just because of the likes of a craven man like Brockenhurst!"

For some seconds the two looked at each other, the understanding total, then Drake broke the silence.

"So what happened to him? Do you know?"

Carr shook his head.

"I don't! It being just before Salamanca, the Peer was too busy, but had he not been, Brockenhurst would have been arrested and shot for cowardice, if the Peer was in the mood. For Brockenhurst, I saw some quote by him in a newspaper when we were in Winter Quarters, making the most of our retreat back to Cuidad. Pack of rubbish it was, but that's all I can say, apart from the fact that he's still in Parliament, of course, debating and deciding our affairs."

Drake's face darkened.

"Well, God rot him, is all I can say."

Then Carr's face brightened.

"Right, so, if I hear you correctly, you think yourself fit enough to be out of here within two days?"

Drake nodded agreement.

"Most certainly, yes. I'm sore right enough, but, like I say, ..."

He lowered his voice to a whisper once again.

".......not as sore as my ears with the incessant prattle about what this bit of text means rather than that, and incessant thanks to Him above for the good fortune that has befallen us all, and every other blessing bestowed upon us by the infinite goodness of His Right Hand!"

Carr laughed out loud.

"We'll get you a horse. There are plenty round about now. Carravoy now has two and D'Villiers three. You can take your pick."

"What about you?"

"Yes, I have one, so has Padraigh and Heaviside, but we prefer to walk. Probably best that I give you mine."

Carr then slapped his hands on his knees and rose.

"Right, best get going and get that letter written, before O'Hare uses up all the candle!"

He gave his friend two gentle pats on his shoulder and then exited the cart, when Sedgwicke sprang to attention and, as Albright at last managed to rise, Carr turned to them both.

"Captain Drake is plainly on the mend. Thank you for the care you have given him."

He did not wait for any reply, but donned his shako and hurried away.

oOo

The dawn light that Colonel Carr slept through, in the pleasant environs of Pamplona, found his Cornet brother up on a hillside staring down at the town of Tolosa, seated on his horse alongside Peterson and Oakwood, the latter studying the view intently, needing to do no more than lean against his saddle horn.

"That I don't like. Walls, gates and blockhouses, all squeezed in between a river and a steep hillside."

Peterson was studying also, in his case the town but not in such detail, because his attention was divided equally with what was beyond.

"Full of French we can suppose, plus there's what looks like two Brigades in reserve in the hills back behind the town, I'd guess beyond the river."

Oakwood now looked rightwards across the steep hillside they were on.

"And there's another Brigade on our hillside opposing us, on that ridge up ahead. The town's full of French, of that you can be certain and most of them are those we chased out of Villafranca and probably a few extra that have marched down from up North. We're no longer all that far from the coast."

He drew out his watch and studied it.

"6 o' clock! This will take some time. I'd not bet on less than 12 hours!"

Above them and slightly further on along the ridge was Anson, with his two Colonels and both Majors, all five evidently studying and worrying about what was in front of them, this done with much arm pointing. A Graham ADC arrived and the arm pointing ceased to be replaced by looks of resignation as the ADC rode away. Then Major Johnson rode down to Smythe of One Squadron and motioned Oakwood and his Cornets to come up and join them.

"I'm telling you this in case you get lost in this tangle of hills. The main column is some way back down the road. Bradford's Portuguese Line are to push away those French that we can see opposing us along the hillside, then they secure that ridge, get along it and get onto the Pamplona road that runs East. Some KGL will be supporting Bradford. Our task is to escort Longa's Spanish on a long sweep out to the right, to get onto the Pamplona road that way and get behind the town. Hopefully, by then the KGL and Portuguese will have come down off their ridge to join us on that road and even be waiting for us."

He spun his horse before riding back to Anson.

"This place will take some chiselling! It's locked down tighter than a Duchess' daughter's bedroom!"

It was almost an hour before the columns began moving in their direction, three in all. In the centre came the Portuguese Line Battalions, advancing directly their way to assault the ridge, and from the ridge height and forming the Portuguese reserve, they could see KGL below and some way behind. Oakwood looked upwards.

"There's ours!"

Five Spanish Battalions were now on the skyline, the first to quickly disappear over the ridge, the remaining four, with arms sloped, marched on to follow, many unfortunately out of step. All in Anson's Brigade who could see, remarked to themselves on the curious mix of uniforms, two all-white with a blue or red facing, one all green, another all brown. The first, now gone, had looked more like the French. Whatever impact this had upon Anson, he led his men upwards towards his Spanish subordinates and directed his 12th to take position out on the right, whilst the 16th cantered up and ahead to lead the way. As they did so, passing the Spanish column, many in the ranks called out, "Que bien, Ingleses", "Ahora matamos a los Franceses", "Viva Vitoria', or simply "Bravo Ingleses." Few of Anson's understood, but the bright grins and brandished muskets gave at least partial translation that these soldiers were fully up for the fight and pleased to see English cavalry alongside them. A Spanish Officer and a local peasant came to the fore as guides and their route soon became what it needed to be, a wide sweep using tracks that ran through hamlets and farms. Peasants ran out to greet the Light Dragoons, but their cheers and applause doubled when they saw the Battalions of their own countrymen advancing forward and their soldiers responded with gusto themselves, cheering and clapping in reply, many enthusiastically embracing any so inclined. Oakwood shook his head during one particular rousing greeting.

"Just as well that this flanking march is not intended to be secret."

A secret manoeuvre or not, the sounds of combat came to them from over the hills and those with a telescope could see, well over a mile away, Bradford's Portuguese attempting to push forward along their ridge, but definitely being held by their French opponents. Their ride continued on, a Noon halt taking place in a large village and the Spanish Battalions, showing good discipline, took themselves to the side of the road and held their places. Some of their number, festooned with canteens, clattered forward to fill them from a large trough which was being continuously refilled by locals very active on the lifting winch of their village well. The march resumed and many noticed that their shadow which had stretched out to their left when they began, now did the opposite to their right. Oakwood drew out his watch, looked at it and then held it up in the direction of Carr and Peterson.

"Six in the afternoon! Do you think we might be late for the ball?"

However, it would seem that Oakwood was about to be proved wrong when the column halted, whilst Anson and their guide studied the hills to their right front, to the North-East of Tolosa. Many then did the same, Oakwood the first to identify the subject.

"A big column of Spanish Irregulars. Coming down from the North and likely to get in behind Tolosa. From what I hear, these or such as these, were badly beaten by the French force on the coast, but they're here despite all that. Seems that French force that gave them a mauling has moved, probably to here, and those Irregulars are taking their chance to get in on the main act."

Their own column moved on, now descending, and the tracks downward from the farms and hamlets now became more definite and well used, until they joined what was obviously the Tolosa to Pamplona road where the 12th and 16th came together in column and allowed the Spanish Division to take the lead. All through the day, they had heard the combat of Bradford's Portuguese as it built up and then faded in the distance, the resulting white gun smoke drifting lazily over the hills, but now they were in a valley which the road made full use of and so nothing could be seen nor heard. After consultation with Longa, Anson took his men up into the hills to their right, that at least in the direction of French held territory and the 12th and 16th found themselves trotting or cantering into valleys and up slopes to perform their role of flank guard as best they could. Oakwood's timepiece was now reading 'seven' when the first buildings of Northern Tolosa came into view and their main road crossed Tolosa's River Oria and then through the solid and high city wall via a sturdy gate. However, the view quickly became crowded by at least eight French Battalions, all holding together, arriving down from the high ridge and the valley slopes above the road. They were formed about half a mile from the town, with the river behind, but they plainly had no intention of retreating, instead they formed line of battle across the Pamplona road.

It became obvious that they had been pushed down off the ridge by Bradford's Portuguese and the KGL Line Battalions. These two, plus the arrival of Longa's Brigades on their flank would have added to their need for retreat down to where they were now. On the road, Longa halted his men and sensibly waited for Bradford himself, who quickly arrived after cantering down the slope. Anson also saw the need to contribute and he took himself down to the road and the three were soon in consultation. In the relative silence, came the sounds of a major assault being made on the far side of the town, but this did not last even as long as the consultation and the ensuing silence spoke of its failure. At last, Anson rode back up to re-join his own men whilst Bradford's Portuguese formed an assault line that stretched across the full width of the shallow valley that contained the Pamplona road. Behind these were arranged the KGL in the same formation, then Longa's alongside in column. The 16th and 12th, on their observation hill had a grandstand view of what came next. It was line against line, each three deep and it continued as a conflict of continuous volleys, each against the other. Oakwood studied the confrontation as well as he could through the smoke.

"The Portuguese don't have our firepower and they've been in action all day. It's blow for blow and the French are holding."

Carr and Peterson could only agree. Bradford's men were not advancing nor the French giving way. For many minutes the fight continued, until trumpets sounded and the Portuguese fell back. The superb KGL, waiting behind, divided their ranks even as they advanced forward, to allow the Portuguese through and then advanced themselves, the two Battalions of Longa's advancing up on the KGL right to complete the line. Faced with fresh Troops the French did not last long and fell back themselves, still holding formation as the KGL inched forward over the dead and wounded of the past half hour. It was not long before the French had their backs to the River Oria, with only two bridges to use as a crossing. At that point the French won the admiration of all that were watching from the hill. French Officers came to the fore, swords aloft and they led their men forward in a gallant charge. The KGL were forced back, but not so far back as Longa's, who almost broke. However, French bugles now blew and the brave French Battalions fell back, this time at a run and they quickly crossed the bridges to reform on the far side in the space between the town walls and the river bank. Then they marched off rapidly downstream.

The KGL were the first to recover and their Brigadier led them over the bridge that served the town gate, whilst the eight French Battalions had almost disappeared, gaining the support of the two French Divisions in reserve behind the town. Perhaps the KGL Brigadier had been hoping that the gate would not be barred, but he was wrong. His men attacked ferociously but beat in vain against the stout woodwork, whilst some fired up at the French on the walls, but the effort was hopeless. The musketry from the battlements above was causing casualties and any effort at gaining entry required cannon to blow in the gate or proper scaling ladders to get over the walls and so, wisely, the KGL Brigadier withdrew his men out of range. Seeing the retreat, spirits sank within all who were watching on the Pamplona road, including Anson's Light Dragoons, because they knew that their attack had stalled and there was little that could be done from where they were. Oakwood summed it up.

"Could be we're camping here for the night!"

They remained sitting on their horses, listening to the distant sounds of combat coming to them from various directions and hoping that it meant progress of sorts, until they heard the roar of cannon, such as would be produced by a whole field-gun battery, then the sounds of continuous musketry. Oakwood spoke again.

"Seems like we are in but from the other end."

However, the force on the road, composed of all three Allies, still did not move.

"Bradford's waiting, just like us sat here, waiting for Graham to flush the place through from his end."

Then the sounds of more intense musketry came to them from their right, seemingly from not too far over from the hill upon which they stood and most likely coming from the direction of the two French Divisions in reserve over there. Within a minute they were moving in that direction; plainly on his own initiative Anson was taking his men over to investigate and to discover what use they could be. All knew that no one amongst them had yet fired one shot, nor drawn one sabre. They were soon over their hill and Anson spurred his men into a canter. They could now see the Northern end of Tolosa very clearly and French Troops were pouring out of the gate at that end. There was a road that ran alongside the river on the Light Dragoons side and their strong canter continued downwards until they were on its surface and Anson led his men further along until they had a clear view over the river of the French opposite. The order came back, "Every fourth man," and soon three-quarters of Anson's men were on the river bank and using their carbines against the mass opposite. The range over the width of the river, plus a few yards more, was perfectly adequate for their Pagets and so all maintained a lively fire. Baxter was alongside Carr's left, with Makepeace beyond Baxter, but it was Carr that spoke as he reloaded his own 'Paget'.

"Shouldn't they have put some men opposite to return our fire?"

"Perhaps, Sir, but these is too keen to make off. There's none as wants to stay, not if it means running into they Spanish Irregulars up over yonder."

Oakwood, on Carr's right, agreed.

"Your Sergeant has the right of it. You saw those Irregulars coming down this way and in strength. They could be getting across their retreat and closing their only way out."

It was not long before the fugitive stream thinned and so the order came to remount. Once back in column they continued downstream and within not half a mile, Oakwood was proved correct. The Spanish Irregulars had arrived in strength and the French force placed up the hillside to hold them back had joined the retreat, leaving open the Irregulars' route down to the river and so they came down in a rush. Now many French stragglers began to fall into their hands and several were very roughly handled, as could be seen by the 16th from across the river. Others, justly terrified at being taken by the dreaded Irregulars, were now wading over the river, hands in the air, musket discarded. The water was above chest height and progress was slow for many and fatal for some, because Irregulars soon arrived at the bank and opened fire at those struggling through the deep water and the not insignificant current, even though it was obvious that they would be taken prisoner by the British now holding the opposite bank. Many of Anson's men were incensed at what they saw as the murder of helpless men and many rode their horses down to the water, some even into it, to give the French some protection and the amount of fire coming from the other side did slacken considerably. Many French were still in the water, with their hands in the air and shouting versions of "Nous vous remercions. Merci, Anglais. Nous rendons a vous!"

Baxter was looking on as many French soldiers collapsed on the shingle of their side as soon as they left the water, several wounded, all lying between the legs of the 16th's horses. Many Troopers were now yelling insults and shaking fists at the Spanish on the opposite bank. Baxter sat his horse, arms folded over the pommel and shaking his head.

"Funny old war, eh Sir? Ten minutes ago we was all doin' our level best to kill as many as we could. Now we'n doin' our best to save as many as we can. Don't seem to make too much sense. Sir."

oOo

"Where are we now?"

"I've absolutely no idea. My sense of geography has entirely escaped me."

"Would've thought you'd have a better idea, sat up there on that horse!"

"Well, I'm sure you are very kind to provide me with so lofty a perch, but, as things are now, I wish you had not have bothered."

Carr grinned and took his attention away from Drake, who was doing his best to make himself more comfortable in the elaborate, but not necessarily well designed, French saddle. Carr turned to the 'recorder' of the Light Company, Lieutenant Richard Shakeshaft.

"Richard, can you help? What have we been up to?"

Shakeshaft pulled his diary out of his tunic pocket, it residing there for easy access.

"Well, Sir, if you want the details, we left Pamplona the day after our arrival to cut off Clausel, all beginning with a forced march to Mendavia. The next day, the 27th, another to a place called Tafalla, via somewhere called Lerin, where Miles annoyed the locals and they threw things at him when he tried to talk to a young lady. They do not like strangers, I have noted. The 28th was spent going nowhere using roads in the middle of nowhere, but we did end up at somewhere called Melida and today we marched out of there and I do believe we are now marching in something close to the opposite direction. I do have a compass, you see."

"Very good, Richard, and what have you said about Clausel?"

"That we've missed him. He's escaped."

Drake had been listening carefully.

"Seeing as we're now going back to where we came from, I'd say that is something on which we can all easily agree. Johnny's slipped through the net."

Carr pulled a wry face.

"I wonder if Wellington shares our view?"

He looked up at Drake.

"Do you have the map?"

"I do, but I would place its provenance at some time during the time of the Spanish Armada."

"Perhaps, but nothing much changes around here. Let me have a look."

The map was handed down and Carr pulled it open.

"So, Richard, the last town we were in was Melida and we have been heading where, since then? In which direction?"

"Sort of North, but a bit East. Sir."

Carr held the map out for him and pointed to its lower right centre.

"There's Melida. Make your best guess."

Shakeshaft placed his own finger on the town and moved it in what he thought was the correct direction of that day's march, until he came to some writing against the road he was following.

"Sanguesa! Assuming that our orders do include a town. Sir."

"A valid question, Richard. Only time will tell."

Time did tell and in the middle of the afternoon they did enter a town called Sanguesa, but the time of the past four days had told also, all mostly spent on forced marches over little more than goat tracks in the hope of cutting off the Corps of General Clausel. It was now common knowledge that he had rashly marched hard to join forces with El Rey Joseph prior to the battle of Vitoria, but was too late to contribute and then also too late in discovering the French disaster. On the fourth day of the pursuit with hope still residing at Wellington's Headquarters, however feint and fading, the 3rd, 4th and Light Divisions marched into Sanguesa and the Officers of the 105th settled into one floor of a large building near the town centre. Dutiful to his men as he was, W. Anson called around to inform all of what he knew and he did not mince his words.

"The Peer has had us charging around, following one rumour after another about the whereabouts of Clausel. So, Lowry-Cole, Picton and Alten have all told him straight that the men have no more forced marches left in them and the reply has just come back that Clausel got away South-East to Saragosa, tens of miles away from here. So, tomorrow we march back to Pamplona, at normal pace."

The same information was circulating around the ranks, but for them as mere rumour, nothing official, Tom Miles being the first to vent his anger, rumour or not, of where they were now going. He well knew what they had just been through and he vented all his anger as he prepared the evening meal, examining for quality the chunks of salt pork as they were passed across to him, cutting off the parts most offensive with his clasp knife.

"So, the whole thing was just a wild goose chase done at top pace. On they tracks as they sent us over, my boots near fell apart and my shoulders is near raw from bouncin' kit as we was ordered to jog and run."

Deakin looked up at him.

"Now I don't know what you'm getting' so vexed about, where's the surprise? Who promised you that there'd be no chasin' after any Frogs runnin' off after Vitoria? No surprise that we was sent off somewer, to catch up with some of the leftovers as is makin' off to some place of safety."

Miles was in no way suppressed, even though the counter came from Jed Deakin.

"Ah, but why us, the Fourth? There's plenty of other Divisions as fired not one shot all that day. Why not they, to be sent off on the roads huntin' for some fast marchin' Frogs?"

"You knows what he's like, as well as I, choosin' those as he fancies, you'm chosen or not as it may be. All I can say is, that he don't throw lives away for nothing, but when it comes to anything else in this war, he just orders and expects, however tall the order."

Miles scowled.

"I'm only sayin', that's all. Don't seem fair, that's a fact, an' that's all I'm sayin'."

Zeke Saunders had been sat by listening, more amused than angered at the spleen-venting outburst from Tom Miles.

"So how's you jaw after you was hit by that flowerpot thrown by that matron back in that village?"

Miles turned on him, annoyance now occupying his face even more, but rubbing the bruise, nevertheless.

"There weren't no need for that! All I was doin' was helpin' her get that heavy bucket up over the edge of that well. Chuckin' stuff like that at a body as is just tryin' to help."

Saunders laughed.

"You're lucky it wasn't her Father as saw you. He'd have thrown a knife! Most around here is pretty handy with the cutlery. You should know by now what they're like with their womenfolk. You've got to go through the whole family before you can even sit in the same room, with everyone else sat around and watching that you behaves yourself."

Miles had by now subsided somewhat.

"Well, I've heard similar, but all that sounds altogether too....... too ...."

John Byford helped him finish the sentence.

"Convoluted!"

Saunders looked at him.

"Well that sounds like the perfect word, if any of us, other than you, had any idea what it meant."

"It means complicated, involved, drawn out."

Saunders turned back to Miles

"There you are Tom. If you wants to get involved with a local girl, then first you've got to get yourself convoluted."

Laughter greeted the comment whilst Miles returned to stirring the pot for their salt-pork, dried pea and biscuit stew. All around the stable that was their billet, there were now grins of amusement and even Tom Miles managed a return to his normal shrew-like expression.

The following day, at the same time as the Corps made up from the 3rd, 4th and Light Divisions embarked upon a leisurely return to Pamplona that would take a day and a half, the advanced guard of General Graham's Corps was advancing up the road from Tolosa, with G. Anson's Brigade at the van, closely pursued by General Longa's Cantabrians at their best speed. This particular combination of infantry and cavalry found full approval amongst the members of Two Squadron, Corporal James Makepeace in particular, now that they were some way into the day's advance, him enjoying one of the fruits of their close co-operation, a length of dried fish.

"Good lads, those Cantabrian boys. Always up for a bit of trade. Seems they'm well off for dried meat and fish. Wine too, but a bit short on tobacco."

Alongside him, Sergeant Baxter grinned.

"Just as well, bein' as you don't smoke and you took half of mine, seein' as I don't much, neither."

Makepeace took the hint and handed over a strip of dried beef as the Brigade trotted on, but wine was not an issue because much was handed up to them as they eased their way unopposed through the villages along the road to San Sebastian. This seaside fortress they passed merely two miles to its South, but unseen behind the surrounding hills. What they did see were the continuing signs of French retreat, less and less discarded equipment, but depressingly the same number of French stragglers as on previous days. Many that had fallen behind, probably because of wounds, were all now hanging from trees by the roadside, thankfully only very few mutilated.

The day finished at the village of Irun, or rather its outskirts, because very obviously it was well populated by French soldiers. The order came to 'pull off and camp' and that they did, Longa's Brigade arriving soon after, with General Graham at their head, to make camp themselves close by, whilst Graham and his Staff collected together at a large farmhouse, where all assumed that, along with Longa and Anson, the events for the following day were being planned. Carr and Peterson took it upon themselves to wander into the Spanish camp, if only from curiosity, but they were soon made aware of the mood of the Spanish, both being waved into the gathering of a group of Officers. Before any words were spoken, both received a large beaker which was quickly filled with red wine, their 'host' standing to fill each to the brim. Fortunately, he spoke a version of English, unlike his companions, but each stood to touch beakers with their English guests. Their host bid them sit on actual chairs vacated by two Spanish Officers who were happy to stand, then their host beamed at them.

"English! Now we, together, have beaten the sucio, dirty, French, si? Is today we can say that ….."

He held up his left hand, fingers spread and he counted two, the forefinger and the middle finger.

"………. dos ligas, of Spain stands under their sucio boots."

Carr nodded and pointed to his own corresponding fingers.

"Two! Two leagues."

The Officer reached across and clapped him on the shoulder.

"Two! Si, two only! And tomorrow will be no ligas. Tomorrow all Franceses back in their own filthy country, in their own filthy holes."

He then turned to his fellow Officers, his beaker held high.

"Larga vida a Espana libre! Un brindis por los valientes, ingleses combatientes!"

All stood, raised their beakers and drank. Peterson had some idea what had been said and felt the need to respond, so he raised his own beaker and Carr followed.

"And to our brave, valiant Spanish allies!"

Their host translated, which words were met with a chorus of approval. With that, he stood and ushered them further into the Brigade camp.

"I am Teniente Cristiano Fortesa, Come, you see, this all, how you say, celabracion!"

Both gave their names in response, then Peterson nodded and replied.

"We say that, too, or nearly, celebration!"

The Spaniard laughed and clapped him on the shoulder, then he held out his arm, indicating forward.

"Come! There is much to see."

He was correct. The Cantabrians had their own Followers and many were very talented and, in several places, a woman and a soldier were up on transport wagons dancing to the accompaniment of guitars and drums, themselves adding to the percussion with curious wooden plates held in the palms of their hands which they clicked as they danced. Carr and Peterson did not fail to notice several Troopers of Anson's Brigade, who had come over to trade and were now all thoroughly caught up in the universal merriment and the carnival atmosphere. All around the dancers, their audience clapped and cheered encouragement and Fortesa pointed to one couple who seemed to have thoroughly mastered the routine involved of one particular dance.

"This is our own dance, tradicional dance, la Romeria Montanesa. When the French were here, they throw in prison all who do! Now we do, right under noses, as you say. Is our way of saying we are here now, you go. Deja nuestra tierra! To France with you."

Carr nodded approval, then he had a sudden thought.

"Is this Cantabria? Here? This region?'

Fortesa nodded.

"Si. Here this place. We first to be taken by Franceses. Was very bad time for Cantabrians.."

However, he still had his beaker and he hurried over to a group, spoke in rapid Spanish and then returned with a bottle of wine, from which he refilled both his own and those of the pair.

"Manana we see Franceses over river, la sagrado Bidassoa, then all Spain libre!"

The beakers of the three were once more clashed together, then Peterson bowed to the Officer.

"We must take our leave. We have duties. We both thank you for your kindness."

The Officer threw out both arms, the wine spilling.

"Stay! We drink some more. See more dancing."

Peterson bowed again, they were plainly in grave danger of returning to their own lines in a very drunken state, that to be avoided and so he declined again.

"Once again, thank you Cristiano, but no. We have duties for this night."

Peterson went through the motions of ordering and presenting arms with an imaginary musket and this time only the palms of Fortesa's hands were displayed, but this time in understanding.

"Ah! El deber centinela."

Both Peterson and Carr nodded vigorously and both shook his hand, this time Carr speaking.

"Teniente Fortesa. We wish you good luck."

A huge grin split the Cantabrian's face.

"And buena suerte to you, to you both, Tenientes Wee loo bee and Dug lass."

They turned and headed back and out of the camp, not forgetting to return their beakers and wave good-bye at their first hosts. When on their way, Carr sighed.

"I cannot remember seeing such happiness as that anywhere in Spain or Portugal, not since we first came here."

Peterson nodded, then sighed himself.

"I can only agree. One can only think how we would feel and react if an occupying power was at last ejected from what we call hearth and home."

The following day the Cantabrians were the first on the road, perhaps not in parade order, but plainly eager to be on with the business of the day. Whatever the eagerness of either, Anson's Brigade were the first to move and they advanced towards the actual village of Irun, but this time it appeared thoroughly deserted, or at least soon to be. A Troop of Chasseurs emerged and spread themselves across the outer garden walls of the town, but they soon spun their horses to disappear back into the streets and alleyways. Smythe's Squadron was sent ahead to also become absorbed into the narrow environs, but the ensuing silence spoke that the town was now deserted and Anson led the rest of his Brigade through the abandoned and dishevelled streets, the only sound the echo of their horses hooves between the narrow walls. However, once through, they rode another mile and Graham himself arrived at their head and immediately halted the column. They had come to another village, much smaller than Irun. Graham turned to Anson.

"Get some men in there."

Anson waved at a Squadron of the 12th, who rode in, but soon rode back out to signal no occupation. They rode through what was now a scene of complete despoliation, more than Irun; this village being what had once been the quiet and prosperous village of Behobia, the last Spanish settlement before the Bidassoa. The place had been pulled apart, no roofs at all, in some cases not even walls remained in place, windows and doors entirely gone. Once through, having picked their way over streets strewn with smashed furniture, Graham halted the column once more and the reason was obvious, they were facing the final French rearguard, so should he attack with his force, or hold back? Over to the right, there was a very high ridge which dominated the whole area, but streaming down from it was a whole French Brigade, the head of which was even then hurrying along the bank of the Bidassoa towards the bridge that crossed into France. This bridge area had been heavily fortified by the French for the rearguard, many telescopes among Anson's Brigade picking out, on the Spanish bank, a solid blockhouse at the bridge and a substantial length of palisade either side. Oakwood closed his own telescope.

"That's for tomorrow. No point wasting men against that. He'll bring up his guns and deal with it that way. Tomorrow's fine, where's the hurry?"

Indeed there was none and this was the mood, as Anson's Brigade, in obedience to Graham's orders, began the circuitous route to the top of the dominating ridge, it now occupied by a Spanish Brigade. Plainly it was these who had earlier dislodged the French from the summit, all of whom were now over the river. The 16th's horses felt the half-hour climb, but the view from the top was remarkable, all Officers immediately taking themselves to the small Church that crowned the highest point. The scene was set out below them, the bridge over the Bidassoa, the village of Behobia, now occupied by their own forces, the French lines on the Spanish side and the massed French forces now within their own country beyond the river. Meanwhile, the tide of the day swirled up the river channel, sending white tracers of foam from around the central supports of Behobia bridge and, down closer to the sea, the tide negotiated the shallows and islands that marked the change to a wide estuary seen a mile downstream, with a walled town on the estuary bank of the Spanish side. Oakwood folded his arms and took a long look from left to right, then he turned to Carr.

"Over there, Willoughby. That's France!"

Carr looked for himself and managed a broad smile, then the order came to make camp and, once again, Anson's men shared camping ground with Spanish infantry, different from those of the previous evening, but of Cantabrian nationality nevertheless. Although they did not have their Followers, celebrations were soon in progress, singing and drinking beginning mid-afternoon and building with the oncoming darkness. Baxter and Makepeace were stood on English sentry duty, drinking illicit wine brought to them by Spanish sentries. Little was said between the two Light Cavalrymen, little was needed, as their comradeship and shared experience stretched back too far over too many years to require any level of convivial conversation. Instead they watched as the lights were extinguished in the houses on the French side and the campfires of the defeated French died in the hills behind.

The following day, they had a grandstand view of events as planned and executed by Graham. He had brought up not one battery, but two, and soon solid shot was battering the blockhouse and the palisades either side of it. Both shot and chunks of masonry were flung back into the waters and the wicker revetments of the palisades were soon battered into a mess of shattered staves and scattered sand. After an hour the French defenders fell back from their lines and an explosion occurred in the blockhouse, but only partially causing anything like serious damage. However, at that point two Companies of French Voltiguers charged across the bridge and the defenders took their cue that reinforcements had arrived and, alongside the Voltiguers, they ran back to the wreck of their position. There they were met by a whole Battalion of Spanish Cantabrians immediately sent forward by Graham and the result was a fierce and brutal exchange, with both sides fighting for possession of the gaping blockhouse and ruined trenches; musket butts, boots and bayonets being used against opponents much more than any standard musketry. The conflict seemed to last longer than expected, the only French now remaining on the Spanish side were the four hundred plus, all contesting the old position, but it crossed the mind of many that the elite French Voltiguers were reluctant to give way, which exceeded good sense, perhaps because giving best to the despised Spanish was more than many could bring themselves to do. However, others French veterans, more experienced, saw what was happening behind them on the bridge, where engineers were spreading tar oil and gunpowder, such that, when the Voltiguers and others eventually did fall back, obeying their bugle-call and having bought the necessary time, burning torches were thrown and the wooden bridge soon became a raging conflagration. Yet this did not in any way deflate the Cantabrians, who now lined the bank either side of the burning bridge, taunting the French now back on the French side, shaking fists, waving muskets and yelling every Spanish insult they had ever learned. All screamed over the turgid water, even through the dense smoke, but no matter, all were eager to let the French know that now only Spaniards stood on their bank of the sacred Bidassoa.

oOo

As the smoke of the burning bridge at Behobia curled inland, this event highly significant within the Spanish conflict, back in London, four men, each of imposing stature, bar one, strode into the grand entrance hall of the Official Residence of the Secretary of State for War. As they marched across it, the echo of their footfalls was deadened by the grand and even daunting paintings covering the walls either side, each having as its subject a heroic English victory, either naval or military and all against the French. In the lead was the Secretary of State for War himself, Henry Bathurst, the 3rd Earl of that name. The two immediately following were military and dressed as such, with many decorations on show, these being General Livermore and Colonel Waters. The fourth was as civilian as Bathurst in his dressing, walking behind all, but this one was slight and unimposing, bar his immaculate black suit and white linen. With his pale, intelligent eyes missing nothing of his surroundings as he followed his superiors, Redeemed Radipole carried the necessary papers. The Official Residence had been given over for the use of the Austrian Ambassador, Maximillian Friedrich, Count Von Merveldt, for his latest visit to England and it was this notable personage that the four had come to visit. The purpose was to discuss the possibility of Austria's entry into the war as part of what would be a Sixth Coalition against Napoleon. Bathurst remained in the lead, as they ascended the wide marble staircase, which split into two halfway up and Bathurst took the right wing when they came to the junction, with Livermore just behind at his right shoulder. Waters and Radipole, were now side by side and almost in step, bringing up the rear.

Livermore made no attempt at conversation with Bathurst, all had been discussed the previous day, all he could do was to weigh up in his head what difference the victory at Vitoria would make for Austrian ambitions. They had just heard that morning of agreement at the Convention of Reichenbach, where the promise of one half million Sterling to Austria and one million each to Prussia and Russia had been confirmed, this being Britain's unequivocal commitment to a Coalition, but, as it was not yet formalised, the group were there to attempt the final agreement. As a fifth member of the Coalition, already signed up, Sweden needed no more persuading, having been promised Norway. The main concern for Bathurst and Livermore was that Austria had agreed at Reichenbach to enter the war as part of a Sixth Coalition, but only if

Napoleon rejected all terms offered to extend the Treaty of Pleischwitz, which had ended the fighting between France and the Alliance of Russia and Prussia during the Spring of that year. However, there was something extra which gave Bathurst greater anxiety, and it always applied to diplomats, this being that Von Merveldt certainly now knew far more about events between the three 'Allies' than they did and armed with such exclusive knowledge, a man with the negotiating experience of Von Merveldt could manoeuvre Great Britain into a position not necessarily to her best advantage.

Bathurst came to an elaborate double door and had the good manners to knock. It opened immediately, as though they had been expected at that second, and the Equerry to the Ambassador bowed to allow entrance. Von Merveldt was sat waiting, occupying one of three chairs, each of such elaboration that anyone would have identified them as pre-Revolutionary French, as indeed they were, as were all the other decorations and furnishings in the sumptuous room. Von Merveldt rose to shake hands with Bathurst, whilst Waters, remaining by the door with Radipole, remarked to himself that the pair who now stood opposite each other could be brothers, each roughly the same height and build and each appearing within one year of 50, which was true, Von Merveldt one before and Bathurst one after. Bathurst then turned slightly to introduce Livermore.

"Count Von Merveldt. May I introduce General Livermore, my Under-Secretary."

Von Merveldt bowed before shaking hands, then he indicated that the two should sit in the vacant chairs. Sherry was then provided, Von Merveldt having developed a taste for the British adopted wine, but three glasses only, for the number now sitting and he raised his glass, yet spoke no toast. With the glasses returned to the silver tray, Bathurst began.

"Count Maximillian, you will have heard of our significant victory at Vitoria. It caused thousands of French casualties and yielded as many prisoners and also a vast amount of captured materiel. Now there are no potent French forces on the Spanish side of the Pyrenees, bar those besieged in Pamplona and San Sebastian. When both those fortresses fall, we will invade France itself and with the French armies of Spain and Portugal now scattered, depleted and under-resourced, having lost so much, there is no reason to suppose that our coming invasion will not be successful. Then, with an enemy standing on French home soil, pressure on Napoleon will be huge, to either transfer men away from the Elbe, thus weakening himself against yourselves, Russia, Prussia and Sweden, or he makes a disadvantageous peace by extending Pleischwitz with Russia and Prussia, which would be equally advantageous to Austria allowing you to assemble your own armies. However, it would also be of some advantage to Napoleon for the same reason, it would, I fear, give him time to rebuild, which must not be allowed. Buonaparte knows that there is now a foreign army as potent as Wellington's on his South-Western border, just beyond the Pyrenees and you three, plus Sweden, massing in the East and then advancing against him, will spell the end of his reign in Europe. He will attempt to delay this by extending Pleischwitz, therefore Excellency, surely the time is now to form a new Coalition against him and not continue the peace, to any degree?"

Bathurst then turned to Livermore.

"So, how do you see the future, General, in South-West France?"

Livermore folded his arms and looked squarely at Von Merveldt.

"Your Excellency, the army as now commanded by General Wellington is, in my opinion, the best we've ever put into a foreign field. It is now unified under Wellington, veteran, well supplied and well commanded, right down to Battalion level. They will be the first Allied army to walk on French soil and I do not see how they can suffer a setback of any description, given the condition of the French army post Vitoria. Militarily, the time has come for Napoleon's final defeat, if the four nations can bring themselves to combine with us against him. We do not need to tell you that His Majesty's Government would far prefer that your noble country become formally part of the Sixth Coalition which we are attempting to construct, rather than retain your current position of 'armed neutrality'."

Von Merveldt smiled and placed the tip of a forefinger vertically against his upper lip, then he thought for some seconds before answering. He spoke perfect English.

"Napoleon still has upwards of 300,000 men on the Elbe, opposing any coalition armies that we could put into the field and they are commanded by Napoleon himself. I do not need to remind you of the humiliations my country has suffered at the hands of him and his forces. The risk of that being repeated still exists."

Livermore sat forward.

"Excellency. We know that what he still calls the Grand Armee is nothing like the one which he took into Russia last year. He is weak in reliable units and especially weak in cavalry. I do not see how the force he has, even commanded by such as himself, could halt, never mind throw back, the kind of force that your own nation, combined with Russia, Prussia and Sweden, could put into the field. If you wish to be rid of him and end the ten years of this continuous war, then the time is now.

He soon will have us at his back, having poured in through his back door!"

Merveldt smiled at the English allegory, but Bathurst had now sat forward and so Von Merveldt turned towards him. Bathurst took a deep breath. The crucial moment had arrived.

"At Reichenbach we made a promise of finance to you and that still stands. Half a million sterling, but let me ask, what response have you had from Prussia and Russia?"

Von Merveldt sat back.

"They think as we do. Especially Prussia, because for them also, victories against the French have been few and far between, so they remain cautious. However, after Napoleon's Russian disaster, Russia and Prussia took the opportunity last March to declare war, but the Armistice of Pleischwitz re-established peace. Extending Pleischwitz now is very tempting for us. In the case of Russia, any advance against the French border will be a long way from home. They have cleared the French from their homeland and do not expect him to return. Why should they now fight our fight having successfully prosecuted their own? As for Prussia, that threat of reinvasion for them is indeed more real as we speak. However, it is diminished I acknowledge, because of the loose, but existing, Alliance that now exists between us three, all sat opposite him on the Elbe. As you say, that Alliance could be formalised into the Coalition you describe, but Buonaparte, needing time, knows this and may agree terms to extend the Pleischwitz Armistice, however onerous to himself."

Bathurst shook his head.

"If we give Napoleon time by extending Pleischwitz, he will recover and try again, especially against you and the Prussians, and then perhaps Russia again, who knows? This is the time, now, to strike whilst his forces are weak. We won against him at Vitoria because they ran out of men, as much as anything. El Rey Joseph had no reserves. He ran out of men because Napoleon removed some from Spain to bolster his Eastern front against you. If you could only occupy him in the East, Wellington could be in Paris by the Autumn, or Napoleon would be forced to send at least a Corps away from you and down to South-West France to add to the defence of France down there, which would substantially add to the chances of your own victory."

Von Merveldt looked at him steadily.

"You have offered finance to us. You have also offered finance to Prussia and Russia. If so, how much?"

Bathurst's face became blank. The terms of Reichenback were not yet common knowledge, all were the product of individual negotiations.

"We have offered, yes, but the final amount is under discussion and dependant, as I'm sure you understand, on the level of commitment that they are prepared to offer."

Bathurst then sat forward even further, he was worried. Von Merveldt's expression and tone gave him warning that he knew something important that Bathurst did not, or that he was engaged in diplomatic dissembling with the aim of avoiding any firm commitment. Bathurst spoke firmly.

"Excellency, Great Britain is doing all she can to end this Buonaparte menace once and for all. Already we are financing Spain and Portugal and clearing those countries using our own armies. Our own blood and treasure. Our financial offers to your country and those to Russia and Prussia are firm. We can only ask that you press your own Government to encourage Prussia and Russia to terminate the Pleischwitz Armistice, by making a firm commitment that your country, Austria, join both in the field if they decide to seriously prosecute a war against Buonaparte. That would make five of us, allied together, when Pleischwitz finally fails."

Von Merveldt smiled, his lips stretching just enough to register pleasure, or perhaps merely registering an understanding of Bathurst's anxiety.

"I'm sure you can appreciate that I cannot commit my country to such an undertaking myself. We have a Government, as you do. What I can say is that I will soon return to Austria and what you have stated to me and what you have again offered will be discussed. Your victory at Vitoria has certainly made a difference."

Von Merveldt now leaned forward slightly, a conspiratorial smile on his lips, his body supported by his right forearm over his knee.

"What I can tell you now, is that only this morning, by fast courier I received word on the Dresden Conference between our Foreign Minister, Prince Klemens Wenzel Von Metternich and Buonaparte himself. The subject was Pleischwitz and it was discussed with a view to achieving an extension. Von Metternich brought peace proposals from Russia and Prussia, which called for the return of Illyria to Russia, this being all the lands on the East coast of the Adriatic. The terms also included the return of pre-Revolution Austrian territories to the South of the Alps, usurped after Marengo; the dissolution of the Duchy of Warsaw; the return of France's eastern boundary back to the Rhine and the break-up of the Confederation of the Rhine, Buonaparte's puppet Governments there."

He paused, whilst Bathurst's and Livermore's spirits sank, then he continued openly grinning.

"The result was that Napoleon rejected the proposals and has refused to compromise."

Both Bathurst and Livermore sat back in their chairs, both stunned by the news, but Bathurst was the first to recover.

"So, Count, that tells us that Pleischwitz will not be renewed. The terms have been rejected, so Austria will place armies into the field alongside those of Prussia and Russia. Also, of course, there is the fact of Russia and Prussia being allied by a mutual defence pact signed at the Treaty of Kalisch. The Sixth Coalition is complete!"

Von Merveldt shook his head.

"Almost, Lord Bathurst, almost, but not quite. Nothing is as yet signed and we, Austria, remain in our position of armed neutrality. You have an English saying, do you not, about slips between cups and lips, but you also have another about events being 'in the bag'."

He then sat forward even further, his voice diminishing in volume.

"What I say to you now must remain with us."

He pointed to Waters and Radipole remaining at the door.

"Their silence is assured?"

Livermore nodded vigorously.

"Absolutely, Excellency."

Von Merveldt nodded and continued.

"After the failure of the Dresden conference, your 'in the bag' is more likely. I should say our joining you is almost certain. Buonaparte has offered to send his Minister Coulaincourt to try to negotiate again to extend Pleischwitz, but Von Metternich has acceded to this only to create time during which we can re-arm. Von Metternich will insist on the ending of the Confederation of the Rhine, the 16 German States controlled by Napoleon. The ending of this he will certainly refuse, so, look to August, then we will formally be on your side. And in the field."

He noticed the pleasure on the faces of the two sat before him, even the smiles crossing the faces of the two stood by the door, then he actually grinned again as he sat back, before signalling to the servant stood behind him. More sherry arrived and the servant even took it upon himself to carry two glasses over to Waters and Radipole. Their own sherry now received, whilst the fine glasses of those sat on the chairs clinked together, these two touched their own glasses for their own toast.

oOo

Oblivious to events miles to the North of them and certainly to those far away in London, on that same day were set in motion some of the details discussed by such influential figures as Bathurst and Von Merveldt. Events debated in London were discussed in terms of the concerns of nations, not the mere affairs of Brigades and Divisions commanded by mere Major and Lieutenant Generals, but as part of the latter, the 3rd, 4th and Light Divisions returned to Pamplona, after their fruitless chase of the escaping Clausel. In the case of the 4th Division, they were required to march straight into the trenches opposite the citadel and for that afternoon, that night and most of the next morning they sat contemplating the formidable defences shown clearly in the morning sunshine. All could now be seen in more detail, three walls in succession extending back towards the central Keep, the second and third walls higher than the one before, such that the outer wall could count on artillery support from the two behind. The 105th sat their trench, all studying the elaborate and very intimidating defences, the French tricolour barely stirring in the heated air currents that ascended from the many warm surfaces of the citadel. As so often, the two Sages of the Colour Company, Deakin and Halfway smoked whilst studying the unmoving view before them, bar the occasional movement of a sentry behind an embrasure, the gap blinking as he passed. This time it was Halfway who began the discussion.

"You reckon he'll send us at that lot, like he did Badajoz?"

Deakin shook his head without removing his own pipe.

"No! Not even him. There's no breaching them walls, and there's no castle on the outside to climb over. That's as tough as we saw down at Elvas. A place like that, you has to starve out. No other way."

Halfway was nothing like so certain.

"Ah, but how far's Johnny up the road? He's back at home now, near enough, and could gather up more men and come back down. Try to relieve this place."

"Could be Tobe, but Vitoria wrecked just about every army he's got. All scattered, bar that Clausel we went chasin' after, but he'll be in no shape to do much too soon. We'll be further up together ourselves an' stronger, afore he's in any way pulled himself up together. I can't see the Frogs comin' back to claim this place again."

His pipe now exhausted, he knocked out the dottle on a nearby stone.

"I may be wrong, but I can't see it. So, I'll be happy to sit here a while, in peace and quiet with Bridie's cookin' twice a day."

He looked at his friend, grinning.

"So how be things with you and Esme?"

Halfway swayed his head from side to side in non-committal fashion.

"Well, she's handy enough with a needle and thread. And glad enough to count herself alongside me!"

Deakin grinned even more.

"Well, if only that, 'tis good to have a good woman up by your side. I'd say we've seen the worst of this, there'll be no more severe worryin' over what could happen to the likes of our own. I can't see another retreat, not like that back to Roger's Town. Nor that for Coruna."

Halfway nodded agreement, adding nothing of his own, but the ensuing silence was disturbed by the sound of marching feet and both turned around to see at least a Brigade marching in behind them. Halfway's brows came together.

"Hello! What's this?"

The answer came in the form of RSM Gibney, now stood behind them.

"We're out of here! These of the 7th is taking over. So, pull the'selves away an' take off back t'camp."

However, Halfway felt the need to pry.

"What do you know, Sar' Major?"

Whilst watching the Colour Company file out of their section of trench, Gibney spoke.

"What ah knows, Corporal Halfway, is that Hill is off to some valley called the Bastan, then up to a place as calls itself Maya. He's off wi' the 2nd, the Light, an' some Portuguese. Tomorrow, these 7th comes out to follow Hill and we goes back in t'here. Then turn and turnabout until some Spanish comes up to relieve us an' then we're out."

"And then?"

"Who knows, Halfway lad? Who knows?"'

oOo

They were making the journey as a result of a debate amongst their group regarding what to do with their store of doubloons gathered from the French baggage camp at Vitoria. The subject was kept secret, the venue of the meeting some way out of camp and the final agreement was that the money could not remain in their dog-cart, a better solution needed to be found before they quit Pamplona, a decision that did not take long to agree on. Therefore, it was five, almost embarrassed, foot soldiers who turned the corner into the main street of Pamplona, embarrassed for the way they stood out amongst the Pamplonians, all going about their business, well dressed and well presented. Pamplona, so near the French border, had largely been spared the brutal attentions of a French army on campaign. The five were conspicuous, not only for their soldiers' uniform but more because of its sheer wear and tear. All had patches on the knees of their trousers with the cuffs of each leg badly frayed and their jackets were now more a greyish pink, rather than the proud red they once had been and all had crude sewing to repair rents and tears and hold on patches of different patterns and shades. However, many men tipped their hats to the four and shook their hands and greeted them warmly. A gypsy woman had given each a sprig of lucky heather, asking no charge, but John Davey gave her an escudo anyway. Most notable was when one woman kissed Tom Miles, to the great amusement of the other four, to which derision he took his usual degree of umbrage.

"I don't see what's so strange about that!"

Holding to that opinion, he then looked around for another woman to sidle up to, but at that point they had arrived at the entrance to the Banco de Coruna which formed part of the banking community of Pamplona and so Miles was pushed in through the door. Inside they were confronted by a long, gleaming mahogany counter and the five walked up to a clerk who was free and each dropped a heavy bag of doubloons onto the worn, but polished surface. Byford had spent some time discovering the correct Spanish.

"Deseamos transferir el valor de estos a un banco inglés."

The others knew exactly what he was saying and nodded vigorously. The clerk nodded also and replied.

"Si, Senor. Coutts de Londres sera satisfactorio?"

That Byford understood well enough, that the value of their doubloons would be lodged to their credit with Coutts and Co. in London.

"Si. Perfectamente."

At this point, Tom Miles, ever suspicious, came up to Byford's shoulder.

"What'll happen now?"

"The clerk here will work out how much our doubloons are worth in sterling and give us a Note of Credit for that amount. He'll send a note to Coutts Bank in London telling them all about it, so that when we walk in with our Note to their London office, we'll be given the value of these doubloons in pounds, shillings and pence."

Miles' face turned to astonishment as he looked at the clerk, then the doubloons, then at Byford as his natural suspicions rose.

"How do we know that these is straight? They could be a bunch of twistin' bastards!"

At that point the Clerk, busy counting the doubloons, looked up and spoke, albeit with a heavy Spanish accent.

"I can assure you, Sir, that all will happen just as your friend here has described."

Byford's face broke into a broad grin as he looked at him.

"You speak English! Why so?"

The clerk grinned back.

"I spent much time dealing with English merchants in Coruna. I even spent some months working in your City of London."

Byford turned to Miles.

"There you are! A London lad, well almost."

Miles was not wholly convinced.

"And this Coutts crowd. Who be they? Have you heard of 'em."

It was the clerk who replied.

"I worked there, Sir, when I was in London. We have very good relations with them."

Then Byford added his opinion.

"They were the bankers of my family during my fall from grace and I would think still are, so I have certainly heard of them. No one there is going to twist us out of the bit of money that applies to us. Coutts has been there for almost two hundred years. They deal in thousands, millions!"

Byford then turned to fully face Tom Miles.

"And there's not a Court in the land that would not enforce the Note of Credit this gentleman is about to give us. Not one!"

Saunders then grinned and spoke up.

"There you are Tom. The law will be on your side. For a change!"

However, Tom Miles was barely listening, his attention was drawn away to the noisy clicking of the abacus as the beads sped across the oak rods and the clerk made his calculations. Once the beads were still, the clerk began writing something below the counter, then he turned to an important looking man sat at a desk behind him and spoke words that even Byford could not understand. Their clerk passed the note back to the man, who studied it and signed it to then pass it back and their clerk handed it straight over to Byford, who nodded his thanks, then spoke in Spanish.

"Gracias, Senor. Estamos agradecidos."

The clerk smiled.

"It is us who should be grateful to you."

With that all five walked away from the counter, but Miles was at Byford's elbow.

"How much?"

Byford held the Note of Credit out for him. Miles could not read the words, but he knew figures. He sucked in a breath.

"Three hundred and ten pounds, five shillings!"

The remaining three, almost as shocked as Miles, craned their necks to see for themselves, but Byford handed the note to Saunders so that both could stare at it, but Miles was still worried.

"What if that bit of paper gets lost!"

This gained him Davey's attention.

"Fair question, Tom, but like we said last night, how long do you think that coin would stay in our cart, when word gets round as to what's in there? On top, 'twas a heavy load for the girls to lug up and down, 'specially as we'n now goin' up into the mountains. We sends that note to my Mother and she'll keep it safe."

The unimpeachable trustworthiness of Davey's Mother was known to all and now even Miles was satisfied, but Byford added some more security.

"We'll not send it normal post, but through the Battalion, who'll send it on to John's Mother. The Quartermaster told me all about it, that plenty of letters and whatnot for the Officers arrive that way. Best way, too, I think, just for a few extra Escudos. And we'll get a full and detailed receipt. That we will have to keep safe, just in case."

With that, they returned to their camp, using the streets they had used to get there, with Miles placing himself in the path of any single woman approaching, but all to no effect, whilst the others discussed the sense of what they had done, easily convincing themselves that they had made a good choice. Once back in camp they bumped into RSM Gibney.

"Where's tha'all been?"

It was Davey who answered.

"Bit of shopping, Sar'major. For the women. A bit of sightseeing, too, we may not be back here again."

Gibney frowned, but said no more on the subject, instead he said something that they wanted to hear.

"The Spanish have arrived to take over in't trenches. Tomorrow, we're off up t'road. Place called Roncesvalles."

oOo

Thus it was, come the following day, that with light feet the partners of the Coutts' Note of Credit began the march up the valley of the River Arga as part of W. Anson's Brigade, this making up one third of Lowry-Cole's 4th Division. Anson and Stubbs remained as his Brigadiers, but Skerret had been replaced by Ross, the former now returned to England. There was little change in the Brigade since Salamanca, this remaining as the 48th, the 27th, the 105th and one Company of the 60th Rifles but, post Vitoria, the Provisional Battalion was now some of the 53rd Shropshire and some of the 2nd Foot, The Queen's Royals. There were few complaining about leaving the heat of the plain in mid-July even with the prospect of a long climb, such that on the second day of their march, the 17th July, they were in the cool of the mountains with running water plentiful, but the mountains brought its own travails, first remarked upon by the newest Officer of the 105th Light Company.

"A lot more up than down, this. Sir."

"Why yes, Lionel, I mean Luttrel. No surprise really, we are, after all, marching into the Pyrenees."

Bettridge almost immediately regretted his almost asinine comment, but not quite. Some conversation had to be better than none, no matter how crass, and there was some truth in what he was saying. Their march up to the French frontier was definitely one third down, into valleys and river basins and two thirds up, although Drake had just pointed out that they were advancing to the summit of the Pyrenees. Therefore, Bettridge continued.

"Rumour has it that our destination is somewhere called Roncesvalles. We've already got two Divisions up there."

"I think I can confirm that, Luttrel. And, if memory serves, it's got a bit of history to it. Something Holy about it too, judging by the number of Pilgrims coming the other way, despite the fact that there's a war on. The name's ringing distant and cracked bells, from where I've no idea. Something literate and legendary, I believe, and it's been nagging since we left Pamplona. Whatever, truth will out from some direction, I feel sure."

The day terminated at Lintzoain, after a march on a road that twisted, turned, dropped and climbed alarmingly, such that each Company was required at some stage to drop back and help with the transport wagons, pushing at the rear or pulling on towing ropes. However, the village itself proved to be very pleasant, sat in a wide, flat valley enclosed by distant peaks. The current situation in each village had not escaped the notice of many in the 105th, including Joe Pike.

"Seems as though everyone's thinking that the French won't be coming back."

His companions looked around and they could only agree as they watched the local people repair their fences, doors and shutters, after the predations of a retreating French army two weeks before. With that, Pike rose from where they were and walked to the nearest dwelling where the man of the house and also what looked like his Father, were attempting to mend an animal pen, which required several rails. Pike picked up a rail and simply offered it up to the space between the uprights and then made a chopping motion with his hand to show where it should be cut, but not exactly matching the space. Pike then went to an upright and motioned with his finger where a hole should be bored, then described a shape with his fingers to show a shaped end of the rail that would fit into the hole. They were bemused at first, but the two worthies soon understood and nodded their agreement. Within five minutes Pike returned with some Battalion tools and set to work. Davey, Saunders, Deakin and Halfway soon joined in and the next two hours turned into a productive time, even if communication was a problem. With the job completed, the rails were thoroughly tested by such as Miles and Davey standing on them and the rails supporting their weight was greeted by the solemn nodding of heads by the farmer and his family.

The following hours became a very jolly time, the yard then becoming their camp and the family adding their own meal to the army rations, which they all ate together, although much food overflowed from the long family table to the soldiers and Followers all sat on benches around the yard. The meal was followed by local children dancing to a tune played on a Basque flute and drum, one performer playing both at the same time. The day ended with the family's sheep being driven into the new pen from the nearby pasture, Deakin, Davey and Solomon taking part and making good use of their past experience. With the sheep thus secured, all those watching, nodded and commented on the healthy sheep in their effective pen, it secure and properly jointed. However, the reason for secure fencing was made clear by one word from the farmer.

"Lobos. Muchos lobos."

Miles turned to Saunders.

"What'd he say?"

"Wolves, I think. Up here, makes sense."

However, the older man was adding his own comment.

"Si. Tambien los lobos franceses."

His face became grim and he passed his hand across his throat, but the group broke up with all smiles and the following day, the 105th were waved on their way by the whole family. The march took not half the day, before the 4th Division was halted in another broad valley and ordered to make a firm camp, with the next village just visible higher up the valley. Tents were pitched and proper hearths of stones and earth were constructed, all under the strict supervision of Nellie and Bridie, who then turned to Jed.

"Is it so we'll be here for some while?"

Deakin halted the filling of his pipe.

"I'd say, unless the French or Wellington thinks different."

"Do you think there's a chance of a few rabbits or hares, at all."

Deakin looked up in to the dear face of his comely 'wife'.

"See John or Tom. They're the boys for shooting that kind of thing."

However, with this she was not satisfied.

"And weren't you raised in some place that was full of rabbits, hares and suchlike?"

"I was, but we weren't allowed to use guns. You'd get arrested. Only the Squire could use such as that."

"So what did you use?"

"Traps, snares and ferrets."

"Well, sure now, haven't you got two out of those three! So why not?"

He stared up at her, but with affection undiminished.

"So, what's wrong with rations?"

Her hands came up to her hips.

"And sure! What's wrong with a bit of fresh meat?"

Deakin nodded, defeated.

"All right. I'll see what I can cobble together, from what's around and what might be with the waggoneers and engineers."

He rose and ambled off to begin his search. The following day, when Deakin began his constructions, they were undisturbed by any Officer's orders, but the mood was somewhat subdued by a distant, but heavy rumbling that came to them barely audible in the still mountain air. Their Officers, Carr, O'Hare and Heaviside were all sat relaxed outside their Headquarters tent, the sun warm but not oppressive, whilst their coffee was hot and fresh. Carr had been listening to the sound for some time.

"San Sebastian, I suppose. Graham seeing what he can do."

O'Hare opened his eyes into the bright, clear sunlight.

"No reason to think otherwise. What else would be getting a drubbing such as that? Is your brother over that way?"

Carr nodded.

"He is and I've not heard from him, but I've heard of no serious cavalry action. So, I can only assume that he is well."

Carr's assumption was absolutely correct, because his brother was at that moment sitting on similar camp chairs with his friend Douglas Peterson and their Squadron Captain Samuel Oakwood. Between periods of contentedly dozing off, they all idly observed the to and fro of French forces and civilians down in the Bidassoa valley, beyond the river. Civilians, these being local fishermen who, despite the threat and sight of an invading army just over the water, continued to fish by the simple method of a small rowboat towing a net out into the incoming tide and then hauling it in, each time with a reasonable catch of silver, struggling fish. With the latest catch now hauled in, Peterson dragged his thoughts back to the fact that they were serving soldiers and the rumble of the bombardment.

"That must be Graham, disturbing the peace at San Sebastian. Anybody heard anything?"

The question was really directed at Oakwood, him being the Senior and more likely to be involved in the spreading of such news, but little was forthcoming.

"From what is being bandied about, it's been a bit of a struggle taking some Convent on the heights above the town, it took two goes at it and our Portuguese then got carried away and attacked the defences across the isthmus, what they call a 'hornwork'. There they got a bloody nose. So, what you can hear now is us battering away at that, the hornwork, still in French hands, one assumes."

Peterson leaned forward. Carr still had his eyes shut.

"Does Graham have better guns than we had at Burgos?"

Oakwood nodded, before easing himself back into his chair.

"New, from what I hear. It shouldn't be long before we get ourselves inside."

At that point, Carr did open his eyes.

"Sir. What's a 'Forlorn Hope'?"

Oakwood now leaned forward himself and stared hard at Carr.

"Willoughby! You don't want to know. You put such questions right out of your head."

oOo

The days passed with the incessant rumble of the guns assaulting San Sebastian coming to the three on the West wind from three miles away. Three days became four, whilst G. Anson's two Cavalry Regiments occupied their lofty perch on the San Marcial heights simply by camping on it. Thirty miles away to the South-West, W. Anson's Infantry Brigade was on a height even loftier, but still down below

Roncesvalles. On the morning of the fifth day, Nellie Nicholls bustled up and sat beside her husband Henry, him sat with Colour Sergeant Harry Bennet. She was accompanied by Bridie, who stood ready to provide any verbal support if required and Nellie launched immediately into her complaint.

"This place gives me the creeps, so it does. What with talk of wolves, sure that's one thing, but there's Devils in them woods, of that I'm sure. Sure now, didn't you hear them last night?"

Nicholls looked across at his wife, wholly perplexed.

"What, by all that's Holy, are you driving at woman? Devils?"

Nellie struck an aggressive pose of her own, even though sat down.

"There's nothin' Holy about them woods. Howlin' Devils is what's over there and where's the surprise? Heathen place that this is! So far from a proper Church and everythin'."

Bennet leaned forward and looked at her, as puzzled as anyone.

"Nellie, this is about the most Holy place we've been to. Hundreds of Pilgrims passing every day. There's a Monastery up above, so I've heard."

Nellie had her own reason, which nicely linked the two.

"Then the wailin' must be the Devils complainin' about the Holy people so far up close and on their way to their own Holy place."

At that moment, Deakin and Halfway arrived, with a brace of rabbits each and Deakin spoke first, having heard something of the argument.

"What's all the worry?"

Henry Nicholls' brows came together in exasperation.

"Nellie here, thinks there's Devils over in the woods."

Nellie now looked aggressively up at Jed Deakin.

"That's right! So there are!"

Deakin dropped the rabbits beside Bridie, who immediately began an examination.

"Well, we've just come out of those woods and we weren't bothered by any kind of Devil."

Nellie was unconvinced.

"Sure now, don't you know such as them only comes out at night!"

Deakin could only shake his head, but Halfway had been stood wracking his brains to explain what was the cause of Nellie's acute discomfort. Eventually, the memory was cudgelled forth.

"Jed. Don't you remember when we was with the Norfolks, they sent us up to Scotland to do to them Scots what they'd ordered us to do to the Irish and every night we heard wails coming out of the woods?"

Deakin looked at him.

"And what did that guide tell us?"

"Wildcats! He said they was wildcats. They sets up a godawful noise come the night-time. Kept us awake, they did."

They both turned to Nellie, but Deakin was speaking.

"There you are, Nellie! 'Tis wildcats. The woods must be full of 'em, in parts like this."

Nellie then adopted her most disgruntled and unconvinced expression.

"Well, Devils or wildcats 'tis all enough to turn your blood to water, so it is. Horrid place this, full of horrid sounds. And cold at night, is another!"

Henry leaned over and kissed her, which did not change her expression, but the sight of the now skinned rabbits did bring some form of pleasure to her face.

It was during the eighth day of watching and waiting on the Bidassoa that the atmosphere of contentment from the triumphs achieved so far was wholly shattered. Oakwood arrived at the Officers' tent of Two Squadron, to find the pair drinking coffee.

"Get ready to move. We're pulling back. The assault on San Sebastian yesterday failed completely. And worse. Johnny's regrouped and he's coming over the Pyrenees at two places, Maya and Roncesvalles with a serious force at both. The Peer's ordered all the San Sebastian guns back to Passages harbour. That's where we're going. If we can't hold them back up in the mountains and they both combine, then that'll be our escape route. No choice. Many are saying we'll be pushed out!"

oOo

The dawn was full when the 105th were called to arms as part of Anson's Brigade, the 105th the furthest up the road that led up to Roncesvalles pass. The cold was bitter, just as Nellie had complained of and rumour was flying around the ranks, with Carr, O'Hare and Heaviside as bemused as anyone, but, nevertheless, all obeying the order to form up on the road, ready for combat. Followers stood beside the column, holding the hands of those important to them who were within reach, these being stood in the outside ranks, whilst others waved helpless hands at those beyond inside the column. The first to know what was happening was Carr, when W. Anson arrived, somewhat breathless, having ridden down from the pass, but his knowledge was reasonably detailed.

"Nothing yet, but the guerrillas tell us there's a large force on its way, coming up from France. They've seen two endless columns on the mountain tracks up to the pass, one either side, so let's hope those tracks are narrow and they'll struggle to deploy quickly, which will give us a fighting chance. Cole sent Ross' Brigade moving up at two this morning, so we've enough in position. As for us, we wait, but the worry is that there's plenty of goat tracks that can be used to get around the main pass and our position. Enough to keep Cole permanently on edge."

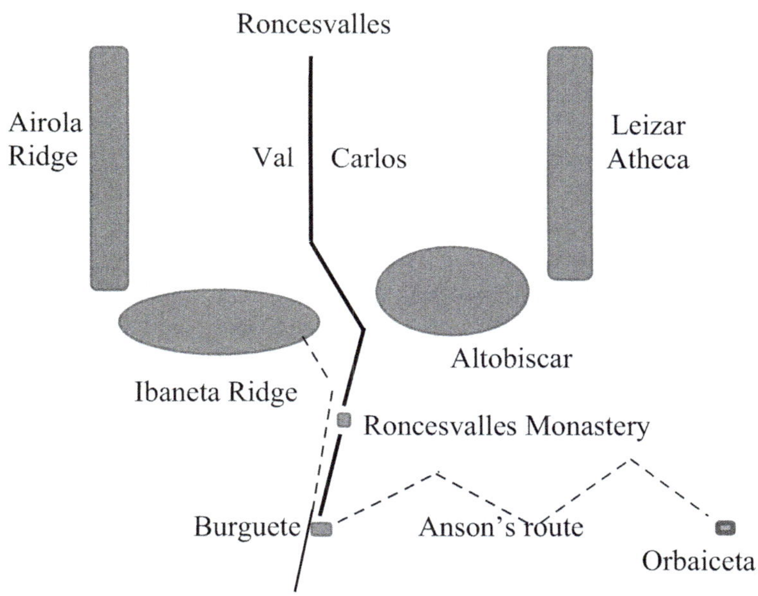

'What's the ground we're holding up there, Sir?"

Anson held out his left hand, palm down, but with the middle and third finger folded back. He pointed to his little finger.

"That's a ridge sticking out of the main Ibaneta ridge into France. One of the French columns is coming along it. That's called the Airola Ridge"

He pointed to the knuckle of the finger and the one next.

"That's the Ibaneta ridge. Ross is defending that."

Then his index finger.

‘That’s the Leizar Atheca. It points back into France. The French are coming towards it, but we hold the far end facing them with a Battalion’s worth of Lights.”

Then he pointed to the knuckle next to it, of the middle finger.

“That’s the highest hill we hold, in fact the highest there, called the Altobiscar and Byng’s holding that. It joins the Ibaneta with the Leizar Atheca.”

Then he pointed to the space between both fingers.

“That’s the Val Carlos. So deep, from up the top you think you’re flying!”

“Right Sir, very clear, thank you. So, from back here, we could be ordered to either side.”

Anson nodded.

“Yes, but we’ll hold here. Johnny’ll not get over up there. Our worry is being outflanked and cut off. This is a serious counter-offensive after Vitoria. My guess is, we’ll hold them here, but then pull back. Johnny perhaps crossing somewhere else, where we are not, and getting behind us, that’s the main worry and almost certainly true.”

The morning wore on, with the 105th remaining formed on the road. The Followers brought over food, there had not been time for breakfast and so Bridie was able to reach Jed Deakin, him at the head of the column. A skillet was thrust at him and so the Colour leant back onto his shoulder, freeing both hands. One more laden skillet was passed in, this to Bridie’s son, Ensign Patrick Mulcahy for both himself and Henri Rasenne to share and both immediately wolfed down the food. Halfway and Deakin also shared one plate and Deakin took the first portion onto his spoon.

“What’s this?”

“Rabbit stew. From that pair what you brought in yesterday.”

The hot food was hurriedly eaten by both, whilst all in the column ate something. No permission had been given, Carr saw no reason to put a stop to his men eating before what could be a serious engagement, nor did he stop them even when the sound of continuous musketry came to them from over the horizon, well over a mile away, through the still mountain air. At the head of the 105th column were four Officers, which included Anson, and all were eating whilst they could, stuffing back coffee and rolls. O’Hare was the one with the most experience and gave his judgement concerning the sounds of conflict rolling at them from amongst the tangle of valleys and hills.

"That's from two directions. One to the front, but another off to the right."

Anson thrust his roll into his pocket and gave his mug to Heaviside, then he produced a map from his right-hand pocket and unfolded it to run his finger rightwards over from where they were.

"My guess is there. Orbaiceta. There's a big foundry over there and another track that crosses these mountains from France comes up there. It's there, for us, would be my guess. Whatever, we're no damn use down here. We'll go up to that village above us, Burguete. From there, we can get to the pass or over to this ...."

He looked again at the map. "....... Orbaiceta!"

He rolled up the map, a determined look on his face.

"Right, Carr! Get yours moving. The rest will follow."

The orders rang out and the final goodbyes flew across the ranks. The road up was steep, but good and the Brigade made a rapid climb, however, they had only got to within a view of Burguete when an ADC came down the road towards them at a fast canter and reined in beside Anson. Carr and his two Majors were close enough to hear.

"Sir. Orders from General Cole. Take yours across to Orbaiceta. You
will find a Spanish Brigade there. Whether or not they are holding, we do not know, but we can still hear fighting. Please to take yours over at your best speed."

Anson did not move.

"And a guide, in this maze of mountains and goat tracks?"

"I'm afraid I have no word on that, Sir, but I'm sure someone in Burguete will be able to guide you satisfactorily."

Anson nodded, but the expression on his face and his tone was mildly ironic.

"Very well. Tell the General that he can count on us. We will do the best we can."

The ADC saluted, turned his horse and spurred him back up the road.

Anson turned to Carr and O'Hare, his map already spread open.

"Look. There's a road that takes the right direction, but then it stops in
the middle of nowhere. To get onto another for Orbaiceta means a mile over
who knows what kind of country. It's four miles as the crow flies, never mind what the roads do. But, that said, we must get on. Orders are orders."

The march began and within five minutes they were in Burguete with many very anxious locals stood outside their houses engaging in worried conversation. Anson went straight up to one that look fit, young and capable, and held a purse of doubloons before him.

"Orbaiceta? Rapido. Si?"

The young man nodded, took the purse and waved Anson forward, but not out of the village, only to a side road directly right and the journey began. The road was good at first, but then it became a rough track that took them through thick woods, but they were not slowed. Then onto a decent road, but it twisted and turned alarmingly, besides dipping and rising and all the while the sounds of combat grew louder with the reducing distance. Anson called up Carr.

"Henry. What do you think? Should I send on the Lights?"

Carr did not hesitate.

"Yes Sir. If this is the only possible road. If there is no other that you could take, which could take you off to God knows where. The guide should come with us, leaving you to find your own way."

Anson turned to their guide.

"Orbaiceta. Solo un camino?'

The guide nodded.

"Si, Senor, solo un camino a Orbaiceta. No puedes perderte."

"I think that means we can't get lost."

Anson then held up one finger.

"Una liga?"

The man shook his head, held up his index finger, then curled it down. Anson turned to Carr.

"I'll take that as half a league, one and a half miles. You lead. I'm giving you all the Lights, including my Rifles."

The orders rang out, reaching the 105th Light Company, being the first of the five Light Companies in Anson's column. They were at the rear of the 105th who were leading the Brigade and Ellis did not wait for any Officer.

"Column of twos. Double up the column."

Miles was not impressed when he saw what they were being asked to do and he was not alone.

"God, he wants his bumps felt!"

Ellis had ordered a column of two because there was so little room remaining on the road alongside the main 105th column and immediately alongside the road was a precipitate drop, which was what so troubled Miles and many others. However, all arrived safely at the head of the column, reformed fours and began their jogging run for the final mile and a half. Soon Drake was suffering and he called out to Carr, just alongside.

"Henry. I'm blown."

Carr nodded understandingly.

"Come on when you can."

The road was merely a track, seemingly endless across steep hillsides and through thick woods, but their guide jogged on confidently, then, merely by turning a corner, they came to the village, to find the streets full of Spanish, with some wounded and being cared for at the roadside. The sounds of continuous musketry came from above and Carr led his men on and up through the village. It was not long before they came to the Spanish position, which was no more than a thick skirmish line spread across the hillside, anchored on a shepherd's hut on the right and two stone-built animal pens on the left. Carr looked across the hillside, then to the heights to his left. He turned to Shakeshaft leading Two Section.

"Richard. With the whole Company, work your way up. Get as much height beyond those stone pens as you can. Deny any Frogs our left flank. The other Lights are coming now and I'll send the 48th up alongside you. The 27th and Provisionals will be behind these Spanish and the Rifles will hold that hut over there. That'll do it. These Dons are in no mood to give ground. I'm going back to the village to await Anson. Good luck."

"And to you, Sir."

Carr descended and passed Bettridge, leading One Section and looking altogether fearful, but reassuringly for Carr, Ellis was with him.

"Good luck, Luttrel!"

Bettridge managed a weak smile but hurried on as best he could, labouring through the thick scrub and heather, but it was Ellis who first came battering his way up to Shakeshaft to receive Carr's orders.

"Fight in files, Sir?'

"No. In pairs. Just take post and fire at any targets. We'll settle in and hold. I'll do that here at these pens with Two and most of One, but Johnny has the height, so you take a file from One up to our left, check that there are no Johnnies up there and establish our flank."

Ellis saluted and ran off, straight to Davey, Miles and Pike.

"You three! Load, then with me. We're going higher."

They all loaded their weapons carefully, then Ellis began a hopeful way up through the gorse and heather to climb a shoulder of the hillside. Like the veteran he was, once there he first halted, removed his shako and then peered over the top, to almost immediately come back down.

"There's a few Johnnies a hundred yards beyond, but none above. Shakeshaft's wrong, it's flat and it's us that has the height, but only just. One's an Officer waving a sword about. John, he's yours."

He then examined the flintlock of his own Baker.

"Weapon check."

They all did and even Miles was not resentful, then Ellis edged his way up, half crawling through the thinning scrub to gain a sight of the French skirmish line, then he gave his orders.

"Miles. First left from the Officer. Pike, first right. Mine, second right. Fire after John."

They all eased forward and took their firing positions. Davey sighted carefully even though it was under 100 yards. He fired and the French Officer jerked sideways to then lean forward and fall to his knees. Meanwhile the others had downed their targets and were rapidly reloading. Miles speaking the obvious, somewhat unnecessarily.

"These is just Line. Not they tassel swingin' bastards."

He was ignored, as they all brought their Bakers up to the ready and searched for targets. At that point Lieutenant Bettridge arrived, with Byford, Saunders and Bailey. Ellis turned around, his puzzled face asking the obvious question, but Bettridge gave his own answer.

"As you're our far left, Sergeant, I thought some reinforcements."

Ellis nodded agreement, which was genuine.

"Yes Sir. Good thinking, Sir."

Then he pointed upwards.

"There's not too many of 'em, Sir. There are some higher than us, but only out beyond 200 yards. Nearer to us, 'tis more or less flat and it's them that's a bit down below."

However, from Bettridge there came nothing further, so Ellis continued.

"So, stay down and come up only to fire, Sir."

Bettridge nodded at the non-question, then a bullet buzzed between them to take off Bettridge's left epaulette.

Ellis grinned.

"Best pick that up, Sir. Something to show the girls. And your grandchildren!"

All around grinned, as Davey fired to bring down a French NCO, who was shouting orders. Ellis rose up to take a look.

"I'd say we was fair set, Sir, with what's opposite us. We can hold here as long as they don't send a lot more forward to push us back and gain our flank."

Bettridge nodded and grinned, he was actually beginning to enjoy himself, being nominally in charge of seven consummately capable soldiers, all busy killing and wounding his country's enemies.

At that moment, Carr was some 200 yards behind, coming to much the same conclusion. The Spanish were determined to hold their ground and, reinforced by veteran Redcoats, they should be able to do just that and there was Anson with the rest of the Brigade who should arrive any minute. He was just turning to walk back down to the village when a Colonel on horseback arrived and reined in.

"Blackstaff, 1st Royal Dragoons. What's your assessment? General Cole needs to know."

"Carr, 105th. You can tell him that this is secure, as things stand. We've a good line on a strong position, so even if they send down another Brigade, Anson along with the Spanish will hold. It'll take a Division to push us back."

Blackstaff gathered his reins, prior to riding off.

"So, you're 105th! That'll provide plenty of excuse then, to go running off! Not that you ever needed much of one!"

With that he spurred his horse away, leaving Carr with his sword now halfway out of its scabbard, he was so angered, but the ADC was soon gone, now disappeared into the village streets. Carr slammed his sword back into its scabbard.

"I'll remember you, just see if I don't."

Still fuming, he strode down the hill to the village where he met Anson around the first corner.

"It's secure, Sir, only needing our Lights and the Spanish. Up above here we hold the higher ground, strange to say, but there's some Johnnies spread out on the hillsides beyond. To show yours in reserve would be no bad thing. They've no artillery and they'll need more than they've got right now to push us back down. If not reinforced, they may well withdraw."

Anson nodded.

"Good! Well done Carr. We'll arrange as you say and await orders. What's happening at the pass, I've absolutely no idea."

Carr took a deep breath at the thought.

"We had Blackstaff of the 1st Dragoons here but minutes ago. I gave him a report for Cole. Did he not say anything?"

"No he did not. Just galloped on through."

Carr nodded, his face again showing his anger.

"I'm not surprised."

Anson looked puzzled, expecting more, but none came.

"Right. Take your 105th up to the left in reserve and I'll arrange the rest."

Carr saluted punctiliously.

"Yes Sir."

Then Drake arrived, just as Anson was leaving, and Carr's mood changed.

"Caught up, then?"

Drake grinned but still breathing heavily.

"Swept up, more like, by the Regiment, but I held on."

He took one deep breath.

"Where are we at, up here?"

"Yours are up on the left, with Shakeshaft in charge. Not much to do but keep your head down, or keep moving if you do have to show it."

"How long till Noon?"

Drake pulled out his own watch to answer his own question.

"One hour. The men will need feeding. And us!'

"Agreed. Relieve by Companies. Grenadiers first. Got to keep Charles busy with something."

The final hour of the morning passed quickly, with no reduction in the heavy skirmishing. Some wounded returned to the village, mostly Spanish, then, whilst most of the 105th were eating back in the safety of the village, another of Lowry-Cole's ADC Colonels arrived with orders that halted all enjoyment of their Noon meal. Anson sent him around to his Colonels and he arrived first at Carr. He was not Blackstaff.

"Your Brigade are ordered up to the pass."

"What's happened?"

"The French have attacked on both sides of the San Carlos valley, but they've been held on the right, at the Altobiscar. The heaviest fighting is now with Ross in front of the Ibaneta, that on the left, on the Airola. That's how it was when I left to come here."

"Will they be held?"

"Almost certainly, especially when you get there, but I must get on."

Via RSM Gibney the order reached Bettridge and Ellis and, with each of the Bettridge's seven sending one more shot at the scattered French, they came back down, passing Spanish Light Troops who came up to take over their position. The first grinned openly as they passed by

"Hola, Ingleses. Hoy matamos a los franceses, si?"

Miles nodded as he passed on down, understanding nothing, but some reply was needed.

"Yes mate. Whatever you say."

The 48th were nearest to the road and led off, with the 105th last. Even though it was their second time over, the road appeared no less dangerous nor less arduous, but an hour of hard marching brought them back to Burguete, then the marching became even harder for the climb up to the pass, which became steeper with each footfall. Within the hour, they came to the Monastery just below the crest, with Monks and Pilgrims holding a ceremony outside, all the Pilgrims and many Monks down on their knees. The Monastery was splendid and carefully built, standing solid, of large grey blocks. Drake studied the scene between laboured breaths, with Bettridge alongside him.

"Let's hope they're praying for us, Lionel, I mean Luttrel. Good to have God on your side."

Elsewhere within the ranks of the 105th, the comments were somewhat less charitable, particularly from the very secular John Davey. He had noticed the pitiable hovels and cottages in Burguete and also on the road up.

"Prayin' that no cannonballs comes over to spoil their fine monastery."

Miles alongside made a comment from his own concerns, he had noticed the wounded being treated at the roadside.

"Why aren't some of our wounded in there? Aren't Monks supposed to be Medicoes an' all?"

Pike, more generous of spirit, answered.

"Perhaps some are, Tom. We can't see inside."

However, Davey had not finished.

"Ah! If you've got a rosary and can say their catechism. I had all that hammered into me with a rod across my back in Sunday School, by a Catholic Priest!"

However, soon Anson's column halted, their Officers now being given orders. With their feet now still, all could now hear the heavy skirmishing coming from above on their left and the even more significant gunsmoke in that direction rising from the long ridge that stretched out into France. Soon, they were moving in that direction, into the steepest climb of all, leftwards up a steep slope of bare scrub, with the road over the pass itself down to their right and wooded hills on the height leftwards being the destination of the leading 48th. Halting in their order of march, the 105th arrived onto the slopes nearest the road and for them the Val Carlos was revealed, deep, and stretching back and beyond into France. For some time they stood as they had marched, in a column of fours, receiving no order to stand down, or form firing line. Nor did any order come for any Company to leave their line to support the conflict on the Ibaneta, the sounds of which were even then dying away and also the lines of wounded were lessening, these unfortunates becoming fewer and fewer.

The Officers of the 105th strolled over towards the road, the better there to observe the view and to take stock of the position on the other side of the pass. Carr was the first to make a judgement on the situation opposite and he was blunt and to the point.

"No one's moving over there, neither us nor them."

There was a block of French infantry at the end of the ridge extending back into France and, at right-angles to these, a line of Redcoats could be seen across the summit of a rounded ridge that barred their way across a valley. Both were now making use of cooking fires. Carr turned away, but he had remembered Anson's 'finger' description.

"We must be on the Ibaneta ridge, the far right of it. So! Stand down. Set sentries and stand down. We're here for the rest of the day at least, probably sleeping up here, so let the men eat and rest. Who knows what tomorrow will bring?"

The orders were given and soon their own cooking fires were started, many men going back down the slope to gather fuel in the thick woodlands. Anson came over and said nothing to countermand Carr's orders, in fact he was soon drinking coffee and eating army biscuits himself, along with Spanish sausage, all in the company of the Officers of the 105th. It was the view there which had attracted them all to that point as a group and even Carravoy was moved to make some comment, stood with D'Villiers and Slade, all watching the shadows of clouds on high change shape as they traversed the undulating countryside.

"I say, this is most stunning. Can't say I've ever seen the like."

St. John Slade turned to him.

"Perhaps Scotland, or the Lakes, but I'll agree this takes some beating."

Close by, Heaviside was sat with Carr, O'Hare and Drake, him also inspired.

"It is He who sits above the circle of the earth and its inhabitants are like grasshoppers, who stretches out the heavens like a curtain, and spreads them like a tent to dwell in. Isaiah 40, verse 22."

It was O'Hare who turned to him, plainly somewhat askance at Heaviside's quote, O'Hare being one of the more sceptical amongst the audience.

"Grasshoppers as may be, but a tent would not come amiss were we indeed ordered to spend a night up here."

The conversation ceased and all stood continuing to admire the view, but after a mere few minutes his thoughts of two days previous were recalled by Drake.

"This Roncesvalles place, dredging in the deepest recesses of my memory it has some significance."

Then he turned to his three superior officers, smiling resignedly.

"But I cannot remember anything more than that."

It was Heaviside who gave the matter the most thought.

"Mentioned in some sort of romantic ode. Or epic. I could not say more."

John Byford was stood sentry close by and he pondered whether he should speak, but he decided that he should, for the simple reason that he knew the subject of their enquiries.

"Begging your pardon, Sirs. Perhaps I can help."

Carr turned to him, but not sternly. He had some regard for Byford from the time when Carr was Captain of the Light Company. Carr felt some affinity with Byford, who was a family outcast just as Carr himself and it was only Grandparents' money and influential uncles that had gained Carr a Commission.

"Help, Byford? How?"

"About Roncesvalles, Sir. The significance of this place."

"Very good, Byford. Do tell!"

With his musket remaining at 'order arms', Byford took a deep breath.

"Well, Sir. The only answer I can give is that this place is the setting for the Song of Roland. An epic poem about a battle here at Roncesvalles, Sir. Although not really a battle, more a brief skirmish and very one sided."

It was Slade who, whilst still sitting, turned around to see Byford, and was somewhat astonished by his answer.

"And you know this, how? Private."

"We had to study the poem at school, Sir."

"And what school was that?"

"Winchester, Sir."

Slade's chin and eyebrows moved in opposite directions, but he soon recovered.

"An English epic, such as Morte d'Arthur?"

"Similar, Sir, only the Song of Roland is in Medieval French rather than Olde English."

Further disbelief grew within Slade, but full consternation within Carravoy. Byford's place of education and its depth surpassed that of both, but Carr spoke encouragingly, wishing to know more.

"So, what's the story?"

Byford took a deep breath.

"Well, Sir. It was in the days of Charlemagne, who invaded Spain through here to plunder Pamplona. The last of his force were retreating back when they were ambushed by Basques. Pamplona was their capital and so they were somewhat aggrieved. The Commander of Charlemagne's Rearguard, Roland, blew his horn to call him back, but they arrived too late and the Rearguard was wiped out, including Roland. An epic was written based on it, Sir."

The response was an astonished silence, so Byford continued.

"Some think it was all about keeping the Muslims out of France, Sir, but it wasn't. It was more about Charlemagne spreading his military influence, Sir, by sacking Pamplona. The Muslim expansion had been long halted by then."

Still no reply.

"It was a skirmish, really. I'd say it takes longer to read the poem, than it took to fight the battle."

A pause.

"I hope that helps, Sir."

"And it happened here?"

"Yes Sir, or very much close-by."

Carr nodded, he well knew the hidden depths of Private Byford.

"Thank you, Byford. That's good to know. You can stand down, there's no need for a sentry here. Get yourself back to your mess."

Byford brought his musket up to 'shoulder arms', saluted, made a sharp turn and marched off. Carravoy was the first to comment.

"Well, I never would have thought it, that such as that could come out of the rank and file."

Carr looked at him sternly.

"I would have thought, Charles, that you've been with us long enough to know that there are hidden depths in any Battalion. The 105th is no exception."

Whilst Carravoy angered, Slade perked up, suddenly in buoyant mood.

"Yes, and I've seen that soldier out walking with a most comely filly, that I wouldn't mind tupping myself!"

Carr now angered and turned on him.

"Major Slade! We do not talk about our Followers in that fashion. Private Byford and Eirin are properly married and have a child. I regard Followers as being vital to our effectiveness, as much as our waggoneers, storemen and bandsmen. Vital and sustaining. Ask Captain Drake here."

Drake immediately spoke up, there was no need for any enquiry from Slade.

“Oh yes! Saved my bacon so they did. Matron Nicholls fighting off Spanish scavengers at Vitoria with nothing more than a soup ladle!”

The tension was broken and all managed a smile or a grin of some degree. Then came fog, rolling in like a theatre curtain to cover the whole area and pickets were immediately sent out, or more accurately down, 200 yards below the ridge summit. One was commanded by Jed Deakin, with Toby Halfway and two privates and all sat on the steep hillside in the eerie light. The light of the sun, a celestial force, continued doing battle with the earthly power of the mountains, but the fog persisted, becoming more dense as the influence of the sun waned with the dying of the day. They were disturbed by heavy footfalls behind them to see a group of Grenadiers led by Sergeant Arthur Bennett. Deakin looked up as they passed by.

“What’s on, Art?”

Bennett halted briefly.

“Carr’s ordered Carravoy to mount some patrols and to take one out himself, so watch out, he’s in no good mood. D’Villiers has got another.”

“Any password?”

Bennett laughed.

“Expect either of them two to think of that? Just give the ‘who goes there’. You’ll recognise the voice of either. Best King’s English, don’t you know!”

Deakin laughed as the Grenadiers disappeared into the murk, now deepened by both the night and the vapour. In the event there were no mishaps, Deakin and his men saw no one, but they could hear calling from the patrols just down over on the slopes below, then they heard what must be a patrol, but could see nothing. Deakin sprang up with bayonet fixed.

“Halt! Who goes there?”

The reply came back, body unseen.

“105th Grenadier patrol. Lieutenant Ameshurst.”

“Pass on, Sir. All’s well.”

“Indeed it is, Colour-Sergeant. I’ve been sent to collect you. We’re pulling out, back down the mountain. Seems there’s a bit of a panic on.”

oOo

Chapter Ten

Sorauren

The order was for immediate withdrawal and Lowry-Cole's three Brigades marched down from their high ridge in total darkness, taking their cue to turn right and down when they arrived at the surface of the road which crossed the pass. Anson's quit their positions in the same order as their arrival, the 48th coming down first from the Ibaneta, then the 27th, then the Provisionals, so that the 105th, along with Anson's Rifles, were the last to leave and begin the descent back to Burguete. They passed through in the dead of night, but there were many lights in the houses and cottages and also lanterns on the hillsides as families abandoned their homes, knowing that the French would be marching through with the coming dawn.

Carr and O'Hare were as perplexed as anyone at the fact of abandoning so strong a position which they had held with ease, but their question was answered by Anson, who, as ever, felt the need to keep his immediate subordinates informed. He was brief and to the point.

"Hill's been pushed back at Maya, the other main pass to the North. He's at least ten miles back down into the Bastan valley. There's talk of more Johnnies coming over a minor pass between us and Hill, somewhere called the Ispegui. Byng was very worried by the fog so he told Cole that staying there was too big a risk and Cole agreed."

Carr turned to him, but could see only a vague shape in the utter darkness.

"How far back do we go?"

"Henry, your guess is as good as mine, but we have to cover the siege at Pamplona. If you want my guess, I'd say it'll be in the hills before Pamplona, where both Hill and Cole can at least support each other to hold what must be a substantial French force; if and when they can combine together. What came at Hill over at Maya must have been overwhelming to push him that far back."

"This is a major setback, then, Sir."

"Yes, Carr. I'd say that it is!"

Behind them, within the column, the conversation was of more immediate and personal concerns, such as between Halfway to Deakin.

"No sleep tonight, then, Jed!"

"I'd say you've the fact of it there, but there's serious fightin' comin' up an' that's another the fact there can be no doubt of.

Halfway's veteran instinct had told him true and it was in the early hours that they passed through another town with the inhabitants abandoning everything, as had those of Burguete, but there was no stopping, all Regiments maintained a brisk march straight through. It was with full light that the whole of Cole's column halted on the road where it wound through a gentle valley and the order was passed back, "Make camp and rest." However, for the Light Companies of Anson's Brigade, this did not apply, the order coming back to the 105th via an Anson ADC riding up to Carr.

Retreat to Sorauren

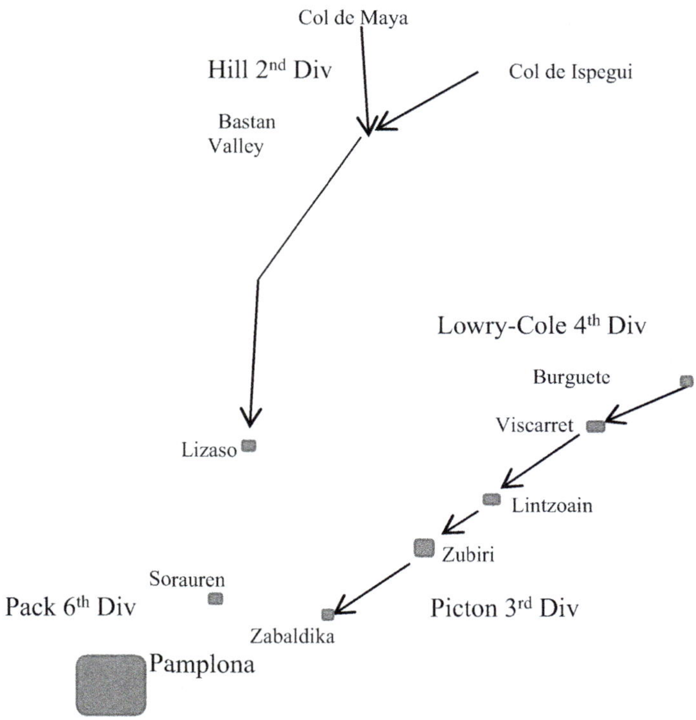

"Sir. All our Lights are ordered back up the road to form a strong picket line. Our Brigade is the rearguard."

Weary himself, Carr nodded.

"We're the rearguard! Why am I not surprised by that? Who'll command?"

"The Brigadier asks if you will, Sir."

"Asks, you say!"

Carr turned away and walked to where O'Hare and Heaviside were beginning their own attempt at rest.

"Padraigh. All Anson's Lights are ordered back up on picket, myself in charge. You have command should anything happen. Get a picket between ours and the Lights to pass on a warning if mine get attacked. There's a whole French army coming down this road."

O'Hare rose to his feet and walked off to the nearest Company, the Grenadiers. The other Light Companies of the Brigade were already on the road and Carr, hurrying to find his own Light Company, felt himself fortunate that the first man he met was Senior Company Sergeant Ellis.

"Ellis! Get the men up, we're on picket along with what's coming up the road behind me. Four Light Companies, including the Rifles, then we to join on."

"Sir! The men are very tired, Sir."

At that, Carr lost patience.

"Then they can bring their blankets!"

At that harsh reply, Ellis hurried off and Carr went to where he could see Drake, Shakeshaft and Bettridge, all of whom, luckily, were not yet asleep.

"No rest yet! We're on picket, back up the road a mile."

With heavy feet, the 105th Light Company toiled back up the road, not a steep climb, but a climb nevertheless and all were tired, sullen and hungry, such that even Tom Miles held his peace. Even he could not bring himself to state the obvious, but Carr did not press the march, instead they halted quite soon, where the valley narrowed and there was a bridge over the valley's brook. He first placed the 105th Lights.

"Nat get over that bridge and up onto that slope, where you have a decent view back up. Send out picket sentries, relieved each hour. Let the men sleep and eat as they choose, but keep a good watch. No fires."

Drake led his men to climb the slope indicated, which did give an excellent view of the road back up to Roncesvalles and from there Drake studied the distance, then he turned to Sergeant Fearnley of Two Section, stood nearby.

"You and three more, Sergeant, keep watch whilst the rest sleep. Don't go far down, stay close up here, to keep a better view back up the road. One hour and you'll be relieved."

He looked left across the valley to see that Carr had given the same orders to the other Companies, they were all where they had halted, but he had sent Bairns' Rifles further up the road. Satisfied, he rolled himself in his own blanket and instantly fell fast asleep. He was awakened not two hours later, by a gentle shaking from Sergeant Ellis.

"Sir! Johnny cavalry, Sir,"

Drake leapt up and took but a few paces forward to see, at a distance of about half a mile, a French cavalry patrol, conspicuous in the green fields by their light blue, or even pink, uniforms.

"Send a runner to tell the Colonel. From down there, he may not have seen them."

Joe Pike was the first athlete that Ellis came to and he ran the quarter mile to Carr, who then hurried back up the same distance, his telescope at the ready.

"Still there?"

"No! They've seen us and gone."

Carr nodded.

"To tell their General and bring down their infantry."

He looked at the men all around, still sleeping.

"We're pulling back to the Brigade. Fast march. I don't want to be caught out here by any cavalry."

Within half an hour of speaking those words, Carr was relating much the same to Anson.

"Cavalry know we're here, Sir, and are coming down the road."

Anson looked worried, but his reply was steady.

"Very good, Henry. Cole's taken Ross' and Stubbs' on down the road, leaving us here. We're still the Rearguard and will follow him immediately, but keep your Lights back. Rearguard to the rearguard."

He turned away, then turned back.

"Oh, and more good news. The San Sebastian siege has been abandoned, with all artillery pulled back to Santander. We said this is serious, and we were right!"

The five Light Companies were waiting on the road, but Carr held them there as Anson rode off to return to his Brigade and, very quickly the rear Battalion of the Brigade, being the Provisionals, could be seen disappearing around a far bend and the road then empty. Carr waited for Bairns' Rifles to arrive and Bairns immediately came up to Carr when he saw him.

"Sir? Any orders?"

"You're the last so keep back and keep a good look behind you. Fire a shot if you see anything, then run. If we hear that, we'll be holding further down in close support."

Bairns smiled at such concern and clear orders and then the rapid march began for all, down through the village of Viscarret, all now abandoned. After an extra mile they crossed a river, behind which was a steep ridge, with the village of Lintzoain at one end, but they ignored the signpost indicating the way in, and keeping to the road at the foot of the ridge they pressed on, but not far. Just across the river, General Byng was waiting and he was plainly as tired, worn out and dispirited as anyone.

"Carr, we're offering battle from that ridge behind. Spread your Lights across the lower slopes, but gain some height. It's only three in the afternoon, so I'm expecting some kind of action. Ignore that river, it's called the Erro and is no barrier at all."

"And if they come, Sir?"

"Give them as tough a time as you can."

Carr took one pace back and saluted, incensed at so vague an order, but Byng was riding off and so Carr was left to study the ridge slope he had been asked to defend. On the right, as he looked straight at it, was the village of Linzoain just off the main road, whilst on the left the slope curved away from him with the road at its foot. Quickly, he made up his mind, going first to Bairns.

"Tom. Cole is setting a main line atop this ridge, we're his skirmishers. Get yours into that village but when it gets too anxious, as you judge, pull back and hold the slope above the village. The rest will be across to your right on the hillside. When we retreat further up the slope, so do you."

Bairns saluted and ran off, then Carr went to his four remaining Companies, still in column on the road. He led them forward, allocating each a section of his line, ordering each Company to form in three ranks, because the slope gave the third rank a good enough view over the first two. When he came to the 105th, who were the last and therefore at the end of the formed line, they were also ordered to stand in three ranks. That done he climbed the slope to better study the ground. The Erro wound its course close to the foot of the slope but it was, as Byng had said, a very insignificant stream at that time of year and it departed the slope in front of the 105th, away into the open fields beyond. Taking all in, he stood for a while, then he thought out loud.

"Well, if nothing else, it's good ground!"

At that point Luttrel Bettridge climbed the slope up to him.

"Sir. Captain Drake sent me up. Any orders, Sir?"

Carr could only smile down at the teenage Bettridge, at a face still awaiting its first shave, who should really be struggling with some passage from Ovid, rather than the deadly business of holding a rearguard against an advancing and powerful army. He noticed the missing epaulette.

"Your missing wing! Have you still got it?"

Bettridge pulled it from his pocket, it plainly damaged from the French bullet.

"Yes Sir. Sergeant Ellis told me to keep it, Sir. To show the girls he said."

Carr laughed.

"Well, in that he's correct, but for now you are improperly dressed. Take your tunic to one of our Followers, when you get the chance. One of them will sew it all back together for you, of that I'm certain. I'd recommend Mrs. Bridget Mulcahy."

That said, Carr pointed to the village down to their left.

"Now, Luttrel. Some will come through that village, but most will issue into the fields in front and advance from there. Stay here, because for the moment there are no new orders. When they come, you must take the message, we will see them first from up here."

Then he remembered that Bettridge was Brockenhurst's nephew and could only imagine the attitude towards the 'common ranker' that had been instilled within him by such as Brockenhurst and Slade. He pointed down the slope to their line.

"Those are our men down there, Luttrel. They are all thorough veterans and they can fight like you won't believe. We are here fully across Spain because of them, they fight and they win. I could make many of them down there into an Officer and they would make a decent fist of it. I'm proud to be their Colonel and it matters to me that I do not let them down, because I know they won't let me down. They fight for the Regiment and our Colours and they fight for each other. In equal measure. Remember that!"

"Yes Sir."

Bettridge was somewhat taken aback by such a sentimental outburst from his Colonel and so, somewhat embarrassed, he turned to study the view, whilst Carr focused his telescope. They had only been there for a few minutes.

"Infantry, Luttrel. No cavalry as yet. Run down and warn the Rifles in the village, then along to each Captain in the line. And good luck!"

As Bettridge descended the slope in huge strides, Carr studied events. The French infantry were leaving the road and spreading across the fields opposite, they had seen the Allied position. Carr waited and watched, his telescope telling him that those leaving the road were Voltiguers, two Battalions strong. Next, what seemed to be two Companies detached themselves, returned to the road and then headed for the village, whilst the rest spread out into skirmish order. There would be no column attack and so he had to change his own positions, lines were too easy a target against skirmishers. He hurried down to his line, coming first to the 48th, centre left, and their Captain.

"Skirmish order. Get forward and hold the river. Send a runner to the 27th on your left."

Carr hurried on, giving the same order to the Provisionals and soon there were no formed troops across the slope between the 105th, who were not yet threatened, and the village. It was from there that the first sounds of conflict came and within minutes it was plain that Bairns' men were making the French pay a high price for even the first buildings, they had made no inroads at all. Not long after, the same crack of many muskets came from down by the river, but he saw no retreat. His line was holding. He returned to the higher ground and studied the fields from where the French had first advanced and then he saw what worried him most, there was a distinctive splash of cavalry colour moving across the landscape, but he was reassured by the fact that there were no metal helmets nor breastplates, which would have meant heavy cavalry. His telescope told him that they were Light Cavalry, probably Chasseurs, French Hussars, this decided by their light blue uniform and squat, black busbies. Almost certainly they would try his flank, where the 105th were and so he descended rapidly to find Drake.

"Chasseurs are on their way, probably coming for us. One Squadron, I'd say. 100 sabres, but I'm sure you already knew that."

Drake feigned indignation.

"I'm disappointed to have to remind you that any form of mathematics has always been my most accomplished forte!"

Carr laughed.

"Just so, therefore prepare to move 50 yards to your right, to the end of the mountable slope. Get them into two ranks before the point where it becomes too steep."

"And leave a gap in our line!"

"Leave me to worry about that. The Provisionals have spread right to hold the river. The cavalry want our flank, so when they come, they'll be at you, so they're all yours!"

Coming on at a good canter the Chasseurs could now be seen and they were, indeed, heading for a flank and so Drake needed to defend the last of the accessible slope on that side. He gave the orders for formation, two ranks. When that was done, he stood behind his men.

"Load!"

Inside 20 seconds, all were at the 'make ready', Baker Rifles vertical above them.

"Fire by ranks. On my order."

The Company were holding a 100 yard front, stood at intervals with the second rank stood back from the gaps in the first line. It was clear that the Chasseurs intended to charge and so Drake waited. He waited until the horsemen were slowed by the steep slope.

"First rank, present!"

The muskets were lowered.

"Fire!"

The volley crashed out but Drake waited a long five seconds. The smoke cleared and then it was plain the charge had been halted, with many fallen men and horses now blocking further progress, but many Chasseurs continued to attempt to struggle through.

"Second rank, present!"

Two second pause.

"Fire!"

Again the same crash of 40 odd rifles and the Chasseur assault was finished, survivors now turning in retreat. The failure of the Chasseurs now caused the Voltiguers to pull back themselves, their Commander content to await reinforcements, as would be necessary to confront the main force higher up on the ridge. Carr took himself to his own Company and to Drake.

"Casualties?"

"None!"

Up on the ridge, it was with relief that they heard the renewed silence from below, which marked the end of any immediate conflict which could involve them, but there was tension from another source. General Picton had arrived up on the ridge and immediately began consultations with Cole and Anson. It had not gone unnoticed by Anson's men that they were now alone on the ridge, Cole's other Brigades were now marching down the back slope, down to the road behind the ridge. Also, Picton's garb had not gone unnoticed, it was well known throughout the army as the presage of a battle whenever he wore such as he wore now, a tall, round civilian hat, a blue frock coat and a furled umbrella, which he used as a riding whip. This was remarked upon by Toby Halfway, in the second rank behind Jed Deakin in the Colour Company.

"See old Tommy's in fighting gear, there behind us, Jed."

Deakin turned to look, but he said just one word, more spat than spoken.

"Picton!"

For over an hour they stood in the heavy heat of the late afternoon, Picton riding the line of Anson's Brigade, these alone and prominent on the ridge, Picton glowering at the 105th, receiving sullen, uncompromising expressions in return. They remembered his insulting comments after the capture of Cuidad Rodrigo when they were attempting to protect terrified civilians and he remembered the replies hurled back at him from within their ranks. It was during this indulgence of mutual dislike that Deakin again studied the far distance.

"If he wants a fight, well, there's one coming his way!"

The main French force had arrived down from Roncesvalles, in a strength that appeared to be a whole Corps of two Divisions, one Division keeping to the road, whilst the other was already marching off to position itself on the pasturelands regularly watered by the Erro and its tributaries. Picton ceased his riding and was soon joined by Cole and Anson and an intense discussion ensued, with much arm pointing both forward to the French and back towards Pamplona. The French soon halted in their positions, but the Command discussion did not. O'Hare and Heaviside were stood together, studying the trio carefully, unfortunately out of earshot, but O'Hare had his own major concern.

"All our Lights are down over and at the bottom of this hill. What of them? What's he going to do about them?"

Heaviside was as worried as O'Hare, but for a different reason.

"This ridge is untenable with this force. We can be outflanked on both sides."

Beneath them, Carr was worried for both reasons. He had a steep climb behind him and if this French force got onto the ridge using the flanks after a full-bloodied assault, then he would be cut off. He continued to study the French intently for the next half-hour, but they did not move. He studied his watch equally intently and the time was nearing six o' clock. Darkness would arrive in under three hours, but that was time enough for a minor battle for which he would be in the centre. He had no choice but to go up himself. Byng had placed him there, but Byng may have gone and, if that were the case, then it may well be that no one in any authority knew they were there. The climb was arduous and took some time and at the top the first figure he saw was Picton, an incongruous sight to any military eyes, sat his horse, slapping his umbrella against his right leg. Carr immediately came to the attention and saluted.

"Sir. Beg to report, Sir."

Seeing Carr, Picton's face immediately changed as though he had a violent toothache.

"You may, Major!"

Picton had ignored Carr's Brevet rank, but he spoke out, nevertheless, clear and firmly.

"Sir. I have placed under my command the five Light Companies of General Anson's Brigade. This by General Byng, Sir. We are at the foot of the ridge. In view of the recent arrival of the French, do you have any orders for us, Sir?"

Picton's face changed. There could be no arguing with the legitimacy of Carr's question, but he frowned down at him nevertheless.

"You've already been in action, so I am told. Seen off one attack."

"Yes Sir. That's true, Sir."

Picton looked into the distance, then down at Carr.

"What would you say he's got out there? Five, six Brigades?"

"More like Divisions, Sir, from what I hear of the action at Roncesvalles. I can see no reason why the whole French force from the pass is not now down here and opposite us."

Picton turned sharply towards him, aware of the contradiction of his own assessment, but also knowing that Carr could well be correct. He was also aware himself that his ridge could be turned at both ends, but he was also tempted by the idea of his own skirmishers softening up any French column attempting a direct assault, helping to defeat that assault and then he could retire at leisure. He looked directly at Carr.

"What would you do if a French column came at you, from where you are now."

Carr looked at him directly, even challengingly.

"Hold back their skirmishers, Sir, until pushed back by the column itself."

There was no reply, so Carr continued to give his opinion with no equivocation.

"That would be the case if required to hold at the bottom of the slope, Sir. However, it would be better to come back up and fight their skirmishers at the top, just below the summit, where we would have a serious advantage. Hold them there at the military crest and then rejoin our main line when their main column arrived. We would be rejoining as whole Companies, Sir, rather than as a scattering of men who've just run up a hill."

Picton's face remained impassive, then he studied the French once more. As before there seemed to be no movement from them, but they were a potent force, probably greater than his own and poised to strike. His jaw came together and he spoke, plainly reluctantly.

"Very well, Carr. I think you have the right of it. Bring your men up and form a line wherever you see fit."

"Do I remain in command, Sir?'

"You do!"

Relieved, Carr descended rapidly, first to the village using a convenient track down. Bairns' Rifles were immediately sent up, carrying their few wounded with them, then he went along the line, sending up each Company, then finally to the 105th where he found Drake.

"Nat, we're going back up. Reform at the military crest from where you can see all the way down, you know what I mean."

The order was given and the men began their climb, many using their rifle butts to lever their way up, because there the slope was at its steepest. At the top, the Rifles were already in the perfect position and the other Light Companies were conforming. However, by the time they had arrived in their new position, the French position had changed, a strong Brigade or even a Division, was now moving far out to the Allied right. This French advance was indeed serious and well understood by O'Hare.

"He's sending a Brigade to outflank our right and it's a pound to get a penny that he's doing the same for our left. It won't be long before he sends something forward to hold us here. Perhaps not a column, but a whole Brigade in open order. We can only hope that Picton is thinking about both flanks. That French General couldn't run a whelk stall if he isn't sending out to both!"

Heaviside was already turning around, to look both ways.

"He must have heard you. The Provisionals and the 48th are moving, in opposite directions, the 48th down to the road. The wisdom of the prudent is to understand his way. Proverbs 14, verse 8."

Ignoring the Religious reference, O'Hare looked himself to indeed see the Provisionals marching off to hold the left flank, the 48th the right.

"One thing I will say is that it is starting to get a mite lonely up on this ridge! Just us and the 27th facing all that's still out in front of us."

He turned to Heaviside.

"The men are in columns of Companies. Get them into a firing line. Creet will do the same with his 27th, if he has the mind. Or if he has different orders! I can't see us marching out of here without some kind of joust with the Johnnies!"

Carr saw the movement of the two Battalions reforming into firing lines behind him on the ridge to O'Hare's prompting and he registered the positions of his own 105th and also the 27th, both now quickly formed into line, but he soon returned to his own concerns. He walked along the top of the slope, giving simple instructions, if attacked to fire when the chances of a hit were good. To the Light troops this simply meant independent action and so all settled into a good firing position, within the open covering of trees. This applied to the 105th Light and, on hearing the order, they found branches, logs and stones which they piled into a barricade, augmented by loose earth. Behind them, Picton's telescope never left his right eye, scanning the full width of the area below, watching both the French at the road and the Brigade marching at French pace to his right, but mostly he studied what was happening at the road in front of him. This anxious examination continued for almost half an hour, his left leg taking punishment all the while from the umbrella, whilst his right hand held the telescope. Finally, both were still and he turned to his ADCs, within earshot of O'Hare.

"We're leaving. He's relying on his flank moves, nothing from the front, and we are secure at both sides by now. So, Bingham; tell Anson down there with the 48th to hold until we are past on the road. Tell him we'll fight a rearguard on the road if needs be and hold them until dark. McMichael; get to the Provisionals and tell them to move now and get themselves back towards Pamplona."

The two spurred their horses away, but whilst he had been giving his orders, a third ADC had been studying the French and he turned to his General, deeply worried.

"Sir! He's coming forward. Standard French attack."

The telescope was back to Picton's eye in an instant, to see a thick skirmishing line advancing before a two Battalion column, with artillery furthest ahead on both flanks. He panned again to the right, the flanking Brigade had by now disappeared behind the end of the ridge. This was a quandary, what to do, allow a French column to cross the ridge and come down onto his retreating Division. That choice meant leaving now, if they were to be safe at all, or otherwise bring the column to a halt and hope there will be time for the force fighting the perilous rearguard on the ridge to escape past the flank assaults? He made his decision; the former was too big a risk and so he chose the latter, even if it meant half a Brigade being badly mauled in such a conflict. He turned to his remaining ADC.

"Get down to Anson with the 48th. Tell him that the ridge is being attacked by a French column. I'm going to halt it before leaving, so he must hold that flank open. The Provisionals will soon be on the road with him."

As the ADC galloped off, Picton used his telescope again to see that the French were hurrying forward and were now closing to within a quarter of a mile. He looked behind him and was reassured. The 105th and the 27th were already in a firing line and he had a good skirmishing line at his front, commanded by Carr, whom he could see at the top of the ridge, overseeing all before him. Meanwhile, back before the 105th firing line, O'Hare remained with Heaviside and they had seen the French movements.

"Picton looks worried!"

"So should he be. I don't like any of this one little bit!"

"Well, we'll soon know."

Picton was riding over, the anxiety on his face intensifying the deeper red of his complexion, which was plain for both to see.

"There's a French column coming our way. Two Battalions."

O'Hare saw no reason to be overly deferential to Picton.

"Yes Sir. We've seen it."

Picton did not react.

"I'm leaving yours and the 27th to bring it to a halt and then pull back. Get your men ready. Creet will be in command. He's a full Colonel."

With that final barb, Picton rode off to the 27th. O'Hare looked along his line, then at Heaviside.

"Well, we couldn't be more ready than we already are!"

Heaviside grinned and nodded, whilst O'Hare waited for the quote, which was not long in coming.

"Be ready and keep ready, you and all your hosts that are assembled about you and be a guard for them. Ezekiel 38 Verse 7."

O'Hare laughed.

"Amen to that, Brother Joshua. Amen indeed!"

Both men shook hands and grinned, before again observing Picton. Having delivered his orders to Creet of the 27th, he was back in front of them, at the top of the slope and no longer alone, because the first two ADCs had by now returned. Picton studied the oncoming column for seconds, then he turned his horse to walk across the front of the 105th to reach the 27th on the left, presumably to give final instructions to Creet. It was at that moment that they heard the distant sounds of musket exchanges from back behind their right, but Picton rode on.

Carr, at the top of the slope, was thinking if there was anything more he could do other than check the positions of his five Companies, but all were perfectly positioned and 'settled'. There was little left to do, other than to make sure that all was well understood and so he took himself to the end of his line and found Captain Bairns of the Rifles.

"You've seen that column, Tom. They'll be here in ten minutes. On the whistle you fall back, yours, the 27th and the 48th Lights to form on the end of the 27th. Good luck."

Bairns saluted perfectly.

"Sir!"

Carr walked on, giving the same instructions to the remaining two Companies, except that the Provisionals and his own Light

Company would form on the end of the 105th. With that, the first solid shot from the supporting French artillery began to arrive, almost all crashing into the trees above and he saw his men crouch down further into their firing positions. He looked behind and was gratified to see the main line of the 105th and the 27th too far back across the ridge to be affected by the six French field-guns, then he looked forward to see that the inevitable French Voltiguers had now reached the foot of the slope. Behind Carr was Picton and he heard the fateful ADC arrive, him somewhat in a panic and speaking loudly.

"Sir, from General Anson. The French have advanced further around our right and are threatening the road. Can he have the 27th? Sir?"

Picton immediately swung his horse's head around and almost galloped over to the 27th. Inside a minute the Regiment was jogging across the ridge to follow the ADC. Many in the 105th turned to watch them go, but there were no insulting comments, the mutual respect between the 105th and the 27th was absolute. Picton came back to his watching position close to Carr and both of them saw what all on the edge of the ridge could see, that the French column itself, with skirmishers before, was now at the foot of the slope. Carr looked at Picton and simply waited, he knew what was to come and Picton walked his horse over to Carr and studied him for a long ten seconds.

"Carr! If that column gets over the ridge, they will cut off the Provisionals and take the 48th and 27th in flank and rear. My aim is to get away into the night. My Third Division is at Zubiri, three miles back, soon to be joined by Ellis' of Lowry-Cole's 4th, who are now on their way. Anson's must fall back on both mine and Cole's intact, then we all retreat together. We cannot afford to lose a whole Brigade. There's no defensible position between here and Pamplona, so we must give them a reverse here."

Then Picton stared hard at Carr, as though acknowledging the fact, "I know we don't like each other", but his face showed neither contempt nor animosity. There was more a sense that Picton hoped that Carr knew that he had no choice, but that was something that Carr had already acknowledged within himself. However, what Picton then said, in his inimitable way, was both serious and sincere.

"For that, I've got to leave yours here. Stop them, Carr! Stop them and then get away as best you can. If there's any collection of whore's melt bastards that can do that, it's yours!"

With that, he used his umbrella to good effect and rode with his Staff over the back of the ridge, leaving Carr to ponder the back-handed compliment. At the head of the slope, the Rifles were now into action as the French Voltiguers used the easier track up from the village, but soon there was fierce conflict all across the slope. Within minutes, Davey and Miles were back down from their parapet for the fourth time, lying on their backs and reloading.

"How many you got, John?"

"Three!"

"Same here. These is sufferin'. 'Tis like fish in a barrel!"

All along the line, assailed by the Light Company marksmen from above them, the Voltiguers were taking heavy casualties, especially on the flanks where both the Rifles and the 105th were using Baker rifles. However, the success of the action in front of him and just below the summit, meant nothing to O'Hare. Now there was only one Regiment remaining on the ridge, their 105th. Anson and Picton had gone, presumably to supervise both the 48th and the 27th on the most obvious flank. Only the Light Companies with Carr remained to boost their numbers, but then came at least some encouragement. It was not long before the conflict on the slope in front died to nothing, the cost to the Voltiguers had proved too heavy to continue any advance. They descended into cover and waited for the main column to arrive, whilst the cannon-shot continued to arrive above, but only damaging the trees. Carr walked his line congratulating all he saw, him well satisfied, as they were also, with the numbers of blue uniformed casualties that now littered the slope below, then he ran back up to his 105th and came up to O'Hare and Heaviside.

"Just us!"

They both grinned and nodded, Heaviside answering.

"Just us! Older men are sober-minded, dignified, self-controlled, sound in faith, in love and in steadfastness. Titus 2, verse 2."

The all laughed, O'Hare especially.

"Well, I'll take that to myself, which leaves out you two!"

Then Carr offered his hand to both.

"Good luck!"

The drums in the French column could already be heard, adding to the urgency. Carr took stock. He had five Companies of Light Troops including his own of the 105th. The nearest 105th Company to him were the Grenadiers and so he called over Simon Ameshurst.

"Simon. Our skirmishing line is just out of sight over the crest, five Light Companies. Tell each Captain what to do when pushed back by the main column. On the whistle, the Rifles, the 27th and the 48th will fall back to the left of our line, the Provisionals and our own to our right. They probably already know that, but, next, when the column arrives and we engage it, at their discretion I want them to push forward onto their flanks. If they can, close up, the closer the better. That understood?"

Ameshurst took a step back and saluted.

"Sir!"

Carr then looked along his own line and took a deep breath.

"Ensigns! Colours!"

Deakin and Bennett immediately pulled off the leather sheaths and handed The Colours to their Ensigns, Deakin noting with dismay the broad grim that now spread across his 'stepson's' face. When he turned, he found Carr stood before the Colour Company, sword drawn and already taking a deep breath.

"Men!"

Silence fell along the line, all that could be heard was the sound of the

French drums down amongst the trees.

"There's a Frog column coming up this slope, two Battalions, thinking they can go through us like we aren't here. They think things have swung back in their favour, so we're going to change their minds about that. We are the fighting 105th, the fighting Rag and Bone Boys!"

He held up his left sleeve.

"We wear the green!"

He took another deep breath.

"There's no gang of Frogs yet born of woman that can go through the 105th and shove us out of their way like we were nothing more than a bunch of half-trained Militia! It's Picton that's given us this job! I know what we all think of Picton, but he needs this done and we're not going to let him down. You know the drill! Half Company volleys. Obey your Captains and like the Sergeants say, get off your ten, boys. Just get off your ten! Now load. Time to show these Crapauds just who they're taking on."

He was met by cheers, brandished muskets and raised fists, but he had turned to face the slope, waiting for the Light Companies to fall back and then it would be up to his own 105th, stood in a two-deep line. Over to Carr's right and just over the edge, Davey, Pike and Miles were up at their parapet. They could hear the drums getting louder and they could see the Voltiguers rising up from cover as the column advanced up to support them. Davey was the first to sight and fire, Pike and Miles soon after and two bodies spun backwards to collide with the feet of the oncoming column, the third slumped to his knees. The conflict was no different to what had gone before between themselves and the French skirmishers, heavy casualties amongst the Voltiguers and soon Carr's men were causing casualties in the front ranks of the column itself. Frenchmen were falling all across the width of their attack, but they came on, 50 yards wide in what seemed around nine or ten ranks deep, fully closed up. Carr, satisfied that his men were in good cover, allowed them to assail the column until the last minute, then he blew his whistle and the five Light Companies sprang up and, led by Bairns and Drake, they sprinted back to form either side of the 105th.

The French drums increased in volume, it was the only sound, because the French artillery had long ceased to fire. All along the line of the 105th, with the Light Companies added, silence reigned. Carr, O'Hare and Heaviside looked along the first rank, stock still, and all almost smiled to see the hard, grim, determined faces of all there, all stood rigid at 'order arms'. The first to be seen of the French was their Eagle standard appearing above the top edge of the slope, then the shakoes of the front rank, then their faces. Carr took a deep breath.

"Make ready!"

Along the whole line, muskets were raised from a butt on the ground to a barrel in the air. Did he see the expression change on the faces of the French, perhaps, but Carr quickly stepped back within the first rank. He then allowed the first two ranks of the French column to gain the crest and step onto the ridgetop which brought them within 40 yards range.

"Present!"

All weapons came to the level, then expressions did change at the front of the French column, but this registered with Carr for not even a second.

"Fire!"

The front ranks of the two centre Companies opened fire with a hard crash, then the front ranks of the Companies either side to them fired and this spread further out to the flanks in quick succession. Within 15 seconds all in the front rank had fired, from a line of well over 200 yards focused onto one of 50. Then, with total steadiness, the Captains of the centre Companies merely waited for the smoke to thin enough to see and the same arrived from the second rank, all to be repeated as though set off by clockwork. Smoke blocked most of the view, but through it could be seen falling and struggling bodies and above the crash of the volleys the cries of wounded men. The column had been brought to a standstill. From the far right, Drake could see that the first two or three ranks had been almost obliterated and those following were now struggling over the bodies of their dead and wounded, but at the same time receiving the same degree of punishment. He saw Carr raise his sword and lead the centre forward, then the order came down to him at the end of the line.

"Ten paces forward."

The line advanced, halted and continued the half-Company volleys. Yet another ten paces brought them to within 20 feet of their struggling opponents. Drake decided that the time had come and he raised his own sword.

"Forward! Forward! Get onto their flanks."

The Grenadier Company were already curling around to improve their own view and Drake led his men over and back into the trees, where each quickly gained cover. The Provisionals followed and soon ragged but continuous volleys were being poured into the outside ranks of the column, which was now no more than a disordered mass. They withstood for not two minutes. Being dreadfully mauled from the front and taking serious casualties from the sides, the column broke and ran. In their place, where they had been, the ground was covered with dead, dying and seriously wounded Frenchmen, but there was no pursuit as the smoke drifted away. Every Redcoat, disciplined and veteran, stood their ground and waited. They all knew that a second Battalion column was yet to arrive and for them, Carr had decided, they would not be allowed to gain the crest. Their skirmishers were now but a pitiful few, so let the column come up into a 'horseshoe' of fire. He issued the order.

"Stand fast and reload. Order arms."

All along the line, men reloaded their weapons and came to 'order arms'. As the last musket butt went down beside the last right boot, Carr heard the drums and spoke to himself.

"Take advantage of any advantage."

They would fight the French from the top, making the most of their height advantage and he decided to leave the Light Companies where they were and rely on the initiative of their Captains.

"Port arms!"

All muskets came up to the diagonal across each chest. Before him was a line of French dead and wounded on the edge of the ridgetop. Just below, on seeing the second column, the Light Companies settled further into their flanking positions. Carr led his men forward, through and over the human wreckage that had once been the leading ranks of the first Battalion column, many wounded reaching up and pleading for aid, but his men marched on. Once able to look down the slope now before them, the second column could be seen below and, using the trees and bushes at the sides as cover, his own marksmen independently opened fire to bring down the last Voltiguers and some Officers in the lead. Davey especially picked out the French Colonel at their head, he took careful aim and when the Baker gave its flat bark, the Frenchman staggered sideways into a tree and then slumped down as his men marched up past him. When the range for his line was down to 40 yards, Carr, heart pumping, took another deep breath.

"Make ready! Present!"

A short pause during which he felt, rather than saw, muskets come to the horizontal all along the line.

"Fire!"

Again the half-Company volleys crashed out, regular and terrifying, the continuous sound echoing back from the trees. From the side, Drake could see the first ranks practically swept away inside a minute by the incessant hail of bullets, and his own men were dealing out the same punishment to the sides of this column, as to the one earlier. The following ranks of the column pushed forward, but they were also brought to a halt and then, after less than three minutes, closer to two, morale inside the column collapsed. They could hear the incessant fusillade from the British line, their brother Battalion merely minutes before had ran down past them as a shocked and defeated mob and now they also had been brought to a halt, caught between fire from three sides. The column dissolved and ran, each man feeling trapped and assailed from all directions, save the rear, where dwelt safety. When he was certain of the column's defeat, Carr turned to his Bugler.

"Bates! Recall!"

The notes rang out and all turned to hurry back from the edge of the slope, all except Major St. John Slade, his head now spinning from the noise and the carnage. For the first time he had been involved in the intense uproar at the centre of a veteran line firing half-Company volleys. To his unaccustomed mind, he had just been through two acts of utter madness, so bad that the incessant crashing of muskets all around him, this and the groans of the wounded and dying, had robbed him of any capacity to respond to what was needed. With Slade stood paralysed with shock, more than once it had been Deakin who yelled out the order to fire. The sulphur smoke still hung in the air, whilst both behind and below was a wall of French dead and dying, this the brutal result of the merciless volleys of his own Regiment, inflicting what had been close to slaughter. He turned from the edge to find himself required to pick a careful way through the results of the first conflict. A Frenchman plucked at his trouser leg, but Slade looked down to see two staring eyes within a mask of blood. He shied away, but he was not moving fast enough for Colour Sergeant Deakin.

"Sir! Sir! We have to fall back. We'll be out of here soon."

Slade turned at the sound of the familiar voice and its urgent words. It brought him back to some level of reality.

"Yes Sergeant. As you say."

Standing further back on the ridgetop, Carr saw the Light Companies emerge from the trees, so he gave another order for a different set of notes from Bugle Bates.

"Form fours!"

His own Battalion quickly formed for order of march and the Light Companies did the same. Carr then looked at O'Hare.

"Take them down."

The order rang out and the column moved, leaving a scattering of red-coated shapes on the grass. Carr had seen a number of wounded being supported in the column, but there was nothing he could do for those remaining, these were either dead or so badly wounded that they soon would be. The 105th and the Lights must quit the ridge and hurry down onto the road to Pamplona. The final Company to pass him were the Rifles and he began walking to match the pace of Bairns.

"Tom. I don't know if the road below is still open. Take yours on ahead and get down to it. You may be needed down there. Take Nat Drake's with you."

Carr was the last to leave the ridge, hearing as he hurried away, only the moans of the dying as they lay amongst those already dead. The route down was merely a rough track through trees and the light was dying but lingered strong enough for him to see his way. He ran at his best pace and came to the head of his column just as it arrived on the road and there he found Anson, closely watching two, perhaps three French Battalions about 300 yards out before him. Plainly these were the French columns that had attempted the outflanking march earlier that afternoon.

"Sir! On the ridge. Both columns have been halted and I'd say were now in a bad state. Sir. They'll not be coming forward again soon. Beyond rallying, I'd say."

"Casualties? Yours?"

"I'd say 40, Sir. Across mine and the Light Companies."

"Very well. Good work. We've had a brisk time of it down here and lost a few ourselves and he still may not be done, although he's pulled back for a while. Have yours got another fight in them?"

"Whatever you order, Sir."

"Right. The 27th and 48th have gone on. I've not seen the Provisionals, but I suspect they found another route out of here. I've heard nothing that makes me think otherwise. I sent an ADC to find them, but he's not yet returned. Johnny's still there, as you can see, he may try once more before full dark, so set yours as a firing line on the edge of the road."

The orders were shouted down the line and the column broke up to reform as a two deep line along 250 yards of the roadside, both the 105th and their accompanying Lights. The evening was now well advanced such that little could be seen clearly beyond 200 yards from the road. The first they knew of the French advance were the inevitable Voltiguers emerging menacingly from the gloom of the trees and hedgerows in the fields out beyond the road. Anson himself gave the order to load and make ready, then they saw the French line, but it halted at 200 yards and then fired a volley which caused not above a handful of men to fall wounded. Anson looked at the static French, with Carr stood beside him.

"We've only to show that we mean to make a stand and hold until dark. He'll not follow."

As if to answer, the French line advanced another 50 yards, which was enough for Anson.

"Firing by ranks. Present."

All weapons came to the horizontal.

"Front rank fire!."

The volley crashed out, followed seconds later by that of the rear. The impact was impossible to see, but the affect was. The French line dissolved back into the darkness and Anson turned to Carr.

"Told you! They don't want a serious fight. Not yet anyway."

He sheathed his sword.

"Form them up, Carr, and get them off to Zubiri. Picton's there and what happens next is up to him. Both you and I are out of here!"

The column formed within a minute, all eager to leave and, with Anson and Carr at their head, the column marched away into the full dark of the Pyrenees foothills, with only a scattering of Summer stars above their heads. Soon heads were nodding but their feet continued the automatic rhythm of the march. The conflict on the ridge had left Carr as mentally exhausted as anyone and he complained as such to Anson.

"The men had little sleep last night, Sir, being pulled back off the ridge at Roncesvalles in the middle of it, and now there'll be none this night."

A voice from a mouth unseen came to Carr from his right.

"Understood, Henry, but this is a retreat and we must get back to where we can make a stand and hold them back. The Peer's up San Sebastian way or some such, so it'll be up to Hill, Cole and Picton just how we play this game out. There's nowhere between here and Pamplona and we must not be caught on the road. Zubiri's not far, I'll give yours three hours there, perhaps more, once we've got Picton's Third between us and the French.

The road twisted and turned to such an extent that, in the dark, the leading ranks almost lost the road, but almost two hours brought them into Zubiri, its main road illuminated by many fires lit along its length by Picton's own men. To his credit, Picton had not retired, but remained waiting, knowing that men under his command were still in contact with the French and unaccounted for, so he walked forward onto the road himself to meet Carr and Anson.

"Carr. Report."

Carr came to a halt and saluted. Picton looked even more malevolent in the light of the dancing flames from the fires nearby.

"Both columns halted, Sir, before we got away."

"Halted, Carr, you say? This is no time for false modesty. Will they be following?"

"Our two won't, Sir, we gave them a mauling, but I cannot say such for those that we found trying to cut us off from the road. General Anson here can speak better about that than I can. Sir."

Anson stepped forward.

"Colonel Carr has the right of it, Sir. We held them off, well enough, those that threatened the road, but they'll be down here well before Noon tomorrow. That would be my guess."

Picton nodded.

"So, not at dawn, at least, which is when we leave and I want yours gone before then.

Carr stepped forward.

"Sir, this is the second night my men have not slept and they have just fought off two French columns. We, that's General Anson and I, had hoped for them to be given some rest, Sir."

Picton glowered at them for a long five seconds, the flames picking out the braid and decorations on his Major General's uniform, but not his eyes, his brows were now lowered too far by a deep frown. He pulled out his watch and spoke the message of the hands.

"It's one in the morning. I want you gone by four!"

Both Carr and Anson took a step back and saluted to follow the route of their men and find them 200 yards down the road, alongside it and all fast asleep. Carr found O'Hare and Heaviside lying side by side, both fast asleep, under their blankets. The only pair still awake were Sergeants Gibney and Ellis.

"Sar' Major and yourself Sarn't Ellis. We can spend three hours here, courtesy of General Picton, but we must be gone by four. Can I trust you to wake us then? Here's my watch."

Carr held out the family heirloom, given to him by his Mother's brother, towards Gibney, who took it and saluted.

"Four it is, Sir."

"Very good. I'll be here."

With that, Carr shed his pack, pulled out his own blanket and was asleep before he was stretched out on the floor, the blanket dropped useless beside him. Gibney bent down and pulled the blanket up and over, until it was properly covering the unconscious form of his Colonel.

oOo

It was Ellis who found himself shaking Carr awake.

"Sir. Sir. 'Tis time, Sir."

Carr propped himself up on one elbow.

"Is it four?"

"Yes Sir, just on. Here's your watch."

"What are the men doing?"

"Getting up themselves, Sir, and moving onto the road."

Whilst Carr levered himself more upright to take the watch, Ellis rolled up Carr's blanket and buckled it under the straps of his backpack.

"There we are, Sir. Dark's just movin' over, like, an' so it should be near light by the time we're movin'. Sir."

Carr now pulled himself to his feet and took a drink of water.

"Very good, Sergeant. And moving should we be."

As no more than a collection of dark, merging shapes, groups of men moved in the direction of the road, to form up where they were required, in their Companies. The order was given and the 105th began their march, the light gaining ascendency with every mile. After two hours of easy downward marching, to the cheerful sound of the River Arga on their left, they came to a steep hill on their right with a Church prominent on the summit, although only the spire was visible, and there they were directed off the road to then climb up and through a small village which surrounded the Church. At the rear, Drake noticed Shakeshaft pulling out his diary.

"Recording where, Richard?"

"Yes. Zabaldika. Six in the morning, 27th July 1813."

Drake grinned and marched on, the terrain becoming increasingly clear. They were now in a deep valley, with steep hills on both sides, but the valley floor sloped gently upwards from the village, which they had already needed to make a sharp climb to pass through. The valley terminated ahead at a steep slope, a solid wall of dark green scrub, spanning the valley from one side to the other, rising up from the valley floor around half a mile to their front, but only half as high as the ridges each side. The climb became more and more arduous, up the right-hand side of the valley to gain what they thought was its end, but it was not, they had climbed onto what could only be described as a 'land-bridge' barely 200 yards wide and once on its summit they used it to cross the valley. On the far side of the land bridge the 105th saw why it could be described as such, because there was another valley, as deep as that containing Zabaldika, only longer, with another village at the far end. Whilst crossing their high perch, they could see on the slope before them, above both valleys, various units of the Allied army, British, Portuguese and Spanish. All had come down from Roncesvalles before them. Carr, however, was not convinced by what he saw.

"Is this their defensible position we've taken up? It can be turned at both ends, the Arga valley that we've just come up from and I bet that place down there has a road that goes straight to Pamplona."

O'Hare was staring rightwards, down the valley.

"I fear you are correct. One can only hope that we will have enough, firstly, to defend the Arga valley, we can assume that Picton will do that, when Johnny does come down. Second, enough to hold this ridge that we're marching onto, and third, to block anything trying to go through that place down there at the far end of the valley and get on to Pamplona. Presumably something must be arriving from somewhere to do that."

They continued across the land-bridge, to be greeted half-way by Anson.

"This is where we're offering battle. You can see the Provisionals there, right in front of you, they got here in the dark, the 27th and 48th next to them, on their left. Stubbs Portuguese are there between this land bridge, the 'saddle', as we're calling it and that hill above Zabaldika. You can see two Spanish Battalions on that. Called locally Spanish Hill, so I am reliably informed, which seems appropriate, wouldn't you say? You get yourselves up behind those Spanish, back of that hill, in reserve of them."

Carr nodded, wearily.

"Yes Sir, but can the men sleep and eat? They're all in."

"Once in position, they can, yes, but we expect the French before nightfall. So, last words, that village down there, at the far end of the valley, that's called Sorauren. I know you like to know these things. A main road goes through it to Pamplona. Oh, and the Followers are up from Pamplona."

Carr smiled at Anson's helpfulness.

"Very good, Sir. Thank you."

He led his men on to leave the 'saddle' and supervise the positioning of their line up the steep slope 300 yards behind the Spanish on their hill. Once in place they all slumped down to the ground, all energy gone and some cooked, some slept, despite the bright sun of the early morning. It was the Followers who found them, rather than the other way around, finding them in the usual haphazard way of walking the area behind the line and asking for any directions that may be useful. They had climbed the back of the ridge, up from the Pamplona to Sorauren road, where the first of the Followers came across Ross' Brigade, these the first to arrive from Roncesvalles and holding the Allied far left. Two of the three 'lookers' did the enquiring, Bridie and Eirin, Consuela's English not being up to the task. Bridie went first to a Corporal of the 7th Royal Fusiliers, all sat above a tiny stone built Chapel, 40 yards down the slope.

"May I beg your pardon, your Honour, but can you be directin' me to the 105th? We've been told that all are gatherin' up to here."

The Corporal, sat just apart from the others of his mess, turned and laughed, but spoke loud enough for all to hear.

"What! The 105th, those runners! Now just what would a comely piece such as yourself be doing with a bunch turntails such as that?"

Bridie showed no reaction, but Nellie did, she sprang forward and had to be halted by Bridie and Consuela.

"Never mind turntails, you gobshite! They're our men and we needs to know their whereabouts and if you cannot help, then you can keep your rotten gobshite words back down your black throat!"

All around laughed at such a tirade and one spoke up.

"They're not this end, Ma. Those up the other have just come down from Roncesvalles. Try up there."

At that moment Eirin arrived and all in the group turned at her arrival, but she addressed her Mother, Bridie, ignoring the looks and the comments.

"I'm told that Anson's is at the far end, Ma. Just been told. Anson's is their Brigade."

With that, they began their journey of almost a mile, but Nellie still had a parting shot.

"Muckrakes, the lot of you. Dirty muckrakes!"

They passed three Battalions of Portuguese placed at the top of where the valley slope was steepest, these holding the Allied centre, then it was not long before they heard the cry of 'Up here! Up here!". Those Followers in the lead had seen the lurid green of the facings of their own Regiment and many men sprang up to greet their loved ones, including Deakin, Byford and Saunders, but the first question came from Bridie, when she looked around at the familiar group.

"Are you alright? You look all in."

Deakin kissed her.

"We're alright, love. Just not much sleep. Have you any rations, all we've got is used up?"

As an answer they pulled up their small cart, which contained baby Ellen and began unloading flour and salt-pork. Meanwhile Bridie pushed Deakin down to the ground.

"You sit now and rest yourself. We'll get some food going."

In no time, using the fires already there, water was soon boiling and a stew being prepared, but there was little sleep because of what could now be seen happening on the far side of the valley. French cavalry were walking their horses on the path up the far slope from Zabaldika, the same one that the 105th had followed earlier in the day, followed by two French infantry Divisions, who marched on to cover the whole of the slope opposite the Allied army. Being in reserve, the 105th were not called to arms, but the rest of Anson's were, these being in the front line, the Provisionals in front, then across leftwards came the 48th and then the 27th. Likewise stood to the alert were Stubbs Portuguese behind the Provisionals and the two Spanish Battalions holding Spanish Hill. However, the 105th were allowed to sit and take their food whilst the two forces stared at each other across a distance of less than a quarter of a mile.

It was at that moment, with the French now static, that loud and raucous cheering broke out from all along the Allied line, starting from the Sorauren end. Campbell's three Portuguese Battalions in the Allied centre to the left of Anson's Brigade shouted loudest when the cheering reached them, which was soon taken up by the 27th and 48th and then by Stubbs Portuguese.

Davey and Miles sat up, with Byford just behind. Miles stared left and right at the cheering and waving men all across the line before them.

"What's stirred them up? 'Specially they Portuguee. What they shouting Byfe?"

"Douro!"

"Douro? B'ain't that the river we was at, back in …… what was it, Oporto?"

"Back in 09 and, yes Tom, Douro was the river and that's the Portuguese nickname for him, Wellington. Seems that he's arrived, at the other end. Making many men happy, it would seem."

Davey was not so sure.

"Nosey's here, is he? Then get ready for a very bloody business on the morrow."

It was not long before Wellington arrived at their own flank and the three Battalions of Anson's in the front line were brought to the attention, as were the Portuguese in reserve above the saddle, but no one came to Carr and so he allowed his men to continue their leisure. Wellington progressed in stages to his right, using his telescope at each halt. Eventually he arrived at the top of Spanish Hill to use that vantage point to study the depth of the valley down to Zabaldika and to also look fully down the Arga valley towards Pamplona, where Picton's Division was holding a low ridge and facing a substantial French force. With all now seen and examined, he rode back, acknowledging the extra cheers and greetings of all his men along the line as he made his way back to the Sorauren end of his position. However, the 105th's idleness did not last long when fighting broke out on Spanish Hill, coming to the 105th's attention as gunsmoke and the sound of volleys. All at that end were immediately called to arms but the Spanish held the skyline after firing several volleys, then they disappeared over the edge of the hill. Carr was stood with O'Hare.

"Seems the Dons are mounting a bayonet charge!"

"What's the odds?"

"Evens!"

However, no bet was placed and within a short time, the Spanish reappeared, waving their arms in triumph, some waving French shakoes. O'Hare turned to Carr, grinning.

"I should have taken you up!"

Carr would have answered were it not for the distinctive sound of cannonfire now coming to them from down the Arga valley, to their right. It was Carr again who commented.

"That's Picton answering the door knocker!"

O'Hare laughed.

"Not today, thank you, would seem to be the answer!"

The day wore on, the Allies observing more French forces arriving, but there was no exchange of fire even though some units were even within long musket shot from each other. Both sides were weary, having fought battles and marched hard. After the Noon meal, all three Senior Officers of the 105th were sat together, sometimes upright, sometimes lying back, often succumbing to the need to sleep. O'Hare was perhaps more energised than the other two, possibly because there was so much to observe amongst the French opposite, not least the arrival of what was obviously a group of French Staff Officers, who merged with another group and could plainly be seen arguing. O'Hare passed his telescope to Heaviside.

"There, in the centre. Could be El Rey again, having another barney with those who do actually know what they're doing."

Heaviside took the instrument and focused it for himself.

"Not as I've heard. Boney's dismissed his own brother after Vitoria and put Soult in charge. One of those must be him, perhaps along with other exalted names; Reille, Foy, Clausel. High ranking Marshalls all. "

He took a deep breath such that both Carr and O'Hare knew exactly what they were about to hear.

"Therefore pride is their necklace, violence covers them as a garment. Psalms 73, verse 6."

Carr laughed. He had heard the conversation but had not seen what was happening opposite, having remained dozing for some half an hour, so now he did sit up, but he did not use his telescope.

"Ney? Do you think?"

"Not that I've heard."

"Amen to that."

The day continued with each side staring at the other and all was still, save the odd lone horseman galloping to the left or sometimes to the right to adjust both armies. More food and sleep completed the day, but the Marshalls of France did not disperse, not until the rain came, a thunderstorm rolling down from the Pyrenees. O'Hare stood and found his blanket.

"This will spoil all that gold braid and finery, unless they've agreed to disagree."

There came a huge peal of thunder, a shot of lightning and the rainfall intensified. Fires were quickly swamped and men reached for their blankets, regretful and even angry that their promised tents, available hitherto, on this occasion were not. The only tent available to the 105th came out of Nellie and Bridie's dogcart, a spare one obtained under nefarious circumstances and was now one of the few erected on the ridge. Many amongst their group expected the shelter to be sequestered by their Officers, but none arrived at the entrance, except Captain Nat Drake, who had been collected and then ushered into the tent with many verbal blandishments, beginning from Nellie.

"Mr Drake, Sir, you're not well and in no fit state to be puttin' up with a soakin', so you're not, as The Lord's my witness."

Drake was shoed inside and found himself bedding down with the Mulcahy and the Nicholls children, including Eirin, with baby Ellen. Drake made no argument and therefore rolled himself in his blanket and, whilst listening to the rain pounding the canvas, he soon fell fast asleep. For the rest of the 105th, indeed for both armies, it was a night of misery, all of the 105th sat on streaming ground with a sodden blanket over their heads which soon dripped as much water through as though they were actually stood out in the heavy rainfall. Saunders and Byford, chosen for sentry duty, were stood out in the rain, staring out into the inky darkness, so black that they could not even see the falling raindrops and with only the memory of what they had seen during the day to convince them that a powerful French army was arranged opposite, because there were no campfires.

"Big one tomorrow, John."

"Big one, yes, but this is the end of the French in Spain."

Saunders turned to him, although he was merely a vague shape beside him.

"How so?"

"When have the French ever pushed us off a hill like this one? They'll come at us and it'll be bloody, but it will be a disaster for them."

"I like the last bit you said, but not the first, the 'bloody' bit."

"It's what we used to call at school 'an irresistible force meeting an immovable object'. The immovable object always wins, even though moved a bit. That's us. This is the one that matters. It will be Vitoria that will go into the history books, this will only be a footnote, but after this, Johnny will be back in France for good. Vitoria didn't do that."

Saunders laughed.

"Have you told Wellington?"

"I think he already knows."

Then they heard footsteps sloshing through the liquid mud behind them, so both turned and Saunders, being the Corporal, called out.

"You our reliefs?"

A gruff and irritated voice came out of the darkness.

"'Sright! Standing here about good enough?"

Byford and Saunders began their climb back up the ridge slope.

"It'll do. We've laid on running water, so be grateful."

"Bugger off!"

The two laughed as they supported each other up the slippery slope, but soon they had little idea if they were amongst the 105th or not, and so they simply sat and waited for the dawn, each sharing a Spanish sausage given to them by Bridie.

In the event, the rain stopped with the very beginning of dawn, this emerging light allowed by the lowering rainclouds finally clearing away to the South and exposing a bright, rising sun. However, before full dawn the army was formed for battle, the order to form of line coming as a relief from being sat under a sodden blanket, wearing soaking clothing. From the French, with the arrival of light, there was no movement forward, instead, surprisingly, for the first hours of the day there was only movement from side to side as their Commander shifted his units to better positions. For Anson's Brigade, the major focus was on two French Brigades, each of three Battalions, these newly placed so that they could mount an assault directly across the saddle. To these Carr paid particular attention, studying them for some while. For some hours he had been sat, as usual with Heaviside and now he pointed with his telescope when O'Hare arrived, who sat and then pulled around his haversack to extract some food.

"Those are for us."

O'Hare did no more than glance up from arranging his biscuits and cheese, that formed part of his prolonged, sparse and delayed breakfast, now approaching lunch. He had been busy all morning with his duties as the Senior Major.

"But in no hurry, it would seem. Not even a cannonball sent across to say good morning."

Carr watched him dissect a portion of cheese.

"All's well amongst the men? All in place?"

O'Hare nodded without looking up, but Heaviside was sat watching all intently, neither eating nor using a spyglass and asked the obvious question.

"The Peer had us ready before dawn, as is his wont, but with M'sieu over there, it seems as though he is in less than two minds to attack at all. Do you think he's waiting for more to arrive?"

Carr did not lower his telescope as he replied,

"I'd say not. Whatever he's got that came over at Roncesvalles will be here by now or very, very close. One piece of good news, I hear, is that Hill's stopped all French progress down the Bastan at a place called Lizaso. So, my guess is General Johnny doesn't much fancy us up here and so he's weighing the odds. Coming against us up here, he has practically zero chance, that he knows, but on the other hand, he knows he must do something. He has the initiative having pushed us back ten miles or more. He must do something, he cannot just pack up and walk back into France. Boney would banish him to run the muck carts!"

O'Hare turned quickly to Carr.

"What about us attacking them?"

Carr guffawed.

"Not in this life. The Peer knows that the French have the initiative and he's waiting for them to make a mistake with it. When we've held their attack, then we may move forward. M'sieu Soult is in a quandary. If Soult fails to push us off from here, that'll count as a defeat.

He cannot stay sat over there for much longer, with no supplies or anything."

Heaviside looked at him quizzically.

"He could simply go back and defend the Pyrenees!"

Carr shook his head.

"Not good enough for Boney. He thinks we're a nothing sort of army, poor quality, too small and only fit for what he'd call a skirmish. He chased us out once, back to Coruna and that's the impression he has. Of us! We don't stand; we always pull back when it gets risky. He expects Soult to deliver a decisive defeat and drive us all the way back into Portugal. Boney's anger is Soult's biggest worry."

O'Hare had been listening intently.

"Aye, and there'll be a lot of good men dead, so's Soult can keep Boney off his back!"

Heaviside looked from one end of the French dispositions to the other, seeing no movement, not even artillerymen tending their pieces, then he turned to Carr.

"Well, at the moment my money would be on what I said, he'll funk it, having seen us up here, and retreat to the passes."

Carr looked at him astonished, mouth agape.

"I never thought for a second, that I would ever hear any reference to gambling spoken by you!"

Heaviside laughed.

"My mouth shall speak wisdom; the meditation of the heart shall be understanding. Psalms 49, verse 3."

Carr grinned.

"As you say, Joshua, but for now I'm going to stand the men down, unless someone tells me to stand them back up."

He pulled out his watch.

"Ten o' clock. They've been stood-to since before dawn and eaten nothing. Allow them to cook what they can, but no man more than twenty paces from his position."

In no time the welcome order ran along the ranks and the 48th and 27th to their left followed Carr's example. Fires were started using the carefully protected kindling that all carried in their backpacks and soon cheery steam and the smells of cooking began to pervade the ridge, so that soon the only occupants on it behaving as though there would soon be a battle were Senior Officers panning telescopes from one end of the French ridge to the other. Well back, yet within sight of their men stood in battle lines, the Followers already had stews prepared of various descriptions and Nellie, seeing their Battalion lighting fires and boiling camp kettles, came to her own conclusion.

"Sure, we should take the men some food, so we should. Even if 'tis only enough for a mouthful or two, 'tis better than just a swallow of tea. We can do that, until someone says we can't!"

The two stewpots were unhooked and carried between Nellie, Bridie, Eirin and Consuela, with Esme carrying two sacks of biscuit. Down on the line their men saw them coming and hastily found their spoons in their backpacks and, as each soldier spooned collectively from the pot, Bridie looked across the valley.

"Jed, is that all the French? There seems a powerful lot of them."

Deakin swallowed a mouthful and waited for Halfway to obtain another spoonful.

"You've never seen the Johnnies up this close before, have you, love? Certainly not just before a battle. You're not to worry, we've seen more than that before."

She looked down at him and then back across the valley, when her tone became more than a little anxious.

"Not this close and that's the truth. Sure, you could shout good morning across that valley, them bein' up so close and all!"

Her eyes now found her Ensign son, sat just ahead.

"Do you think there will be a battle here, now, Jed?"

"There'll be something, love. Either a set piece or a runnin' fight, with rearguards and what have you, but there'll be something."

"Well now, you just take good care of my Patrick down there and mind you don't get your awkward selves into too much of a scrape. You hear me now!"

With that she pulled Deakin's pannikin out from the straps of his backpack and then did the same with Halfway, but at least with him she asked a form of permission.

"I'll be needin' yours, too, Toby."

Then Deakin was relieved of his spoon for Bridie to spoon out two good shares onto the pannikins and take them down to Patrick and his fellow Ensign, Henri Rasenne. The food was immediately seized upon and quickly consumed by the pair of hungry teenagers. At that point, RSM Gibney was touring the line of the 105th, worried that the distraction of food did not go on for too long, because almost all of the Followers were now down with their men. He arrived at Nellie and her companions.

"'Tis time tha got th'sens back on up now, girls. This could all start off any time now, cannon-balls 'an all. Best get back an' ready all for what comes next when t'all begins, tha' knows. There'll be plenty of such for thee to do, if ah'm not mistaken an' ah don't think ah am!"

The Followers knew exactly what he was referring to, the tending of the wounded and they quickly obeyed, carrying their pots and biscuit sacks back up the ridge and beyond serious danger to prepare or check that they were ready for the likely stream of wounded. It was then that they found Gibney's warning justified because not long after his tour, all of the 105th heard the first sounds of conflict, but coming to them from afar, seemingly from the back left of their ridge and down in the valley below Sorauren. The order 'stand-to' immediately ran along the line and so plates and spoons were hastily wiped and stowed away, for the ten Companies of the 105th to form at 'Order arms'. Carr looked at his watch.

"Twelve-thirty! He's wasted half the day!"

O'Hare looked mournfully across the valley.

"Well, it looks as though he's going to make the most of the rest of it!"

All along the French position, the French forces were rising to their feet, with Eagle Standards rising prominent above their ranks. No telescope was needed to see that Soult was sending three strong assaults forward, because against the British left, held by Ross' Brigade, down the French slope came a four Battalion column and another of five, closely side by side. Against the Allied centre, this held by Campbell's Portuguese Brigade, he was sending two columns side by side, each of three Battalions. Finally, advancing down to the saddle came a column formed by one of the three Battalion Brigades the 105th had been watching all morning. The continuous sounds of combat from their far left in the Sorauren valley still drifted up to their ears and it was not long before the sharper sounds came to them over the shorter half mile when the first two French attacks met fierce resistance first from Ross' and then Campbell's Brigades. However, the sound never slackened which told the story that the heavy French columns were holding the ground they had gained and were even making progress further up and onto the Allied ridge. That some French success had occurred was confirmed when an ADC galloped up and Stubb's Portuguese Brigade disappeared leftwards to support that flank.

However, O'Hare especially was watching the column destined for the saddle, not only watching but hearing.

"There've got somebody there very good at winding them up!"

In front of the first Battalion there was a cavorting Officer, waving his sword as they advanced, whirling his free arm and dancing as he shouted, the replies from the column reaching the ears of the 105th from across the valley, bellowed from the throats of 2,000 men.

"Vive la Revolution! Vive l'Empereur! En avant! En avant! A Lisbon! Les Anglais sont tout des laches! Nous sommes des soldats de France! Nous sommes des soldats de l'Emperor. Vive la France! Vive l'Emperor!"

Battle of First Sorauren

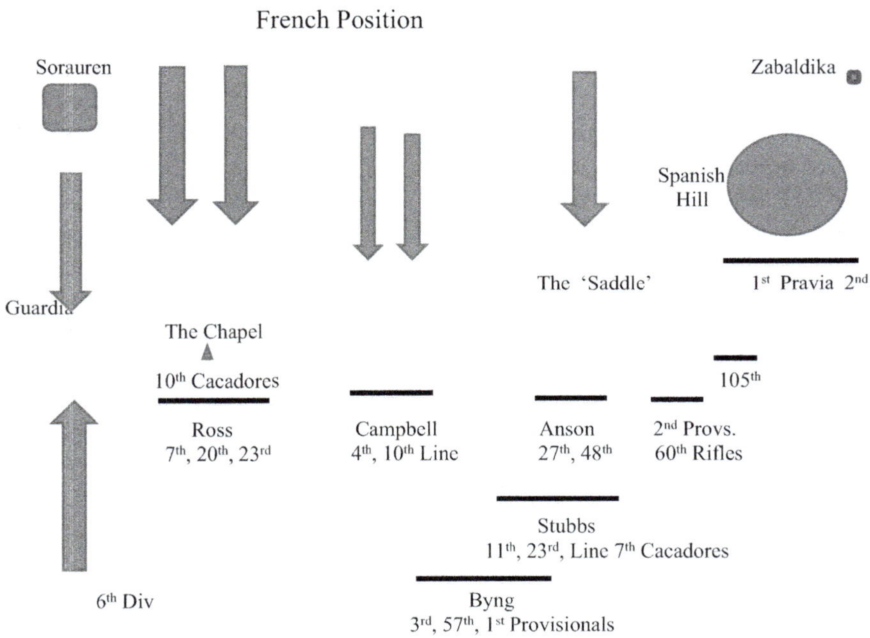

All shouts continued, as the column advanced on, but remaining audible, despite competing with the increased sound of the ferocious firefights that had broken out all along the Allied line, as the two French assaults against the Allied left and centre gained ground and held it against the defenders on the ridge. At the same time French howitzer shells began to sail up and over Spanish hill, the smoke trails from their fizzing fuses marking their passage as they arced up, but too high and too far to do any damage, exploding far behind the two Spanish Battalions on the hill and far beyond the right of the 105th.

Meanwhile, the French column had finally traversed the 400 yards or so of the saddle and were at the foot of the ridge slope. They would be engaging the 27th and the 48th, sometime after the conflicts had begun further down the valley towards Sorauren. Carr looked over to study those who were awaiting them, those whom he knew to be two of the steadiest, the most proficient and the most destructive Regiments in the whole Allied army. Nearest were the 48th Northamptons, their

Regimental Colour of deep buff, fluttering unconcernedly above their ranks, alongside their equally insouciant King's Colour. Further along, to their left, was the paler buff of the 27th Iniskillings' Regimental and also their King's Colour, both showing the odd, indifferent movement. Within the ranks, however, there was no movement at all, all were stood stock still at 'Order arms' with Officers stood out in front as statues, their swords tilting back over their right shoulders. Anson was furthest forward before them. Carr looked at the column, then to the British line and swallowed hard. The first French Battalion was Line, with their Grenadiers at the fore, their wide cross-belts and broad epaulettes emphasising their height and size. Carr spoke softly to himself, to him there could only be one outcome.

"This is going to be appalling!"

Anson called out 'Make Ready', then he raised his sword and led his men forward a dozen paces to come to the top of the steepest part of the slope. If that did not cause dismay within the French column, then what came next certainly did, when Anson ordered 'Present", and around 1,400 muskets came down to the horizontal. Carr saw the whole column visibly shiver in the following brief seconds during which all observing involuntarily held their breath, when time seemed to stand still. Anson allowed the range to come down to a terrifying 30 yards and many in the front ranks of the column fired at that moment but the weight of fire that hit them from the first volley was horrifying. The whole of Anson's first rank fired together and Carr saw all the uniforms of the French front rank, both tunics and shakoes, jerk and jolt with the impact of around 700 musket balls, such that almost all were thrust backwards into the second rank. Then the second rank of the 27th and 48th fired and now the number of falling bodies actually tumbled back those of the following ranks, for them to also go rolling down the slope. It was now impossible for the first French Battalion to make any progress, but Anson waited until all his men had reloaded, then he led them even further forward and then the half-Company volleys began, the ruthless 27th and 48th inching forward as their flanks closed in around the sides of the increasingly helpless column.

The first French Battalion broke and ran, then the second came forward over the wreck of what remained of the first, but the fire of the implacable and viciously competent British Battalions did not slacken, so there was no reduction in the punishment the column continued to receive, shown by the number of French bodies falling down onto the stony track or backwards down the slope. The ordeal inflicted on the column lasted for less than three minutes before all French assaulting across the saddle broke and fell back. The third French Battalion simply halted and retreated, despite the vocal efforts and gestures of their Officers, the one sided contest was too horrific to become entangled in. The two victorious Redcoat Battalions then advanced down the slope as they maintained close contact with the struggling Frenchmen, but now, with the column vanquished, having reached the beginning of the saddle, they calmly halted and awaited orders. However, Anson quickly ordered them back and they ascended the slope to the cheers of the Spanish on Spanish Hill, the 105th and the Provisionals, all cheering, grinning and brandishing muskets. Both Regiments reformed on their original position, the air being thick with both musket smoke and the cries and moans of the badly wounded. Amongst these, there was barely a handful wearing a Redcoat and all these, both wounded and dead, were brought back up the hill, but one of the wounded was General Anson, him now being carried back to the rear, his left leg bloody, this not unnoticed by Carr, "Who now holds command?", he spoke out loud to himself.

Total as the defeat had been, Carr's attention was then drawn leftwards to the continuing sounds of combat on that side, its ferocity undiminished from the time before the attack that came across the saddle and also what he could now hear. The anxious question crossed his mind, "Has our left been turned?" A partial answer came in the form of Wellington himself, who had ridden across and must have seen the defeat of the column across the saddle, or at least the final throes. Carr sprang to attention and saluted, but Wellington was in a hurry.

"Carr. I'm taking the 48th and 27th across the slope in a flank attack against what's come up at Campbell and Ross at the Chapel. Stubb's Portuguese are already over, they're needed in the centre with Campbell, which is giving way. If they try again across the saddle, then it's up to yours and the Provisionals to repeat what's just been done. This saddle and that Spanish Hill must be held."

"Yes Sir, but General Anson is wounded and has been taken back. Who will be in command of this flank?"

Wellington stared down whilst controlling his horse, who seemed to be anxious to be away, as was Wellington and so, to quickly establish command, he immediately appointed the only Colonel within earshot.

"You will, Carr!"

Carr's heart missed a beat.

"Yes Sir. Are there any reserves?"

"There were, Carr. Byng's were back up the hill, but they've gone, I've had to move them down to the left to support Ross at the Chapel. You hold this with what you've got."

Neither meant anything to Carr, where General Ross or the Chapel was, but Wellington had hauled his horse's head around and was on his way over to the line of the 48th. Carr watched as soon, in obedience to Wellington's orders, the 48th, still in line, descended the hill some way down and the 27th extended the line back up. They would act as a door swinging across the slope into the side of the French columns who were presumably attacking Campbell's Portuguese in the centre and also Ross' Brigade beyond them. Both advanced into the drifting smoke with ported arms and after no more than three minutes Carr heard a volley and a cheer, then all sound was absorbed into the sound of the original firefight which had not slackened.

Carr looked around at what he was expected to cope with. The Provisionals were on the slope immediately above the saddle with Anson's Company of Rifles, his own 105th were in support behind the two Spanish Regiments who were holding Spanish Hill, and these were in position just back from its crest. He knew that at least a French Division was down in Zabaldika, which, so far, had not been engaged at all. He ran straight over to O'Hare and Heaviside.

"Anson's wounded and the Peer's taken the 27th and 48th off to sort out what's happening on the left. We lost Stubb's Portuguese a while ago, as I'm sure you saw."

He took a deep breath to catch his breath.

"He's placed me in charge. We've the Rifles and Provisionals above the saddle, then us and those two Dons there in front on the hill. There's no reserves, he's moved them all off to the left. Things must be getting pretty desperate if he's had to move Byng's and our two of Anson's, all gone to follow Stubbs' Portuguese."

He studied the pair.

"What's likely?"

They both stared back, but O'Hare was the first to look across the saddle, it now covered in French dead and with many wounded now attempting to drag themselves back to their lines.

"Nothing will come over that saddle again. After that massacre, even Boney himself couldn't get that reserve Brigade to move. They can see us and the Provisionals stood guard and fresh. If anything comes, it will be over Spanish Hill, against those two Dons."

Carr looked downwards and then across, at the ground between them and Spanish Hill, studying both sides, left and right. It was a narrow neck of land that joined the ridge to Spanish Hill, with a definite but not impossible slope either side, making the feasible area for a firing line a mere 100 yards across, perhaps a little more, giving no room for a full, two rank firing line. He turned to both.

“Right! Two wings, one behind the other, left in front, then right. That puts us in four ranks. We practiced that back in Garda, remember, before the Long March. The front wing delivers a volley then engages with the bayonet, the other maintains musket fire through the spaces, then exchange as and when Officers judge possible. It may well be needed, those Dons held yesterday when Johnny came up to feel us out, but this is the real thing, this will be serious. Capturing that hill is his last throw!”

As if to emphasise his words, the howitzer shells fired from Zabaldika began once again, sailing up and over their heads to explode ineffectually some 200 yards back from the 105th, but the three Officers now exchanged serious looks, O’Hare speaking what they all thought.

“Looks like he’s going to try the hill. Should we close up behind the Dons, do you think?”

Carr considered for a moment and then shook his head.

“No. That’s their position and they should be given a chance to hold it, as they did yesterday. Where we are here, halfway up this slope, is as good as it gets if we have to counter-attack, if and when the Dons fall back. Formed on this slope where we are, all four ranks can fire.”

Heaviside had been studying the two Spanish Battalions on the hill and was the first to see them all get to their feet.

“Seems as though your ideas are about to be put to the test.”

The two Spanish Battalions were climbing to their feet, with several Spanish Officers now running back from over the far side of the hillcrest, plainly in alarm. Spanish drums beat out the order and both Battalions formed into their customary four-deep line, which gave a perfect length to cover the whole hill. The drums beat again, the white standards of both were raised with their bright designs and both moved forward, their Officers swords raised up as they led their men on. In less than a minute both Battalions had disappeared and Carr turned back to his own men, beginning with O’Hare and Heaviside.

“As we said, left wing behind the right. Now.”

The pair ran off as Carr continued to anxiously study the now virtually deserted hilltop and soon the 105th drums beat out and the Battalion formed as ordered. Whilst that was happening, the sound of an intense musketry exchange came to them from over the far side of the hill. It lasted no more than four minutes before fading to nothing and the Spanish came back over the hill, all plainly once again cock-a-hoop at their victory, laughing, waving and slapping each other’s backs and shoulders in the joy of their triumph. Then the difference between the two became apparent, the Regiment on the right, their uniform all blue with white facings, reformed immediately, whilst the other, a paler blue with white trousers needed to be screamed at by their Officers, despite the beating of the drums. Within ten minutes, they were called forward again to disappear over the ridge, plainly another attack was on its way up and within a minute the sounds of a furious musketry exchange came back, loud and ferocious to the 105th standing on their slope. O'Hare was stood with Carr.

"That previous was just the start. Johnny's making a serious effort at this hill and this time they won't hold."

Carr's mouth was set in a grim line.

"Give the order to load and uncase The Colours."

The order was passed along the line and Jed Deakin, the precious Colour now in the hands of his stepson, sub-consciously went through the process of loading, whilst exchanging a few words with Halfway, him stood behind and loading equally automatically.

"Big set-to this one, Tobe. He's got a Division as fancies that hill, got more down there than them Dons can handle."

"Can't say you'm wrong, Jed, let's just hope we both comes out the other side. Good for Bridie and Esme."

Deakin laughed as he returned his musket to order arms.

"They'll be fine, Tobe, no matter what happens. You knows how it works, there'll be others, as'll take our place, but here we go, not long now. Seems the Dons have had enough."

Both Spanish Regiments, now broken, were streaming back over the hill, with French Eagles visible behind them, their column coming forward in steady pursuit, with the usual encouraging shouts and Revolutionary chants. Of the two Spanish Regiments, the soldiers with the white trousers were plainly in a blind panic and many sprinted up to the line of the 105th, many weaponless, to blunder, even crawl, through the 105th ranks, whilst others fled to either side, running almost anywhere. The 'all blue' were more together, falling back in full retreat but remaining as a Battalion, holding to their Officers. These ran to the 105th right, but Carr was now intent on the oncoming French, these still coming over the hillcrest, rank after rank, as if a blue tide. He raised his sword.

"Fire by ranks. Front, two, three and four. Make ready!"

Almost eight hundred muskets came to the vertical, amongst them their two Colours, the King's and the Regimental, brazen and challenging above the centre.

"Present!"

All responded to the order, the menacing sweep down, all weapons now pointing downwards into the dip below. Carr waited, but the first volley must come from his men, not from the French. The first

French muskets from the front rank came up at 50 yards range, but many were still reloading after their encounter with the Spanish.

"Front rank, fire!"

The first muskets crashed out, smoke, flame and burning cartridge paper emitting from their ranks and the front rank of the French column collapsed and also some of the second. Carr needed to give no more orders, as each rank counted the three seconds and then fired, second, third, then fourth, after that it was load and fire at your best speed and from the 105th it was incessant. The column's progress had been halted but there were many ranks behind still pressing forward, encouraged by their Officers, climbing over the bodies of their dead. Carr looked along his line, to see every man smoothly and rapidly reloading his weapon to send yet another bullet into the oncoming French. He was judging his moment and after some three minutes during which each of his men had probably fired at least ten bullets point blank into the column, he turned slightly to his right.

"Bates! You there?"

"Sir!"

The front of the column was now complete chaos, any Frenchman who tried to advance and gain more ground was quickly felled, many being also hit as they struggled over the writhing bodies of earlier casualties.

"Sound advance."

The notes rang out above the screams and the musketry. The front two ranks of the 105th ceased firing and fixed bayonets, while the rear two reloaded. O'Hare was to the left and turned to face his men.

"Fix the brummagem, boys. It's down to cold steel now, they've had lead enough."

Heaviside was on the left and nothing so military came out of him as he stood before his men, sword aloft.

"Let no man's heart fail because of him. Thy servant will go and fight with this Philistine. Samuel 17. Verse 32."

Whilst the response to O'Hare had been grim faces, for 'Bible' Heaviside came cheers and brandished bayonets, but for Carr in the centre with The Colours, the response was a simple advance forward as he waved his sword towards the column, there was no time for three cheers, simply one loud Huzzah! It took fewer than 10 paces before they were amongst the French and the conflict became so close that Carr could neither swing his sword or thrust, he could only punch forward with the steel bell-guard. This was the press of Towton and Agincourt, as the air was filled with grunts, screams and curses, backed by the crash of muskets from the 105th rear ranks. The cries of 'En avant' were heard less than what came from both the men and Officers of the 105th as they shouted to encourage each other. The French were tired from their long and difficult climb, the firefight with the Spanish and now they had faced the appalling ordeal inflicted on them by the 105th, but the column was endless, three Battalions, and so the whole hilltop was covered in blue uniforms and beyond. The bayonets of the 105th were doing destructive work, but equally and probably more destructive was the continued musket fire from the rear two ranks, firing through the first two ranks of their comrades, not just through but over, because the 105th remained still on their original slope. The smoke creating an eerie fog in which men felt themselves engaged in individual combat, but eventually the 105th were over and beyond the pile of French dead and were amongst the oncoming French ranks who were fresher and had had a chance to recover from their climb. Thus, the fighting continued as intense as before, on an equal front but over a distance which could often be measured in inches.

St. John Slade felt as though he was fighting for his very life, even though the men around him were fighting their way forward into the column, fighting as pairs or even trios. He was being pushed forward, his arms whirling in defence more than attack, avoiding levelled bayonets, musket butts and even punches. Suddenly, he could see a French Eagle before him being carried by a French Lieutenant, with protecting Serjents de Porte-Aigles close by. One saw Slade as a severe threat to his Standard and he swung his axe down onto him, but Slade had been pushed forward so that only the corner of the blade connected and that behind his shoulder. The greater blow was from the shaft meeting Slade's left epaulette, the blow buckling his left leg, such that he tripped and fell over a prone body when he tried to regain his feet. The Serjent came forward, the axe-head poised for a brutal downward thrust, when Slade was aware of a figure springing over him to hammer the butt of his musket full into the face of the menacing Serjent. Bayonets were thrust forward above him, but then the French column gave a surge forward and Slade was aware of many Redcoat legs around him and someone dragging him back by the collar.

"Sir! Get up, sir!"

Slade looked up and back to see Henry Nicholls, musket in one hand, the other obviously on his collar. Immediately above him was the soldier who had wielded the musket butt, a Colour Sergeant's Badge prominent on his left sleeve. The group fell back into the Redcoat ranks and a musket blast from somewhere in the two 105th rear ranks halted the French advance. Now that the fighting was on level ground those in the rear two ranks had more difficulty, they had to wait for a gap or barge one open to fire through, so now their fire was having less impact, but, once reloaded, they were determined to send a bullet into any Frenchman confronting their own front rank.

As their Captains ordered and where possible, the men of the 105th were exchanging places such that many of the rear ranks were now in the front, bayonets having been quickly fixed or removed. This included the Light Company out on the left, and now One Section were face to face with the column, the wicked, extra-long, Baker rifle bayonets giving an advantage that they made full use of. The giants Saunders and Solomon were at the point of a wedge, both maiming and slaying at will, whilst either side of them, taking advantage of the distraction that both behemoths caused, came Miles, a particularly good bayonet fighter, with Davey, Ellis, Pike, Byford and Bailey. The Provisionals above the saddle had not stood idle and two Companies had wheeled right and were sending fire, albeit at maximum range, into the right-hand side of the French column. Thus, on this side the French column began to give way, the 105th musketry at no range at all, with the bayonet charges, were both having their effect, fewer members of the column were now so eager to advance forward. The four ranks of the 105th had by now inevitably merged into one solid line, all now fighting their way forward, either with a bayonet or a loaded musket. In the centre of his men, Carr sensed this and knew that this was the time, so he half turned to Bates, obediently just behind him.

"Bates. Full charge!"

The strident notes sounded out and Carr raised his sword.

"Into them, boys! Into them. Charge, charge! Into their faces. Hurrah for the King! Hurrah for the 105th!"

Very few heard him above the din, but all four lines, albeit now nothing like so orderly, surged forward over the short distance, merely feet in some cases, and the column began to thoroughly break, those in the front turning to run and take back with them those still attempting to come forward. The mass heaved and dissolved, all running back over the crest of the hill, followed by the now triumphant Redcoats. Carr, as tired and out of breath as much as anyone, ran hard to stay in the lead and over the hillcrest he turned again to Bates.

"Recall and reform, Bates. As many times as you can manage."

The notes sounded out, penetrating the din and just in time, because many of the 105th were following the French down the hill and, at the sound of the bugle call, their Sergeants began screaming at them to stop and return. All breathless and many bloodied, the 105th reformed their four ranks across the crest and watched the French disappearing down the steep slope. Carr did not want to remain there exposed for too long to artillery fire, but he took the chance to walk along the line and say "Well done, boys" as often as he could. The replies were mostly exhausted grins, but some held up the sleeve of their left arm to show the lurid green of their cuffs, of which they were plainly very proud. Satisfied, almost elated, Carr turned again to Bates.

"Sound 'Fall back'."

The 105th obeyed, but only as far as just beyond the crest. Carr went immediately over to the Light Company, to see Nat Drake on his knees, supporting his head with his sword, this stuck into the ground. He ran over.

"Nat! Are you alright?"

Drake levered himself upright and then to his feet.

"Never better! Hungry, perhaps."

Carr managed a short laugh.

"So what's new? But, get yours down over the hillside in a skirmishing line. Not too far, just enough to see Zabaldika. Johnny has plenty of reserves down there and he'll come again. I want full warning."

Ellis was nearby and had heard all. He needed no order.

"Right, you lot. Forward and down the hillside. Pairs, not files."

The Light Company advanced forward and spread themselves across the hillside some 100 yards down over the crest, across the 200 yard width. However, Miles and Bailey were not in the best of moods, Miles especially.

"Just think of all that French loot back thur, t'other side of this hill."

Bailey was on one knee, his Baker rifle projecting down the hillside.

"There'll be time, Tom. 'Sides, there's more'n a few lyin around here, after that set-to with the Dons."

Miles looked around and his face brightened when he saw that Bailey's words were true, so he went over to the body of a Voltiguer Officer and turned it over to search the pockets, but he was seen by Ellis.

"Miles! You get back on watch and keep watch, or I'll see you on the triangle, see if I don't!"

Miles rose and sullenly returned to Bailey and adopt his position on one knee, grumbling the while, worried that the Spanish who ran would now be engaging in very rewarding pillaging back over the hill. Just across from them were Pike and Davey, both studying the French force on the valley floor, just above Zabaldika.

"He's still got a lot down there, John."

Davey nodded indulgently at the obvious comment.

"You'm not wrong there, Joe. Enough for one more go, probably two. You heard what Nosey said to Carr, this hill's got to be held. I don't know how things went on over to the left, but I'd say we held at t'other end, but we're pretty much played out all along the line. If they takes this hill and then comes again over that saddle, then they can roll up the whole line. Nosey wants it held, even if it means each one of us lyin' dead on top of it!"

Subdued at Davey's words and also by the disturbing thoughts they caused to surface, Pike stared down the slope and was amongst the first of the Company to see French Voltiguers again ascending the only accessible slope of the hill.

"John. Look!"

He pointed down and Davey saw a thickening line of French skirmishers stretching across the hillside. Drake was already screaming orders.

"Single line. Independent fire."

Ellis was already running back up the hill to warn Carr and soon the first shots were fired. Using Baker rifles, the marksmen of the Light Company began bringing down their opponents at will, but the survivors continued to struggle upwards and soon the main column came into view, as dense as the previous. The climb was too steep for the normal shouts of encouragement and so the front ranks silently slogged on, their Eagle prominent but way back in the centre of the column. In the centre of his own line, Drake was watching intently, standing with Shakeshaft and Bettridge. His men were bringing down Voltiguers all across the hillside, but they could not hold for much longer before the full column arrived, and then the Company would have to split into their Sections and run to join the end of the now inevitable 105th firing line. Drake looked behind and up. He could not see the 105th, but he knew that Carr would be choosing his moment, so he immediately chose his.

"Pull back! One Section form right, Two Section left."

All rose and hurried back up the hillside, those of One Section tending to their left as they ran up to join on the right of the 105th line. Just over the crest the 105th were formed, now in a three-deep line, stood steady and waiting and so Bettridge watched his men gather themselves on the right end of the line. They were no sooner in place than Saunders, as a Corporal at the end of the line, heard shouting and looked over to see the 'all blue' uniformed Spanish Regiment now reformed and re-entering the fight. Their Officers were to the fore and shouting encouragements, the nearest could be heard as they came up to extend the line of the 105th down over the hillside.

"Somos los Guardias Espanoles! El Segundo. Hoy los Guardias mueren junto a los Ingleses!"

Miles, close to Saunders turned around to Byford.

"What he say, Byfe?"

"Something like they are the 2nd Spanish Guard and today they die alongside the English."

Miles snorted.

"Well, he can bloody well die if he wants to, just don't expect I to lie down and do the same!"

At that moment the line was ordered forward, all with weapons at the 'make ready'. They tramped forward, eerily, the only sound being the swish of the scrub and gorse against the coarse canvas of their trousers. The ridge crest came and they advanced over, to find that Carr had timed their advance perfectly, the leading French ranks were just over 50 yards down the slope. Carr raised his sword for halt and gave his first order.

"Front rank kneel."

They dropped to one knee.

"Present!"

All muskets came to the horizontal.

"Fire!"

The volley from the kneeling front rank echoed across the hillside, followed at intervals by that of the second and third ranks, then it was independent fire, a non-stop fusillade sweeping the front ranks of the French column. As before it shuddered to a halt, the men exhausted by their climb, these had been the rear Battalion of the column that had just been defeated and now they were being asked again to take this hill against massed Redcoat firepower. For those in the left of the French column life became even more difficult because the Segundo Guardias Espanoles, led by their Officers, began to close in from the 105th right, the elite Spanish vengeful in their assault upon the left flank of the column. The Frenchmen stood their ground for mere minutes, ineffectually attempting to return fire, in fact any who brought their musket to the 'present' immediately became a target for two or three British muskets. Inevitably, the column recoiled and withdrew, not headlong but the effort was hopeless, they knew it and men were falling fast, lying two, even three deep, before them. Carr called 'cease-fire', but the Principe continued to fire, even at maximum range, intent on causing the last possible French casualty. Eventually, those on the right of the 105th heard the order, "Alto el fuego", then the sound of musketry was replaced by loud Spanish cheering and shouting, accompanied by the waving of muskets in the air, many with a Spanish shako on its muzzle. Miles looked over.

"Seems like we cheered them up!"

Carr was of the same opinion, but recognised the necessity of showing thanks in some way and so he walked the 100 yards or so to the Guardias ranks and was pleased with the reception he received from the Spaniards as he walked across, although he could barely understand a word, except the inevitable "Bravo Ingleses". Their Colonel noticed his approach and strode to meet him, ignoring Carr's outstretched hand to then grasp him in a fierce embrace and only then to shake hands. Somewhat discomfited, nevertheless Carr spoke first.

"Thank you for your support."

He was almost certain that the Guardias Colonel had some understanding of Carr's meaning, but the reply from the Spaniard had little bearing on what Carr had said, being spoken in broken English, probably the only English the man knew, which soon ran out.

"Is good, yes, hoy, all juntos como uno, battala los franceses."

Carr nodded vigorously, he was certain that, whatever was said, he would agree with. All was made easier when a Spanish Major arrived who spoke much better English.

"Do you think, Colonel, that the French will try again?"

Carr nodded.

"Yes. I think they will and I hope that we can stand together again."

The Major translated and the reply came in the form of his Colonel beating his chest, pointing to the two Colours just behind him, then inflicting another bear hug. Carr had by now had quite enough of that sort of thing and so he smiled, saluted and took his leave, back to the 105th, who were already, on O'Hare's orders, back behind the crest. Carr jogged back over himself to see firstly the Colour Company and just before their ranks he saw St. John Slade, his left arm in a sling.

"Major Slade, please be so good as to take yourself over to the Light Company. Give Captain Drake my compliments and ask him to re-establish the skirmishing line."

Slade hurried away to reach Drake, him now busy eating, as were most of his Section, much of it taken from dead Frenchmen's haversacks.

"Captain. Colonel Carr wishes the skirmishing line to be back in place."

Drake nodded, after a swallow of wine from a French 'waterbottle'.

"Expected as much."

He pointed to the sling.

"Anything broken?"

"I don't think so, but bad bruising and a bit of a cut. I was battered to the floor."

Drake immediately knew the implications of the latter.

"And who got you out of that?"

"Colour Sergeant Deakin I believe."

"Then you should thank him. Could well be that he saved your life!"

With that, Drake hammered in the stopper of his French water bottle and walked forward.

"Light Company. With me."

The line was quickly re-established, Miles and Bailey taking great pains to return to their original spot. Miles looked around to see that Ellis was over on the far side.

"Len! Watch for Ellis. He's some way off."

Miles hurried to the dead Voltiguer Officer and the silver buttons were off in a trice, then the silver belt buckle. He was looting the pockets, when Bailey called out urgently.

"Tom, he's comin' back over."

Crouching, Miles came back to Bailey's side and they shared out the buttons, buckle and money, more for ease of carrying, for all would go into the 'Community Chest' that evening. That done, both settled into their positions and ate what they had in their haversacks, all washed down with two swallows of brandy each, this gained from a nearby dead Frenchman. Just back from them, Carr, O'Hare and Heaviside were stood alone at the top of the slope, at a useful vantage point, each taking what refreshment was available, this provided by Sergeant Bryce taking advantage of the halt in the conflict. The three were stood together, oblivious to the fact that they were stood in a field of carnage, the hillside covered in French dead, with some Spanish from both previous conflicts. All were too tired to talk, eating mattered more, but talking did resume, when they once more saw French skirmishers appear on the slopes lower down. O'Hare was the first to empty his mouth.

"He must want this hill very badly. That's a whole Division coming up this time."

Heaviside was immediately incensed at seeing again what would inevitably be a futile attempt.

"Well, he can go to Hell!"

He then took a deep breath.

"Oh you who dwell by many waters, rich in treasures, your end has come, the thread of your life is cut. Jeremiah 51, verse 13."

Carr and O'Hare looked at each other astonished, laughing in turn, until O'Hare was able to speak.

"Joshua, if even you is using bad language, then we should all take cover!"

It was not long before their own skirmishing line opened fire, with the same result, maximum casualties amongst the French. Ellis ran over to John Davey, pointing down the hill as he arrived.

"John! I reckon that's their own General leading them up himself."

Davey had noticed himself a lone figure in an elaborate uniform, sword in one hand and out in front. Behind him Officers were everywhere yelling encouragement and what must be every drum in the Division beating out the advance. Davey took the trouble to load carefully, this time wrapping the ball in a small piece of leather and tapping the ball down the barrel using his small mallet on the ramrod. He set the sights for 50 yards, firing downhill the ball would barely drop at all, and then he took careful aim. Ellis rolled over to one side as Davey fired, this taking him away from the smoke. Ellis saw the Officer's leg jerk from under him and he fell sideways.

"You've done him a lot of no-good, John. He'll not be climbing hills for a while."

The French attack had no shape at all, simply a mass of men forcing themselves forward up the steep slope, through the thick gorse and heather, with every French Officer who was still available out in front, waving swords and breathlessly yelling encouragement. Carr sent O'Hare to bring up the 105th line, then he turned to Bates, because he was now concerned for his Light Company still engaged with a thick line of skirmishers.

"Sound recall Bates. Bring them back up."

The notes sounded and the Sections split as before. As the 105th came forward, so did the Guardias Espanoles, up from the slope to the right. Carr saw no reason not to use what had worked before, other than to give the French an earlier sighting of the same line that had beaten them before, the same green Regimental Standard and the same King's Colour. With his three ranks halted very visibly over the crest, he gave his orders.

"Front rank kneel. Make ready."

The Guardias had already opened fire, at maximum range but they were closing rapidly with the side of the column. At 50 yards, Carr took a deep breath.

"Present! Fire!"

The three volleys crashed out, then independent fire began again and from the 105th this meant well over three shots per minute per man, most often over seven in two. By sheer firepower, the French mass was battered to a standstill, 25 yards from the crest. Carr had no intention of mounting any kind of bayonet charge, the musketry alone of his veteran Battalion would end this last, desperate French effort and so it proved. Like a slow wave, the French had bravely inched up as far as they could, only to be halted by the solid, obdurate wall of the 105th line, sending a hail of ¾ inch lead balls into their ranks. It was not long before the mass fell back, Officers last, these still attempting to wave their men forward, but eventually, for even these, the tide of their courage ran out and all fell back. The Guardias broke out into mad cheering, but the 105th stood silent, their thoughts the duplicate of what Carr spoke out loud.

"That's it. This is done!"

However, his final, blunt words were to Captain Lord Carravoy, him filthy, sweat streaked and with a cut on his face.

"Yours to provide picket. No more than a dozen men."

oOo

The final events of the battle petered out below Sorauren, these last few exchanges heard, as before, from a distance far over to the left and rear for the 105th. First, a sudden explosion of fire on the Pamplona road below Sorauren, which lasted merely fifteen minutes, then, finally, sporadic fire in the valley extending up from Sorauren itself, which died first on the French side, causing the Allies to quickly comply and the valley at last fell silent. With the final ending of the day's conflict, leaving the Guardias to occupy Spanish Hill, the 105th lifted themselves further back up the ridge to where the Followers had made camp. However, on arrival, there they were found tending the wounded of the 105th and laying out the dead, with keening women and children knelt beside the prone figures. Apart from a consoling pat on the shoulder for those who were at least acquaintances, there was little that could be done. As soon as they came to their campfires, food was ladled out and all sat quietly to eat and drink, bar Zeke Saunders, who had a head cut and Joe Pike who had a bayonet puncture wound in his chest, which could have been far worse had not a bullet from the rank behind taken half of that particular Frenchman's head away at the time of the thrust. Bridie and Consuela fussed over both in turns, but Nellie was attending to Lieutenant Bettridge, him with a black eye and a cut to his left thigh, which required the lowering of his breeches, neither of which he can remember receiving. That he was an Officer of King George meant nothing to Nellie, what she saw was an bemused teenage boy, still in shock, with his breeches around his ankles.

"Now just what would your Mother be thinkin', Mr Bettridge, Sir? Gettin' yourself into such scrapes!"

However, they had not been settled in for much more than half an hour, before the drums beat 'fall in'. All climbed wearily to their feet, donned equipment and hefted their muskets onto their right shoulders. Walking down alongside Deakin, Halfway was as weary and irate as anyone.

"What's this for, Jed? Be all startin' up again?"

Deakin shook his head.

"Search me, Tobe, but I'd say not. If 'twer' all kickin' off again we would have heard somethin' loosin' off. Cannons or whatever. I'm certain that all's finished for this day."

However, the parade formed, with all Officers out front, then the order came, 'present arms'. All muskets were swung through the precise arcs for all to then be still. What happened next was that a tall, thin Officer, in a green Hussar uniform and on a huge horse, with two attendants, rode up to the centre of the 105th and halted opposite The Colours. Carr saluted elaborately with his sword which the Officer acknowledged with barely more than a wave of his riding crop. Halfway was stood behind Deakin.

"That's Slender Billy. What's he want?"

It wasn't Deakin who answered, instead it was Henry Nicholls.

"Give us all six months' leave!"

There were sniggers all around, but the young, angular figure had begun to speak, whilst remaining on his horse.

"I am the Prince of Orange, on Lord Wellington's Staff and he has sent me over here to you so that I may pass on his thanks and congratulations for the performance of the 105th during today's fighting. He asks me to make you aware of his admiration for your courage and steadfastness under difficult circumstances. He told you that Spanish Hill must be held and, virtually alone, you did exactly that, whilst our other flank at the Chapel was under immense pressure. Yours was a performance for which the whole army owes thanks. So, once again, well done, you have the admiration of the whole army and the genuine thanks of its Commander in Chief."

With that he required his horse to back up two steps, before he swung its head around and walked it off, back from whence he came. Whilst those in the ranks remained generally unconcerned by the words of praise from a Staff aristocrat, although they well remembered the insults that had been thrown at them over the past months, the words had a far more profound effect on Brevet-Colonel Carr, particularly those contained in the final sentence, 'admiration of the whole army'. Perhaps not exactly admiration, perhaps not the whole army, but many now knew what they had achieved and so the shame heaped onto the 105th by Brockenhurst's debacle was now purged. Any comments such as that from Blackstaff up at Roncesvalles, were thrust back down his throat. When was the last time that the 1st Royal Dragoons had received a personal thanks from a Commander in Chief? Whilst he savoured the thought, thoroughly lost in the notion, RSM Gibney approached and saluted.

"Beg pardon, Sir, but do I dismiss the men, Sir?"

The strong Yorkshire accent dragged Carr out of his reverie and he turned to the evidently worried Gibney.

"Dismiss the men? Why yes, of course Sergeant Major. And well done and thanks to you for your conduct this afternoon."

"Yes Sir. Thank you, Sir, but should tha' not say a few words th'sen? Sir? The lads did well, tha' knows. Sir."

Gibney's words hit home. Carr had not thought of it himself but he knew that he should. His face was already showing that he was straining for the words.

"You are correct, Sergeant Major. I will do that directly."

Gibney took one pace back and wheeled off a perfect salute. Then, thinking furiously Carr walked to stand before The Colours, where he performed an exaggerated salute with his sword, before carefully sheathing it, then he took a deep breath.

"Well done, lads. There's not many that get a personal thanks from their Commander in Chief for their achievements in any battle. There are few that could have done that, it needed the likes of us to hold that hill and that's what we did. We took it back and then held it, twice, against ten times our number. The Dons are back on it now, it is, after all, called Spanish Hill."

Another deep breath.

"And I'm sure a certain Colonel Brockenhurst will get to hear of it. One way or the other."

As grins broke out all along the ranks, Carr turned to Gibney who took his cue and the parade was dismissed, so that all, including Officers, took themselves wearily back to where they had a 'home fire' and where, thankfully, the tents had arrived. They sat round campfires for the rest of the day, most nursing minor wounds and there were many comments about Wellington's message, several similar to that of Tom Miles.

"Why not a double issue of rum? What's the use of a few odd words from that spindly gawk?"

With the following dawn, the 105th were called awake and paraded at the very earliest light to stand ready to advance down the slope to their previous positions and counter any renewed French advance. However, after one hour, then two, it was obvious that none would come, the French were in their same positions as they had been at the end of the previous day, all secure around campfires, sleeping, eating or simply lounging with comrades. There was no French force anywhere that could be described as being formed into 'battle-array'. That decided, the 105th were stood down and so Miles and Bailey sat looking enviously, as the Spanish, of all descriptions, cleared the battlefield of casualties, the mournful carts being hauled up the slope by hangdog horses.

"There'll be a fair shake of French coin jinglin' in Spanish houses, this eve, you can be sure."

Bailey looked at his predictably miserable and perpetually unsatisfied scavenging companion somewhat impatiently.

"No need for too much complainin', Tom. We've done alright. B'ain't nothin' here that'll come up to what we got in Vitoria. That's the loot as matters!"

"Ah, an' now 'tis in the hands of a lot of twistin' bank bastards as'll shiv the likes of me and you, an' not lose one wink of sleep."

Bailey shut up and shook his head, deciding that there was nothing more mournful and inconsolable than Tom Miles denied the opportunity of battlefield loot. For Carr, O'Hare and Heaviside, the day of idleness presented an opportunity to take a stroll along the line and perhaps find out what all the desperation had been about on the far left during the previous day. They collected Drake and began the journey and the first Regiment they came to were the Provisionals, called to their previous place of the day before and it took some time after the introductions and handshakes before they could pass along. Then came the Portuguese, three Battalions and then the ridge summit began to descend towards Sorauren and they found themselves amongst Byng's Brigade, the 1/3rd Buffs and the 1/57th. The four stood for a while, somewhat surprised by the feverish activity all around, as guns and ammunition were hauled up the back of the ridge from the road in the valley that ran down from Sorauren, this valley now being full of British and Portuguese Troops. The idle four were then approached by a Captain of the Buffs, who quickly introduced himself.

"Good morning. Rigden. First Third."

They all introduced themselves and shook hands but Rigden was smiling the most.

"We hear you 'Rag and Bone Boys' did sterling work over there on the right. All got a bit fraught, did it?"

Drake was the one most at ease with the language of the aristocracy and so he was the first to reply.

"A little, yes, but, you know, one copes!"

However, Carr, by nature more direct, began with the questions.

"What happened here?"

Rigden cleared his throat and pointed down the hill to where a tiny stone-built Chapel stood incongruously in the middle of the slope.

"Well, Johnny came on in two columns, one each side of that, which were thrown back by Ross' Brigade, but they came back up, reinforced and got to here, which would have been alright again, but the Portuguese on the right buckled up and the Frogs got onto Ross' right. We, Byng's that is, had to come over and down and what I hear is that two of yours, from Anson's, came sweeping across the slope and sent the whole lot packing. But the Frogs were right up to here and past, even. Much higher. If it wasn't too fraught at your end, it certainly was here!"

Carr nodded agreeably.

"Yes, well, we all did our bit, yourselves no less than anyone else. It was our 27th and the 48th that came across the slope. We watched them go."

Meanwhile, Drake had been studying the activity happening on the rear slope, as another field-gun arrived at their position.

"So what's happening here? What's doing the rounds?"

Rigden pointed down the valley.

"That's the 6th Division down there, all ready to go at Sorauren and just out of sight beyond that hill are Lord Dalhousie's 7th; that being Barnes' and Inglis' Brigades, who've just arrived from the Bastan. Tomorrow, so the rumour has it, we go at them!"

The final word was emphasised and on hearing that, Carr turned to go.

"Our thanks to you, Captain Rigden. Always handy to know what each bit of the army we belong to is up to. We wish you good luck."

Handshakes were exchanged and the four started back, with O'Hare the most worried.

"We go at them? Across the same valley, against a similar ridge as they failed against us? And Soult's still plenty of troops over there. Yesterday made barely a dent in his force, desperate as it all was and this time it'll be us going across that saddle!"

Drake was immediately subdued at the truth of O'Hare's words.

"Well, at least we've got cannon up on our line. Johnny got nothing from his artillery yesterday."

However, Carr was shaking his head.

"You're right, Padraigh. It would be madness to try an assault across the same valley where the French had failed, against an enemy settled in, as those are."

He pointed across the valley but no one replied, yet it was with a little more cheer that they returned to find three field-guns now deployed on the level ground to the left of the saddle. They returned to their tent and Bryce organised some tea.

Elsewhere, Major St. John Slade was taking a deep breath to prepare himself for what he was about to do. The breath now released, he walked forward the short distance to the mess camp of Jed Deakin and Zeke Saunders. When it was obvious that they were the object of his journey, all sprang to their feet and came to the attention. It never occurred to Slade to stand them at their ease and so he began anyway, addressing Jed Deakin.

"Colour Sergeant. It seems that I have you to thank for me coming out of that fight yesterday in one piece. My thanks to you again."

He did not offer his hand, but he did remain standing there and so Deakin felt obliged to reply in some way, and he spoke the only words he could think of.

"It's alright, Sir, it's what we do. You're 105th. One of our own, Sir. We takes care of each other. You're a Rag and Bone Boy, Sir. Same as we are."

Having stumbled for something like the right words, Deakin immediately regretted describing this aristocratic Officer in such a fashion and so he paused and spoke what he hoped would reduce the possible insult of what he had just said.

"If you takes my meanin', Sir? No offence."

However, his words, all of them, had brought an smile to St. John Slade's face, but not one of mirth. The simple words describing him as being unquestionably regarded as an accepted member of these most dauntless and steadfast of veterans had a profound effect on Slade, such that he swallowed hard, but said nothing, and so Deakin continued.

"But it was Sergeant Nicholls there, Sir, as pulled you back, 'till you got back onto your feet, Sir."

Henry Nicholls was stood nearby and so Slade turned to him.

"My thanks to you also, Sergeant Nicholls."

Nicholls said nothing, but did reel off a blistering salute, but Nellie was also stood nearby and had noticed the obvious sling.

"We're all hopin' that your wound is not too troublesome for you, Major Slade, your Honour, Sir."

Slade bowed towards her.

"It is somewhat stiff, Mrs. Nicholls, but less troublesome than I could have hoped."

"'Tis grand to hear that, Sir. So, will not you take a drop of tea with us, now?"

This was a step too far for Slade and so he bowed again.

"I thank you, Mrs. Nicholls, for the kind offer, but I have my duties to attend to, you understand.

Nellie curtsied as Slade turned to go, but all the soldiers stood there had now saluted and so he felt honour bound to at least make a return and so he did, very carefully and perhaps a little more drawn out than necessary, but he felt the gravity of the occasion and wished to show it. However, as he returned to the Officers' lines, Deakin's words still hung in his mind, 'one of our own'. There was not one occasion in all his aristocratic background or experience that even came close to such words of absolute inclusion or acceptance, all too often the exact opposite. Still somewhat emotional, he wandered back to his tent, to find Carravoy, D'Villiers and Ameshurst in there, all fast asleep. With no-one to confide in, he sat outside the tent, pondering the implications of what had just been said to him and, with the other half of his mind, pondering the attitude that he had carried into Spain with him, as Brockenhurst's Militia Major.

With the dying of the light, Cyrus Gibney came into the mess camp of Jed Deakin and his companions.

"Jed. Brigade orders. They wants NCOs on watch all through t'night. You and Henry two till four. He wants us all stood-to afore dawn, in case another French attack."

Deakin nodded.

"Right, Sar' Major. Two till four."

Military business done, Bridie spoke up.

"Mr. Gibney. Will you not take a drop of tea with us? 'Tis fresh made."

Gibney halted his departure. Like many in the Battalion, he could not say no to Bridie Mulcahey.

"That'll be grand, Mrs. Mulcahey. Most welcome, ah'm sure."

Thus, Cyrus Gibney spent the last hours of daylight and some of the evening, sat amongst old comrades talking over old campaigns and events with such as Deakin, Nicholls, Hill and Halfway. With the arrival of full dark, he took his leave.

"Ah'm thankful for the tea, Mrs. Mulcahey, ah'm sure. So, best check ont' pickets. Good night to all, could be a big day tomorrow."

All bid him the same and so Deakin and Henry Nicholls took themselves away to sleep and be woken later by Sergeant Obediah Hill and Ethan Ellis when they came off watch, Hill passing on his concerns.

"There's goin's on across the valley, Jed. They'm movin', I'm certain. Makin' changes in the dark."

The relieving pair, Deakin and Nicholls walked the 200 yards down to the saddle to watch and listen. It was Nicholls who first voiced the obvious question.

"Why are there good campfires in the middle of the night. 'Tis like they was still cookin' rations."

Deakin did not reply, he was listening, using his countryman's ability to discern one sound from another.

"I can hear wheels. Carts or guns, can't tell, but he's movin' his articles around, that's for sure. Shouts of men, too."

"There's fires still burnin' bright over to the left. 'T'ain't natural, them's bein' tended, or stoked up and left to burn."

"Right. Who's Officer of the Watch?"

"O'Hare."

"You stay here. I'll go over. We may not be the only one's as've heard all this, but maybe we are."

Deakin hurried over to where O'Hare was, stood before his own campfire and staring into the dark.

"Beg Pardon, Sir, but there's a lot of movin' opposite. Men and guns."

"Very good, Colour Sergeant, I can hear them also, but you did right to report. I've sent a message across, but we'll all be stood-to soon and we'll see what's what with the daylight. Now return to your post."

Whilst all the pocket-watch hands present on the ridge crawled around to show four in the morning, and then beyond, so the daylight gradually grew over the valley and Deakin and Halfway could see the dark shapes on the hillside opposite. A Grenadier Sergeant and Corporal came to relieve them but Deakin and Halfway remained there anyway, Deakin giving the reason.

"We'll all be stood-to in a few minutes anyway."

The shapes over the valley took better form, one a long French column moving across the hillside directly above the saddle and also two stationary columns, each of Brigade strength, sat on the hillside to the right of it, one behind the other, above and to the left of Zabaldika. Carr, O'Hare and Heaviside were now up and examining for themselves what could be seen across the valley, Carr as bemused as anyone.

"What the Hell is he trying to do? That's madness, to march an army across an enemy's front."

He turned to O'Hare and Heaviside.

"Warn the men. It will be us doing the attacking this day!"

O'Hare and Heaviside were still staring at the long column labouring sideways across the steep slope opposite, whilst they could see another whole French Division, the two Brigades, sat doing nothing, occupying the bare hillside directly opposite Spanish Hill. It was not long before a Staff Officer came galloping up to their end of the Allied position and reined in opposite Carr.

"Sir! General orders are to stand to. The whole army. General Wellington is issuing rapid orders to take advantage of what we can see happening opposite. You may have to make it up as you go along, Sir, but yours and the Provisional Battalion are to attack across the saddle, supported in reserve by the 27th and the 48th. When you hear the cannons open up on Sorauren, that will be your signal to attack. Sir.

"And General Anson?"

"Still wounded Sir. And fretting!"

Carr laughed, as did O'Hare and Heaviside.

"A good sign, I feel. Thank you, Major."

"Thank you, Sir. And good luck to you and to your men, Sir, especially after your efforts on that hill over there, the day before yesterday."

With that he saluted and rode off to the 48th and 27th, these someway further up the slope. Carr looked at the other two, but it was Heaviside who came out with the inevitable.

"I will tell of your name to my brothers. In the midst of the congregation I will sing your praise. Hebrews 2. Verse 22."

"Most appropriate, Joshua, but meanwhile we must assemble our own congregation. Beat 'stand to' and form opposite the saddle."

It was not long before the drums beat out the order and, all too briefly, the men of the 105th spoke their goodbyes to their loved ones, Consuela adjusting Zeke's head bandage before she kissed him and all other couples, married or 'army', sharing a firm, if brief, embrace. Once formed up, Carr looked along his line, the men stood firm and steady at 'Order arms', their 'uniforms' barely conforming to that description at all, but the Officers were out front with swords drawn and tilting back onto their right shoulders. Heaviside and O'Hare were stood before their respective wings and the shocking 105th Colours stretched out above the centre, held open by the firm breeze. With that picture absorbed and considered, Carr spoke softly to himself, his voice quavering with emotion.

"We are the 105th. The Prince of Wales Own Wessex Foot. There's none like us! They call us the Rag and Bone Boys and more besides, but we wear the green and we make it count. None like us!"

At that appropriate moment the guns above Sorauren opened fire and Carr was able to look down the length of the valley to see shells and cannonshot begin to deluge the unfortunate village and also a battery in the centre of the Allied line then began to send accurate shot into the column moving across the hillside opposite. The three guns 100 yards to their left soon joined in, beginning a bombardment of the two Brigades squatting on the hillside opposite Spanish Hill, for these to immediately all spring to their feet when the shot began to arrive and begin a rapid retreat up the hillside. From their left, far up the valley at Sorauren, there came the sounds of ferocious fighting. Carr ignored it, instead he raised his sword and took a deep breath.

"One Hundred and Fifth!"

He swung his sword forward and began a brisk trot down the slope onto the beginning of the saddle. His line followed, soon adopting a 'V' formation as they crossed, but reforming into a line on the far side. Then began a steady advance upward, against an enemy that could not retreat fast enough. Carr led his men on and upwards, no one had yet fired a shot, such was the eagerness of the two French Divisions to escape. Soon, his breath ran out, he was nearing the top and he found himself being overtaken by the two young Ensigns. He pointed to the highest peak on the once French held ridge, not 200 yards distant.

"There! Take The Colours up there and once there, you wave them, for all you are worth!"

oOo

Footnotes

Chapter One

Captain Scovell deciphering captured coded French dispatches was one the of the major intelligence coups of the Peninsular War. Scovell was the Cipher-Secretary at Wellington's Headquarters. Three duplicates were captured, one by Portuguese Ordenanca, two others by Julian Sanchez men between Salamanca and Cuidad Rodrigo. They told a great deal about Marmont's army and his plans for the future, giving Wellington sufficient reassurance about his own advance into Spain, which resulted in the victory of Salamanca.

One of Wellington's most dangerous moments was his entry into the city, where the joyous populace almost pulled him off his horse and he had to be rescued by the 14th Light Dragoons. Also, he was forced to rescue himself and quickly retire, when he and his Staff came under heavy artillery fire on San Cristobal ridge some weeks later.

Chapter Two

Literary Licence - The 40th 2nd Somerset did not retreat before the French column at Castrillo de la Guarena. With the 27th they halted and threw back a whole French Division in three columns, the 17th Leger, 2 battalions; 65th Ligne, 3 battalions and the 22nd Ligne, 3 battalions. The cavalry attack at the same time was met by Alten's 14th Light Dragoons and the 1st Hussars KGL, and not G. Anson's Light Dragoons.

There are several versions of what Wellington was doing when he exclaimed, "By God, that will do!", during the Battle of Salamanca. Three witness statements give an account, one, that he had his mouth full of beef; two, of ham; and three that he was spreading some mustard onto some ham. The story of throwing a chicken leg over his shoulder would seem to have been made up by someone to add extra drama to the crucial moment.

The fighting against the French rearguard was probably the fiercest of the whole battle. The 32nd of Hinde's Brigade lost 137 out of 600 present, but the 11th Devons of Hulse's lost 340 out of 516 and the 61st 366 out of 546. For the final attack the 61st had no Officer standing who could carry The Colour, two privates bore them forward. These losses are exceeded only by those suffered at Albuera by such as the 57th Middlesex, who, from this, earned the nickname 'The Diehards'. The Devons became the 'Bloody Eleventh'.

Chapter Three

The failure of the Spanish General Carlos D'Espana to hold his position at Alba de Tormes was, indeed, one of the most unfortunate tactical mistakes of the war. The number of French who escaped probably lengthened the war in Spain by several months.

The achievements of the KGL Dragoons at Garcia Hernandez are recognised as being amongst the most remarkable of all the Napoleonic Wars.

Chapter Four

Wellington's effort to capture Burgos by escalade alone, without siege artillery, is looked upon as one of his worst mistakes. However, after the French disaster of Salamanca, Napoleon poured veteran troops into Spain to restore the situation and Burgos, even if captured, could probably not have been held anyway, being so far Eastwards into Spain. Therefore, heavily outnumbered, retreat was inevitable.

Chapter Five

The retreat from Burgos to Cuidad Rodrigo was all the more disastrous because it was so avoidable, being that the rations could easily have been divided over the three columns and the extreme starvation avoided, rather than be sent on a route so far North so as to make the Commissariat convoy doubly safe from the French. The supply column being directed so far Northwards by Quartermaster-General James Willoughby Gordon undoubtedly turned a simple retreat into a near catastrophe. Losses were almost 5,000 from an army of 50,000, but this does not convey the dreadful state of the army when it reached Cuidad Rodrigo. However, as his highly critical letter to all Officers after the retreat shows, Wellington lay most of the blame onto his men, which incensed many, and it was not forgotten.

Gordon was probably the most incompetent and disruptive of all Wellington's Senior Officers and was later sent home because he sent sensitive letters back to England, facts from which appeared in the British press. Before being dismissed, Wellington decreed that should not be shown any more high level Staff documents, yet he was not criticised for the retreat fiasco.

The experience of Anson's Brigade above Miranda D'Azan before the full retreat, was indeed one of the most ghoulish of the war. Nothing had been done to clear the French dead from the ridge, they remained as they fell after being virtually annihilated by the 3rd Division.

Chapter Six

There is no record of any intelligence scheme to persuade the Americans that the British were about to invade, or that a whole Division was to be transferred to Canada to enable that. However, it is possible that it happened and will probably never be revealed if it is true, but the Americans did capture Fort Erie early in 1813 and El Rey Joseph was ordered to transfer 40,000 troops to his brother in Germany.

Chapter Seven

The advance across Spain from the Portuguese border to Vitoria is one of the most rapid advances in military history, certainly of the Napoleonic War. On the 24th May Hill's column advanced on Salamanca and on 18th June both forces confront each other at Vitoria. It was an advance of 250 miles in 24 days, to clear virtually the whole of Spain of French forces.

Chapter Eight

The Battle of Vitoria marked the end of all French ambitions in Spain; all of El Rey Joseph's significant armies were destroyed. The two undoubted turning points of the battle were the Rifles being guided to the unguarded bridge at Tres Puentes by a Spanish peasant, which cost him his life from a French cannonball and the achievements of the 88th Connaught Rangers and the 45th Nottinghamshires. The feat of arms of the 88th at Vitoria surpassed even their achievement at the Battle of Busaco, both a triumph against huge odds.

The pillaging of the French baggage park after the battle is one of the salient events of the whole Peninsular War. Besides so many on the Allied side enriching themselves, many priceless works of art were rescued, not least being the Water Seller of Seville by Velasquez. In all 200 were rescued and 83 hang in Apsley House, the Duke of Wellington's London residence. The paintings come from the Spanish Royal Collection and were officially given to Wellington by King Ferdinand of Spain, when Wellington offered to give them back.

It was merely days after the battle that Wellington wrote his infamous and generally unjustified letter to Bathurst which included the phrase, "We have in service the scum of the earth as common soldiers." This was not an unusual statement for Wellington, in fact, long years afterwards, he officially informed a Commission on the Army that, "He had no idea of any great effect being produced on British soldiers by anything but the immediate fear of corporal punishment." However, he would not have his men disparaged in any way. After Napoleon had abdicated for the first time, there was a victory parade in Paris where a Battalion of Redcoats was inspected by an Austrian General. Having walked the ranks the General commented to Wellington, "Not very big, are they?" The reply came, "No, but they've never been beat!"

Chapter Nine

Besides Wellington's infamous letters, the arrest of Norman Ramsey was a scandal which absorbed the whole army and kindled additional animosity towards Wellington himself. Confusion and bad staff work were rife during the advance after Vitoria, but a very irate Wellington targeted Ramsey as his 'whipping boy'. He found Ramsey moving East, against his wishes and ordered him to halt and not move until he received further orders from Headquarters. Ramsey was mistakenly following Anson, as he had been ordered, although Anson was to the North, which few Staff knew. The next morning the Assistant Quartermaster General, Captain Campbell, found Ramsey and asked him if he had received direction. Ramsey answered 'No', and so Campbell ordered him to follow Anson, who so many thought was on his way to Pamplona. Ramsey took Campbell's instruction to be the necessary orders from Headquarters, but Wellington found the guns again moving in the wrong direction and had Ramsey arrested for disobeying a verbal order.

Ramsey remained under arrest for several weeks whilst many interceded for him to be pardoned, whilst Ramsey, as a matter of honour, said nothing. He was cut out of the reward given to all Officers after Vitoria, did not receive the advance his brevet rank merited and he fell to the bottom of the promotion list. He remained silent, not so his comrades who branded Wellington as being in perpetual dislike of the artillery. Ramsey fell at Waterloo, still a Battery Commander.

Ramsey's Battery's escape at the Battle of Fuentes D'Onoro is the subject of the splendid painting by William Barnes Wollen.

Chapter Ten

The achievements of the 40th 2nd Somerset at Sorauren rank amongst the highest of the whole Peninsular War. They had suffered considerable loss from the rearguard at Lintzoain such that when the two Spanish Battalions lost Spanish Hill, the 40th were required to re-capture it with just 400 men and 10 Officers. The French had 2,000 men on the hill, which the 40th stopped by sheer firepower and then threw back with a desperate bayonet charge, which cleared the summit. Another three Battalion French Regiment renewed the attack, which was repulsed by firepower alone, this with the aid of one of the Spanish Regiments, who had rallied. Clausel, the Divisional Commander, then sent up a third, which contained every man that he could muster, advancing with 'drums beating and Eagles to the front', which was also beaten back by firepower and the threat of the bayonet. Wellington always held the 40th in high regard and he fully appreciated the importance of Spanish Hill being held, as all reserves had been drawn over to the left. He sent the Prince of Orange to pass on his thanks and congratulations.

oOo

Printed in Great Britain
by Amazon

35118326R00351